INVITATION TO THE CLASSICS

INVITATION TO THE CLASSICS

EDITED BY

LOUISE COWAN AND OS GUINNESS

Library at Versailles during the eighteenth century,
containing the archives of the Ministry of Foreign
Affairs.

Baker Books

A Division of Baker Book House Co
Grand Rapids, Michigan 49516

Published by Baker Books
a division of Baker Book House Company
P.O. Box 6287, Grand Rapids, MI 49516-6287

Library of Congress Cataloging-in-Publication Data
Invitation to the classics / edited by Louise Cowan and
    Os Guinness.
        p. cm.
    Includes bibliographical references and indexes.
    ISBN 0-8010-1156-6 (cloth)
    1. Literature—History and criticism.
    2. Christianity and literature.   I. Cowan, Louise,
1916–   II. Guinness, Os.
PN49.I69   1998
809—dc21
                                                        97-43058

Designed by Three's Company, London

Worldwide coedition organized and produced by Angus Hudson Ltd, Concorde House, Grenville Place, Mill Hill, London NW7 3SA, England
Tel: +44 181 959 3668
Fax: +44 181 959 3678

Printed in Hong Kong / China

"Never Again Would Birds' Song Be the Same" from *The Poetry of Robert Frost* edited by Edward Connery Lathem, Copyright 1942 by Robert Frost, © 1970 by Lesley Frost Ballantine, © 1969 by Henry Holt and Company, Inc. Reprinted by permission of Henry Holt and Company, Inc.

For current information about all releases from Baker Book House, visit our web site:
http://www.bakerbooks.com

For information about the Trinity Forum, visit the Forum's web site:
http://www.ttf.org

Picture acknowledgments
Picture research by Image Select
AKG Photo: pp. 131, 133, 225, 309
Ann Ronan at Image Select: pp. 3, 27, 34, 36, 38, 59, 64, 72, 79, 81, 85, 87, 89, 93, 97, 104, 107, 108, 109, 113, 115, 117, 119, 121, 128, 135, 137, 139, 144, 145, 151, 153, 157, 159, 161, 163, 165, 171, 173, 175, 177, 179, 185, 188, 191, 193, 197, 203, 211, 221, 227, 229, 237, 239, 247, 257, 261, 269, 277, 293, 295, 296, 303, 313, 317, 351
Art Resource: pp. 147, 181, 199, 209, 287
Chris Fairclough Colour Library/Image Select: pp. 213, 281, 325, 355
Edimedia: pp. 345, 347
e.t. archive: pp. 43, 103
Fotomas Index: p. 275
Georgia College: p. 353
Hulton Getty: pp. 289, 335
Image Select: pp. 15, 21, 29, 31, 39, 46, 47, 48, 52, 61, 63, 67, 73, 76, 83, 91, 99, 105, 123, 141, 149, 155, 166, 169, 183, 187, 195, 201, 205, 215, 216, 219, 231, 233, 235, 241, 243, 245, 249, 251, 259, 267, 271, 279, 283, 285, 291, 297, 299, 305, 307, 315, 319, 323, 327, 329, 331, 341, 343, 359, 364
Image Select/C. Vroujard: p. 254
Image Select/Fragment Collection: p. 311
Jonathan Cape: p. 362
Mary Evans: pp. 51, 55, 56, 77, 126, 127, 143, 146, 273, 301, 339, 361
National Tourist Office of Greece: p. 53
Peter Wyart: pp. 69, 95, 129, 207, 263, 265, 321, 336, 337
SCM: p. 349
Shone/Image Select: p. 357
Tim Dowley: pp. 44, 49, 65, 71, 98, 101, 129, 223

To
Mr. and Mrs. Henry J. "Bud" Smith
Originators and patrons of this project
Great friends
Great lovers of faith, freedom,
and the riches of our heritage
With deep gratitude and appreciation

Contents

Contributors

Larry Allums (Ph.D., University of Dallas) is chairman of the Humanities Department at the University of Mobile and director of the Fairhope Institute of Humanities and Culture. He has published articles on Dante and Southern literature and has edited a recently published collection of essays, *The Epic Cosmos.*

Glenn C. Arbery (Ph.D., University of Dallas) teaches literature at Thomas More College in Merrimack, New Hampshire. He has published essays and poems and is currently completing a book on the *Iliad.*

Virginia L. Arbery (Ph.D., University of Dallas) teaches in the Humanities Program at St. Anselm College, Manchester, New Hampshire, and is a Richard Weaver Fellow. A consultant to The National Center for America's Founding Documents at Boston University, she writes on American politics and literature.

Lionel Basney (Ph.D., University of Rochester) teaches literature and writing at Calvin College. His essays and poems have appeared in a wide range of periodicals, including literary journals, scholarly journals, and religious magazines. He has written social criticism, including *An Earth-Careful Way of Life.*

Beatrice Batson (Ph.D., Vanderbilt University) is professor emerita of English and former chair of the department, as well as the coordinator of the Special Shakespeare Collection and the director of the Shakespeare Institutes

at Wheaton College. Her most recent publications include *John Bunyan's Grace Abounding* and *The Pilgrim's Progress, with Critical Essays and Annotated Bibliography of Scholarly Works, 1964–1987.*

Sharon Coolidge (Ph.D., Duke University) is professor of English at Wheaton College. Her most recent scholarly work has been an article on *Eliduc* in *Mediaeval Studies* and as a contributor to *The Dictionary of Biblical Tradition in English Literature.*

Bainard Cowan (Ph.D., Yale University) teaches English and comparative literature and civilization at Louisiana State University and directs the Comparative Literature Summer Institute. He is the author of *Exiled Waters: Moby Dick and the Crisis of Allegory* and the coeditor of several books, including the LSU Press series Horizons in Theory and American Culture.

Louise Cowan (Ph.D., Vanderbilt) is former chairman of the English Department and dean of the Graduate School at the University of Dallas and a founding fellow of the Dallas Institute. She is the author of two books on the Southern literary renaissance and of numerous essays on literary and educational topics. Currently, she is the general editor of a series entitled Studies in Genre, which includes *The Terrain of Comedy* and *The Epic Cosmos.* In 1991 she received the Charles Frankel Award for her contribution to education in the humanities.

John F. Crosby (Ph.D., University of Salzburg) is professor of philosophy at Franciscan University of Steubenville in Steubenville, Ohio, as well as chairman of the department and director of graduate philosophy. He has published books and essays on John Henry Newman and Karol Wojtyla. His most recent work is *The Selfhood of the Human Person.*

Robert S. Dupree (Ph.D., Yale University) has taught in the English Department at the University of Dallas since 1966. He studied French literature at the University of Paris and the University of Caen, France. His most recent book is an annotated anthology of seventeenth-century English poetry.

Edward E. Ericson, Jr. (Ph.D., University of Arkansas) is professor of English at Calvin College. He is the author of *Solzhenitsyn and the Modern World,* and, with the author's cooperation, abridged *The Gulag Archipelago.*

C. Stephen Evans (Ph.D., Yale University) is professor of philosophy at Calvin College. He is the author of numerous books, including *Passionate Reason: Making Sense of Kierkegaard's Philosophical Fragments* and *The Historical Christ and the Jesus of Faith: The Incarnational Narrative as History.*

Harold Fickett (A.M., Brown University) is a writer and speaker. He is the author of three novels, *The Holy Fool, First Light,* and *Daybreak,* a collection of short stories, and a short, critical biography of Flannery O'Connor, *Images of Grace.* He serves as senior editor of *Image: A Journal of the Arts and Religion.*

Bruce Frohnen (Ph.D., Cornell University) is senior research fellow at Liberty Fund. He is the author of *Virtue and the Promise of Conservatism: The Legacy of Burke and Tocqueville* and *Saving Liberalism from Itself: Communitarianism and the Uses of Civil Religion.*

Margaret Gardner (M.A., University of Virginia) has taught English literature and composition at the high school and college levels. As a researcher and editorial assistant, she has worked for *Newsweek* magazine, the National Museum of American History, and Time-Life Books.

Dona S. Gower (Ph.D., Vanderbilt) is the director of the Teachers Academy and fellow of the Dallas Institute. She has coedited *Teaching the Teachers* and has published essays on multiculturalism, genres, and literary paradigms for teaching, leading, and learning.

Roger J. Green (Ph.D., Boston College) is professor and chair of biblical and theological studies and holds the Terrelle B. Crum Chair of Humanities at Gordon College. His most recent work is *Catherine Booth: A Biography.*

Eileen Gregory (Ph.D., University of South Carolina) is professor of English and chairman of the department at the University of Dallas. She has recently completed a book on H.D. (Hilda Doolittle), *Classic Lines: H.D. and Hellenism.*

Os Guinness (D.Phil., Oxford University) is a writer and senior fellow of the Trinity Forum. He has served at the Brookings Institution, the Williamsburg Charter Foundation,

and L'Abri in Switzerland. His books include *The American Hour* and *The Call.*

Stephen Gurney (Ph.D., University of Maryland) is professor of English at Bemidji State University. He has written *Alain Fournier* and *British Poetry of the Nineteenth Century,* and is presently writing *British Poetry of the Seventeenth and Eighteenth Centuries.*

Christopher Hodgkins (Ph.D., University of Chicago) is associate professor of English at the University of North Carolina, Greensboro. He is the author of *Authority, Church, and Society in George Herbert: Return to the Middle Way* and is currently at work on *Reforming Empire: The Protestant Imagination, Colonialism, and Conquest in British Literature.*

Thomas T. Howard (Ph.D., New York University) is professor of English at St. John's Seminary College. He teaches the history of English literature as well as the works of the Inklings, Evelyn Waugh, Flannery O'Connor, and others. He is the author of many books, including *The Achievement of C. S. Lewis* and *Lead, Kindly Light.*

Mary Lou Hoyle (Ph.D., University of Dallas) is an associate professor in the Performing Arts Department at Texas Woman's University in Denton, Texas. She has contributed articles on literary theory to *The Terrain of Comedy, The Epic Cosmos,* and *The Muses.*

Alan Jacobs (Ph.D., University of Virginia) is associate professor of English at Wheaton College. He has written extensively on modern literature and literary theory, and has just completed *What Became of Wystan: Change and Continuity in Auden's Poetry.*

Gail Kienitz (Ph.D., University of Notre Dame) is assistant professor in the English Department of Wheaton College. She teaches specialized courses in nineteenth-century British literature, women writers, and autobiography as literature.

Elizabeth Franklin Lewis (Ph.D., University of Virginia) is assistant professor of Spanish at the University of Tennessee, Knoxville. Her recent publications include two articles on eighteenth-century women writers Josefa Amar y Borbón and María Gertradis Hore.

John Lowe (Ph.D., Columbia University) is professor of English at Louisiana State University, where he teaches African American, Southern, and ethnic literature and theory. He is the author of *Jump at the Sun: Zora Neale Hurston's Cosmic Comedy,* editor of *Conversations with Ernest Gaines,* and coeditor of *The Future of Southern Letters.*

Roger Lundin (Ph.D., University of Connecticut) is professor of English at Wheaton College. He is the author of *The Culture of Interpretation* and a biography of Emily Dickinson in The Library of Religious Biography series.

Telfair J. (Ted) Mashburn, III (D. Phil., Oxford University) is associate professor of philosophy and religion at the University of Mobile in Alabama and assistant director of the Fairhope Institute of Humanities and Culture. An ordained Southern Baptist minister, he teaches and preaches in churches.

Mary Mumbach (Ph.D., University of Dallas) is a founder of the Thomas More College of Liberal Arts in Merrimack, New Hampshire, where she serves as dean of the college and associate professor of literature. Recently she has contributed to *The Epic Cosmos* and *The Terrain of Comedy*.

Jude V. Nixon (Ph.D., Temple University) is professor of English at Wayne State University. His publications on Hopkins and other Victorian writers have appeared in scholarly journals and collections of essays. His most recent publication is *Gerard Manley Hopkins and His Contemporaries: Liddon, Newman, Darwin, and Pater*.

Mark A. Noll (Ph.D., Vanderbilt University) is McManis Professor of Christian Thought at Wheaton College. He is the author of *Princeton and the Republic, 1768–1822* and *A History of Christianity in the United States and Canada*.

Daniel E. Ritchie (Ph.D., Rutgers University) is professor of English at Bethel College in Minnesota. He has edited two books on Edmund Burke. His most recent book is *Reconstructing Literature in an Ideological Age*, which treats English literature from Milton to Burke.

Arthur A. Rupprecht (Ph.D., University of Pennsylvania) is professor of classical languages at Wheaton College. He has contributed to *The Expositors Bible Commentary* and *Dictionary of Paul and His Epistles*.

Daniel Russ (Ph.D., University of Dallas) is headmaster of Trinity Christian Academy in Dallas, Texas. He also is a fellow of the Dallas Institute of Humanities and Culture, where he founded and directs the Institute's Studies in Leadership Program. He contributed recently to *The Muses* and *The Olympians*.

Leland Ryken (Ph.D., University of

Oregon) is professor of English at Wheaton College, where he has taught since 1968. Author of over twenty books, he has recently written books on Milton, the Bible as literature, and the classics in Christian perspective.

Peter Sampo (Ph.D., University of Notre Dame) is the president and cofounder of Thomas More College in Merrimack, New Hampshire. He has contributed to *The Recovery of American Education* and *Liberty, Life and Family*.

Robert Martin Schaefer (Ph.D., University of Dallas) is chairman of the Department of Social and Behavioral Sciences at the University of Mobile. He is coeditor of *American Political Rhetoric* and *The American Experiment*.

Gary D. Schmidt (Ph.D., University of Illinois) is chair of the English Department of Calvin College. His most recent book, *The Iconography of the Mouth of Hell*, reflects his medieval interests, but his retelling of *Pilgrim's Progress* and his *The Blessing of the Lord* reflect his interest in children's literature as well.

Dennis Patrick Slattery (Ph.D., University of Dallas) is interdisciplinary coordinator of the Masters in Counseling Psychology program and core faculty member of the Mythological Studies program at the Pacifica Graduate Institute in Carpinteria, California. He has recently published *The Idiot: Dostoevsky's Fantastic Prince* as well as many essays on literary figures, criticism, and contemporary culture.

Marilyn Gump Stewart (Ph.D., University of Dallas) teaches at the Greenhill School in Dallas and in the summer program of the Teachers

Academy of the Dallas Institute of Humanities and Culture. She has contributed essays to *Teaching the Teachers, The Terrain of Comedy, The Epic Cosmos,* and *The Analecta Husserliana*.

Charles R. Sullivan (Ph.D., Columbia University) teaches early modern and modern European history at the University of Dallas. He has written on eighteenth-century Scottish and French political economy and is currently writing on social science in early nineteenth-century France.

Henrietta Ten Harmsel (Ph.D., University of Michigan) is emerita professor at Calvin College, where she taught in the English Department for twenty-five years. She has written *Jane Austen: A Study in Fictional Conventions* and numerous articles on English novels. Her other specialty is translations of Dutch poetry into English.

G. B. Tennyson (Ph.D., Princeton University) is professor of English at the University of California, Los Angeles. He is the author and editor of numerous books on Victorian literature and coeditor of the journal *Nineteenth-Century Literature*. He recently wrote, narrated, and produced the documentary film *Owen Barfield: Man and Meaning*.

Carsten Peter Thiede (C.M.A., Berlin University) is director of the Institute for Basic Epistemological Research, Paderborn, and life member of the Institute for Germanic Studies, London University. He edited the works of Stendhal in German and organizes studies in modern European Christian Literature. A trained historian and papyrologist, he is coauthor of a book about the origins of the gospels, *Eyewitness to Jesus*.

John H. Timmerman (Ph.D., Ohio University) is professor of English at Calvin College. He is author of fourteen books, including *T. S. Eliot's Ariel Poems: The Poetics of Recovery* and *The Dramatic Landscape of Steinbeck's Short Stories.*

Dean Ward (Ph.D., University of Virginia) teaches English literature at Calvin College, where he also directs the college writing program. He is author of *Tradition and Adaptation,* a book on writing across the curriculum.

Robert E. Wood (Ph.D., Marquette University) is professor of philosophy at the University of Dallas. He is the author of *Martin Buber's Ontology: An Analysis on* I and Thou, *A Path into Metaphysics,* and *Approaches to Aesthetics: Studies in the Philosophic Tradition.*

Ashley Woodiwiss (Ph.D., University of North Carolina) teaches in the Department of Political Science at Wheaton College and is active in the American Political Science Association. His current research considers how a Christian conception of politics responds to the recent intellectual developments in liberal, communitarian, and postmodern thought.

The Purpose of
Invitation to the Classics

A classic, according to Mark Twain, is "a book that people praise and don't read." But perhaps Twain's wit needs a little revision for our time. For when many people hear the word *classic* today, they think not of a book at all but of a Coke, a 1950s roadster, an early Beatles' song, or even a CD-ROM game.

This, however, is the least of the challenges facing an advocate of the classics today. For the grand and inescapable tradition of Western literary classics confronts us with fundamental choices over our understanding of words, reading and art, as well as citizenship, civilization, faith, and the whole notion of the true, the good, and the beautiful. In answer to these foundational issues, the contributors to *Invitation to the Classics* uphold one tradition of response, standing clearly over against others. We seek to be "custodians" of this heritage—grateful heirs and stewards—and not, like so many others, as either "creators" or "cannibals."

At one level, the purpose of *Invitation to the Classics* is straightforward with the title speaking for itself: to introduce the Western literary masterworks in a clear and simple style that is mature in seriousness and tone and Christian in perspective—and in doing so, to help reawaken Western people to the vibrant heritage of these classics that are rich in themselves and in their two-thousand-year relationship to the Christian faith.

Each year the Trinity Forum holds a series of forums offering those in European and American leadership circles the opportunity to engage with readings selected from classic texts of the world. Almost invariably the staff is asked to suggest a list of further texts to be read. *Invitation to the Classics* is the answer to countless such requests and to the wider interest in the revival of the classics that they represent.

The immediate occasion of this volume was the farsighted vision and generosity of a Texas businessman and his wife, and in particular their hosting a gathering of professors of literature to discuss such a guide. Happily this diverse group of scholars, distinguished in their fields and Christian in commitment, found surprising agreement over the purpose and approach and the classics to cover. Their goal was to produce a volume unmatched for its comprehensiveness, scholarly authority, Christian commitment—and unabashed love for the classics.

At another level, *Invitation to the Classics* is written with broader cultural considerations in mind. In particular it is inspired by five burning convictions about the worth of the classics and our responsibility to them.

First, in a day when words seem to be supplanted by images and the printed page by the electronic screen, we may be enthusiastic users of the best modern technology but we should remain unregenerate readers. The contributors to this volume believe in the supreme value of words and their inescapable importance for the life of the mind and the human spirit.

Second, with the Western world at large urgently needing renewal, we should all remember that great periods of renaissance and reformation spring from a return to first things. Once we recognize the classics' lyric beauty, their aching tragedy, their probing intellectual inquiry, their profound imagination, sympathy, and wisdom, we see that their capacity to restore is fundamental to our continuing liberty and vitality.

Third, despite the deadening effect of our modern preoccupation with "success" and the "bottom line," we can be assured that the classics have an intrinsic human, cultural, and spiritual worth. Their value far transcends such commonly claimed benefits as adult education or personal self-improvement—let alone such false motivations as "culture snobbery." The classic works are a "great conversation," the Western contribution to the ongoing discussion of the primary themes of life and death, right and wrong, triumph and tragedy, which we all confront in being human.

Fourth, with the passing of the post–World War II generation that advocated a rediscovery of the great books, it is time and past time for a new championing of the great literary classics of our Western civilization.

Fifth, with endless controversies swirling around the Western masterworks, individual followers of Christ and the church of Christ as a whole have a unique responsibility to guard, enjoy, and pass them on. Christians should stand alongside people of many faiths and allegiances who treasure the priceless heritage of this three-thousand-years' conversation of imagination and ideas—not least because they are privileged to share the faith that animated the majority of these masterworks.

Subcreators, Not Creators

Where do we contributors to this guide differ from the other main attitudes toward the classics today? On one side we stand over against the "creators"—those who go too far in treating literature and art as an end in itself and who emphasize human creativity, whether in the writer or the reader, too strongly.

The older version of this tendency grew out of the romantic movement and still holds sway over the popular understanding of great artists and writers. It falsely elevates art, making it a substitute religion. Thus literature becomes "divine" and "redemptive"; the writer a "genius" with a pioneering mission of "self-expression"; the museum is "temple" of the arts; and the critics are the priests who mediate the mysteries to the masses. Ironically, it might

appear unwise to refer to this inflated view of art because it provides an alibi for religious people who reject the arts. But the proper answer is not a dismissal, but rather a replacement of a bad view of art with a good one.

A more recent version of this tendency emphasizes the creative role of the reader over the writer—just as the exaltation of art objects has led, ironically, to the exaltation of art observers. Many contemporary literary critics undermine the author's intentions by questioning whether a text has any intrinsic meaning. Others claim that a classic is just the product of historical, economic, and social forces rather than a masterpiece born from an individual's brilliance. Both groups emphasize the reader's role in determining the meaning of a work. And among readers at large, the critic in particular is elevated to the position of creator.

This recent tendency leads to a debunking of the genius and inspiration of the classics. The works are to be read only as products of their time or, worse still, as the texts of "dead, white European males." The public then sees the great books as no longer worth reading—or only to be read through the lenses of academic interpretation. To adapt Shakespeare to speak of the effect of some critics, "They come to bury Shakespeare, not to praise him." Or as C. S. Lewis argued a generation ago, the glorification of art—and now its creator, the critic—results in a confusion of second things with first things, of a lesser good with a greater good, and thus the dislocation of the classics from ordinary life. Consequently, Lewis said, "little is left for us but high-minded works which fewer and fewer people want to hear or read or see, and 'popular' works of which both those who make them and those who enjoy them are half-ashamed."

In contrast to the creators' theory of genius and its idolizing of pretensions to absolute originality and spontaneity, we hold the view that humility should be a precondition of all creating and learning. Unlike God, the human artist does not create "out of nothing." Human creativity is derivative and reflective, working within the bounds of what God has formed.

So in terms of making art and writing lit-

"The Deification of Homer," by Ingres, 1827. Homer is surrounded by other literary figures of Western civilization, such as Plutarch in the blue headdress at Homer's shoulder and Molière at bottom left of the steps.

erature, we are subcreators rather than creators. In terms of reading the classics, we recognize the worth of a classic with humility, including the author's intention and accomplishment; we do not rule on its place in the canon by overemphasizing our own response. Ours is an interpretation born of admiration. As Lewis concluded about the creator's responsibility, "an author should never conceive himself as bringing into existence beauty or wisdom which did not exist before, but simply and solely as trying to embody in terms of his own art some reflection of eternal Beauty and Wisdom."

Custodians, Not Cannibals

On the other side we stand against the "cannibals"—those who go too far in treating literature and art as commodities to be consumed. This tendency, which results from modern consumerism, turns works of art into products for the all-devouring market of images. Ours is a world of tie-ins, cash-ins, credits, spin-offs, hard sell, soft sell, recognition opportunities, "cross-promotions," "cause-related marketing," and a manic creativity in licensing anything and everything.

"Market totalitarianism" takes control as market forces invade and colonize more and more of human life, subjecting it to the constraints and criteria of money. Thus the human is reduced to the economic, behavior to self-interest, success to productivity, public life to a marketplace—and of course, art to investment and advertising, museums to shopping malls, and literature to best-selling merchandise. (The market equivalent of Twain's "classic" is today's "best-seller" that is hyped into being the most bought but least read book of its time.)

In contrast, when the Metropolitan Museum in New York was dedicated in 1880, trustee Joseph C. Choate pointed his audience in a very different direction. "Think of it, ye millionaires of many markets," he told his audience of industrialists and financiers, "what glory may yet be yours." If you convert your railroad shares and mining stocks into the canvases of old masters, he exhorted them, you will help adorn these walls for centuries. "The rage is to hunt the philosopher's stone, to convert all baser things into gold, which is but dross; but ours is the higher ambition to convert your useless gold into things of living beauty that shall be a joy to a whole people for a thousand years."

Whatever the motivation, such high-minded sentiments are rare in an era schooled in the consumer lifestyle of ceaselessly buying, using, and discarding. Regardless of its truth, meaning, history, and value, anything and everything can be grist for the mill of the all-consuming market. Late nineteenth-century citizens were commonly called to be custodians of culture. But we today—all of us, not simply the rich—are well-trained as cannibals of culture. Our challenge, therefore, is to sustain the calling to be heirs and stewards.

The Battle of the Books

The contributors to *Invitation to the Classics* know that the job of the custodian has its own pitfalls—Ralph Waldo Emerson warned that a too-reverential study of great books would produce only great bookworms. More importantly, the powerful alternatives of the "creators" and "cannibals" represent forces that cannot be dispatched by a rhetorical wave of the wand. And the challenges facing those who desire to be stewards of the Western literary classics are greater than ever. The guide is not the place to wage the controversies or seek to settle the outcome. But candor demands that we at least identify the main obstacles.

One obstacle to a proper appreciation of the classics is the centuries-old strain of cultural philistinism within the community of faith itself. Philistinism rejects the importance of literature and art and instead glories in an unadorned irrationality of faith. The influential nineteenth-century evangelist Charles Grandison Finney displayed this disdainful attitude. Though well-educated, he still said, "I cannot believe that a person who has ever known the love of God can relish a secular novel. . . . Let me visit your chamber, your parlor, or wherever you keep your books. What is here? Byron, Scott, Shakespeare and a host of triflers and blasphemers of God."

Such philistinism stands in direct contrast to the classicism that helped develop Christian culture in the West. The apostle Paul, for example, was thoroughly trained in classical languages, literature, and philosophy. He always addressed the classical pagan world but never trimmed his message to fit its mold. Nor was he an early Christian "know-nothing."

In the church, however, a misguided philistinism has flourished because most Christians lack a Christian aesthetic, an agreed Christ-centered philosophy of the arts. Christians therefore tend to swing between two extremes—puritanically dismissing the arts as irreligious or seeking to exploit them as a means of promoting faith and morals. In the latter case the church's temptation is then to support religious painters and writers whose work more closely resembles propaganda than true art. This false art is designed to sway the heart and mind to predetermined ideas rather than to inspired truth.

But ironically, Dorothy Sayers argues, the Christian faith provides a key to understanding human creativity that far surpasses the classical understandings of art, such as those of Plato and Aristotle. The Greek saw art as *techne*—manufactured products meant only to teach or entertain. The Christian, in contrast, should see the connection between human creation and divine creativity—between the artist's inspiration and God's divine revelation as Creator, Word, and Spirit. The threefold act of creation—experiencing, expressing, and recognizing—is not only a single, indivisible act of the creative human mind but directly reflects the divine Creator's trinitarian nature. This view provides a welcome alternative to the unattractive options—viewing art as either entertainment or indoctrination.

A second obstacle to a proper appreciation of the classics is the movements within the Western world that assault the very notion of the classics and their entire tradition. Currently the most prominent example is "the battle of the books" that embroils many universities—with its sometimes serious, sometimes shallow but noisy attacks on the Western "canon" of classics. The movement is commendable for drawing attention to neglected writers and traditions, but, paradoxically, it overlooks the diversity of the traditions within the West as well as the West's characteristic curiosity about traditions outside itself. It was epitomized for many by the infamous rallying cry at Stanford University, "Hey, hey, Ho, ho! Western culture's got to go!"

The relentless drive toward a specialized life is a third reason why the defense of the classics is difficult in the modern world. In the eighteenth and nineteenth centuries, many common people in America had a knowledge of the Bible, Shakespeare, and Italian opera that people today would view as the preserve of the theologian, the literary scholar, and the musicologist. There was almost no cultural elite, especially when it came to reading. In 1772, Jacob Duché wrote of the American colonies, "The poorest laborer upon the shores of the Delaware thinks himself entitled to deliver his sentiment on matters of religion or politics with as much freedom as the gentle man or scholar. . . . Such is the prevailing taste for books of every kind, that almost every man is a reader."

But this old "high average" has gone and a "battle between the brows" (highbrow, lowbrow, and middlebrow) has broken out. At one end, everyday knowledge has sunk far below the old high average—the so-called "dumbing down" of thinking. Everyday knowledge is now determined more by television, advertising, and news headlines than by literary pursuits. At the other end, today's elite knowledge, requiring multiple academic degrees, is far above the old high average—because it is so specialized. Technical jargon renders various fields uninteresting and inaccessible to the lay reader, creating a world where only other specialists can understand specialized knowledge. A chasm is opened between experts and ordinary people— and experts in one specialty are automatically lay people in the field next door. This in turn leads to a myth of expertise and professionalism that creates a disabling dependency for anyone but the professional, whether rocket scientist, trial attorney—or writer, artist, and critic. In literature, the end is the disastrous idea that the classics are only for scholars.

A fourth obstacle to appreciating the classics is our modern preoccupation with the present at the expense of the past. As television superjournalist Bill Moyers lamented, "We Americans seem to know everything about the last twenty-four hours but very little of the past sixty centuries or the last sixty years." Television is biased against memory and history with its very pace and style—the ceaseless, breathless flow of the *now* renders viewers incapable of remembering.

This bias against history is representative of the modern world as a whole. With our passion for progress, for choice and change, for relevance, for the newer-the-truer and the latest-is-the-greatest, the past—by definition—is fated to be outmoded, irrelevant, and out-of-date. The twentieth century, as G. K. Chesterton observed at its beginning, is "marked by a special cultivation of the romance of the future." The result is frankly odd: "The modern man no longer preserves the memoirs of his great-grandfather; but he is engaged in writing a detailed and authoritative biography of his great-grandson."

A fifth obstacle to a proper appreciation of the classics lies in the modern tendency to abuse rather than use the past. Remembering has always been one of the most important modes of human thinking; it is a key to identity, faith, wisdom, renewal, and the dynamic of a living tradition. Remembering, therefore, is much more than mental recall. It makes the difference between tradition as the living faith of the dead and traditionalism as the dead faith of the living.

Understood this way, remembering is never nostalgia, which is a symptom of the sickness of homelessness. Nor must it be confused with such other modern abuses of the past as tourism and historical theme parks, which seek access to the past without allowing the tradition of the past to exercise authority over the present. When the past becomes reduced to products and images by entertaining, advertising, and selling, we know about the past, yet are not a part of it. We can be cut off from our tradition by things that claim to put us in touch with our past.

The Best Argument
for the Classics Is the Classics

We could argue for the classics on many grounds. Education, for example, is a primary beneficiary of the classics. As Chesterton noted, tradition is essential to "the one eternal education; to be sure enough that something is true that you dare tell it to a child. . . . Obviously it ought to be the oldest things that are put to the youngest people; the assured and experienced truths that are put first to the baby."

Another argument for the classics could be the corrective wisdom that flows out of the past. Every age has its own outlook, talent at seeing certain truths, and proneness toward particular mistakes. As C. S. Lewis wrote, "we all, therefore, need the books that will correct the characteristic mistakes of our own period. And that means the old books. . . . The only palliative is to keep the clean sea breeze of the centuries blowing through our minds, and this can be done only by reading old books." His concluding advice was practical: "It is a good rule, after reading a new book, never to allow yourself another new one till you have read an old one in between. If that is too much for you, you should at least read one old one to every three new ones.

But rather than rely on such arguments or defend a certain canon, we offer a straightforward statement (in the next essay) of what is a classic, why we should read the classics, and how we should set about reading them. We do not seek to resolve the controversies or the works themselves would get lost in the battle over the books. Similarly, we do not seek to prove the value of the classics prior to reading them. Their value will be proved in the reading.

In short, *Invitation to the Classics* assumes that the best argument for the classics *is* the classics themselves. If the great classics of Western imagination and ideas are really what we believe them to be—and what they have shown themselves to be—they have their own authority and speak best for themselves. When this happens they will always outlast their critics, open the eyes of those unfamiliar with them, surprise the blasé, delight the enthusiast, and lead generation after generation to fresh levels of discovery and appreciation.

—Os Guinness

The Importance of the Classics

*S*ometime back, when I was a young instructor teaching *Hamlet* to a freshman class, a few lines from the play struck me with peculiar force: "Not a whit; we defy augury," Hamlet proclaims in response to his friend Horatio, who has cautioned him to call off a coming duel. Hamlet refuses and proceeds to make a rather strong profession of faith: "There is special providence in the fall of a sparrow," he declares. "If it be now, 'tis not to come; if it be not to come, it will be now. If it be not now, yet it will come. The readiness is all."

This mention of providence struck me as being in marked contrast with Hamlet's earlier anguished irony. It took on the aura of something momentous. What did Shakespeare intend his readers to think of so radical a turnabout? Did it not in fact imply that the author himself saw and understood the change wrought in Hamlet by faith? Yet my graduate professors and other scholarly authorities considered Shakespeare a nonbeliever—almost, it would seem, a freethinker. They agreed that he was a practical man, not in any sense an idealist. Hadn't his plays been composed for money, not for art? Certainly he could not have intended by them anything profound. Granted, they allowed, he was a genius: his comedies, though light bits of froth, were charming; his tragedies, though nihilistic, were powerful. And as for his own outlook on life, most of them assumed, it was implied most cogently in King Lear, in the bitter speech of blinded old Gloucester:

> As flies to wanton boys are we to the gods;
> They kill us for their sport.

But in *Hamlet* I saw a new key to Shakespeare's work. Hamlet's quest for faith roused in me a kindred feeling. I remember going over the young prince's soliloquies, tracing the movement from his despairing "Oh that this too, too solid flesh would melt" to his meditative "To be or not to be," and on to his affirmative "There's a divinity that shapes our ends, rough-hew them how we will."

At this moment I was standing at a crossroads. The Christian belief in which I had been reared had been seriously damaged during my college years and finally demolished—ironically—by a required course in religion that had brought about my complete capitulation. None of the biblical sources could be considered reliable, the experts of the day argued. And for me, once the seeds of doubt had been sown, the entire gospel was called in question. The account was surely a fable, enlarged and considerably embellished by a few followers—for what motive, it was hard to say. But belief in so strange and mysterious a tale asked for more credulousness than I was willing to grant. By the time I entered graduate school I had put aside the entire question of faith. But then, when reading *Hamlet* to my class, I saw incontestable evidence that Shakespeare—or his chief protagonist, at least—had come to rely on divine power.

I pored over *Hamlet* several times during the ensuing months, each time finding further evidence of Shakespeare's spiritual outlook. And gradually it became apparent that his perspective was not simply spiritual, but overtly Christian. Sacrificial love was evident everywhere in his dramas. *Grace* was one of his key words; *evil* was its darker counterpart. His comedies in particular were virtual illustrations of themes and passages from Scripture. By today, of course, several scholars have come to acknowledge and even explore Shakespeare's Christian faith; but at that time my discovery seemed monumental. It meant recognizing the secularism of our day and discerning the bias of most scholars. And it started me on the process of reading all serious literature more closely.

It was a year later, in teaching Dostoyevsky's *The Brothers Karamazov,* that I rediscovered Christ in his fullness—and came to see the urgency of his teachings. The resulting protracted study of Scripture and theology eventually led to my overt profession of faith.

Before literature came to my aid, I had perused theology in vain. Even the Bible was unconvincing. Not until a literary work of art awakened my imaginative faculties could the possibility of a larger context than reason alone engage my mind. I had been expecting logical proof of something one was intended to recognize. What was needed was a way of seeing. I had to be transformed in the way that literature transforms—by story, image, symbol—before I could *see* the simple truths of the gospel.

Above all else this seems to me the chief value of what we call the classics: they summon us to belief. They seize our imaginations and make us *commit ourselves to the self-evident,* which we have forgotten how to recognize. Four centuries of rationalism have led us to expect empirical evidence and logical coherence for any proposition. Even for the things ordinarily considered certain, we moderns require proof. In this state of abstraction, we are cut off from the fullness of reality. Something has to reach into our hearts and impel us toward recognition.

Though there are other media for this impulsion, one of the most effective is what the ancients called poetry, meaning literature in general. Poetry is language used primarily to express universals; as Aristotle wrote, poetry is truer than history. Cut loose from the sagas of personality and the prescriptions of factuality, poetry can witness to the timeless and immortal. It elevates our consciousness so that we learn how to exercise discernment. And, as Hamlet declared, "the readi-

ness is all." If we are restored to ourselves and made ready, then we can begin to establish the kingdom of Christ in our own lives and in those we touch.

How Do We Value the Masterworks?

We don't often wish to make so grand a claim for the power of the great books, however, being more likely to defend them as desirable rather than necessary. We let ourselves be persuaded that their chief value lies in their capacity to enculturate. Admittedly, the ability to "read" the society we live in—to interpret the web of meanings in which we all find ourselves enmeshed—is not a minor advantage.

Over the centuries, the books known as the classics have formed intricate bonds among men and women who have grown up within the radius of a civilization that began to flower nearly three thousand years ago. Young people have understood the ideals of their society through the classics and have come to love something intangible: the quest for wisdom and insight, generated in ancient Greece and Rome. What Plato called the eros of the beautiful and Virgil considered an amor for humane virtues were changed in their encounter with the caritas of the gospel and spread outward through Europe and the New World, transforming human imaginations.

There is more to it, however, than feeling at ease with one's fellows. It is not simply a matter of understanding the society in which we live, even though such comprehension is a distinct benefit. More importantly, from these great books society has gained its ideas of justice and freedom; from them it has shaped its concept of honor and beauty. And although the content of this body of writings alters almost imperceptibly as epochs come and go, its core remains surprisingly constant. For centuries the Greco-Roman classics have been taught in Europe and the New World on an equal basis with Shakespeare and the Bible. Fully as much as the Book of Exodus and *Pilgrim's Progress,* the *Iliad* and the *Aeneid* have stood in Western minds as model accounts of heroism. These and other masterworks have been so intricately woven into the fabric of daily life as to provide a kind of second nature not only for political and intellectual leaders but for ordinary citizens who by their sense and virtue determine the character of social order.

Even so, for all their cultural value, the classics function not simply as great books but as something closer to spiritual exercises. It is not enough for them to be known *about*; they need to be truly *known* in the fullness of their intimacy. Taken in and savored, they become a way of understanding oneself in relation to larger powers of the human soul. But as William Butler Yeats has written: "because the divine life wars upon our outer life, and must needs change its weapons and its movements as we change ours, inspiration has come to them [the poets] in beautiful startling shapes." The great books speak to us of honor and love and sacrifice; but they do not always speak in familiar phrases. They do not tell us what we already know. Transcending current opinion and fad, through symbol and metaphor they reveal a clear and uncluttered access to the realities that determine our lives.

But too often in our day, the very term classics is suspect. The classics tend to be regarded as symbols of elitist culture rather than as the vital and broadly democratic forces that they are. Surrounded by an aura of adulation on one hand and apathy if not frank disapproval on the other, they are likely to repel rather than attract the intelligent reader. Surely we ought not approach them as a "canon" of prescribed writings, as sacred and unchangeable as Holy Scripture. Neither should they be thought of as antiques, to be carefully guarded in locked shelves.

The classics are no canon, designated by either divine edict or human experts, nor are they fragile untouchables. They are the formed thought and imagination of humanity, tested over time, altering their perspective and sometimes their entire meaning with every new work that challenges their stature and every new reader courageous enough to wrestle with their inexhaustible vitality. They occupy their position because of the persistence and fidelity of readers. They have no life except in their read-ers; in them, they are living presences that come to be known from the inside—with the heart as well as the head.

What Is a Classic?

How do we recognize a classic? Tradition has held that classics are works of a very high order that touch on matters of immense importance. They are not mere skilled works of whatever category; they establish a category of their own. In fact, when we examine those works that readers have agreed upon as classics, we find a surprisingly constant set of characteristics:

1. The classics not only exhibit distinguished style, fine artistry, and keen intellect but create whole universes of imagination and thought.
2. They portray life as complex and many-sided, depicting both negative and positive aspects of human character in the process of discovering and testing enduring virtues.

Plato and his pupils, from a mosaic at Pompeii, Italy.

3. They have a transforming effect on the reader's self-understanding.
4. They invite and survive frequent rereadings.
5. They adapt themselves to various times and places and provide a sense of the shared life of humanity.
6. They are considered classics by a sufficiently large number of people, establishing themselves with common readers as well as qualified authorities.
7. And, finally, their appeal endures over wide reaches of time.

Given the rigor of such standards, to call a recent work a classic would seem something of a prediction and a wager. The prediction is that the book so designated is of sufficient weight to take its place in the dialogue with other classics. The wager is that a large number of readers will find it important enough to keep alive. Strictly speaking, as we have indicated, there is no canon of great works, no set number of privileged texts. People themselves authorize the classics. And yet it is not by mere popular taste—by the best-seller list— that they are established. True, books are kept alive by readers—discriminating, thoughtful readers who will not let a chosen book die but manage to keep it in the public eye. They recommend it to their friends, bring it into the educational curriculum, install it in institutional libraries, order it in bookstores, display it on their own shelves, read it to their children. But something more mysterious makes a work an integral part of the body of classics, however well-loved it may be. It must fit into the preexisting body of works, effecting what T. S. Eliot has described as an alteration of "the whole existing order." The past, he maintains, is "altered by the present as much as the present [is] directed by the past."

The body of these masterworks thus shifts and changes constantly in the course of time. Plato, who was passed over in the late medieval world in favor of his disciple Aristotle, became a dominant philosopher in the Renaissance; Thomas Aquinas, the learned founder of Scholasticism, has been in

modern times largely relegated to seminaries; Francis Bacon has declined to the role of a minor eccentric. Even Shakespeare, now often described as the world's greatest poet, has not always been considered a classic author; the eighteenth century decried his lack of taste and rewrote several of his plays. John Donne's lyrics lay neglected for two centuries before the twentieth century found in him a kindred troubled soul. John Milton's *Paradise Lost* was almost dethroned in the 1930s and 1940s, but its author's position is more secure now than before. Alexander Pope, whose greatness as poet was unchallenged in the eighteenth century, has been in the twentieth virtually deposed. Herman Melville's *Moby Dick* encountered several generations of readers who dismissed the novel entirely; not until the 1920s did it suddenly attain its full status in the curriculum. Virgil's *Aeneid* seems, regrettably, to be losing some of its position in recent times. But the *Iliad* and the *Odyssey* hold their foremost place as firmly as when Plato cited Homer nearly twenty-five hundred years ago, or when, at the turn of the last century, most college students read them in the Greek.

To place a contemporary writing among the classics, then, is to make a bold conjecture. That conjecture is based on the judgment of a sufficiently large body of readers in current society who consider the work a masterpiece. But the book in question has to be worth their endorsement. All the popular acclaim in the world will not make a classic of a mediocre text.

The masterpieces are not confined to their own peoples or to their own epochs. The organic order of literature that makes up the Western tradition exists essentially in a timeless realm, by which we mean a kind of communal memory. We could argue that, since the real existence of masterpieces is beyond time, we should not have to wait for time to make its judgment on newcomers. A recently published work might be seen by perceptive readers to take its place among its predecessors and to converse amicably with them. The sensitive reader should be able to judge.

And remarkably enough, a surprising degree of agreement exists among literary people about twentieth-century classics. The editorial consultants for this volume all expressed a strong agreement about the inclusion of such writers as Eliot, Yeats, Frost, Joyce, Faulkner, Solzhenitsyn, and numerous other recent authors whose ideas and images have already entered into that communally shared web we call culture.

Why Read the Great Books?

Why is it necessary for everyone to read the classics? Shouldn't only specialists spend their time on these texts, with other people devoting their efforts to particular interests of their own? Actually, it is precisely because these works are intended for *all* that they have become classics. They have been tried and tested and deemed valuable for the general culture—the way in which people live their lives. They have been found to enhance and elevate the consciousness of all sorts and conditions of people who study them, to lift their readers out of narrowness or provincialism into a wider vision of humanity. Further, they guard the truths of the human heart from the faddish half-truths of the day by straightening the mind and imagination and enabling their readers to judge for themselves. In a word, they lead those who will follow into a perception of the fullness and complexity of reality.

But why in particular should followers of Christ be interested in the classics? Is Scripture not sufficient in itself for all occasions? What interest do Christians have in the propagation of the masterworks? The answer is as I indicated at the beginning of this essay: Many of us in the contemporary world have been misled by the secularism of our epoch; we expect proof if we are to believe in the existence of a spiritual order. Our dry, reductionist reason leads us astray, so that we harden our hearts against the presence of the holy. Something apart from family or church must act as mediator, to restore our full humanity, to endow us with the imagi-

nation and the heart to believe. My serious encounter with Shakespeare and then with all the riches of the classics enabled me to see the splendor of him who is at the center of the gospels. In a time when our current culture is increasingly secular in its aims, one of the most important resources Christians possess is this large treasure trove of works that have already been assimilated by readers and commentators in the nearly two thousand years of Western Christendom.

How to Read a Classic

Classics are not always easy to read. Some may not be immediately entertaining; yet when properly read they all offer deeply enjoyable experiences. To find this joy, one must persist in the reading process, not stopping inordinately to look up words, but assuming meaning from context. Aristotle tells us that the artist "imitates an action" in his making of a work; and by the word *action* he means not plot but an interior movement of the soul. Hence it is not so much facts and information that one derives from reading a great book as it is an underlying and sustaining insight—which is always a new and profound interpretation of life.

Classics reach out to involve the reader in the process of interpretation, so that the experience becomes authentic. We have to "listen as a three-year child," to use Coleridge's line from *The Rime of the Ancient Mariner*. Otherwise, if we attempt from the beginning to impose our own opinions on what we read, we miss the wisdom it has to offer. Interpretation and evaluation should come after a full reading of the work—after we too have learned enough from the journey to interpret the landscape.

One should read a classic with pencil in hand. Such a work is so dense and complex as to require its readers to participate in the unfolding of its thought. The very act of underlining and annotating serves to engage the reader in a conversation with the text. And afterwards, when the linear experience of reading is complete, one can easily scan back over the marked pages—and thereby fix their pertinent ideas firmly in the mind. This retrospection, in fact, is a necessity if one is to grasp these writings in any depth. The act of putting the parts together leads to contemplation and hence to a deeper experience of the work.

When reading, one needs to remember that poets and philosophers are not prescribing courses of action but exploring aspects of existence. To the extent that they are significant writers, they are letting us know that certain inexorable laws exist in the human makeup—and in the universe—and that we'd better be aware of them. A classic does not dispute or sermonize; Tolstoy, for instance, neither exculpates or condemns his heroine in *Anna Karenina;* instead he shows his readers the tragic effects of a life lived entirely for self-fulfillment.

One should come to such works, then, with what Coleridge has called a "willing suspension of disbelief," a susceptibility to being led into a mental experience that will prove, in the end, enlightening. A classic beckons to thought, not action. Hence readers are free from the pressures of manipulation or propaganda in their approach to the great books; they are introduced to a realm above the ordinary hurly-burly of life, where they can reflect on their own insights and come to some sense of the powers of the mind and heart.

The classics constitute an almost infallible process for awakening the soul to its full stature. In coming to know a classic, one has made a friend for life. It can be recalled to the mind and "read" all over again in the imagination. And actually perusing the text anew provides a joy that increases with time. These marvelous works stand many rereadings without losing their force. In fact, they almost demand rereading, as a Beethoven symphony demands replaying. We never say of a musical masterpiece, "Oh I've heard that!" Instead, we hunger to hear it again to take in once more, with new feeling and insight, its long-familiar strains.

And, as I found with *Hamlet* on that blessed day some forty years ago, I couldn't really say I'd *read* it before in quite that light. I've read it every year since, as I've read the *Iliad* and *Oedipus Rex,* the *Divine Comedy,* and other classics. And in the fresh encounter with old acquaintances, with each reading I find a clearer revelation of him whom St. Augustine addressed when he asked, "As You fill all things, do You fill them with Your whole self, or, since all things cannot contain You wholly, do they contain part of You? . . . or are You wholly everywhere while nothing altogether contains You?"

—Louise Cowan

The "Classics" Are Not the "Canon"

*I*n the spring of 1997, NBC broadcast a contemporary adaptation of Homer's *Odyssey*. In a preview of the program, a critic for the *New York Times* concluded his largely favorable review with a simple summary of the Greek warrior's twenty-year journey that finally brings him home: "Moral: There's no place like home. Classics are not necessarily complicated."

With this tongue-in-cheek conclusion, the commentator nicely reminded his readers of an important reason why the classics have endured. They are great stories, often brought to life with vivid narratives and splendid metaphors. For all that we understandably make of them, the classics are, after all, riveting accounts of mothers and daughters, fathers and sons, and husbands and wives; they tell of the heights of human aspiration for God and the good and of the depths of human misery and depravity. "Man is broad," says a character in Fyodor Dostoyevsky's classic novel, *The Brothers Karamazov*. "Here the devil is struggling with God, and the battlefield is the human heart." Although there is endless complexity in the classics and in their influence over culture, they are not necessarily complicated because they deal in the most fundamental human realities in God's world.

A Canon for the Canonless

In spite of their enduring power and widespread appeal, in recent years the classics have been the subject of much controversy. They have been accused of everything from the creation of oppressive patriarchy to the instigation of racist actions and genocidal impulses. Some see the classics as trivial; others view them as hopelessly exclusive; still others question the very idea of distinguishing between supposedly classic works and all other forms of human creation.

In many instances, these disputes about the nature and worth of the classics are needlessly confused by a failure to distinguish between the question of the classic and the question of the canon. As the contemporary literary scholar Joel Weinsheimer points out, we have come to treat the classic and the canon as though these two very different things were the same. It is a mistake to do so, because although the canonical and the classical have a number of things in common, the differences between them are real and essential to understanding the classics properly.

According to the *Oxford English Dictionary*, the term *canon* means "any collection or list of sacred works accepted as genuine." The term, of course, has its roots in the history of the Christian church, for it named the body of diverse works that came to make up the Old and New Testaments of the Christian Scriptures. For almost two thousand years, whether in Eastern Orthodoxy, Roman Catholicism, or the many branches of Protestantism, the scriptural canon was a closed body of books considered to be inspired by God, revelatory, and authoritative.

Only in the nineteenth century did the idea of a canon of literary works emerge in a way to supplant the ancient biblical model. Especially in the second half of that century, there arose a body of criticism that argued in favor of the idea of poetry, drama, and fiction serving as a form of "secular scripture"—a canon for the canonless in a post-Christian world. In a time when orthodox faith and practice seemed to be losing their authoritative hold over the minds of many people, some thought that a literary canon might replace the discredited biblical canon.

The Victorian poet and man of letters Matthew Arnold was a pivotal figure in the move for literary works to assume such canonical status. In his famous formulation, we in the modern world must be about the business of "acquainting ourselves with the best that has been thought and said in the world."

For almost a century, Arnold's ideal held sway over the study of literature in the English speaking world, as scholars and publishers promoted the idea of a fixed canon of great books. In the last decades of the twentieth century, however, that idea was subjected to a withering critique. Under the influence of what has been called the "hermeneutics of suspicion," postmodern theories of interpretation questioned the claims made on behalf of the canon to truth and universal value. Because the canon largely contained works written by white males in the Western tradition, it was frequently portrayed as an instrument of oppression and exclusion. Rather than revealing truth and universal values, it was held, the canon concealed the relations by means of which men controlled women, the white race dominated people of color, and the industrialized West exploited the third world.

Both the attackers and defenders of the canon have often confused the question of the classic and the canon. Postmodern critics have been prone to see all works of literature as texts to be decoded for their concealed messages of power, while traditionalists have too often reacted as though any criticism of the traditional canon was an assault upon the very foundations of truth, rationality, and virtue. To a certain extent the confusion of both sides is understandable, for some of the works in the literary canon celebrated by Arnold and his cultural descendants were ones that we would call classics. They included the epics of Homer and Greek tragedy, Virgil's *Aeneid* and the Latin poets, as well as such undisputed monuments of English literature as Chaucer's *Canterbury Tales*, Milton's *Paradise Lost*, and certain of Shakespeare's plays. But the canon as the modern literary establishment defined it also included works that we no longer think of as classics, because their lasting significance has come into question.

Passing Fashions, Enduring Foundations

The interesting fact has been noted that as a noun *canon* is a collective term for a group of works but that no word exists in English to designate a single canonical poem, play, or novel. At the same time, *classic* as a noun applied only to individual works, and we have no word for the collective group of works made up by individual classics. From this curious verbal fact, a literary critic draws the conclusion that a canon is plural but determinate; that is, literary canons include a number of works but are inherently exclusionary. The classic, by contrast, is essentially singular, but the number of classics is potentially unlimited. By its very nature, the classic is a more inclusive and flexible concept than the canon.

In the canon, any number of works go in and out of fashion with each passing generation, while classics endure from age to age. Because it is so readily affected by shifts in judgment, taste, and values, the canon constantly undergoes realignment. Over the last several decades, for instance, a heightened sensitivity to historical exclusion and injustice has served to bring a number of hitherto neglected works by women and minorities into the canon. To make room for these new additions, other works once considered canonical lose their standing and are dropped from the canon. The poetry of a number of mid-nineteenth-century New England men, for example, has all but disappeared from the anthologies that catalogue the canon. Longfellow, Lowell, and Whittier are out, and Phyllis Wheatly, Frederick Douglass, and Toni Morrison are in.

The case is very different with the classic. It is inconceivable that at any time in the future Homer's *Odyssey,* Dante's *Divine Comedy,* or the tragedies of Shakespeare will fall completely out of favor and no longer be read, taught, or imitated. They are too much a part of history ever to be removed. The role of the classics in the formation of modern culture is so foundational that in a very real sense, we know the classics before we read them. Their values, visions, stories, and metaphors have shaped our culture and

The Pardoner, from Chaucer's *Canterbury Tales:* engraving after a manuscript in the University Library, Cambridge.

our self-understanding in myriad ways that are undeniable but impossible to quantify.

As a case in point, we might consider the example of one of the key classical genres, the epic. Homer's *Iliad* and *Odyssey* and Virgil's *Aeneid* stand unarguably as the greatest of the classical epic narratives in the Western tradition. And though written in pagan cultures, these works have had an incalculable influence on the history of the Christian church and Christian culture. In the first centuries of the Christian era, Homer and Virgil shaped Christian reflection in complex ways, and in later centuries, they directly influenced some of the greatest enduring works of Christian culture. Dante's *Divine Comedy,* Milton's *Paradise Lost,* and Wordsworth's *The Prelude,* to name but a few, are unimaginable without the guiding influence of Homer and Virgil. At the heart of the classic's enduring power is its irreplaceable role in shaping the history of culture.

If the classic were only important as a general influence on culture, it might be of little more than academic concern. What makes the classic vitally alive is its power to speak directly to us across the span of centuries. Because it comes down to us from a distant time and unfamiliar culture, the classic always has some qual-

ity of strangeness; yet because it has shaped so significantly the culture we inhabit, it also has a ring of the familiar. The German philosopher Hans Georg Gadamer argues that the classic "speaks in such a way that it is not a statement about what is past . . . rather, it says something to the present as if it were said specifically to it."

Questions for Each of Us

One of the classic's greatest powers is its ability to question us and our most cherished values— to "talk back" to us when we interrogate. The nineteenth-century German philosopher G. W. F. Hegel spoke of the classic as "a question, an address to the responsive breast, a call to the mind and the spirit." Like the Scriptures, the classic makes a claim upon us to which we must respond. It challenges our understanding of God, our values, and our very sense of ourselves.

The Bible, especially the Old Testament, contains many accounts of God's questioning of humanity. In fact, the very first time God speaks to Adam and Even after the fall, he addresses them with questions: "Where are you? Have you eaten from the tree of which I commanded you not to eat? What is this that you have done?" By means of questions, God calls us to account and makes us responsible for the thoughts of our minds, the deeds of our hands, and the inclinations of our hearts.

In a similar way, when we read a classic we are not simply critics who ask questions of the text; we are also the subject of the work's own scrutiny as it requires us to review our deepest beliefs. The Christian student of culture would never wish to confuse the power of the classic with the authority of the Scriptures. The Bible is the Word of God while the greatest classics are only supreme embodiments of human insight. Nevertheless, there is something like a divine weight to the questions that the clas-

sics ask of our lives. The writer of the letter to the Hebrews in the New Testament says that "the word of God is living and active, sharper than any two-edged sword, piercing until it divides soul from spirit, joints from marrow; it is able to judge the thoughts and intentions of the heart" (NRSV).

In an age such as ours, when cynicism and suspicion can make it difficult for us to take seriously anything that fails to meet our own standards or to gratify our desires, the great classics of literature have a unique power to speak to us of our potential and our peril. For that, we should be ever grateful.

—Roger Lundin

HOMER

The Iliad and *The Odyssey*
c. 750 B.C.

he *Iliad* and the *Odyssey*, Homer's two magnificent epics, far exceed all but a handful of literary works of the past two thousand years. They are prized for their beauty of conception, verbal subtlety and consistency, soaring imaginative power, and the drama of their depiction of human existence. While recognizing the historical importance of these epic poems, readers cannot help feeling the serene and generous surge of their artistic creativity. In many ways the Western literary tradition is a series of astonished encounters with the greatness of Homer.

The Composition Controversy

Homer probably lived in the eighth century B.C. and composed the *Iliad* near the middle of that century, the *Odyssey* somewhat later—*composed,* but perhaps did not *write* the poems. Many scholars now assume that these epics were originally oral compositions. One widely accepted theory holds that they were composed orally by Homer, then memorized and

Homer (eighth century B.C.); Roman copy of a Greek bust of second century B.C.

passed on with slight changes—perhaps for centuries—until they were finally written down in their present form.

Some scholars question whether an historical "Homer" ever existed, suggesting several poets who successively contributed to the Homeric poems. It is far more likely, however, that a single poet of genius whose name the tradition accepts as Homer composed the poems. If so, he combined the resources of a vital oral tradition with his visionary recognition of the artistic potential in the new way of preserving language in

writing. Perhaps, like the blind John MILTON who dictated *Paradise Lost* to his daughters, Homer did not actually do the writing himself. Whatever the origin, the poems unquestionably have the coherence of texts rather than of transcribed performances. At the same time, they retain the speed and engaging clarity of spoken language.

The Trojan War

The perennially fresh appeal of the *Iliad* and the *Odyssey*, generation after generation for the past twenty-seven centuries, reflects the poet's ability to uncover the enduring conflicts of human existence. For Homer, the definitive condition of life is not peace but battle.

Homer sets his poems in the time of the Trojan War, which historically was about 1200 B.C. The *Iliad* takes place in the last year of the Greek siege of Troy. The *Odyssey* occurs ten years after the successful but distressing completion of the siege, when Odysseus, a Greek leader, is still trying to return to his wife and home.

There have been countless wars in human history, but Homer makes the Trojan War stand for them all—those already long past in his day and those still to come for our children's children. In attempting to explain Homer's universality, we could mention honor, courage, wrath, love, friendship, grief, vengeance, forgiveness, fidelity, endurance; but these words together do not seize the imagination so much as one name: Helen. The city of Troy uneasily and unjustly harbored this half-divine, imponderable beauty, so dangerous to those who fought for her.

Not all Trojans were like Paris, who caused the war by stealing Helen from her husband, Menelaus, king of Sparta. Most of the Trojans actually hated Paris and repudiated his deed. Their great representative figure, Hector, finds himself committed to the defense of an injustice when Paris refuses to give Helen back. But Hector also fights justly, since the Greeks, who have assembled a vast host to reclaim Helen, now threaten his own parents, wife, and son.

In their long siege of Troy, the Greeks, who set out to punish a crime against the inviolability of marriage, forget the pieties of home. They themselves are gradually transformed into becoming the violators. Those who were outraged by the breach of Menelaus's marriage in turn ravage households, slaughter children, and enslave a multitude of other wives as they conquer Troy. Through Homer's art we encounter the inescapable reality of paradox in human experience.

The *Iliad:* Mortality and the Weight of Glory

At the opening of the *Iliad,* the original selfish offender, Paris, is replaced in the reader's imagination by Hector, the model Trojan. Similarly the originally righteous Greek defenders of Helen slowly fade from prominence as the besieged forces concentrate on the son of Peleus and the goddess Thetis—Achilles, that "most terrifying of all men." Huge, swift, immortally beautiful, he keeps the Trojans penned inside the city for years through the sheer terror of his prowess and seeming invincibility.

It is something of a scandal to sensitive readers that the most violent Greek of all is the hero of the *Iliad,* Achilles. Even more troubling, perhaps, is the action of the poem, which concerns Achilles' wrathful insistence on his personal honor at the expense of his army's welfare. When the Greek leader Agamemnon seizes the captive woman Briseis as his war-prize thereby insulting Achilles in front of the army, the infuriated Achilles withdraws from the battle. He uses his divine mother's intervention to insure that Zeus will make the Greeks lose to Hector's Trojans in his absence. Even after the Trojans press the Greeks back against their own ships and Agamemnon offers Achilles great gifts for his return, he refuses. Only the death of his close friend Patroclus at the hands of Hector brings Achilles back into the war—with a vengeance that even the Olympian gods consider excessive.

Many see in Achilles' actions either an adolescent rebellion against authority or an unforgivable pride. But Homer carefully undercuts the grounds for these objections. He presents Achilles' warlike greatness as a dangerous but beautiful extreme in the same way that Helen's beauty is an extreme.

For Achilles, honor and mortality are uniquely related. As the son of a goddess fated to bear a son greater than his father, he is des-

---

Achilles to the embassy urging him to fight:

I carry two sorts of destiny toward the day of my death.
  Either,
if I stay here and fight beside the city of the Trojans,
my return home is gone, but my glory shall be everlasting;
but if I return home to the beloved land of my fathers,
the excellence of my glory is gone, but there will be a long
  life
left for me, and my end in death will not come to me
  quickly.

—*The Iliad*
Richmond Lattimore, trans.

tined either to live a long life with no out-standing glory or to die young but win ever-lasting fame. The imperishable shining of his glory can be purchased, ironically, only by his return to battle—thus, to his death. He rejects the gifts of Agamemnon and the conventional honor that they represent precisely because such things mean nothing to a dead man.

Although gifts and pleas cannot move Achilles to return to battle and forfeit his home-coming, Hector's killing of Patroclus overrides every other consideration. Achilles accepts his own death as the price of avenging his friend. This unselfishness eventually leads him, after a period of unbearable anguish for Patroclus and inhuman brutality toward his hated enemy Hector, to return Hector's body to his father, King Priam, and so to achieve a solemn wis-dom, a kind of peace. Forgetting himself, para-doxically, brings Achilles more honor than he asked for.

The *Iliad* piercingly raises the question of what it means to be human and have to die. Homer elicits the deep intuition that death is a terrible deprivation and a metaphysical *wrong,* not a natural part of life. In this respect, the poem agrees with the biblical revelation that death is abnormal and incongruous, fol-lowing only from the sin committed by our original parents.

Achilles' longing for immortality—terrible as its consequences are for his friends, Troy, and himself—powerfully engages the fiery spiritual hunger within all human beings. In the pain of his glory, he gives some foretaste in the Greek imagination of the transfiguration of humanity brought about by Christ. Achilles, carrying into battle the divinely forged shield that cannot protect him, shows even Christians who are con-fident of the promise of heaven how to be strong enough to bear the weight of glory.

The *Odyssey:* The Enduring Good

For Achilles, glory means the loss of his home-coming; for Odysseus, returning home is pre-cisely what defines him. Achilles burns to appear as what he is, but Odysseus wins fame through his willingness to hide his plans and

Priam to Achilles, asking for the body of Hector:

Honour then the gods, Achilleus, and take pity upon me
remembering your father, yet I am still more painful;
I have gone through what no other mortal on earth has
*   gone through;*
I put my lips to the hands of the man who has killed my
*   children.*

—*The Iliad*
Richmond Lattimore, trans.

seem less than he is. A kind of trickster, the master of disguises and artful deceptions, Odysseus also is able to cleave to a single vir-tuous purpose and endure countless hardships in bringing that driving motive to a success-ful conclusion.

More accessible than the *Iliad,* the *Odyssey* is a varied book of wonders, full of fantastic and memorable incidents. Yet from the begin-ning it also centers with complete sobriety on the need to reestablish the household as the enduring human good.

Illustrated manuscript c. A.D. 300 of Homer's *Iliad,* showing a battle.

Athene with Odysseus when he first returns to Ithaca:

The goddess, gray-eyed Athene, smiled on him,
and stroked him with her hand, and took on the shape of
*   a woman*
both beautiful and tall, and well versed in glorious
*   handiworks,*
and spoke aloud to him and addressed him in winged
*   words, saying:*
"It would be a sharp one, and a stealthy one, who would
*   ever get past you*
in any contriving; even if it were a god against you.
You wretch, so devious, never weary of tricks, then you
*   would not*
even in your own country give over your ways of deceiving
and your thievish tales. They are near to you in your very
*   nature."*

—*The Odyssey*
Richmond Lattimore, trans.

Odysseus has still not returned home in the tenth year after the end of the war. In his absence, his household in Ithaca is beset with suitors for his beautiful and accomplished wife Penelope—or, more accurately, *besieged* as much as Troy ever was. Odysseus's son Telemachus grew up in Odysseus's absence and needs his father to learn who he is as a man. If Odysseus does not return soon, Penelope will be forced to relent and marry one of her suitors.

The goddess Athene is instrumental in recognizing this crucial moment. With the approval of her father Zeus, she sets Telemachus on a journey in search of his father to free Odysseus from his entrapment on the obscure island of the goddess Calypso. She also strengthens Penelope's hope with dreams and omens. Athene embodies a beautiful and imaginative cunning but also a terrible grace. Coupled with Odysseus's homecoming is the uncompromis-

ing severity of punishment for the impious suitors and the unfaithful servants.

St. AUGUSTINE wrote one of the best commentaries on the *Odyssey*'s relation to Christian life in his work *On Christian Doctrine*. Without mentioning the poem by name, he summarized its plot to illustrate the difference between use and enjoyment of this world's goods:

Suppose we were wanderers who could not live in blessedness except at home, miserable in our wandering and desiring to end it and to return to our native country. We would need vehicles for land and sea which could be used to help us to reach our homeland, which is to be enjoyed. But if the amenities of the journey and the motion of the vehicles itself delighted us, and we were led to enjoy those things which we should use, we should not wish to end our journey quickly, and, entangled in a perverse sweetness, we should be alienated from our country, whose sweetness would make us blessed.

Odysseus's long journey homeward after the war is, in effect, a symbol of his reeducation into the sweetness that makes us blessed; the suitors' deaths are retribution for their dalliance in perverse sweetness. But Odysseus's return to blessedness is not his alone: Telemachus, Penelope, and Odysseus—not to mention the faithful servants of the household—converge to rediscover and celebrate the complex reality of love. Like Odysseus's marriage bed rooted in the earth, this reality is solid and strong amid shifting appearances. It will endure.

Issues to Explore

Questions about the central character of the *Iliad* will help to draw out the poem's major themes of honor and mortality. (1) In the *Iliad,* what just claim does the army have on Achilles? (2) What roles do the other great warriors—Agamemnon, Menelaus, Nestor, Diomedes, Ajax, and Odysseus—play in the story of Achilles' wrath? (3) Does Hector represent everything ordinary (marriage, family affection, civic responsibility) that Achilles scorns? Or is he the "other self" that Achilles must reject because of his decision to avenge Patroclus? (4) What is the significance of the meeting of Achilles and Priam at the end of the poem?

The poem of Odysseus opens itself to questions from a more comic perspective. (5) In the *Odyssey*, what does it mean for Telemachus to "look for his father"? (6) Why is the reality of feminine things so much more prominent in this poem? (7) How is Penelope comparable to Helen? (8) Does Odysseus ever become "entangled in a perverse sweetness" during his voyages? (9) What is the significance of his own storytelling—and of storytelling in general—in the course of the poem? Is deceit justifiable? (10) What does it mean to refound a household and a city?

(11) Judging from her portrayal in both poems, are we to consider Helen to blame for the suffering of the war and its aftermath? (12) What is the role of the gods in the *Iliad* and the *Odyssey*? (13) Does Athene have the same relation to Achilles that she has to Odysseus?

—Glenn C. Arbery

For Further Study

The best translation of the *Iliad*—perhaps the best ever done in English—is still Richmond Lattimore's (University of Chicago, 1951). Of the *Odyssey*, many prefer Robert Fitzgerald's lively translation (Doubleday, 1961).

On Homer in general, Cedric Whitman's *Homer and the Heroic Tradition* (Harvard, 1958) is excellent. On the *Iliad*, a good starting place is Seth Schein's *The Mortal Hero* (University of California, 1984). Slightly more technical, James Redfield's *Nature and Culture* in the *Iliad* (University of Chicago, 1975) offers a profound view of Hector's place in the poem. On the *Odyssey*, George E. Dimock, *The Unity of the Odyssey* (University of Massachusetts, 1989) and Norman Austin, *Archery at the Dark of the Moon: Poetic Problems in Homer's Odyssey* (University of California, 1975) are recommended.

AESCHYLUS
The Oresteia
458 B.C.

Aeschylus (525–456 B.C.).

The *Oresteia* by Aeschylus, the father of Greek tragedy, is a trilogy of plays that is a masterpiece of the tragic form and a powerful dramatization of the human longing for the just city. The three plays are *Agamemnon,* the *Choephoroe* (The Libation Bearers), and the *Eumenides* (The Kindly Ones). Together they depict a single action: the fall of a dynastic order obsessed with revenge and the emergence of a democratic civilization searching for both justice and mercy. They constitute the only trilogy from the thirty-three surviving Greek tragedies and serve both as a glimpse of the threefold pattern of tragic action and as a myth of the birth of democracy, or what has been described as "a grand parable of progress."

The Oresteia:
The Violence of Grace

Aeschylus (525–456 B.C.) was an aristocrat, soldier, and poet. He fought at the battles of Marathon, Salamis, and Plataea and viewed those Greek victories as warnings as well as triumphs. As early as the *Persians* (472 B.C.) he portrayed the *hybris* (excessive pride) that can lead to downfall. And his succeeding tragedies continued to warn an unheeding Athens that the violence from without was also present within.

Aeschylus wrote about ninety plays, creating many of the conventions that moved the Greek festivals of Dionysus from dramatic liturgy to sacred drama. His plays are the earliest known works that use soloists from the Greek choruses and stage multiple individual parts around which the chorus moves. In a very real sense, he imagined a theater that would give place to individual characters just as the *Oresteia* depicts a world where the individual's rights could be honored by the many. Seven of his plays survive, among which *Prometheus Bound* and *Seven Against Thebes* rank with the *Oresteia* in poetic power. SOPHOCLES (c. 497–406 B.C.) and EURIPIDES (480–406 B.C.) may have written more fully dramatic works, but they did so on the shoulders of this great originator of the tragic imagination.

The *Oresteia* presents a pattern for the breadth of the tragic vision that has been described in three moments: the tragedy of the fall, the tragedy of suffering, and the tragedy of reconciliation. The first of the plays, *Agamemnon,* renders an act of vengeance on a king by his queen that brings down not only a great warrior and monarch but, with him, the kingdom of Argos. *The Libation Bearers,* the second play, tells the story of

Agamemnon's son, Orestes, who seeks revenge against his mother for his father's murder; he then takes flight to escape the Furies, who rise against him for murdering his own mother. The last play, the *Eumenides,* offers a final vision of reconciliation as Orestes flees to Athens, where the goddess Athene intervenes in a trial by jury. In the totality of the trilogy, the reader grasps both the full sweep of tragedy envisioned by Greek dramatists and the always painful and original story of the birth of democracy.

A Vision for Civilization

Most readers agree that Aeschylus was too modest when he described his work as "slices from the banquet of Homer." Certainly he incorporates in his work the fatal homecoming of Agamemnon, the king of kings who led the Greek allies in defeating the Trojans, to whom Homer refers in his two great epic poems the *Iliad* and the *Odyssey.* But the father of Greek tragedy profoundly transformed the story of Agamemnon and his family from a bloody tale of betrayal and revenge into a vision of civilization. Accordingly, the *Oresteia* surpasses the actual democratic experiment of Aeschylus's Greek contemporaries. In short, what Aeschylus gave the world in these three plays is not merely a dramatization of historical reality but an image of what a just civilization might become.

The first play takes the name of Agamemnon because it focuses on the longing of the people of Argos for their king, who has been away for more than a decade. His queen, Clytemnestra, has conspired with her lover, Aegisthus, the son of Atreus, to satisfy their mutual lust for vengeance for the separate acts of Agamemnon toward the blood-kin of each conspirator. Clytemnestra would avenge Agamemnon's sacrifice of their daughter Iphigenia to the gods in order to expedite the Greek fleets on their way to Troy. Aegisthus would avenge atrocities against his father and brother.

In the second play, *The Libation Bearers,* Agamemnon is long dead, Clytemnestra rules the city with Aegisthus, and the citizens of Argos are described as slaves and wanderers in their own city. Young Orestes, exiled from his native city and kingdom at his father's assassination, returns by orders from Apollo. He is to avenge his father's death and liberate the city from this tyranny of blood lust. What Orestes does not realize is that the ancient hags, the Furies, will rise up to demand the destruction of those who commit matricide. As Orestes himself confesses before killing his mother and Aegisthus: "Now force clash with force—right against right!" Thus the end of the second play does not resolve the conflict but rather deepens it; the issue moves from vengeance and right against wrong to the issue of justice and right against right.

Only in the *Eumenides* does the resolution reveal itself in the person of Athene and the city of Athens. Orestes flees to Athens to discover that the goddess has a more complicated and profound resolution to the conflict than he had anticipated. She proposes that a jury of Athenian citizens convene to hear the concerns and resolve the conflict between Orestes and the Furies. The jury is torn. Athene must intervene with persuasion and her own vote, granting acquittal to Orestes and honor to the Furies, transforming them from Erinyes, powers of darkness, to the Eumenides, the "kindly ones" who will bless Athens. The final vision is one of mercy based on human compassion and divine wisdom, both of which are necessary if democratic justice is to prevail.

Suffering into Truth

The conflicts and insights in these three plays echo in everyday life and throughout our reading of the Scriptures. On the most elementary

> *You wish to be called righteous rather than to act right.*
>
> —Athene from the *Eumenides*
> Richmond Lattimore, trans.

Artist's impression of a theatrical performance in ancient Greece. In front of the raised stage is the masked Chorus (from a nineteenth-century French illustration).

level, no one can deny the goodness and power of blood ties. What is more basic to the human condition than that people love their family and want to protect it? Therefore the audience can understand and sympathize with the unspeakable horror that has motivated both Clytemnestra and Aegisthus to avenge their loved ones. At the same time, the passion of Clytemnestra and the detachment of Aegisthus suggest more of a lust for vengeance than a love of justice. This vengefulness leaves the reader with the deep sense that whatever goodness exists in the family, blood ties cannot be the source of justice for all. In fact, mere blood loyalties are the root of many wars.

Let them render grace for grace.
Let love be their common will;
let them hate with single heart.
Much wrong in the world thereby is healed.

—Chorus from the *Eumenides*
Richmond Lattimore, trans.

In *The Libation Bearers,* Orestes' vindication of justice seems to be a step forward. Here at least is a young man who, responding to divine command, is caught between the contending rights of his two parents. Strictly speaking, Orestes acts justly, not glorying in his mother's death. But the reality of the situation rises up to face him. The ancient Furies remind him that killing one's own blood in the name of justice is itself a deep kind of injustice that must be avenged.

The final play is the final vision: by the mercy of fellow human beings with the aid of the goddess who is "ever near," people can each be given their honor without being given their due. Unlike the distant Apollo or the manic Furies, Athene is willing to be close to the human community when justice and love demand her intervention. And Athens is the city based on neither the blood ties of Argos nor the pure prophetic word of Delphi; rather it is a place where the divine and the human, mercy and justice, meet. The Christian hears the resonance with St. John's words that "the law was given through

Moses; grace and truth came through Jesus Christ" and feels the longing for the New Jerusalem, the city where "justice will roll down" and grace will prevail. But, anticipating the cross of Christ, the *Oresteia* warns that human beings must "suffer into truth" and that "grace comes somehow violent."

Issues to Explore

(1) The *Oresteia* makes its readers or viewers ponder the meaning of justice. The play speaks of a "spirit of revenge," frequently designated as a "curse" on the House of Atreus (Agamemnon's father, who had committed an unspeakable atrocity against his brother, Thyestes). If justice is not conceived of as simple retribution ("an eye for an eye"), then how is it to be determined? Can there be true justice without a concept of God?

(2) Apollo, the god of light and abstract principle, despises the Furies as hounds of guilt and devourers of blood. He represents one extreme, while the Furies represent another. Why is neither satisfactory for the rehabilitation of Orestes? Why must Athene, the goddess of practical wisdom, cast the final vote for Orestes? Can the Christian look on this process as symbolically representing the element of divine atonement that must be present in the redemption of the sinner?

(3) Is the transformation of the Furies believable—from dark pursuing spirits who track down the murderers of kin into the "Kindly Ones" who guard the process of reproduction and family life in the city?

—Daniel Russ

> *The* Oresteia *is a rite of passage from savagery to civilization.*
>
> —Robert Fagles

For Further Study

Two superb and readable translations of the *Oresteia* can be found. One is by Richmond Lattimore in volumes 1–3 of *Greek Tragedies,* edited by David Grene and Richmond Lattimore (University of Chicago Press, 1968). The other is Robert Fagles's translation in the Penguin Classics series, 1979). Fagles's translation includes a fine introduction, which illuminates the implications of these classic plays.

A comprehensive and clear treatment of Aeschylus and his world may be found in Herbert Weir Smyth's *Aeschylean Tragedy* (University of California Press, 1924, reprinted 1969); a good survey of critical interpretations of his work is *Aeschylus: A Collection of Critical Essays,* edited by March H. McCall (Prentice Hall, 1972). Finally, William Lynch's *Christ and Apollo* (University of Notre Dame, 1975) elucidates the distinction between the Greek worldview as understood through the Apollonic light and the Christian vision as experienced through the incarnation of Christ.

HERODOTUS

History of the Persian Wars
c. 430–425 B.C.

Herodotus (484–c. 424 B.C.).

erodotus's *History of the Persian Wars* is the first surviving Greek history, written by one of the greatest storytellers of all time. Cicero called Herodotus the "father of history" mainly because of the beguiling charm of his description of people, customs, and events throughout the ancient world. Herodotus represents an important bridge between Homer's epics in the eighth century B.C., with his emphasis on story and saga, and Thucydides' cool, rational analysis of the Peloponnesian War in the fifth century B.C.

A Traveler, Not a Fighter

We only briefly glimpse Herodotus's life in his monumental *History of the Persian Wars*. Born of a noble Greek family in 484 B.C., he was eminently qualified to write about the Persian Wars, having spent his early life in Halicarnassus on the south coast of Anatolia, which was the scene of the earlier conflicts between the Greek colonies and the Persians.

Unlike many other early writers of history, Herodotus did not par-

ticipate in the conflict at a high level. In contrast, the historians Thucydides and Polybius were generals and Xenophon was an officer and war correspondent in the later campaign against Persia. Although Herodotus showed little knowledge of military strategy, he knew the Greek side of the struggle from his homeland and through living much of his life in Athens. There he became a friend of the playwright SOPHOCLES, who addressed a poem to him.

Herodotus drew his great store

of information about other cultures in large part from his travels in Egypt, Cyrene, the Black Sea region, the Tigris-Euphrates basin, and all of Asia Minor. As he traveled he collected historical, geographical, and archeological information to include in his history. At the end of his life he joined a colony in Thurii in Southern Italy, dying there in about 424 B.C.

The History of the Persian Wars

The "Inquiry," the best translation of Herodotus's word *historia,* narrates the momentous struggle of the Greeks against the Persians, beginning with the Ionians of Asia Minor and then including all of Greece. The greatness of Herodotus's account is not rooted solely in the events of the period he covers—the late sixth and early fifth century B.C. Instead his delightful tales of life in Egypt, Arabia, Babylon, and even in Scythia render him one of the superb storytellers of all time. Sometimes he enhanced his factual accounts by adding literary elements, such as references to popular

Relief from the Royal Audience Hall of Darius I, Persepolis, ancient Persia, c. 500 B.C., showing subjects bearing gifts.

mythology. He named each of the nine books in his *History* after one of the Muses, the sister goddesses who were seen to preside over poetry, song, the arts, and science.

Book 1 begins with his statement of purpose: to present a record of the great events of the past, most particularly the war between the Greeks and the Persians. He recounts the beginning of the struggle, the abduction of women, which led to the Trojan War. The hostilities intensified when King Croesus of Lydia, who himself had subjugated the Greeks, made war on Persia with the help of the Greeks.

In describing the origins of Persian power, Herodotus reveals much about Cyrus the Great, the founder of the Persian Empire. Because of a prophecy that Cyrus would usurp his father's throne, he was left exposed on a mountain by a herdsman of the king's chief of state. But he survived because the herdsman's wife, who was childless and had just suffered a miscarriage, wanted to keep him. Ultimately, his bearing revealed his royal lineage; he fulfilled the prophecy by avenging the death of the herdsman most hideously and overthrowing his father.

Book II tells the story of how Cambyses succeeded his father, Cyrus, and invaded Egypt. The customs and religion of Egypt and Arabia come alive in Herodotus's graphic detail. Book III begins with a depiction of Cambyses' campaigns and the rise of Darius to power. It digresses to describe India and Arabia, and then parts of Darius's empire. This portion ends with the conquest of Samos and the revolt of the Babylonians. Book IV outlines an expedition against the Scythians and another against Cyrene and Libya. Passages characterizing the geography of the region and the customs of the people make up a large part of this section.

Herodotus's interests change dramatically in his last five books. No longer is he interested in great stories from the East and Africa. In Book V he tells of the Ionian revolt and the Greeks' early attempts to help their kin in Asia Minor.

When wrongs are done, the gods will surely visit men with great punishment.

—*History of the Persian Wars*
From Moses Hadas, *The Portable Greek Historians*

Book VI describes the advance of the Persians through Greece and their defeat at Marathon in 490 B.C. Ten years transpire before the Persians return. In Book VII we learn of Darius's death in the midst of his preparations to attack again. Xerxes, his successor, builds a bridge of ships across the Hellespont and a canal for the Persian fleet at the base of the peninsula of Athos. The Persians advance and defeat the Spartans in their heroic but unavailing stand at Thermopylae in 480. (Their Prince Leonidas's last message: "Stranger, tell the Spartans that we behaved as they would wish us to have behaved and are buried here.")

Book VIII gives an account of the preliminary success of the Greeks in a sea battle at Artemesium, but then describes their defeat as the Persian forces advance and destroy the Acropolis of Athens. And the final section, Book IX, describes the nearly miraculous Greek success in routing the Persians at Plataea on land and at Mycale by sea in 479. After one victory the awed Greek response was: "It is not we who have done this."

The great struggle that Herodotus depicts is important in representing the last effort of the East to overwhelm classicism—and ultimately Western civilization—until the Turks reach the gates of Vienna in the fifteenth century. The Greeks saw the Persian Wars as a struggle between Hellenism and barbarism. Because of these struggles, they realized that their fledgling culture was superior and particularly cherished the freedom and democracy that flourished immediately after the Wars in the Golden Age of Athens under Pericles.

God gives men a gleam of happiness and plunges them into ruin.

—*History of the Persian Wars*
From Moses Hadas
The Portable Greek Historians

Fact, Fiction, or Fantasy?

Herodotus should be appreciated for several important reasons. The first is the style of his narrative, which has similarities to that of the Old Testament. Both describe events directly and straightforwardly, contain few abstract nouns, and employ a relatively simple style. As in the Old Testament, Herodotus outlines historical details with little interest in their immediate causes because he believes they result from divine intervention.

A second reason to appreciate Herodotus is for his overall account of the Persian Wars and the triumph of Greece. He consulted previous historical accounts, public monuments, official Persian documents, records at Delphi, and official sources at both Sparta and Athens in assembling his history. But because he is not only a historian but a storyteller, his *History* mixes fact with near fact and fantasy. His chronology is sometimes vague and inconsistent and he greatly exaggerates the number of the Persian troops. Herodotus includes speeches that cannot have been made and encounters that cannot have taken place. But what he provides, in the end, is a history true to the spirit of the events if not always to factual details. He writes a good *story*.

A third reason for appreciation is that Herodotus represents a stage in the human attitude toward war. He comes halfway between the cruelty of HOMER's *Iliad*, however heroic, and the abhorrence of violence in EURIPIDES and VIRGIL that is the backdrop to the proclamation of peace in the gospels. Herodotus's genuine interest in other cultures reflects his insight that all human beings have nobility and worth, a necessary first step toward the universal promise of the gospel of Christ. He does not distinguish pejoratively between Greeks and barbarians—the Persian kings are as noble as the best Athenians and are as prone to *hybris* as the Greeks. In this sense Herodotus is theological: War brings intense and personal suffering; individual suffering is punishment from the gods. He still sees the heroic in war, however. He does not abhor the bloodshed as Euripides did only a half century later.

Because Herodotus is both bard and historian, the reader will always have difficulty separating fact from fiction in his work, particularly in the first four chapters of the *History of the Persian Wars*. Herodotus will always be read as much for his fantastic tales of Africa, Mesopotamia, and Europe as for his account of the Persian Wars. His worth must be measured in both spheres.

Issues to Explore

(1) Because Herodotus saw human events as the work of the gods, he reports human affairs without critique or question. This is also the attitude of the Old Testament writers. Should we view these works as more accurate than those of such writers as Thucydides, who looked for the causes of history by reason and analysis?

(2) Herodotus sees equal worth in all people—especially, and surprisingly for a native of Asia Minor, in both Greeks and Persians. How much further has the Christian faith brought us in our attitudes toward others who are unlike ourselves, and often hostile to us?

(3) Christian readers should also ask how much human kindness results from the grace of God that is common in all life. Does the outworking of faith in a believer's life represent an advance over the noble piety of people like Herodotus?

—Arthur A. Rupprecht

For Further Study

One difficulty in reading Herodotus is that he writes in the Ionic dialect, a close relative of Attic Greek, which developed in the wealthy colonies of Asia Minor. But numerous editions of the *History of the Persian Wars* are available in both Greek and English. The Loeb Classical Series edition presents the Greek text in the Ionian dialect and the English translation on facing pages. The best overall translation of Herodotus is by A. de Selincourt (Penguin, 1972). G. Rawlinson's translation, the most accurate, has appeared in a number of editions, most recently in the New English Library series (1963). Also of note is David Grene's *History of Herodotus* (Chicago, 1987), which attempts to reproduce Herodotus's style.

The *Commentary on Herodotus* by W. W. How and J. Wells (Oxford, 1912) is now out of date on many points, but is still quite useful and has not been surpassed. J. Hart, *Herodotus and Greek History* (St. Martin's, 1982), and J. A. S. Evans, *Herodotus, Explorer of the Past* (Princeton, 1991), have excellent discussions and bibliographies. The special bibliography by Hart is particularly helpful.

Western Histories

As records of the exploits of heroes and saints, or the military successes and moral failures of kingdoms and empires, histories remain sources of private inspiration and public recollection. Through the ages historians have used a variety of methods to examine the past—from personal narrative to critical analysis—in seeking to capture the spirit of an age or the fate of a civilization. Early historians focused on the careers of exceptional individuals while contemporary historians emphasize the plight of a common humanity.

History is the interpretation of the record of human action. The study of history, consequently, imposes two tasks upon the historian. The first is to reconstruct an accurate account of past events. The second is to give meaning or significance to these events. However straightforward these tasks may appear, they can never be completely fulfilled. On the one hand, history includes all of what has been. Like playwrights, historians cannot show everything; they must impose dramatic coherence on their selections from the infinity of particulars. On the other hand, the traces of the past have not all been preserved. Like archaeologists, historians must imaginatively straddle gaps in the record. Every history, in short, remains provisional. As one historian put it, history is "argument without end."

Think . . . of the great part that is played by the unpredictable in war: think of it now, before you are actually committed to war. The longer a war lasts, the more things tend to depend on accidents. Neither you nor we can see into them: we have to abide their outcome in the dark. And when people are entering upon a war they do things the wrong way round. Action comes first, and it is only when they have already suffered that they begin to think.

—Speech of the Athenians
in Thucydides, *History of the Peloponnesian War*
Rex Warner, trans.

Greek Histories of War

Like the Western philosophical tradition, the Western tradition of historical writing was shaped as a response to a series of crises in the Greek world of the fifth century B.C. From the start, these two traditions proceeded on divergent courses. Where philosophers worked with first principles and mathematical axioms, historians worked with changing perceptions and opinions. Where philosophers sought a more permanent reality behind the flux of appearances, historians observed and interpreted humanity's play of passions and interests. For philosophers, virtue began with certain knowledge of the truth; for such early historians as HERODOTUS (c. 480–425 B.C.) or THUCYDIDES (c. 460–400 B.C.), virtue began with a prudent skepticism.

The aim of Herodotus's *History of the Persian Wars* is to "preserve the memory of the past by putting on record the astonishing achievements" of both the Greeks and the Asiatic peoples. It is also to "show how the two races came into conflict." For a first-time reader of Herodotus, these two aims may seem to interfere with one another. The wide-ranging inquiry (historia) into the diversity of human institutions often distracts from the thematic conflict between Persian despotism and Greek autonomy; these digressions do, however, offer some of the best stories of this narrative.

Thucydides' *History of the Peloponnesian War*, by contrast, possesses an unmistakable unity. One of the chief achievements of Greek culture, it tells the story of this "greatest war of all" that pitted the "self-control" and "well-ordered life" of Spartan laws and customs against the restless versatility and free liberality of Athens under the great democratic leader Pericles. Thucydides, a leading participant in the affairs himself, pursues this theme with a new scrupulousness regarding the reliability of his sources. But more remarkable still is Thucydides' "new realism." Unlike earlier histories that saw the gods as a powerful force, here the gods fall silent and human actions have human causes. Thucydides' notion of fate is not the unavoidable destiny that Herodotus believes in, but the discrepancy between intentions and their consequences—a discrepancy that grows tragically as the Peloponnesian War progresses and the defeat of Athens becomes increasingly clear.

Greek vessel, decorated with the figure of a hoplite, or Greek warrior.

Rome offer complementary accounts of the republic's success. The former attributes the rise of Rome to the excellence of its institutions: a balance of power among monarchical, aristocratic, and popular principles had forestalled the dangers of tyranny, oligarchy, and mob rule. The latter credits the excellence of its moral constitution: from the patriotic myths of the rape of Lucretia, the oath of the Horatii, and the geese of the Capitoline Hill came an edifying balance of respect, courage, and religious devotion.

Roman Histories of Civic Life

Three broad frameworks have dominated much of the Western tradition of historical writing. For Herodotus and Thucydides, as well as for their successors the Greek Polybius (c. 202–120 B.C.) and the Romans Titus Livius (59 B.C.–A.D. 17) and Cornelius Tacitus (c. 55–117), historical writing revolves around the civic life of the *polis* with its story of founding and fall, virtue and corruption. Polybius's *Histories* and Livy's *Early History of*

We must conclude then that specialized studies or monographs contribute very little to our grasp of the whole and our conviction of the truth. On the contrary, it is only by combining and comparing the various parts of the whole with one another and noting their resemblances and their differences that we shall arrive at a comprehensive view, and thus encompass both the practical benefits and the pleasures that the reading of history affords.

—Polybius's introduction to
The Rise of the Roman Republic
Ian Scott-Kilvert, trans.

But the virtues of a new nation can be easily corrupted by money and power. To the second-century historian Tacitus neither Roman moral or institutional excellence had withstood the increasing wealth or size of the Empire. He exposes this corruption in *The Annals*, his record of the events from the death of Augustus—the first emperor of Rome—to the year A.D. 69: "Augustus won over the soldiers with gifts, the populace with cheap corn, and all men with the sweets of repose, and so grew greater by degrees, while he concentrated in himself the functions of the Senate, the magistrates, and the laws."

Early Christian Histories

The first framework of historical understanding in the West gave way to the second when the Christian faith triumphed in the fourth century. To the ancient Hebrew view of history as God's providential plan for his chosen people the authors of the gospels and the apostle Paul added the central event of Christ's coming. Thus the old history of the covenant with Israel was completed, and a new history and a new covenant with all humankind was inaugurated. Although it developed linearly, this new history centered on God's eternal vision for humanity and thus set a new standard of historical significance.

The Christian historians Eusebius, Bishop of Caesarea (c. 264–340), and AUGUSTINE of Hippo (354–430) both adopted this new vision of history. But because of the circumstances of their times they had differing approaches to historiography. Eusebius, our principal source of the history of the Christian faith from the apostolic age down to his own day, is a particularly valuable witness because he lived through such experiences as the Diocletian persecution (303–310), the "conversion" of Constantine (312), and the Council of Nicaea (325). In his *Ecclesiastical History* he links the expansion of Rome to the success of the Christian faith. In contrast, Augustine, writing after the Visigoths' sack of Rome in 410, had to defend the Christian faith from accusations that it caused the fall of the Empire. Thus in *The City of God* he separates the cyclical histories of cities and empires from the progress of the church.

Nevertheless both Eusebius and Augustine base their writing of history on the imperatives of religious apologetics. Although these imperatives encourage the composition of often forced and unwieldy universal chronologies and open the door to a return to supernatural explanations, they add a new motive for historical accuracy. The conviction that history is a record of God's incessant supervision of human affairs could, in a work like the *Ecclesiastical History of the English People* by the Venerable Bede (c. 673–735), provide a powerful incentive for both a careful reproduction of primary sources and a scrupulous regard for narrative detail.

Modern Histories

The breakdown of Christian unity during the sixteenth-century Reformation and the ensuing Wars of Religion led in the eighteenth century to the third framework, a new "philosophical history." This history largely abandoned the civic framework of classical historiography and the ecclesiastical framework of Christian historiography for the secular and naturalistic framework of the

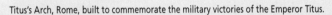
Titus's Arch, Rome, built to commemorate the military victories of the Emperor Titus.

history of the progress of civilization. It was to be, in the words of Edward Gibbon (1737–1794), a "history related to and explained by the social institutions in which it is contained." Gibbon wrote a masterpiece of encyclopedic erudition and literary style, his six-volume *The History of the Decline and Fall of the Roman Empire* (1776–88). In it he brings together two dissimilar modes of thought: those of the French philosopher Baron de Montesquieu and Italian historian Giambattista Vico and of Scottish philosophers David Hume and Adam Smith. Although Gibbon shared an Enlightenment faith in progress, his work, with its emphasis on the decline and fall of a great civilization, also fed an undercurrent of historical pessimism.

This pessimism has come increasingly to the fore in the twentieth century. Chastened by the experiences of the "great democratic revolution" turning into "an age of totalitarianism," contemporary historians have rediscovered Herodotus and Thucydides. Historians today are turning from "structures" to narratives, from the total history of universal civilization to "wonder" and "pure curiosity about the specific," and from the idea of inevitable progress to the unintended consequences of human action.

—Charles R. Sullivan

For Further Study

Recommended texts for the works mentioned include:

Herodotus: *The History,* David Grene, translator (University of Chicago, 1987).

Thucydides: *History of the Peloponnesian War,* Rex Warner, translator (Penguin, 1972).

Polybius: *The Rise of the Roman Republic,* Ian Scott-Kilvert, translator (Penguin, 1979).

Livy: *The Early History of Rome,* Aubrey de Sélincourt, translator (Penguin, 1982).

Tacitus: *The Complete Works,* Alfred John Church and William Jackson Brodribb, translators (Modern Library, 1942).

St. Augustine: *The City of God,* Henry Bettenson, translator (Viking Penguin, 1984).

Bede: *A History of the English Church and People,* Leo Sherley-Price, translator (Penguin, 1978).

Edward Gibbon: *The History of the Decline and Fall of the Roman Empire* (Penguin, 1995).

Donald R. Kelly, editor, *Versions of History from Antiquity to the Enlightenment* (Yale, 1991).

I have taken upon myself the task of defending the glorious City of God, against those who prefer their own gods to the Founder of that City. I treat of it both as it exists in this world of time, a stranger among the ungodly, living by faith, and as it stands in the security of its everlasting seat. This security it now awaits in steadfast patience . . . , but it is to attain it hereafter in virtue of its ascendancy over its enemies, when the final victory is won and peace established.

—The opening lines of *The City of God*
by Augustine
Henry Bettenson, trans.

SOPHOCLES

Oedipus Rex
c. 429–425 B.C.

*S*ophocles' *Oedipus Rex* (Oedipus the King) is generally considered the supreme example of the tragic form. It was the chief model for ARISTOTLE's *Poetics,* the famous fourth-century B.C. philosophical treatise on the literary arts, which ranks tragedy as the highest genre. *Oedipus Rex* has shaped the conception of the tragic vision in the West and therefore has influenced all subsequent attempts to produce a tragic work of art.

A Model for Tragedy

The flowering of dramatic art that took place some twenty-five hundred years ago in the Greek city of Athens produced tragedies that have remained unmatched in the world's literature. The plays of AESCHYLUS (525–456 B.C.), Sophocles (c. 497–406 B.C.), and EURIPIDES (c. 480–406 B.C.) are generally accepted as the prime examples of the tragic genre. Only thirty-three of their works have survived, out of the hundreds written by various playwrights of the time.

According to Aristotle, tragedy

Sophocles (c. 497–406 B.C.).

presents the action of a protagonist who, aspiring toward high achievement, is ultimately undone by a spiritual blindness. The tragic hero's struggles with divine rather than human powers generate a unique response of pity and terror in the audience. But rather than having a negative effect, the experience of the play leads to purgation of these emotions and clarification of the mind and spirit (called by the Greeks *catharsis*). Thus the effect of tragedy, despite its portrait of ruin and devastation, is exaltation rather than depression.

The Oedipus Cycle

Sophocles, the second in the sequence of great Athenian tragedians, focuses on the internal conflicts within his tragic protagonists. Of his 123 plays, only seven survive. The most famous of these are the three that center on Thebes, the accursed city that continually offends the gods.

The first play of the Theban cycle, *Antigone* (442–441 B.C), offers the moving portrayal of a young woman's conflict with the ruler of Thebes and her consequent martyrdom. The plot of *Antigone* actually comes latest in the time scheme of the cycle. It takes place some years after the death of Oedipus, which is depicted in the third play, *Oedipus at Colonus* (produced posthumously, 401 B.C.). The second play is the drama that begins the story, *Oedipus Rex* (429–425 B.C.).

Together, the two Oedipus plays portray the completed pattern of tragic suffering, which appears in its fullness in only two other works in the entire body of Western literature—Job and *King Lear*. Seemingly unjust affliction leads these protagonists to an utter desolation of spirit in which they face the darkness and ignorance of their own souls. Each sufferer works through the tribulation to find the sustaining power of the divine will.

The Search for Truth

In *Oedipus Rex* Sophocles explores the tragic courage of one who struggles toward truth against overwhelming odds. The grandeur and stubbornness of this quest have fascinated and appalled viewers and readers throughout history. What gives the drama its sublimity, however, is its universal theme of the illusion of innocence shattered by the reality of guilt. Oedipus's relentless search for the knowledge of his true condition makes him the ideal image of the tragic hero.

The play represents one day in Oedipus's life: "This day will bring your birth and your destruction," as the prophet Tiresias declares. This one day, however, takes place twelve years after Oedipus has already fulfilled his dreadful destiny of killing his father and marrying

Pride breeds the tyrant
violent pride, gorging, crammed to bursting
with all that is overripe and rich with ruin—
clawing up to the heights, headlong pride
crashes down the abyss—sheer doom!
No footing helps, all foothold lost and gone.
But the healthy strife that makes the city strong—
I pray that god will never end that wrestling;
god, my champion, I will never let you go.

—*Oedipus* Rex
Robert Fagles, trans.

his mother. Thus the plot concerns not the doing of the horrifying deeds, but Oedipus's discovery that he *has* done them. By the end, the clear-seeing hero has discovered himself to be the person most in the dark. He has destroyed all order: the king has become the beggar; the father, the brother of his sons; the husband, the son of his wife. The prophecy has been fulfilled—despite Oedipus's efforts. And he who would endure no imperfection now sees himself to be the most vile and unfortunate of humanity. But rather than taking his own life, Oedipus blinds himself to make amends for his unwitting crimes against his city, his kin, and the gods.

Oedipus Rex and *Oedipus at Colonus* are best considered as a unit. Read by itself, *Oedipus Rex* depicts a chain of events that, like most misfortunes, is mysterious, apparently arbitrary, and seemingly unjust. Why did such dreadful things happen to a noble and well-meaning man? But *Oedipus at Colonus* reveals the end of the action, unveiling something of the divine plan. It is as though the gods posed the problem to themselves: "How can we get this man to the sacred wood of the Furies in Colonus? How can we bring him to our own bosom?" And the answer, which appears cold and uncaring, comes paradoxically from the heart of love: Make him see himself as the pol-

Blind Oedipus is led by his daughter, Antigone; a scene from Sophocles' tragedy *Oedipus Rex.*

Opposite: Classical Greek theater at Nysa, modern Turkey.

The celebrated classical Greek amphitheater at Epidauros, Greece, looking down from the top of the seating area across the theater.

lution of the earth, the one who has done the unthinkable and broken all the taboos. Then see (as Satan says of Job) if "he will curse you to your face."

But in what manner
Oedipus perished, no one of mortal men
Could tell but Theseus. It was not lightning,
Bearing its fire from God, that took him off;
No hurricane was blowing.
But some attendant from the train of heaven
Came for him; or else the underworld
Opened in love the unlit door of earth.
For he was taken without lamentation,
Illness or suffering; indeed his end
Was wonderful if mortal's ever was.

—*Oedipus at Colonus*
Robert Fagles, trans.

After years of wandering, Oedipus reaches the hallowed sacred grove at Colonus and is far from cursing. Here, like Moses, he is enfolded into a mysterious and benevolent divinity. "Indeed his end," we are told, "was wonderful if mortal's ever was."

Sophocles carried the image of Oedipus in his mind for some twenty years—between his composing *Oedipus Rex* and *Oedipus at Colonus*. At last, when he was ninety, the old playwright knew and understood. Oedipus would be brought to wisdom not by having his spirit broken and becoming a craven figure, but by having his magnificent qualities turned in another direction. Oedipus's burial in Colonus outside the city of Athens marks his transfiguration into Oedipus the hero. He finally brings about a blessing for the sacred city.

Of the two plays, the first is brilliant, passionate, rapid, and violent; the second is slow, stately, somber, and transcendent. Both portray the same Oedipus—impatient, headstrong, and finally holy. Together they reveal a glimpse of the divine order behind the social order, moving toward a good beyond the aims of human justice.

So,
you mock my blindness? Let me tell you this.
You with your precious eyes,
you're blind to the corruption of your life,
to the house you live in, those you live with—
who are your parents? Do you know? All unknowing
you are the scourge of your own flesh and blood,
the dead below the earth and living here above,
and the double lash of your mother and your father's curse
will whip you from this land one day, their footfall
treading you down in terror, darkness shrouding
your eyes that now can see the light!

—*Oedipus Rex*
Robert Fagles, trans.

For Further Study

Oedipus Rex is part of the genre of classical tragedy, which has a somber and elevated tone. It is neither long nor difficult to read. But to apprehend its meaning requires considerable reflection. Its language is fairly simple, although the stark poetic imagery of its lines—even in translation—provides a complex reading experience. It is frequently taught, however, both in high school and in the first year of college.

Some good translations are Robert Fagles, *Sophocles: The Three Theban Plays* (Penguin Classics, 1984); David Grene, *Sophocles I* (University of Chicago, 1968); and Dudley Fitts and Robert Fitzgerald, *Sophocles, The Oedipus Cycle* (Harvest Books, 1949). Helpful commentaries are Cedric Whitman, *Sophocles: A Study of Heroic Humanism* (Harvard University, 1951); Bernard M. W. Knox, *Oedipus at Thebes* (Norton, 1971), and *The Heroic Temper: Studies in Sophoclean Tragedy* (University of California, 1965); and Charles Segal, *Tragedy and Civilization: An Interpretation of Sophocles* (Harvard University, 1981). Comprehensive general introductions to Greek culture and mythology are Mark P. O. Morford and Robert J. Lenardon, *Classical Mythology* (Longman, 1985), and Edith Hamilton, *The Greek Way* (New American Library, 1960).

Issues to Explore

For the Christian, the chief action in *Oedipus Rex* symbolizes the unveiling of the roots of pride and self-righteousness. It reveals the tendency to govern one's life by setting up a structure of virtues rather than by submitting to God's will. Like the Book of Job, *Oedipus Rex* deals with the mysterious ways of the divine. It vindicates the person who bears the suffering sent by what the Greeks viewed as the incomprehensible will of the gods.

In this light, Oedipus's struggles to subvert the prophecy by the oracle of Apollo are best understood as the work of a proud leader who tries to avoid the will of God. Some questions to ask are: (1) Is Oedipus free, or does "Fate" determine his destiny? (2) What is the role of the prophet Tiresias? (3) Why does Oedipus choose to learn the truth? Why does he not conceal the unpleasant and unsettling evidence as it starts to unfold? (4) Why does Oedipus strike out his eyes instead of killing himself? (5) What is the total outlook of the drama? (6) With its emphasis on suffering and the punishment of pride, can *Oedipus Rex* teach anything to Christians, who base their ultimate faith in the good news beyond tragedy?

—Louise Cowan

EURIPIDES

The Bacchae
c. 406 B.C.

O f the more than thirty surviving Greek tragedies, Euripides' *Bacchae* is uniquely powerful and shocking in gaining the tragic effect that ARISTOTLE describes in his *Poetics*—the arousal of pity and fear in the audience and the purgation of these emotions. In the *Bacchae,* Dionysus, the god of wine and ecstasy and of the Greek theater itself, is portrayed as a character onstage who orchestrates this pattern of tragic action in a horrifying and bloody spectacle. He causes the fall of King Pentheus and of his city Thebes, a political order that because of the illusion of human self-sufficiency has lost its sense of divine connection.

Dionysus brings about this fall when, manifesting a "spirit of revel and rapture" conflicting with the restraints of human institutions, he appears suddenly and demands the city's worship. But Pentheus refuses and so becomes both the *pharmakos,* the tragic scapegoat, taking on the collective sin of his people, and the *sparagmos,* the dismembered victim. Further, beyond the hideous death of Pentheus, the city too must suffer

Eurlpides (c. 480–406 B.C.); engraving by Hinchcliff.

for its impiety; not only the hero but his people as well are therefore implicated in the pride—the *hybris*—that is at the heart of all tragedy.

The *Bacchae* is concerned, then, with the dangers of self-deception, particularly the Thebans' foolish attempt to impose limits on divinity—which is limitless and therefore largely inscrutable, mysterious, and even terrifying. In it Euripides insists that the realm of spirit, the holy sphere of the

gods to whom piety is due as an acknowledgment of mortal deficiency, lies beyond rational understanding. The gods exist as they are—not as humans in their "rage for order" would render them. Thus even in its terrible unfolding, the play affirms the reality of divinity in a world that would deny this reality in favor of a comforting ideology.

A Golden Age Tragedian

Euripides was born between 485 and 480 B.C. in Athens, shortly before the two great battles of the Persian Wars—Salamis in 480 and Plataea in 479—that secured Greece from foreign invasion. This was the "Golden Age of Greece," and Athens was the leader, particularly in the arts. Euripides was the last of the three great tragedians of Athens, after AESCHYLUS (525–456 B.C.) and SOPHOCLES (497–406 B.C.). Eighteen of Euripides' nearly ninety plays survive, compared with seven each of Aeschylus and Sophocles.

I have no wish to grudge the wise their wisdom;
But the joys I seek are greater, outshine all others,
And lead our life to goodness and loveliness:
The joy of the holy heart. . . .

—The Bacchae
Philip Vellacott, trans.

Although Euripides was popular, he was less honored in his day than his two older contemporaries, winning the Athenian prize for tragedy only five times. He was perceived as radically different from Aeschylus and Sophocles; some thought that, in being less reverent of Athenian traditions and more skeptical toward the gods, he demeaned the proper loftiness of drama.

An artist's impression of a scene from *Medea* (431 B.C.), Euripides' most famous play other than the *Bacchae*.

Euripides entered his period of creative maturity just as Athens entered her period of decline and fall. *Medea* (431 B.C.), his most famous play other than the *Bacchae*, was produced at the onset of a savage civil war among Greek city-states; it depicts a ruthlessness in conquest that parallels Athenian cruelty at the height of power. The *Bacchae* closes this period, reflecting Athens's perilous situation on the eve of its destruction in 404 B.C. by Sparta, its ally against the Persians just seventy-five years earlier.

Coming when it did, the alarming production of the *Bacchae* turned out to be not only politically relevant but also prophetic. The Athenians, like the Thebans, came to believe in themselves so strongly that they thought they could do no wrong; they sought to dictate their own moral and spiritual codes.

A God of Joy, a God of Violence

The Thebans' denial of the Dionysian divine life force is reflected in their king's worldview and his style of governing through a perpetual restraint of human desire. Along with inflicting this repression, Pentheus feels morally superior to anyone who deviates from Theban custom. So when Dionysus appears in the city disguised as a mortal, the king foolishly abuses and imprisons him.

But the god, also known as Bacchus, already has his followers—mostly women who are known as *maenads*. When the play begins, the women of Thebes have succumbed to the lure of Dionysus, cast off their domestic roles, and entered into a rapturous celebration of nature outside the city. But, as a shepherd reports, the Bacchic worshipers are not wanton, instead displaying a "modest comeliness." His description indicates an idyllic harmony between nature and humans, resembling the biblical image of the "peaceable kingdom."

Meanwhile Dionysus demonstrates his power by freeing himself from prison and destroying the walls of the palace. Despite such evidence of supernatural power, Pentheus refuses to acknowledge Dionysus's divinity. The god remains patient, first asking "Can you, a mortal, measure your strength with a god's?" and then suggesting that "a happy settlement may still be found." But when Pentheus is still obstinate, Dionysus concludes that Pentheus —and Thebes—may acquire wisdom of "truths more than mortal" only through suffering and death.

To affirm the presence of the very impulse that the king denies, Dionysus easily entices Pentheus to dress like a woman and spy on the revelers in the hills. Freed from the tyrannizing "curb of reason," Pentheus enters slyly into the spirit of Bacchic joy, only to be discovered by the celebrants as an intruder to the sacred rites and ripped to pieces. Pentheus's own mother, in her madness, carries his severed head back to the city There Dionysus presides over the final sorrow of the tragedy and the bloody evidence of the Thebans' impiety.

The specific challenge of the play is to understand Dionysus, the god of joy, laughter, and dancing who "joins soul with soul in mystic unity" and whose gifts include wine, which banishes "the sufferings of our unhappy race" and "soothes the sore regret." Thus he represents a powerful impulse, a deeply imbedded urge within humanity to transcend the rigid structures of society. In this respect, the revelation of the god's appearance is a summons not unlike the desire to break forth spontaneously in feasting and song—in carnival celebration.

Dionysus presents a threat only when a society denies his existence by making reason the absolute rule: no carnival, no communal joy, none of those rejuvenating interludes of true community that actually give meaning to structure itself. When a person (Pentheus) or an entire people (the city of Thebes) ordains a joyless social life for the sake of a purely rational order, Dionysus exacts his due by inciting madness and violence.

And so Dionysus is often called the god of duality, for the joy he brings bears within it a disturbing contrast. As one commentator says, when Dionysus comes, "all tradition, all order must be shattered. Life becomes suddenly an ecstasy—an ecstasy of blessedness, but an ecstasy, no less, of terror." Dionysus's province,

A mosaic representation of the Greek god Dionysus.

the primal realm of nature that continually threatens to overwhelm humanity's frail structures, goes hand in hand with death.

Issues to Explore

Although the *Bacchae* may seem alien to some Christian readers, many avenues to the work may be explored fruitfully. (1) Some scholars have compared Dionysus to Christ himself, because in various tales of Greek mythology

Can you, a mortal, measure your strength with a god's?

—*The Bacchae*
Philip Vellacott, trans.

When mind runs mad, dishonors God,
And worships self and senseless pride,
Then Law eternal wields the rod.

—*The Bacchae*
Philip Vellacott, trans.

For Further Study

The *Bacchae* is a disturbing but readily accessible play. It is normally collected in volumes of Euripides' work, the best of which are *The Bacchae and Other Plays,* translated by Philip Vellacott (Penguin, 1973), and *Euripides V* in *The Complete Greek Tragedies,* translated by William Arrowsmith (University of Chicago, 1959). Helpful commentaries include Vellacott's introduction to the Penguin edition, Charles Segal's *Dionysiac Poetics and Euripides' Bacchae* (Princeton, 1986), and C. H. Whitman's *Euripides and the Full Circle of Myth* (Harvard, 1974). Walter Otto's *Dionysus: Myth and Cult* (Indiana University, 1965) is valuable, as is his introduction to Greek religion in *The Homeric Gods* (Thames and Hudson, 1954). In addition, C. Kerenyi's *The Gods of the Greeks* (Thames and Hudson, 1951) contains an excellent account of Dionysus.

he has a miraculous birth and is pursued, dismembered, and then restored. Beyond such parallels, is there a connection between the "message" Dionysus brings to Thebes and the message of the New Testament? (2) Is the judgment of Dionysus similar to the Christian injunction not to limit God in terms of law or human institutions? (3) Might there be a link between outbreaks of social violence and the repression or absence of communal expressions of festive joy?

(4) The exposure of pride in the play is another valuable source of reflection. The Thebans are a "stiff-necked" people, too proud of their society and disdainful of those who believe differently. In what way does Thebes embody the timeless human tendency toward the pride that often precedes the tragic fall, in either an individual or an entire culture? (5) Is the Dionysian punishment of an entire city for impiety similar to the Old Testament wrath of God? (6) How does the impulse toward rigid suppression of human desire gain its ascendancy in the soul? (7) How should one show proper piety to the liberating but potentially destructive spirit of Dionysus?

—Larry Allums

ARISTOPHANES

Comedies
425–388 B.C.

The Greek playwright Aristophanes (448–387 b.c.) is generally agreed to be the keenest, merriest wit the world has known. His comic masterpieces have survived through their intrinsic merit, although his frank absurdity, apparent coarseness, and bitingly satiric references are sometimes misunderstood in the modern age. His fundamental vision, however, is profoundly spiritual. Aristophanes was the first to see the full implications of comedy—to recognize that the comic imagination is essential in the movement toward hope and love. In fact, as he shows, those who choose a comic sprightliness and optimism in difficult situations are thereby enabled to renounce self-absorption and hence to endure and prevail.

The Roots of Greek Comedy

The brief glory of Athens's Golden Age was declining when Aristophanes wrote his forty-odd plays. Comedy had been introduced into the Athenian festivals as early as

The Greek playwright Aristophanes (448–387 B.C.) engraved by T. F. Viquet.

486 B.C. and for about a hundred years thereafter flourished as both folk entertainment and serious religious liturgy. Plays were performed in honor of Dionysus, who as the god of wine and corn symbolically represented the destruction and the regeneration of the human community—the first in tragedy and the second in a marriage festival, a *komos,* from which the word *comedy* derives.

Hundreds of comedies were produced in these years of "Old Comedy" before Athens surrendered to Sparta at the end of the Peloponnesian War. When Aristophanes was producing his comic masterpieces, Athens was in dire straits, suffering not only from war but from plague and scarcity, with its trade cut off from other city-states. Although Aristophanes' dramas contain frequent caustic references to civic and military leaders of the day, far more numerous are their delicately lovely lyric passages that indicate the triumph of the human spirit.

During the centuries after the decline of Athens, Aristophanes' comedies continued to survive. Further, when scholars of the Alexandrian library were seeking to preserve the best of the past, they included eleven plays of Aristophanes, whereas they chose only seven each of the tragic dramatists SOPHOCLES and AESCHYLUS. After the fall of Constantinople in 1453, Aristophanes' texts were brought to Italy, where they were translated into Latin. They were thus made available to European readers

Satyr play featuring
Dionysus and
Ariadne, from a
vase in the Museo
Nazionale, Naples.

several years before the works of the Greek tragedians. Over the centuries, the Western world has fully assimilated into its corporate imagination Aristophanes' particular mode of comedy.

A Sharp and Apocalyptic Wit

In the face of imperfect conditions in a deteriorating society, Aristophanes posits a fantastic world in which the imagination can freely operate. Within this imagined realm, the reader glimpses human nature from an alternative perspective. Problems that appear insoluble in actual life can become quite clear in the fictional comic crucible in which aspects of a situation may be exaggerated or slanted and thus more easily recognized. Many comic distortions would be shocking and disgusting if they were not portrayed as ridiculous and absurd. Thus comedy performs an important civic task in engendering recognition and good

*Satire denounces
the world; wit penetrates it;
humor accepts it;
but nonsense transforms it.*

—Cedric Whitman

humor. As Cedric Whitman, longtime classics professor at Harvard, has written, "Satire denounces the world; wit penetrates it; humor accepts it; but nonsense transforms it." Aristophanes' plays contain all four comic modes; but in his use of nonsense—sheer fantastic absurdity—he most excels.

Aristophanes creates two possibilities—two cities—in his plays, both fictional, though one of them is presented as the actual Athens. This is the city he seeks to save: warlike, litigious, venal, debauched, corrupt. The other is the potential city of the enlightened heart: peaceful, harmonious, festive, and full of innocent pleasures. In each of his surviving eleven plays, the corrupt Athens is shown as yielding to the peaceful and innocent new city. The means of its redemption is nearly always a little comic hero who has a nonsensical "happy idea" and attempts the audacious task of bringing it into being.

Comic Renewal

All of Aristophanes' comedies are concerned with the theme of renewal. The heroes—poor, downtrodden, impotent, and old—become rich, successful, potent, and young. In the first play, the *Acharnians*, for instance, the protagonist Dikepolis, a little old Chaplinesque figure, makes a separate peace with the city's enemies, agreeing to trade with them despite the city's embargo. During the course of the play, he gains resourcefulness, wisdom, and the ability to dominate any situation. At the end he is happy with his private peace for himself, family, and friends.

Or in *Clouds,* the hero is an old farmer, Strepsiades, who is not as innocent as Dikepolis. Strepsiades has married a city woman and thus has been introduced to luxury and acquisitiveness. In the course of the play, he goes against his own interests and burns down the newfangled Sophists' think tank, where his son has been learning "Unjust Logic"—inventive ways of legal lying and deceiving. Athens is thus spared the threat of further demoralization.

Another play, *Lysistrata,* is a bawdy graphic comedy in which women take over the Acropolis and vow to end the war by denying their beds to their husbands. The outcome is peace and harmony not only domestically but between enemies, the Athenians and the Spartans.

The Three Comedies
of the "Other World"

But the plays that most express Aristophanes' comic genius are *Peace, Birds,* and *Frogs:* those in which the comic rogue escapes to an imaginary world. In the first, *Peace,* Aristophanes addresses the subject of war and its unsavoriness. A little old Athenian citizen, Trygaeus, trains a dung beetle to carry him on its back as they fly to Mount Olympus, the residence of the gods, so that he can implore Zeus to save the city. When Trygaeus arrives on Olympus he finds that the gods have all departed after they buried the goddess Peace, leaving the god of War in charge. Trygaeus digs up Peace, who emerges with two lovely young women, Theoria (City festival) and Opora (Rural festival). When he turns to go back to earth, Trygaeus finds that his dung beetle has joined the horses in Zeus's train and is now fed on ambrosia instead of dung. This transformation of the earthiest and most unsavory fare into the delicate food of the gods symbolizes the entire action of the play; in it one learns that life is meant for festivity and delight, for peace and joy. The comedy ends with the wedding festivities of Trygaeus and one of the beautiful

*Naught is better, naught more pleasant, than to grow a
    pair of wings
At the theater, for instance, they'd be quite convenient
    things;
Bored with tragedies and hungry . . . never mind, you
    needn't stay;
You could wing it home, eat luncheon in a comfortable
    way,
Then, replete, fly back among us for a comic matinee.*

—*Birds*
R. H. Webb, trans.

maidens, Opora. The promised future is one of agrarian prosperity and joy.

Birds is a remarkable lyric comedy that celebrates the spiritual supremacy of mortals over the gods. In it two friends, Pisthetairos and Euelpides, in disgust with Athens, decide to "go to the birds." They persuade the birds to build a city, Cloudcuckooland, that will prevent all communication between the earth and Mt. Olympus. Prometheus, ever the friend to humankind, informs Pisthetairos that the gods are ready to negotiate. In acknowledging defeat, Zeus relinquishes his royal scepter and his handmaiden Basileia, whose name means Royalty. In this beautifully apocalyptic play, the old depraved city and the corrupt gods are both renounced in favor of the "birdlike" spirituality that makes human beings supreme in the universe.

In *Frogs,* the decay of Athens is so far advanced that Dionysus himself (the god of comedy) travels down to Hades, the realm of death, to bring back the tragic dramatist EURIPIDES. In Hades, however, the contest between Euripides and Aeschylus over the best idea for saving the city ends in a tie and Dionysus himself must decide who wins. He chooses Aeschylus because of the elder playwright's sober wisdom. The play leaves us with

Let honor and praise be the guerdon, he says,
of the poet whose satire has stayed you
From believing the orators' novel conceits
wherewith they cajoled and betrayed you;

. . . .

By this he's a true benefactor to you,
and by showing with humor dramatic
The way that our wise democratic allies
are ruled by our state democratic.

And therefore their people will come overseas
their tribute to bring to the City,
Consumed with desire to behold and admire
the poet so fearless and witty,

Who dared in the presence of Athens to speak
the thing that is rightful and true:
And truly the fame of his prowess by this
Has been bruited the universe through.

—*Acharnians*
B. B. Rogers, trans.

the possibility that poetry may indeed be able to save the city.

Aristophanes' fantastic absurdities force his reader to see things in terms of their symbolic significance, rather than staying with the literal meaning of the action. On the lowest level, his plays are about physical survival; on the highest, they imply the soul's yearning for salvation.

For Further Study

The most readily available edition of Aristophanes' plays is edited by Moses Hadas: *The Complete Plays of Aristophanes* (Bantam, 1962). The best critical study by far is found in Cedric Whitman, *Aristophanes and the Comic Hero* (Harvard, 1964). Other helpful commentary is found in: Louise Cowan, "Aristophanes' Comic Apocalypse," *The Terrain of Comedy* (The Dallas Institute of Humanities and Culture, 1984); Kenneth McLeish, *The Theatre of Aristophanes* (Taplinger Publishing, 1980); Alexes Solomos, *The Living Aristophanes* (University of Michigan, 1974). To understand the role of Dionysus in Greek theater, see Walter Otto, *Dionysus: Myth and Cult* (Indiana University, 1965).

Issues to Explore

(1) Does comedy assume a higher vision of life than almost any other genre? (2) Can one distinguish between the immoral—that which advocates an erroneous and sinful way of life—and the merely shocking and indecent that make up so much of the material of comedy? (3) What function do these latter materials have? Can they be seen purposely to include the body and humanity's "lower" nature in order to lift up the whole person, not just the higher elements? (4) What function does the "happy idea" serve in each of Aristophanes' plays? Because it is not rooted in any human origin, could it be called a gift of grace? (5) Could the audacity of the comic rogue in pursuing the happy idea, then, be considered a kind of heroism?

—Louise Cowan

PLATO

The Republic
c. 375 B.C.

*P*lato's *Republic* is the most thought-provoking and influential philosophical text in the Western world, one that has shaped Western civilization as well as the Western intellectual tradition. In it, Plato, through his mentor Socrates, speculates on what constitutes the best commonwealth, making a lasting contribution to our understanding of education, politics, the virtues, justice, and the *summum bonum* (supreme good). Through the *Republic* and his other writings, Plato has been highly influential although roundly criticized throughout the centuries. He has been called an impractical idealist, a utopian, a nondemocrat, and even a totalitarian. Such thinkers as ARISTOTLE, Cicero, AUGUSTINE, MACHIAVELLI, and NIETZSCHE might debate Plato's arguments, but all have responded to the issues he raises in the dialogues begun over twenty-three hundred years ago by his spokesman Socrates.

Real Philosophers

Plato (c. 428–c. 347 B.C.) was born in Athens to a prominent political

Plato (c. 428–c. 347 B.C.).

family a year after the death of the great leader Pericles. He aspired to politics but became disgusted by the corruption and violence of Athenian democracy, which culminated with the execution of his friend and teacher Socrates in 399 B.C.

Believing that philosophy is fundamental to human happiness and security, Plato became convinced that justice would not arrive "until either real philosophers gain political power or politicians become by some miracle philosophers." In response to both this belief in philosophy and Socrates' execution, Plato founded the Academy in 385 B.C., his new school for the "philosopher-ruler" statesman. The *Republic* sets forth the aims of the Academy.

A Dialogue for Justice

The *Republic* is an unusual work, both a treatise and a drama. It is a dialogue in which the characters interact with each other, sometimes vigorously. This style of writing is in itself significant, for it demonstrates the active nature of thought, bringing to life the issues under discussion. As in most of the Platonic dialogues, the principal character in the *Republic* is Socrates. Thus, though Socrates did not write books or dialogues, his ideas live on through his famous student. Consequently his teachings cannot be easily distinguished from those of Plato.

Socrates . . .

Who, well inspir'd, the oracle pronounced
Wisest of men.

—Milton
Paradise Regained

The setting of the *Republic* is both magnificent and tragic. Around the year 411 B.C. Athens was the greatest and most prosperous city in existence. Yet the Golden Age of Pericles was over—Athenian democracy was being undermined and in a few short years would succumb to Spartan might. But paradoxically it was in this setting, while Athenian glory was still strong, that SOPHOCLES and EURIPIDES wrote their most searching tragic dramas and Plato attempted to understand why human beings—during great prosperity—can undermine political order.

At the beginning of the *Republic* Socrates is detained—kidnapped, as it were—by a number of young men who succumb to the persuasive words of their captive. The "setting" informs the work as a whole: human beings are capable of acting unjustly but are equally capable of inquiring into the nature of justice. As Socrates makes clear, "justice" is not simply a virtue but a state of harmony; when human beings act in a truly human way, they are just. The young men speaking with Socrates struggle to answer the question of how they ought to act. In their conversation, real choices are presented: ought one pursue a life of wealth-getting, glory, or, perhaps, injustice? The *Republic* is not merely a dialogue, but an alternative way of life—a life of inquiry in defense of wisdom and justice. What begins in Book I is a sometimes animated discussion as to why such a life is desirable.

Socrates argues that only when a city is built "in speech"—in extended conversation—can we begin to see justice. He leads his young interlocutors into such a conversation. Socrates further suggests that justice requires an understanding of imagination, virtue, and the good.

Plato examines these and other themes in greater detail in his other, shorter dialogues. For

example, love is the subject in the *Symposium,* virtue in the *Meno,* immortality in the *Phaedo,* philosophy as a civic good in the *Apology,* and practical aspects of politics in the *Laws.*

Justice, Knowledge, Ideas

As Socrates and his colleagues discuss justice, the question arises concerning whether a true difference exists between a vulgar life devoted to pleasure and a nobler one in pursuit of a "just and holy life."

Socrates' attempt to determine the just life culminates in his famous depiction of the soul. According to Socrates, the spirited part of the soul, anger and honor, and the passions should work together in deference to the highest part of the soul, the intellect. Like the soul, all of existence presupposes a hierarchy: God rules humanity, and humans rule themselves and the beasts.

But a problem arises. Socrates indicates that justice, comprehended by the intellect, can never be grasped by the many. The ordinary person is not a philosopher. Passions, combined with self-interest, cause most people to act unjustly. Socrates depicts this situation in Book X of the *Republic* through his famous analogy of the Cave. Human beings are like prisoners in a cave: their sense of reality is based on the unclear shadows that flicker on the cave's wall. Truth lies outside the cave, but it is difficult to grasp because of our imperfection—we remain in the cave.

In likening the city to a cave, Socrates suggests that the lives of the many are formed and directed in terms of shadows or myths—large interpretative fables that designate the individual's place in the city and in the afterlife. But, he says, images perpetuated by the right kinds of myths can persuade human beings to act within laws that reflect the reality outside the cave.

Images, Socrates continues, are far more pleasing than simple narration. For instance, a poet such as HOMER or SHAKESPEARE is more influential than philosophers, whom most people distrust. Philosophers tend to question the opinions on which the city is grounded. But, for the sake of justice, Socrates insists that there must be an alliance between the poets and philosophers.

In Plato's scheme, potential rulers are actually "guardians" whose strength of character and talents are put at the service of the public good. In Socrates' ideal state, which is neither a democracy nor a tyranny, the guardians rule over the soldiers, who control the workers. People fall naturally into one of these three classes. True political justice confines each person to his or her proper function in the city.

As preparation for ruling, guardians receive a comprehensive education that includes mathematics, poetry, gymnastics, music, and an understanding of the "Ideas" or "Forms" themselves. The Ideas, Socrates teaches, are pre-physical forms of things. A specific cat, for instance, is less perfect than the Idea of the cat. The actual cat naturally degenerates and dies but the Idea of cat is eternal. Ideas include all physical objects, as well as such non-physical objects as courage, moderation, prudence, and justice. Socrates suggests that Ideas are more real than the physical objects of this world.

One may grasp these Ideas through reasoned speech. The Socratic goal is to make life correspond to the Ideas. But the genuine pursuit of knowledge requires one to follow Socrates' famous dictum: "I know that I know nothing." Such an ironic claim offers an important teaching: the beginning of knowledge demands that inquirers understand their fundamental ignorance.

Plato's Influence on Christian Thinking

Plato has been highly influential on many later streams of thought, especially Neoplatonism, through the writings of the Egyptian thinker Plotinus (204–270), and early Christian theology, as articulated by St. Augustine. Describing God through our imperfect human language is difficult, Augustine argued. But using Plato's "language" and method of examining nature, by which he had been influenced as a young man, Augustine articulated a profound Christian philosophy of God, love, evil,

Roman copy of a Greek bust of Socrates (469–399 B.C.) of about 370 B.C.

and salvation that has been echoed down the centuries by Christian thinkers and apologists, including the Protestant reformers in the sixteenth century and C. S. Lewis in the twentieth century.

Thomas Aquinas, the thirteenth-century giant of Roman Catholic theology, was more influenced by Plato's most famous student—Aristotle. But although great differences exist

Not unless the philosophers rule as kings or those now called kings . . . philosophize . . . will the regime we have now described in speech ever come forth from nature.

—*The Republic*
Allan Bloom, trans.

The just man is happy and the unjust man wretched.

—*The Republic*
Allan Bloom, trans.

between the master and the student, their similarities outweigh their differences.

Beyond Plato's general understanding of the true, the good, and the beautiful, the *Republic* offers even more to the Christian reader. The Bible does not seek to resolve all the issues and problems to be faced in such areas as politics, economics, and art—for example such questions as: What type of city do we create? What rights do we really possess? Through Plato's conversation and philosophic process followers of Christ can take part in a fruitful deliberation over what is good for humanity.

Issues to Explore

Like any drama, the *Republic* portrays an attractive and compelling action. Yet one must be willing not only to read the text but to reread it. One will benefit from such an effort by reflecting on the text—sometimes for years—and questioning Socrates' arguments in the process. Plato's great achievement lies in his ability to inspire learning through the *maieutic* method, a name derived from the Greek

For Further Study

Some good translations are Allan Bloom, *The Republic of Plato* (Basic Books, 1968), and Richard W. Sterling and William C. Scott, *Plato: The Republic* (Norton, 1985). Helpful commentaries are James A. Arieti, *Interpreting Plato: The Dialogues as Drama* (Rowman and Littlefield, 1991); Paul Friedlander, *Plato* (Princeton, 1970); Mary Nichols, *Socrates and the Political Community* (State University of New York, 1987); and Leo Strauss, "On Plato's Republic" in *The City and Man* (Chicago, 1964).

word for "midwife." Through his "Socratic method" he brings ideas to birth in others.

The *Republic* constantly raises the question, "What is the best way of life?" Observant readers will begin to see the nature and extent of Socrates' proposals. Most likely they will respond by considering the alternative ways of life proposed by the other speakers in the text. We should ask of Socrates: (1) Is the city "in speech" actually meant to be created? (2) What is the relationship between poetry and philosophy? (3) Can human beings truly possess wisdom, or are we forever subject to ignorance and chance?

—Robert Martin Schaefer

ARISTOTLE

Nichomachean Ethics
c. 384–322 B.C.

*A*ristotle's *Nichomachean Ethics,* one of the greatest ethical treatises of Western philosophy, has had a deep and lasting effect throughout the centuries, including an inestimable influence on Christian moral thought.

Socrates, Plato, and Aristotle

Greek moral philosophy begins with Socrates (469–399 B.C.), who taught that it is better to suffer injustice than commit it. Socrates held that committing injustice defiles or pollutes human beings in their innermost selves, or in their souls, whereas suffering even the worst injustice never pollutes the soul. But the soul is made sound and healthy by doing what is just. Socrates' greatest disciple, Plato (c. 428–c. 347 B.C.), and Plato's greatest student, Aristotle (384–322 B.C.), both follow this Socratic understanding of the moral life as *caring for one's soul.*

Aristotle studied for twenty years in Plato's Academy in Athens; hence his earlier work reflects a more Platonic cast than

Aristotle (384–322 B.C.), Plato's greatest student.

does the work of his maturity. His early *Eudemian Ethics* shows its Platonic influence in having a religious basis. He is less dependent on Plato in his later *Nichomachean Ethics,* which, although in no sense an antireligious ethics, has a more humanistic direction.

This difference reflects a larger difference between the philosophies of these two Greek giants. It has been captured memorably by Raphael in his famous painting,

"The School of Athens," in which Plato is gesturing upward, whereas Aristotle, walking at his side, points downward. Plato is animated by longings for eternity; Aristotle, although not insensitive to eternity, is more concerned with this world. Therefore his moral philosophy in the *Nichomachean Ethics* is based on man and his spiritual well being on earth and has much less to say than the Platonic ethics about serving God and preparing one's soul for judgment after death.

Approaching the *Ethics*

In the *Nichomachean Ethics* Aristotle continually tests his generalizations against the experience of living the moral life, always ready to modify them so as to take account of the rough edges of reality. He disapproves of philosophers who defend a theory at all costs; for his part, he shows great respect for the moral common sense of mankind. For instance, Greek moral thought ever since Socrates tends to see moral evil as resulting only from error. Aristotle understands the reasons why

Socrates holds this thesis, but at the same time he has the realism to know that we often *deliberately* do wrong. Thus Aristotle struggles to bring the Socratic theory into closer harmony with our moral experience.

But we must not follow those who advise us, being men, to think of human things, and, being mortal, of mortal things, but must, so far as we can, make ourselves immortal, and strain every nerve to live in accordance with the best thing in us {reason}; for even if it be small in bulk, much more does it in power and worth surpass everything.

—*Nichomachean Ethics*
William David Ross, trans.

When reading the *Nichomachean Ethics* one must bear in mind the difficulty of finding English equivalents for Aristotle's terms. This is especially true of the central Aristotelian term, *eudaemonia.* Although most translators settle for "happiness," this word has overtones foreign to Aristotle. Something like "complete well-being" is more exact in avoiding the un-Aristotelian modern resonance of "happiness." Readers should approach this great work in the awareness that Aristotle's intellectual world is very different from ours, and they should be ready to exercise some imagination to enter into the mentality of ancient Greek culture.

Happiness and Virtue

Aristotle opens the *Nichomachean Ethics* by inquiring, What is the supreme human good? He answers that this can only be *eudaemonia,* or happiness, because it is the only good that we always desire for its own sake and never as a means to anything else. It consists not in just any gratification but in the special spiritual satisfaction that comes from performing well the activities proper to human beings. Because Aristotle, like all the

Artist's impression of Aristotle teaching Alexander the Great.

Greek philosophers, sees the glory of man as lying in "reason" (taken in a much broader sense than the technological reason of the modern world), he believes that happiness comes primarily from acting in accordance with reason. For example, in discussing the virtuous use of anger, he says, "The man who is angry at the right things and with the right people, and, further, as he ought, when he ought, and as long as he ought, is praised." This man lives according to reason and so fulfills the best part of his nature.

But for Aristotle it is not enough that we act in accordance with reason; such acting must be a matter of "habit"—a matter of character. The habits whereby we become ourselves as rational beings are called by Aristotle the virtues. He divides them into the "moral" virtues, such as justice, courage, liberality, and temperance, and the "intellectual" virtues, such as philosophical wisdom. In the former he says we extend the dominion of reason over the unruly appetites and passions of our lower nature, and in the latter we perfect reason itself.

The ethics that most modern Christians are familiar with centers around "moral law" and "obligation" and sometimes "God's will"; but in his ethics Aristotle expresses himself in terms of virtue and of the happiness born of virtue. An Aristotelian virtue-ethics has the advantage of portraying the moral life as not coming from the outside but as being deeply "congenial" to us, the fulfillment of our own being.

Aristotle surprises many twentieth-century readers by claiming that intellectual virtue ranks above moral virtue. For him the highest spiritual activity is contemplation. Because intellectual virtue can be exercised contemplatively, whereas he sees moral virtue as always practical, he places moral virtue below intellectual.

When he discusses the attainment of happiness, Aristotle says that it derives primarily from the possession of moral, and especially intellectual, virtue. But he also deviates somewhat from Plato in teaching that virtue is not the exclusive source of happiness. If some disaster befalls us or those whom we love, we cannot be fully happy, he says, even though we will never be miserable as long as we persevere

The Parthenon, Athens.

in virtue. Thus certain external goods are also required for the fullness of happiness.

A Christian can appreciate the humanistic focus of Aristotle's ethics. For according to Christian revelation human beings are by nature moral beings; they have a conscience to live by even before they encounter Christ. The fall has damaged but has not completely extinguished the moral sense; ethical wisdom such as that of Aristotle is still possible.

Issues to Explore

(1) The *Nichomachean Ethics* contains a splendid discussion of friendship in Books VIII and IX. How are the great themes of Aristotle's moral philosophy reflected in his account?

(2) The first chapters of Book VII contain Aristotle's response to the Socratic teaching that no one knowingly does wrong. What exactly are his criticisms of Socrates?

A man is said to have or not to have self-control according as his reason has or has not the control, on the assumption that reason is the man himself.

—*Nichomachean Ethics*
William David Ross, trans.

For Further Study

Aristotle's *Nichomachean Ethics* is quite accessible because of Aristotle's talent for staying close to moral experience. But the text may not be altogether easy to follow because, unlike a Platonic dialogue, it is not a finished composition. Some think the work is either the notes from which Aristotle lectured or those compiled by an assistant.

In an elementary way Mortimer Adler explains the basic ideas of Aristotle's ethics in his *Aristotle for Everyone* (Bantam Books, 1980), chapters 9–15. On a higher level, but still accessible to the general reader, is the work of the Italian, Giovanni Reale, whom some consider the greatest living historian of ancient Greek philosophy. See the chapter on Aristotle's ethics in his *Plato and Aristotle* (State University of New York, 1988), which is volume II of his *History of Ancient Philosophy.* Also important is his chapter on the Socratic ethics in volume I, *From the Origins to Socrates* (State University of New York, 1987). These two volumes give an excellent survey of all ancient Greek philosophy through Aristotle.

A solid and reliable survey of the *Ethics* can be found in chapter 7 of Sir David Ross's *Aristotle* (Methuen & Co., 1953). Ross also gives an excellent translation of the *Nichomachean Ethics,* available in Richard Peter McKeon, editor, *Introduction to Aristotle* (University of Chicago, 1973). Terence Irwin has done a good translation more recently (Hackett, 1985). Its notes are more extensive than Ross's, and it includes a glossary.

(3) In Book III, chapters 1–5, Aristotle gives one of the most remarkable defenses of free choice in Greek philosophy. How would he respond to our contemporaries who say that human action is completely determined by genes and environment?

(4) Should happiness be the ultimate aim of all our striving? Does not a certain self-centeredness infect the Aristotelian moral life as a result of the centrality that the perfection of our nature occupies in his system?

(5) It has been said that the moral life has a certain imperative element missing in Aristotle. The *Nichomachean Ethics* could be read as teaching that *if* we want to be happy, *then* we should cultivate virtue. But is there not a Christian imperative to grow in virtue that is independent of our desire for happiness? Are we not aware of an unconditional "ought" in our conscience that cannot be cast into these if-then terms? With this "ought" we are on the threshold of that religious dimension of the moral life that is well known to Christians, but not only to them; it was already known to Plato, who is in this respect deeper than Aristotle.

(6) Why does Aristotle in Book X rank the intellectual virtues over the moral virtues? Does moral virtue require an unruly lower nature, making no sense apart from the task of governing it? Are the excellencies of contemplation found only in intellectual virtue and never in moral virtue?

—John F. Crosby

VIRGIL

The Aeneid
19 B.C.

irgil's *Aeneid* is *the* epic of Western civilization just as HOMER's *Iliad* and *Odyssey* are the epics of Greek culture and DANTE's *Divine Comedy* and MILTON's *Paradise Lost* are the epics of the Christian faith. Our political institutions and our ideas about leadership and about the public good versus private interests clearly bear the imprint of Virgil's great story of the origins of Rome.

Virgil (70–19 B.C.) was chosen for his task by Caesar Augustus, who envisioned a grand poem that would glorify Rome. Virgil, however, was unable to write mere propaganda, and his story of Rome's founding is an account of "civilization" that is both triumphant and troubling. When the poet fell ill and was on his deathbed after returning from a voyage to Athens, he is said to have asked for the unfinished *Aeneid* to be destroyed.

A New Civilization

Virgil begins the story of Rome with the same event that Homer wrote about—the Trojan War. It was fought at Troy over the

Virgil (Publius Vergilius Maro), (70–19 B.C.).

beautiful Helen, stolen wife of Menelaus, and won after ten years when the Greeks offered the Trojans a wooden horse as a gift but deceptively hid their soldiers inside. Virgil's story traces the journey of Aeneas and the small remnant of Trojan survivors who escape the burning city as they make their way across the sea to Italy and attempt to build a new home.

Those familiar with the *Iliad* and the *Odyssey* will notice that Virgil

seems to draw heavily on Homer's poems. Aeneas sails past many of the places visited by Odysseus, and the graphic war scenes are similar to those at Troy. Virgil's purpose, however, was not to imitate but to go *beyond* Homer: Whereas the earlier epics depicted two distinctive Greek institutions—the city and the home—the *Aeneid* was to portray Rome's unique achievement—civilization, which encompassed both city and home.

The figure of Aeneas was adopted throughout the Roman Empire as the pattern of the Roman hero. During the Middle Ages, Christians interpreted the Roman conquests depicted in the *Aeneid* as part of God's plan for bringing peace to the world in anticipation of Christ's birth and for establishing a government in which the individual could freely pursue salvation. In his *Divine Comedy* Dante, the greatest medieval poet, even made Virgil his guide through the underworld. He believed that Virgil's work, though accomplished in spiritual darkness, led toward the light of God's love. Virgil continues to be influential though with some controversy in our time.

*. . . so hard and huge
a task it was to found the Roman people.*
—*The Aeneid*
Robert Fitzgerald, trans.

Part of the Forum,
ancient Rome.

Out of the Ashes—Destiny

The *Aeneid* begins with the famous line announcing its hero: "Arms and the man I sing." Led by Aeneas—"the man"—the small band of Trojan exiles first finds refuge in the city of Carthage, which is being built by beautiful Queen Dido. At a feast Aeneas tells his story of Greek deception and Trojan defeat in a way that gives us the first glimpses of the cosmic proportions of Virgil's epic.

As Aeneas recounts it, one day during the

Aeneas's father Anchises tells him in the Underworld:

*Roman, remember by your strength to rule
Earth's peoples—for your arts are to be these:
To pacify, to impose the rule of law,
To spare the conquered, battle down the proud.*
—*The Aeneid*
Robert Fitzgerald, trans.

siege of Troy he believes that the Greeks have left his city. Then, however, he has a disturbing dream in which the slain Trojan hero Hector declares that Troy is doomed. Aeneas awakes to find the city in flames, the situation hopeless. After witnessing the brutal murder of Troy's King Priam he intends to slay Helen, whose fatal beauty has caused the war. He is prevented, however, by the goddess Venus, his mother. She reveals to him the mysterious purposes of the gods: Troy's fall is fated, but he is to lead the survivors to an even greater destiny. These two supernatural events are reinforced by a third. As Aeneas takes his family through the city toward safety, his wife Creusa is lost; when he searches for her, she appears as a spirit and says that he will find a new wife among a people in a land far away.

Aeneas is "born great" and until now has been a noble warrior and citizen. He is reluctant to take on the responsibility of leadership because he knows he will have to submit completely to something much larger than himself—something so large, in fact, that it must be seen as the work of heaven, affecting all humankind. Nevertheless, Aeneas assumes the role, choosing the "public" role over the "private." In hearkening to the call of the gods, he also assumes his distinctive character as a leader—Virgil describes him as "greathearted" and "pious." Aeneas achieves true greatness only when he submits to the will of the gods and devotes himself with absolute piety to his mission.

Yet Virgil is honest about the hardship and suffering that accompany sacrifice of the self to the good of the whole. Readers are not spared Aeneas's grief, despair, and uncertainty as he guides his people toward a goal that he only dimly perceives. The son of a goddess and a mortal father, he is ultimately human.

Nor does Virgil spare us Aeneas's tragic flaws. With the influence of the goddesses Juno and Venus, Dido and Aeneas fall in love, and Aeneas lets himself believe that Carthage can be the Trojans' new home. But their love proves disastrous. When Jupiter, chief among the gods, recalls Aeneas to his mission, the queen's desperate act of suicide leaves her people without a leader. The tragedy is one of the most celebrated love stories of Western civilization. But it is impossible to read without judging: Aeneas fails the divine purpose and causes great suffering; Dido betrays her own mission and the people she has led. In spite of its consequences, Aeneas's abrupt departure reveals both his weakness and his strength, for though it brings sorrow, it is the right response to his grievous error.

Aeneas's final enlightenment comes only when he journeys to the underworld and receives a vision of the future. There his father Anchises shows him the unborn souls of his own offspring, generations of heroes eager to engage the heroic task of establishing the empire that Aeneas is to bring into being. Knowing the sorrows of life, he cannot believe their desire to leave the serenity of the Elysian Fields: "The poor souls, how can they crave our daylight so?" Anchises responds with what became known as the Roman Mandate: "Remember by your strength to rule Earth's peoples —for your arts are to be these: to pacify, to impose the rule of law, to spare the conquered, battle down the proud."

With these words, Virgil proclaims the true work of all Roman leaders, from Aeneas to Caesar Augustus. Through the vision Aeneas realizes that his personal sacrifice is for the good of the largest whole, the earth itself, whose vast potential may be realized only within a new, comprehensive, and inclusive order— civilization. To be civilized, Virgil is saying, is to live within a political order that promotes universal peace, thereby allowing pursuit of virtue and the good life.

Aeneas arrives in Italy with a new clarity of purpose. Tragic suffering, however, continues to haunt his efforts to found this new civilization. Led by the noble but fiery Turnus, the native Italians resist the Trojans' "colonizing" invasion, especially when King Latinus announces that his daughter Lavinia, betrothed to Turnus, will instead marry Aeneas to unite the two peoples. Unable to achieve peace with Turnus, Aeneas fights back and for a time becomes as savage as they are. After single combat between Aeneas and Turnus, the *Aeneid* ends darkly and shockingly with Aeneas's fatal response to Turnus's request for mercy.

Bronze head of the Roman Emperor Augustus.

Issues to Explore

Critics of the *Aeneid* often ignore the complex questions that Virgil's poem raises. (1) Is the concept of civilization—of a structure that rules justly and enforces peace among various groups —a valid one for modern times? (2) Is Aeneas the ideal type of leader for today—one willing to count the costs of both necessary personal sacrifice and necessary use of force for the

After lingering in Carthage with Dido, Aeneas is commanded by Jupiter to continue the mission:

As the sharp admonition and command
From heaven had shaken him awake, he now
Burned only to be gone, to leave that land
Of the sweet life behind.

—*The Aeneid*
Robert Fitzgerald, trans.

Aeneas's response to the war in Italy he has tried to avoid:

> *Never should I have come here had not Fate*
> *Allotted me this land for settlement,*
> *Nor do I war upon your people.*

> —*The Aeneid*
> Robert Fitzgerald, trans.

good of the whole? (3) What are the sobering implications of the final scene?

(4) Christians should especially examine the way Virgil connects human labors in civilization to the realm of the gods. Which determines more of the suffering and circumstances of the *Aeneid:* the gods and fate or the characters and their choices? (5) Could Dido, though in love, still have chosen duty over Aeneas? (6) Does the gods' concern for the human drama foreshadow the Christian's understanding that God's providence controls all? (7) Why does Virgil insist on Jupiter's beneficence and Aeneas's flawed but persistent piety?

> —Larry Allums

For Further Study

The *Aeneid* is stirring and fast-paced, filled with intense human experiences from gory war scenes to tender stories of love. Robert Fitzgerald's translation (Vintage, 1984) is the best; its glossary and "Postscript" are helpful.

The interested reader should also consult two essays by T. S. Eliot, "Vergil and the Christian World" and "What Is a Classic?" in *On Poets and Poetry* (Farrar, Straus, 1957); Brooks Otis, *Virgil: A Study in Civilized Poetry* (Oxford University Press, 1963); W. S. Anderson, *The Art of the Aeneid* (Prentice-Hall, 1969); Henry Steele Commager, editor, *Virgil: A Collection of Critical Essays* (Prentice-Hall, 1966); Mario A. DiCesar, *The Altar and the City: A Reading of Virgil's* Aeneid (Columbia, 1974); W. R. Johnson, *Darkness Visible* (University of California, 1976); and Gordon Williams, *Technique and Idea in the* Aeneid (Yale, 1983).

Roman and Italian Classics

Roman and Italian writings form one of the most powerful and influential streams within Western classics—not least because the geographical region we call Italy has nurtured the longest continuous tradition of writing in Western Europe and the language of Latin has flourished far beyond Italy.

From early times, long before the power of Rome extended across the whole of the Mediterranean and beyond, the region was multilingual. Etruscan and various Latin languages were spoken in the northern and central areas, Greek in the south. Thus, on the one hand, languages other than Latin flourished in Italy, and a number of influential writers whom we normally think of as Greek—such as Theocritus, Archimedes, and Lucian—were also, in a certain sense, Italian writers. Even long after Latin had became a full-fledged literary language, such bilingual writers as Cicero and the Emperor Marcus Aurelius were still composing works in Greek.

On the other hand, Latin flourished far beyond Italy. Although the use of Greek waned in the West after the fall of Rome, Latin continued to be the official language of the Western church and state for well over a millennium afterward. During the Middle Ages in Italy, as elsewhere

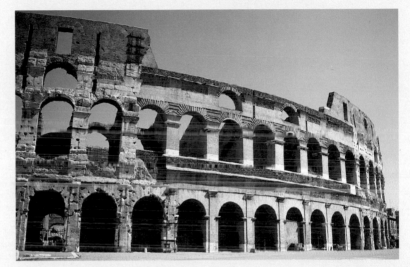

The Colosseum, Rome.

in Europe, it was universally used for both trade and schooling. Latin continued to be the language of scholarly treatises until the end of the eighteenth century and still is the official language of the Roman Catholic Church. Italian humanists emphasized the break between ancient Rome and medieval times, but a substantial linguistic and cultural influence continued well into the seventeenth century.

Greek Writers in Ancient Rome

A clear illustration of this continuity can be seen in the way certain philosophical trends of Greek origins, which were popular in ancient Rome, were absorbed into early Christian thought and thus into the mainstream of European intellectual life. For example, Epictetus, a Greek-speaking philosopher living in Rome during the first century A.D., was a leading exponent of Stoicism. His ethical teaching about the human will in his Discourses influenced such Roman disciples as Arrian, Seneca, and Marcus Aurelius (whose *Meditations* was one of the most influential books of antiquity) as well as early Christian thinkers. And the versatile Stoic philosopher Seneca—the scientist, poet, dramatist, and satirist who invented the philosophic essay—influenced such church fathers as Tertullian, Lactantius, and Jerome. His tragedies were imitated by fifteenth-century Italian playwrights and, in the following centuries, by French and English dramatists, including Shakespeare. Along with the Roman comedy writers Plautus and Terence, Seneca was a major influence on the European theater.

Likewise, the philosophy of Epicurus (c. 340–c. 270 B.C.), whose letters to his followers seem similar to St. Paul's epistles, offered a message of religious salvation popularized by such Roman writers as Lucretius, author of *On the Nature of Things*. Epicureanism, however, differed from the Christian faith in too many respects to be other than a rival doctrine. Nevertheless, its attractiveness to those who sought peace of mind doubtless obliged early Christians to address its claims and present alternative paths to the same goals.

Finally, the Neoplatonic tradition had an enormous influence on Christian thought. Drawing its inspiration from PLATO, though more directly religious, it spoke of the union of the soul and the absolute (the One) and provided an intellectual basis for a religious life. The most notable representative was another Greek thinker, Plotinus, who lived in Rome during the third century A.D. and influenced the notable Christian writers Ambrose, AUGUSTINE, and, later, Boethius. Plotinus's impact was also felt over a millennium later when Platonic thought was rediscovered by the Italian humanists in Florence, particularly by Marsilio Ficino.

Another Greek-language writer who traveled all over the Roman Empire may be included in the company of these philosophers. Lucian (c. 120–200) was a rhetorician and satirist whose works were mostly forgotten in the

Tomb of the Latin poet Virgil (70–19 B.C.).

West after the fall of Rome, but who remained influential in Constantinople throughout the Middle Ages. He was rediscovered and taken up enthusiastically by such sixteenth-century writers as Erasmus, Thomas MORE, and François Rabelais. Likewise, Plutarch (c. 49–c. 120), the prolific author of the famous *Parallel Lives* from which Shakespeare drew for his Roman plays, was neglected in the West until the Renaissance. His comparative approach to history transformed the writing of biography in Europe up to the end of the eighteenth century.

The Great Latins

Among historians writing in Latin, Livy (c. 59 B.C–A.D. 17) is considered the most accomplished prose writer of Augustan Rome. He is the source of our stories of Romulus and Remus, Horatius, Cincinnatus, Hannibal, and the

I sing of warfare and a man at war
From the seacoast of Troy in early days
He came to Italy by destiny
To our Lavinian western shore,
A fugitive, this captive buffeted
Cruelly on land as on the sea
By blows from powers of the air—behind them
Baleful Juno in her sleepless rage.
And cruel losses were his lot in war,
Till he could found a city and bring home
His gods to Latium, land of the Latin race,
The Alban lords, and the high walls of Rome,

—Virgil
The Aeneid
Robert Fitzgerald, trans.

sack of Rome by the Gauls. His *History of Rome* has been called the prose counterpart of VIRGIL'S *Aeneid.* An influence on all subsequent Roman historians, he continued to be read as late as the twelfth century and then was rediscovered during the Renaissance.

The greatest of the Roman historians is Tacitus (c. 55–117), who may have studied with the educator Quintilian; his *Annales* and *Histories* are important primary sources for our knowledge of the Roman emperors from Tiberius to Nerva. He is equally important as both a prose stylist and a penetrating analyst of historical and psychological causes.

History in antiquity was closely related to oratory. The most famous orator of ancient Rome was Cicero (106–43 B.C.), statesman, philosopher, and poet. He successfully shaped Latin into a subtle literary and philosophical language with a long and distinguished life. Never forgotten in the West, Cicero became the primary model for correct Latin during the Renaissance. The other major figure for Latin rhetorical style and educational theory was Quintilian (c. 35–c. 100), who has been ranked only a little below Socrates as a teacher. His one existing work, the *Institutes,* has influenced European letters enormously, beginning with Tacitus and continuing with such Christian authors as Jerome, Lactantius, Cassiodorus, and Isidore of Seville.

Three great Roman poets have also served for nearly two millennia as models in European literature. The impact of Ovid (43 B.C.–A.D. 18) on art, music, and literature has been enormous. The witty style

The Roman poet Ovid (Publius Ovidius Naso) 43 B.C.– A.D. 17.

of his love poetry was imitated continuously for eighteen centuries. His greatest contribution, however, was his long mythological poem, the *Metamorphoses,* to which generation after generation of writers, artists, and composers has been indebted. Horace (65–8 B.C.) holds the distinction of being Rome's greatest lyric poet. Indeed, he has been studied by scholars and students virtually without interruption from the first century B.C. to our own. Apart from famous odes, epistles, and satires that have been imitated and translated by some of the greatest European poets, he was influential as a literary theorist through his classification of aesthetic principles in his so-called "ars poetica"

("Letter to the Pisos"). Likewise, Virgil (70–19 B.C.) was never neglected in the West. Indeed, during the Middle Ages he was regarded as a great pre-Christian writer and visionary. DANTE Alighieri (1265–1321) in his masterwork the *Divine Comedy* even made Virgil his guide in the *Inferno.*

From the Middle Ages to the Renaissance

After the fall of the Roman Empire in 476, students in ecclesiastical schools continued to study and imitate the great Latin writers. The center of literary activity, however, shifted to France by the twelfth century. When literary works in Italian began to appear alongside

The soul, which is created apt for love,
The moment pleasure wakes it into act,
To any pleasant thing is swift to move.

Your apprehension draws from some real fact
An inward image, which it shows to you,
And by that image doth the soul attract;

And if the soul, attracted, yearns thereto,
That yearning's love; 'tis nature doth secure
Her bond in you, which pleasure knits anew.

And as fire mounts, urged upward by the pure
Impulsion of its form, which must aspire
Toward its own matter, where 'twill best endure,

So the enamoured soul falls to desire—
A motion spiritual—nor rest can find
Till its loved object it enjoy entire.

Now canst thou see how wholly those are blind
To truth, who think all love is laudable
Just in itself, no matter of what kind.

—Dante
The Purgatorio
The Divine Comedy
Dorothy L. Sayers, trans.

Latin writings, they betrayed a French rather than classical influence. The lyric forms that emerged during the eleventh century in southern France, along with the heroic romances from the north, continued to be important models up to the time of Dante. After 1250, nevertheless, an independent native Italian literature began to emerge, brought to fulfillment in the *Divine Comedy* in the first decades of the 1300s. Rather than following a classical model, Dante chose a unique structure for his poem. Although he wrote the *Comedy* in Italian, he produced other works in Latin. His successors were often bilingual as well.

For example, Francesco Petrarca (Petrarch, 1304–1374), sometimes considered the first humanist, thought of himself primarily as a Latin writer. His Italian love sonnets, which derived from medieval sources, did have an enormous influence throughout Europe, but his contemporaries honored him more conspicuously for attempting to revive ancient Roman models of eloquence. Unlike his predecessor Dante, he rejected the scholastic philosophers of the Middle Ages, instead taking as his guides the early church fathers along with the great classical Roman authors. His epic, the *Africa,* inspired by Livy and Cicero, was not only written in Latin but followed closely the form of Virgil's *Aeneid.* In addition, he wrote numerous letters, philosophical and autobiographical works, prayers, and poems in both Latin and Italian.

His younger contemporary and friend, Giovanni Boccaccio (1313–1375), also wrote in both languages. His writings tend to follow medieval rather than classical models, though he did compose a Latin treatise on the classical gods. Apart from a large number of commentaries, treatises, epistles, and poems in Latin, he created several verse romances and allegories in Italian. Two of them were imitated by CHAUCER. His masterpiece, however, is *The Decameron,* a collection of a hundred stories in Italian prose that offers a truly comprehensive picture of life during this period.

In the course of the fifteenth century the major Italian humanists began a full-scale revival of the classical past, setting the tone for the next centuries of European literary history. Yet the unique character of Italian literature was much more than a mere scholarly imitation of the past. The melding of medieval and classical elements introduced by fourteenth-century Italian authors was continued in the late fifteenth- and sixteenth-century romance-epics of Matteo Boiardo (*Orlando Innamorato*), Ludovico Ariosto (*Orlando Furioso*), and Torquato Tasso (*Jerusalem Delivered*). They served as important models for English writers from Spenser to MILTON. Niccolò MACHIAVELLI, in addition to his famous *The Prince*, also wrote a commentary on the Roman historian Livy that reveals his own understanding of the relationship between the classical and contemporary worlds.

Continually attentive to the great literary achievements of their past yet open to influence from the north, postclassical Italian writers illustrate in exemplary fashion the way in which diversity and absorption—the accommodation of pagan achievement within a Christian perspective—have shaped Western European literature.

Later Italian Literature

Although Italian influence was at its height during the Renaissance period, in the centuries to follow a number of writers continued to make their mark on European letters. The extravagant baroque style of Giambattista Marino (1569–1625) set the tone not only for seventeenth-century Italian poetry but for much of other European poetry as well. Further, the invention of opera early in the period had an impact far beyond its original goal of emulating

Pygmalion loathed the vices given by nature
To women's hearts; he lived a lonely life,
Shunning the thought of marriage and a wife.
Meanwhile he carved the snow-white ivory
With happy skill: he gave it beauty greater
Than any woman's: then grew amorous of it.
It was a maiden's figure—and it lived
(You thought) but dared not move for modesty.
So much did art conceal itself. The sculptor
Marvelled, and loved his beautiful pretence.
Often he touched the body, wondering
If it were ivory or flesh; he would not
Affirm it ivory. . . .

—Ovid
Metamorphoses
Gilbert Highet, trans.

ancient Greek drama; and in the eighteenth century, it was above all the poet Pietro Metastasio (1698–1782), the greatest Italian literary figure of his time, whose reform of the operatic libretto gave Italian drama a hearing all over Europe. At the same time, the reform of comedy was carried out by Carlo Goldoni (1707–1793) in an attempt to replace the improvisatory, farcical style of the *commedia dell'arte* with more sophisticated scripted plots.

During this period such original philosophical thinkers as Giordano Bruno (1548–1600) and utopian poet Tommaso Campanella (1568–1644) had an outstanding successor in Giambattista Vico (1668–1744). His *The New Science* (1725–1744) marks the emergence of a modern sense of historical consciousness in opposition to Cartesian rationalism.

Just as the Italian Renaissance represented a new way of looking at the past, so Italian writers after Vico gained a new vision of the present through the growing interest in political unity and national independence. These new ideals are given fresh expression in Alessandro Manzoni's great novel *The Betrothed* (1825–27), in the pessimistic romanticism of the philosophical poet Giacomo Leopardi (1798–1837), and, later in the nineteenth century, by the important poets Giosuè Carducci (1835–1907) and Giovanni Pascoli (1855–1912). Carducci's and Pascoli's work, along with Francesco De Sanctis's groundbreaking history of Italian literature, extended historical awareness back to the Roman heritage even as it imagined a greater Italian nation in the future.

For Further Study

Burckhardt, Jacob, *The Civilization of the Renaissance in Italy*, second edition, S. G. C. Middlemore, translator (Penguin, 1990).

Copley, Frank O., *Latin Literature* (University of Michigan, 1969).

De Sanctis, Francesco, *History of Italian Literature*, two volumes, Joan Redfern, translator (Barnes and Noble, 1931; 1968).

Garin, Eugenio, *Italian Humanism*, Peter Munz, translator (Greenwood Press, 1965; 1975).

Kenney, E. J., and Clausen, V. W., editors, *The Cambridge History of Classical Literature* (Cambridge, 1982).

Whitfield, J. H., *A Short History of Italian Literature*, revised edition (Manchester University and Greenwood Press, 1980).

Wilkins, Ernest H., *A History of Italian Literature*, revised edition by Thomas G. Bergin (Cambridge, 1974).

The Italian playwright Luigi Pirandello (1867–1936), awarded the Nobel Prize for Literature in 1934.

This peculiar combination of romanticism and classicism in the emerging sense of an Italian identity also characterized twentieth-century writing, though in a mode different from that going back to Dante. Novelist, poet, and playwright Gabriele D'Annunzio (1863–1938), for example, was a latter-day romantic but also a political activist, at once a disciple of Friedrich NIETZSCHE and of the French symbolists. Likewise, the very different scholarly activities of philosopher, historian, and critic Benedetto Croce (1866–1952) served to emphasize the continuity between the Italian past and its literary present.

More to the point, however, after the Fascist period and the aftermath of World War II a new awareness emerged. Its roots lay in the spiritual protests of the earlier secret gnostic movement and a rejection of the grand political gestures of D'Annunzio's generation. The resulting intense, if frequently melancholy, lyricism led, on the one hand, to the poetry of Giuseppe Ungaretti (1888–1970), Eugenio Montale (1896–1981), and Salvatore Quasimodo (1901–1968); and, on the other, to the psychological realism of such novelists as Alberto Moravia (1907–1990) and Cesare Pavese (1908–1950).

Throughout the twentieth century, Italian literature displays a wide range of styles, from the avant-garde dramas of Luigi Pirandello (1867–1936) to the fantastic linguistic worlds of Italo Calvino (1923–1985). Yet it still possesses the same nature that has always characterized the Italian imagination in its union of earthy humor and visionary extravagance with a comfortable commitment to the burden of an ancient past.

—Robert S. Dupree

Early Christian Writers

The early period in Christian history (A.D. 100–451) is the most significant and creative age for the articulation of the Christian faith. Beginning with the death of the last apostles and ending with the Council of Chalcedon (451), this period witnessed the development of the major theological doctrines of the Christian faith. All mainstream Christian churches regard this period as the definitive landmark in the development of Christian doctrine.

During the first part of this period, in the second and third centuries, the church was misunderstood and often persecuted by the state. Thus the earliest development of the Christian faith involved Christians explaining and defending their beliefs and practices to a hostile pagan public. Justin Martyr, Irenaeus, Tertullian, and Origen are leading representatives of this age. They came to be known as apologists or defenders of the faith.

The conversion of the Emperor Constantine to the Christian faith and the subsequent reconciliation of church and state in the fourth century enabled theology to become a matter of public interest and concern throughout the Roman Empire. The fourth and fifth centuries may therefore be regarded as a time of immense theological activity with divergent views being articulated, debates abounding, and councils convening to discuss theological matters. Athanasius was a leading figure in the most intense debate of the fourth century—the trinitarian controversy at the Council of Nicaea—in which he defended the divinity of Christ. Although theological debates received maximum notoriety, most Christian writers' efforts were then more pastoral and practical in nature. Two excellent examples are the letters of Ambrose and Jerome.

Justin Martyr (100–165)

Justin, a Gentile philosopher born in Palestine, was the most famous apologist for the Christian faith in the second century. Born of pagan parents, he came to faith after a long search in pagan philosophies. His *First Apology,* written from Rome, directly appeals to the Emperor Antonius Pius for justice on behalf of Christians who face Roman persecution. In the course of his defense of the gospel, Justin shows himself to be both churchman and philosopher. As churchman, he argues for the uniqueness of Christ as the Messiah of the Old Testament and Son of the true God and, subsequently, for the claims that this belief places on Christians. The *Apology,* in this respect, is

Justin Martyr (100–165).

something of an early manual for converts. After addressing his *Second Apology* to the Roman Senate, Justin and his disciples were denounced as Christians; when they refused to sacrifice, they were scourged and beheaded.

As philosopher, Justin is speculative and somewhat daring. He is the first Christian thinker to seek to reconcile the claims of faith and reason, emphasizing the role of reason in guiding human beings toward the truth. Further, he demonstrates that the charge of atheism leveled against Christians is similar to that unjustly leveled against the famous philosopher, Socrates. Finally, and perhaps most daring of all, Justin defines "Christians" as those who are given to and led by reason *(logos)*.

> We have been taught that Christ is the first-born of God, and we have declared above that He is the Word of whom every race of men were partakers; and those who lived reasonably are Christians, even though they have been thought atheists; as among the Greeks, Socrates and Heraclitus, and men like them.

Irenaeus (140–202)

Born in Smyrna (present-day Turkey) and perhaps a student of Justin's in Rome, Irenaeus was first a missionary to and later a bishop of Lyons (France). His *Against All Heresies* is a detailed attack on gnosticism and a pastoral attempt to establish clearly the belief in the one God and in his only begotten Son, Jesus Christ, who is truly God and truly human. He promotes orthodoxy in a culture rife with heretical teachings that threaten the truth of the gospel.

Irenaeus is the first great catholic theologian. Perhaps the greatest contribution he makes involves his identification of those authorities that collectively constitute a tradition for determining the true Christian faith. After Christ's resurrection, according to Irenaeus, the apostles were those who preached the gospel publicly and later handed down the Scriptures to be the ground and pillar of the faith. Next, the Scriptures and apostolic testimony were preserved and passed down through a succession of leaders of the churches, the bishops.

> It is within the power of all, therefore, in every Church, who may wish to see the truth, to contemplate clearly the tradition of the apostles manifested throughout the whole world; and we are in a position to reckon up those who were by the apostles instituted bishops in the Churches, and [to demonstrate] the succession of these men to our own times.

Finally, the church of Rome came to be recognized as the preeminent authority for preserving the true faith. "For it is a matter of necessity that every Church should agree with this Church [of Rome], on account of its preeminent authority."

Tertullian (160–225)

This North African theologian is often regarded as the father of Latin theology because of the impact of his writings—some thirty-one books—on the Western church. Brought up in Carthage as a well-educated pagan, Tertullian converted to Christ as an adult; his advice in dealing with heretics is honest, practical, passionate, and even somewhat comical. He is brilliant and masterly in style and argues for a pure Christian theology that would have nothing to do with Greco-Roman philosophy or other sources beyond the Bible. "What has Jerusalem to do with Athens, the church with the Academy, the Christian with the heretic?" Or more bluntly: "a plague on Aristotle, who taught them dialectic. . . ."

Although he recognized the ambiguities inherent in biblical interpretation ("arguments about Scripture achieve nothing but a stomachache or a headache"), Tertullian appeals to the *Regula Fidei*—literally the rule of faith, a summary of the essential affirmations of apostolic preaching such as God the creator, the divinity of Christ and the Holy Spirit, the second coming, and so on—as the authoritative guide in matters of faith and practice.

Origen (185–254)

A biblical translator, expositor, preacher, philosopher, devotional writer, and theologian, Origen is considered by many to be the greatest of the early church fathers. Superbly educated in a Christian home, Origen lost his father in the Alexandrian persecution of 202 and

When it is said that "the last enemy shall be destroyed," it is not to be understood as meaning that his substance, which is God's creation, perishes, but that his purpose and hostile will perishes.

—Origen in *Documents of the Christian Church* (Oxford, 1967)
Henry Bettenson, ed. and trans.

escaped martyrdom himself only because his mother hid his clothes. His *Contra Celsum* is an authoritative reply to perhaps the most devastating intellectual assault ever brought against the Christian faith, the second-century Greek philosopher Celsus's book, *The True Doctrine*. Origen moves point by point through Celsus's argument in answering such criticisms as the following: Christians are basically unintellectual; the virgin birth did not take place; Christians are polytheists; the resurrection of Christ is superstition; Jesus performed miracles by practicing magic; the incarnation is a most shameful doctrine. Origen closes his work by suggesting to Ambrose, who sent him the copy of Celsus's book, that if Celsus ever wrote a sequel as promised, to "search out

There are three ways in which the meaning of the Holy Scriptures should be inscribed in the soul of every Christian man. First, the simpler sort are edified by what may be called the "body" of scripture . . . ; Secondly, those who have made some progress are edified by, as it were, the "soul." Thirdly, the perfect . . . are edified by the "spiritual" Law, which has the shadow of the good things to come.

—Origen in *Documents of the Christian Church* (Oxford, 1967)
Henry Bettenson, ed. and trans.

and send the treatise that we may make to that also the reply that is given to us by the Fathers of the truth, and may refute the false opinions in that as well."

Jerome (Eusebius Hieronymus Sophronius) (347–420).

Athanasius (295–373)

This bishop of Alexandria for forty-five years is best known for his defense of Christ's divinity in light of the Arian movement, which held that Christ was not fully God. Exiled five times and often in hiding, Athanasius was indomitable through the long, bitter controversies and was described as standing alone against the world *(Athanasius contra mundum). On the Incarnation*, written in his twenties, is one of his earlier works, coming before the Arian controversy and the Council of Nicaea of 325. In it, Athanasius offers a powerful, passionate, and reasonable defense of the idea that God assumed human nature in the person of Jesus Christ. God comes down to our level, Athanasius suggests, like a teacher who speaks in a way that pupils can understand. The incarnation was necessary in order for God to heal that which suffers. In other words,

God had to become human to heal the human condition. Finally, and perhaps most provocatively, Athanasius states that God or the Word of God was made man so that we might be made God. Historic orthodoxy owes much to both the resolute character and theology of Athanasius.

Ambrose (339–397)

A high-ranking government official in the midst of a successful public career, Ambrose was pressed into the office of bishop by the popular demand of the citizens of Milan. He neither desired nor was trained to administer this office, but through hard work, study, and courage, Ambrose came to be one of the most brilliant and influential bishops ever, celebrated both as a preacher and a champion of orthodoxy. Along with Jerome, Augustine, and Gregory the Great, Ambrose is one of the four traditional doctors of the Latin church.

The letters of Ambrose illustrate not only a practical concern within his ministry but also one of the leading themes in the faith—the relations between church and state. The letters show Ambrose at work dealing with such issues as idolatry, heresy, appropriation of church funds, and excommunication, all within a church-state context. One of the letters contains the remarkable account of Ambrose's excommunication of the Roman Emperor, Theodorius. He is also famous for his key role in the conversion of St. Augustine, who studied rhetoric under him and revered him.

For Further Study

One way to approach these writers is to read them in order of importance. This method is, admittedly, extremely subjective. One could start with Origen, who is perhaps the greatest theologian and the most daring and speculative; then move to Tertullian, a fiery spirit, uncompromising by nature but easy to read; next Irenaeus, who emphasizes structure and authority and may justly be called the first biblical theologian; then Justin Martyr and the rest. Another approach might be to read the writers chronologically. This would tend to situate the . author and establish a sense of history.

The recommended editions for each text follow.

Justin Martyr: *First Apology* in *The Ante-Nicene Fathers,* volume I, Alexander Roberts and James Donaldson, editors (Eerdmans, 1965).

Irenaeus: *Against All Heresies* in *The Ante-Nicene Fathers,* volume I.

Tertullian: *Prescriptions against Heretics* in *Early Latin Theology,* The Library of Christian Classics, S. L. Greenslade, translator and editor (Westminster Press, 1956).

Origen: *Contra Celsum,* Henry Chadwick, translator (Cambridge, 1953).

Athanasius: *On the Incarnation of the Word* in *Christology of the Later Fathers,* The Library of Christian Classics, E. R. Hardy, editor (Westminster Press, 1954).

Ambrose: *Letters,* in *Early Latin Theology.*

Jerome: *Letters,* in *Early Latin Theology.*

Jerome (347–420)

Jerome's name is etched in Christian annals forever because of his Latin translation of the Bible—the Vulgate—and his numerous commentaries. But his *Letters* invite a closer view of his personal concerns and pastoral relationships.

Ascetism was at the center of Jerome's life. He believed that the disciplined life of renunciation was needed to offset worldliness in a church that was gaining political power and continually being tempted to compromise with secular authorities. In one letter, Jerome invites his friend, Heliodorus, to become a hermit in the desert. Later some used this appeal as a kind of apology for the ascetic life. In another, Jerome cautions a young church leader against accepting gifts: "Let us never seek for presents and rarely accept them when we are asked to do so . . . the very man who begs leave to offer you a gift holds you the cheaper for your acceptance of it." And Jerome shows a capacity for what could be called a modern approach to education, in his words to parents on teaching their young daughter: "You must not scold her if she is slow to learn, but must employ praise to excite her mind. . . . Above all you must take care not to make her lessons distasteful to her, lest a dislike for them conceived in childhood may continue into her maturer years."

—Telfair J. Mashburn, III

AUGUSTINE

The Confessions
A.D. 401

Augustine of Hippo (A.D. 354–430).

By any one of a number of standards the *Confessions* of Augustine is a classic. It is generally considered the first full-scale autobiography of the ancient world and one of the most influential spiritual autobiographies of all time. As a devotional text, the *Confessions* also confirms Augustine's place as one of the greatest thinkers of the Christian church. His extensive writings influenced the development of both medieval theology and the Protestant Reformation. The *Confessions,* however, is not simply one man's story. As readers throughout the centuries have noted, it is the story of everyone who has journeyed from worldliness, ambition, and despair to salvation and joy by the grace of God.

In writing about his life, the man known to us as St. Augustine also captured a historical moment of great importance, for he stood at the crossroads of history—the collapse of the Roman Empire. In A.D. 324 Constantine was crowned Emperor and the Roman Empire officially became a Christian empire. By the time Aurelius

Augustinus was born thirty years later in the North African town of Tagaste, the foundations of both the Roman Empire and the early Christian church had already begun to crumble. During the span of Augustine's lifetime (A.D. 354–430) both church and state proved to be increasingly unstable entities. Following invasions by

the Goths and Vandals, the Roman Empire eventually fell; the Christian church, however, was largely reunified through the efforts of Augustine, whose writings formed the intellectual and theological foundations of the medieval church.

As a philosophical text, the *Confessions* is also a classic treatise on time, memory, beauty, ethics, and the problem of evil. On these important philosophical issues, Augustine modifies the fourth-century Greek philosopher PLATO and anticipates the seventeenth-century French philosopher René Descartes.

Even if Augustine had not secured a high place in the intellectual history of Western civilization via his other writings, the simple, beautiful, readable prose of the *Confessions* would have earned him a place as the writer of a work of classic spiritual devotion. For as the opening and closing sentences attest, Augustine's primary purpose in writing the *Confessions* is to offer prayer and praise to God, who inscribes his being into individual lives and history.

He serves you best who is not so anxious to hear from you what he wills as to will what he hears from you.

—*The Confessions*
Rex Warner, trans.

An Unlikely Saint

Augustine's early years, as portrayed in the *Confessions,* reveal him as an unlikely candidate for such an esteemed position within the history of the church. Born to a Christian mother and pagan father, he spent most of his youth and early manhood satisfying his own and their worldly ambitions. Success as a student at Carthage led to his success as a teacher first in Tagaste, then in Carthage, and later in Milan. Increasingly prestigious appointments led him further and further from the simple faith and pietism of his mother. Intellectually he found the philosophy of Platonism and the dualism of Manichaeism (which sees good and evil, light and darkness as equal oppositional forces) far more palatable than the Christian faith. Rhetorically he preferred the eloquence of Cicero to the seemingly offensive simplicity of Scripture.

Augustine's personal life offered no better indications of his eventual sainthood. As a student he took a mistress—an accepted practice by the moral conventions of the day—who bore him a son. Years later he dismissed the woman, whom he apparently loved very much, in anticipation of an arranged marriage that never came to be. But Augustine also had outstanding virtues as a young man. He was by all accounts brilliant, and during his highly successful appointment as an instructor of rhetoric in Milan, he generously arranged to have members of his family as well as friends join him in his household.

The people Augustine gathered in Milan would witness one of the most dramatic and influential conversion stories of history. In Milan, he gradually became disillusioned with the philosophy of Manichaeism, and he was mildly compelled to admit the persuasiveness of Bishop Ambrose's exegesis of Scripture. He

was nonetheless loath to give up his individual will and desires in order to attempt the Christian life. Increasingly, however, he was convinced that worldly success had not and could not guarantee happiness or peace.

One day Augustine, sick in heart and mind, was sitting alone in a garden in Milan, with his friend Alypius a short distance from him. As he agonized over his inability to resist the temptations of the flesh, he heard what seemed to be the voice of a child singing "Take and read, take and read." He picked up the Scriptures and his eyes fell on Romans 13:13–14. He understood the passage to be a startlingly direct command for him to "put on the Lord Jesus Christ and make no provisions for the flesh in its concupiscences."

At that moment, the battle that had raged in Augustine's heart and mind, about himself and against himself, was over. He committed his life to God's will and purpose and allowed himself to be remade in the image of Christ. Augustine recorded these events in the *Confessions* with a dramatic intensity and honesty that remain undiminished by frequent readings.

The Heart's True Peace in God

Eleven years after his conversion, Augustine began writing his *Confessions.* It is an account of his life, which reached a turning point in the momentous experience of that day in the garden in Milan. The *Confessions* as such serves a number of purposes and should be understood in a number of contexts; indeed, the very title suggests the multiple meanings. The text is a confession (an acknowledgment) of sins and a confession (a profession) of faith. It is also a confession (a declaration in the manner of the Psalms) of God's grace, beauty, and providence.

These overlapping purposes help clarify the somewhat confusing structure of the *Confessions*. The first nine books tell the story of Augustine's past, his life prior to his conversion. Book 10 is a discourse on memory and an examination of the present state of his conscience and soul. Books 11–13 offer a meditation on time and eternity, which begins

Milan Cathedral, Italy.

with an examination of the opening verses of Genesis. The scope of Augustine's *Confessions* thus encompasses various configurations of the past, present, and future—personal and universal.

Augustine also has multiple audiences for the *Confessions*. Primarily he addresses God directly and intimately, but he addresses himself as well and the "kindred race" of humankind, who will recognize in his experience the universal cry of the human heart. If a single conviction guides Augustine's choice of narrative incidents, it is to be found in his powerful and celebrated cry to God: "Our hearts are restless until they can find peace in you."

The remaining events of Augustine's life, useful to understanding the *Confessions,* can be

My sin was all the more incurable because I imagined that I was not a sinner.

—*The Confessions*
Rex Warner, trans.

*There is no doubt in my mind, Lord, that I love you.
I feel it with certainty. You struck my heart with your
word, and I loved you.*

—*The Confessions*
Rex Warner, trans.

For Further Study

The recommended translations are Rex Warner's *The Confessions of St. Augustine* (New American Library, 1963) and Henry Bettenson's *The City of God* (Penguin, 1984). Robert Ottley's *Studies in the Confessions of St. Augustine* (Robert Scott Publishers, 1919) and Peter Brown's *Augustine of Hippo* (University of California Press, 1967) are good biographical studies. Roy Battenhouse's *A Companion to the Study of Augustine* (Oxford, 1955) is a useful guide to the works of Augustine. Jaroslav Pelikan's *The Mystery of Continuity* (University Press of Virginia, 1986) is a more advanced, but highly readable, philosophical and historical analysis of Augustine's work.

summarized chronologically as follows: his conversion took place in 386; he was baptized at the age of thirty-three on the Saturday before Easter in 387 (his mother, a strong influence in his life, died that same year); he was ordained as a priest in the Catholic Church in 391; he was appointed Bishop of Hippo in 396; he wrote the *Confessions* from 397–401 and he wrote another one of his great works, *The City of God,* from 413–426. He died in Hippo in 430, the same year the Vandals attacked the North African city.

Issues to Explore

Asking questions is vital to enriching the experience of reading Augustine's *Confessions*. In considering these questions and encountering the profoundly simple, heartfelt, and beautiful prose of the man whose spiritual autobiography has become a foundational text of Christendom, we discover the significance of Augustine's *Confessions* to Christians of all ages and traditions.

(1) Consider the ways in which Augustine's story is the story of every Christian. How do the conversion experiences of the New Testament—including Paul's—compare with Augustine's? (2) Why do particular incidents

and images from the text achieve symbolic significance outside the immediate context of the entire *Confessions* (such as Augustine's stealing pears as an adolescent or his encounter with the drunken beggar in Milan)? (3) What are the effects of Augustine's directly addressing God as an audience in the *Confessions*? (4) What are the purposes of his own questions in his text? Note his courage in posing answers to difficult theological and philosophical questions. (5) Numerous quotations from the *Confessions* have served as memorable reminders of the power of Augustine's life story and Christian witness, including "I believe in order to understand" and "Late it was that I loved you, beauty so ancient and so new." What other lines encapsulate the experience of Augustine?

—Gail Kienitz

BEOWULF
c. 700–750

Beowulf, by an unknown poet, is the first great English epic poem and a dramatic portrayal of the tensions arising from the impact of the Christian faith on a warrior society. Probably recorded in the early eighth century, this work of alliterative verse cuts to the center of heroic values in the Anglo-Saxon culture. Its central character, Beowulf, embodies the Anglo-Saxon sense of aggressive honor, stout-hearted and open acceptance of what is fared, and moral and physical strength pitted against a chaotic world. These qualities can be seen in the three central scenes in the poem: Beowulf's fight with the monster Grendel, his battle with Grendel's mother, and the final bloody confrontation with the fire-breathing dragon.

Viking helmet and mask from the Sutton Hoo Treasure, England.

A Single, Unknown Poet

Although the author was almost certainly not the originator of the poem, he was more than a mere adapter or editor. He probably decided to connect the stories of Beowulf's victorious fight against Grendel with the final mortal battle against the dragon. It was he who most likely put the noble and heroic Beowulf at the center of the narrative, casting him as a larger-than-life character whose epic proportions dominate the action of the poem. And scholars believe he added the intensely Christian elements to the pagan epic that recast the brooding Anglo-Saxon sense of *wyrd,* or fate, into a Christian acceptance of judgment and providence.

The author of *Beowulf* was a *scop,* an Anglo-Saxon court poet who shaped poetry and recited long narrative poems. He was probably of noble birth and may have been a chaplain or an abbot who was supported by the Anglian court. He was a man well-versed in both Scandinavian stories and the epic poetry of the Anglo-Saxons.

The Warrior Society and the Christian Faith

The *Beowulf* poet wrote in a world struggling with two very distinct influences. One was the warrior society in which he lived. Here one's place in the culture was determined by loyalty to kings and nobles. The most significant relationship was between a lord and thane (one who freely served in mortal combat). The thane owed complete fidelity to the lord and, in return, the lord was obliged to reward the loyal thane. Anglo-Saxon poetry celebrated the thane's epic feats of strength and fierce devotion, as well as the lord's generosity.

[Beowulf] was the kindest of worldly kings,
Mildest, most gentle, most eager for fame.

—*Beowulf*
Charles Kennedy, trans.

Opposite: A page
from a tenth-
century manuscript
of *Beowulf*,
describing Beowulf's
reception in the hall
of King Hrothar.

But the *Beowulf* poet also wrote in a world that was fast becoming Christian. This influence brought in by missionaries and scholars was spread by various writers through the Anglo-Saxon kingdoms. Christian *scops* turned their poetic techniques to new subjects, creating epic characters out of Old Testament heroes and applying their techniques toward understanding the work of the one God instead of the various Germanic deities.

The creative tension between these two influences dominates much of *Beowulf*. For instance, the hero Beowulf fights dragons and saves his people, but he is also aware of the role of fate in his life. Another example of this double outlook can be seen in how the poet celebrates marvelous elements of setting and fabulous creatures but is not above moralizing and preaching at times. Hrothgar, the king whom Beowulf saves from the monster Grendel, is not only a noble ruler but a wise Christian who can warn the hero against pride. The success of the poem rests on the balance between the traditions of a warrior society and Christian beliefs.

By the side of the barrow abide you to see
Which of us twain may best after battle
Survive his wounds. Not yours the adventure,
Nor the mission of any, save mine alone
To measure his strength with the monstrous dragon
And play the part of a valiant earl.

—*Beowulf*
Charles Kennedy, trans.

The Four Tones of *Beowulf*

The *scop* of *Beowulf* blended together four different tones to create an intricate tale. The dominant tone in the epic is heroic. It encourages the reader to marvel at the man Beowulf. "Behold the hero," the *scop* seems to say, and we see an extraordinary hero who both performs deeds of tremendous strength and portrays moral courage and faithfulness to others. With this heroic tone the poet celebrates the themes of fame and renown. The hero's reputation is made not only through strength, but through honor, generosity, and loyalty.

A second tone running through much of the poem, connected to the heroic, is the elegiac—a sorrowful and mournful tone. Here the *scop* stresses the ultimate failure of all human victories. Even as Beowulf enters the battle with the dragon he knows that he must lose. Victory or loss, however, is less important than fighting on the right side. The poet weaves in such themes as the necessity of bravery and the demands of friendship, honor, kinship, and one's position in this world.

The poet also orchestrates a third tone, which is pensive and reflective. At times the narrator reflects on the implications of Beowulf's actions, weaving in a major theme of Northern myth—that the world is only a transient place, soon to fade away. All of Beowulf's glory, and even the treasure of the dragon, will vanish. One should still fight, but with the knowledge that the material world is fleeting.

The fourth tone is moral and didactic. Because of this tone some argue that the poem is essentially Christian. Throughout the poem the narrator and sometimes the characters deliver pithy speeches about moral questions. In general these seem to be insertions in the larger pagan story, but are connected to the greater theme of how one lives in a world of monsters who breathe disorder and chaos.

Determining Destiny: Character or Fate?

The *scop* of Beowulf answers the question of how to live in a world of darkness and disarray.

On one level, one should live life heroically and honorably—fight the monsters and keep commitments. This path seems easy for Beowulf, who can battle with monsters effectively because he has the strength of at least ten men.

Yet the poet also creates a character who represents the common person. Wiglaf is an unextraordinary fellow who sees the dragon about to maul Beowulf and rushes through the fire and smoke to preserve his kinsman and king. Although Wiglaf is unable to kill the dragon or afford much protection for the stricken Beowulf, he heartens his lord by acting courageously and dutifully—as, the poet suggests, we all should.

For the Christian, *Beowulf* poses a paradox. The heroic code prized by Beowulf and his followers is essentially pagan, without elements of grace or redemption. And yet God's presence is consistently felt within the pagan worldview. Beowulf is acutely aware of his finiteness; his drive for glory is based on his desire to be remembered after his death. But the narrator gives the sense that his actions are controlled by divine will. Fate, Beowulf claims, will not destroy an undoomed man. This conviction illustrates the tension between an individual's actions and providence.

As the poem progresses, the *scop* seems to suggest that battles are never fully won and issues never completely clarified in this world. Age and wisdom bring greater difficulties, not greater ease. Life grows harder for Beowulf as he moves from the friendly hall of King Hrothgar to the hostile underwater den of Grendel's mother and then on to the isolated and windy headland of the dragon's cave. The relatively easy victory over Grendel is followed by the fierce battle with Grendel's mother and then by the mortal fight with the dragon. Even the battles Beowulf faces grow murkier: he seems justified in the struggle against Grendel, less so against Grendel's mother, and much less so in his combat with the dragon. As Beowulf fights according to the code he knows best, he is aware of the forces larger than himself that control—or at least influence—his life.

Better for man
To avenge a friend than much to mourn.
All men must die; let him who may
Win glory ere death. That guerdon is best
For a noble man when his name survives him.

—*Beowulf*
Charles Kennedy, trans.

For Further Study

The original language of *Beowulf* is virtually impenetrable to a reader unfamiliar with Anglo-Saxon. Much of its vocabulary is unique to this poem; some of the words—such as the very first *(Hwæt we gardena / in geardagum)*—have no modern equivalent. Also, the poet's creative metaphors (called "kennings") and compound words are unknown to our present-day culture. For example, "Hammers' leavings" suggests a sword, "swan's bath" the ocean. Because of these difficulties most readers must turn to a translation of the poem, which presents the problems of recreating the poetic effects of one language in another.

The best edition of the poem is Frederick Klaeber's *Beowulf and the Fight at Finnsburg* (Heath, 1950). Howell D. Chickering has published a dual-language edition, in which the original Anglo-Saxon is printed side-by-side with a modern poetic translation: *Beowulf* (Anchor, 1977). The best known poetic translation is Charles W. Kennedy's *Beowulf: The Oldest English Epic* (Oxford, 1978). The most popular prose translation is E. Talbot Donaldson's *Beowulf* (Norton, 1966). David Wright's *Beowulf* (Penguin, 1957) is a close competitor.

The best general literary history of the period is Stanley Greenfield's *A Critical History of Old English Literature* (New York University, 1965). A more pointed analysis of the poem within its context is Edward Irving's *A Reading of Beowulf* (Yale, 1968). A facsimile of the manuscript has been published by the Early English Text Society as *Beowulf* (Original Series 245, 1959, reprinted 1981). The original manuscript is on view in the British Museum.

Tore him in pieces, bit through the bones,
Gulped the blood, and gobbled the flesh,
Greedily gorged on the lifeless corpse,
The hands and the feet.

—Beowulf
Charles Kennedy, trans.

Issues to Explore

(1) In what way does *wyrd* or fate play a strong role in Beowulf's decisions? Does his sense of predetermined fate affect his actions? (2) *Beowulf* is in many ways a poem about a culture in conflict with itself; there are at least two competing claims for how one ought to live. Does Beowulf successfully juggle these two claims? (3) *Beowulf* presents alternating visions of youth (the young Beowulf versus Wiglaf) and age (Hrothgar versus the old Beowulf). Are we as readers to choose one over the other as appropriate, or do both visions have something to tell us about how we are to live? (4) In an age when gold and glory are much prized, what are Beowulf's real goals? Why is he so eager for fame? What benefits does he imagine the treasure will bring to his people? (5) In what way is story and narrative important in this poem and in this society? Does story play a similar role in our own time?

—Gary D. Schmidt

Medieval Christian Writers

Medieval Christian thought remains vital beyond its own time for two supreme reasons—its penetrating spiritual insights and its grand endeavor to harmonize faith and reason. "Faith seeking understanding" is the way Anselm describes the effort. Virtually all the Christian writers during this period between the fifth through the fourteenth centuries sought to explain the world and human existence by reference to God and the major tenets of revealed truth. They also gave us some of the deepest classics of spiritual devotion.

The period begins with AUGUSTINE, the theological giant of the era whose shadow looms so large as to merit one historian's praise: "St. Augustine, it would be generally agreed, has had a greater influence upon the history of dogma and upon religious thought and sentiment in Western Christendom than any other writer outside the canon of Scripture." And the period reaches an apex with Aquinas's synthesis of reason and revelation in the thirteenth century. In between are writers of lesser stature whose contributions are nonetheless significant. Boethius is one of the last Christians to hold to Roman philosophy; his emphasis on the merits of philosophy is heroic. Anselm's argument for the

Boethius (Anicius Manlius Severinus) (c. 480–524), Roman statesman and philosopher.

existence of God and his defense of the incarnation have become classic proofs. And the works of Bernard of Clairvaux and Bonaventure are definitive explorations of Western spirituality.

Boethius (c. 480–524)

Boethius was perhaps the greatest of the thinkers who followed Augustine. A statesman and philosopher, he studied at Rome and Athens, became consul to Theodoric the Ostrogothic king of Italy, and later was imprisoned and ultimately executed on grounds of treason and sacrilege. During his lengthy imprisonment Boethius wrote *The Consolation of Philosophy*. Despite the absence of specifically Christian teaching, the work became one of the most widely read books of the Middle Ages.

The *Consolation* records the triumph of reason and hope over misfortune and disaster. It begins with Boethius recounting the causes of his despair: his reputation destroyed, liberty lost, and execution imminent. In the midst of his misfortune, Lady Philosophy comes to Boethius and offers consolation by challenging him to think, to reason. The problem, she suggests, is not outside of Boethius but rather within him. "You have not been driven out of your homeland; you have willfully wandered away. Or, if you prefer to think that you have been driven into exile, you yourself have done the driving. . . ."

Lady Philosophy then causes Boethius to reflect on the fundamental questions of human existence. What constitutes true happiness? Happiness is not found in wealth, honor, or power. Rather true happiness is to be found in the philosophical quest for the supreme good, God. "Grant, Oh Father, that my mind may rise to Thy sacred throne. Let it see the fountain of good; let it find light, so that the clear light of my soul may fix itself in Thee."

The *Consolation* poses two other questions: How can there be evil in a world governed by a good and omnipotent God? How can there be free will if God already knows the course of events? Boethius's answers are complex and paradoxical, perhaps meant to be secondary to the reverence and awe that his thoughts tend to produce.

Anselm (1033–1109)

In his writings Anselm, a Lombard who became Archbishop of Canterbury, achieves the best expression of the harmony of faith and reason since Augustine. He departs from the medieval practice of collecting, examining, and harmonizing authorities, instead exhibiting a certain freedom to speculate. His contribution to the Christian faith is most clearly expressed in his proof of the existence of God (*Proslogion*, A Discourse) and his defense of the incarnation (*Cur Deus Homo*, Why God Became Man).

The *Proslogion* sets forth what has come to be known as the "ontological argument," the proof of God from being/existence (ontos). Anselm begins by defining God as "a being than which nothing greater can be conceived." He then considers the argument against the existence of God by citing the fool, who says in his heart, "There is no god." But the fool has a concept of God even while denying that such a being exists. For Anselm, the fool's ability to conceive of God is itself a testament to the reality of his existence.

In *Cur Deus Homo*, Anselm addresses criticism against the Christian doctrine of the incarnation. Opponents charged that Christians dishonor God by affirming that he became man. Because feudal thinking emphasized the roles of hierarchy and subordination, actions were evaluated in terms of status. Stealing from a peasant was different from stealing from a king. Therefore the incarnation was dishonorable to God in that the indignity of Jesus' life and his shameful death are incompatible with God's majesty. To this charge, Anselm develops an argument that includes the following: Men and women who sin dishonor God and must pay the penalty for not fulfilling their obligations to God; it is not proper or just for God to forgive the debt incurred; humans cannot repay the debt they owe ("a sinner cannot justify a sinner"); therefore, in order to satisfy the debt "which none but God can make and none but man ought to make, it is necessary for the God man to make it."

Anselm's interpretation of the atonement has been profoundly influential, especially in repudiating an earlier notion that the devil had rights over fallen human beings, which the cross satisfied.

Bernard of Clairvaux (1090–1153)

In 1098 a group of monks founded a new monastery in the swamps of Cîteaux, France, to protest the growing laxity of monastic life. By the twelfth century, the Cistercians were the most renowned reform movement in Europe. This success was largely due to its most famous member, Bernard of Clairvaux. The son of a Burgundian nobleman, Bernard had an influence in religious, political, and social affairs that was so dominant as to merit the title, "the uncrowned ruler of Europe." He is celebrated, for example, as the preacher for the Second Crusade. But Bernard made his greatest and most lasting contribution in the area of spiritual development.

The *Selected Works* traces Bernard's understanding of spiritual development through several key themes. Exploring humility and pride, Bernard recounts Benedict's twelve steps of humility and then, because, as he maintains, human beings experience pride most intensely and comprehensively, he develops his own twelve steps of pride. In analyzing pride Bernard thus considers its opposite, humility.

> I can teach only what I have learned. I did not think I could fittingly describe the steps up when I know more about going down than going up. . . . I have nothing to set before you except the order of my descent. But, if you look carefully, you will find there the way up.

Regarding the knowledge of God, Bernard wrote five books to Pope Eugenius III entitled *De Consideratione* (On Consideration). The books are like pastoral letters in which Bernard encourages, stimulates, challenges, and even teaches the pope about consideration, which he defines as "searching for truth, active thinking and balancing and judging." Book V charts the movement of the soul as it considers that which is ultimate, God. Such consideration leads one up "not by steps but in great leaps beyond our imagining" until one reaches a mystical contemplation of God.

What, then, is God? He is the purpose to which the universe looks, the salvation of the elect. What he is to himself, only he knows. What is God? All-powerful will, benevolent virtue, eternal light, changeless reason, supreme blessedness. He creates minds to share in himself, gives them life, so that they may experience him, causes them to desire him, enlarges them to grasp him, justifies them so that they may deserve him. . . .

On the subject of love, Bernard's "Sermons on the Song of Songs" emphasizes God's love for his people. In a way reminiscent of Origen in the third century, Bernard offers a spiritual interpretation of

For I do not seek to understand that I may believe, but I believe in order to understand. For this also I believe,—that unless I believed, I should not understand.

—Anselm, *Proslogion*
S. N. Deane, trans.

sexual imagery. He understands the bond between bridegroom and bride to represent that of Christ and the church. And in perhaps his most famous illumination of the erotic, Bernard takes the passage from the first chapter of the Song of Songs, "Let him kiss me with the kiss of his mouth" to be symbolic of Christ.

> The mouth which kisses signifies the Word who assumes human nature; the flesh which is assumed is the recipient of the kiss; the kiss, which is of both giver and receiver, is the Person which is of both—the Mediator between God and man, the Man Christ Jesus.

Bonaventure (1217–1274)

This thirteenth-century friar, professor, administrator, cardinal, and papal adviser continues an outlook that can be traced back through Bernard and Anselm to Augustine. Simply put, this tradition is described as the primacy of faith. Bonaventure reaches a certain culmination of Augustine's position, which regards all knowledge as depending on revealed truth.

Bernard of Clairvaux (1090–1153) leads a procession of monks at Clairvaux monastery, France.

After being elected as minister general of the Franciscan Order, Bonaventure was meditating on the vision of the six-winged Seraph, which St. Francis, founder of the order, had received some thirty-five years earlier. The result was *The Soul's Journey into God*, which symbolically interprets that vision. "The six wings of the Seraph can rightly be taken to symbolize the six levels of illumination by which, as if by steps or stages, the soul can pass over to peace through ecstatic elevations of Christian wisdom." The soul moves along its journey by contemplating God as reflected in the material world, bodily senses, the natural mind, and the heart as renewed and reformed by grace. In the fifth and sixth stages, the soul turns to God and contemplates him as Being itself and as the Good. The seventh and final stage results in a mystical union with Christ:

> he passes over the Red Sea, going from Egypt into the desert, where he will taste the *hidden manna*, and with Christ he rests in the tomb, as if dead to the outer world, but experiencing, as far as is possible in this wayfarer's state, what was said on the cross to the thief

For Further Study

It is probably best to read the writers in order of importance, beginning with Boethius, who is simple, provocative, heroic, and philosophical. Move next to Anselm—theological and more difficult to understand—and finish with the spiritual writers, Bernard and Bonaventure. Or consult any standard introduction to the writers, works, and historical period. Recommended editions follow.

Boethius: *The Consolation of Philosophy*, Richard Green, translator (Macmillan, 1962).

Anselm: *Proslogion* and *Cur Deus Homo* in *St. Anselm: Basic Writings*, S. N. Deane, translator, introduction by Charles Hartshorne (Open Court Publishing, 1962).

Bernard of Clairvaux: *Bernard of Clairvaux: Selected Works*, The Classics of Western Spirituality, G. R. Evans, translator (Paulist Press, 1987).

Bonaventure: *Bonaventure*, The Classics of Western Spirituality, Ewert Cousins, translator (Paulist Press, 1978).

who adhered to Christ: *Today you shall be with me in paradise*.

The *Tree of Life* also issues an invitation to journey. But this journey proceeds not by contemplation of the mysterious but rather by contemplation of the historical events in the life of Jesus. The goal of the true believer is absolute conformity to Christ; in order to conform, one must understand the life, ministry, suffering, death, resurrection, and glorification of Jesus. So Bonaventure describes in vividly imagined detail major events in

Christ's ministry. About the cross, Bonaventure writes, "Thrown roughly upon the wood of the cross, spread out, pulled forward and stretched back and forth like a hide, he was pierced by pointed nails, fixed to the cross by his sacred hands and feet most roughly torn with wounds." He not only evokes human feelings that range from love to anguish but, more importantly, challenges believers to appropriate in their own lives those same virtues so evident in the life of Jesus

—Telfair J. Mashburn, III

THOMAS AQUINAS

Summa theologica
c. 1265–74

One work from the Middle Ages that towers above all others through its enduring influence is the *Summa theologica* of the Dominican friar and professor, St. Thomas Aquinas (1224–1274). As his "summary" of theology, it not only gathers together the preceding tradition, it also provides an interpretation that assimilates the best of the philosophy of his day. At the Council of Trent (1545–63), which formulated basic Catholic teaching for succeeding centuries, his *Summa* was placed on the altar alongside the Scriptures. The work clearly dominated subsequent Roman Catholic tradition.

St. Thomas Aquinas (1224–1274).

Learning through Questioning

The *Summa* expresses an approach to thinking about faith that is rooted in the work of French philosopher Peter Abelard (1079–1142) and Italian theologian Peter Lombard (c. 1100–c. 1160). In a culture based on theological authority, Abelard showed that authorities could be quoted on differing sides of basic

questions in theology. Following Abelard, Lombard in his *Sentences* created a logical pattern of questions about the whole field of faith and gathered a comprehensive set of quotations from authorities, mainly St. AUGUSTINE. For over three hundred years theologians were trained by writing commentaries on this work.

Aquinas began his own training by writing such a commentary. He wrote commentaries throughout

his life: on Scripture, on the sixth-century Syrian monk Dionysius, on the Roman senator Boethius, and especially on ARISTOTLE. He penned several works on disputed questions, such as *On Truth* and *On the Power of God*. And he wrote two summaries of theology: the *Summa contra gentiles*, written for missionaries to the Muslims, and the *Summa theologica*.

Making Sense of It All

In the Summa theologica Aquinas borrowed the most general framework of questions from the pagan Greek philosopher Plotinus as mediated by Dionysius the pseudo Areopagite, an early Christian philosopher. Plotinus saw all things as going forth from God and returning to God through the interior development of the soul. To Plotinus's framework Aquinas added questions concerning Jesus as the actual way back to the Father.

Overall the *Summa* contains 604 main questions, each with several subquestions, totaling over three thousand. Methodically Aquinas raises a question and develops

The state of the soul is more perfect embodied than disembodied.

—*Summa theologica*
Robert E. Wood, trans.

objections to his position before he cites an authority who held the position he then develops in the body of the article. At the end he replies to the initial objections. The massive set of questions, objections, and replies allows us to glimpse the lively debates of the universities at that time. Thus we should see the *Summa* as a continually evolving organism, responding to the questions that emerge, and not as a finished cathedral, chiseled in stone.

A key principle in the *Summa* is that faith presupposes a rational nature that it helps to perfect: "The soul is the subject of grace because it belongs to the class of intellectual or rational natures." A rational nature seeks to "make sense," to be coherent and comprehensive, to understand how a thing fits together with others in order to find its place in the larger scheme of things. Theology is an attempt to "make sense" out of faith—to see how what is revealed in Scripture relates to what we know through our experience, both in everyday life and in science.

The Greek philosophers made two great attempts to comprehend human experience: one rooted in PLATO as interpreted by Plotinus, the other in Aristotle. The Platonists tended to consider the body as a prison, earth as an exile, and the "other world" as the place where we belong. Through Augustine and Dionysius, Platonic thought dominated the Middle Ages.

Aristotle's works became influential during Aquinas's life as they were translated for the first time into Latin. In contrast to Plato, Aristotle argued that the human being belongs essentially to "this world." While most of Aquinas's contemporaries were Platonists, Aquinas followed Aristotle. He used Aristotle's approach to explain the incarnation, the sacraments, and the resurrection of the body, three essential Christian doctrines. He claimed

that embodiment is such a good thing that God himself became a man living in this world, and that the sacraments prolong God's presence in bodily form. He even held that "the state of the soul is more perfect embodied than disembodied." This approach made many Platonist theologians and bishops nervous. Several bishops, in fact, issued condemnations of the rising Aristotelianism, including Aquinas's thought.

Organization of the *Summa*

The organization of the *Summa* follows a two-step process. First Aquinas draws on both Aristotelian and Platonist sources to explore philosophy independent of Christian revelation. He then extends and perfects philosophy by incorporating revelation. Following Plotinus's pattern, Part One (I) deals with God and creation. Aquinas derives indications of God's existence from the nature of everyday experience. He claims—against most believers and with most of the ancient pagan philosophers—that one cannot *prove* a beginning in time. But he shows that, whether having a temporal beginning or not, our world is an ever created universe, always dependent on God's creative power.

Aquinas then moves to divine revelation where God breaks the philosophic deadlock, declaring that he started the universe. Furthermore, beyond having the wisdom and power to create, the God proclaimed in revelation is a Trinity—Father, Son, and Spirit. Aquinas then explores created beings, from angelic intelligences to material beings. He focuses on human beings, who are both rational animals and incarnate spirits, "on the border between time and eternity." Part One ends with a treatment of divine providence that governs both nature and history.

The first part of Part Two (I-II, following the Latin *prima secundae*) determines philosophically the goal of human existence. Through our intellect we view things in the light of the notion of being, a notion that includes everything in its scope. "The human soul is, in a way, all things." Fundamental human desire follows from the all-exclusive

The great gothic cathedral at Cologne, Germany, where Thomas Aquinas spent part of his life.

orientation of the intellect. God is the only one answering to the desire for fullness of being. Revelation shows how that desire can be fulfilled. The materials we have to work with are our own actions and passions through which we develop habits leading us to or away from our final end. We are aided generally in the development by both human and divine laws and, from moment to moment in our lives, by the workings of grace.

The second division of Part Two (II-II) becomes more concrete. Humans commence the journey back to God with the cardinal virtues introduced by Plato and Aristotle: temperance, courage, and justice guided by prudence. Aquinas distinguishes between practical, prudent intelligence and the blind compulsory feelings sometimes incorrectly called conscience. Revelation completes and elevates these virtues with the theological virtues of faith, hope, and love. Contrary

The human soul is, in a way, all things.

—*Summa theologica*
Robert E. Wood, trans.

The soul is the subject of grace because it belongs to the class of intellectual or rational natures.

—*Summa theologica*
Robert E. Wood, trans.

to many Christians, but following the ancient pagan philosophers and the monastic tradition, Aquinas argues for the superiority of the contemplative life in our return to God—a life absorbed in thought about God, living in his presence—over a life dedicated to activity, wholesome and necessary though that might be. Aquinas's own life was a mixture of the contemplative and active lives, with the aim of presenting to others the fruits of contemplation.

In Part Three (III) Aquinas considers Christ's incarnation, life, and death as the way back to the Father. He also explores the relationship between the sacraments and the incarnation. Aquinas had completed his work on baptism, confirmation, and the Eucharist when he suffered a stroke. The rest of the treatment of the sacraments and the concluding treatment of the resurrection of the body, the last judgment, and heaven, hell, and purgatory were added from his early commentary on Lombard's *Sentences*.

For Further Study

The *Summa* in paperback is available from Christian Classics in a five-volume version (1981) and in an abridged volume (1991). For secondary sources see G. K. Chesterton's *St. Thomas Aquinas: The Dumb Ox* (Image, 1956); Josef Pieper's *Guide to Thomas Aquinas* (Mentor-Omega, 1962); Etienne Gilson's *The Christian Philosophy of St. Thomas Aquinas* (Random House, 1956); and M. D. Chenu's *Toward Understanding St. Thomas* (Regnery, 1964).

Issues to Explore

The reader is encouraged to thumb through the *Summa,* exploring the questions of most personal interest to gain a sense of the whole. One might focus on a few key issues: (1) How is philosophic reason related to faith? (2) How does Aquinas understand embodiment as essential to humanness? How does this relate to the resurrection? (3) How are general human virtues related to the theological virtues?

—Robert E. Wood

Dante

The Divine Comedy
c. 1307–21

Many consider Dante's *Divine Comedy* the supreme literary work not only of medieval Christendom but of the Christian faith in general, rivaled only by Milton's *Paradise Lost*. Never has a poet given a more compelling vision of Christian love than Dante in his *Commedia* (the *Divina* was added after Dante's death). This massive and intricate structure of almost fifteen thousand lines, or one hundred "cantos," is divided equally into three large sections—*Inferno, Purgatorio,* and *Paradiso*—that correspond to Dante's conception of the states of souls not only after death but in life as well. They form what Dante himself called "the sacred poem," a stirring drama of the human soul discovering the life of faith in a faithless world.

Pilgrim and Poet

Using himself as a fictional character, Dante the poet relates what happens to Dante the pilgrim in the *Comedy* when, "midway in the journey of our life," he awakes to find himself lost in a dark and

Dante Alighieri (1265–1321) from a portrait published in 1521, thought to be from a miniature by Giulio Clovis.

savage wood. He has somehow "left the straight way" but is delivered from death when a figure of great importance in his life appears from the dead to intervene. Sent by Beatrice, who has descended from heaven into hell to call him to this task, the pagan poet Virgil comes to guide Dante back to the true path. The lost pilgrim must travel through Hell, Purgatory, and Heaven, the three

realms of the afterlife that reveal God's justice and his love.

As Dante travels he glimpses things unknown to people in this life. He relates the story of his sometimes perilous, sometimes pleasurable journey: the souls he encounters in each realm; the sights he sees, from the dismal gloom of hell to the blinding light of heaven; and the wisdom he gains as he is finally prepared to resume his earthly trials. The poem ends with one of the most memorable images in Western art when Dante beholds the Beatific Vision and comes face to face with God.

No Home for the Exiled

Born in Florence, Dante Alighieri (1265–1321) grew up in an Italy torn by opposing political and religious factions. Indeed, throughout Medieval Europe during this period princes, kings, and would-be emperors battled sometimes with and sometimes against the papacy in Rome in a long chronicle of strife between church and government.

In 1295, Dante threw himself into these struggles and early in

In the middle of the journey of our life
I came to my senses in a dark forest,
for I had lost the straight path.

—The *Inferno*
The Divine Comedy
H. R. Huse, trans.

The Pilgrim's Guides
to Divine Love

Dante chronicles his love for Beatrice in the *Vita Nuova* (the "New Life"), a slender, readable volume of thirty-one love poems interspersed with prose commentary. Approaching thirty years of age, he recalls his first sight of Beatrice when he was almost nine and she had just turned eight. This visionary experience stirred within him an enduring love and forever changed his life.

The impression was deepened when, nine years later, she greeted him on the street. From that point onward, he says, he placed himself in the service of love as he sought to understand her extraordinary impact. When she turned on him her beautiful eyes and remarkable smile, he was moved to a nobility that he had not felt before. Although they were not intimate at all—she married someone else—he came to regard her as a manifestation of God's grace and love that he alone could discern. After her death at the age of twenty-four, he concluded from a "marvellous vision" that he should compose no more until he could write of her what had never been written of any woman. That composition was the *Comedy.*

The other seminal influence in Dante's life was Virgil's epic story of Rome's origins. Medieval theologians regarded the *Aeneid* as a masterpiece and employed the hero Aeneas and the events of the poem to shed light on the Bible. Like all other poetry, however, Virgil's great work was held to be fictional and thus greatly inferior to Scripture.

But Dante chose Virgil as his guide to the threshold of heaven in the *Comedy,* describing him as journeying in darkness but lighting the way for those who follow. In so doing he began a movement that broke down the presiding scriptural elitism and then reclaimed non-Christian achievements as aspects of God's truth worthy of study. In this sense Dante bridges the Medieval and Renaissance worlds, gathering up the former and stepping prophetically into the latter.

The central roles of Beatrice and Virgil reflect Dante's "sacramental" view of the world and history. Dante sees God revealing his abun-

1302 he found himself on the losing side—exiled from his beloved city and condemned to death. He never saw Florence again, but wandered from patron to patron in Italy even as his literary fame grew during the last two decades of his life. He wrote the entire *Comedy* in exile, and his pride would not allow him to accept the conditional offers of pardon issued by Florentine officials once his poem became known.

The *Comedy* alludes to these events frequently, but by far the greatest influences from his earlier life were the two figures already mentioned: Beatrice, a young woman of Florence, and Virgil, the famous Roman poet who lived just before the birth of Christ and wrote the epic poem the *Aeneid.*

The Baptistery,
Florence Cathedral,
Italy.

"The Meeting of Dante and Beatrice" by Henry Holiday.

dant love everywhere and at all times in his creation. Nothing is lost, no life lived or action performed in futility, because both the greatest good and the greatest evil show forth divine truth and advance his plan. The *Divine Comedy* exemplifies the meaning of the word *catholic*—inclusive and redemptive—as no other poem does.

A Journey of Love

The single, unified theme of the entire *Comedy* is love, or *amor*. God *is* love, and every aspect of his creation, especially humanity, is infused with this divine attribute. According to Dante, people cannot live without loving; because they have free will, however, they may choose to love the wrong object or to love the right object too much or too little. In the very middle of his poem, on Mount Purgatory, Dante has Virgil speak at length on this truth of life's drama: the arduous search to love the right things in the right way. Thus Dante the pilgrim journeys toward a full understanding of the love in which God intends for him to live

and find joy, not only in this life but in the next. He must come to see his love for Beatrice as merely an imperfect reflection of the abundant love to be found in the blessedness of God's will.

Each main section of the poem portrays a different stage in this human understanding of God's love: the *Inferno* reveals the most horrid consequences of love perverted or defective; the *Purgatorio* depicts flawed souls actively seeking perfection in love; and the *Paradiso* shows the absolute happiness of perfect love achieved.

As Dante's vision ends, he concludes his poem thusly:

For the great imagination here power failed;
but already my desire and will
were turning like a wheel moved evenly
by the Love which turns the sun and the other stars.

—The *Paradiso*
The Divine Comedy
H. R. Huse, trans.

Piccarda's description of what it's like to be in Heaven:

And His will is our peace;
it is that sea to which wholly moves
what He and Nature create.

—The *Paradiso*
The Divine Comedy
H. R. Huse, trans.

And as Dante moves through the three realms—observing, acting, suffering, and learning—the drama of his own salvation unfolds. Because he is alive he is an alien in the strange landscape, but he steadily gains the needed maturity in love to return to the fallen world.

Inferno

Virgil first leads a terrified Dante into Hell. He relieves Dante's fears, however, with his news that Beatrice, herself the last link in a chain of "blessed ladies" beginning with the Virgin Mary, summoned Virgil to be Dante's guide. Thus Dante sees that Heaven itself bends to his distress, calling on him, an ordinary person, to become a hero.

Dante learns that in Hell he will see "the woeful people who have lost the good of the intellect." These souls of the damned reside within the *Inferno's* ten levels that lead downward in ever-tightening circles to Satan, fixed in ice at the center of the earth. After observing the sad mystery in the first circle of those seemingly innocent—the unbaptized infants and virtuous pagans who sought but missed the good—Dante witnesses on other levels souls twisted by incontinence, violence, and fraud during their earthly lives. This terrifying, often grotesque spectacle is punctuated by the stories of people from the past and present. After going past Satan, the two travelers climb upward and finally emerge "to see again the stars."

Purgatorio

Once out of Hell, Dante has to ascend Mount Purgatory, the abode of souls saved but not yet pure enough to enter Paradise. Here the pilgrim must actively purge his own sins as he mounts the seven terraces, each prescribing a different method of cleansing. On the third ledge, for instance, he must endure the blinding smoke of wrath, or on the level of the lustful, he must join the souls by entering a "refining fire" that seems to him hotter than "boiling glass."

In the journey up the mountain he continues to mature in God's love, becoming aware that Beatrice herself awaits him at the peak. Once there he discovers the marvelous Garden of Eden, inaccessible on earth to mortals after the fall but here the entrance to Heaven for the redeemed. Contrary to what he expects, Dante suffers further anguish, first from Virgil's sudden departure and then from Beatrice's stern rebuke for his forsaking her after her death. After they are reconciled and he is commanded by her to write this very poem, she prepares him "to mount to the stars."

Purgatory most resembles our earthly existence. Whereas the souls in the *Inferno* are occupied with self-centered and fruitless activity, those on the mountain move arduously upward toward God through their suffering. The "purgatorial virtues" abound: forgiveness, humility, generosity, and community, all of which flow from an increasing commitment to love. Thus Dante depicts the joy in suffering of those who struggle to live within God's circle of love. The great "Lecture on Love" in Cantos 16–18 expounds Dante's belief that although life is perilous, people are not only capable of but ultimately responsible for the choices that determine their eternal destiny.

Paradiso

This last portion of the *Comedy* is a grand feast of light, song, and movement. By far it is the most detailed, abundant image of heaven ever composed. With Beatrice as his guide and companion, Dante rises through the ten heavens toward the Empyrean, the highest heaven, again pausing in each circle to speak to the inhabitants and witness spectacular expressions of God's glory.

These thirty-three cantos depict the pilgrim's spiritual refinement as he ascends with the specific goal of reaching the unparalleled Beatific Vision at the poem's conclusion. With every sight he sees and soul he hears, his understanding increases. The final four cantos take place in the Empyrean, described by Beatrice as "the Heaven of pure light, / a light intellectual, full of love."

Here Dante bends to drink from the river of life and witnesses its transformation into the celestial rose, alive with the activity of the saints and the angels—the "holy company" who abide eternally in God's presence. What Dante writes in Canto 33, when he beholds the Beatific Vision, is arguably the high point in Christian poetry. Even as he attempts to discern the divine mystery of this vision, he is thrust back to the earth. Now, however, he is in a decisively different state from that in which Virgil first found him lost in the dark wood; his "desire and will" now turn in harmony with "the Love which turns the sun and the other stars."

Beatrice to Dante in the highest heaven:

*We have advanced
from the greatest body to the Heaven of pure light,
a light intellectual, full of love,
love of the good, replete with joy,
a joy that transcends all sweetness.*

—The *Paradiso*
The Divine Comedy
H. R. Huse, trans.

Issues to Explore

Like all classics, the *Comedy* opens itself fully to those who return to it often. Dante himself says that one should not lightly "venture on the deep" of his poetry; but to miss its riches completely would be an immeasurable loss, especially for the Christian reader. In spite of its length and complexity, the poem may be easily entered from several angles.

(1) Each realm is so graphic and detailed that the literal story captures the imagination quickly, but Dante's method demands the

The Ponte Vecchio, Florence, Italy.

On the threshold of the Terrestrial Paradise, Virgil says to Dante:

. . . free, upright, and whole is your will;
it would be wrong not to do as it pleases.
Therefore, over yourself, I crown and miter you.

—The *Purgatorio*
The Divine Comedy
H. R. Huse, trans.

For Further Study

The *Divine Comedy* is available in numerous translations, the best of which is Charles Singleton's three volumes with facing-page Italian text and valuable commentary (Bollingen Series, Princeton, 1970, 1973, 1975). The best one-volume translation is H. R. Huse's (Rinehart Editions, 1954), but the serious reader should be wary of accepting Huse's rather simplistic notes.

Biographies and critical commentary abound. The most helpful studies include: Michele Barbi's *Life of Dante*, translated by Paul Ruggiers (University of California, 1954); Erich Auerbach's *Dante: Poet of the Secular World* (University of Chicago, 1961); Francis Fergusson's *Dante's Drama of the Mind* (Princeton, 1953); and, for a more contemporary treatment, John Freccero's *Dante: The Poetics of Conversion* (Harvard, 1986). The commentaries and notes of Dorothy L. Sayers in the three-volume Penguin edition (1949–62) remain some of the most helpful aids to an understanding of Dante and his epoch.

question: to what beyond themselves do specific episodes point? For example, in the *Inferno*, what do the great lovers Paolo and Francesca (Canto 5), the suicide Pier delle Vigne in the form of a thorn tree (Canto 13), Dante's own teacher Brunetto Latini (Canto 15), or the Greek hero Ulysses (Canto 26; known to the Greeks as Odysseus) reveal about misdirected love? (2) How are Dante's many encounters with individual souls in the *Purgatorio* and the *Paradiso* likewise memorable both in themselves and as pointing toward universal truths?

(3) The pilgrim himself is another important focus of the poem. In Hell he succumbs on occasion to its vices but then submits himself to Purgatory's ordeal and participates in heaven's joy, thus seeming to experience the entire range of human possibility in this life. Specifically, how does Dante's understanding change and grow during this progression? (4) And how does this incredible vision of the *other world* reveal so much about God's will for one's life in *this world?*

(5) The riches of the *Comedy* are inexhaustible and do not depend on arriving at definitive answers in order to be enjoyed. Ponder, for example, such issues as the guidance of Virgil and Beatrice, the impotence of Satan, the humble joy of the mountain, or the incomparable Beatific Vision of the poem's conclusion.

—Larry Allums

SIR GAWAIN AND THE GREEN KNIGHT
c. 1370

*S*ir Gawain and the Green Knight, a charming Middle English alliterative poem by an anonymous author, is the most important existing English account of the adventures of King Arthur's court. A romance adventure, it is brief and comic in tone, focusing on the heroic spirit and its renewal of a society. The story is told by a narrator who follows the common self-effacing medieval practice of claiming to be a mere instrument for transmitting his tale, not its inventor.

The Gawain poet probably wrote three other poems—*Patience, Purity,* and *The Pearl*—which are preserved with *Sir Gawain* in one manuscript. Not much is known about this poet, who wrote in a West Midland dialect and was probably CHAUCER's contemporary. But even if he wrote only *Sir Gawain,* he would still rank as one of the most accomplished English poets in his century.

Courtesy as a Virtue

Sir Gawain falls in the Arthurian tradition, which exalts courtesy as

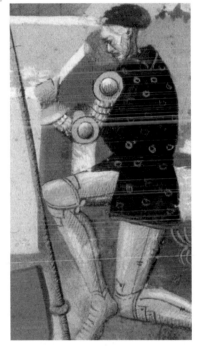

"Gawain kneeling at the fountain" from Romance of the Grail, France.

an art of embodying charity in even the most ordinary circumstances of life. Originally an imitation of Christ's humbling himself even to death, courtesy extends this "saving grace" to every person. The characteristic manifestation of this virtue in the Arthurian tradition is designated

gentilesse, the knight's or gentleman's dedication of his superior strength to the honor and service of those with less worldly power than he.

Such gentilesse is frequently taken for granted and sometimes even despised as hypocritical; to the worldly, the gentle person may appear manipulative. *Sir Gawain and the Green Knight,* on the contrary, presents its young hero's actions as efficacious, forward-looking, and redemptive. It places this code of courtesy among the glorious accomplishments of civilization; through it all people —even the most lowly—can practice heroic virtue.

Yet Sir Gawain also acknowledges the specific dangers that necessarily accompany any high and noble calling. The best knights find themselves in the greatest danger of losing their way spiritually by attaching too much significance to their successes. And because manners may become corrupted, a knight's virtue must occasionally be tested. If he finds himself betraying his beliefs, he must acknowledge his fault and rededicate himself in humility.

About the shield:

His one thought was of this, past all things else,
That all his force was founded on the five joys
That the high Queen of heaven had in her child.
And therefore, as I find, he fittingly had
On the inner part of his shield her image portrayed,
That when his look on it lighted, he never lost heart.

—*Sir Gawain and the Green Knight*
Marie Borroff, trans.

Losing One's Life to Gain It

As *Sir Gawain* begins, Arthur's court at Camelot has become well established, but its very success could tempt its knights to forget valor. Apparently out of danger, its members might become self-satisfied and soft. Perhaps aware of this peril, while celebrating Christmas with prayer and feasting, King Arthur declares at table that he will not partake of the feast until some contest is held or some tale of valor told. As though on cue, a gigantic green knight enters the hall, challenging any volunteer to a "little game" of trading blow for blow with an ax.

The knight's power and size suggest that he will easily be able to behead anyone who accepts his challenge, but he will concede the first blow to King Arthur's representative. When the company allows Sir Gawain, the youngest knight, to accept, they jeopardize the very future of the Round Table in the next generation. Only later do they discover that the Green Knight is an agent sent by a sorceress to test their moral strength. Gawain does indeed decapitate the stranger with his

Illustration from the 1529 edition of Sir Thomas Malory's *Mort d'Arthur*, printed by Wykyn de Worde.

blow. But the awesome knight picks up his severed head and reiterates his challenge. He will return the blow to Gawain on the following Christmas. The Green Knight must be sought out and satisfied.

A year later Gawain sets out to keep his word. Along the way, he is tested repeatedly in chivalric virtue. For instance, when a married noblewoman tempts him, he must not only avoid adultery but refuse a lady graciously. His solution is to pretend to mistake her seductive proposals for polite flattery. Gawain's conduct demonstrates that the true virtues of Camelot have been passed on to his generation. He protects the lady's honor as carefully as his own.

Though not succumbing to the worst temptations, Gawain reveals weakness when he breaks an agreement with his host to exchange everything gained during the day and keeps back a green girdle that will supposedly protect him from physical harm. When he meets the Green Knight on the appointed day, he does not lose his head as he would have if he had succumbed to temptation completely. But he does receive a slight wound on the neck from the Green Knight's ax as a penance for failing somewhat in the practice of courage, truth, and chastity. He keeps the green girdle, but only as a reminder of his shameful weakness. Upon his return to Camelot, his fellow knights share willingly in his humiliation, adopting green sashes as part of their official garb.

Thus the story is about the testing and self-sacrifice that are needed for civilization. To build a civilization people must subdue nature. Despite human effort, nature renews itself, springing back to life seasonally and again growing wild. Like the top of a plant, the head of the magical Green Knight grows back when cut off.

Gawain's head, however, would not grow back. His risk of losing it is therefore an act of considerable courage. To make and protect such a complex institution as Camelot, the knight must be willing not only to use the renewable life of nature but also to risk his own life for the sake of honor and virtue. By losing his life, he may gain it and bring a boon to his people.

King Arthur, the semi legendary Christian British king of the sixth century.

Serving Is Better than Watching

Sir Gawain tells the story of the initiation of a youth into the responsibilities of his high calling. It shows the paradoxical situation of the Christian who must resist temptation without despising the person through whom temptation comes. Finding himself in situations where he might escape his responsibility without being blamed or even caught, Gawain persists, nevertheless, in a seemingly futile task.

The Green Knight expresses the efficacy of Gawain's penance:

I hold you polished as a pearl, as pure and as bright
As you had lived free of fault since first you were born.

—*Sir Gawain and the Green Knight*
Marie Borroff, trans.

He is called to resist flattery, practice chastity, keep a promise that he would like to retract, and persevere beyond the limits of what could be expected of someone in his situation. Finally, he must do penance for his failure to achieve perfection.

Of particular interest to the follower of Christ is the poem's depiction of the virtues as rooted in the hearts and habits of those who live a life of grace. The young knight is able to uphold his beliefs wherever he travels—far from the protection of his elders and even where the laws of the land seem markedly different from his own. Further, *Sir Gawain* distinguishes between the mere avoidance of sin and the actual practice of charity. It makes clear that the Christian does better to serve, even at the risk of making errors, than to remain a mere spectator in life. But the hero is not excused from the sins he may commit in the course of his extraordinary efforts. If he repents seriously and humbly, however, each fall may prove a *felix culpa* (a happy fault) that gives rise to greater progress toward spiritual maturity.

Issues to Explore

In translation from Middle English, *Sir Gawain* is not difficult to read, even for those of high-school age, but provides a rich opportunity for discussion. Questions to ask include: (1) One of the accusations that virtuous people face when they refuse to succumb to a temptation is that they appear to look condescendingly on those who do not share their standards. How does a mixture of wit and formality, as well as courage and fidelity, help Sir Gawain resist the lady's advances without insulting her? (2) Would the directness and frankness of today's conversational style (often praised for freeing us from the "bonds" of formality) actually have hampered Gawain? (3) How is the image of Mary on Gawain's shield connected to his heroic acts? (4) What is the role of magic in the story? (5) And what is the poet's view of the necessity of sacrifice in maintaining the world of Camelot (or any civilization)?

—Mary Mumbach

For Further Study

The edition translated and edited by Marie Borroff (Norton, 1967) is excellent, giving a sense of the alliterative verse form of the original Middle English. The introduction by the translator is most helpful in alerting the reader to the significance of various details.

For further reading about the knights of the Round Table, see *King Arthur and His Knights: Selected Tales* by Sir Thomas Malory (Oxford, 1956), edited by Eugene Vinaver. Although much more loosely constructed than the Gawain poet's verse, this version presents a variety of adventures. For an introduction to the nature of chivalric love, see M. C. Darcy's *The Mind and Heart of Love* (Meridian Books, 1956).

GEOFFREY CHAUCER

The Canterbury Tales
c. 1386–1400

The Canterbury Tales is a vivid and lively medieval poetic work, the major literary achievement of Geoffrey Chaucer (1343–1400). He has long been considered the third most important English writer after SHAKESPEARE and MILTON. Chaucer belongs to the High Middle Ages, when the English were still deeply religious and thoroughly Catholic in their doctrine and practices. In Chaucer, this religious outlook blends with a delightful preoccupation with human personality to produce a humanistic prevailing spirit.

The Canterbury Tales embodies these two sides of his genius. Written in a variety of verse forms and genres, *The Canterbury Tales* is an unfinished collection of twenty-four stories. A pilgrimage from Southwark, a suburb of London, to Canterbury sets the narrative framework of the stories, in which the twenty-nine pilgrims in the traveling group tell stories to pass the time more pleasantly. The pilgrimage becomes the symbol of the human journey on the way to final judgment.

Geoffrey Chaucer (1343–1400); portrait from an early fifteenth-century manuscript.

The Unity of the Collected Stories

Two structural devices unify the collection of stories. One is the pilgrimage itself. Pilgrimages became so common in the Middle Ages that Chaucer could have looked out from his home in suburban London to see pilgrims headed to the shrine of Thomas à Becket in Canterbury. The institution of a pilgrimage enabled Chaucer to bring together a complete cross-section of English society, from the nobility and clergy to the commoner. Moreover, Chaucer made the pilgrimage a dramatic device in which characters interact with each other and in which the physical journey gives a sense of progression toward a spiritual goal.

Another unifying device is the tension between the secular and the religious, the worldly and the spiritual. The pilgrims themselves are an ambiguous mixture of these two qualities. Their stories either mingle the two elements or fall clearly into one category or the other. The prioress, for example, shows the imperfect submergence of the woman in the nun: she goes on religious pilgrimages and wears a rosary, but her actual preoccupations are making herself attractive to men and imitating the manners of the court. Similarly, the monk fits into the religious routine of monastery life, but his obsessions are hunting, fine clothes, and gourmet food.

When April with his sweet showers has
pierced the drought of March to the root,
and bathed every vein in such moisture
as has power to bring forth the flower;
when, also, Zephyrus with his sweet breath
has breathed spirit into the tender new shoots
in every wood and meadow . . . :
then people long to go on pilgrimages,
and palmers long to seek strange shores,
and far-off shrines known in various lands,
and, especially, from the ends of every shire
in England they come to Canterbury.

—*The Canterbury Tales*
A. Kent and Constance Hieatt, trans.

Chaucer's Greatness

Several elements constitute Chaucer's greatness as a writer. *The Canterbury Tales* will fall into place more readily when we are aware of these right from the start. One is Chaucer's affectionate understanding of human nature. In *The Canterbury Tales* this genial acceptance takes the form of skillful character portrayal, including an ability to visualize characters, an acquaintance with an immense range of characters both socially and morally, and an adeptness at portraying universal types that gives us the impression of having met the person before.

A second aspect of Chaucer's genius is his storytelling ability. He gravitates to entertaining and comic stories that both allow for a maximum of character development and clashes between characters and include the story material that audiences through the ages have enjoyed most—romantic love, sex, adven-

Opposite: An engraving of the Wife of Bath, after a manuscript in the University Library, Cambridge.

Right: An illustration of Canterbury pilgrims from a manuscript of around 1420.

ture, conflict, violence, suspense, mystery, fantasy, heroism, villainy, and vividness of setting. Within the course of the various tales, Chaucer develops the Christian virtues of faith, hope, and charity—the three summarized especially in *gentilesse,* which is a lovingkindness and courtesy toward one's neighbors.

A third feature that has endeared Chaucer to centuries of readers is his comic spirit. Much of Chaucer's comedy belongs to the realm of satire—the exposure of human vice or folly. In it the social and religious abuses of the day are laughed at, not because Chaucer took these abuses lightly, but because he believed that laughter—not loathing—is the best way to discredit the vices and foibles of the human race.

Getting Started: *The General Prologue*

The place to start reading *The Canterbury Tales* is with "The General Prologue." The prologue begins and ends with the narrative structure— that is, the story of the assembling of the pilgrims in London and their agreeing to the story-telling competition on the pilgrimage. Character sketches of the individual pilgrims are enclosed within this narrative framework.

Although "The General Prologue" is one of the inspired performances of English literature, we need to have the right expectations if we are to approach it properly. Characterization—not plot—is the key component of the prologue. Readers should not come to this brilliant panorama looking for a story line, for it introduces the cast of characters who will participate in the drama that follows. The underlying genre is the character sketch.

The individual portraits come alive through Chaucer's techniques of description. Chaucer himself claims to mingle three ingredients in his portraits—external appearance, social standing, and inner character. The portraits combine individualizing traits, such as the Prioress's nickname "Madame Eglantine" and her education in a specific convent school located in a London suburb, and universal or typical traits, such as her flirtatiousness that fits the medieval social type of the wayward nun. Chaucer's economy of expression is breathtaking. In a few sharp lines a whole personality comes to life in our imaginations. He builds most of the portraits around an essential trait, sometimes accompanied by a quick glimpse into the inner person. Also noteworthy is a planned randomness in the structuring of the portraits, so that the description seems natural and artless. The portraits combine idealization and satire, often related to the overriding theme of the *Tales* as a whole—the tension between the worldly and the spiritual. Also prominent is irony or discrepancy—between what a character is and should be, or between what the narrator says about a character and what we as readers know to be true. Comedy pervades the whole, based on an amiable acceptance of human faults and eccentricities.

One further comment on "The General Prologue": Chaucer himself is one of the pilgrims in the story. Thus Chaucer the pilgrim is a conscious fictional creation, and part of the irony of Chaucer the author is to make his alter ego an unreliable narrator. When the narrator

Middle English:

Whan that Aprill with his shoures sote
The droghte of Marche hath perced to the rote
And bathed every veyne in swich licour
Of which vertu engendred is the flour;
Whan Zephirus eek with his swete breeth
Inspired hath in every holt and heeth
The tendre croppes, and the yonge sonne
Hath in the Ram his halfe cours y-ronne,
And smale fowles maken melodye,
That slepen al the night with open yë
(So priketh hem Nature in hir corages):
Thanne longen folk to goon on pilgrimages. . . .

—*The Canterbury Tales*
A. Kent and Constance Hieatt, trans.

praises various characters extravagantly, therefore, we are expected to protest the exaggerated praise as unwarranted.

Reading the Individual Tales

"The Pardoner's Prologue and Tale" makes perhaps the best starting point. On approaching any of the individual narratives, the reader should reread the storyteller's portrait in "The General Prologue" for its revelations about the person telling the tale. The pardoner is the most depraved person on the pilgrimage, guilty of such offenses as fraud, greed, hypocrisy, and sexual perversion.

"The Pardoner's Prologue" is both a sample sermon, in which he describes his typical preaching style, and a confession, in which he admits his greed and fraud as a seller of relics. After just beginning his story his preacher's instinct takes over and he launches into a homiletic digression on four sins of the flesh. The pardoner's story is much praised for its clear structure, its vivid portrait of three young rioters, its evocation of setting and mystery, and its irony (the basic premise itself is an ironic impossibility—the quest to slay death).

Next on the list should be "The Nun's Priest's Tale," a fable about a rooster named Chaunticleer and his wife Pertelote. The story begins with the utmost realism in a widow's farmyard, but then launches into a fantasy with talking animals. The story is the first notable instance in English literature of mock epic—a form that treats trivial everyday reality in the high and elevated style of epic literature. The primary aim is simply comedy. The rooster and hen do, however, become the archetypal husband and wife with contrasting temperaments struggling for dominance.

In another tale, the Wife of Bath tells the laugh-provoking history of her five marriages. She thereby introduces the subject of marriage and sex into the discussion. Her stories and several others make up the so-called marriage group, which includes stories by the "Oxford clerk" (student), the merchant, and the franklin (a nonaristocratic property holder). Together these stories raise the contemporary issue of

> *It befell that one day in that season,*
> *as I was in Southward at the Tabard Inn,*
> *ready to go on my pilgrimage*
> *to Canterbury with a most devout heart,*
> *at night there came into that hostelry*
> *a company of nine-and-twenty people—*
> *all sorts of people, who had met by chance;*
> *and all of them were pilgrims*
> *who were riding toward Canterbury.*
>
> —*The Canterbury Tales*
> A. Kent and Constance Hieatt, trans.

whether the husband or wife should hold the "mastery" in a marriage. Another cluster of stories deals with frankly bawdy and obscene materials in the best comic tradition. Chaucer renders these *fabliaux* (short, largely indecent comic tales) more humorous than offensive through his skillful use of poetic narrative.

Issues to Explore

Reading Chaucer imparts a sense of life that has three main ingredients. One is the comic spirit that pervades *The Canterbury Tales*. We can legitimately speak of the refreshment value of such literature, along the lines of C. S. Lewis's comment that "the Christian . . . has no objection to comedies that merely amuse and tales that merely refresh. . . . We can play, as we can eat, to the glory of God." So in exploring a tale, consider: (1) What are the literary pleasures of this passage? (2) What accounts for one's enjoyment of the material? (Answers are likely to include such elements as humor, richness of human personality, vivid description, and plot devices like conflict, irony, and satire.)

A second feature of Chaucer's art is his celebration of the richness and diversity of human personality, communicated skillfully by character portrayal. The seventeenth-century English poet John Dryden looked at the sheer abundance

For Further Study

Chaucer wrote in Middle English, but most people prefer to read him in translation. The Bantam edition entitled *The Canterbury Tales by Geoffrey Chaucer* (edited by A. Kent and Constance Hieatt) contains the Middle English text and a modern English translation on facing pages.

Even in translation, Chaucer is somewhat difficult for a modern reader. He wrote in poetry rather than prose; he preferred fantasy to realism. Many of the details that Chaucer included presuppose a reader's acquaintance with medieval symbolism. But his tales can be read and enjoyed on many levels.

Helpful sources include: Muriel Bowden, *A Commentary on the General Prologue to the Canterbury Tales* (Macmillan, 1948); Trevor Whittock, *A Reading of the Canterbury Tales* (Cambridge, 1968); Donald R. Howard, *The Idea of the Canterbury Tales* (University of California, 1976); and Helen Cooper, *The Canterbury Tales* (Oxford Guides to Chaucer, 1989). Robert M. Lumiansky, *Of Sondry Folk: The Dramatic Principle in the Canterbury Tales* (University of Texas, 1955), explores the links between tale and teller, and Leland Ryken, *Realms of Gold: The Classics in Christian Perspective*, chapter 2 (Harold Shaw, 1991), discusses the comic element.

of human personality in *The Canterbury Tales* and exclaimed, "Here is God's plenty." To explore Chaucer's techniques of characterization further, the reader may ask, (3) What do the physical traits of this pilgrim tell me about his or her moral character? (4) Does this religious figure represent a character worth emulating? What about this secular figure?

Chaucer's third outstanding quality is his compassionate reproof of human weakness, with satire serving as the vehicle. Two objects of satiric exposure are particularly relevant to Christians. Chaucer is adept at capturing the hypocrisy that infiltrates the life of religious people and institutions. Another of his great themes is *eros* defiled—the power of sex in people's lives and its capacity for perversion. Good questions to ask are, (5) What human failings does Chaucer present for our understanding? (6) Following the hints laid down in the text, what does Chaucer offer as a corrective to those failings?

—Leland Ryken

THE SECOND SHEPHERDS' PLAY AND EVERYMAN

c. 15th Century

*T*he Second Shepherds' *Play* and *Everyman* are the two most celebrated examples of medieval drama—drama that grew out of the church and is prized for its depiction of the mysteries of the Christian faith and its exploration of vice and virtue. *The Second Shepherds' Play* is a complex mystery play that stands out for its engaging charm and poetic exuberance. *Everyman* is the most famous morality play, which has become a classic because of its forceful simplicity.

Origins of Medieval Drama

Medieval drama grew out of the church, but not straightforwardly. Because of the association with brutality and bloodshed, the church had actually banished drama in the fourth century but resurrected it in the ninth and tenth centuries as a tool for teaching the uneducated. Used initially within the liturgy of the church service itself, drama enhanced the parishioners' understanding of the gospel

A wheeled pageant vehicle in the market square, Coventry, for the medieval mystery plays.

lessons. The story of Christ's death and resurrection was dramatized in the tenth century; the Christmas story in the eleventh. With time, these individual dramatizations developed into mystery cycles, so called, some think, because they were sponsored by the craft guilds *(misteres)*. But, more likely, the name was given them because they depict the sacred biblical mysteries that culminate in the life and death of Christ. They encompass the whole biblical story from

creation through Old Testament prophecy to the nativity, passion, and finally the last judgment.

As the cycles grew in complexity, they were removed from the church service itself, first to the courtyard, and eventually out of the hands of the church entirely, becoming the responsibility of various guilds to perform. With such a move, the language and action became more secularized, and the emphasis began to shift from teaching to entertainment although the cycles continued to celebrate the mysteries of the Christian faith. There was even a day set aside for their performance, Corpus Christi day, established to honor the mystery of Christ's flesh and blood in the Eucharist. In many communities these cycles were performed over a day or two, with individual plays dramatized on pageant wagons that paraded throughout the city.

In addition to mystery cycles, there were also miracle plays—plays that celebrated the lives of saints—and morality plays, such as *Everyman, Mankind,* and *The Castle of Perseverance*. Although morality plays also grew out of the church,

Everyman responding to Death's summons:

Full unready I am such reckoning to give.
I know thee not. What messenger art thou?

—*Everyman*

they were influenced most directly by homilies and sermons rather than the liturgy. Whereas the mystery plays were charmingly realistic, portraying high sacred mysteries as they pertained to ordinary people, the morality plays typically were dramatized allegories of vices and virtues. Most often they dealt with temptations in this life and the inevitability of death.

Two Dramas of Redemption

The Second Shepherds' Play is one of two shepherds' plays in the Wakefield cycle and clearly the best in the group of thirty-two plays that comprise this group. Much of this reputation comes from the distinctive hand of its author, the Wakefield Master, who wrote six of the plays in the cycle and who is known for his broad humor, his biting social criticism, and his unique nine-line stanza with its tumbling rhythm. In *The First Shepherds' Play,* the author celebrates an Eden-like innocence. In *The Second Shepherds' Play,* he portrays the imperfect human condition, vividly demonstrating the need for redemption and celebrating the mystery of Christ's incarnation.

While *Everyman* also presents the need for redemption, it does so through the use of personification allegory. In other English morality plays, the focus is typically on the figure of humanity, who is tempted to sin by a comic vice character. Through his struggles, the figure of humanity eventually finds salvation. In *Everyman,* by contrast, the unknown author heightened the play's intensity by focusing on one overpowering threat: Everyman's confrontation with death.

The Second Shepherds' Play: The Stolen and Sacrificed Lamb

Through the structure, comic devices, and symbols of *The Second Shepherds' Play,* this delightful comedy celebrates Christ as the lamb of God, slain for the salvation of humanity to restore what Satan stole. The play is structured in three parts, which are separated by three songs. It begins with a clear depiction of a fallen world as seen by three shepherds who complain about social unrest and misuse of power, domestic strife, and cosmic disturbances. These issues suggest the disorder that results from sin and the need for redemption.

The second section focuses on Mak the sheep stealer, a comic devil figure. In the night while the other shepherds sleep soundly under a spell he has cast, Mak steals a sheep and carries it to his wife, who swaddles it in cloths and hides it in a child's cradle. When the shepherds awake to find their sheep missing, they search Mak's house in outrage but cannot find the stolen animal. But as they leave, they remember that they have not yet given a gift to Mak's new baby. Their act of charity leads them to discover the lamb in the cradle. Although Mak insists that the child has been bewitched to look like a sheep—a supernatural birth—the shepherds punish him and his deceitful wife by tossing them in a blanket.

In the last part of the play, the shepherds hear the call of the angels to adore the true supernatural child in the animal's manger. When they see the Christ child, they offer him gifts of cherries, a ball, and a bird—all symbols of different aspects of the Trinity.

The play's significance emerges from the relation of these three sections. Most notable is the way in which the sheep-stealing scene provides a comic inversion of the actual adoration of the Christ child. In both accounts the "child" is announced and adored. There is also the obvious inversion of a lamb in a child's cradle and Christ in an animal's manger.

The deeper meanings emerge from a consideration of the medieval doctrine of the Eucharist, or Communion. Both Mak and his wife claim to know nothing about the lost

Death: after the allegorical print by Hans-Sebald Beham (1500–1550).

sheep and swear that they will eat the child who lies in the cradle if they are lying. This adds to the comedy but more importantly underscores the central mystery of faith: Christ is the lamb of God who was born in a manger to give his life for us. When we partake of the Eucharist, we symbolically eat his body and blood and celebrate our salvation through him. Through his supreme act of charity, Christ reorders and redeems the fallenness of the world, as depicted at the beginning of the play.

Everyman: Live Uprightly to Die Uprightly

Everyman is a stark and terrifying allegory in which God on high sends word to Everyman that he must meet Death. Frightened, Everyman unsuccessfully tries bribes and persuasion to avoid Death. He is equally unsuccessful in convincing Fellowship, Kindred and Cousins, and Material Goods to go with him. They all vow to help but flee quickly when they discover his goal. Only Good Deeds and Knowledge will agree to go along. Good Deeds, however, is too feeble to walk because Everyman has failed to nurture her. To empower Good

Deeds, Everyman confesses his sins and does penance. He then sets off to meet Death accompanied by Discretion, Strength, Beauty, and the Five Wits (or senses), as well as his two original companions.

As Everyman prepares to descend into his grave after receiving the last sacraments, all but Knowledge and Good Deeds desert him; Knowledge will part at the moment he descends. Only Good Deeds will follow him into the grave. At the play's end, Knowledge stands over the grave and asserts the reality of Everyman's salvation as he listens to the angels singing, welcoming Everyman to heaven.

Preserved in four manuscripts from 1508–37, *Everyman* was probably written before the end of the fifteenth century. What it lacks in color and comedy, *Everyman* makes up for in

From the prologue:

> *Ye think sin is the beginning full sweet,*
> *Which in the end causeth the soul to weep.*
>
> —*Everyman*

Everyman praying to God:

O eternal God, O heavenly figure,
O way of righteousness, O goodly vision,
Which descended down in a virgin pure,
Because he would every man redeem,
Which Adam forfeited by his disobedience:
O blessed Godhead, elect and high divine,
Forgive my grievous offence; . . .

—Everyman

For Further Study

Although both plays are brief, their fifteenth-century English will present some difficulties, if a great deal of delight, to the modern reader. Using editions with good glossaries or reading in a good translation is recommended. *The Second Shepherds' Play* is light and playful in tone; *Everyman* is straightforward and somber.

Good editions of both plays are in David Bevington, *Medieval Drama* (Houghton Mifflin, 1975), along with commentary on both the plays and an excellent background to medieval drama. The best translation of *The Second Shepherds' Play* is in John Russell Brown, *The Complete Plays of the Wakefield Master* (Heinemann, 1983). Very readable versions of *Everyman* are in John Gassner, *Medieval and Tudor Drama* (Bantam, 1963), and A. C. Cawley, *Everyman and Medieval Miracle Plays* (Dutton, 1959).

sobering devotional thought. Whether we are readers or an audience, the play forces us to reexamine life and to realize how little of this world we can take to the grave. Just as Everyman received word that he needed to prepare to meet God, so too do we receive a message through the play.

Issues to Explore

As both *Everyman* and *The Second Shepherds' Play* contain many different levels, questions will help the reader explore more deeply aspects of the comedy, allegory, and symbolism within the plays. Questions to ask in *The Second Shepherds' Play* include: (1) How does music function in the play? Why is some music harmonious and some out of tune? (2) How does the author characterize the sheep-stealer Mak? What is the significance of the spells he casts and of his commending himself into the hands of Pontius Pilate? (3) What is the significance of the three gifts that the shepherds bring to the Christ child? (4) Why do you think the author chose to use comic inversion as a way to

celebrate the mysteries of faith? What makes it effective?

Questions regarding *Everyman* include: (5) What is the role of confession, penance, and sacrament in Everyman's salvation? (6) Why are the Good Deeds weak before confession? (7) Why do Beauty, Discretion, Strength, and the Five Wits go with him as far as the grave and then depart, whereas Fellowship, Material Goods, and Kindred do not go with him even that far? (8) What is the role of Knowledge in the play?

—Sharon Coolidge

THOMAS MORE

Utopia
1516

homas More's *Utopia,* which he wrote in Latin in 1516, is the masterpiece of a man his fellow-Englishman Samuel JOHNSON described as "the person of the greatest virtue these islands ever produced." In *Utopia* More established a literary form that has exerted inestimable influence on the modern political imagination. By reshaping the classical genre into a form in which imaginary societies offer examples for philosophical and practical guidance, More both signaled and helped create the modern epoch. Since More's day, fictional accounts of utopias have appeared in rapid succession throughout Europe and America. In the nineteenth and twentieth centuries in particular, the fiction has become reality as attempts have been made to found actual regimes free of the ills that traditionally plague society. The recently failed Marxist attempt is most notable among many.

More lived during the Renaissance, when a fresh awareness of the philosophic and artistic triumphs of classical Greece and Rome led to fresh efforts to perfect the human condition. In one sense,

Sir Thomas More (1478–1535), after the portrait by Holbein.

then, *Utopia* can be seen as a revival of such classics as PLATO's *Republic,* which contains its own utopian vision, and AUGUSTINE's *City of God.* But the Renaissance discovery of the New World also brought with it a sense of possibility for new political and social orders. The time was right for the imaginative creation of an ideal cosmos that served to measure the realities of the day.

A Man for All Seasons

Born in 1478, well educated in the Greek and Latin classics, law, and Christian theology, More fully participated in the projects of Renaissance humanism—the study of those subjects most endowed with moral significance. His wit and learning facilitated his quick rise to knighthood and, even further, to an appointment by Henry VIII that made him Lord Chancellor of England.

This precarious combination of the spiritual and active life, however, came to an end when the king unsuccessfully sought from the pope an annulment of his marriage to Catherine of Aragon so that he could marry Anne Boleyn. Although a long-time friend of Henry, More resigned the chancellorship when Henry declared that he, and not the pope, was the head of the Church of England, whereby he could marry Anne. Two years later, More courageously refused to take an oath supporting the Act of Supremacy, which officially made Henry the head of the Church of England and declared his supremacy over all foreign kings, including the pope. More refused

Raphael Hythloday:

As long as private property remains, by far the largest and the best part of mankind will be oppressed by a heavy and inescapable burden of cares and anxiety.

—*Utopia*
Robert M. Adams, trans.

A Stifling of Individuality

Hythloday's tale is part of a larger discussion between the character More and Hythloday on the best way to respond to the evils of European society. Hythloday's account of Utopia counters More's observation that "it is impossible to make all institutions good, unless you make all men good, and that I don't expect to see for a long time to come." Hythloday unreservedly affirms the features of Utopian society: "So I reflect on the wonderfully wise and sacred institutions of the Utopians who are so well governed with so few laws. Among them virtue has its reward, yet everything is shared equally, and all men live in plenty."

Particularly beneficial to the Utopians, Hythloday states, is the institution of common property. There is no need for money. Basic necessities are available to all at public expense. Luxuries are eliminated. This system is possible through the most productive economic institution—the one pursuit common to all—which stipulates that all citizens must work periodically on the social farms. Besides this common labor, they all learn a trade or craft of their own choosing to produce common goods.

Supposedly no pleasure is forbidden in Utopian society provided it does no harm. But Hythloday is so enthusiastic about Utopia that he fails to notice how distasteful and distinctly *un*pleasurable the institutions of this state are. Utopian laws and conventions are shaped with a view to curbing not only pride but physical urges as well. For instance, the required uniforms distinguish male from female, married from unmarried. And all citizens are carefully observed to circumvent unlicensed behavior. Further, although all the houses are alike, they must be traded every ten years; the mandate to alternate farm and city life in two-year cycles, while meant to counter the attachment to things, ends by creating a virtually nomadic way of life. The hard manual labor on these farms is not only forced but is at times dealt out as punishment.

Other examples of the state's rigid moralism include the penalty of slavery for the first commission of adultery, death for the second. Citizens may follow their religious conscience

on the grounds that the king and Parliament had no legal authority to act in this manner. He was imprisoned and, after a subsequent act of Parliament interpreted as treason any refusal to take the oath, was beheaded on July 6, 1535.

The Meaning of "No Place"

Utopia, written in Latin nineteen years before More's execution, when he was at the height of his favor in the court, is an engaging satire on human pretensions. It recounts a tale that the narrator, the well-traveled Raphael Hythloday, tells to Thomas More, who is himself a character in the book. In the tale Hythloday makes observations regarding the institutions established on Utopia, a remote island ruled by King Utopus.

The tale is not easily interpreted, partly because of the meanings of the names. For instance, the name Raphael means "healing of God" and the name Hythloday means "dispenser of nonsense." Are readers thus supposed to understand this narrative as a divine healing effected by a dispensing of nonsense? As Hythloday is the only source of information, should his whole account be taken as nonsense? Translating other names only adds to the complexity: More's own name in Greek is *moriae,* which means "folly." King Utopus means "King of no place"; Anydrus, the principal river of the island, is "no water"; the governor, Ademus, signifies "peopleless." And because Utopia has an indefinite location and a vague history, it appropriately translates as "no place." Clearly, these names alert its readers to the playful spirit at work and preclude any mistaking of *Utopia* for a straightforward account of the cure for society's ills.

but may not preach openly against official religious dogmas that teach immortality of the soul and reward or punishment after death. To contest these two dogmas publicly would mean public infamy and, if repeated, death. Even those whose lives are coming to a painful end are seen as reproofs to the pleasure principle in Utopian society: they are exhorted to commit suicide or submit to euthanasia.

When Institutions Rule the Spirit

In *Utopia* Thomas More presents an answer to the following question: What would a society look like after an institutionally determined attempt to root out the consequences of pride, particularly in the form of attachment to private property?

Many disparate interpretations have been advanced concerning More's answer. For some communists of the early twentieth century, *Utopia* previewed Marxist communism. Other interpreters have understood *Utopia* as a medieval manifesto that affirms Catholic solidarity, agrarian economy, and the monastic life. Still others find in it a model for the good society, lacking only Christian revelation to perfect it. In each case, however, the stumbling block for these interpretations is More's keenly satiric tone.

We must ask what More is satirizing. Actually, different historical epochs may be said to have discovered different facets of the work since its publication. For the modern age, for instance, Raphael Hythloday fits the mold of a familiar figure—the ideologue who identifies all ills in society as stemming from one particular institution, whose elimination will eliminate evil. In his enthusiasm for a single cause, he sees nothing but his good aims while missing the obvious costs. More's *Utopia* satirizes this dispenser of nonsense, this utopian thinking. By this "healing of God" he cures us of thinking that the ills of the world can be eliminated by the Hythlodays of the world. And it returns us to the belief that we must change the heart of the individual to change society. The limitations present in human nature must be deeply considered by all who

wish to bring Christian principles to bear in an imperfect world.

Plan of the island of Utopia, from the 1518 edition.

Thomas More, the character:

This one thing alone {communal living and property} takes away all the nobility, magnificence, splendor, and majesty which {in the popular view} are considered the true ornaments of any nation.

—*Utopia*
Robert M. Adams, trans.

Yet I confess there are many things in the commonwealth of Utopia that I wish our own country would imitate— though I don't really expect it will.

—*Utopia*
Robert M. Adams, trans.

For Further Study

One of the best translations is by Edward Surtz, S.J., *Utopia* (Yale University, 1964). For many differing interpretations, see the Norton Critical Edition edited and translated by Robert M. Adams, *Utopia* (W. W. Norton, 1992). For a good biography see R. W. Chambers, *Thomas More* (Newman Press, 1935).

Issues to Explore

More's book is subtle, delightful to read, and rewarding to the careful reader. Questions that arise from the reading of *Utopia* include: (1) Why has the work received so many conflicting interpretations? (2) How and why does More employ the use of satire? (3) What does *Utopia* tell us about the nature of modern politics, much of which has been conditioned by utopian thinking? (4) Can the truth of Christ become institutionalized into the truth of society? (5) Why do attempts to implement a utopian dream often turn into nightmare existence? (6) Are there good features to utopian thinking that can serve as necessary paradigms for society? (7) Why is the modern world so fascinated with utopian thinking and projects?

—Peter Sampo

MARTIN LUTHER

The Babylonian Captivity of the Church (1520)
The Small Catechism (1529)

Martin Luther (1483–1546), the great Protestant reformer, theologian, and hymn writer, is as a person as much a classic as are any of his writings. His role as spark of the Reformation in the sixteenth century has made him one of the most honored figures in Protestant history. This has also long made him a reviled figure among Roman Catholics, who have held him responsible for destroying the godly synthesis of the High Middle Ages. In the last generation, however, Catholics and Protestants have reached new levels of mutual understanding. Luther still remains a larger-than-life figure, but one whom Protestants now see as a man of his times and Catholics recognize as a serious contributor to the understanding of the gospel.

A Monumental Figure

Many of the products of Luther's teeming pen deserve special consideration. As an adult, Luther published on average one writing (some very brief, some very long) every three weeks of his life. The fullest English translation of his

Martin Luther (1483–1546).

works totals fifty-five volumes, but this represents less than half of what he actually published in Latin or German. After Jesus Christ, he has inspired more studies (pro and con) than any other figure in Western history. Of the many superlative treatments, a half-century-old study by Roland H. Bainton, *Here I Stand: A Life of Martin Luther,* has justly

won a reputation as a classic work on a classic subject.

At the end of his biography, Bainton evaluates Martin Luther by comparing him with similar figures in English religious history. His judgment suggests why it is so difficult to take the measure of the man:

> If no Englishman occupies a similar place in the religious life of his people, it is because no Englishman had anything like Luther's range. The Bible translation in England was the work of [William] Tyndale, the prayer book of [Thomas] Cranmer, the catechism of the Westminster divines. The sermonic style stemmed from [Hugh] Latimer; the hymnbook came from [Isaac] Watts. And not all of these lived in the one century. Luther did the work of more than five men.

An Imperfect Saint

Luther's parents belonged to what we today call the rising middle class; they wanted him to have a better life than they had. So they sent him to the University (at Erfurt). But just after Luther received the Bachelor of Arts in 1502, he threw the family into consternation by entering a monastery. Why did he do so? Fear of lightning during a thunderstorm perhaps. But more certainly because the death of close friends had shown him his own mortality and because he wanted to find God.

Luther was a diligent monk for over fifteen years, during which time he undertook advanced theological study. After becoming a doctor of theology in 1512 he began lecturing on the Bible in a small, new university at Wittenberg. For the rest of his life he taught students the Scriptures while preaching frequently in the town churches.

For more than his first decade as a monk Luther was in constant turmoil. He was especially driven to question his own motives for seeking God. Why did his scrupulosity as a monk not bring rest to his soul? Finally, with the advice of his supervisor, Johannes von Staupitz, and through constant attention to the Scriptures—especially the Psalms and the Epistle to the Romans—Luther found an answer. The "righteousness of God" that so terrified him should not be regarded as a divine standard that measures sinners in their unworthiness. Rather, it is a gift that God offers to those who exercise faith in Jesus Christ. When this insight flooded his heart, Luther said it was as if he had been "reborn and . . . gone through open doors into paradise."

To begin with, I must deny that there are seven sacraments, and for the present maintain that there are but three: baptism, penance, and the bread. All three have been subjected to a miserable captivity by the Roman curia, and the church has been robbed of all her liberty. Yet, if I were to speak according to the usage of the Scriptures, I should have only one single sacrament (i.e., Christ), but with three sacramental signs.

—*The Babylonian Captivity of the Church*
A. T. W. Steinhäuser, Rev. F. C. Ahrens, and A. R. Wentz, trans.

Efforts to reform the church followed naturally from this personal discovery. Where Luther felt the institutional church blocked the gospel of free grace in Christ, he protested. Such a protest led him in 1517 to post ninety-five theses for academic debate against the practice of selling indulgences (whereby souls might be remitted penalties for sins).

Luther's vision of the gospel nerved him to debate some of the church's leading defenders and, in 1521, to proclaim before the Holy Roman Emperor, Charles V, at the Diet of Worms: "Unless I am convicted by Scripture and plain reason—I do not accept the authority of popes and councils. . . . My conscience is captive to the Word of God. I cannot and I will not recant anything."

The same commitment drove Luther into whirlwinds of activity—translating the Scriptures, writing hymns, trying to restrain those he considered radicals, preaching continually, answering letters by the score, eventually helping set up territorial Protestant churches, and all the while keeping small armies of printers at work.

Luther was not a perfected saint. Of special damage in the history of the West were his harsh denunciations of Jews. In 1543 he called on rulers of Germany to drive them out of the land and forbid their rabbis to teach. Luther was acting on what he considered legitimate theological grounds, because he had heard that Jewish teachers were enticing Protestants and Catholics away from the Christian faith. His violent arguments, however, nurtured the ground from which much evil has sprung.

In short, Luther was not impeccable. But he was a man gripped by a mighty vision of God. It was this vision of God that shook him to the depths of his own being, broke through the religious conventions of his day, and compelled nearly the whole world to pay attention.

The Works

Although Luther was not a systematic writer, his works have coherence. Almost all of them express what it means for God to liberate humanity through Christ's work on the cross.

One of his great early expressions of that teaching was a treatise of 1520, *The Babylonian Captivity of the Church*. This work laid down a fearsome gauntlet. Its thesis was that the Catholic Church used its seven sacraments to enslave the conscience of Christians. There were, Luther argued, only three true sacraments, that is, rites to which Christ himself had attached promises with a visible sign: baptism, the Lord's Supper, and confession. Protestants later reduced the number even further to include only baptism and the Lord's Supper.

As devastating as this critique was, even more shocking was Luther's revision of the mass, the heart of Roman Catholic piety. He particularly attacked the teachings that the mass renewed Christ's sacrifice on the cross and that through "transubstantiation" the substance of the bread and wine becomes the body and blood of Christ. He retained the idea of a "real presence" in the Lord's Supper but held that its nature was mysterious; it could not be tied down to Aristotelian categories of substance. Most important, it was critical to restore the mass, not as a means by which we present ourselves to God, but by which God freely draws us into his love in Christ. Luther's argument in *The Babylonian Captivity* was stunning, both for what it said about the sacraments but also for how it demonstrated a revolutionary willingness of individual conscience to question the authority of the church.

A very distinct work, revealing a different side of Luther's character, is his *Small Catechism* in 1529. Luther's prince had asked him to help with a visitation of churches in the countryside of Saxony. When Luther and his colleagues found an appalling ignorance about the most basic Christian teachings, he asked his learned friends to prepare a simple set of questions and answers to use for basic instruction. When they delayed, Luther prepared some wall charts that presented simple explanations for the Ten Commandments, the Lord's Prayer, the Apostles' Creed, and the Christian sacraments. When his colleagues delayed even further, Luther gathered his wall charts into a "Small Catechism." This book, which has been translated almost everywhere that Lutheranism has

Martin Luther (left), with John Oecolampadius, John Frederick the Magnanimous, Elector of Saxony, Huldreich Zwingli, and Philip Melanchthon; painting by Lucas Cranach, c. 1530.

taken root in the globe, is down-to-earth, mostly free from polemics, and entirely successful at presenting the Christian faith in a memorable, fresh, and straightforward way.

The spirit of the work is suggested by a short instruction that Luther offers to assist heads of families in leading daily prayers. He provides a form of evening prayer that includes this petition: "I give Thee thanks, heavenly Father, through thy dear Son Jesus Christ, that Thou hast this day graciously protected me. I beseech Thee to forgive all my sin and the wrong which I have done. Graciously protect me during the coming night." The characteristic note is what follows: "Then quickly lie down and sleep in peace."

For Further Study

Any one book by or about Luther is not enough. But we can understand Luther's character when we see how casually he treated his own writing. Late in his life Luther's friends began to collect his widely scattered works to publish a definitive edition. The old man was not impressed. He thought that maybe his Small Catechism and his reply to Erasmus in 1525, which defended God's grace as the sole source of salvation, were worthy of being saved. He reckoned that some of his biblical exposition might still be useful (he may have been thinking of his work on Galatians—the work he called, out of love for his wife, his "Katie von Bora"). But the rest he was willing to let go, because what mattered most was nothing that he had done but what God had done for him.

Standard English texts are found in the fifty-five-volume American Edition, *Luther's Works*; *The Babylonian Captivity* is in volume 36, edited by A. R. Wentz (Fortress, 1959). An authoritative translation of *The Small Catechism* may be found in *The Book of Concord*, Theodore G. Tappert, editor (Fortress, 1959). There are countless editions of Luther's individual works. A good one-volume anthology is Timothy F. Lull, *Luther's Basic Theological Writings* (Fortress, 1989).

Besides Bainton's biography, a few other notable English-language works are worth mentioning, including Philip S. Watson, *Let God Be God! An Interpretation of the Theology of Martin Luther* (revised, Fortress, 1970); H. G. Haile, *Luther: An Experiment in Biography* (Doubleday, 1980); and Heiko A. Oberman, *Luther: Man between God and the Devil* (Yale, 1990).

Actually, during the mass, we should do nothing with greater zeal (indeed, it demands all our zeal) than to set before our eyes, meditate upon, and ponder these words, these promises of Christ—for they truly constitute the mass itself—in order to exercise, nourish, increase, and strengthen our faith in them by this daily remembrance. For this is what he commands, when he says: "Do this in remembrance of me."

—*The Babylonian Captivity of the Church*
A. T. W. Steinhäuser, Rev. F. C. Ahrens, and A. R. Wentz, trans.

Issues to Explore

(1) What is the relationship between Luther's personality, his dramatic career, and the nature of his theology? (2) What is Luther's basic point? Is it one that needs to be announced today? (3) Why have historians sometimes seen Luther as an unwitting factor in the rise of modern secularism, as well as the father of Protestantism? (The answer concerns Luther's promotion of the individual conscience over against the traditions of church and state.) (4) How has the growth of Protestant churches followed along the course that Luther first outlined? How has it diverged from his interests? (5) What might a modern Roman Catholic say about Luther's protest against the late-medieval form of the Catholic Church? (Roman Catholics, including the pope, took part to good effect in recent commemorations marking the 450th anniversary of the Augsburg Confession [1980] and the five hundredth anniversary of Luther's birth [1983].)

—Mark A. Noll

Devotional Classics

Devotional literature has been central to the life of the Christian church since its beginning, although the influence of such writings has often been felt most powerfully during times of religious and social upheaval. Testifying to an ardent faith, these works are a constant reminder of key Christian truths often forgotten by a wayfaring church or a shallow culture.

In the popular imagination, writing that deals overtly with the religious life is often seen as appealing to the heart alone and thus void of serious rational or theological considerations. Yet the best of the superb devotional classics remind their readers of the necessity of the clear light of reason and a steadfast mind. The greatest writers of these works, although from various denominational traditions and national backgrounds, are all doctrinally grounded. Their authors rely on the written Word to give meaning to the enfleshed Word, Jesus Christ. Consumed with a love for God, they rejoice in a life of service to others, especially the poor. Thus they often emphasize the simplicity of life, moderation in all things, and disregard for possessions.

Nor are these writers withdrawn from life. Some of them take refuge out of the world, it is true;

but others are thoroughly involved in the events of their times. Yet all bear witness to a deep belief in the sacredness of life and in a peace of heart and mind that the continual presence of God can bring.

Speaking to the minds and hearts of Christians in all ages, devotional literature encompasses universal and edifying biblical, theological, and personal themes. Its authors wish to lead their readers, as it were, gently by the hand to God. Many of the great devotional works are classics by any standard—for example, Augustine's Confessions. But one can easily name others that richly repay closer acquaintance.

Julian of Norwich (c. 1342–1416)

What we know of Julian of Norwich, the greatest of the English medieval mystics, comes largely from her writings; and even with those, certain conclusions have to be inferred. Educated under the auspices of the Benedictine Order, she may have taken the vows of a Benedictine nun. She lived a cloistered life at the Church of St. Julian in Norwich, England, and drew her name from that affiliation.

At the age of thirty Julian was stricken with a serious illness, from which she nearly died. During this

time of extreme suffering she experienced sixteen visions, or "shewings," from God within a twenty-four-hour period. Recovering quickly, she dedicated the remainder of her life to meditating upon those visions, eventually writing of them in Revelations of Divine Love. This classic work should be read not so much for a demonstration of theological precision as for an impassioned plea that all believers seek God "earnestly and diligently, . . . abide in Him steadfastly for His love, . . . and trust in Him mightily. . . ."

Julian often meditates vividly on the bleeding and suffering Christ and the meaning of his passion for the salvation of the world. In the cross was love revealed, "for endless love made Him to suffer," and in our lives is love continued. Julian takes refuge in that love and from an ever grateful heart thanks God for his provision of salvation in Christ. "We know in our faith," she wrote, "that when man fell so deep and so wretchedly by sin, there was none other help to restore man but through Him that made man."

Thomas à Kempis (c. 1380–1471)

Thomas, born in Kempen, Germany, was educated by the Brethren of the Common Life and later entered the Augustinian order near Zwolle in the Netherlands, where he remained the rest of his life. He labored as a copyist and wrote devotional literature; his *Imitation of Christ,* the famous manual of spiritual devotion published in 1441, points the way toward achieving communion with God.

Some scholars question whether Thomas wrote the *Imitation* or was merely the copyist of someone else's writing. In any case Thomas was responsible for the popularization of this work, which reveals wisdom for Christians traveling their spiritual journey and provides devotional direction for all who "would be truly enlightened, and be delivered from all blindness of heart."

The Imitation of Christ has universal appeal in honestly and forthrightly recognizing the sin and subsequent frailty of the human family, "so much inclined to outward things, so negligent in things inward and spiritual." It deals with such practical problems in the Christian pilgrimage as bearing with harsh criticism, adversity, and spiritual dryness. The work, however, is centered primarily upon Christ and his death on the cross. Following him means "giving thyself up with all thy heart to the divine will, not seeking thine own interest, either in great matters or in small, either in time or in eternity."

Francis of Sales (1567–1622)

John Calvin's Geneva was also the home of Francis of Sales, a prolific devotional writer whose works have been influential on subsequent spiritual writing. Born in the nearby town of Sales to a family of privilege, Francis later

Thomas à Kempis (c. 1380–1471).

studied in Paris and was trained as a lawyer. He followed another calling, however, more in keeping with his preference for theology over law. He was ordained to the priesthood in 1593 and served primarily in Geneva, over which he became the bishop in 1602. He was a diligent defender of the Roman Catholic faith.

Francis's most enduring work, entitled *Introduction to the Devout Life,* was immediately popular when published in 1609. It is the compilation of letters and papers written to a woman who had dedicated her life to God after hearing Francis preach in 1607. In it Francis clearly states that his aim is to assist the reader to "advance in devotion"; he opens the work in

this practical way: "I shall begin with the preparation, which consists in placing yourself in the presence of God and imploring His assistance. Now, to assist you to place yourself in the presence of God, I shall set before you [the] principal means."

Francis calls for self-examination, followed by resolutions and the practice of the Christian virtues. His *Introduction* is filled with images of the natural world and vivid pictures of what the Christian life is intended to be. Christians, he says, are like eagles flying aloft to God.

Like many devotional writers, Francis is primarily concerned for the reader to become aware of the presence of God in the sacredness of everyday life, primarily through

FRANCISCVS SALESIVS

Francis of Sales (1567–1622).

humously as *The Practice of the Presence of God,* a humble work that gives great insight into how the devotional life sustains a person in the ordinary events of everyday life.

In his "practice of the presence of God," Brother Lawrence sought to live a life of simplicity and straightforwardness and therein found genuine joy. He was resolved "to make the love of God the end of all his actions."

Even in the kitchen Brother Lawrence's continual experience of God's presence enabled him to do his work well—as unto God. As his biographer says, "He was more united to God in his outward employments than when he left them for devotion and retirement." Finding God in the ordinary, the humble, and the mundane, he engaged in his "practice of the presence of God" with ease and naturalness. He advised others to do the same: "That time of business does not with me differ from the time of prayer, and in the noise and clatter of my kitchen . . . I possess God in as great tranquility as if I were upon knees at the blessed sacrament."

prayer and meditation. In this way, the believer sets "a higher estimation on the favor of heaven than on the honor of this low and perishable world."

Brother Lawrence (c. 1605–1691)

The Practice of the Presence of God is probably the most popular devotional classic today. Its author, Nicholas Herman, was an obscure saint who had served as a soldier, witnessed combat, and endured hardship as a prisoner of war before joining the Carmelite order in 1651 as a lay brother. He was assigned as a cook in a Parisian monastery and thought of himself as "a servant of the servants of God."

After his death the world learned about Brother Lawrence from two brief biographies, sixteen letters, and a short paper entitled *Maxims.* The biographies and letters were published post-

Jesus commands us to mark his footsteps, to tread where his feet have stood; and not only invites us forward by the argument of his example, but he hath trodden down much of the difficulty, and made the way easier and fit for our feet. For he knows our infirmities, and himself hath felt their experience in all things but in the neighborhoods of sin; and therefore he hath proportioned a way and a path to our strengths and capacities.

—Jeremy Taylor
The Great Exemplar of Sanctity and Holy Life

Jeremy Taylor (1613–1667), seventeenth-century Anglican priest and devotional writer.

François Fénelon (1651–1715)

If some people are called to minister to the "cultured despisers of religion," this seems to have been true of François Fénelon, born into an aristocratic French family and educated in philosophy and theology. His ministry in Paris was to the nobility; King Louis XIV called Fénelon to tutor his grandson and then appointed him Archbishop of Cambrai in 1695.

Fénelon fell out of favor with the church because of his defense of Quietism, a movement stressing detachment from the things of this world, but official papal decree did not deter him. He became highly regarded for his pastoral ministry to people of both high and low birth. His letters amount to eleven volumes, the heart of his devotional literature. He is best read for his very practical advice, such as that found in *Christian Perfection,* the best known of his works. In it he writes, "Let us pray God to uproot from our hearts all that we want to plant there ourselves, and that he plant there with his own hand the tree of life loaded with fruit."

This life of faith, as he points out, leads to Christian perfection and increases benevolence. Herein is the practical side of spiritual life, always an important key to reading Fénelon—the life of faith aids the suffering believer who has lost a friend to death or who falls into doubt. In spite of circumstances, his readers are told, "Renew within you often the feeling of the presence of God."

Jeremy Taylor (1613–1667)

A seventeenth-century Anglican priest who served in England and Ireland, Jeremy Taylor was a prolific writer of fifteen volumes, many of which are devotional. He was born to a barber, graduated from Cambridge, and became a teaching fellow at Oxford. His fame today rests on his devotional works, which he wrote with a forcefulness and eloquence praised by voices as divergent as Samuel Taylor Coleridge and John Wesley.

Taylor in his writing insists that all of life be made holy by the disciplined believer and admonishes his reader to "make religion the business of your life," the pattern for such a life being Christ. His best known works, *Rule and Exercises of Holy Living* (1650) and *Rule and Exercises of Holy Dying* (1651), constitute more a challenge to the individual Christian than a call for a private faith. Prayer and meditation, Taylor felt strongly, are not to be isolated from the life of the church and the communion of saints.

His books should be read as guidelines for practical piety, offering rules for reading Scripture, the practice of prayer, and meditation. But his most persistent advice is to "press after Jesus" and therein find one's high calling. Jesus "commands us to mark his footsteps, to tread where his feet have stood; and not only invites us forward by the argument of his example, but he hath trodden down much of the difficulty, and made the way easier and fit for our feet."

John Wesley (1703–1791).

John (1703–1791) and Charles (1707–1788) Wesley

John and Charles Wesley, together with a band of friends, changed the face of religious and cultural life in Britain and America in the eighteenth century. Two of nineteen children, the brothers Wesley were reared in a religious Anglican home and educated at Oxford.

The year 1738 was significant for them; they had been missionaries briefly in America, but found themselves unfit for that service and returned to England where they were influenced by genuine Moravian piety. Both brothers then experienced an evangelical conversion—first Charles, and then three days later, John. On May 24, 1738, John's heart was "strangely warmed" when he listened to the reading of Luther's preface to the Epistle to the Romans in a religious meeting on Aldersgate Street near St. Paul's Cathedral, London. From

that time onward the Wesleys gave themselves to the work of evangelism.

John's published *Sermons* are a wealth of classic devotional literature as well as a source of theological education, appealing to both the heart and the mind. His sermons provide a theological textbook that points to the glory of God. "All the blessings which God hath bestowed upon man are of his mere grace, bounty, or favour: his free, undeserved favour, favour altogether undeserved, man having no claim to the least of his mercies," he wrote in "Salvation by Faith." In addition to his sermons, one should read his *Journal,* which gives his own account of his work under the guidance of God.

Charles was a gifted preacher, but is best remembered for his hymns, over six thousand written during his lifetime. They are filled with rich biblical vocabulary and whether sung or read enhance the devotional life of the Christian. Among the best known are "And Can It Be," "Love Divine, All Loves Excelling," "O For a Heart to Praise My God," and "Hark! The Herald Angels Sing."

Charles Wesley (1707–1788).

John Woolman (1720–1772)

Born to devout Quaker parents in Northampton, New Jersey, John Woolman was a minister who wrote deep, sincere, unadorned expressions of his faith. He ministered to the Indians and pioneered in the campaign against slavery in America until his untimely death from smallpox. A selfless Christian, he abhorred all that is contrary to the teachings of Scripture.

He that gives alms to the poor takes Jesus by the hand; he that patiently endures injuries and affronts, helps him to bear his cross; he that comforts his brother in affliction, gives an amiable kiss of peace to Jesus; he that bathes his own and his neighbor's sins in tears of penance and compassion, washes his Master's feet. We lead Jesus into the recesses of our heart by holy meditations; and we enter into his heart when we express him in our actions.

—Jeremy Taylor
The Great Exemplar of Sanctity and Holy Life

Woolman rejoiced when he recognized "that true religion consisted in an inward life, wherein the heart doth love and reverence God the Creator, and learns to exercise true justice and goodness, not only toward all men, but also toward the brute creatures."

His classic is his autobiography, *The Journal of John Woolman.* We can read this work as another example, much like that of Brother Lawrence, of the life of devotion to which all are called in the circumstances of their lives and times. The work portrays a man who in his simple and unencumbered life bears witness to the strength and freedom of sacrificial living. To Woolman the genuine Christian faith consists of this: "To keep a watchful eye towards real objects of charity, to visit the poor in their lonesome dwelling-places, to comfort them who, through the dispensations of divine providence, are in strait and painful circumstances in this life, and steadily to endeavour to honour God with our substance, from a real sense of the love of Christ influencing our minds thereto."

Evelyn Underhill (1875–1941)

Mysticism (1911) and *The Mystic Way* (1913) demonstrate Evelyn Underhill's brilliant acquaintance with many Christian mystics. An Englishwoman reared an Anglican and educated at King's College, London, she eventually became attracted to mysticism and great devotional literature. Her own writings have provided spiritual nourishment for thousands.

Under the spiritual care of

For Further Study

These writers may be read chronologically, as they are presented here. A better approach, however, is to read the most popular, beginning with *The Practice of the Presence of God* and *The Imitation of Christ.* These could be followed by *Holy Living* and *Holy Dying,* and perhaps by Julian of Norwich and John Woolman. With this background, one is ready to read the Wesley brothers and, lastly, Francis of Sales, François Fénelon, and Evelyn Underhill.

The recommended editions for each text follow.

Julian of Norwich: *Showings,* Edmund Colledge and James Walch, editors (Paulist Press, 1978).

Thomas à Kempis: *The Imitation of Christ* in Bernard Bangley, *Growing in His Image* (Harold Shaw, 1983).

Francis of Sales: *Introduction to the Devout Life,* John K. Ryan, editor (Harper, 1950).

Brother Lawrence: *The Practice of the Presence of God* (Revell, 1981).

Jeremy Taylor: *Jeremy Taylor: Selected Works,* Thomas K. Carroll, editor (Paulist Press, 1990).

François Fénelon: *Christian Perfection,* Charles F. Whiston, editor (Harper, 1947).

John Wesley: *Sermons,* Vols. 1–4 in *The Works of John Wesley,* Albert Outler, editor (Abingdon, 1989).

Charles Wesley: *Charles Wesley: A Reader,* John R. Tyson, editor (Oxford, 1989).

John Woolman: *The Journal and Major Essays of John Woolman,* Phillips P. Moulton, editor (Oxford, 1971).

Evelyn Underhill: *The Evelyn Underhill Reader,* Thomas S. Kepler, editor (Abingdon, 1962).

Baron Friedrich von Hugel she came to believe that all of life is sacramental. Underhill came to accept each day with its many trifling duties as a gift from God and another opportunity to worship him. She provides the theological grounding for such devotion through her books, such as her 1937 classic *Worship.* In it she reminds us that worship is not some kind of private religious experience, but the goal of the genuine devotional life. Through these writings and her work with spiritual retreats, Evelyn Underhill might be called a director of the souls of the saints.

Those reading her works or hearing her lectures have been challenged by her clarion call for

the long and costly struggle that "makes the human creature a pure capacity for God." She writes that "Spiritual achievement costs much, though never so much as it is worth. It means at the very least the painful development and persevering, steady exercise of a faculty that most of us have allowed to get slack." In *Concerning the Inner Life* she likewise calls for works of genuine charity among the poor and dispossessed, "to love and save not the nice but the nasty, not the lovable but the unlovely, the hard, the narrow, and the embittered, and the tiresome, who are so much worse."

—Roger J. Green

NICCOLÒ MACHIAVELLI

The Prince
1532

*N*iccolò Machiavelli's *The Prince,* the pioneering work of modern political science, is one of the best known, most widely quoted, and most often emulated political works of all time. Machiavelli wrote *The Prince* with specific political motives while in forced exile. In this slim volume he formulates a view of politics perfectly attuned to a world in which mutual loyalty, faith, and honest intentions cannot be assumed to exist. Because of this quite unclassical cynicism that drove a sword between virtue and realism, focusing instead on power, success, image, and efficiency, Machiavelli is said to be the founder of modern *realpolitik,* ushering in a completely new stage in political philosophy.

Niccolò Machiavelli (1469–1527); portrait by Santi di Tito.

The End Is All That Counts

The Prince makes a case for the acquisition and maintenance of power by a strong-willed monarch who has the necessary intelligence to carry out his ambitions. In it Machiavelli distinguishes between a state ruled by an autocrat and one operating as a republic, in which people rule themselves. He cites as the outstanding example of a republic the political order of Rome before the rule of Caesar Augustus.

Machiavelli's advice to such a leader is practical and sometimes cunning: Use unethical means as necessary to gain political ends. "In the actions of all men and especially princes, where there is no court of appeal, the end is all that counts." In ruling, princes must recognize the essential amorality of the political situation, their knowledge allowing them to build and rule a unified state by sheer force of will. Demonstrations of such a strength of will increase their power, avoid disorder in the state, and gain glory for themselves.

In response to the disintegrating conditions of his own time, Machiavelli sought to justify the need for unethical political practice. He thereby clearly breaks with classical and Christian theorists, who advocate that leadership of the state serve to build moral virtue in the life of citizens. "Machiavellianism," as the Elizabethans contemptuously termed this deviant view, became an entire way of thinking.

Secular and anti-religious realism in politics had been present several generations before Machiavelli, a loss of concern for eternal salvation having gradually led to the search for ultimate meaning in worldly matters. Machiavelli brought this burgeoning movement clearly into focus.

It is not, therefore, necessary for a prince to have all the above-named qualities {faithfulness, integrity, loyalty}, but it is very necessary to seem to have them.

—*The Prince*
Luigi Ricci, trans.

A Time of Crisis

Born in Florence in 1469 and educated in the classics, politics, and religion, Machiavelli soon exhibited a desire and talent for administrative and political work. At the age of twenty-nine he became secretary to the chancery in Florence, the office that managed the republic's foreign affairs. By this time he had witnessed the invasion of Italy by Charles VIII of France, the rise and fall of the monk Savonarola, the fall of the Medici family, and the establishment of a new Florentine republic. During the next fourteen years, he represented the republic in embassies to many of the important powers with whom Florence had diplomatic relations.

In 1512, the republic fell and the Medicis once again ruled Florence. Machiavelli lost his post and was arrested for treason, tortured, and exiled. While living among peasants and woodcutters he immersed himself in the classics and cultivated his own considerable writing talents. After his daily duties in more menial tasks, Machiavelli would put on the costume of the royal court in the evening and enter—through books—the classical court of the ancient thinkers and writers. "They welcome me warmly, and I feast on the nourishment for which I was born and which is mine *par excellence.*"

By the time of Machiavelli's death in 1527, he had composed not only *The Prince* and his *Discourses* on the Roman republic but also dramas (the most important being *Mandragola*), satires, poetry, a treatise on the art of war, a history of Florence, and several other works. But above all his other writings, *The Prince* struck the imagination of its Renaissance readers, arousing both attraction and repulsion. On this work his fame chiefly rests.

Machiavelli's thought responded to a crisis in Western civilization—the disintegration of Christendom into church and national states. He saw a spiritually animated whole break into national jurisdictions as the pursuit of dynastic and institutional interests led to the destruction of the large harmonious order of the Middle Ages. Because of the Roman Catholic Church's emphasis on temporal power, the pope could be viewed as another monarch and understood in terms of power politics. The growing national enclaves of France, England, and Spain asserted an increasing strength that challenged established order. The balance that existed in Italy among the five power centers—Milan, Florence, Naples, the Papal States, and Venice—was upset by the invasion led by Charles VIII.

The Practices of a Prince

In *The Prince* Machiavelli unmasks the reality of power drives in political life behind the appearance of pious intentions. Unlike such thinkers as PLATO, ARISTOTLE, and AUGUSTINE, who lamented this state of affairs and sought reform, Machiavelli was unique in actually advocating power politics and emphasizing the importance of appearances in its acquisition: "So a prince need not have all the aforementioned good qualities," he writes, "but it is most essential that he appear to have them. Indeed, I should go so far as to say that having them and always practicing them is harmful, while seeming to have them is useful."

Machiavelli argues that the state originates in the will of the founder. Statecraft is therefore the greatest act of the great man because first, the prince increases his power and glory exponentially and, second, the ruler masters fortune *(fortuna)*. Fortune for Machiavelli is that fickle combination of hard-to-foresee and hard-to-control forces that "is the arbiter of one half of our actions," although "she still leaves the control of the other half, or almost that, to us."

Fortune can be the harsh ruler of a harsh world. No providential hand of God rewards virtue in this world as no providential hand

Machiavelli's writing desk during his time of exile.

of God saved civilized Italy from the trauma of being invaded and looted by the barbarians of Charles VIII. Machiavelli does not speak of heaven. But he does see people overcoming *fortuna* through power and calculation—those with Machiavellian *virtù* (talent and vitality) sufficient to permit the crafting of a political order. At the slightest miscalculation or failure to stay alert, however, fortune can destroy plans and states as a raging flood can destroy everything in its path. Founders and maintainers of the power of states should be held in awe because of their almost miraculously successful efforts against what appears to be the insuperable forces of fortune.

In *The Prince* Machiavelli has created a myth of the Savior Prince. Though many historians have pointed out that historical accuracy in his treatise is suspect, his aim, however, is not a scientific account of history but the creation of a myth of explanation that transcends historical accuracy. Machiavelli hopes to sway the emotions of both prince and people by calling them to imitate the glories of ancient Rome, and he shows that the promise held out by this

Therefore it is necessary for a prince, who wishes to maintain himself, to learn how not to be good, and to use this knowledge and not use it, according to the necessity of the case.

—*The Prince*
Luigi Ricci, trans.

new infused myth can save Italy from its fragmentation and weakness only if a man of outstanding *virtù* takes this myth into himself to become the savior of Italy. In this way, *The Prince* continues the long tradition of literature called the "mirror of princes," although Machiavelli replaces the classical exhortation to virtue with *virtù* of his own defining—power politics.

Much of modern political life can be understood only in Machiavellian terms. Machiavelli's views on politics have endured because the conditions that formed them are still present. The loss of spiritual knowledge with the

Whence it is to be noted, that in taking a state the conqueror must arrange to commit all his cruelties at once. . . .

—*The Prince*
Luigi Ricci, trans.

accompanying emphasis on the material world characterizes the modern age. We confront, therefore, a world obviously subject to crushing power, whether economic, political, or military. Consequently the modern world seeks a person of power who can meet adverse fortune and conquer it—a Savior Prince. Accordingly, we tend to look on modern politics as a source of salvation.

Issues to Explore

The Prince is deceptively short and fairly easy to read. Machiavelli's arguments are subtle, however, and, although easily condemned, should not be easily dismissed. Questions that the reader may ask in understanding this complex work include: (1) Are modern political conditions similar to or different from those that brought Machiavelli's *Prince* into the world? (2) Is today's political practice as flawed

For Further Study

The literature on Machiavelli is extensive. The most thoughtful analysis is Leo Strauss's *Thoughts on Machiavelli* (University of Chicago, 1958). For a translation of Machiavelli's *The Prince* and *Discourses,* see Niccolò Machiavelli, *The Prince* and *The Discourses,* translated by Luigi Ricci (Random House, 1950). For the life of Machiavelli, consult Roberto Ridolfi, *The Life of Niccolò Machiavelli,* translated by Cecil Grayson (University of Chicago, 1963). For the differing interpretations of Machiavelli, see De Lamar Jensen, editor, *Machiavelli: Cynic, Patriot, or Political Scientist?* (D. C. Heath, 1960).

as Machiavelli sees it universally? (3) In the world of *realpolitik,* what is the role for people who take faith and virtue seriously? (4) Is power politics all of politics? (5) What are the dangers of politicizing the whole of life and asking politics to do more than it can? (6) What are the limits of realism and cynicism after which they become—ironically—very unrealistic?

—Peter Sampo

JOHN CALVIN

Institutes of the Christian Religion
1536, 1559

*J*ohn Calvin's *Institutes of the Christian Religion* is one of the two or three greatest and most influential Protestant writings; it ranks among the classic summaries of the Christian view of God and the human condition. Yet nearly five centuries after his life, Calvin's name still evokes strong reactions. To some he symbolizes all that is repressive in Western society. To others he is a hero who powerfully recovered the Bible's true meaning concerning the fate of humanity and the glory of God. Whether friend or foe, all who know Calvin recognize his *Institutes of the Christian Religion* as the great summary of his thought. It is a learned book written for beginners, a simple book extending more than a thousand pages, a grand summary that Calvin hoped his readers would eventually set aside in order to engage directly with the Bible itself.

A Marked Man

John Calvin (1509–1564) was born in Noyon, France. His father was a cathedral official who wanted his

John Calvin (1509–1564), from an engraving by Konrad Meyer (1616–1689).

son to become a lawyer. Although Calvin prepared for the law, his great interest was always ancient literature. Increasingly, the agitation created by Martin LUTHER and like-minded reformers drew Calvin's attention to the Bible. Unlike his older contemporary Luther, who explained several times how he had been led away from Catholicism, Calvin wrote

cryptically about his own spiritual journey only once. Sometime, probably in 1529 or 1530, God "by an unexpected conversion . . . tamed to teachableness a mind too stubborn for its years." Immediately Calvin intensified his work with the Bible. "The rest of my studies," he said, "I pursued . . . more coolly."

Calvin's ability quickly earned him a reputation among early French Protestants. To aid in his teaching, he brought out in March 1536 a short Latin work, *Christianae Religionis Institutio,* expounding the basic nature of Christian faith. He prefaced it with a letter to his king, Francis I, refuting charges that the new Protestant teaching was innovative or incendiary. The work's six parts briefly explained the Ten Commandments, the Apostles' Creed, the Lord's Prayer, the two sacraments retained by Protestants (baptism and the Lord's Supper), the reasons why Protestants gave up the other five Catholic sacraments, and the meaning of "Christian liberty"—especially on issues of church and state.

So successful was this little book that Calvin immediately became a marked man.

Now we shall possess a right definition of faith if we call it a firm and certain knowledge of God's benevolence to us, founded upon the truth of the freely given promise in Christ, both revealed to our minds and sealed upon our hearts through the Holy Spirit.

—Institutes of the Christian Religion
Ford Lewis Battles, trans.

He had already fallen under suspicion of Catholic authorities in France and now was forced to move regularly to remain at large. From Protestants the danger was exactly opposite. Calvin, who always longed for the quiet of uninterrupted scholarship, was beset by further requests to explain the Scriptures. When he passed through Geneva in August 1536, the fiery reformer William Farel would not let him leave. Calvin was reluctant to stay, but did so when Farel told him that God would blast Calvin's scholarly leisure if he left. He then endured two difficult years as pastor of one of Geneva's churches. When mounting tension forced Calvin to leave Geneva in 1538, both he and the city fathers were delighted.

Calvin moved to Strasbourg where he spent the most enjoyable period of his life. He led a French church, married the widow of an Anabaptist, published an important commentary on the epistle to the Romans, and prepared an expanded Latin version of the *Institutes* (1539). Partly because of that new edition and partly because of his willingness to defend Geneva's move from the Catholic Church, he was recalled to Geneva in 1540.

For the next quarter century, Calvin preached and taught regularly. He guided the city's ministers and lay elders in his reforms. Only when his elite opponents blundered in 1553 by backing the heretic Michael Servetus did Calvin's reforms finally win the day.

For the last decade of Calvin's life, Geneva served as a model for much of the rest of Protestant Europe, as Calvin and his colleagues received refugees and Calvin's expositions of Scripture circulated ever more widely. Amid his other labors, he regularly produced new editions of the *Institutes*. French translations of the work, beginning in 1541 with one prepared by Calvin himself, exerted a considerable influence on the development of modern French. In 1559 Calvin published his last, definitive expansion, again in Latin.

The Shape of the *Institutes*

Unlike modern systematic theologies, the *Institutes* does not begin with lengthy sections canvassing what needs to be known before approaching theology itself. Rather it is oriented toward experience, "piety with truth." In broad outline the *Institutes* follows the shape of Paul's epistle to the Romans. Consideration of the knowledge of God in himself leads to a study of the human condition, then to the person of Christ, the salvation Christ offers, and finally to practical questions.

The volume is divided into four books. First is a section on "The Knowledge of God the Creator." It concerns what people may know of God through nature and then why the Scriptures are necessary. In Book II, "The Knowledge of God the Redeemer," Calvin considers sinful humanity's need for a savior, the law of God as moving us to see our need of a savior, and the person and work of Christ as the coming of that savior. Two powerful sections from this book—one on the universal moral value of the Ten Commandments and the other on Christ as priest, prophet, and king—have been reprinted individually. Book III turns to "The Way in Which We Receive the Grace of Christ." It considers faith and redemption and also spells out Calvin's teaching on election and predestination. In Book IV, "The External Means by Which God Invites Us into the Society of Christ," Calvin considers the church, the sacraments, and the state.

Knowledge of God and of Ourselves

Although the little book of 1536 grew considerably by 1559, its purpose did not change.

Calvin wants his readers to gain an integrated picture of the Bible as it demonstrates God's love to the human race in Christ. He also wants them to understand that the hope for a genuinely good life is found only in the Christian message of salvation.

Later readers have studied Calvin for all sorts of reasons. Some desire guidance on particular teachings of the Christian faith. Some, like G. K. Chesterton in his biography of St. Thomas AQUINAS, *The Dumb Ox*, want to discover why Calvin vented such anger on the Roman Catholic Church. But the best reason for reading the *Institutes* today is the same as it was in the sixteenth century—for its probing, diligent, immensely learned, clearly expressed, and extraordinarily thoughtful presentation of biblical teaching on the nature of the human condition before a God who combines perfect righteousness and perfect love.

Although the subjects covered by the *Institutes* extend far and wide, Calvin never deviates from his goal of showing how the Bible illuminates who we truly are and what God has truly done to rescue us from our sin. The first sentence of Book I illustrates this major purpose compellingly: "Nearly all the wisdom we possess, that is to say, true and sound wisdom, consists of two parts: the knowledge of God and of ourselves."

The *Institutes* presents Calvin's controversial teaching on predestination. He is completely unabashed in arguing that some people believe the gospel and others do not because of the electing power of God. But unlike some later "Calvinists," Calvin himself hedged the doctrine of predestination with many safeguards. He warns that when people "inquire into predestination they are penetrating the sacred precincts of divine wisdom" and must therefore speak with great care. He also cautions against trying to push Scripture beyond its own logic. All qualifications having been made, Calvin's statement of the doctrine remains a classic—either of profound biblical insight for those who read the Scriptures as he did or of profound offense to the moral sensibility of those who disagree.

A view of Geneva, showing a galley and sailing ship in the harbor, from Hartmann Schedel, *Liber chronicarum mundi*, 1493.

We shall never be clearly persuaded, as we ought to be, that our salvation flows from the wellspring of God's free mercy until we come to know his eternal election, which illumines God's grace by this contrast: that he does not indiscriminately adopt all into the hope of salvation but gives to some what he denies to others.

—*Institutes of the Christian Religion*
Ford Lewis Battles, trans.

Calvin's *Institutes* is a classic because its presentation, hammered out in the life-and-death disputes of real life, came from one of the great minds in one of Europe's formative transitional ages. It is a classic because its subject matter, the timeless and yet always timely words of Scripture, can never be exhausted. But most of all it is a classic because its theme, nothing less than the rescue of human beings by the ever-living God, is as fundamental as life itself.

Issues to Explore

(1) Calvin did not have an easy life—forced travel when younger, much strife in Geneva during his mature years. How do you think his life circumstances affected his theology? (2) Why do you think that Protestant groups following theologies like Calvin's (sometimes called Reformed Protestants) expanded much more rapidly than any other Protestant bodies for the two centuries after Calvin's life? (3) After thinking about Calvin's organization of material in the *Institutes,* can you propose a better way of putting things than he did? (4) What purposes did Calvin feel his understanding of biblical teaching on predestination fulfill? (5) Why is Calvin's reputation so controversial?

—Mark A. Noll

For Further Study

The best modern English translation of the *Institutes* was made by Ford Lewis Battles and published in two volumes with extensive notes by John T. McNeill (Westminster, 1960). Battles also prepared a translation of the first edition of 1536 (Eerdmans, 1986). Reliable abridgments have been prepared by Tony Lane and Hilary Osborne (Baker, 1987) and Hugh T. Kerr (revised, Westminster/John Knox, 1989).

The best biographies and theological studies include full attention to the *Institutes*. They include *John Calvin: A Study in French Humanism* by Quirinus Breen (revised, Archon, 1968), *The Constructive Revolutionary: John Calvin and His Socio-Economic Impact* by W. Fred Graham (John Knox, 1971), *A Life of John Calvin* by Alister McGrath (Basil Blackwell, 1990), *The History and Character of Calvinism* by John T. McNeill (Oxford University Press, 1954), *John Calvin: A Biography* by T. H. L. Parker (Westminster, 1975), *John Calvin: His Influence in the Western World* by W. Stanford Reid, editor (Zondervan, 1982), and *Calvin: The Origins and Development of His Religious Thought* by François Wendel, translator (Harper & Row, 1963). William J. Bouwsma's *John Calvin: A Sixteenth Century Portrait* (Oxford, 1988) is important for showing how much the considerable tensions of Calvin's theology reflect the major intellectual strains of the Renaissance and Reformation age.

MIGUEL DE CERVANTES

Don Quixote
1605, 1615

iguel de Cervantes's *Don Quixote* is the first modern novel—and one of the funniest and most entertaining books ever written. Like all literary classics, *Don Quixote* captures the reader's imagination and provides a context for serious reflection on the meaning of human existence. It also bears witness to the clash between Christian ideals and the conflicting images of reality in a rapidly changing world. The background for the novel's action is the merging of Spanish, Latin, Germanic, Arabic, and Jewish cultures in Renaissance Spain. All of these peoples are duly represented in the narrative, which fuses elements from classical epic, chivalric romance, and popular adventure stories into a new mold.

The Struggles of a Military Hero

Miguel de Cervantes Saavedra was born near Madrid around 1547 of a family with noble traditions but financial difficulties. Records show that he enlisted in the Spanish army led by John of Austria and was

Miguel de Cervantes Saavedra (1547–1616).

acclaimed a hero in the Battle of Lepanto in 1571. But he learned how quickly fortunes can change when Algerian pirates captured him as he made his way back to Spain in 1575. He made several unsuccessful attempts to escape and was finally ransomed five years later.

Once home, the former military hero had difficulty finding a job. Given a series of petty bureaucratic posts, he led a life of poverty and instability, imprisoned at least twice for debts. Yet in his late

fifties, after a series of failures as a poet and dramatist, he began his masterpiece, *Don Quixote of La Mancha, the Ingenious Gentleman.* He published the first part in 1605 and its sequel in 1615, a year before his death.

The Ingenious Gentleman's Quest for True Adventure

After a long satirical preface, the story of Don Quixote begins when a middle-aged, middle-class gentleman decides that it is "fitting and necessary" that he should become a hero—specifically a knight-errant like those in the chivalric romances he has loved reading. Wearing a homemade suit of armor, he mounts his horse and sets off on a series of adventures. Before leaving, he dedicates himself to a lady, Dulcinea, "for a knight-errant without a lady-love was like a tree without leaves or fruit, a body without a soul." Dulcinea, however, is no lady at all. Actually she is Aldonza Lorenzo, a peasant woman dubbed Dulcinea by the knight.

> *"I know who I am," said Don Quixote,*
> *"and who I may be, if I choose."*
>
> —*Don Quixote*
> Samuel Putnam, trans.

Opposite: An early twentieth-century illustration of Don Quixote.

The symbolic image of the journey—the movement toward identity, order, and salvation—forms the basis for the plot. In each of three "sallies," Don Quixote ventures out into the world and then is returned home again to La Mancha. His friends, the village priest and barber, bring him home from the first sally. Undaunted, he sets off again, this time with a squire, Sancho Panza, as his companion. He is captured and brought home in a cage at the end of the first part of the novel. The third sally, which forms the basis of the second part of the novel, takes the two now-famous companions by invitation to the castle of a polished and urbane Duke and Duchess. It concludes when a disillusioned and tired Don Quixote, once again returned by friends to La Mancha, makes his will and dies peacefully in bed.

Satirical Comedy, Tragic Romance, or Social Commentary?

Don Quixote's humor made the novel an immediate best-seller in Renaissance Spain. On one level, it is the story of a lovable madman whose amusing adventures in the "real" world mock the one-dimensional seriousness of melodramatic romances to which many people turned in his day for escape. The second part of the novel thus may seem to be a kind of cautionary tale in which the hero recovers his sanity when he renounces the romance of chivalry as a dangerous illusion.

In the nineteenth century, however, a different dimension of meaning became popular in interpretations of Cervantes's work. Like all great comedies, this novel has a tragic undertone. Thus Don Quixote began to be seen as a misunderstood idealist—a fool for Christ—whose quest to destroy the evils of hypocrisy

and banality is defeated by the harsh literalism that dominates the modern world.

More recently, thoughtful readers have recognized that the novel is neither purely satirical nor tragically romantic. It is, however, quite obviously serious. Such social issues as the divine right of kings, the rehabilitation of criminals, the question of prostitution, the ethics of warfare, and the relation of art to society are examined and debated in *Don Quixote*. Cervantes neither vindicates nor condemns established society's point of view; he has no "plan" for social progress, only questions for the human community.

Romance and Reality

The major issue raised in *Don Quixote* is the undeniable complexity of reality. Cervantes sets the action of this great novel in motion after carefully explaining his intention to tell "the truth" about the famous Don Quixote of La Mancha and his squire Sancho Panza. The playfully ironic attitude of the narrator is crucial; therefore neither sentimentality nor cynicism is an appropriate response to the narrative. Instead, readers are called to enter the novel's imaginary world ready to reflect thoughtfully on the multiple dimensions of what we take to be reality. Similarly, the narrator's seeming digressions must be carefully attended to if, as Cervantes apparently intends, neither Don Quixote's nor Sancho Panza's point of view is to cancel out the other. Even the views of the priest and barber are to be given their due.

Because the magic of narrative art can capture its audience so completely, Cervantes continually interrupts the main course of the story as if to demand that his readers think. He orchestrates a clash between the real-seeming history of imaginary characters and the at-times intrusive presence of details that playfully mock an eagerness to follow the make-believe adventures. For example, the exciting story of the great duel between Don Quixote and a Basque traveler abruptly stops because, the narrator informs us, the history as told in the original manuscript ends.

Readers must wait patiently while the narrator relates the fantastic account of his search for the history's conclusion and his discovery of the documents written by the Arab scholar Cide Hamete Benengeli.

Our readiness to return to the story of the duel, as if it were the more engaging reality, sheds light on the predicament of the novel's central figure. Information in the form of "facts" is not so fascinating as the imaginative transformation of experience through story. Like Don Quixote, we begin to see a broken-down nag as the chivalrous steed Rocinante, a homely inn as a castle, a windmill as an evil giant. The world of romance, which no doubt represents a dream of heroic existence, articulates ideals that elevate the human enterprise: courage, strength, courtesy, beauty. The narrator's presence affirms those ideals but adds another dimension: attachment to the homely, prosaic details (like windmills or barber's basins) that ground poetic idealism in the critical company of mundane reality.

The classic comic pairing of Don Quixote and Sancho Panza deliberately brings opposites together. It reveals the superficial distinctions between "the ideal" and "the real" that cover human experience. When Don Quixote sees a knight on a steed wearing Mambrino's helmet, Sancho sees a barber on an ass carrying his basin on his head. The narrator intervenes with the "truth" that lies between the two: the barber wears the basin *as if* it were a helmet. This last view, which accepts the presence of multiple perspectives, calls on readers to question and enlarge their first impressions.

Issues to Explore

The beauty of the novel, its essentially Christian core, emerges from its affirmation of the human enterprise on earth. Like the gospel narratives, the novel moves between all layers of human experience, attending to the lowly as well as to the great. On one level Don Quixote's adventures trace the journey of the soul toward salvation. Though placed in the context of foolishness and eccentricity, Chris-

The priest reviewing the books in Don Quixote's library:

For when he has witnessed a comedy that is well and artfully constructed, the spectator will come out laughing at its humor, enlightened by the truths it contained, marveling at the various incidents, rendered wiser by the arguments, made more wary by the snares he has seen depicted, and more prudent by the examples afforded him.

—*Don Quixote*
Samuel Putnam, trans.

"He who retires," said Don Quixote, "does not flee. I would have you know, Sancho, that valor not based upon prudence can only be termed temerity, and the triumphs of the foolhardy are to be attributed to good luck rather than to courage. I admit that I retired, but not that I fled."

—*Don Quixote*
Samuel Putnam, trans.

tian virtues prevail. The action of the novel as a whole affirms the truth that spiritual ideals can be incarnated on earth in the most unlikely places and unexpected situations. For however eccentric, Quixote's vision is understandable to the other characters as well as to contemporary readers; Cervantes's protagonist is not an alienated or isolated figure.

Questions about Don Quixote's vision are rooted in modern doubts about invisible realities. (1) Is Don Quixote a figure of the Christian saint? If so, why is he so laughable? Why are his friends so intent on disenchanting him? (2) Why is the presence of Sancho so necessary to Quixote and vice versa? (3) What forms does evil take in the novel and how effectively does Quixote deal with them? (4) What are we to make of the novel's conclusion?

—Marilyn Gump Stewart

For Further Study

Though *Don Quixote* is undeniably long, it is quite easy to read in a recent edition, as schoolchildren all over the world can testify. Four modern English translations of *Don Quixote* are easily available: the Norton Critical Edition contains the (1885) Ormsby translation as well as helpful background material and critical interpretations; Signet Classics offers the (1965) Walter Starkie translation (an abridgment); Penguin Books publishes the (1950) J. M. Cohen translation as well as a reissue of the (1978) Samuel Putnam translation originally published by Random House. All are reliable and highly readable. The best introduction to the novel's philosophical implications is Jose Ortega y Gasset's *Meditations on Quixote* (Norton, 1963), while A. J. Close's *The Romantic Approach to Don Quixote* (Cambridge, 1990) details current critical controversy.

Spanish Classics

Born of a diverse culture and a turbulent history, Spanish literature is known for its poetic exuberance, tragic sense of life, and concern for issues of social justice and religious faith. Spain's melding of Catholic and Moorish cultures and its strong individualism despite its oppressive political institutions produced the first great European novel *Don Quixote*, the beautiful lyric poetry of Lope de Vega and José de Espronceda, and the profound mystical writings of Teresa of Avila and John of the Cross. Although Spanish literature was deeply influenced by European literary trends, from Renaissance neoclassicism to romanticism, its best authors have adapted generic forms to create their own original expression of Spain's struggles and triumphs.

Heroic Tradition

Spain's early history is characterized by attempts at conquest and occupation of the peninsula, most notably by the Romans, Visigoths, and Moors. This early period ended in 1492 when King Ferdinand and Queen Isabella won the south back from the Moors, unifying the kingdoms of Spain and ending seven centuries of Moslem rule. In part an expression of medieval religious zeal, the wars of reconquest established the political,

El Cid and the lion; an incident from the medieval epic.

cultural, and religious dominance of Castile and set Castilian as the official language. Yet throughout the history of Spain, and particularly during this medieval period, many individuals resisted the power of those ruling the political and ecclesiastical institutions. In literature this challenge was first posed by Spain's great medieval epic *The Poem of the Cid*.

The earliest copy of this anonymous poem dates from the first half of the fourteenth century. *The Poem of the Cid* differs from other European epics in its adherence to historical facts—there are no dragons or sorcerers here. Based on the life of Ruy (Rodrigo) Díaz de Bivar (c. 1043–1099), also known as the Cid Campeador, the action of the poem begins as the unjustly exiled Cid and a small group of his followers leave the town of Burgos and set off into Moorish territory, conquering city after city as they go. Throughout the poem, the Cid's admirable qualities are underscored by the repetition of various epithets such as "the loyal Campeador" and "he of the noble beard." The citizens of Burgos suggest the theme of the poem when they exclaim— "God, what a worthy vassal, had he but a worthy lord!" Despite the presentation of the Cid as the ideal champion, his qualities are not overexaggerated. The poem's simplicity and attention to exact detail make it a unique and compelling epic.

Love, Labyrinths, and Dreams

In the sixteenth century, Spain became an international power. King Carlos I, grandson of Ferdinand and Isabella and of King Maximilian of the Austrian Hapsburg dynasty, became the "Holy Roman Emperor," proof of his alliance with the Church in Rome. This period also marked the commencement of Spain's Golden Age of literature and art, during which CERVANTES composed *Don Quixote*. Yet in the midst of this glorious prosperity, deep religious

Baroque poet and playwright Lope Félix de Vega Carpio (1562–1635).

tensions divided Christians during the Protestant Reformation and the Catholic Counter-Reformation. In this setting the mystic Teresa of Avila (1515–1582), though deeply loyal to the Catholic Church, challenged its worldly power and defended the individual's right to a personal relationship with God.

Baroque poet and playwright Lope Félix de Vega Carpio (1562–1635) was one of the most prolific and successful artists of his time, having composed over two thousand plays and poems. His personal life was equally frenetic, and his many loves, both worldly and divine, are captured in his lyric verse. Although Lope de Vega experimented with various poetic forms, his preference for the traditional ballad and Petrarchan

sonnet places him firmly in the Spanish lyric tradition and connects him to a larger European context. The tumultuous love affairs of his youth are reflected in the collection *Moorish and Pastoral Ballads*. In it Lope de Vega, like many of his contemporaries, romanticizes the life and loves of the ancient Moors. Although in form, setting, and character names these ballads resemble their medieval predecessors, they are more sentimental than historical.

After becoming disillusioned with his former romantic vision of life, Lope de Vega joined the priesthood. During this period he published a collection of sonnets entitled *Sacred Rhymes*. The first poem, "When I sit down to contemplate my plight," introduces the self-reflective tone of the collection. This sonnet is organized around the metaphor of life as labyrinth, taken from the classical legend of the Cretan minotaur slain by Theseus. Yet the monster at the center of this maze can be slain only by divine guidance, as summarized in the last three lines of the poem:

> My darkness, though, quite
> vanished by your light,
> The monster of my blind decep-
> tion slain,
> Lost reason to its home returns
> content.

Toward the end of Spain's Golden Age its political and economic power plummeted. The traglcomedies of playwright Pedro Calderón de la Barca (1600–1681) reflected the turmoil of this period; his 1635 play *Life Is a Dream*, for instance, dramatizes the spiritual questions of men and women who feel trapped by destiny in lives of misery. The play tells the story of Segismundo, the unwitting heir to the throne of Poland, who is imprisoned by his own father, King Basilio, after signs read at the young prince's birth foretold imminent destruction under his rule. When the king allows Segismundo the opportunity of proving himself, the angry young prince fulfills every bad prophecy. After being imprisoned again, he is informed that his experience was but a dream, thus explaining the metaphorical importance of the title:

> What is this life? A fantasy?
> A prize we seek so eagerly
> That proves to be illusory?
> I think that life is but a dream,
> And even dreams not what they
> seem.

Once Segismundo learns the proper perspective of his power, he is able to break the force of his unlucky stars and become the good ruler his father desired.

Pages from *Autos Sacramentales* by Calderón.

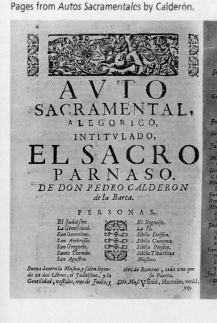

The Sleep of Reason

In 1700 the last Hapsburg king of Spain, Carlos II, died without an heir. His grandnephew Phillipe D'Anjou was named successor, bringing the French house of Bourbon to Madrid. The new rulers introduced ideas from the Enlightenment, and a decadent Spain began to dream of greatness again. A few Spanish intellectuals responded by undertaking ambitious plans to reform all aspects of Spanish society and culture.

One of the most successful plays of this era, written within the strict formal confines of neoclassic comedy, is *The Maiden's Consent*, by Leandro Fernández de Moratín (1760–1828). It tells the story of a young girl, Francisca, who is being forced to marry the much older don Diego, the uncle of the man she really loves. Francisca refuses to disobey her mother, but when Diego discovers the love between the young couple he gracefully steps aside and insists that they marry, saying to Francisca's mother: "This is what happens when authority is abused and when youth suffers under its oppression...."

Although in the play the elders are brought back to reality and reason by those they govern, in real life Moratín and his generation saw their dreams shattered by the Napoleonic invasion of 1808. Despite attempts to carry out their reforms through the Constitution of Cádiz (1812), the conservative and oppressive Bourbon Fernando VII returned to the throne after Napoleon's defeat in 1814.

Rebellion and Reconciliation

In 1833, the rebellious young Spanish poet José de Espronceda (1808–1842) returned from exile in France after general amnesty was granted upon the death of Fernando VII. Espronceda has been likened to a Spanish Byron, and indeed both his life and his works exemplify romantic defiance of authority and convention. His poem "Pirate's Song" (1835) portrays many of the characteristics of Spanish romanticism. Foremost, it emphasizes absolute freedom; thus the hero is an outlaw and an outcast, accountable to no one:

> My only treasure a pirate ship,
> My god but liberty,
> My law, brute force and a hearty
>   wind,
> My land, the open sea.

This symbolic rupture with convention is also discernible in the poem's formal aspects, which break the strict rules of neoclassic poetry.

By midcentury Spain's new industrial economy recreated its social structure, adding both a formidable upper-middle class and a large sector of citizens living in abject poverty. Just as DICKENS, Balzac, and TOLSTOY had done in their countries, the realist novelist Benito Pérez Galdós (1843–1920) analyzed the historical development of this new divided Spain. *Fortunata and Jacinta* (1887) traces the tumultuous years of the 1860s and 1870s in Madrid through the lives of some two dozen characters from different levels of society. Fortunata, the real protagonist, imagines she can escape her working-class destiny to become the legitimate wife of the wealthy Juanito Santa Cruz as the

Pedro Calderón de la Barca (1600–1681).

mother of his only heir. She expresses this "idea," as she calls it, on her deathbed, and it transforms into a profound desire that her son be both the reconciliation of two divided worlds and the hope for Spain's future:

> Ah! What a wonderful idea—
> With this thought I'll not need
> the Sacrament, that's certain,
> because it came to me from on
> high. Here in my heart I can hear
> the voice of the angel who told
> it to me. . . . It is the key to the
> door of Heaven. . . .

Her dream is fictionally realized when her son is taken into the Santa Cruz household as its legitimate heir; but historically Pérez Galdós's ideal of bridging the gap between these classes was never realized.

A Leap of Faith

Spain's political and social turmoil continued through the end of the century, culminating in 1898 with the loss of its last colonies in the Philippines and the Caribbean

The Andalusian poet Federico García Lorca (1898–1936).

I don't know whether I believe or do not believe; I know that I pray. I don't know very well what my prayer is. There are a certain number of us who meet here at nightfall to tell the rosary. I don't know who they are, and they don't know me, but we feel that we are one and in intimate communion with one another.

Another group of writers reflected the political turmoil of their time—the Generation of 1928. These avant-garde artists endured through the bloody Spanish Civil War (1936–39), which brought fascist leader Francisco Franco to power for almost forty years. One of the first writers to fall victim to Franco was the Andalusian poet Federico García Lorca (1898–1936), who was murdered early in the war by Nationalist troops. His collection of ballads, the *Romancero gitano*, borrowed formal elements from the traditional Spanish ballad, combining them with Andalusian legend and surrealistic imagery to create a "dream-world" through verse. The poem "Sleepwalking Ballad" demonstrates Lorca's poetic mastery:

Islands. In the years that followed, a group of young writers known as the Generation of 1898 reflected the political and philosophical crisis of their nation. One of these was author and intellectual Miguel de Unamuno (1864–1936), who attempted to reconcile Spain's devastated present with its glorious past. In *Mist* (1914) he explores the existential angst of modern Spain through his pitiable character, Augusto Pérez, who wanders through the streets of Madrid, daydreaming his way through life.

Through his main character, and through a departure from formal elements of the traditional realist novel, Unamuno raises many questions about the nature of fiction and reality, of existence and nonexistence, and of humankind's tragic relationship to God and the universe. Rooted in the thoughts of Søren KIERKEGAARD, *Mist* expresses the idea that religion is not based on reason but rather on an irrational "leap of faith." As a friend of Augusto says to him:

Green grows my love, my love
    grows green.
Green wind. Green-branching
    tree.
Stallion on the mountain heights
    And ship upon the sea.

Through its complex imagery, the poem escapes the purely narrative and remains lyrical in expression and metaphorical in intent. Thus the story of two gypsy-men's futile struggle to flee from the imminent danger of the civil guard becomes a universal symbol of the human condition in a modern world.

An Empty Soul

The years immediately after the Civil War were difficult ones for all Spaniards. In 1942 a young novelist named Camilo José Cela (b. 1916) published perhaps the most important book of the postwar generation, *The Family of Pascual Duarte.* Written primarily in the first person, the book recounts the unfortunate life of the criminal Duarte. Cela's novel exemplifies the postwar style of "tremendismo," which represents through grotesque imagery the degraded existence of modern humanity. Time and again Pascual's claims of being a victim of circumstance are betrayed by his cruel actions, yet the reader remains curiously sympathetic to this very human character. The narrative begins nostalgically with a description of his youth. But as Pascual recounts a hunting trip with his loyal dog Chispa, his idyllic narrative is abruptly destroyed:

> [Chispa] trotted back with me and lay there gazing into my face again. I realize now that her eyes were like those of a priest listening to confession, that she had the look of a confessor, coldly scrutinizing, the eyes of a lynx. . . .

> I picked up the gun and fired. I reloaded, and fired again. The bitch's blood was dark and sticky and it spread slowly along the dry earth.

Pascual is unable to face his own shortcomings, reacting violently to

For Further Study

Most of these works are quite approachable for the thoughtful lay reader, and many of the editions named below also include introductions with critical commentary. The five-part series *A Literary History of Spain* is also recommended. This list should serve not only as an introduction to the riches of Spanish literature, but also as an inspiration to explore these and other fine texts further.

Poem of the Cid: Lesley Byrd Simpson, translator (University of California, 1957). This prose translation accurately represents the original text.

Lope Félix de Vega Carpio: *Moorish and Pastoral Ballads* and *Sacred Rhymes* in *Desire's Experience Transformed: A Representative Anthology of Lope de Vega's Lyric Poetry,* Carl W. Cobb, translator (Spanish Literature Publications, 1991).

Pedro Calderón: *Life Is a Dream,* Gwynne Edwards, translator (Methuen Drama, 1991).

Leandro Fernández de Moratín: *The Maiden's Consent,* Harriet de Onís, translator (Barron's Educational Series, 1962).

José de Espronceda: "Pirate's Song," Alice Jane McVan, translator, in *Ten Centuries of Spanish Poetry,* Eleanor Turnbull, editor (Johns Hopkins,

1955). This book contains a great selection of translated Spanish poetry from its beginnings to the twentieth century.

Benito Pérez Galdós: *Fortunata and Jacinta,* Lester Clark, translator (Penguin, 1973).

Miguel de Unamuno: *Mist,* Warner Fite, translator (Knopf, 1928).

Federico García Lorca: "Sleepwalking Ballad" in *Lorca's Romancero Gitano: A Ballad,* Carl W. Cobb, translator (University Press of Mississippi, 1983).

Camilo José Cela: *The Family of Pascual Duarte,* Anthony Kerrigan, translator (Little, Brown and Company, 1964).

Critical Studies: *A Literary History of Spain* (Barnes and Noble). A series of six books:

> *The Middle Ages,* A. D. Deyermond (1971).

> *The Golden Age: Prose and Poetry,* R. O. Jones (1971).

> *The Golden Age: Drama 1492–1700,* Edward Meryon Wilson (1971).

> *The Eighteenth Century,* Nigel Glendinning (1972).

> *The Nineteenth Century,* Donald Shaw (1972).

> *The Twentieth Century,* Gerald Griffiths Brown (1972).

those who get too close to his empty soul.

From the heroic battles of the Cid to the meaningless violence of Pascual, the upheavals of Spanish history set the tone for a literature

marked by cynicism and tragedy, yet also by idealized dreams and profound hope.

—Elizabeth Franklin Lewis

WILLIAM SHAKESPEARE

Hamlet; King Lear; Midsummer Night's Dream; and *The Tempest* 1601–11

*S*hakespeare is the supreme English poet and dramatist, considered by many the greatest writer the world has known. His achievement is so massive as to make of the man an enigma; how could any one person produce so many plays of such unrivaled quality? This question, combined with the scarcity of details known about his personal life, has led a few enterprising literary sleuths to advance the theory that Shakespeare's work was written by someone more learned—Sir Francis Bacon, for instance, or the Earl of Oxford. But such literary hypotheses are based on highly dubious conjecture, leaving the scholarly world with its few though irrefutable—facts that establish the identity of Shakespeare the man.

William Shakespeare was baptized in Stratford-on-Avon on April 26, 1564, married a local woman named Ann Hathaway when he was eighteen, had three children, and went to London a few years later. There he joined the Globe Theatre's troop of actors, probably associated with poets and playwrights at the Inns of Court,

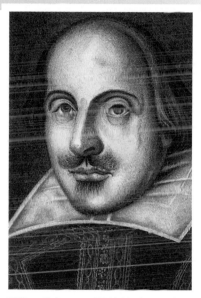

William Shakespeare (1564–1616); portrait in oils dated 1609.

and composed plays that are mentioned by several contemporary writers. He apparently drafted his will in his own hand, leaving his wife his "second-best bed," and was buried in Stratford-on-Avon on April 25, 1616. During this seemingly uneventful life, he gave poetic form to the very soul of Britain, raising it to a height that enables everyone everywhere to participate in its grandeur.

Unchallenged English Classics

Shakespeare lived at a time of enormous energy and burgeoning possibility—sixteenth-century England. The English Renaissance reached its peak during the reign of Elizabeth I (1558–1603), an epoch of geographical, naval, commercial, and intellectual expansion. Yet, although new ways of thought were beginning to modify the medieval Christian culture that had dominated England for four or five centuries, the Elizabethan era was still solidly God-centered. Even so, the appropriate role for humanity was considered to be the active rather than contemplative life. Exuberance, talent, and extravagant display characterize the dominant style. The arts, particularly those of language, flourished.

Elizabethan drama marks the high point of English literature. It was a communal art, played to an eager audience of all classes. Shakespeare was an actor, part of a group that built its own theater, the Globe; in this atmosphere he wrote all his plays. Several

To be or not to be; that is the question:
Whether 'tis nobler in the mind to suffer
The slings and arrows of outrageous fortune,
Or to take arms against a sea of troubles,
And by opposing end them. To die, to sleep—
No more—and by a sleep to say we end
The heartache, and the thousand natural shocks
That flesh is heir to! 'Tis a consummation
Devoutly to be wished. To die, to sleep—
To sleep—perchance to dream: ay, there's the rub,
For in that sleep of death what dreams may come
When we have shuffled off this mortal coil
Must give us pause.

—Hamlet

playwrights before him and during his time established the conventions and themes for the Elizabethan audience—George Peele, John Lyly, Robert Greene, Thomas Kyd, the brilliant Christopher Marlowe, and the classical Ben Jonson. Their experimentation with dramatic and linguistic techniques enabled Shakespeare to use an already existing form and, writing from within the actual production of dramas, to bring to it his unique genius.

Shakespeare's total body of work consists of thirty-seven plays, two narrative poems *(Venus and Adonis* and *The Rape of Lucrece),* and 154 sonnets. All of these, in varying degrees, manifest the charged energy of expression that renders the Shakespearean style unique. Written at a time when the English language was in its glory—this was the age that produced the King James translation of the Bible—Shakespeare's poetry makes use of a balance of Anglo-Saxon and Latin, creating an instrument of miraculous power and versatility. Scholars are not certain of the exact dates of some of his plays because Shakespeare was apparently not interested in publication and left to others the task of arranging his works

in chronological order. Eighteen of his plays were published during his lifetime in quartos (large sheets folded twice into four leaves); after his death John Heminges and Henry Condell put together thirty-six plays in the first folio (sheets folded once into two leaves). *Pericles,* a thirty-seventh play, is also regarded as part of the Shakespearean canon.

Shakespearean Tragedies

Because Shakespeare's imagination worked within the Christian frame of redemption, he saw life as leading to a final end of reconciliation and love. But just as clearly he saw that experiences of loss that the serious artist cannot evade occur on the way. The first of Shakespeare's great tragedies is *Hamlet* (1600–1601), followed in rapid succession by *Othello* (1603–4), *King Lear* (1605–6), and *Macbeth* (1605–6). In each of these, after the tragic hero has suffered his downfall, he freely chooses his own final destiny—either to submit to a power higher than his own pride or to continue with himself as the center of existence. Othello and Macbeth choose self; Hamlet and Lear allow themselves to be destroyed and remade.

Hamlet

Hamlet has greatly puzzled its critics: it is in fact the most discussed work in the English language. And the speculation has mainly centered on the strange, troubling "problem" of its central character. But, as C. S. Lewis has pointed out, *Hamlet* is about a situation, not a character. It concerns, as he says, "a man given a task by a ghost." Hamlet, already melancholy from the hasty marriage of his recently widowed mother, Gertrude, is faced with a startling revelation conveyed to him by his dead father's tormented spirit: the man whom, Gertrude has married, Claudius—Hamlet's uncle—is the elder Hamlet's murderer. The ghost's threefold command is complex and difficult. He demands that his "foul and most unnatural murder" be avenged and the royal bed of Denmark cleansed of "luxury and damned incest"; that Hamlet's own mind not be tainted; and that Hamlet's mother not be harmed:

> Leave her to heaven
> and to those thorns that in her bosom lodge
> to prick and sting her.

This task requires, as Hamlet recognizes, not only courage and the ability to act but also a clear spirit. And behind the cleansing of the royal bed lies the rehabilitation of a demoralized society. The rottenness of Denmark is highlighted in the play from the beginning. The secrecy of Claudius's regicide hovers like a dark shadow over Elsinore, its capital. Denmark is "an unweeded garden," Hamlet exclaims in his first soliloquy, "things rank and gross in nature possess it merely."

Ill and disturbed though he is, Hamlet knows that his very salvation is at stake: he cannot *act* with the wrong motive. His task becomes, then, the transformation of himself; and if Hamlet commits atrocities while he is in the grip of his "antic disposition," his audience tends to forgive the young prince because of his obvious anguish. By the end of the play, Hamlet has come to understand that "the readiness is all"—that he cannot carry out the action himself but must leave all to "the divinity that shapes our ends." He avenges his father by killing his murderer in the full light of the court. Dying himself, Hamlet gives a final commission to his friend Horatio:

> Absent thee from felicity a while
> And in this harsh world draw thy breath in
>   pain
> To tell my story.

It is a story of the committed life—and of the difficulty of giving one's will over to divine guidance.

King Lear

If *Hamlet* is the tragedy of a young man, depicting the inevitable disillusion of innocence, then *King Lear* is the tragedy of the elder, who, feeling himself increasingly powerless, attempts to shore up his strength by a kind of bribery. Lear stages a public pageant in which he will divide his kingdom into three parts, one for each daughter, giving the largest portion to the one who ceremonially praises him most. His vanity and hunger

The only known genuine illustration of Shakespeare's Globe Theater, London, showing the stage of the second Globe Theater, built on the foundations of, and in the same style as, the first Globe.

We are such stuff
As dreams are made on, and our little life
Is rounded with a sleep.

—*The Tempest*

for affection render the old king unable to credit his truthful child Cordelia and leave him deceived by his two hypocritical daughters. He banishes Cordelia, who cannot "heave her heart into her mouth" to exaggerate her filial love. Lear's loyal servant Kent, too, is exiled for defending Cordelia. To Lear's angry command "Out of my sight!" Kent responds, "See better, Lear!" He thus states the underlying motif of the play—vision—which will be reinforced in the play by metaphor, symbol, and an actual blinding. The goal of life, to be sought in old age, is to "see" truly.

In the course of time Lear is turned out by his two cruel daughters. The suffering undergone by this formerly absolute monarch drives him out of his senses. In a raging storm on the heath, in what Coleridge has called "the world's convention of agonists"—Kent in disguise, a fellow sufferer masquerading as a lunatic, and the Fool—the old king starts on his painful path toward wisdom as his "wits begin to turn." In his madness he comes to recognize his abuse of power, seeing at last his responsibility as monarch to "poor naked wretches, wheresoe'er you are / that bide the pelting of this pitiless storm." He gains not only a new understanding of authority, but of fatherhood, wisdom, and love. Just as the king must be servant, the father must give way to the child, the wise must be taught by the foolish, the strong must be helped by the weak.

Lear's reunion with Cordelia, wherein he declares his love for his faithful daughter, is one of the high lyric points in all literature, even though both are shortly thereafter to die. Holding the dead Cordelia, Lear's final test is to "see better." Can he finally see in her a testimony of love and truth? "Look there!" he says, pointing to her lips, "Look there." And this old man,

who has been afraid to make friends with dying, crosses over the line to follow his beloved without a thought of his own death.

Shakespeare's Comedies

Shakespeare achieved his height in the genre of tragedy in the midst of a lifelong vision that was essentially comic. His career as playwright began with comedies; it reached its fullest power, however, in his four great tragedies. From these magnificent and tormented works, his imagination moved on to his dark comedies before emerging in the profound spirituality of the last plays, which make up a category of their own. But in all his comedies, Shakespeare depicts a world in which music, revelry, love, and forgiveness point the way to a happy outcome. In nearly every comedy, the plot requires two worlds of action—one of them usually in a forest, constituting a retreat from an unbearable public situation. In this "green world" the problem is somehow solved; and a return to the public world and right order is the undeviating result. On a deeper level, however, Shakespeare's comedies are about love and community as the tragedies concern individual salvation.

A Midsummer Night's Dream

Shakespeare's most spirited and delightful play is *A Midsummer Night's Dream* (1594–96), which addresses the relation of poetry and imagination to the public life. The play is set around Athens, which is noted for its high political achievement, its justice and democracy—the model of the ancient world. Its chief masculine character is Theseus, the legendary ruler of Athens, who is depicted throughout Greek mythology as one of the great heroes, a good and just man. Before becoming king of Athens, Theseus endured many ordeals—among them an encounter with the Amazons, whose queen Hippolyta he has captured. *A Midsummer Night's Dream* takes place in the threshold time before their marriage, which heralds the coming of a new era of peace and unity.

The plot is set in motion by a father's for-

Alonso, King of Naples, shipwrecked with his court on Prospero's enchanted island, amazed by fairies, goblins, and strange creatures preparing a banquet; from a chromolithograph of *The Tempest* published 1856–58.

bidding his daughter, Hermia, to marry the man she loves, Lysander; the father resorts to an old law that gives the father absolute power over the life of his daughter. The two lovers set out to escape in the forest outside Athens. A second pair of lovers follows and will learn in this night in the forest to distinguish true love from "fancy." Another layer of the theme concerns the King and Queen of the Fairies, Oberon and Titania. All nature has been disturbed by their quarrels, but during this magical night they are brought back into harmony with each other. Their reconciliation is accomplished primarily through the agency of Bottom, a weaver, who comes to the forest with a group of guildsmen to rehearse an artless play designed for Theseus's wedding celebration. After the play is performed the next morning, King Theseus sets aside the old law and blesses the coming marriage of the two young couples, which coincides with his own union with Hippolyta. Thus the magic encountered in the forest, representing poetry, sets all things right; and the play makes clear that the political order must be refreshed from time to time by the imagination.

The Tempest

The two high points of transcendence in Shakespeare's work, wherein he resolves all his themes, are *King Lear* and *The Tempest* (1611). One is tragedy, one is comedy; both deal with old men—fathers—who at the end must reevaluate their lives. *King Lear,* the tragedy, depicts that revisioning as prerequisite to entering, in death, a higher kingdom of love. *The Tempest,* the comedy, depicts renunciation as prerequisite to spiritual rebirth and a return to life. Considered by most authorities his supreme play, *The Tempest* is one of the two or three great visionary works of the world.

The play takes us to Prospero's island, a site of endings and beginnings—a place seemingly at the very edge of creation where a primordial life exists, a life in darkness, prior to order. It is the *Nadir* to which one comes after utter defeat. Prospero and his daughter Miranda have been brought here by the monstrous sea, set adrift in a leaky boat by traitors. Prospero has been in a realm of sleep and dreams ever since, where his own imagination and the magic of his books are aided by Ariel, the airy spirit who represents providence and grace. Through Ariel's agency, Prospero's enemies are brought

Poor naked wretches, wheresoe'er you are
That bide the pelting of this pitiless storm,
How shall your houseless heads, and unfed sides,
Your looped and windowed raggedness, defend you
From seasons such as these? O I have ta'en
Too little care of this!

—*King Lear*

For Further Study

The body of writings on Shakespeare is so immense that one simply has to choose a few that shed light on important aspects of his work. See the three-volume edition of the plays edited by John F. Andrews (Doubleday, 1989) and the *Shakespeare Handbook* by Levi Fox (G. K. Hall, 1987). Theodore Spencer, *Shakespeare and the Nature of Man* (Macmillan, 1942), is a good general study; A. L. Rowse's *Shakespeare the Man* (St. Martin's, 1988) is a readable and authentic biography; G. Wilson Knight's *The Wheel of Fire* (Oxford, 1930) remains provocative and profound; and C. L. Barber's *Shakespeare's Festive Comedy* (Princeton, 1959) provides helpful insight into the comedies. The Signet paperback editions of individual plays are well edited and useful, with good introductions and critical commentary.

to the island by a terrifying yet unharming tempest. "Not a hair perished," as Ariel reports: "On their sustaining garments not a blemish / But fresher than before. . . ." Prospero thus has his foes in his power; the experience, however, teaches him to forgive rather than seek vengeance. As one of the court party Gonzalo says of the experience on the island, "each of us [found] ourselves, when no man was his own." And, in particular, Miranda finds a husband in Ferdinand, the Prince of Naples.

But the necessary prelude to this creative state is the tempest. All one can do after being destroyed by chaos is to be reborn; this metaphor of rebirth is finally the chief motif in the drama. *The Tempest* is the culmination of all the concerns of Shakespeare's plays, gathered together and viewed from another plane of reality. Here the clustered analogies of rebirth may be seen in relation to one dominant metaphor: the resurrection effected by love.

Issues to Explore

For the Christian, Shakespeare's plays are a mine of instruction, revolving around the actions of grace in a fallen world. The reader could trace the way in which his four great tragedies mark a path through sin toward either the loss of the soul or salvation. (1) How does pride blind each tragic hero? (2) What is the turning point for each protagonist? (3) What role do the feminine characters play in the action?

Examine the way in which *The Tempest* addresses the perennial problems raised by the other Shakespearean dramas. (4) What can mortals do, having a limited knowledge and living in a world marred by evil? (5) Is knowledge a good in itself? Then how did Prospero lose his dukedom? (6) Is education a good? Then why is Caliban made more corrupt by learning? (7) Does Miranda represent a kind of wholeness of knowledge to be striven for? (8) Is genuine selfless love the nearest approach the plays show to wisdom?

—*Louise Cowan*

JOHN DONNE

Poems
1572–1631

*J*ohn Donne's stunning wit and probing spirituality place him at the forefront of English lyric poets. Today he is best known for his love poetry and later religious verse. But his reputation was not always based on his lyrics. Donne's renown when he died in 1631 at the age of fifty-nine rested on his decade as Dean of St. Paul's Cathedral in London. Many believed Donne (pronounced "Dun") to be the greatest preacher England had ever known; certainly he was one of the most dramatic and exciting.

The Recovery of a Lyric Genius

Few people had read Donne's poems in his lifetime because only a handful had been published. The rest Donne had shown just to his friends; others knew them only through handwritten copies passed among poetry-lovers. Two years after his death a book of his poems was printed, and even then they were not universally admired. Donne clearly wrote original and distinctive lyrics, but many thought

John Donne (1573–1631).

they were too strange and rough-edged. Before long he was thought of as merely a minor poet and by the turn of the twentieth century even highly educated people were unlikely to know his work.

In 1912, however, a new edition of Donne's poetry was issued, and the literary public began to take notice. What earlier generations had thought too odd, readers in the twentieth century found exciting and adventurous. A neglected genius had been rediscovered.

The Two John Donnes

John Donne was born in London in 1572 to Roman Catholic parents. Catholics were severely persecuted in England then, and many social and occupational doors were closed to them. Thus many think that Donne quietly rejected Catholicism in his twenties for worldly rather than religious reasons. Young John clearly had difficulty finding his place in the world. Although he attended both Oxford and Cambridge and studied law in London, he never took a degree; he traveled broadly in Europe; he served as a soldier with the flamboyant Earl of Essex; he eventually made a secret marriage, which proved idyllically happy although initially disastrous to his fortunes. As an older man, Donne thought of his life as falling into two distinct phases, almost as though he were two people: first Jack Donne, the wild young rake, and later the Reverend Doctor John Donne, man of God.

One short sleep past, we wake eternally
And death shall be no more: Death, thou shalt die.

—Holy Sonnet 10

Opposite: Old St. Paul's Cathedral, London, where John Donne was Dean and preached his celebrated sermons.

Poems for Lovers

The poetry of Jack Donne is sometimes satirical, but his most common subject is love—or often, mere sensuality. For instance, in "The Flea" the speaker addresses a woman he hopes to seduce, telling her she will lose no more honor by submitting to his desires than she lost life when bitten by a flea. Or in "The Sun Rising" he rails at the morning sun for marking the end of a night of love-making. But in "The Canonization" Donne treats love more seriously. The speaker sees himself and his beloved as "saints" of love because they have dedicated themselves to each other, just as the saints of the church dedicate themselves to God. They are thus "canonized for love," and after they die earthly lovers will pray to them.

Not all of Donne's love poems are written to imaginary or real mistresses. One of his greatest lyrics, "A Valediction Forbidding Mourning," was written for his wife, Ann, as he was about to depart for an extended visit to France. Near the end of the poem he compares true lovers to a compass used for drawing circles:

If they [our souls] be two, they are two so
　As stiff twin compasses are two:
Thy soul, the fixed foot, makes no show
　To move, but doth if th' other do.

And though it in the center sit,
　Yet when the other far doth roam,
It leans, and hearkens after it,
　And grows erect, as that comes home.

Such wilt thou be to me, who must
　Like th' other foot, obliquely run;
Thy firmness makes my circle just,
　And makes me end, where I begun.

This passage shows why so many readers admire Donne's striking originality as a poet. Here is one of the most famous images of faithful love in English poetry; but it is an unusual image, not universally appreciated. In the eighteenth century, for instance, Samuel JOHNSON labeled such poets as Donne "metaphysical poets," declaring that in their work "the most heterogeneous ideas are yoked by violence together; nature and art are ransacked for illustrations, comparisons, and allusions; . . . but the reader . . . , though he sometimes admires, is seldom pleased."

Loving God above Women

For many years Donne's influential friends tried to convince him to become an Anglican priest. He refused until 1615, when he finally was ordained. What changed his mind is unclear. He began giving his attention to explicitly Christian poetry as early as 1608; perhaps his frequent serious illnesses turned his thoughts to spiritual matters. Further, his greatest outpouring of Christian poems, including most of his "Holy Sonnets," follows the 1617 death of his beloved wife, Ann, in childbirth.

From the time of his ordination until his death some sixteen years later, Donne no longer pursued the themes that occupied the young Jack Donne. He remained preeminently a love poet, but he sought to describe the love of God instead of the love of woman. He may have come to see his earlier poems as either frivolously worldly—for instance, "The Flea" or "The Sun Rising"—or, more dangerously, inclined to establish an idolatrous religion of love, as in "The Canonization" or "The Ecstasy."

Yet his later religious work continued the "metaphysical wit" of his secular love poetry. For instance, in one of his sonnets, "Batter my heart, three-personed God," he first takes on the role of a city that God must attack and overthrow. Then he makes the shocking portrayal of himself as the unwilling lover whom God must similarly overcome:

Take me to you, imprison me, for I
Except you enthrall me, never shall be free,
Nor ever chaste, except you ravish me.

The idea of God as a rapist is shocking, to say the least. Yet Donne has an important theological message: we are so profoundly sinful that we cannot turn to God; God must take the initiative and bring his gracious love to our unwilling hearts.

Donne's Christian poems combine originality with spiritual depth. These lyrics include his most famous poems, such as the sonnet "Death be not proud," which celebrates the Christian's ultimate victory over death. In "Goodfriday, 1613, Riding Westward" he first regrets the motion of life that pulls him westward, toward sunset, when his "soul's form bends toward the East." But his meditation makes him aware that the original sunrise was darkened; "sin had eternally benighted all" except for the saving death of Christ. Remembering the divine agony, he now finds appropriate his riding away from the rising sun, which recalls the Rising Son whom he cannot face:

> O Savior, as thou hang'st upon the tree;
> I turn my back to thee, but to receive
> Corrections. . . .
> . . . .
> Restore thine image, so much, by thy grace
> That thou may'st know me, and I'll turn my
> face.

The pun on "sun" and "son" is characteristic; Donne apparently relished all sorts of word play. In what may have been the last of his poems, "A Hymn to God the Father," he used not only that same pun but also one on his own last name. Here is the last of three stanzas, in which he addresses God:

> I have a sin of fear, that when I have spun
>   My last thread, I shall perish on the shore;
>   Swear by thyself, that at my death thy
>   Sun
> Shall shine as it shines now, and heretofore;
>   And having done that, thou hast done,
>   I fear no more.

In his *Confessions,* St. AUGUSTINE had written to God, "Our hearts are restless until they find their rest in you." In the later poetry of John Donne we see a restless spirit, kindred to Augustine's, finally achieving peace.

Batter my heart, three-personed God; for You
As yet but knock, breathe, shine, and seek to mend;
That I may rise and stand, o'erthrow me, and bend
Your force to break, blow, burn, and make me new.

—Holy Sonnet 14

We then, who are this new soul, know,
Of what we are composed, and made,
For, th'atomies of which we grow,
Are souls, whom no change can invade.

—"The Ecstasy"

Sermons and Meditations

As great as John Donne is a poet, he is an equally great writer of prose. His is the notable phase "No man is an island, entire of itself. . . ." Although difficult for the modern reader, his sermons are uniquely imaginative—including the last he ever preached, just weeks before his death. Those who heard it were shocked by his cadaverous appearance and hollow voice, and believed they saw a man preach his own funeral sermon. Indeed they had, and he did so with complete sincerity and great spiritual power. Yet Dr. John Donne retained at the end what Jack Donne possessed at the beginning—a remarkable flair for the dramatic.

Issues to Explore

The thoughtful Christian reader of Donne's poetry should keep a few questions in mind: (1) Why should we read poems that appear to celebrate mere sensuality? (2) Are the poems what they appear to be? If so, what value is there in reading them? (3) How do we evaluate the quality of poems whose craftsmanship is admirable but whose message seems disturbing? (4) In what ways do the later, explicitly Christian poems of Donne resemble the earlier erotic poems? (5) Do Donne's occasional

For Further Study

For an introduction to Donne's poetry the reader should begin with the poems mentioned in this essay, as well as "The Relic," "A Nocturnal Upon Saint Lucy's Day," "The Funeral," "A Valediction of Weeping," and "Air and Angels" among his love poems. For the religious poems one should begin by reading the Holy Sonnets, "Goodfriday, 1613, Riding Westward," and "A Hymn to God the Father."

Donne's poetry is widely available; almost any edition will do. But for a selection of Donne's poetry and prose, including letters as well as sermons and other devotional work, choose John Carey's excellent collection in the Oxford Authors series, simply called *John Donne* (Oxford, 1990). A good critical and historical introduction is William Zunder's *The Poetry of John Donne: Literature and Culture in the Elizabethan and Jacobean Period* (Barnes & Noble, 1982). Also, Helen Gardner has edited the useful *John Donne: A Collection of Critical Essays* (Prentice Hall, 1962), which includes her fine essay on Donne's religious poetry.

"shock tactics" in his Christian poems achieve their desired goals? Do they cause readers to see familiar truths in new and vivid light? Do they make us aware of spiritual values we had neglected?

—Alan Jacobs

GEORGE HERBERT

The Temple
1633

George Herbert's collection of poetry, *The Temple,* has a sustained brilliance and an intimacy that make him the foremost and most influential English devotional poet. Only his older contemporary John Donne and his Victorian Jesuit admirer Gerard Manley HOPKINS can compare with Herbert for heartsearching eloquence and technical mastery. But Herbert's thematic variety and his combination of complementary opposites make his work unique: he brings together wrenching struggle and quiet resolution, earthy imagery and cosmic reach, plainspoken directness and musical dazzle. Herbert has been beloved across the spectrum of Christendom because he is the most catholic of Christian poets. He animates the symbols and cycles of the ancient liturgy with the evangelical fervor of the Reformation, answering Christ's grand imperative, "You must be born again."

The Holy Mr. Herbert

Herbert is so much a poet of spiritual struggle—and hard-won

George Herbert (1593–1633).

harmony—that it helps to know something of the ambitions, frustrations, and transformations of his life. He was born in 1593 to Sir Richard and Lady Magdalen Herbert. True to his family's competitive nature, Herbert had ambitions for a high secular position at the English court, even though he was a Cambridge

divinity student. But his would-be career ran afoul of the shifting political and religious currents of the 1620s. As Puritan and high-church factions vied to enforce their opposing ideals, King James I died and the high-church party gained control. The balances of the old Elizabethan "middle way"—strongly Protestant in doctrine and reformed Catholic in worship—began to collapse. Loyal to this *via media,* Herbert saw his political hopes crumble along with it; even within the church, his prospects were bleak.

As his fortunes declined, Herbert floundered. A younger son, he inherited no fortune or assured income. He picked up the thread of his church career, but hesitated a long time—perhaps six years—to become a priest, apparently burdened with unworthiness. By the time he resolved his inner dilemmas and was ordained in 1630, he had composed many of the poems in *The Temple.* The rest were written during the brief three years left to him as he ministered to the obscure Wiltshire village of Bemerton, near Salisbury.

Having been tenant long to a rich Lord,
  Not thriving, I resolved to be bold,
  And make a suit unto him, to afford
A new small-rented lease, and cancell th' old.

In heaven at his manour I him sought:
  They told me there, that he was lately gone
  About some land, which he had dearly bought
Long since on earth, to take possession.

I straight return'd, and knowing his great birth,
  Sought him accordingly in great resorts;
  In cities, theatres, gardens, parks, and courts:
At length I heard a ragged noise and mirth

  Of theeves and murderers: there I him espied,
Who straight, Your suit is granted, *said, and died.*

—"Redemption"

He threw himself so fully into his work that the parishioners who filled tiny St. Andrew's called him "the holy Mr. Herbert." In 1633, dying of tuberculosis, he handed the manuscript of *The Temple* to a friend, who published this collection of 160 poems posthumously. So, forgotten at the centers of power, Herbert died famous in a small place. But his little book soon spread his fame through the kingdom and the world.

Herbert's poetic reputation rests almost entirely on *The Temple* and some Latin poems. His main English prose work, *The Country Parson,* is a concise and extraordinarily practical manual for rural pastors; his advice on preaching and congregational relations is still valuable.

The Temple: A Chorus of Varied Voices

For all of its autobiographical echoes, *The Temple* is not primarily about Herbert. Nor is it merely a loose gathering of poems. As its title implies, the work is an intricately built structure, made for the worship of God. It has three major sections: (1) *The Church-Porch* is a place of preparation, a collection of proverbial wisdom for outward behavior; leading into (2) *The Church,* a large "congregation" of short poems probing the believer's bittersweet inner life; leading on to (3) *The Church Militant,* a prophetic vision of sin and redemption competing throughout history on a global scale. The longest section, *The Church,* is organized in part around architecture with such poems as "The Altar," "The Church Floor," and "The Windows," and in part around the church year, including "Good Friday," "Easter," "Whitsunday," and "Christmas." But like the Psalms, it is mainly a chorus of varied voices—struggling, thanking, complaining, praising.

A few of Herbert's poems in *The Temple* are directly autobiographical. "Affliction" (I) is his most personal, tracing the course of his early, naive religiosity, his courtly ambitions, his disappointments and illnesses. It ends with a near threat to abandon Christ but rebounds with the tortured paradox,

  Ah my deare God! though I am clean for
    got,
  Let me not love thee, if I love thee not.

Realizing that he has "loved" Christ mainly for the promised "benefits," he pleads with the Lord to free him from mercenary motives. Significantly, Herbert wrote *five* different poems titled "Affliction"—the numbers were added to the titles by the printer. "Employment" (I) and (II) express his frustration at his secular failure. Then in "The Priesthood" he explains his long hesitation in entering the ministry—he fears that God's wrath will consume him for seizing holy office. Finally, in "Aaron" his fears have been resolved—unholy in himself, he can put on Jesus' righteousness to serve.

The young George Herbert with his mother; a Victorian illustration.

The Cycle of Grace

Though most of the poems are not so auto biographical, Herbert's life permeates his art. He writes as a man humbled and exalted by hard experience. "Sermons are dangerous things," he often said, and so is his poetry— it is aimed at the reader's heart. His great theme is *grace:* unmerited and unsought by the self-righteous and self-sufficient; offered by Christ with blood and tears and rejected by sinners as an insult. Yet grace is finally irresistible, embraced by the heartbroken like a buoy in a storm and enjoyed like a feast in a famine.

This repeated cycle of grace—offer, rejection, humbling, embrace—is established immediately in *The Church,* which begins with a sequence of poems about Christ's sacrifice and humanity's response. "The Altar" (shaped like its title) presents the believer's stony heart as the place of sacrifice. Then in "The Sacrifice" the crucified Christ offers himself, repeating in agony "Was ever grief like mine?" The misguided speaker in "The Thanksgiving" eagerly answers with programs of good works to erase his debt to Jesus, but is finally struck dumb by the infinity of the passion. "The Reprisal" repudiates such "dealing," embracing the healing humiliation of the atonement. A few poems later, "Redemption" revisits the crucifixion under the cloak of a shocking parable about a tenant seeking to renegotiate his lease, only to find his landlord dying for him in a city slum. "Easter" relapses by attempting to repay Christ in song, but proclaims its own failure. Then, in "Easter-Wings" (shaped like *its* title), the speaker prays to fly with Christ and participate in *his* victory.

This same cyclical struggle with divine grace is repeated in varied ways throughout *The Church,* stressing both the inconstancy of the believer and the constancy of God. "Jordan" (I) and (II) lampoon self-important religious poetry that calls more attention to its own eloquence than to the gospel's simple beauty. In "The Holdfast" a comic zealot seeks spiritual security in strict behavior and seems disappointed when told he can do nothing Christ has not already done for him. In "The Collar," a religious man rages at a god of delays, denial, and niggling rules, only to have his ravings transformed by a single loving word from the heavenly Father:

Me thoughts I heard one calling, "Child!"
And I reply'd, "My Lord."

"The Flower" puts such ups and downs in perspective. It pictures the believer's life as a series of seasonal deaths and resurrections until we come to the garden of paradise, "where no flower can wither." *The Church* concludes with the sublime "Love" (III), in which the guilt-laden "guest" insists on shutting himself out of the heavenly inn.

> Love bade me welcome; yet my soul drew
>   back,
>   Guiltie of dust and sinne,
> But quick-ey'd Love, observing me grow
>   slack
>   From my first entrance in
> Drew nearer to me sweetly questioning
>   If I lack'd anything.
>
> A guest, I answer'd, worthy to be here:
>   Love said, You shall be he.
> I the unkinde, ungratefull? Ah, my deare,
>   I cannot look on thee.

In the final lines, the guest loses—and so wins—a witty debate with the innkeeper Jesus, a host so irresistibly gracious that he refuses to take no for an answer. Indeed, in a final twist, the host offers a meal that turns out to consist of himself—for in retrospect we see the poem backlit by a surprising, deeply serious pun linking innkeeper, guest, and consecrated eucharistic bread in communion.

Issues to Explore

As when reading any lyric poetry, the reader should ask: (1) Who is speaking to whom (or what) and in what circumstances? (2) Does the speaker's mind or attitude change during the course of the poem? If so, how and why? (3) What comparisons—especially extended comparisons—does the poem use? Also, specific to Herbert: (4) How does this poem relate to those before and after it? Is it part of a pattern or sequence? (5) To what does the title

For Further Study

For a reader familiar with the language of SHAKESPEARE or the King James Bible, Herbert is not difficult; his vocabulary is highly concrete, often conversational. The authoritative text of *The Temple* is found in *The Works of George Herbert,* edited by F. E. Hutchinson (Clarendon Press, 1964); the best affordable paperback version is in *The English Poems of George Herbert,* edited by C. A. Patrides (Rowman, 1974). Some helpful studies include Joseph H. Summers, *George Herbert: His Religion and Art* (Harvard University, 1954; reprint *Medieval and Renaissance Texts in Studies,* 1981); Richard Strier, *Love Known* (University of Chicago, 1983); Gene Edward Veith, Jr., *Reformation Spirituality* (Bucknell University, 1985); and Christopher Hodgkins, *Authority, Church, and Society in George Herbert: Return to the Middle Way* (University of Missouri, 1993). The standard Herbert biography is by Amy M. Charles, *A Life of George Herbert* (Cornell University, 1977). Izaak Walton's famous *Life of Herbert* (Oxford, 1927) is to be enjoyed rather than trusted.

refer? (6) Does the poem have any particular stanza form or unusual shape? How does this affect its meaning? Probing more deeply: (7) What is Herbert's usual stance toward God? Is he too intimate? (8) Does Herbert conceive of God as a stern judge or a passionate lover? (9) What is the significance of Herbert's extraordinary use of common objects? (10) Does his poetry constitute in itself a religious experience somewhat like the Psalms?

—Christopher Hodgkins

JOHN MILTON

Paradise Lost
1667

Paradise Lost stands alone as England's great epic. The last in the classical epic tradition inherited from the Greeks and Romans, it is admired for both its religious stature and the grandeur of its style and structure. Widely acknowledged as one of the monumental poems of the world, it celebrates human freedom and "justif[ies] the ways of God to men." Its author, John Milton (1608–1674), is important both as a writer and a person. Literary scholars generally regard him as the second greatest English author, after SHAKESPEARE. His importance lies partly in the way, as a Christian humanist, he synthesizes the entire intellectual and cultural history of the West up to his time. The most learned of English authors, Milton fills his works with allusions to the Bible, classical mythology, and history.

John Milton: Christian, Poet, Statesman

Milton's life falls into three well-defined periods: the first, childhood and education (1608–40), during which he wrote his lyric

John Milton (1608–1674).

poems; the second, his twenty-year public career (1640–60), in which he served as Latin Secretary to Cromwell and wrote polemical prose in support of the Puritans; the third, the period of his major works (1660–74), in which he wrote *Paradise Lost, Paradise Regained,* and *Samson Agonistes.*

There is something for everyone in Milton. Experts in theology, music, education, politics, history, science, and literature have studied

his writings and written about them. His *Of Education* is a landmark document among educational treatises, defining the ideal of a Christian liberal arts education with unmatched clarity. *Areopagitica,* his defense of the right to publish ideas for public discussion, is still the classic essay on freedom of the press. Milton is also a primary source for the ideas of the Puritan theologians.

Milton's Short Poems

The best introduction to Milton's poetry is some of his lyric work— short, song-like poems. Examples of his lyric genius are "Song on May Morning," his Christmas poem "On the Morning of Christ's Nativity," and "On Time." The companion poems "L'Allegro" and "Il Penseroso" are justifiably famous, as is the pastoral elegy "Lycidas."

The human side of Milton is equally accessible in some of his sonnets (fourteen-line poems with an intricate rhyme scheme). Milton wrote Sonnet 7, his graduation poem, on his twenty-third birthday. It wrestles with the

what in me is dark
Illumine, what is low raise and support;
That to the height of this great argument
I may assert Eternal Providence,
And justify the ways of God to men.

—*Paradise Lost*

problem of the swift passing of time. Sonnets 9 and 14 celebrate the spiritual virtues of two women, showing the falsity of claims that Milton disliked women. Sonnet 18 expresses Milton's prayer for justice and redemption on the occasion of the massacre of the Waldensians—Italian Calvinists—by Catholics in 1655. Sonnet 20, a verse epistle that invites a former student to dinner, provides a glimpse of Milton as advocate of enlightened leisure. Sonnet 23 is a moving vision of Milton's deceased wife, whom he portrayed as a glorified saint in heaven. Greatest of all is Sonnet 19, which expresses Milton's coming to terms with his blindness at the age of forty-three or forty-four. The reader will benefit from studying these poems before tackling *Paradise Lost*.

Paradise Lost: The Fundamentals

Paradise Lost was Milton's attempt to do for his nation what HOMER did for the Greeks and VIRGIL for the Romans. Reading Homer and Virgil is a good preparation for reading *Paradise Lost*. Elements common to *Paradise Lost* and other epics include the narrative material originating in ancient stories, a hero—Milton added a heroine as well—of national or racial importance, a cosmic scope that includes the supernatural world, and an action built around a central feat, usually military or political.

A good strategy for reading *Paradise Lost* is to ask how Milton used various motifs inherited from the tradition of epic poems going back to Homer. Milton's general pattern was to "Christianize" the classical tradition wherever possi-

Opposite: "Satan resting on the mountain," illustration by Gustave Doré (1866) for *Paradise Lost*.

ble. For his story he reaches back in history—as epic poets have always done—but his source is the Bible (especially Genesis 1–3) instead of classical mythology. Milton's supernatural cosmology, or theory of the natural order of the universe, is specifically Christian. Heaven, earth, and hell are the main scenes of action. The gods of classical epic are replaced in Milton's epic by angels and, above all, by God.

Sometimes Milton's Christianizing of the epic tradition is so radical that scholars speak of *Paradise Lost* as not only an epic but an anti-epic. Whereas the classical epic hero was a model of virtue, Milton's epic protagonists—Adam and Eve—are the archetypal sinners. Their epic feat is a crime—falling from innocence. The crucial struggle in Milton's story does not occur on the battlefield but within the human soul. Conquest consists not in military action but in obedience to God and coming to trust in Christ as Savior. Whereas the classical epic celebrated such masculine virtues as military strength and political rulership, Milton replaces them with pastoral and domestic values. He portrays Adam and Eve's life of spiritual contentment and virtue in paradise.

Much of the power of *Paradise Lost* stems from what Milton called its "great argument": its structure of ideas and themes. These ideas include the moral and spiritual conflict between good and evil; the Christian view of history, which unfolds as a sequence—eternity, life before the fall, fallen human history, eternity; and the human-divine relationship. Further, *Paradise Lost* emphasizes the importance of hierarchy (which Milton's age pictured as a Great Chain of Being); reason as the means to virtue, achieved by governing the emotions and appetites; and the conception of evil as disobedience to God.

Milton was attracted to stories and characters from Scripture because he believed that they embodied the deep significance of life. Instead of arguing with Milton's version of biblical events, we should accept them as poetic images of reality, both earthly and supernatural. Milton provides partly fictional images of the familiar realities of the Christian faith to make them come alive.

Of man's first disobedience, and the fruit
Of that forbidden tree, whose mortal taste
Brought death into the world, and all our woe,
With loss of Eden, till one greater Man
Restore us, and regain the blissful seat,
Sing, Heavenly Muse.

—*Paradise Lost*

Paradise Lost also appeals to the emotions—Milton achieves his effects by causing his readers to *feel* a certain way toward the settings, characters, and events. Most generally, he wishes to arouse positive feelings toward good and aversion toward evil. We can profitably analyze how Milton makes the good attractive and the evil ultimately unattractive, despite its initial powers of seduction.

Christian readers will find themselves very much at home with Milton. After all, he wrote for a "fit audience, though few" (invocation to Book 9). His "fit audience" is familiar with the Bible and sympathetic to the Christian faith. In fact, Milton's epic masterpiece lays out the whole vast fabric of Christian doctrine. Milton aims, further, to impart a vision of the good life, contrasting it with a vision of life marred by weakness and sin.

Images of Hell

Paradise Lost is divided into twelve books. One of several structural schemes by which Milton arranged his story is the principle of six pairs of books. Books 1 and 2 plunge into the sordid world of hell, where Satan and his fallen angels have just landed and are debating what they should do in light of their predicament. In these books we encounter images of such recognizable experiences as defeat, pain, suffering, tyranny, revenge, hatred, confusion, loss, ambition, futility, defiance, and delusion. The pride and consequent debasement of Satan provides a glimpse of the aspiring mind forced to confront its own crushing failure. Milton's hell is a portrait of "darkness visible," a picture of the bondage of evil.

Milton wrote *Paradise Lost* in two distinct styles, which scholars call the "demonic" (or "infernal") style and the "heavenly" (or "celestial") style. The demonic style is baroque (a fleshy, ornate, highly involved style), weighed down with allusions to classical mythology and ancient epic. It has an abundance of epic similes (in which a character or event in the story is compared at length to something from history or nature) and an elaborate sentence structure that demands intense concentration. This is a heroic style, designed to mimic the form and subject matter of the old epics that celebrate human self-reliance and conquest.

Images of Heaven and Paradise

The first half of Book 3 is Milton's story of life in heaven, in which he employs the images of light and transcendence. His celestial style is relatively simple. It consists mainly of the absence of things that make the style of the first two books so complicated. To those familiar with Scripture, this part of the poem is fairly easy to read because Milton fills it with allusions to the Bible and familiar Christian ideas.

Book 4 is the best part of *Paradise Lost*. Milton gives a picture of life in the Garden of Eden, which is also his vision of how God intended human life to be lived— at any time, in any place. Milton's vision of the good life is a distinctly Puritan vision in which marital life is portrayed as joyous and blessed. *Paradise Lost* is both a great love story and nature poem.

War in Heaven and the Creation

Books 5 and 6 tell the story of the war in heaven. Here, too, Milton recounts a partly fictional story, which is based on a biblical framework, as a way to depict eternal spiritual realities. It chiefly centers on the character of Satan and God and the battle between good and evil. This epic contest itself is an exciting story— unsurpassed as a war story among all epics that portray battles.

Satanic destruction is balanced by the story of divine creativity in Books 7 and 8. Milton's descriptions are built on the creation accounts in the Bible and a mass of commentary that had grown up around those accounts. His imagination runs deep and rich as he imagines God creating the universe and humankind.

The Fall and Its Effects

Book 9 is the story of Adam and Eve's fall into sin, and Book 10 recounts the immediate consequences of the fall. It is not primarily a story of what *happened* on the fatal day of the fall, but

The world was all before them, where to choose
Their place of rest, and Providence their guide:
They hand in hand, with wandering steps and slow,
Through Eden took their solitary way.

—*Paradise Lost*

rather how the fall into sin *happens* in our own and other people's lives.

The final two books use a convention known as the vision of future history. Milton's vision of fallen human history is based on a paradox of loss balanced by restoration, grief balanced by consolation, pessimism mitigated by hope. Milton built this "doubleness" into the fabric of Books 11 and 12. The vision itself moves toward the incarnation and atonement of Christ. The purpose of these books is to teach Adam and Eve—and us—how to live in a fallen world.

Opposite: Oliver Cromwell (1599–1658) Lord Protector of England 1653–58.

Issues to Explore

Milton is a difficult poet. He writes in an exalted style that is almost a language to itself, using dignified vocabulary and long sentences. Milton would have agreed with the Greek dramatist ARISTOPHANES that "high thoughts must have high language." The best strategy is to read Milton's elevated language in this spirit, not worrying about unusual words or allusions. If his style becomes too difficult, much of it will be made intelligible when the words are read aloud.

Reading *Paradise Lost* provides a rich opportunity for discussion and reflection. (1) Books 1 and 2 are based on an ironic contrast between the apparent grandeur of Satan and the actual evil and futility of his enterprise. Where are evidences of this paradox of evil? (2) Milton's images of hell are designed to tell us the truth about evil. What specific things does Milton reveal about evil by means of his partly fictional story of life in hell? (3) Looking at Books

For Further Study

Paradise Regained tells the story of Christ's victory over Satan in the temptations in the wilderness. It may be a more readable poem than *Paradise Lost*, but most people find it inferior. *Samson Agonistes*, however, is as excellent a dramatic tragedy as *Paradise Lost* is an epic.

Milton's works are available in many editions. The best edition for the general reader is the Everyman's Library edition, edited by Gordon Campbell and entitled *John Milton: Complete English Poems, Of Education, Areopagitica* (1994). The Norton Critical Edition of *Paradise Lost* (edited by Scott Elledge, 1993) contains the text of the epic, a few of Milton's sonnets and prose passages, and selections from literary criticism.

The best book on Paradise Lost is C. S. Lewis's *A Preface to Paradise Lost* (Oxford, 1942). Stanley Fish's *Surprised by Sin: The Reader in Paradise Lost* (St. Martins, 1967) provides a sequential reading of the poem in a Christian understanding of the story. The biblical element in Paradise Lost is discussed by James Sims, *The Bible in Milton's Epics* (University of Florida, 1962), and Leland Ryken, *Realms of Gold: The Classics in Christian Perspective*, chapter 4 (Harold Shaw, 1991). Milton's doctrine is outlined in C. A. Patrides's *Milton and the Christian Tradition* (Oxford, 1966). The definitive modern biography of Milton is William Riley Parker's *Milton: A Biography* (Oxford, 1968).

Henceforth I learn that to obey is best,
And love with fear the only God, to walk
As in his presence, ever to observe
His providence, and on him sole depend,
Merciful over all his works, with good
Still overcoming evil. . . .

—*Paradise Lost*

3 and 4, what are the cornerstones of Milton's theodicy (his attempt to reconcile God's goodness and power with the fact of evil in the world)? (4) How *does* God intend human life to be lived: In harmony with nature? In continuous worship and gratitude to God? With every human longing (including the sexual) satisfied? With work to do? (5) According to Books 5 and 6, what is the origin of evil? What are its characteristic ways of working? What does God do about the presence of evil in the universe? (6) In Books 7 and 8, what would Milton have us understand about our physical world? About the people in this world? (7) What are the effects of sin as portrayed in Books 9 and 10? How *does* the fall into sin happen in our lives? How should we live, in light of this? (8) In Books 11 and 12, what have Adam and Eve learned? What have we learned?

—Leland Ryken

BLAISE PASCAL

Pensées
1670

laise Pascal's *Pensées*, although fragmentary and incomplete, is a penetrating, original, and stylish defense of the Christian faith and one of the supreme Christian writings of all time.

Pensées (the French word for "thoughts") forms Pascal's work up to his death on his audacious plans for a comprehensive *Apology for the Christian Religion.*

Celebrated in his lifetime as a mathematical genius and inventor, Pascal through the *Pensées* has become an incomparable spiritual guide to millions. Although he wrote at the dawn of the scientific age, he strikes themes whose resonance grows louder in light of scientific theories three centuries later.

Few authors have captured the human predicament so poignantly; almost no other Christian author has conveyed the response of the Christian gospel so searchingly. *Pensées* endures because the work both mirrors Pascal's remarkable mind and provides an astonishing window into the human heart.

Blaise Pascal (1623–1662).

A Genius and a Saint

Pascal's writings are inseparably tied to the short, intense flame-burst of his life (1623–1662). Born at Clermont in France, the son of a successful lawyer, he was bereft of his mother when he was only three. Pascal was therefore left between an older and a younger sister to be raised by them and his father and educated at home.

Giving the boy special treatment because of poor health, Pascal's father recognized early that his son was a precocious genius—especially in mathematics. Indeed in his own day Pascal's reputation rested on his extraordinary scientific and technical innovations. Famous for his work on conic sections, the cycloid, probability theory, and the problem of the vacuum, he is heralded as the father of the modern computer because he invented a calculating machine. As the peer of such Enlightenment leaders as the philosopher René Descartes, Pascal truly was a Renaissance thinker who was one of the greatest prose stylists in the French language.

Pensées, however, was born of a very different and originally little-known stream of influence on Pascal's life. In 1646, Pascal's father was treated by two amateur bonesetters who introduced him and his family to their faith as well as their art—Jansenism, a Catholic puritan movement centered at Port Royal near Paris. Rooting their belief in St. AUGUSTINE, the Jansenists protested the spiritual

The heart has its reasons of which reason knows nothing:
we know this in countless ways.

—*Pensées*
A. J. Krailsheimer, trans.

lukewarmness and moral laxity of the contemporary church, especially among the Jesuits.

Pascal's "first conversion" when he was twenty-three was more a new way of life than a dramatic experience. But it was followed eight years later on the night of November 23, 1654, by his "second conversion"—an intense two-hour mystical experience that he recorded in "The Memorial," the opening lines of which follow:

Fire
"God of Abraham, God of Isaac, God of
    Jacob," not of philosophers and scholars.
Certainty, certainty, heartfelt, joy, peace.
God of Jesus Christ.
God of Jesus Christ.
My God and your God.
"Thy God shall be my God."
The world forgotten, and everything except
    God.

This "night of fire" became decisive for Pascal's remaining eight years of life. It was so precious and pivotal to him that he sewed the parchment record of it into the lining of his doublet—and into every new doublet he bought for the rest of his life. After years of chronic sickness, depression, and mounting pain, Pascal died at the age of thirty-nine.

Sketches for an
Unfinished Cathedral

Drawn into the forlorn struggle by the Jansenist community to rebut Jesuit accusations and attacks, Pascal wrote a stinging but anonymous reply in *The Provincial Letters* in conditions of real danger and great secrecy. His cause was eventually lost and the Jansenist movement obliterated, but his work became a classic of French satirical polemic. Following that publication, Pascal realized the need for

a full-scale apology (or defense) for the Christian faith. He began its composition in 1657, working on it slowly and painfully over the last four years of his life.

In the *Pensées* Pascal clearly aims at cultured, intelligent free-thinkers with refined manners and easy-going morals. But the full purpose and final order of the completed book cannot be worked out satisfactorily from the existing preliminary sketches. This incompleteness makes the *Pensées* both easier and harder to read. On the one hand, Pascal's thoughts are often cryptic and tantalizingly unfinished. Occasionally they are in nearly final form—for instance, the "Wager," which is Pascal's celebrated argument for faith in God couched in gamblers' terms. But sometimes they are incomprehensible. More often they are terse, prompting the thought that if the notes are this remarkable what might the completed work have been?

On the other hand, Pascal's thoughts have a distilled essence, a diamond-like sharpness, and an explosive suggestiveness precisely because they are *not* weighted down with more leisurely pages of argument. In particular, Pascal is a master of aphorisms; for example, his celebrated saying that is far more than a play on words: "The heart has its reasons of which reason knows nothing." Equally, his brief reflections on such topics as "the folly of indifference" and "diversion" are masterpieces of deep human observation, reflection, and provocative argument: "If man were happy, the less he were diverted the happier he would be. . . . I have often said that the sole cause of man's unhappiness is that he does not know how to stay quietly in his room."

Pensées, however, is not a book to be read through like other books; it is better approached as a series of reflections to be pondered at their own pace. And certain background considerations are needed for the best understanding of the book. First, as far as we can tell, Pascal composed the bulk of the *Pensées* in the following way. Using large sheets of paper, he jotted down his entries and separated them with a horizontal stroke. Then he cut the large sheets into as many strips as there were entries, arranged them by subject, and threaded the strips together to form a bundle. Each bundle corresponds to our chapters. Our modern editions are based on the two copies made of Pascal's original soon after his death.

Second, Pascal employs an argument in the *Pensées* that is not linear but cumulative; and, although profoundly rational, it depends on more than reason alone. Eschewing a rational "proof" for God's existence, Pascal uses an approach that is at once more profound, more popular, more concrete, and more effective. He appeals to human misery in awakening self-knowledge, raising the riddle of human existence, and spurring a search that can lead to the only possible answer—Jesus Christ. Because the whole person must be saved, the whole person must be moved on the spiritual pilgrimage.

Third, Pascal strategically argues from false alternatives. Somehow fated always to be caught in the middle—between the priests and the free-thinkers, between the philosophies of the skeptic Montaigne and the stoic Epictetus, and between the worlds of the convent and the gambling saloon—he uses dualisms to argue for the higher truth of the Christian faith.

Thus people are caught between the finite and the infinite, between misery and grandeur, between reason and the heart, between reason and authority. As he says, "Man is neither angel nor beast, and it is unfortunately the case that anyone trying to act the angel acts the beast." In each case Pascal uses the polar opposite to cancel out each side. He then shows that the contradictions can be reconciled only by introducing a third truth whose fullness contains the half truths of the faulty extremes. This third truth is the Christian gospel.

Thus Pascal's relentlessly rational arguments point beyond reason and pivot on the same passionate logic as the "Memorial" that he wrote after "the night of fire." Philosophy, science, logic, poetry, common sense, and ordinary human experience—he uses them all in driving to the same overwhelming conclusion: "Jesus Christ is the object of all things, the center toward which all things tend."

Blaise Pascal.

Issues to Explore

For the Christian, the *Pensées* is a classic to be read and reread, for it is a gold mine of Christian reflections on the human condition. It is also a brilliantly effective example of how to present the Christian faith and a humbling example of a hero-saint whose intellectual integrity is matched perfectly by his lonely courage in suffering and by the ardor of his love for God.

If man were happy, the less he were diverted the happier he would be. . . . I have often said that the sole cause of man's unhappiness is that he does not know how to stay quietly in his room.

—*Pensées*
A. J. Krailsheimer, trans.

Man is only a reed, the weakest in nature, but he is a thinking reed. There is no need for the whole universe to take up arms to crush him: a vapour, a drop of water is enough to kill him. But even if the universe were to crush him, man would still be nobler than his slayer, because he knows that he is dying and the advantage the universe has over him. The universe knows none of this.

—*Pensées*
A. J. Krailsheimer, trans.

Some questions to ask are: (1) Which of the individual aphorisms throughout the book do you find the most helpful and memorable? (2) How do such topics as "diversion" illuminate modern lifestyles and busyness? (3) Do you find Pascal's argument from human self-knowledge more compelling than the rational proofs of God's existence? Why? (4) Why do many readers of *Pensées* find some of the second half (for example, on biblical prophecies) less compelling than Pascal's treatment of the human predicament? (5) What must it have been like for Pascal to sketch the *Pensées* so feverishly and in such pain, knowing that he would not complete his work?

—Os Guinness

For Further Study

Several English translations of the *Pensées* are available. The Penguin edition, translated and introduced by A. J. Krailsheimer (1966), is generally reckoned to be the best. Krailsheimer has also translated the *Provincial Letters* (Penguin, 1967) and written a longer introduction to Pascal in the "Past Masters" series by the Oxford University Press (1980).

Among a vast critical literature on Pascal, T. S. Eliot's introduction to the *Pensées* (E. P. Dutton, 1958) is particularly interesting because it comes from one great Christian writer on another. Two more recent books have fascinating applications of the *Pensées* to the defense of the faith today: Peter Kreeft, *Christianity for Modern Pagans* (Ignatius, 1993), and Thomas V. Morris, *Making Sense of It All: Pascal and the Meaning of Life* (Eerdmans, 1992).

JOHN BUNYAN

The Pilgrim's Progress
1678, 1684

*J*ohn Bunyan's classic work *The Pilgrim's Progress* has long been the best read and most enduringly cherished religious allegory in the English language. Published in 1678, the work passed through eleven editions during Bunyan's lifetime, and when he died in 1688 it had been translated into Dutch, French, and Welsh. The book has now been translated into more than seventy languages and dialects.

The Pilgrim's Progress

The Pilgrim's Progress has been widely influential throughout the centuries since its publication. The famous allegory is one of the chief avenues by which the Puritan spirit entered the mainstream of the English Reformation. Like any classic, however, the work transcends its historical era and embodies universal truths that are always contemporary. Through the metaphor of a journey Bunyan shows the stages of a pilgrimage from the City of Destruction to the Celestial City, or the stages of a solitary pilgrim on his way from a

John Bunyan (1628–1688).

state of misery to a state of blessedness.

Such names from the allegory as Slough of Despond, Mr. Worldly-Wiseman, Mr. Money-Love, and Hill Difficulty are familiar to people in various cultures. Vanity Fair gave William Thackeray a title for his greatest novel; Nathaniel HAWTHORNE appropriated the allegorical structure for his tale "The Celestial Rail-road." The artist William Blake painted a number of watercolors illustrating

scenes from the work, and composer Ralph Vaughan Williams wrote an opera entitled *Pilgrim's Progress*. Mr. Valiant-for-Truth's song quite often appears in hymnals today.

Preacher, Prisoner, Author

John Bunyan (1628–1688) was the son of a Bedfordshire tinker. In his autobiography Bunyan describes his father's family as being "of that rank that is meanest and most despised of all the families in the land," but points out that his people were once landed yeomen. Bunyan's emphasis on his humble birth is not inverted snobbery; it is his way of attributing to God credit for what he had become. Although his formal education was undoubtedly slight, he had read and studied such intellectually demanding books as Martin LUTHER's *Commentary on Galatians*.

Bunyan joined the Baptist church in Bedford when he was about thirty and began preaching in nearby villages. Because he refused to follow an Elizabethan act against Nonconformists—those not associated with the official Church

This Book will make a Traveller of thee.

—Preface
The Pilgrim's Progress

of England—he was imprisoned. The three-month sentence was extended to twelve years, with a brief respite during the sixth year. Bunyan spent most of the time preaching to prisoners and writing books. He wrote *The Pilgrim's Progress* when he was imprisoned a second time for a few months in 1675. Part II, his less familiar sequel, was published in 1684, sixteen years after Part I. Altogether, Bunyan was the author of more than sixty books.

Layers of Meaning

As a literary form, allegory has a long and reputable history. C. S. LEWIS held that it belongs "not to medieval man but to men or even to mind in general." During the Middle Ages DANTE and CHAUCER wrote splendid allegories, but since then the popularity of the form has declined considerably. Dorothy L. Sayers referred to Bunyan as "the last of the English allegorists in the great tradition."

It is important to think of allegory as a narrative that has layers of meanings in addition to the literal or surface meaning. Although the story in an allegory may have its own appeal and the images their own beauty, the major emphasis is on the ultimate meanings that the story and images unfold.

Bunyan describes the nature of allegory and builds a strong argument for figurative expressions in his rhymed preface to the work. He contends that he, as allegorist, has the highest authority for using images, metaphors, or any literary figure because Old Testament writers, Christ, and the apostles used images, metaphors, and parables. In *The Pilgrim's Progress* he employs the distinctive features of allegory, including the dream framework, the use of characters to personify vices and virtues, and dialogues between characters.

One Pilgrim's Journey

Bunyan develops his allegory in *The Pilgrim's Progress* within the framework of a dream-vision. He depicts the steps of the traveler who seeks "the everlasting prize" on his pilgrimage from his lost state to his arrival in the New Jerusalem. Although the narrative is presented as a dream, one of the strengths of Bunyan's work is the realistic story of this journey.

The central character in Bunyan's allegory is Christian, who flees his family and the City of Destruction to begin his adventuresome pilgrimage to the Celestial City. Along the way he wallows in the Slough of Despond, contends with Mr. Worldly-Wiseman, and loses his burden at the Cross. But this is barely the beginning of the pilgrimage. Christian clambers up the Hill Difficulty, struggles with Apollyon, trudges through the Valley of the Shadow of Death, endures persecution at Vanity Fair, and sinks into despair in Doubting Castle. These, too, are only a few of his experiences. Near the end of the pilgrimage Christian catches a glimpse of the ultimate goal from the Delectable Mountains. He then crosses the River of Death and finally enters the New City where he receives "ten thousand welcomes."

As Christian travels across a terrain of roads, hills, and valleys, he experiences both times of action and interludes of contemplation. Following his wanderings in the Slough of Despond, confrontations with Mr. Worldly-Wiseman and Mr. Legality, and the chastening interview with Evangelist, he enters a time of study and reflection at the Interpreter's House. Similarly, his persecution at Vanity Fair and suffering in Doubting Castle precede the quietness and peace of the Delectable Mountains.

Bunyan gives rich descriptions of the surrounding landscape along Christian's pilgrimage. Consider the view from the House Beautiful: "he saw a most pleasant Mountainous Country, beautified with Woods, Vinyards, Fruits of all sorts, Flowers also, with Springs and Fountains, very delectable to behold."

Bunyan also masterfully creates his characters. Often he shows the essence of a personality with only a few strokes. The character Obstinate, who has no patience with "Crazed-headed Coxcombs," begins almost every comment with a ringing note of finality. His mind is made up; he needs no help from books or people. When Pliable wishes to follow Christian, Obstinate scornfully replies: "What! more Fools still? be ruled by me and go back." Another example is Mr. By-ends' arrogant—and ironical—account of his family connections: "Mr. Two-tongues was my Mother's own Brother by my Father's side"; Mr. Facing-both-ways and Mr. Anything are also relatives. By permitting By-ends to be his own satirist, Bunyan shows how thoroughly hypocrisy has saturated the little man's being.

Bunyan includes numerous debates or dialogues in his allegory. The dialogue between Christian and Mr. Worldly-Wiseman is especially sharp. In a few paragraphs Christian reveals that he is not quite ready for Wiseman's insidious counsel, and Wiseman shows that he has only contempt for Christian.

The Pilgrim's Progress has truly become a classic in English-speaking homes. The issues it raises are still contemporary. Human weaknesses abound: lust for riches, desire for rank, display of pride, physical abuse, prejudiced juries, self-destructive melancholy, overwhelming doubt. More positively, there are also the joys of companionship, strength in belief, might of hope, and the redemptive role of the church.

Equally contemporaneous is the fallibility of Christian's behavior: he falls prey to Wiseman, loses his parchment roll, falls into the net of flattery, leads another astray through vain-confidence, and wanders around in bypaths. But this pilgrim does nevertheless make progress and reach his goal of the Celestial City through grace.

Christian (Bunyan's pilgrim) encounters the cross; from a Victorian chromolithograph.

Issues to Explore

Although the allegory is relatively easy to read, the work raises many profound issues worth pondering. (1) In suggesting a biblical model for his narrative, Bunyan believes that parables, metaphors, and other figures are fresh ways to reveal important truths. What advantages are there in telling the Christian story through fictional representation?

(2) A study of the historical and moral levels in the work also offers rich rewards. A central question is how the allegory depicts the thinking of the Protestant Reformation: to what extent does Christian's journey reveal patterns of Lutheran, Calvinist, and Separatist theology?

Above all, we can ask questions concerning the metaphor of the journey as the organizing

I saw a man . . . with his face {turned away} from His own House, a Book in his hand, and a great burden upon his back.

—*The Pilgrim's Progress*

I am reading old Bunyan again . . . and am profoundly struck with the true genius manifested in the simple, vigorous rhythmic style.

—George Eliot

For Further Study

Good primary sources are: N. H. Keeble, editor, *John Bunyan: The Pilgrim's Progress* (Oxford, 1976); J. Blanton Wharey, editor, *The Pilgrim's Progress,* second edition, revised by Roger Sharrock (Clarendon, 1960). Helpful commentaries are: Roger Sharrock, *Bunyan: The Pilgrim's Progress* (Casebook Series, Macmillan, 1976); Henri Talon, *John Bunyan: The Man and His Works,* translated by Barbara Wall (Harvard, 1951). For a biography of Bunyan, see John Brown, *John Bunyan,* notes and emendations by Frank Mott Harrison (Banner of Truth, 1964).

principle of the allegory: (3) Why does the journey theme seem particularly effective for Bunyan's purposes? (4) What temptations does Christian encounter on the pilgrimage? Is there a special significance to the sequence? (5) About two-thirds of the way through Part I, the narrator is jolted awake, even though he subsequently resumes sleep. What is the significance of his awaking, only to resume sleep? (6) If Mr. Great-heart and Mr. Valiant-for-truth are ideal Christians, how do they differ from Christian and from us? (7) If the allegory depicts a coherent view of the progress of human life to a new and blessed state, how does each episode support this allegorical scheme? (8) What specific values could *The Pilgrim's Progress* hold for the reader who does not share Bunyan's religious convictions?

—Beatrice Batson

JONATHAN SWIFT

Gulliver's Travels
1726

*J*onathan Swift's *Gulliver's Travels* is a masterpiece of satirical literature written in an age rich in satire. Published in 1726, this and Swift's other writings held up a standard of knowledge, common sense, and humane reasoning against the moral obtuseness, windy abstraction, and simple-minded optimism of his day.

Satire as Moral Knowledge

Like all satire, *Gulliver's Travels* presupposes that the world is a battleground, and that the reader understands the norms of good and evil. When a satirical world or character collapses, as Gulliver ultimately does, the breakdown happens because of a massive failure of moral decision-making. In this respect satire differs from tragedy. Tragedy presents a hero or heroine who undergoes suffering entirely out of proportion to his or her failings. The reader shares the struggle of the tragic hero in comprehending the moral world. In satire, by contrast, suffering or absurdity becomes a guide for the

Jonathan Swift (1667–1746); Anglo-Irish satirist and clergyman.

reader but generally remains unperceived—or wrongly perceived—by the characters. Few characters in satire may be considered "heroic."

The theme of human vanity in *Gulliver* is part of a tradition that extends from Ecclesiastes through the Latin satirists, down through Swift, Evelyn Waugh, George Orwell, and Walker Percy. The

Old Testament prophets have strong satirical elements as well. Like satirists, the prophets believed in a moral norm, cast derision on human folly, and above all assumed that the outcome of the battle would determine the course of the future. Christian and Jewish writers are notable in the satirical tradition precisely because their faith provides a standpoint for evaluating the spirit of each age.

An Age Ripe for Satire

Jonathan Swift was born in Ireland in 1667 to English parents. After an unhappy academic career, he joined the English household of the distinguished diplomat Sir William Temple in 1689. This year proved fortunate for Swift, as would later be reflected in *Gulliver's Travels,* for Temple was then criticizing modern thinkers for some of the very tendencies that Gulliver would exhibit.

Ordained a priest in the (Anglican) Church of Ireland in 1695, Swift shortly afterward began writing satires of the "moderns"—*A Tale of a Tub* and *The Battle of the Books* (1704).

From Voyage 2, to Brobdingnag:

The Learning of this People is very defective; consisting only in Morality, History, Poetry and Mathematicks; wherein they must be allowed to excel. But, the last of these is wholly applied to what may be useful in Life; to the Improvement of Agriculture and all mechanical Arts; so that among us it would be little esteemed. And as to Ideas, Entitles, Abstractions and Transcendentals, I could never drive the least Conception into their Heads.

—Gulliver's Travels

These works established his reputation and reputedly ruined his chances for high advancement in the church. He served small Anglican parishes in largely Catholic Ireland, worked on behalf of church causes, and engaged in political journalism until being installed as dean of St. Patrick's Cathedral in Dublin in 1713.

Swift formed his literary friendships with Alexander Pope, John Gay, Thomas Parnell, and other notables, establishing the Scriblerus Club in the 1710s. During the next decade his reputation as an effective apologist for Ireland grew, culminating in the satire *A Modest Proposal* (1729). Swift died in 1745 and is buried in St. Patrick's Cathedral.

As learned societies in London and Dublin optimistically laid the foundations of modern science, they sometimes neglected the human purposes that should attend science. Swift shaped his writing in response to his time—the European Enlightenment, sometimes called the "Age of Reason." In France René Descartes had developed a method of abstract reasoning that ignored the significance of experience and common sense. Swift's satire was directed against rationalism and the contemporary optimism concerning human perfectibility, which omitted any consideration of human sinfulness.

Gulliver's Travels: Voyages into Human Frailty

Swift's work satirizes all of these "modern" tendencies, and nowhere is his bite more powerful than in *Gulliver's Travels*. Lemuel Gulliver shares most of the beliefs and hopes of an Enlightenment European. He recounts his four voyages in first person, the typical perspective of travel literature. This perspective allows Swift to exploit the powerful ironic contrasts between the Enlightenment perceptions of Gulliver and those of a more insightful observer—namely the reader. Although Gulliver's observations suggest many specific shortcomings, his overall failure may serve as an indictment of the Enlightenment generally, pointing up the inability to recognize one's own pride.

The first voyage takes Gulliver to Lilliput, whose inhabitants are one-twelfth his size. The second takes him to Brobdingnag, the land of the giants, who regard Gulliver as Lilliputian in height. Swift's irony partly works in these sections by exploiting the literal differences in size. The large pretensions of the Lilliputians appear ridiculous by virtue of their small stature. Gulliver describes the emperor, for instance, as being "taller by almost the Breadth of my Nail, than any of his Court; which alone is enough to strike an Awe into the Beholders." Similarly, Gulliver's pretensions seem ridiculous in Brobdingnag, where he is mortally threatened by a giant wasp and deeply humiliated by a monstrous frog.

Swift's satire unflinchingly exposes the dark side of national pride, honorific titles, human beauty, and the compromises people make to rationalize cruelty and injustice. In the third voyage, to the floating island of Laputa, Gulliver lives among crazed, abstract reasoners who take his Enlightenment assumptions to exaggerated conclusions. Almost unbelievably, their scientific projects—setting a spider to spin silk stockings and extracting sunbeams from cucumbers, for instance—were actually conducted by members of the Royal Society in London. Even in this voyage, however, Gulliver apparently learns nothing about the limits of human reason and the benefits of traditional ways of life. Like the Laputans, Gulliver is a "modern." He fails to question their expectation that the next technological innovation will forever remove the fundamental problems that face humanity.

In each of the first three voyages, Gulliver adopts the perspective of his hosts at some point with ridiculous but generally harmless consequences. In the fourth voyage, however, to the land of the horses (or "Houyhnhnms," pronounced "whinnums"), the results are disastrous. On the one hand, Gulliver is confronted with the utterly rational lives of the horses, who govern the land. On the other, he sees the complete bestiality of the brutish, human-like apes, the Yahoos, who also live there. The horses live in the manner that Gulliver's "modern" assumptions have told him was appropriate to human beings. He then realizes that such a life is beyond human beings. Never having learned how to question his assumptions, Gulliver can only reject humanity altogether.

Gulliver does not change his views; instead he goes mad. He is unable to choose an alternative Christian view (held by Swift) that acknowledges human rationality while recognizing human depravity and that remembers the corruptions of sin while applauding the advances of science. Instead, Gulliver wrongly concludes that the human beings of his acquaintance are Yahoos. On his return home he prefers to his family the company, conversation, and smell of his English horses.

When Pride Breeds Self-Deception

Although Gulliver's hatred of humanity at the end of his travels should not be taken as Swift's own view—as it was in the nineteenth century—neither should its satire be dismissed. Much of what Gulliver learns about human corruption from the Houyhnhnms is true. A powerful Christian mind (like that of Swift himself) or a secular mind skeptical of secular forms of salvation (like that of George Orwell) can truly appreciate the searching critique of human shortcomings in *Gulliver's Travels*.

For Christians, the searing moral clarity of *Gulliver's Travels* has its parallels in biblical prophecy and wisdom literature. Like the audience of the Hebrew prophets, Gulliver and other characters in the book are capable of the greatest self-deception when they face the most obvious instances of cruelty and greed that ultimately stem from their pride. Lest we become

Gulliver captures the fleet of the Blefuscudians, from an early twentieth-century chromolithograph of *Gulliver's Travels*.

> [I]nstead of seeing a full Stop put to all Abuses and Corruptions, at least in this little Island, as I had Reason to expect: Behold, after above six Months Warning, I cannot learn that my Book hath produced one single Effect according to mine Intentions.
>
> —Letter from Capt. Gulliver to his cousin Sympson

From Voyage 2, to Brobdingnag:

*As for yourself (continued the King {of Brobdingnag})
who have spent the greatest Part of your Life in
travelling; I am well disposed to hope you may hitherto
have escaped many Vices of your Country. But, by what I
have gathered from your own Relation, and the Answers
I have with much Pains wringed and extorted from you;
I cannot but conclude the bulk of your Natives, to be the
most pernicious Race of little odious vermin that Nature
ever suffered to crawl upon the Surface of the Earth.*

—*Gulliver's Travels*

complacent, however, the "gentle reader" of
Gulliver's Travels is forced to examine his or her
own pretensions, no less than the reader of the
Old Testament.

Issues to Explore

When reading Swift's rich satire, one should
bear the following questions in mind: (1) The
irony of *Gulliver's Travels* depends on the
reader's ability to sense the gap between Gulliver's faulty impressions and an agreed-upon—
but often unstated—moral norm, which the
reader shares with Swift. What are some examples of this gap? What do we learn from the
humorous presentation of this gap? (2) What
character or description within each voyage
seems to be morally normative? What is Gulliver's reaction? (3) What is the difference

For Further Study

Gulliver's Travels is an enormously funny
book, especially when read aloud to a
group of students or friends. Its language is simple, and it is often taught in
high school. The Norton Critical Edition
of *Gulliver's Travels*, edited by Robert
Greenberg (1970), contains a wide
variety of excellent critical essays as well
as Swift's relevant correspondence. The
Riverside Edition of *Gulliver's Travels*
(Houghton Mifflin, 1960) has good notes
and a useful introduction by Louis Landa.

The standard biography of Swift is the
three-volume *Swift: The Man, His Works,
and the Age* (Harvard, 1962–83) by Irvin
Ehrenpreis. Richard Quintana's biographical works, *Swift: An Introduction*
(Oxford, 1955) and *The Mind and Art of
Jonathan Swift* (Oxford, 1936), are still
held in high esteem as well. Frank
Brady's *Twentieth Century Interpretations
of Gulliver's Travels* (Prentice-Hall, 1968)
is a useful collection of critical essays. A
more recent collection, edited by Claude
Rawson, is *The Character of Swift's Satire*
(Delaware, 1983).

between the mental anguish that afflicts Gulliver (especially in the final voyage and the
"Letter from Captain Gulliver") and that of a
tragic figure such as Job, Oedipus, or King
Lear?

—Daniel E. Ritchie

JONATHAN EDWARDS

A Treatise Concerning Religious Affections 1746

*J*onathan Edwards's *A Treatise Concerning Religious Affections* is a masterful and influential analysis of religious emotions, written with extraordinary theological profundity, philosophical skill, and psychological astuteness. Along with the English pastor George Whitefield, Edwards was instrumental in bringing about the Great Awakening of the 1700s. He was a brilliant preacher and theologian who was especially concerned that believers practice true religion. Although he was deeply philosophical he manifested a childlike piety. And though he wrote about subtle, complex, and profound matters, he was able to communicate the gospel simply. *A Treatise Concerning Religious Affections* reflects his unique combination of gifts.

Thomas Chalmers (1780–1847), Scotland's greatest preacher of his era, was especially aided by this provincial New England pastor of the previous century. Reflecting on Edwards's remarkable qualities, he wrote: "he affords, perhaps, the most wondrous example in modern times of

Jonathan Edwards (1703–1758), by Amos Doolittle, after Joseph Badger, 1793.

one richly gifted both in natural and in spiritual discernment; and we know not what most to admire in him."

A Communicator of Divine Glory

Jonathan Edwards (1703–1758) was the only son in the large family of a New England clergyman. He graduated from Yale

College at age sixteen and then studied theology privately for several years. During that period he underwent a conversion that he later described in a "Personal Narrative." This account of a young man's gradual awakening to the greatness of God became immensely influential when it was published after his death. As he put it in that narrative with characteristic emphasis, "there came into my soul, and was diffused through it, a sense of the glory of the Divine Being." To communicate this divine glory became the burden of his life as pastor and theologian.

Edwards served briefly as the minister of a Presbyterian church in New York City (1722–23) and a tutor at Yale College (1724–26) before beginning his long association with the Congregationalist church in Northampton, Massachusetts, in 1726. Under Edwards, Northampton experienced waves of revivals: first in 1734–35, after he preached a series of sermons on justification by faith, and again in 1740–42, in the wake of a visit from the passionate preacher George Whitefield.

[I]t is God's manner of dealing with men, to lead them into a wilderness, before he speaks comfortably to them, and so to order it, that they shall be brought into distress, and made to see their own helplessness, and absolute dependence on his power and grace, before he appears to work any great deliverance for them.

—A Treatise Concerning Religious Affections

In 1750 Edwards was dismissed from his charge in Northampton when he offended prominent members of the community by insisting that their children make their own coherent statement of personal faith before being admitted as full members. Thereafter he lived with his large family in frontier Stockbridge, Massachusetts. Here he preached to Native Americans and was pastor of a small English congregation while also writing many of the treatises for which he won theological renown. Edwards died from an inoculation against small pox on March 22, 1758, only weeks after answering a call to become the president of Princeton College in New Jersey.

The unifying center of Edwards's concern was the glory of God. The dynamic activity of the Godhead, especially as manifest in the Trinity, was ever in the forefront of his work. Against the eighteenth-century optimism about an ever-improving world, Edwards defended Augustinian convictions about the lostness of humanity and the need for divine grace to initiate the process of redemption. Yet in tune with the spirit of his age, Edwards also promoted a view of reality in which "the sense of the heart" (one of his favorite phrases) was foundational for thought and action alike.

As a revivalist, Edwards shared the burden of Whitefield for the conversion of the lost. As a promoter of holiness, he shared—despite major philosophical and theological differences—points of contact with John Wesley, who edited some of Edwards's writings for publication in Britain. But as a Christian thinker, Edwards most resembled his near contemporaries, the Catholic French philosopher Nicholas de Malebranche and the Anglican philosopher George Berkeley, who also developed forms of theistic idealism in response to the materialist drift of their age.

That perspective was fleshed out in a series of works that are still studied today. Edwards edited the diary of a young missionary, David Brainerd, whose intense self-examination and exultant spirituality established a model for later Protestant piety. In 1754 he published *Freedom of the Will,* which defended traditional Calvinism with arguments drawn from the eighteenth century. A twofold work, published posthumously in 1765, revealed Edwards's fullest thoughts on the nature of the good life. *The Nature of True Virtue* reveals the difference between doing right because it is practical and prudent and doing right for God's glory alone. And *The End for Which God Created the World* mines the Scriptures to show that pursuing the glory of God is the proper goal for all existence.

The Great Awakening and *Religious Affections*

From Edwards's earliest involvement with the revival of his own congregation he pondered how to distinguish true religion from its artful counterfeits. The task grew doubly urgent when in the flush of New England's Great Awakening (1740–42) some of the revival's friends verged off into enthusiastic excesses, such as burning books and conducting riotous public meetings. Detractors quickly seized on these excesses to condemn the Awakening as a whole.

Edwards defended the Awakening and examined the best and worst of religious experience in two earlier works—*Narrative of Surprising Conversions* and *Some Thoughts Concerning the Present Revival.* But his most mature examination of the subject is *A Treatise Concerning the Religious Affections.* It has been likened, with justice, to William James's *Varieties of Religious Experience* because of its acute examination of the psychology of religion. In his treatise Edwards argues that true religion resides in the heart, or the seat of affections, emotions, and inclinations. A major portion of the volume is given to painstaking scrutiny of religious

Jonathan Edwards's home in Northampton, Massachusetts.

behaviors that are largely irrelevant to determining true spirituality.

Truly religious affections, he affirms, are shown through solidly rooted "marks" or signs. The first of these is religious affection (or inner turning) arising "from those influences and operations on the heart, which are spiritual, supernatural and divine"—that is, which come from God rather than from a human source. Other "marks" of truly Christian inclination are a sense of "evangelical humility," a concern for "excellence of divine things," a manifestation of "the temper of Jesus," a softening of the heart, and a "beautiful symmetry and proportion" in attitudes and actions. The last and most definite of the signs is long-term faithfulness in Christian practice for the glory of God. Edwards's analysis, in sum, emphasizes that presence of true spirituality is not indicated by the quantity of emotion, but by the origin of such emotion with God and its outworking in a life styled in conformity with God's being.

The Heart of True Religion

Edwards often cuts too close for comfort in his analysis of what does *not* count as true religion, even now after more than two centuries. Today we live in an age that gives too much attention to the quality of feelings, especially "comfort" with an idea or a situation. We also place a great deal of stock in "performance." We are prone to value the glib over the conflicted, the polished over the uncouth, the professional over the amateur. In other words, we are as eager in our own way as the would-be Christians of Edwards's day to mistake surface appearances for inner realities.

If Edwards poses a stiff challenge to transient, self-deluding spirituality, so too does his guide to genuine religion. *Religious Affections* is a sharp reminder—nearly unparalleled in Western literature—of where the heart of true religion resides. As Edwards describes it, the heart of religion is precisely the heart. Moreover, the heart is not abstracted from day-to-day reality but is everywhere in touch with that reality; and not for one glowing moment only, but for a lifetime.

This picture of true religion is demanding indeed. But Edwards would say that it is not an impossible ideal, because the God whose standards are so high has also bent low to us in

Affections that are truly spiritual and gracious, do arise from those influences and operations on the heart, which are spiritual, supernatural, and divine.

—*A Treatise Concerning Religious Affections*

'Tis no sign one way or the other {of the presence of true religion}, that religious affections are very great, or raised very high.

—*A Treatise Concerning Religious Affections*

the beauty of his Son. Understanding that beauty is the key to Edwards's closing injunction in this great work: "We should get into the way of appearing lively in religion, more by being lively in the service of God and our generation, than by the liveliness and forwardness of our tongues, and making a business of proclaiming on the house tops, with our mouths, the holy and eminent acts and exercises of our own hearts."

Issues to Explore

(1) How does Edwards distinguish between true and false religion? Does he emphasize the most important things for that discrimination? (2) How would Edwards respond to someone who holds that the essence of religion is ethical, moral behavior? (3) What connections can you draw between Edwards's own life (with its dramatic moments and its occasions of strife) and his religious thought? (4) Is it possible to go overboard in seeking the kind of true religion of the heart that Edwards promoted? (5) Edwards stands at the head of the revival tradition in American history. How has that tradition lived up to Edwards's teachings, or where could it be improved by taking Edwards more seriously?

—Mark A. Noll

For Further Study

The best text with the most helpful critical tools has been prepared by John E. Smith as the second volume in the Yale edition of *The Works of Edwards* (Yale, 1959). Cheaper texts are available from several publishers including the Banner of Truth Trust.

Introductions and notes to the Yale edition, which now includes more than a dozen volumes, provide the best guides to Edwards. Of several good one-volume anthologies, the best two are edited by Harry S. Stout in connection with the Yale edition (1995), and C. H. Faust and T. H. Johnson, *Representative Selections with Introduction, Bibliography, and Notes* (revised, Hill and Wang, 1962). Nathan O. Hatch and Harry S. Stout, editors, *Jonathan Edwards and the American Experience* (Oxford, 1988), collect important articles; Norman Fiering's *Jonathan Edwards's Moral Thought and Its British Context* (University of North Carolina Press, 1981) is an outstanding intellectual history for the questions that led to *Religious Affections*. Edwin Scott Gaustad's *The Great Awakening in New England* (Harper & Bros., 1957) remains a fine study. Harold P. Simonson's *Jonathan Edwards: Theologian of the Heart* (Eerdmans, 1974) is an excellent all-around introduction.

SAMUEL JOHNSON

Essays and *Rasselas*
1759

JAMES BOSWELL

The Life of Samuel Johnson, LL.D.
1791

*S*amuel Johnson is the dominant literary figure of mid-eighteenth-century England, partly because of his moral essays, poetry, and prayers, as well as his *Dictionary of the English Language* and *Lives of the English Poets,* and partly because he was the subject of a uniquely fascinating biography—*The Life of Samuel Johnson, LL.D.* by James Boswell.

By themselves, Johnson's essays and his philosophical romance, *Rasselas,* constitute the most searching body of Christian moral reflection between Blaise PASCAL in the seventeenth century and Søren KIERKEGAARD in the nineteenth. But Johnson is even better known because of Boswell's biography, which historian Thomas Macaulay pronounced the best biography ever written. Through it "Dr. Johnson"—or the biography's overwhelming cartoon of him—has become as much a classic as his

Johnson and Boswell return home after a night on the town; caricature by Rowlandson.

writings. His wisdom—and idiosyncrasies—are known to millions who have never read *Rasselas* or the essays.

A Prodigy of English Letters

Born in Lichfield, England, in 1709, the son of an unsuccessful bookseller, Johnson demonstrated a precocious intelligence early in his life, but left Oxford University without completing his degree when his money ran out. He worked all his life as a freelance writer in the London literary market, mastering all the genres—translation, biography, poetry, political pamphlets and parliamentary reports, fiction, drama, criticism, sermons, and travel books. He composed three volumes of letters and a set of incomparable prayers. The twentieth-century philosopher Ludwig Wittgenstein called these prayers the most "human" writing he knew and gave copies of them to his friends. In an age of great conversationalists, which included Edmund

Truth, such as is necessary to the regulation of life, is always to be found where it is honestly sought.

—*Rasselas*

Burke and John Wesley, Johnson was recognized as supreme in that art. As one friend said, "How he does talk! Every sentence is an essay."

Johnson compiled his celebrated *Dictionary of the English Language* in seven years, working alone except for secretarial help. It set the standard of usage for a century and made him famous across Europe. When Lord Chesterfield tendered a belated offer of patronage as a way to climb into Johnson's spotlight, Johnson fought him off with a notorious letter. Then, unexpectedly, he poured out his heart in his preface to the *Dictionary:* "Most of those whom I wished to please have sunk into the grave. . . ."

These deep friendships, sparkling conversations, enormous intellectual labor, and poignant personal revelation are Johnson's hallmarks. He never lived in an ivory tower, but rather intended his writing to serve his community. Nor did he ever detach his character and feelings from his work.

Johnson's Essays: Wisdom Literature

Besides the *Dictionary,* Johnson is best known for his essays, such as those in *The Rambler,* published twice weekly between 1750 and 1752 (a total of 208 essays). Johnson considered these his favorite work ("pure wine" he told Boswell). Unlike newspaper columns, the *Ramblers* seldom discuss contemporary events. Instead they concern moral topics—the questions, duties, and urgencies of living. Some of the *Ramblers* are parables; some literary criticism. In most, however, Johnson pondered a general topic of the moral life. He contributed similarly to *The Adventurer* (1753–54) and *The Idler* (1758–60).

These essays are not always easy to read. Johnson's style is dignified, sober, often somber, meticulous, and reflective. Sometimes the essays tell stories about people Johnson observed. Under fictional names ("Hilarius," "Mrs. Busy"), Johnson explores the lives of people his polite readers might neglect, such as a prostitute or a "modish lady" miserable in her isolation.

Johnson's essays fall into the category of "wisdom literature." They teach what Johnson called "the regulation of common life"—how to live in a moral and sensible way. The essays draw on biblical and classical sources, including Aristotle, Cicero, and Horace. Where the two traditions conflict—as in the Stoic counsel to ignore pain—Johnson explains why the Christian counsel is better. We should bear pain with love and patience, he says, not because it is Christian to do so, but because it is more practical and humane.

Wisdom writings have traditionally been divided into two kinds, and Johnson treats both. One category is concerned with practical wisdom, prudence, good sense; in this vein, various *Ramblers* focus on marriage, business, and schooling. The other is spiritual wisdom, knowing what goodness is and how to attain it; with these ends in view, other *Ramblers* treat hope, selfishness, egotism, and repentance.

Although Johnson addresses moral subjects, he seldom preaches. He often begins by stating a general rule—we "should never suffer [our] happiness to depend upon external circumstances." He then investigates why this maxim became a rule, considers whether it is reasonable and possible to obey it, and explores the difficulty of putting it into practice. Sometimes the essays are startlingly modern in their psychology. Their explorations of anxiety and our disguises for immoral motives have been compared to Freudian analysis.

Perhaps more than any other theme, Johnson returns to hope and its frustrations. We always seem to imagine more than we can eat, do, or control, he points out; consequently we are disappointed. Here, however, Johnson shows pity and realism. He points out that hope itself is a kind of happiness. And we can learn to hope for things that will not disappoint us.

Samuel Johnson (1709–1784), English lexicographer, writer, critic, conversationalist. After portrait by Sir Joshua Reynolds.

A Fable of False Hope versus Truth

In 1759 Johnson wrote—in the evenings of one week, he tells us—a short "novel" about an Ethiopian prince named Rasselas. The book is too exotic and too little interested in setting and plot to be a real novel. Rather it is a fable, a story told for the purpose of its moral.

At the start, Rasselas is cooped up with his brothers and sisters in a place known as Happy Valley—a utopia of pleasure and quiet where the young prince must stay until he succeeds his father as emperor. Desperate to see the world, however, Rasselas escapes with his sister and tutor. Wealthy and cultivated, the travelers are able to investigate many realms with little difficulty. Everywhere they pose the same question: What is the perfectly happy life? Everything they see leads to the same answer, that no perfect "choice of life" exists. As Johnson writes in conclusion, "human life is a state where there is much to be endured and little to be enjoyed."

Much has been made of the gloom of Johnson's story. He is credited with a "tragic" view of life. But *Rasselas* is not a tragedy; rather it falls in the tradition of the wise and sober Ecclesiastes. The fable suggests that if people expect money, fame, beauty, political power, or length of life to make them perfectly and permanently happy, they will be disappointed. Yet the lesson of this revelation is hopeful: "Truth . . . is always to be found where it is honestly sought." Mortals can learn to bear disappointment with love, constructive work, and the hope of heaven.

> *His mind resembled the vast amphitheater, the Coliseum in Rome. In the centre stood his judgment, which, like a mighty gladiator, combated those apprehensions that, like the wild beasts of the Arena, were all around in cells, ready to be let out at him.*
>
> —*The Life of Samuel Johnson, LL.D.*

Pour forth thy fervours for a healthful mind,
Obedient passions, and a will resign'd.

—*Vanity of Human Wishes,* 1749

Boswell and *The Life of Samuel Johnson, LL.D.*

Because Johnson was one of the most famous people of his time, several biographies of him were written before his death, and more soon after. The finest is undoubtedly that of Johnson's Scottish friend, James Boswell. It provides a detailed and moving picture of Johnson, through which the great man seems vitally alive in its pages.

Most of the familiar Johnson stories come from Boswell. Here is Johnson the great talker of "the Club"; Johnson sleeping until noon, muttering under his breath, sticking his fingers in the pudding; Johnson roaming the London streets, "tossing and goring" people with his wit, putting pennies in the hands of homeless children as they sleep; Johnson crying out that he is terrified of death.

Boswell drew the biography from a lifelong journal, which is a classic in its own right. Unpublished until the twentieth century, its appearance has raised doubts about the reliability of the biography. The journal reveals the way in which Boswell fleshed out notes of events and conversations to mold them for his purposes. Is his Johnson an accurate portrayal or merely a half-fictional creation?

Boswell's Johnson does indeed deviate at times from the man of Johnson's own work—exaggerating, for instance, his respect for authority in politics and religion. But what we find in Boswell is generally compatible with what we read in Johnson. In the end, then, we have two Johnsons, both invaluable: the Johnson of the *Ramblers* and *Rasselas,* whose wisdom has become "a permanent part of the conscience of mankind," and the Johnson of Boswell's *Life,* a wise and powerful presence from the past.

Celebrities of eighteenth-century England at Tunbridge Wells, Kent; Samuel Johnson is in front of the second pillar on the left. From a print published in London, 1904.

For Further Study

A selection of Johnson's essays, drawn from the enormous Yale edition of all his work, is *Selected Essays from the Rambler, Adventurer, and Idler,* W. J. Bate, editor (Yale, 1968). The prayers, free of nineteenth-century censorship, can be found in *Dr. Johnson's Prayers,* edited by Elton Trueblood (Prinit Press, 1980). *The Story of Rasselas, Prince of Abissinia,* edited by D. J. Enright, is available from Viking Penguin (1976).

Modern biographies of Johnson include those by James Clifford (Heinemann/McGraw-Hill, 1955, 1979), John Wain (Macmillan, 1974, 1980), and W. J. Bate (Harcourt Brace Jovanovich, 1977). Donald Greene's *Samuel Johnson* (Twayne English Authors Series, 1989) is a fine introduction to all of Johnson's writing. The best commentary on Johnson as a moralist, however, is still W. J. Bate's *The Achievement of Samuel Johnson* (Oxford, 1955).

The standard edition of *The Life of Samuel Johnson, LL.D.,* edited in six volumes by L. F. Powell (Oxford, 1934, 1950), may be found in many libraries. Two good paperback abridgments have been published by NAL-Dutton (1968) and Viking Penguin (1979). All the many volumes of Boswell's journal, originally published by McGraw-Hill, are now out of print. Boswell's own life has been written by Frederick Pottle and Frank Brady (McGraw-Hill, 1984).

Issues to Explore

Reading Samuel Johnson or reading about Johnson can be very rewarding. Among questions to ask in the process are the following: (1) Setting aside the hope of heaven, what does Johnson see as goals or strengths that people may reasonably hope for in this life? (2) What kinds of truth are "always to be found" in the ordinary course of life? What kinds—philosophical, scientific, political, ethical, imaginative—do we most need? (3) Johnson thought that biography was the most pleasurable and profitable form of writing because the stories of what human beings have done and suffered always "come home to us." What uses can we make of such stories of the past, including the story of Johnson himself? (4) Is Johnson right to conclude, in *Rasselas,* that we typically "choose our lives" by chance without knowing what will ultimately, or rationally, be the best choice to make?

—Lionel Basney

Western Social and Political Philosophy

Three centuries of influential political writing from the 1600s through the 1800s have contributed decisively to the rise of the modern world. One defining feature of this age is the increasing drive of political philosophers to replace the Christian faith with a new authority, the natural sciences. The leading thinkers and their works are pivotal in themselves, but they also raise important issues for Christians. Their political philosophies, often identified with modernity, undermined the previous Christian foundation for justice and a well-ordered society. The main ideas of this period incorporate the rise of science, the social contract, the Enlightenment, and the ideologies of the nineteenth century.

René Descartes (1596–1650), author of *Discourse on Method* (1637).

Science as the Starting Point

The scientific revolution of the sixteenth and seventeenth centuries had a profound impact on the social and political thought of the day. Two of the most important works of this period are Francis Bacon's *The New Organon* (1620) and René Descartes's *Discourse on Method* (1637). In the *Organon,* Bacon (1561–1626), an English politician as well as scientist, presents his inductive scientific method that advocates the study of experience to reach a general conclusion. He claims: "We must begin anew from the very foundations, unless we would revolve forever in a circle with mean and contemptible progress." His series of aphorisms (short, pungent assertions) is quite readable.

Like his contemporary Bacon, the French philosopher Descartes

> *It is idle to expect any great advancement in science from the superinducing and engrafting of new things upon old. We must begin again anew from the very foundations, unless we would revolve forever in a circle with mean and contemptible progress.*
>
> —Francis Bacon
> *The New Organon*

(1596–1650) also believed that a new foundation for human knowledge had to be found. In his *Discourse* he gives a brief autobiographical account of how his method of reasoning formed the foundation for his philosophical system: "Since this truth, *Cogito ergo sum* (I think, therefore I am), was so firm and assured . . . I judged that I could safely accept it as the first principle of the philosophy I was seeking."

Two key terms associated with the thought of Descartes are *dualism* and *rationalism*. The former refers to his division of reality into two substances, mind (or spirit) and body (or matter). The mind, the home of thought and self-reflection, is free and based on the self-knowledge of the thinking person. But body or matter is subject to mechanistic laws knowable to reason unaided by revelation. Rationalism, then, refers to the perspective that everything in the visible world can be explained by reason as the result of mechanical causes. Thus Cartesian rationalism expelled mystery and miracle from the language of science.

Descartes was concerned with how his *cogito* could square with traditional Catholic theology; the net effect of Baconian empirical science and Cartesian rationalism, however, was to deal a heavy blow to the classical tradition of natural law beginning with ARISTOTLE and to Christian theology in general. Classical natural law taught that a moral law, knowable by properly trained human reason, held the world of politics and society together. This tradition, when wedded to Christian theology by the work of such medieval theologians as AQUINAS, came to

serve as the foundation for the study of law, politics, ethics, and theology. Reason and revelation worked together as regulative principles, being the "two books" whereby people knew how they ought to live their lives. Consequently, the scientific revolution's challenge to Aristotle in the fields of natural and moral-political philosophy formed a two-front campaign that was much more than a mere intellectual contest. The very character and shape of Western society—and the public place of religion within that society—was at issue.

The Social Contract

The first development of the new learning in political thought was the social contract. Between 1651 and 1762 five major political thinkers explored this idea of an agreement between individuals to form a society with rights and duties clearly defined for both the community and the ruler.

The first was Thomas Hobbes (1588–1679), who was directly influenced by Descartes. In his *Leviathan* (1651) he applies the new learning to the political situation in an England whose foundations had been rocked by civil war. He employs the biblical metaphor of the Leviathan ("nothing on earth is his equal," Job 41:33) to argue that human security can rest only under an absolute political sovereign who also controls religious affairs. In this massive volume Hobbes dismantles both the classical natural law tradition (parts I and II) and traditional Christian theology (parts III and IV). Though his writing is dense and difficult to understand,

In such a condition there is . . . worst of all, continual fear and danger of violent death, and the life of man, solitary, poor, nasty, brutish, and short.

—Thomas Hobbes
Leviathan

it has been nonetheless highly influential in later thought.

On the continent, the Dutch philosopher Benedict Spinoza (1632–1677) extended Hobbes's argument for a natural right to self-preservation to that of a natural right to self-fulfillment through discovering God's presence in and around us. The father of pantheism, Spinoza renounced the Cartesian dichotomy of mind and matter in favor of a thoroughgoing mechanistic materialism; for him God, nature, and the universe were one. He offered his *Treatise on Religious and Political Philosophy* (1670) as an encouragement to those "who would philosophize more freely if they were not prevented by this one thought: that reason must be the handmaid of theology."

Back in England, John Locke (1632–1704) in his *Two Treatises of Government* (1690) modified Hobbes's account by employing the language—though not the substance—of traditional natural law. Believing in the natural goodness of people, he advocated that the state operate on the natural laws of reason and toleration—including religious toleration. Thus Locke contributed

But I soon noticed that while I thus wished to think everything false, it was necessarily true that I who thought so was something. Since this truth, I think, therefore I am, *was so firm and assured that all the most extravagant suppositions of the skeptics were unable to shake it, I judged that I could safely accept it as the first principle of the philosophy I was seeking.*

—René Descartes
Discourse on Method
Laurence J. Lafleur, trans.

to the American concept of the separation of church and state. In his brief *A Letter Concerning Toleration* (1690), he claims: "[T]here is absolutely no such thing under the Gospel as a Christian commonwealth."

These secularizing tendencies of social-contract thought were reinforced in the eighteenth century by the skepticism of David Hume (1711–1776) and the romanticism of Jean-Jacques ROUSSEAU (1712–1778). Hume's "Of the Original Contract" appeared in 1748. In it he argues against Locke's notion of a social contract based on natural law, though he accepts Locke's view that society should be understood merely as the effort to secure the individual's private property. Rousseau in *The Social Contract* (1762) contends that justice and morality cannot be limited to traditional Christian understandings. Rather he stresses the complete freedom of the human will to create the values by which to live.

In each case the religious affiliations of these thinkers is critical: Hobbes and Hume were considered atheists; Spinoza was a leading proponent of pantheism; Descartes a skeptical Catholic; and

Locke a Unitarian. These positions determined their attempt to provide a secular basis for their models and to bypass Christian theology and traditional scriptural interpretations.

But, overall, the combined effect of these social-contract writings was breathtaking in its importance. In the United States (influenced directly by Locke and Hume) this body of thought led to the establishment of a constitutional system that, for all its achievements, sometimes encourages a rootless and materialistic individualism. On the European continent (influenced more by Spinoza and Rousseau), social-contract theory has supported an equally materialistic but collectivist tendency.

The Enlightenment

A second development of the scientific turn in political thought occurred in the latter eighteenth century with the philosophical and cultural movement that called itself the Enlightenment. Principal political and economic thinkers of this group include Charles de Montesquieu (1689–1755), Adam

Smith (1723–1790), Immanuel Kant (1724–1804), and Jeremy Bentham (1748–1832). Much of the thinking of this period worked toward creating a "science of man" modeled after the natural sciences, one that promised social progress through the expansion of personal liberty and the increase of material wealth. By this time most social and political thought assumed a nonreligious starting point.

Montesquieu in his huge and rambling *The Spirit of the Laws* (1748) sounds some of these themes by a systematic, orderly, and comprehensive presentation of law. He sees law as the essential condition governing all of life and ordering "the necessary relations deriving from the nature of things." His view reflects the belief that all human relations are determined by certain observable laws similar to the laws of physics that rule falling bodies. Discovering these human laws and arranging society accordingly became the central aspiration of this period.

The Enlightenment confidence in human progress through scientific knowledge is seen in Adam Smith's *Wealth of Nations* (1776). Here and in his *Theory of Moral Sentiments* (1759) Smith rests social progress on the idea of the "invisible hand" of a free-market economy that maximizes wealth through dynamically guiding self-interest. Thus, although Smith was a Christian believer and a deeply moral man, his theory of the economic sciences replaces the will of God with the "invisible hand" of the market as the authoritative guide in determining the just and the good.

Jeremy Bentham applied the same concern to the area of law. In

Immanuel Kant (1724–1804), author of *Critique of Pure Reason* (1781).

(literally "dare to be wise") as the motto of the Enlightenment, meaning the willingness and moral courage individuals should possess to think for themselves apart from any institutions of authority and tradition.

Age of Ideology

The third great development in modern political thought occurred in the nineteenth century, the "Age of Ideology." Political thinkers of the time sought to advance the Enlightenment project by means of specific political ideologies that were understood as a system of political philosophy. The most important were the nationalism of G. W. F. Hegel (1770–1831), the liberalism of John Stuart Mill (1806–1873), and the communism of Karl Marx (1818–1883).

In his *Philosophy of Law* (1821) and *Philosophy of History* (1824) Hegel rejects the abstractness of Kant's metaphysical system in order to ground human freedom in the state. For him the state is the source of all spiritual reality, the "Divine Idea as it exists on Earth." The result is a powerful philosophical boost for nationalism.

In his *On Liberty* (1859) Mill

his *Introduction to the Principles of Morals and Legislation* (1789) he claims, "Nature has placed mankind under the governance of two sovereign masters, pain and pleasure." For him the key to social progress is to structure legislation and the enforcement of morals so that the "principle of utility" or "the greatest happiness of the greatest number" can be achieved.

Kant, the great figure of the Enlightenment, defined this period as "man's emergence from his self-incurred immaturity." He was more concerned with philosophy than politics (see his *Critique of Pure Reason* of 1781), but strongly supported the Enlightenment dream of freedom and peace in his *Idea of a Universal History* (1784) and *Perpetual Peace* (1795). Influenced by Rousseau and following the principles of the American and French revolutions,

Kant grounded the rights of the common person on his portrayal of a secular natural order, the order of right based on principles of pure reason. As a modern he possessed great hope that the progress of science and philosophy would usher in a universal and cosmopolitan age of perpetual peace and justice. He invoked the ancient Latin motto *Sapere aude*

To understand political power right, and derive it from its original, we must consider, what state all men are naturally in, and that is, a state of perfect freedom, to order their actions, and dispose of their possessions and persons, as they think fit, within the bounds of the law of nature, without asking leave, or depending upon the will of any other men.

—John Locke
Second Treatise of Government

For Further Study

Excellent, up-to-date versions of each of the texts mentioned can be found through either the current Cambridge University series, Texts in the History of Political Thought, or the Hackett Publishing Company, which specializes in philosophical literature.

For a brief and helpful survey of the scientific literature of the scientific revolution, consult Michael R. Matthews, editor, *The Scientific Background to Modern Philosophy* (Hackett, 1989). A fuller and richer account is E. A. Burtt's *The Metaphysical Foundations of Modern Science* (Doubleday, 1952).

An engaging and readable source for the Enlightenment is Peter Gay's aptly subtitled *The Enlightenment: An Interpretation; the Rise of Modern Paganism* (Knopf, 1966).

The literature of the age of ideology period can be quite engaging in its direct dealing with political issues of the day. Both Marx and Mill make for stirring and thought-provoking reading. Hegel is much more difficult. For a readable collection that includes thin volumes on each of these authors, see Oxford University's Past Masters series.

For the literature of American political thought, which is usually straightforward and readable, consult Michael Levy's *Political Thought in America: An Anthology,* second edition (Waveland Press, 1988).

---

makes a moving appeal for a very different idea: the maximization of individual freedom. He pushes the idea of absolute freedom to its furthest limits while remaining within the bounds of a constitutional order: "the sole end for which mankind are warranted, individually or collectively, in interfering with the liberty of action of any of their number, is self-protection."

Marx's idea is most revolutionary of all. Claiming to have "stood Hegel on his head," he rejected Hegel's idealist nationalism for what he called "scientific socialism." In his most famous work, *The Communist Manifesto* (1848), Marx proclaims, "Communists everywhere support every revolutionary movement against the existing social and political order of things." Seeing religion as an instrument of oppression, Marx represents the Enlightenment project in its fullest secular and, finally, atheistic form.

—Ashley Woodiwiss

A Note on American Political Thinking of the Period

The history of American political thought from 1776–1865 can be understood as the effort to balance the modern promise of liberty with the order necessary for social life. Though decisive in the United States, the American framers, such as Thomas Jefferson and James Madison, are closely tied to their European counterparts. Two important later Americans who reflect this tension in the mid-nineteenth century are Henry David Thoreau (1817–1862) and Abraham Lincoln (1809–1865). Thoreau in *Civil Disobedience* (1849) celebrates the idea "that government is best which governs not at all"; Lincoln, in contrast, in his Inaugural Addresses (1861, 1865) wrestled with the divine meaning of democracy. It is ironic but perhaps symptomatic of the period that Lincoln, a nonordained political office-holder, would become America's greatest public theologian.

JEAN-JACQUES ROUSSEAU

Confessions
1781, 1788

*J*ean-Jacques Rousseau (1712–1778), forerunner of the French Revolution, father of romanticism, author of the influential political tract *The Social Contract* and of the educational program second only to Plato's—*Émile or On Education*—also wrote a shockingly frank autobiography. Rousseau's *Confessions*, the recollections of his first fifty-three years (1712–65), radically departs from Christian confessional literature that began with St. AUGUSTINE's great autobiographical work. Published only after his death, at his insistence, Rousseau's *Confessions* disclosed intimate details about his life, allowing him to vindicate himself against circulating charges and then to cite the even worse sins of his detractors.

Seeing himself as heroic, both a lover and a teacher of humanity, Rousseau opens his candid twelve-book memoir with the modest claim that he has "resolved on an enterprise which has no precedent, and which, once complete, will have no imitator." Factual details provide the backdrop for the more important reality—his feelings. To read the

Jean-Jacques Rousseau (1712–1778); aquatint by Pierre Michel Alix after portrait by Jean Francois Garneray.

Confessions is to understand the introspective, self-absorbed, exhibitionist, and psychology-centered modern world that Rousseau helped to initiate.

Read Thyself

What is the power of the work? The *Confessions* has profoundly influenced biographical, psychological, and fictional explorations of the self. Leo TOLSTOY, like many others, examined himself in light

of Rousseau's *Confessions*. Rousseau intended his personal revelations to be a new sacred writing, a paradigm for sensitive souls. Portraying himself as an innocent, a witness to humanity's inherent goodness, he unveiled his heart as the authoritative script of human meaning. The intense subjectivity of the work provides a lens through which to interpret the objective meaning of his political writings, particularly *Émile* (1762) and *The Social Contract* (1762).

Rousseau followed the lead of Thomas Hobbes, the seventeenth-century political philosopher, who replaced Socrates' "Know thyself" with "Read thyself." He completed the modern reversal of the classical and Christian view that reason should order the passions. Because the passions are more powerful than reason and truly natural to human beings, Rousseau claimed, they dictate how we feel about—not know—the world. In Rousseau's view, reason serves existence only secondarily; it allows one to discern or "read" the human impulses that write the script of one's life.

I have only one faithful guide on which I can count: the succession of feelings which have marked the development of my being. . . . The true object of my confessions is to reveal my inner thoughts exactly in all the situations of my life. It is the history of my soul that I have promised to recount, and to write it faithfully I have need of no other memories; it is enough if I enter again into my inner self. . . .

—*Confessions*
J. M. Cohen, trans.

Early Years

A Swiss, who was born in Geneva and brought up Calvinist, Rousseau lost his mother to fever soon after his birth. He presents her as a prototype of Sophy in *Émile,* a figure of feminine simplicity, virtue, and intelligence—in contrast to the Parisian women he comes to abhor. During his first eleven years, Rousseau lived in his imagination. His father, an unsuccessful watchmaker, swung from tear-filled extremes of love and anger toward his son. The emotion surrounding his early years grew as Jean-Jacques devoured all the romances from his mother's library at the age of seven. These primers filled Rousseau with the "strangest and most romantic notions of human life, which neither experience nor reflection" could rectify.

Romance novels were superseded by political biography, however, when Rousseau discovered Plutarch's *Lives.* Moved by patriotism, he wrote, "I took fire by his example and pictured myself as a Greek or a Roman." Figures of romantic love and ancient political greatness thus inform his views of sexual relations in the private realm and patriotism in the public realm.

At sixteen Jean-Jacques began his life of wandering. Neglectful of the time one evening, he was locked outside the city gates. The future "solitary walker" decided to leave Geneva and strike out on his own. The difficulty with his choice, however, was that he had no guidance to obtain true "moral freedom." As he explains in *Émile,* "The first of all goods is not authority but freedom. The truly free man wants only what he can do and does what he pleases."

Of all his writings, Rousseau was the proudest of *Émile,* which details the lack of moral restraint of his early years. (In the *Confessions* he expresses dismay that *Émile* was banned by the Archbishop of Paris, condemned by the French Parliament, and triggered outrage in his native Geneva.) He presented his five-book novel as a treatise on humanity's natural goodness. His work shows how the individual is transformed into a citizen as private passions are redirected toward patriotism; through education, individuals are ushered from natural freedom into civil society. "In all matters," he wrote, "constraint and compulsion are unbearable to me."

A Saint or an Interesting Madman?

As a middle-aged suitor, Rousseau was described by Sophie d'Houdetot, the only woman he truly loved, as "an interesting madman." His oddly varied series of occupations might confirm her view. The *Confessions* detail how, during a fourteen-year period (1728–41), Rousseau served as a lackey, untrained music teacher, servant, unschooled tutor, and notably, pupil to himself. From 1742, his private studies galvanized him. They resulted in his first success, as a respected music copier. He then became a diplomatic aide, opera composer, playwright, novelist, encyclopedist, and major political thinker. All of his efforts were centered on reconciling natural freedom and society's constrictions.

"If he wasn't a saint, who was?" exclaimed Thérèse LeVasseur, an illiterate laundress whom Rousseau married in 1768 after twenty-three years of living together. Her admiration for a man who abandoned to an orphanage their five babies, each unnamed, is hard to fathom. Showing his remarkable capacity for abstraction, Rousseau argued in the *Confessions* that his decision was not negligence; it showed that he was a good "citizen," "a member of Plato's *Republic.*"

Spanning the nursing years to marriage and citizenship, *Émile* can be seen as a debt owed to the children he never educated or nurtured. Along with his enormously popular novel, *Julie, or the New Heloise* (1760), the two works fictionalize the personal tension between duty and desire Rousseau keenly felt. Is it possible to inculcate morals without jeopardizing natural freedom? If not, then a legitimate political order based on consent is—in Rousseau's view—not possible.

A Political Resolution

Perhaps Thérèse's elevated estimate of Rousseau was due to his relentless paring away of whatever weighs down humanity's native freedom. *The First Discourse* (1750), his earliest political writing, argues that the establishment of the sciences and the arts has corrupted morals. Conventional life, he claimed, results in lack of fulfillment in marriage, dilettantism in education, hypocrisy in religion, and self-serving in politics. Indeed, as he concluded in *The Second Discourse* (1755), institutions fragment a person's unity with nature, causing self-alienation, a theme he explores more fully in *The Social Contract*. Thus, as he states in its much-quoted opening line: "Man is born free, and everywhere he is in chains."

Many read Rousseau's famous words as a call to arms. Edmund Burke, like Louis XVI, Robespierre, and Napoleon, vigorously argued that Rousseau's works and self-portrait were the source of the thought and sensibilities of the French Revolution. Rousseau, however, would not have acknowledged responsibility.

In *Émile*, Rousseau, who claimed he read the Bible every night, denied original sin, replacing grace and truth with fidelity to feeling. He tried to refocus self-love, which through comparison with others can lead to envy and divisiveness—so that the disadvantaged are seen as one's potential self. Therefore in feeling pity for the less fortunate, one feels pity for oneself. Thus the natural love of oneself, through pity, becomes a source of social virtue and cohesiveness.

Class-bound French society, in Rousseau's view, was incapable of this kind of pity and

The destruction of the aqueduct; an incident from Rousseau's *Confessions*.

thus made impossible a socially unified political order. The simple republics of antiquity, particularly Sparta and the early Roman republic, offer a model of citizen virtue to be replicated on this new term of pity. The legislator

I regard all the particular religions as so many salutary institutions which prescribe in each country a uniform manner of honoring God by public worship. These religions can all have their justifications in the climate, the government, the genius of the people, or some other local cause, which makes one preferable to another according to the time and place. I believe them all to be right as long as one serves God suitably. The essential worship is that of the heart.

—*Émile*
Allan Bloom, trans.

or founder of these republics supervises the transformational process whereby the individual wills are unified into "the general will" to form a legitimate government.

Both the *Confessions* and *Émile* suggest that Rousseau's interest in politics was that of an artist, a crafter of malleable human souls. "Everything is rooted in politics," he wrote in his mid-thirties, and "whatever might be attempted, no people would ever be other than the nature of their government made them." This growing and abiding interest in the best government for the best people aligned Rousseau with the ancients, who saw politics as comprehensive. But Rousseau believed that people are not political by nature; instead, they are shaped to be so. The most lasting, and perhaps most devastating, effect of his thought was to show how political leaders can attract others to their causes through infusing romantic emotion into politics.

Issues to Explore

The *Confessions* are over six hundred pages of engaging, sometimes lyrical, often unreliable, self-revelation. *Émile* should be read to see the close relation between Rousseau's autobiography and education. A few key questions to consider include the following. (1) How have Rousseau's views of education and natural religion influenced the shift from Christ-centered

For Further Study

The standard translation of the *Confessions* is by J. M. Cohen (Penguin, 1953). Roger Masters in *The Political Philosophy of Rousseau* (Princeton, 1968) and Leo Strauss in *Natural Right and History* (Chicago, 1953) interpret his political teaching. Allan Bloom's translation and commentary on *Émile or On Education* (Basic, 1979) are superb. Jacques Maritain offers the best Christian critique of Rousseau in *Three Reformers* (Thomas Y. Crowell Co., 1929; Apollo, 1970). Ernst Cassirer's short book *The Question of Jean-Jacques Rousseau* (Yale, 1954) is comprehensive in its concerns. Jean Starobinski's *Jean-Jacques Rousseau: Transparency and Obstruction* (Chicago, 1971) finely analyzes Rousseau's own psychology.

to psychologically centered education and religion? (2) What is the effect of placing feelings prior to reason? (3) Is Rousseauan freedom at odds with the Christian faith? Is it one with modern sensibilities?

—Virginia L. Arbery

ALEXANDER HAMILTON, JAMES MADISON, AND JOHN JAY

The Federalist
1787–88

The Federalist stands as the greatest single work in American political thought. Its eighty-five letters were drafted by Alexander Hamilton, James Madison, and John Jay and published in four New York newspapers in a campaign from October, 1787, to May, 1788. Their intent was to persuade the New York state convention, which met in the summer of 1788, to ratify the proposed U.S. Constitution. The letters soon became known as the authoritative source for understanding what Thomas Jefferson called "the genuine meaning" of the Constitution. Further, George Washington declared that *The Federalist* would "merit the notice of posterity" because the letters so ably discuss the principles of free government.

Charting Destiny

The Federalist can be understood fully only in its historical context.

James Madison (1751–1836).

These collected essays form an explicitly political argument in the midst of an intense political struggle. They were written at the precise moment that America's political destiny was being

decided—after the Constitutional Convention had met in Philadelphia and set forth the Constitution for ratification by the states. For acceptance, nine states were needed to ratify the document.

The three authors wrote under the single pseudonym of "Publius," an ancient hero who saved the Roman republic. They demonstrate "a lesson of moderation" by showing that the principles set forth in the Constitution correspond to the self-interest of New York—and the other twelve states. They were writing against their opponents, the Anti-Federalists, who charged that the Constitution was a dangerous innovation breaking with the traditional understanding of what forms a true republican government. As the best expression of the constitutional ideals for which the revolutionary generation fought, most of the Anti-Federalists looked to the Articles of Confederation, which were written in 1776 but not ratified until 1781. After

The accumulation of all powers, legislative, executive, and judiciary, in the same hands, whether of one, a few, or many, and whether hereditary, self-appointed, or elective, may justly be pronounced the very definition of tyranny.

—*The Federalist,* Number 47

heated and prolonged debate, New York narrowly accepted the Constitution on July 26, 1788, by a vote of thirty to twenty-seven.

Three Men, One Voice

The three authors—Alexander Hamilton (1755–1804), James Madison (1751–1836), and John Jay (1745–1829)—were towering figures in the American political landscape when the Constitution was ratified. Hamilton, a New York lawyer, was a personal friend and aide to George Washington during the Revolution. Under President Washington, Hamilton was the first and greatest Secretary of the Treasury, setting America on its course as the world's leading commercial empire. A delegate to the Constitutional Convention in Philadelphia, he coordinated the efforts to ratify the Constitution in New York. Intensely committed to the Constitution's passage in New York, he wrote the greatest number of the papers—fifty-one.

Madison, who was active in Virginia politics, is known as "the father of the Constitution" because of his monumental efforts in Philadelphia. He went on to become a leader in the House of Representatives, Secretary of State for eight years, and then President of the United States for two terms. Madison wrote twenty-nine of the papers.

Jay, like Hamilton, was a prosperous New York lawyer. He had written that state's 1777 constitution and served as Secretary for Foreign Affairs under the Articles of Confederation. Because he became ill during the ratify-

ing period, Jay contributed only five of the eighty-five essays. He subsequently became the first Chief Justice of the U.S. Supreme Court.

Keeping a Free Society Free

The essays of *The Federalist* were written in the learned style of eighteenth-century political elites. They combine biblical, classical, and recent history with contemporary European political affairs, philosophy, and discoveries from the emerging natural sciences. The text is organized around four major topics: first, America's need for a stronger union than had existed under the Articles of Confederation (Numbers 1–14); second, the particular weaknesses of the existing confederation (Numbers 15–22); third, the proper powers that a national government should possess and exercise (Numbers 23–36); fourth, the proposed Constitution's conformity with the principles of the Revolution (Numbers 37–85).

In Number 39 of *The Federalist,* Madison acknowledges that the chief question concerning the Constitution is whether "the general form and aspect of the government be strictly republican." Only a republican form of government, he maintains, would reflect the nature of the American people and correspond "with the fundamental principles of the Revolution." If the Federalist supporters of the plan cannot prove its republican character, "its advocates must abandon it as no longer defensible."

This question of what constitutes a "republican form of government" was the central point of debate between the Federalist supporters of the Constitution and their Anti-Federalist opponents. Madison believed a republic to be "a government which derives all its powers directly or indirectly from the great body of the people, and is administered by persons holding their offices during pleasure for a limited period, or during good behavior." The Anti-Federalists may have seen the necessity for this definition but found it insufficient. Arguing from history, they charged that a republican government was more than a mere institutional design for representation. Rather,

flourish, thus serving as a kind of social check and balance.

American society is thereby conceived by *The Federalist* as a pluralist society where self-interested political behavior is to be expected, but to be checked by both social and institutional arrangements. Madison sets out his institutional solution to the threat of factions in perhaps the most oft-quoted paper, Number 51. There he claims that government is "but the greatest of all reflections on human nature." After describing human nature in Number 10, he asserts in Number 51 that the only institutional design allowing a free society to remain free is a structure based on the separation of powers. Checks and balances assure that "ambition must be made to counteract ambition."

The Federalists branded their opponents as people "of little faith." As they won the argument and achieved the ratification of the Constitution, they secured their vision of an expansive, acquisitive, and free society for generations to come. *The Federalist* became the great record of this vision.

Issues to Explore

The prescription for a free society and government as set out in *The Federalist* may strike the Christian reader as surprisingly secular. The "new science of politics" that *The Federalist* celebrates thus appears to diminish or neglect a worldview central to many citizens of this modern commercial republic. (1) Considering the Anti-Federalist stress on virtue, the place of religion in public life, and a more participatory

Alexander Hamilton (1755–1804), a New York lawyer and, under President Washington, the first and greatest Secretary of the Treasury.

they said, it must also touch the character of the citizen. The Anti-Federalists believed in the positive role of government in both public morality and religion. Self-interest, they argued, could be overcome through education and religion, thereby fostering a sense of civic virtue.

Madison considered the Anti-Federalists' remedy unlikely to be put into practice and countered it with the Federalist vision for American society, which can be seen most succinctly in such essays as Numbers 10 and 51. In the former, Madison paints the picture of a free society irredeemably beset by the problem of "factions," self-interested groups bent on controlling political power for their own narrow ends. He contends that the only proper social remedy for such disunity is to structure society so that as many factions as possible can

> *A NATION without a NATIONAL GOVERNMENT, is in my view, an awful spectacle. The establishment of a Constitution, in time of profound peace, by the voluntary consent of a whole people, is a PRODIGY, to the completion of which I look forward with trembling anxiety.*
>
> —*The Federalist*, Number 85

For Further Study

The Federalist is an impressive rhetorical work, although its sentences tend to be lengthy and complex in structure. The text may thus present difficulties to contemporary readers, but patience and a good edition can prove quite rewarding. Certain essays of *The Federalist* have been considered as truly capturing the essence of the work. Historian Clinton Rossiter states that "the common consent of learned opinion" holds the following to be the most important: 1, 2, 6, 9, 10, 14, 15, 16, 23, 37, 39, 47, 48, 49, 51, 62, 63, 70, 78, 84, and 85. This listing may prove to be a helpful guide for those who lack the time or endurance to read the text from cover to cover. Madison's Numbers 10 and 51 and Hamilton's Number 78 should certainly be read and appreciated.

Edited versions of the complete text of *The Federalist* currently available are by Jacob E. Cooke (Wesleyan University Press, 1961), Clinton Rossiter (New American Library, 1961), and, more recently, a student edition by George W. Carey and James McClellan (Kendall/Hunt, 1990). For those who want to trace the frequency of citations, occurrences of ideas, and so on, see Thomas Engeman, Edward Erler, and Thomas Hofeller, editors of *The Federalist Concordance* (Wesleyan University Press, 1980).

For the political and intellectual background to the text, two readable histories are Forrest McDonald's *Novo Ordo Seclorum: The Intellectual Origins of the Constitution* (University of Kansas, 1985) and Gordon Wood's *The Creation of the American Republic, 1776–1787* (W.W. Norton, 1972). The latter is a central text in the recent scholarly rehabilitation of Anti-Federalist thought. Herbert Storing's little volume, *What the Anti-Federalists Were For* (University of Chicago, 1981), is the best summary of their views. For Anti-Federalist writings see his massive collection, *The Complete Anti-Federalist* (University of Chicago, 1981), seven volumes.

form of government, why have conservative churches in America accepted the vision set out in *The Federalist* and the political economy it inspired? (2) Can Anti-Federalist themes of community and virtue hold a political vision whereby churches can find strength to resist the ravages of a secularizing modern society?

And as to the text of *The Federalist* itself, some questions may be asked. (3) Does this text give us insight into the "original intent" of the framers of the Constitution, or must we read it as a *political* text and hence a more slanted account of what the Constitution is about? (4) Does this text reflect any dominant intellectual influence(s), or is it best read as a patchwork of authorities and sources put together ad hoc for the purposes of an immediate political task? (5) If contradictions between the three authors emerge from the text, how do we reconcile their differences? (6) What specific vision of America's future do these authors hold? Has this vision been realized? (7) Is the America of our day consistent with the American vision set out by the authors of *The Federalist*?

—Ashley Woodiwiss

JANE AUSTEN

Pride and Prejudice
1813

*J*ane Austen's *Pride and Prejudice* is an eighteenth century comic romance of such psychological depth and literary beauty that many consider it the finest novel by the greatest female novelist. It is one of six novels by Austen (1775–1817), whose brilliant wit, subtle moral insight, and exquisite style make them enduring classics of domestic comedy.

Novels of Domestic Comedy and Social Change

Austen's writings—*Sense and Sensibility, Pride and Prejudice, Mansfield Park, Emma, Northanger Abbey,* and *Persuasion*—form a unique link between the novels of the eighteenth and nineteenth centuries. They broach not only the individual and family concerns of England's early novelists, such as Samuel Richardson, but also the larger social issues that preoccupied such nineteenth-century practitioners of the craft as Charles DICKENS and William Thackeray.

Surprisingly, Austen's quiet life as a single woman in the small

Jane Austen (1775–1817).

village of Chawton in southwest England equipped her perfectly for achieving such a distinction. She read prodigiously in the great "originators" of the English novel, such as Richardson and Henry Fielding (and also in their numerous cheap imitators), and trained her keen eye and sharp wit on the quiet drama and superficial social standards of "a few families in a small country community." Austen perceived the rise of money as

society's new supreme standard of evaluation in its shifting class-based structure. She drew witty critiques of contemporary society's changing values, traditional class biases, and individual follies and self-deceptions.

Within the provincial setting, Austen most often uses the theme of marriage to disclose the false standards of society and individuals. As her novels reveal, woman's place is precarious in a society that values economic standing over personal virtue. Thus the marriage of a daughter to a man of "fortune" becomes the central action around which everything else revolves. Enveloping this concern is the larger drama of a changing village culture. Among Austen's wise and rueful novels adhering to this pattern, *Pride and Prejudice* is preeminent.

Early Influences and Novel Experiments

Samuel Richardson (sometimes called the "mother" of the novel) and Henry Fielding (sometimes called its father) are the most apparent eighteenth-century

It is a truth universally acknowledged, that a single man in possession of a good fortune, must be in want of a wife.

—*Pride and Prejudice*

influences on Jane Austen. Although she parodies Richardson's sentimentality and didacticism, she maintains the advantages of his probing psychological analysis but avoids the limitations of his subjective, first-person approach. And while avoiding the sometimes almost sardonic critique and objectivity of Fielding, she maintains his ironic viewpoint and comical running commentary on human folly.

Austen uses the new technique of a partially omniscient point of view—she enters the mind of only one character, the heroine. Through this method she preserves the "internal vision" that Richardson mastered. But by becoming the "objective" narrator, she drops the limitations of the first-person point of view, allowing herself—like Fielding—to comment from the outside. Thus she moves closer to the modern novel by showing not only the face of the clock (in the manner of Fielding) but also the inner workings behind the face (in the manner of Richardson).

In various ways, then, Austen sets the stage for the truly modern novel: its psychological realism; its critique of both the individual and society; its emphasis on the protagonist's character development; its often domestic and local setting; and its placement of romantic love and happy (or unhappy) marriage at the center of the plot. She achieves these traits by focusing on her heroines. They are sometimes mocking, sometimes oversentimental, always marriageable, and often—as in *Pride and Prejudice*—superbly characterized through irony, contrast, and a realistic overcoming of personal flaws.

Intertwining Ironies and Personal Insight

Pride and Prejudice tells the story of two very different sisters from a middle-class family,

Elizabeth and Jane Bennet, and their troubled courtship by two friends of aristocratic birth, Darcy and Bingley. At the center of this novel is the bright, sparkling Elizabeth Bennet. Austen presents the intricate influences of family, friends, suitors, financial status, and class distinctions not only on the obviously vulgar, stupid, pompous, and bitter characters but even on the witty, sensitive heroine herself.

Elizabeth's father and mother stand in stark and ironic contrast to each other. Mr. Bennet's intelligent and humorous personality has become almost totally embittered by his early marriage to a vulgar, foolish woman. Mrs. Bennet's embarrassing attempts to marry off her five diverse daughters continually amuse and annoy Elizabeth. The sad match of her parents acts as a comic but sober reminder of how devastating a loveless marriage can be.

This marriage makes credible the vast differences among the five daughters—clever Elizabeth, conventional Jane, lovesick Lydia, moralizing Mary, and colorless Kitty. Although Elizabeth is clearly superior, she comes to see that her sisters are all inevitably a part of her. She must learn to restrain her sometimes sharp wit to avoid living—like her father—only to laugh at others. She has to understand that embarrassing relatives are not limited to her family. And she finally realizes that the handsome but heartless "villain" who seduces her foolish sister Lydia was once well on his way to seducing her.

Many British novels preceding *Pride and Prejudice* featured seductions in all their scandalous details and effects. In her treatment of the theme, however, Austen demonstrates her moral and artistic superiority. Even clever Elizabeth could possibly be "seduced" into a loveless marriage because her social and financial standing makes marriage mandatory. And though she avoids such a destiny, she has several narrow escapes. Elizabeth emphatically turns down a marriage proposal from the pompous Rev. Collins. And when her admired friend Charlotte Lucas gladly decides to marry him, Elizabeth cruelly remarks to her, "Engaged to Mr. Collins! Impossible!" But later when the "charming" Wickham appears

Jane Austen's home at Chawton, Hampshire, England.

in the neighborhood, Elizabeth is almost taken in herself. She escapes, but is overwhelmed with shame by the scandal of her sister's elopement with him.

After this disgrace Elizabeth feels that her growing love for Darcy, the wealthy and proud man she once swore never to marry, will never be reciprocated. But an ironic switch comes into play: because Darcy once rescued his own sister from Wickham's manipulations, he feels deep sympathy for Elizabeth.

Another delightful but painful irony occurs when Elizabeth must tell her sister Jane and her father that she is engaged to Darcy, whom she had once hated. Both echo almost exactly Elizabeth's words to Charlotte: "Engaged to Mr. Darcy! Impossible!" This response causes Elizabeth to shed truly repentant tears.

Thus through a superb intertwining of ironies the apparently incompatible Elizabeth and Darcy move toward a happy and humane marriage. Elizabeth will have to bear the vulgarity of her now overjoyed mother, but Darcy will have to accept the similar vulgarity of his snobbish aunt. Through the mellowing influence of true love, they both learn to see their own faults and overcome pride, prejudice, and the superficial criteria of a money-mad, class-conscious society. In fact, they now demonstrate the joyful validity of the comically ironic opening sentence of the novel: "It is a truth universally acknowledged, that a single man in possession of a good fortune, must be in want of a wife."

"I am happier even than Jane: she only smiles, I laugh."

—*Pride and Prejudice*

Charlotte and Elizabeth on Mr. Darcy:

"I dare say you will find him very agreeable."
"Heaven forbid!—That would be the greatest misfortune
of all!—To find a man agreeable whom one is determined
to hate!—Do not wish me such an evil."

—*Pride and Prejudice*

For Further Study

Good paperback editions with helpful introductions are Dell's (1959), introduced by Mark Shorer, and Penguin's (1983), introduced by Toby Tanner. The definitive hardcover edition was published by R. W. Chapman in 1923 (Oxford). Helpful critical commentaries include Marvin Mudrick, *Jane Austen* (Princeton, 1952); Andrew Wright, *Jane Austen's Novels* (Chatto and Windus, 1953); A. Walton Litz, *Jane Austen: A Study of Her Artistic Development* (Oxford, 1965); Kenneth L. Moler, *Jane Austen's Art of Allusion* (University of Nebraska, 1968).

Issues to Explore

Its wit, irony, romantic plot, and captivating heroine all make *Pride and Prejudice* a delight to read. Twentieth-century readers may initially find the action somewhat slow, but if they persist they will soon be swept away by the sheer pleasure of the book.

For the Christian, the plot of *Pride and Prejudice* offers notable issues for reflection. One involves what Austen originally planned to name the novel, *First Impressions*. This title applies to Elizabeth Bennet, who must learn to overcome her unfavorable first judgments of others—especially Darcy—and see that she is not always right. The novel also dramatizes the significance of maintaining high personal standards of love and charity in a society where money, marriage, and social status have become the measure of all morality. Both of these insights indicate that we live in an imperfect world and that we ourselves contribute to that imperfection. Finally, however, the novel conveys a truth central to Christian living—love makes it possible to love the unlovable in an often unlovable world, for it can "endure all things."

We should ask several questions as we read: (1) Why does Elizabeth make a more intriguing heroine than her beautiful sister Jane? (2) How do her parents and her other sisters compare and contrast with Elizabeth? (3) Does a spirited and intelligent young woman, caught in a superficial social system, almost inevitably fall into irony and mockery? (4) What can bring her to the good judgment and kindness such a society needs? (5) What is the effect of grace and compassion on arrogance and pride, especially in Darcy and Elizabeth? (6) What are some of the subtle influences in our own society that lead to superficial values, unhappy marriages, and a general weakening of the Christian faith and its moral code?

—Henrietta Ten Harmsel

JOHANN WOLFGANG VON GOETHE

Faust
1808, 1832

*G*oethe's *Faust* is the cornerstone of classical German drama and a seminal work in the Romantic movement. The two-part play is based on the historical figure of Georg Faust (c. 1480–1540), a German amateur alchemist, astrologer, and charlatan whose strange practices inspired a host of tales, legends, and dramas. His contemporaries described him as a magician who invoked ghosts, attempted to fly over Venice, and was finally caught by the devil disguised as a dog. In 1587 the popular folktale introduced the motif of a bargain with the devil, according to which, after Dr. Faustus's wishes were fulfilled, his soul would fall to the devil.

Further developments of the story highlighted deeper moral, philosophical, and theological issues current in sixteenth-century Europe. One theme, for example, concerns the Renaissance fear of the dangers of a reckless exploitation of knowledge, in particular the rapid and spectacular progress of the natural sciences. Behind this modern anxiety, however, lay several centuries of legends

Johann Wolfgang von Goethe (1749–1832); statue at Frankfurt am Main, Germany.

concerning a godless, devil-inspired magician; these tales can be traced back through the Middle Ages to second- and third-century accounts of Simon the Magician, first mentioned in the New Testament.

Two hundred years before Goethe, the English dramatist Christopher Marlowe wrote the *Tragical History of Doctor Faustus*,

first performed in 1594. Marlowe included such characteristic elements as the famous introductory monologue of Faust that explains his inner turmoil and aspirations and the conflicts between the magician's craft and the Christian faith, between sin and repentance, between tragedy and comedy. But Marlowe, unlike Goethe, insisted on the tragic outcome of Faust's refusal to heed the consequences of sin; in the English play, Faust is finally and irrevocably damned. The drama ends with a choir deploring the tragic fall of a highly gifted man who rebelled against God. More than two hundred years later, Goethe was to reinterpret the outcome of the story.

Goethe's *Faust*

Johann Wolfgang von Goethe (1749–1832), poet, playwright, and novelist, was also a scientist (researching plant biology and optics) and an internationally active official at the court of Weimar. He reluctantly studied his father's profession—law—but after qualifying turned to his true passion and wrote his first drama.

Goethe took up the subject of Faust, devising a so-called *Urfaust* in 1775. This was his first and fragmentary attempt at coming to terms with the image of Faust in the era of European Enlightenment—his portrayal of a character whose qualities should be seen on a universal all-too-human level, beyond the confines of "doctrine" or "reason." His first draft of 1775 was never published, but a revision under the title of *Faust, a Fragment* appeared in 1790. The poet's friendship with Friedrich von Schiller (1759–1805), one of the most important German dramatists of the classical period, inspired Goethe to revise the subject again. He wrote the first and most famous part of *Faust* (later called *Faust, The First Part of the Tragedy*) between 1797 and 1806. Then twenty-one years after the completion of Part I (and fifty-four years after the *Urfaust*), Goethe used earlier notes and drafts to write a philosophical and poetic sequel, *Faust, Part II,* influenced by his desire to reconcile his own classical thought with the sentiments of Romanticism.

A Pact with the Devil

Goethe's Faust is a disillusioned scholar who turns to search the world of experience when his intellectual pursuits become dry and lifeless. Nearing despair, he makes a pact with Mephistopheles, a devil who appears first as a black poodle. The agreement is that Faust will be given infinite knowledge, a knowledge with godlike power, to last until he reaches a stage of satisfaction. If he ever declares, "Oh stay; you are so fair!" to any given moment, he will immediately be required to surrender his soul to the devil.

The play continues with a series of temptations that take Faust to the brink of moral degradation. In the first, after Mephistopheles restores Faust's youth, he presents the reinvigorated scholar with an innocent young maiden, Gretchen (also called Margarete). Faust seduces her and she bears a child, whom she drowns when she is overcome with remorse. Facing execution for her crime, she refuses to flee with Faust, instead choosing to accept the justice of humanity and the mercy of God.

Faust II is more visionary, fantastic, and symbolic than Part I. It is about change, metamorphosis, evolution, science, poetry. If the first part of Goethe's poem is tragedy, the second is, like DANTE's *Divine Comedy* and JOYCE's *Finnegan's Wake,* a drama of the mind. Most scholars agree that while Part I deals with the microcosm (the small human cosmos), Part II depicts the macrocosm (the great cosmos of the universe). It opens with no period of penance, no anguish or grief on Faust's part. He has been cleansed and purged by airy spirits while he slept. He is free to ransack ancient Greece and bring back Helen of Troy, to go to the realm of the "mothers," those archetypal feminine figures of creativity, as well as to strive to make the world beautiful in any way he can.

Faust reads from the Bible:

It says: "In the beginning was the Word.*"*
Already I am stopped. It seems absurd.
The Word does not deserve the highest prize,
I must translate it otherwise
If am well inspired and not blind.

. . . .

The spirit helps me. Now it is exact.
I write: In the beginning was the Act.

Geschrieben steht: "Im Anfang war das Wort!"
Heir stock ich schon! Wer hilft mir weiter fort?
Ich kann das Wort so hoch unmöglich schatzen,
Ich muss es anders übersetzen,
Wenn ich vom Geiste recht erleuchtet bin.

. . . .

Mir hilft der Geist, auf einmal seh ich Rat
Und schreibe getrost: Im Anfang war kie Tat!

—*Faust*
Walter Kaufmann, trans.

"Goethe in the Campagna" by Tischbein, 1787.

After many years have passed, Faust, in old age, has almost achieved the completion of a project to reclaim land from the sea. One old couple, Philemon and Baucis, however, will not relinquish their simple cottage on their small plot of land. They attend church nearby, and the sound of the church bells is a torment to Faust. He commands, finally, that the pair be removed from their land by violence if necessary. In the process they are killed, the house is burned, the church destroyed. When Faust is alone that evening, Care, Distress, and Sorrow come to his room; all depart except Care, who leaves Faust blinded.

Unseeing, Faust commands his workers to finish the task at the seashore. They begin digging his grave; he thinks they are continuing work on the project. The sound of their work, the sense of his accomplishment for the human race—this moment of high achievement—are such supreme satisfaction to him that he exclaims, "Oh stay; you are so fair!" and immediately falls dead. Mephistopheles stands over his body and prepares to take him away. But choirs of angels appear, proclaiming, "He who exerts himself in constant striving, / Him we can save"—thus preventing Mephistopheles' triumph. They are joined by all the forces of good; and finally Gretchen herself, the wronged young woman whose death he caused, welcomes Faust into the regions of the blessed. The play ends with a choral song, the last lines of which are: "The Eternal Feminine / Leads to perfection."

Eternal Striving

What did Goethe mean by his famous play? Authorities are divided on this issue. Some see the ending as bitter and ironic, condemning rather than approving Faust. Others see it as a portrayal of universal mercy, given to those who never relinquish the aspiration for noble achievement, even though their actions may be destructive. Whatever else may be said, it seems clear that Goethe intended the play to be thought-provoking. A letter he wrote to his friend Johann Peter Eckermann in 1827, shortly before his death, characterized Faust as "a man who out of grave confusion constantly strives for the better."

Goethe's *Faust* enables the reader to look with admiration on the passionate search for knowledge and at the same time to understand the horror implicit in perpetual striving that has no goal but infinite progress. It shows the nobility of the quest for beauty and at the same time the degradation brought about in riding roughshod over human values in its pursuit. Further, the drama portrays the lure of the Faustian striving that attempts to penetrate nature's secrets with magical techniques. It is this fundamental ambivalence that has made *Faust* a peculiarly modern poem and has rendered it perpetually challenging. From the quest for knowledge exhibited by this one literary character, the idea of "Faustian striving" has become proverbial in Germany and throughout the West.

Thus Goethe's *Faust* has a haunting quality and is something of a prophetic work that discerns and diagnoses the fundamental illness of modern times. Apparently, Goethe spent sixty years pondering the great dilemma: could that very striving in the modern soul (which makes moderns damage the feminine, take advantage of the helpless, and sin against the earth) still be the agent of their salvation? Can humanity find mercy, devoted as it has been to science and the gospel of infinite progress?

Issues to Explore

From a Christian point of view, the recurring theme of *Faust* in world literature and music remains a fascinating challenge. (Apart from Goethe's *Faust,* consider Marlowe's tragedy of 1594, Alexander Pushkin's Russian treatment

For Further Study

The books and articles on Goethe's *Faust* are inexhaustible. Stimulating insights may be gained from E. M. Butler, *The Fortunes of Faust* (Cambridge, 1952), and J. W. Smeed, *Faust in Literature* (London, 1975). George Steiner contributed thought-provoking forays into Goethe's *Faust* as drama in his controversial but durable *The Death of Tragedy* (London/Boston, 1961). For those who want to read the German original of Goethe's play, an outstanding new edition is Albrecht Schoene, editor, *Johann Wolfgang von Goethe: Faust,* two volumes (Frankfurt/Main, 1994). The recommended translations in English are *Faust* by Walter Arndt (Norton Critical Edition, 1976) and Walter Kaufmann (Doubleday Anchor, 1961).

of 1826, and Thomas Mann's novel *Dr. Faustus* of 1946.) The quest for absolute power over living beings and nature accompanied by a desperately guilt-ridden conscience retains a disturbingly modern appeal. (1) Why have Goethe's dramas appealed to readers and theatergoers for more than two centuries as the most thought-provoking approach to the subject? (2) How integral is a Christian perspective to understanding the play? (3) How is our own era's attitude to knowledge and power infected with a sense of Faustian bargaining?

—Carsten Peter Thiede

WILLIAM WORDSWORTH AND SAMUEL TAYLOR COLERIDGE

Lyrical Ballads
1798

*N*o single work in English poetry has had more lasting influence than *Lyrical Ballads,* coauthored by William Wordsworth and Samuel Taylor Coleridge and published anonymously in 1798. Following a remarkable, intense literary friendship that began in 1797, *Lyrical Ballads* was the only one of several joint projects to come to fruition. A group of lyric and semi-narrative poems, it was envisioned as an exploration of a new subject matter in a simplified poetic diction, with an unprecedented emphasis on the faculty of imagination.

The importance of the volume, however, goes beyond what either man initially thought. Its opening and closing poems—Coleridge's *The Rime of the Ancient Mariner* and Wordsworth's "Lines Composed a Few Miles above Tintern Abbey"—establish two central elements of a romantic "credo," a belief in an

Samuel Taylor Coleridge (1772–1834).

William Wordsworth (1770–1850).

immanent spirit within nature and in the power of the imagination to apprehend it. Moreover, they open a distinctive interior landscape that persists even now—a subjective emphasis that has, since the romantics, seemed not only normal but unavoidable.

Political and Literary Revolution

In the context of the turmoil of the late eighteenth century, *Lyrical Ballads* appears at once revolutionary and conservative. When Coleridge and Wordsworth first met in 1795, both men had been active partisans of the French Revolution (1789) and supported radical reform in England. By 1797, however, each had separately rejected many of the premises of the French Revolution. Not only were they disgusted with the bloody aftermath of the Revolution, but they increasingly saw its abstract humanitarianism as dangerous.

The French Revolution was a culmination of the spirit of the Enlightenment in eighteenth-century Europe, characterized by its elevation of the claims of reason and science. By employing the scientific method, reason could discover the laws ruling nature, human relations, and social institutions, and, accordingly, correct the imperfections of society. This rationalist spirit, although originally theistic and aristocratic in its conception of the "laws of nature," eventually took the form of the atheistic, abstract democracy that fueled the French Revolution. It sought to destroy all "superstition" associated with the tyranny of the past—not only religious belief, but customary order, such as familial institutions and inherited systems of law.

At the time of their early friendship, while England was at war with France, both Coleridge and Wordsworth were suspected of being agents for political revolution in England. Some early reviewers thus took *Lyrical Ballads* as a subversive document—a claim for which there is some truth. These two poets were

> . . . *this prayer I make,*
> *Knowing that Nature never did betray*
> *The heart that loved her; 'tis her privilege,*
> *Through all the years of this our life, to lead*
> *From joy to joy.*
>
> —Wordsworth
> "Lines Composed a Few Miles above Tintern Abbey"

rightly seen to have a "levelling muse" that participated in the spirit of revolution: they chose incidents from common and rural life, adopted the "language really used by men," and portrayed sympathetically those suffering from destitution.

In many ways, however, *Lyrical Ballads* is firmly directed against the aims of the Revolution. Its central concern is not the injustice of the class system, but rather contemporary conditions, such as how an urban environment, as Wordsworth's Preface points out, reduces the mind "to a state of savage torpor." Modern life

produces a "degrading thirst after outrageous stimulation," which "rapid communication" of information gratifies instantly. *Lyrical Ballads* attempts to counter this degradation by affirming the dignity of the human in particular instances that point to the beauty of endurance, piety, and fidelity. It aims to create for a skeptical audience *the capacity to believe,* rather than promoting any specific version of an *object of belief.*

The Rime of the Ancient Mariner: A Tale of Transgression and Suffering

The Rime of the Ancient Mariner begins the first edition of *Lyrical Ballads* and presents a recurrent romantic figure—an outcast whose transgression dooms him to special suffering. But Coleridge, unlike other romantics, does not glorify the heroism of this outlaw. Because he was shaped by traditional Christian piety—more than any other romantic—he emphasizes, against rationalist claims for essential human goodness, the fallen human reality of pride, perversity, and self-destruction.

The long poem tells how a ragged mariner finds a man going to a wedding and, by the power of his "glittering eye," holds him in a spell so that he will hear his story. During a voyage to the Southern seas the mariner has killed an albatross, a white bird of good omen. His arbitrary act represents the human assumption of willful mastery over nature; it also suggests a fundamental impiety toward nature's creatures. As punishment his fellow mariners hang the dead albatross around his neck. Eventually the other mariners die, but he is doomed to suffer Life-in-Death, a torment of thirst and hallucination. Then, with sudden imaginative insight, he beholds the beauty of the lowliest of creatures, water snakes playing on the water by moonlight. "A spring of love gushed from [his] heart, / And [he] bless'd them unaware." At the "self-same moment," the albatross drops from his neck.

Though the mariner's original pride has been broken in contrition and love, he must endure a sea-journey as penance, conducted by

The ruins of Tintern Abbey, subject of Wordsworth's poem.

invisible angelic "spirits." Later, when he asks a Hermit to absolve him of his sins, he is seized by a permanent penance—the compulsion to wander forever, telling his tale to a few chosen people. He ends with a moral message of piety:

> He prayeth best who loveth best,
> All things both great and small:
> For the dear God, who loveth us,
> He made and loveth all.

Though this poem is undoubtedly Christian in its piety, its daring innovations must be emphasized. The belief in a creation animated by spirits was not common in Coleridge's time; instead the dominant attitude was disbelief or hostility. Coleridge's poem tested the possibility of creating the feeling or attitude of faith, so that one has "a willing suspension of disbelief for the moment, which constitutes poetic faith."

"Lines Composed a Few Miles above Tintern Abbey": A Romantic Credo

"Tintern Abbey" closes *Lyrical Ballads,* highlighting the underlying themes of the whole collection of poems in the volume. The poem begins with a contemplation of a landscape that Wordsworth had visited five years earlier. The question he addresses concerns the meaning this landscape has assumed as an image in his conscious and unconscious life. Within the poem,

Wordsworth claims that this image of the river Wye has been a healing and soothing memory, while he dwelt "in lonely rooms, and mid the din / Of towns and cities." Moreover, as an unconscious presence, it may have influenced his capacity for charity, for "little, nameless, unremembered acts / Of kindness and of love." Finally, this image contributes to moments of illumination and ecstasy, when "we are laid asleep / In body, and become a living soul [and] . . . We see into the life of things."

Wordsworth claims so much from a single, ordinary moment of perception because of his overarching belief that nature's presence guides us invisibly throughout life. Wordsworth's perception of spirit in nature is not a simple pantheism, the conception that everything is divine. Rather he emphasizes the primacy of sensory, experiential knowledge. When we perceive the world, we also take in the spirit of nature that resides both in the mind and in things. This unconscious spirit works on us in manifold and profound ways; memory especially serves as a reservoir of spirit, waiting to come to consciousness.

Wordsworth believes that our interchange with this vital spirit is most intense in youth and diminishes with age; but youth, though intensely alive to nature, is "thoughtless." With greater consciousness in age nature gives an ability to understand the larger dimension of its beauty, to hear "the still, sad music of humanity." Thus youth and age can have a constant interchange. A fidelity to the spirit of

Enough of Science and of Art;
Close up those barren leaves;
Come forth, and bring with you a heart
That watches and receives.

—Wordsworth
"The Tables Turned"

nature working within the mind and heart leads one to wisdom and to a sense of piety toward nature as "the nurse, / The guide, the guardian of my heart, and soul / Of all my moral being."

Paving the Way

Lyrical Ballads attempts to render a poetry of piety in the aftermath of generations of skepticism directed at supernatural belief. The divine object of this piety is not a Christian God who transcends creation but a creative spirit that resides invisibly within nature and thus is embedded within human experience. In this romantic recovery of meaning, the imagination, rather than analytical reason, provides the means of grasping the invisible presences within nature.

Unlike the Christian poetry by George HERBERT or John DONNE, *Lyrical Ballads* prepares a path toward belief for those entangled in the skepticism of modern life. As such its poems remain pertinent today.

Issues to Explore

Wordsworth and Coleridge allow the reader to formulate questions about the very nature of belief, and the way in which belief works within a literary work and in relation to a reader. (1) What does it mean to believe or to have faith? (2) Are these simply matters of the "assent of reason" or do they also involve imag-

For Further Study

Those wishing further study of Wordsworth should see the Oxford Authors Edition edited by Stephen Gill (1984). A good biography of Wordsworth is Stephen Gill's *William Wordsworth: A Life* (Oxford, 1990). Geoffrey Hartman's study, *Wordsworth's Poetry 1787–1814* (Harvard, 1971), provides a reliable introduction. The Oxford Authors Edition of Coleridge, edited by H. J. Jackson (1985), gives a good selection of poetry and prose. And W. Jackson Bate's *Coleridge* (Harvard, 1968) represents a fine critical biography. For intellectual background, see Basil Willey, *Coleridge* (Norton, 1973); a sound introductory treatment of the poetry and prose is given by Humphrey House in *Coleridge* (Rupert-Hart Davis, 1953).

ination? (3) What is the relation between the "poetic faith" engendered within a poem and the doctrinal faith we may profess as traditional believers? Questions to ponder concerning *Lyrical Ballads* itself include: (4) What are the implications of the emphasis in *Lyrical Ballads* upon the common person, often seen in destitute circumstances? Is this sympathy for the ordinary a debasement or an enrichment of literary tradition? (5) When we use the word "nature" we are probably doing so in a romantic sense. What is this sense of nature? Is it a true one? Is it limited? (6) Both Wordsworth in "Tintern Abbey" and Coleridge in *The Rime of the Ancient Mariner* attend to enunciate a certain faith in humanity and in the powers of nature. What are the strengths and limits of this faith?

—Eileen Gregory

German Classics

Power, aspiration, brilliance, and despair—these have been the defining traits of the German literary mind. Until the late eighteenth century Germany had an uneasy relationship with other European literatures, attempting in its first instances to reconcile the stark poetic fatalism of the old Germanic heroic tradition with the gentler and more hopeful tenets of the Christian faith. This labor, one might say, has never been fully accomplished. Thus a peculiar ambivalence has characterized German writing from the start.

Romancers and Mystics

Literature in the German language began in the eighth century, encompassing the area of what today is Germany, Austria, northern Switzerland, Liechtenstein, the northwestern Czech Republic, western Poland, eastern France, eastern Belgium, Luxembourg, and parts of the Netherlands. But it was not until the twelfth and thirteenth centuries that it produced lasting contributions to European literature. The single most popular work of the period was the *Nibelungenlied*, an epic poem written between 1190 and 1200 that recounts a legendary version of the historical conflict between the Burgundians and the Huns under Attila. Richard Wagner later immortalized it in his operatic cycle *Der Ring des Nibelungen*.

The great medieval romancers were Wolfram von Eschenbach (c. 1170–1200), author of the idealistic poem *Parzival*, a quest for the Holy Grail; Hartmann von Aue (c. 1170–1215), writer of romances celebrating trials of Christian virtue (*Erec, Der Arme Heinrich*), and Gottfried von Strassburg, glorifier of passionate love denied (*Tristan*). Wolfram and Gottfried were Minnesangers, lyric poets of the German courts who were influenced by the French and Provençal troubadours. The courtly love lyric, with its cult of devotion to the noble lady, flowered in the hands of these poets. Most renowned was Walther von der Vogelweide (c. 1170–1230), whose lyrics express wit, self-confidence, and patriotic devotion as well as the transports of love.

The mystical aspect of the German mind was expressed in the writings of Meister Eckhart (c. 1260–c. 1329), Heinrich Seuse (c. 1295–1366), and Johannes Tauler (c. 1300–1361). Eckhart as the speculative mystic went so far as to suggest the divinity of humanity; Seuse as the poetic mystic described his insights in an exuberant language; and Tauler as the public preacher and missionary linked the popular idea of contemplative mysticism with a call

Title page of Luther's Wittenberg German Old Testament.

for action. But lasting success, even in terms of world literature, has been granted to a less mystical and more practical book of devotions, *The Imitation of Christ* by Thomas à Kempis (1379–1471).

Second String to Philosophy and Theology

For the German language, the Renaissance and Reformation era was an epoch of philosophy and theology, of textual criticism and natural sciences rather than of imaginative literature. And more often than not, literature—poems, novels, plays—was used in a social, political, or religious context. Its vigor, however, began anew in Martin LUTHER (1483–1546), when he established the modern German language by translating the Bible. Since then the national poetic imagination has been at once dogmatic and speculative—deeply questioning, absolute in its response, reliant on subjectivity, troubled with demons, and musically expressive.

But that very language, which rang forth earthy and authoritative in the early sagas and in Luther's Bible and hymns, became a source of difficulty in the neoclassical age when symmetry, order, and "the golden mean" were dominant. Again, as during the Renaissance era, imaginative literature was less widely received than philosophy and its sister arts. Two exceptions to this rule, however, gave birth to true classics: Gotthold Ephraim Lessing (1729–1781) and Christoph Martin Wieland (1733–1813). Lessing, a precursor of German classicism, can be said to have invented the "bourgeois tragedy" in Germany. Today one of his dramas, *Nathan the Wise* (1779), is still widely regarded and performed, not only in Germany, as the first example of monotheistic ecumenism—the belief in the unity of Judaism, the Christian faith, and Islam, which most orthodox Christians reject.

Wieland, in contrast, was an educator and rediscoverer of classical literature who almost single-handedly made Greek and Latin texts widely read in Germany. He translated these classics in an accessible and yet precise enough way to remain exemplary for the famous German schools of classical

philology in the nineteenth and early twentieth centuries. With his *Story of Agathon* (1766) he introduced the new genre of the *Bildungsroman* (apprenticeship novel); he also wrote the text used by Carl Maria von Weber for his fairy tale opera *Oberon* (1780).

This epoch of neoclassic reason and disciplined enlightenment soon engendered a counterreaction of sentimentalist poetry in the second half of the eighteenth century. The term "sentimental," however, as applied to a range of less reason-orientated authors, tends to detract from the vital effect of this group on German literature. Two names in particular remain important: Friedrich Gottlieb Klopstock (1724–1803) and Matthias Claudius (1740–1815).

Matthias Claudius (1740–1815).

Klopstock was the popular author of odes, dramas, and above all *The Messiah* (1773), which was justly praised as the first truly classical work in German since Luther's translation of the Bible. The poet Claudius still has a remarkable fame that rests on his personal, intimate, sincerely Christian poems, some of which, such as "The Moon Is Risen," are among the texts that many Germans know by heart.

The Flowering of Germanness

The German literary genius came into its own in the late eighteenth century, exporting to the rest of the world a mood, a depth of soul, and an entire new vocabulary. At that time the *Sturm und Drang* (Storm and Stress) movement sent a shock wave throughout Europe and America. This movement consisted of authors who regarded themselves as exemplifying original genius, placing inspiration and innovativeness above reason or philosophical enlightenment. The young Friedrich Schiller (1759–1805) with his plays *The Brigands* (1781) and *Intrigue and Love* (1784), the young Johann Wolfgang von GOETHE (1749–1832) with his plays, his poems, and his sensationally successful novel *The Sufferings of Young Werther* (1774), Johann Gottfried Herder (1744–1803), and Friedrich Maximilian Klinger (1752–1831) are the most notable representatives of this movement.

This explosion of German self-discovery and its imaginative outpourings in the late eighteenth and early nineteenth century had social and historical roots in Germany's recent liberation from the alien rule of the Holy Roman Empire. Thus Goethe's language gave a new definition to independence, power, and the balance of the human faculties. The high serenity of reason that had found expression earlier in the mysticism of Meister Eckhart and Jakob Böhme now encountered an opposite defining trait, the extremism of interiority and passion. This later movement was represented fervently in Goethe's and Schiller's time by the *Sturm und Drang* poets and by Herder's philosophically reasoned embrace of all forms of folk expression.

Goethe and Schiller in particular gave the language, and hence the German mind and sensibility, its "third" birth, making it follow one

Work of seeing is done,
now practise heart-work
upon those images captive within you; for you
overpowered them only: but now do not know them.
Look, inward man, look at your inward maiden,
her the laboriously wrested
from a thousand natures, at her the
creature till now only wrested, never yet loved.

Werk des Gesichts ist getan,
tue nun Herz-Werk
an den Bildern in dir; jenen gefangenen; denn du
überwältigtest sie: aber nun kennst du sie nicht.
Siehe, innerer Mann, dein inneres Mädchen,
dieses errungene aus
tausend Naturen, dieses
erst nur errungene, nie
noch geliebte Geschöpf.

—Rainer Maria Rilke
"Wendung"
Michael Hamburger, trans.

of Goethe's own maxims: "Become what you are." Their works have been virtually enshrined as the national heritage: Goethe's *Faust,* his two Wilhelm Meister novels of education (1796, 1829), and his novel *Elective Affinities* (1809); Schiller's three-part Wallenstein tragedy (1800), his drama *Wilhelm Tell* (1804), which is still Switzerland's national play, and such poems as his "Ode to Joy," now officially Europe's "national anthem" in Beethoven's setting.

Yet other German writers of this period deserve recognition, such as Herder. A qualified theologian and churchman, historian and physician, he was the first to

recognize the literary importance of "folk songs"—a term he coined in German that was later translated into other languages. His edition of *Volkslieder* (1778) was the first work of its kind, including authentic regional songs from practically all European languages. Herder was the first to analyze the Hebrew Bible as literature and poetry, finding it the oldest, simplest, and most sublime poetry ever written (*On the Spirit of Hebrew Poetry,* 1782).

Another figure, little noticed outside Germany, is Heinrich von Kleist (1777–1811)—the greatest German classical playwright and novelist. His comedies *Amphitryon*

(1807) and *The Broken Jug* (1811), his tragedy *Penthesilea* (1808), such dramas as *Kathie of Heilbronn* (1810), and such short stories or novels as *Michael Kohlhaas* (1810) are unsurpassed masterpieces. Using the whole range of German, they employ an imaginative repertoire of words and rhythms, provide profound insights into human characters, and reveal often surprising but purposeful effects. Kleist has been called the single most important paragon of German literature.

"Classic" versus "Romantic"?

Although German literary history distinguishes sharply between "classic" and "romantic" authors, readers of translations may have difficulty in seeing such an exact distinction. Both movements—if in fact they were separate—found ways to harmonize the two opposite cravings of pure reason and dark brooding. Goethe's was knowing, large, and imaginatively daring. He was appalled by the "senseless violence" of the young Kleist's dramas and did what was necessary to keep Kleist from a theatrical career. Kleist, unable to lead a successful public life, committed suicide a few years later.

Like Novalis (pen name of Friedrich von Hardenberg, 1772–1801), Kleist took an opposite direction from Goethe, embracing the extremes of classic and romantic at once. He expressed the irrational as though it made sense and formulated paradox as the equation that engenders the world. Novalis, who died at the age of twenty-eight, has become quite topical once more with his essay "Christendom

or Europe" (1799), which describes the ideal of a united Europe reconciled by the Christian faith. His emphatic, mystical poems (*Hymns to the Night,* 1800) combine a sense of unquestioned faith with a longing for death, inspired by the early death of his fiancée.

Ludwig Tieck (1773–1853) and E. T. A. Hoffmann (1776–1822), on the other hand, were less interested in religious questions than in exploring the unconscious and often dangerous and sinister side of genius. Tieck drew on the tradition of fairy tales, highlighting the strain of dark fable that inhabits the German folk imagination, which Jacob and Wilhelm Grimm (1785–1863, 1786–1859) were bringing to light in their retellings. A novelist and playwright, but more than anything an organizer and inspirer, Tieck acquired lasting influence by his translations of SHAKESPEARE's complete works.

Two further authors of the classical period are Friedrich Hölderlin (1770–1843) and Jean Paul Friedrich Richter, called Jean Paul (1763–1825). Whereas Jean Paul's role was that of the idealistic, humanistic, and often humorous novelist, producing brilliant examples of the educational novel in *Titan* (1800–1803) and *The Awkward Age* (1804–5), Hölderlin was and perhaps still is the archetypal classical poet. His poems, particularly his odes and hymns such as "Bread and Wine," "Patmos," and "Celebration of Peace," embody the typically German attempt at reconciling the heritage of Greek and Roman antiquity and the classical gods with the Jewish-Christian concept of divinity and faith. His odes and hymns express the highest lyrical

achievement of what the philosophers of his time called the "transcendental" and the "absolute."

Literature in German is unimaginable without an intimate link to philosophy at its highest pitch. Immanuel Kant (1724–1804), F. W. J. von Schelling (1775–1854), and G. W. F. Hegel (1770–1831) subjected romantic insight to a technically proficient, formally disciplined analysis and transplanted the entire growth of Western philosophy from the soil of religion to the muddy and uncertain ground of the "I"—the "subject." Four later great minds writing in German, all of them originators of world revolutions of different kinds, tried to nail down the radical instability of that same romantic subjectivity. Karl Marx (1818–1883) and Sigmund Freud (1856–1939) built systems defining it according to some predictable mechanism—the means of production or the biological drives. Friedrich NIETZSCHE (1844–1900) and Carl Gustav Jung (1875–1961) took the opposite path of grounding it in universal concepts denied rationalism, the first emphasizing the "Dionysian"—an elemental unity with nature—and the second an archetypal realm underlying conscious thought.

To varying degrees, most of the authors who called themselves romantics departed from the Greek focus of classicism. Amplifying the mysterious and undefinable dimensions of the medieval Christian faith and of current folk culture, they often still retained the culture's medieval as well as pagan roots. Many of these were committed Christians such as the Catholics Joseph von Eichendorff

(1788–1857) and Clemens Brentano (1778–1842), author of fairy tales, poems, and a three-volume collection of folk songs, *The Boy's Miracle Horn* (1805–1818).

Novels and Poetry

The German novel has a varied history. As an "idea" it positively scintillated; it was to unite all the greatest traits of all the genres from the Greeks to the English, according to Novalis and his fellow writers in the "Athenäeum" group, Friedrich and August Wilhelm Schlegel (1772–1829, 1767–1845). But no German novel actually written ever seemed to please them. They considered those conceived in the romantic movement too quirky and capricious. Yet at this same time German writers gave to the world the dominant structure for the novel in the form of the *Bildungsroman,* a narrative of education that recounts the growth of a youth's sensibility through adventures, misadventures, musings, and a bourgeois rite of passage into maturity.

Among the poets of the nineteenth century during or after the decline of the romantic movement, the Protestant vicar and poet Eduard Mörike (1804–1875) has influenced generations of young and old readers with his comforting and comfortable poems, short stories, and fairy tales, among them "The Gnome of Stuttgart" (1852) and *Mozart on His Journey to Prague* (1855). More aggressive and innovative, Georg Büchner (1813–1837) irritated the literary world with his social-revolutionary

plots, as in his play *Danton's Death* (1835). His posthumously published drama *Woyzeck* (1879) scandalized opera lovers in Alban Berg's piercingly expressionistic opera of 1925.

Somewhere between Mörike and Büchner is Heinrich Heine (1797–1856), whose collections of poetry and essays describe individual feelings and social and political moods and events with a unique blend of sensitivity and irony, sometimes called mock-heroic poetry. Heine, a Jew who converted to Protestantism in order to "obtain an entrance ticket to society," never forgot his religious roots. His writing is most moving whenever he incorporates his old Jewish tradition with his new Christian experiences.

One of the few remarkable female authors of the period was Annette von Droste-Hülshoff

Thomas Mann (1875–1955).

(1797–1848). A Catholic with deep faith, she wrote ballads, penetratingly searching spiritual poems, and the novel *The Jews' Beech Tree* (1842)—all appreciated as unparalleled examples of sensuous, faith-inspired realism in an austere, often dark and somber language.

At the turn of the century the realistic movement progressed to the naturalistic movement, employing detached narration and minute detail to describe the lives of the impoverished. Foremost among the German naturalists was Gerhart Hauptmann (1862–1946), whose "social drama" *The Weavers* (1892) highlighted the plight of the lower classes in a society with slowly disintegrating pillars. Later in his life Hauptmann wrote such plays as *Hamlet in Wittenberg* (1935) and was celebrated as a kind of reincarnation of Goethe. Surprisingly, however, he turned into an admirer and supporter of Hitler's Nazis.

Simultaneously, anti-naturalistic tendencies were exemplified by such writers as Rainer Maria Rilke (1875–1926) and Hermann Hesse (1877–1962). Rilke, considered the most important figure in twentieth-century German poetry, still commands a worldwide readership around his poems and the novel *The Notes of Malte Laurids Brigge* (1910). And Hesse's popularity in German-speaking countries rose again in the sixties and seventies as the American youth culture sought new, esoteric experiences inspired by Buddhism, exemplified in his novels *Siddhartha* (1922), *Steppenwolf* (1927), and *The Glass Bead Game* (1943).

As Somber as the Century

German literature of the twentieth century is necessarily somber and chaotic. In a time when politicians and many artists opted to replace the human image with angel, monster, or machine, strong notes of condemnation of the increasing inhumanity were struck by such Christian authors as Ricarda Huch (1864–1947), Gertrud von Le Fort (1876–1971), Werner Bergengruen (1892–1964), and Reinhold Schneider (1903–1942). Schneider, for instance, wrote the much translated novel *Las Casas vor Karl V.* (1938; translated as *Imperial Mission*), a passionate protest against the persecution of minorities that is widely understood as an attack against the anti-Jewish politics of the Nazis. Other authors, however, offered determined resistance, including the pagan existentialist Ernst Jünger (b. 1895) with his heroic war diary *In Tempests of Steel* (1922), the anti-Nazi resistance novel *On the Marble Cliffs* (1942), and almost countless editions of novels and diaries that have made him the most highly recognized German author in France.

The twentieth-century German novel has been dominated by two paths, near opposites of each other and punctuated by the Nazi years and the destruction of Germany. Thomas Mann (1875–1955), whose Nobel Prize–winning novel *Buddenbrooks* was published in 1901, exemplifies the tradition of the novel as exploration of interiority, of states of consciousness colored by the unconscious, and of reason as a

For Further Study

Selected criticism includes: Wolfgang Beutin et al., *History of German Literature: From the Beginnings to the Present Day,* Clare Krojzl, translator (Routledge, 1993); Andrew Weeks, *German Mysticism from Hildegard of Bingen to Ludwig Wittgenstein: A Literary and Intellectual History* (State University of New York Press, 1993); Werner Kohlschmidt, *A History of German Literature, 1760–1805,* Ian Hilton, translator (Holmes & Meier, 1975); Eric A. Blackall, *The Novels of the German Romantics* (Cornell, 1983); Erich Heller, *The Artist's Journey into the Interior and Other Essays* (Random House, 1965) and *The Disinherited Mind: Essays in Modern German Literature and Thought* (Harcourt, 1975); Michael Hamburger, *A Proliferation of Prophets: Essays on German Writers from Nietzsche to Brecht* (Carcanet, 1983) and *After the Second Flood: Essays on Post-War German Literature* (Carcanet, 1986).

sublime achievement of balance before the abyss. Mann's subsequent works, among them *Death in Venice* (1912), *The Magic Mountain* (1924), and the biblical tetralogy *Joseph and His Brothers* (1933–43), secured his reputation as one of the few German authors of worldwide renown. Other distinguished novelists of consciousness were Hermann Broch (1886–1951), author of *The Sleepwalkers* (1932) and *The Death of Virgil* (1945), and Robert Musil (1880–1942), who wrote *The Man without Qualities* (1930–60).

The opposite path for the novel is defined by Franz KAFKA, who renews the intensity of the experience of human life as paradox: inexplicable, unjustifiable, and an endless source of wonder. Kafka and Walter Benjamin (1892–1940), perhaps the greatest essayist of the century (*One-Way Street; Illuminations,* 1961), stand as reproachful reminders of the quickening presence of Jewish writers in German literature.

Significantly, the reputations of both rose after World War II, when a new generation reflected on an era of debased representations of the human spirit to discover these authors who kept alive the tradition of serious questioning, interior wandering, and paradoxical response as a vital antidote.

Undoubtedly, some contemporary authors have already secured a place for themselves in the canon of German and world literature: Heinrich Böll (1917–1985), Nobel Prize winner in 1972, with such novels as *House without Guardian* (1954) and *Billiards at Half-Past Nine* (1959) and Günter Grass (b. 1927) with his internationally successful novels, such as *The Tin Drum* (1959). At the end of its most violent century, German literature reflects in its constant attempts to reconcile darkness and light the crucial questions not only of Germany but of the human heart in general.

—Carsten Peter Thiede

JOHN KEATS

The Great Odes
1819

Five of the supreme odes of the English language were written by one man, John Keats, in one of the precious twenty-five years allotted for his life.

These poems—"Ode to Psyche," "Ode on Melancholy," "Ode to a Nightingale," "To Autumn," and "Ode on a Grecian Urn"—have engaged endless commentary among reflective minds and affected the imagination of virtually every serious writer since their day.

"The odes are so germinal to English literature," one authority has written, "that they have been used as a standard to determine its nature."

As a unified sequence, the odes are concerned with the relation of poetry to truth and of truth to life. Their exploration of the center of creativity connecting sense and the intellect, "teases us out of thought" and engulfs us in what Keats spoke of as the "dark mysteries of human souls." Keats's letters, written at the same time as the odes, are important parallel documents that provide a prose basis for his theory of imagination.

John Keats (1795–1821), engraving after the portrait by Walter Hilton.

A Terrible Urgency, a Lasting Legacy

John Keats was born in London on October 31, 1795, and died in Rome on February 23, 1821—not quite four months after his arrival there on his twenty-fifth birthday. Those months in Rome were miserable, like most of his life. His father had died when he was eight,

his mother when he was fourteen. He was apprenticed to an apothecary at fifteen and entered medical school when he was twenty. He nursed his brother Charles during the last stages of tuberculosis and contracted the disease himself two years later.

The determining choice of his life, however, occurred when he gave up medicine for poetry. His friendship with the writer Leigh Hunt had introduced him to the poetic stir all about him; it was a time when, under the influence of the new "spirit of the age," the lyric was again assuming primary importance. In one early poem, "Sleep and Poetry," Keats indicated his urgency:

> O for ten years that I may overwhelm
> Myself in poetry; So I may do the deed
> That my own soul has to itself decreed.

At this point, however, he had only six, not ten, remaining years. But he can hardly be matched in any language for the speed and energy with which his poetic talent unfolded. At first he wrote rather ordinary verse in the inherited

Darkling I listen, and, for many a time
  I have been half in love with easeful Death,
Call'd him soft names in many a mused rhyme,
  To take into the air my quiet breath;
Now more than ever seems it rich to die,
  To cease upon the midnight with no pain,
While thou art pouring forth thy soul abroad
  In such an ecstasy!

—"Ode to a Nightingale"

style of the day. Then suddenly, after reading the Iliad, he composed the magnificent "On First Looking into Chapman's Homer," the sonnet that uses the discovery of the Pacific Ocean as a metaphor for the "wild surmise" of discovery itself.

Keats then began a huge project, *Endymion,* the story of a mortal in love with the moon. Dissatisfied with the poem before he finished it, however, he nevertheless persisted with it while conceiving his next long poem, *Hyperion,* an epic modeled on MILTON's style in *Paradise Lost*. This too displeased him; he saw the danger of being so strongly influenced by any predecessor and no doubt discovered the difficulty of writing an epic in the modern era. About this time he developed his theory of the poet's essential "negative capability"—the ability to put aside self in order to participate in the identity of another being.

In the following year, 1819, he composed his great poems: "The Eve of St. Agnes," "La Belle Dame sans Merci," "Lamia," the sonnets, the five odes, and another, "Ode to Indolence," not published until after his death. During the last year of his life, 1820, he was unable to write because of his illness. In search of a warm climate, he traveled to Rome with his friend, the painter Charles Severn. The agony of his dying was heightened by isolation, the cold dankness of Rome, his hopeless love of his betrothed, Fanny Brawne, and his despair at not accomplishing what he intended in poetry.

On his epitaph are the words (at his direction): "Here lies one whose name was writ in water."

Lyric Classics: The Five Odes

But his prophecy proved untrue: his name is forever "writ" in that repository of highest poetry that makes up a people's consciousness and memory. It is hard to imagine that he would have surpassed his best poems, even had he lived to an old age.

Keats's great odes were actually written in six months—from April to September, 1819. The ode, a traditional classical form rooted in the dissimilar styles of the Roman poet Horace and the Greek lyricist Pindar, had been given new vigor by eighteenth-century English poets; and several of the romantics had used the form to examine their commitment to the poetic vocation. Keats's odes departed from the two traditional modes, being written in regular stanzas. They are, in effect, the dialogue of an intense soul with itself, each exploring in a different context an aspect of the poet's ardent search for the real.

Though of course each ode stands alone, the five may be viewed as succeeding stages in the poetic process, which, for Keats, also represents the journey of the soul. The first, "Ode to Psyche," could be said to depict the discovery of the *eros* of poetry, with the nymph Psyche representing the quest for union with divine love. The poet vows to build an altar to Psyche in "some untrodden region" of his mind. The second in the series, "Ode on Melancholy," discovers that the "wakeful anguish of the soul," the longing of the poet for vision, leads to the shrine of the goddess Melancholy, who dwells in the "very temple of delight." Only those who taste the fullness of joy can experience her somber depths. The third poem, "Ode to a Nightingale," traces the actual poetic experience, following the path of imagination as it enters the dark forest, carried there not by "the dull brain," but by "the viewless wings of poesy." In this hallowed realm where the nightingale sings across time to all sorts and conditions of humanity, the poet seeks insight and briefly achieves it. The

Part of the ancient forum, Rome.

fourth, "To Autumn," depicts the ripeness—the dream-like state of fertility   that precedes the making of the poem, using harvest as its metaphor. Finally, "Ode on a Grecian Urn" concerns the finished work of art and its relation to the viewer, embodying its testimony to beauty as a mode of truth. Keats resolves each of his odes with the completeness and all-embracing repose of a feminine symbol: Psyche, Melancholy, the nightingale (Philomela), the goddess of harvest (Cybele), and finally the "still unravished bride of quietness" (the urn).

"Ode on a Grecian Urn"

"What the imagination seizes as beauty must be truth," Keats wrote in an oft-quoted letter. This theme is central to the most famous of the odes, the "Ode on a Grecian Urn," in which the poet demonstrates the validity of the claim that truth is beauty and beauty truth.

Like many other Keats poems, "Ode on a Grecian Urn" begins with a direct address in which the speaker ostensibly invokes the urn, a "foster-child of silence and slow time." Keats's lyric voice elicits a dreamlike meditation on the mystery and timelessness of the urn—this "sylvan historian"—transforming the concrete situation into a universal truth. Readers observe the silent urn from the perspective of the poet, the viewer, and humanity in general.

One side of the urn depicts a festival, with a musician playing an instrument and a young man pursuing and almost overtaking a maiden. "Yet do not grieve though thou hast not thy bliss," the speaker advises the lover: "Forever wilt thou love and she be fair!" The work of art has thus caught and preserved human feeling at its most intense. On the other side of the urn, a crowd has come to celebrate a different kind of ritual—a sacrifice. And here Keats performs a truly marvelous feat: he creates in the reader's imagination the empty town that has been deserted by all the people on the urn. The celebration of the two most sacred rituals of a com-

Heard melodies are sweet; but those unheard
Are sweeter; therefore, ye soft pipes, play on;
Not to the sensual ear, but, more endear'd,
Pipe to the spirit ditties of no tone. . . .

—"Ode on a Grecian Urn"

munity—those surrounding love and sacrifice—thus gives immortality to an entire way of life.

By the end of the poem, the urn's permanence, deriving from its high beauty, "teases us out of thought as doth eternity." Although we lack factual knowledge concerning the figures on the urn—their village, religion, or festivals—we have nonetheless come to partake of a different kind of truth about them. And this truth has been conveyed through nobility of form. The urn has outlived the past—and will outlive us because of its beauty. It has been preserved through all the ruin of time; and though silent it nevertheless powerfully expresses a verity: "Beauty is truth, truth beauty. That is all / Ye know on earth and all ye need to know."

Issues to Explore

(1) If poetry is considered, as it was in the romantic age, to be a means to the spiritual life, do Keats's stages of progression in his odes seem applicable to the ordinary person as well as to the poet? (2) In what sense is the Grecian urn a "foster-child of silence and slow time"? How has it been fostered by these two? (3) Quite obviously, the Grecian urn's pronouncement that "Beauty is truth, truth beauty," does not refer to either beauty or truth in the literal sense. Can these two ever be the same thing? (4) In what way does the imagination function differently from the process of rational thinking?

—Louise Cowan

For Further Study

The best edition of Keats's poetry is Jack Stillinger's *The Poetry of John Keats* (Harvard, 1978). Hyder E. Rollins has edited in two volumes *The Letters of John Keats, 1814–1821* (Harvard, 1958). The standard biography is by W. J. Bate: *John Keats* (Harvard, 1963, 1979), though an early account of Keats's life by Amy Lowell is sympathetic and readable (Houghton Mifflin, 1925). Helpful and important studies of the poetry are Helen Vendler, *The Odes of Keats* (Harvard, 1983), and Earl R. Wasserman, *The Finer Tone: Keats's Major Poems* (Johns Hopkins, 1967).

ALEXIS DE TOCQUEVILLE
Democracy in America
1835, 1840

*A*lexis de Tocqueville's *Democracy in America* is arguably the most penetrating and certainly the most quoted analysis of Americans and their government. It has been called "the standard source for generalizing about America" (historian Daniel J. Boorstin); Tocqueville as a commentator has been pronounced "possibly beyond rivalry" (President Woodrow Wilson). Though written by a foreigner, *Democracy in America* was required reading in secondary schools throughout the United States for many decades. In it Tocqueville framed principal issues of American politics, from the dangers of the tyranny of the majority to the problems of excessive individualism.

An Adventurer in Democracy

Born in 1805 to French nobility, Tocqueville lived in a time of great turmoil in his homeland. Revolutionaries who professed democratic values had overthrown the old monarchy in 1789. Instead of installing a free government,

Alexis de Tocqueville (1805–1859), by Theodore Chassériau, 1850.

however, they instituted a series of tyrannies, guillotining thousands, including Tocqueville's grandfather and aunt. Tocqueville's father Hervé was only twenty-four years old when released from prison, but his hair had turned completely white.

But personal tragedy did not make Tocqueville an enemy to democracy. Instead, convinced that its spread was inevitable, he strove to make democracy peaceful and

friendly toward liberty. As a writer and statesman (he served in the French judiciary and parliament for a number of years, eventually becoming France's foreign minister), he sought to protect the people's rights while fostering a sense not only of community but of independence. He equally opposed both those who would destroy tradition in the name of democracy and those who would destroy freedom in the name of tradition.

On May 11, 1831, the twenty-five-year-old Tocqueville landed in Manhattan. He sought to escape political turmoil and intrigue by traveling to America with his friend and colleague Gustave de Beaumont. Officially he came to the New World to report on American prison reforms. But his real reason was more adventurous—to analyze the young American democracy as a backdrop for proposals to develop freedom in France.

During the next nine months Tocqueville traveled seven thousand miles by steamer, stagecoach, and horseback, conducting hundreds of interviews and filling fourteen notebooks. He and Beaumont journeyed across most of what would become the eastern United States. They observed local customs, conversed with typical and atypical Americans, and prepared general interpretations of the American character. *Democracy in America* was born as a result.

No Mere Flattery

The first volume of Tocqueville's work was hailed a classic as soon as it was published in France in 1835. An English translation followed at once, with accompanying praise. But readers received the second volume less warmly in 1840 because of the mistaken assumption that it was unfriendly toward democracy. As Tocqueville himself observed, he always intended to serve as a true friend to democracy, offering constructive criticism rather than mere flattery.

The free institutions of the United States and the political rights enjoyed there provide a thousand continual reminders to every citizen that he lives in society. At every moment they bring his mind back to this idea, that it is the duty as well as the interest of men to be useful to their fellows. Having no particular reason to hate others, since he is neither their slave nor their master, the American's heart easily inclines toward benevolence. At first it is of necessity that men attend to the public interest, afterward by choice. What had been calculation becomes instinct. By dint of working for the good of his fellow citizens, he in the end acquires a habit and taste for serving them.

—*Democracy in America*
J. P. Mayer, ed., George Lawrence, trans.

Although a lover of democracy, Tocqueville hated democratic *revolution.* He saw in it the potential for tyranny and the tearing of people from their familiar and accepted beliefs, practices, and institutions. His second great work, *The Old Regime and the French Revolution,* stud-

ied the causes of democratic revolution in France. His posthumously published *Souvenirs* is an acerbic commentary on the weaknesses of France's democratic governors during the socialist revolution of 1848.

Tocqueville died in 1859 during a self-imposed exile after yet another dictator took over the French government. He was working on what surely would have become another classic: *The European Revolution,* which survives in draft form and examines the consequences of the revolution of 1789. In it, Tocqueville argued that the drive for equality produces violence and tyranny when divorced from the decent customs of local life.

Fifty Years On

Democracy in America offers a wide panorama of American democracy fifty years after the Revolution. In the first volume, Tocqueville outlines the dangers of a democratic tyranny of the majority. In the second he warns of a new, soft form of despotism (ultimate rule) that would make American life easier but would destroy its meaning. Democracy, he maintains, tends to flatten people's personalities, making them creatures of mass opinion and enslaving them to the drive for material security, comfort, and equality.

Tocqueville also fears an "individualism" that would force Americans to withdraw from public life into the comforts of private and family life. The government would then oversee an increasing number of the tasks originally carried out by families, churches, and local associations. Towns would become mere slaves to state and federal officials. Local, voluntary associations in which citizens learn to treat others decently would wither and die. Americans would no longer serve their neighbors. Instead they would bow to the faceless majority and the state, which would care for their needs as it told them how to live and what to believe.

These concerns, however, merely point to the central questions Tocqueville raises: What moral habits are necessary if a people are to remain free? And, even more fundamentally, why is it good to be a free people? Here he differs distinctly from modern observers. The

"Liberty Leading the People," 1830, by Eugene Delacroix.

secret of American democracy, Tocqueville says, lies not in the abundance of its natural resources or in the genius of its laws and Constitution, but in the mores or "habits of the heart" formed in the American townships. Only with the proper feelings and habits can a people remain free.

Tocqueville praises American local self-rule and individual rights—property rights in particular—precisely because they "provide a thousand continual reminders to every citizen that he lives in society." Citizens need to share responsibility because "it is the duty as well as the interest of men to be useful to their fellows."

The First Political Institution

Tocqueville's comments on religion in American public life are particularly astute. Whereas in France he has "always seen the spirit of religion and the spirit of liberty marching in opposite directions," in America they are "intimately united." The reason lies in the separation of church and state, which dissociates religion from government but not religion from society or public life. Indeed, precisely because of this separation, for Americans reli-

gion "must be regarded as the first of their political institutions."

Independent of state control, religion has played a dominant role in shaping the people's customs and habits. It has provided answers to the fundamental questions of life, teaching Americans that some issues, such as God's will, cannot be voted on "democratically."

> *The great object of justice is to substitute the idea of right for that of violence, to put intermediaries between the government and the use of its physical force.*
>
> —*Democracy in America*
> J. P. Mayer, ed., George Lawrence, trans.

Churches have also been important participants in social life. They have given religious sanction to the daily charitable and other social acts performed by Americans. Religion forms good characters, making people capable of ruling themselves, instead of being ruled by kings or dictators. In this way religion has also taught people how to use their freedom—by serving

Local institutions are to liberty what primary schools are to science; they put it within the people's reach; they teach people to appreciate its peaceful enjoyment and accustom them to make use of it.

—*Democracy in America*
J. P. Mayer, ed., George Lawrence, trans.

For Further Study

Democracy in America is a very readable book, filled with descriptions of local customs and the countryside. Although it is quite long—two volumes and over seven hundred pages—it is well worth reading in full. One volume can be read at a time. No abridged edition exists that does justice to Tocqueville's vision.

Two standard translations are available: Henry Reeve, revised by Francis Bowen, *Democracy in America,* two volumes (Vintage, 1945), and George Lawrence, *Democracy in America* (Anchor, 1969). Helpful commentaries include Jean Claude Lamberti, *Tocqueville and the Two Democracies* (Harvard, 1989), and Ken Masugi, editor, *Interpreting Tocqueville's* Democracy in America (Rowman and Littlefield, 1991). A useful biography that also provides commentary on Tocqueville's work is J. P. Mayer, *Alexis de Tocqueville: A Biographical Essay in Political Science* (Viking, 1940). The most complete biography is Andre Jardin, *Tocqueville: A Biography* (Farrar, Straus, Giroux, 1988).

their friends and neighbors according to the Golden Rule.

Democracy in America is not only a fascinating snapshot of an earlier America but an important yardstick for measuring contemporary America. It analyzes the workings of a free society and religion's critical role in ensuring that it remains free. It shows that when the Christian faith is protected from state interference it can provide both the possibility of salvation in the next life and the rules and habits to lead decent lives in this life. Only those shaped by religious understanding and experience will consistently seek to follow the Golden Rule, serving their families and neighbors.

Issues to Explore

Tocqueville analyzes the habits of the heart necessary for a good life and a free society. Some questions to ask are: (1) Is faith merely a useful tool to most Americans, providing rules by which to lead productive lives? Or does faith set people on the true path, whatever the day-to-day consequences? What would Tocqueville think? (2) Tocqueville saw local control over daily life as the key to virtue. Is he correct? Can we have a national government that takes care of all of our needs and still lead decent lives? (3) Tocqueville describes the American political system in detail. Is his description still relevant? Why or why not?

—Bruce Frohnen

RALPH WALDO EMERSON

Essays
1841, 1844

he need was never greater of new revelation than now," Ralph Waldo Emerson told a group of Harvard Divinity School students in 1838, and from that point on, he set to fill that need by writing and by inspiring others. In essays written over three decades, Emerson preached a gospel of steadfast faith in the innocence of the self and exhorted Americans to believe that they could retain Christian morality and spirituality even as they abandoned the creeds of the Christian faith. The works in which Emerson set about this task are models of creative, poetic prose. They have endured because of their enormous influence on later writers and because they provide one of the best keys we have to unlock the mysteries of the American psyche.

The Evangelist of the American Self

Born into a long line of New England clergymen, Emerson trained for the pastorate and served for a short period as a minister. After only three years in the pulpit, however, he broke with his

Ralph Waldo Emerson (1803–1882).

church in 1832 over the administration of the Lord's Supper. He was offended by the particularity of the gospel and church rituals. Instead of proclaiming a gospel rooted in the life of Jesus and the history of the church, he longed to proclaim a message about the universal spiritual principle residing in every human being.

When Emerson exchanged his pulpit for a lectern and the sermon

for the essay, he helped to change the course of American literature dramatically. He became the foremost American evangelist of the gospel of the innocent, infinite self. Emerson died in 1882, less than a month before his seventy-ninth birthday.

The Sacred Integrity of the Human Mind

The heart of Emerson's thinking appears in the essays he wrote in the decades after leaving the Unitarian church. In these works, Emerson developed a distinctly romantic understanding of God, culture, and the self in a philosophy that has come to be called "Transcendentalism." The hallmarks of his creed included belief in the divinity of the self, the spiritual significance of nature, and the centrality of the poet in human life. Although Emerson wrote scores of important essays, the core of his thought may be found in four of the most accomplished and widely read: "The American Scholar," "The Divinity School Address," "Self-Reliance," and "The Poet."

To believe your own thought, to believe that what is true for you in your private heart, is true for all men,—that is genius. Speak your latent conviction and it shall be the universal sense; for always the inmost becomes the outmost—and our first thought is rendered back to us by the trumpets of the Last Judgment. Familiar as the voice of the mind is to each, the highest merit we ascribe to Moses, Plato, and Milton, is that they set as naught books and traditions, and spoke not what men thought but what they thought.

—"Self Reliance"

Belief in the essential goodness of the self underlies all the essays. If "man has been wronged," Emerson writes in "The American Scholar," it is because "he has wronged himself. He has almost lost the light that can lead him back to his prerogatives." Like key figures before him in the Enlightenment and romantic movement, Emerson saw the self as born innocent in the state of nature. "Trust thyself," he argues in "Self-Reliance": "every heart vibrates to that iron string." Emerson would say that we can attribute our traumas and dilemmas to our failure to follow the dictates of that pure self. Because "society everywhere is in conspiracy against the manhood of every one of its members," "Self-Reliance" argues that we must trust the self's deepest intuitions. We must "believe that what is true for you in your private heart, is true for all men,—that is genius."

Emerson's view of the self is a radical distortion of the Protestant view. That is, it carries certain insights or impulses of the Reformation to extreme conclusions. For instance, by scaling back the number of sacraments from seven to two and by stressing the vital importance of the will in the process of salvation, the Reformation removed some of the mystery of the faith and granted unprecedented importance to the human spirit. In "Self-Reliance," Emerson continues the process of removing the

sacred and takes it as far as it can go: "Nothing is at last sacred but the integrity of our own mind. . . . A man is to carry himself in the presence of all opposition as if every thing were titular and ephemeral but he."

That is not to say, however, that Emerson dismissed nature as a trivial reality. On the contrary, he thought of the natural realm as a source of boundless meaning. "Nature is the opposite of the soul, answering to it part for part," he explains in "The American Scholar." "Its laws are the laws of his [humanity's] own mind." The enlightened person can see that "the ancient precept, 'Know thyself,' and the modern precept, 'Study nature,' become at last one maxim." As Emerson asserts in "The Poet," "the world is a temple, whose walls are covered with emblems, pictures, and commandments of the Deity. . . ."

All we need to do, Emerson believed, is to interpret the myriad messages God has written on every page of the book of nature. To help us decipher the meaning of the world and our experience, we have the poet. "For, as it is dislocation and detachment from the life of God that make things ugly, the poet, who re-attaches things to nature and the Whole, . . . disposes very easily of the most disagreeable facts." Past religions granted priests or pastors the power to interpret sacred texts. But in Emersonian romanticism, such holy men are a hindrance and must step aside to clear the way for the poets.

A Challenging "Prophet"

Emerson's essays raise provocative questions for the Christian understanding of the self, nature, and God. They especially challenge Protestants to confront the potential of certain tendencies in the Reformation tradition. In reacting against what is perceived as a mechanical understanding of grace in Catholic practice, Protestants have stressed the centrality of personal response in faith. But Emerson has done to Protestants what Protestants did to Catholics. Because his essays promote the "divine sufficiency of the individual," all the traditions and texts of the Christian faith

"Emerson in ecstasy over Nature," sketch from the notebooks of Richard Church.

become mere repositories of dead wisdom and discarded practices.

At the same time, Christians need to recognize the truths embodied in Emerson's critique, for at the heart of Judeo-Christian belief has always been a tradition of prophetic judgment. In his iconoclasm and skepticism about all dogmas and rituals, Emerson gives voice to that prophetic cast of mind. For example, when he writes in "The Divinity School Address" that the "prayers and even the dogmas of our church . . . [are] wholly insulated from anything now extant in the life and business of the people," he states an ever-present danger in Christian ministry.

In the end, the temptations facing Emerson are the same ones that assail all prophets. Prophets can forget that they are mere messengers and not the source of the message they have to convey. Believing the self to be a great repository of truth, an Emersonian can too easily fail to distinguish that self from God. Emerson himself took such a distinction—between God and humans—to be meaningless. As he explained to the group of Harvard Divinity School students, Jesus Christ himself taught the doctrine of the human as God: "He saw that God incarnates himself in man, and evermore goes forth anew to take possession of his world."

The Poetry of His Prose

Emerson's essays are studded with sentences that read like lines from great poems. Their arresting imagery has the ability to seize the attention of readers and prompt them to undertake a fresh assessment of their lives. Although Emerson also wrote poems, it was in his essays that he accomplished most as a poet; the metaphors, analogies, and stylistic surprises of the sentences mark him as one of the great masters of American prose.

Emerson's accomplishments as a writer of stunning sentences, however, also point to the problems that readers may encounter when imagining how the world might look if governed by Emersonian principles. One critic stated the problem well: "The problem of Emerson's prose was the same as that of his philosophy, how to reconcile the individual with society, how to join his sentences into a paragraph." At times it is as difficult to detect how Emerson's paragraphs and whole essays cohere as it is to imagine how a group of fallen individuals believing in their own divinity could live in peace in community.

Issues to Explore

The reader of Emerson's essays can profit by asking questions such as these: (1) In what way does Emerson depend on the images and insights of the Scriptures and the Christian tradition, even as he seeks to be free of the authority of the Christian faith? (2) How does Emerson attempt to reconcile his celebration of the individual with the realities of life in community? (3) For what reasons does Emerson see the artist or poet as the central figure of the modern age? (4) Because Emerson places such great faith in the innocence and power of the self, what are the consequences if one loses faith in that self?

—Roger Lundin

For Further Study

Emerson's essays are available in a number of affordable formats. The Library of America volume, *Emerson: Essays and Lectures* (1983), is the most comprehensive single-volume collection of his major works. Gay Wilson Allen's biography, *Waldo Emerson* (Viking, 1981), is essential reading for an understanding of Emerson's life. For the cultural background to his work, one can profitably consult F. O. Matthiessen's *American Renaissance* (Oxford, 1941) and Lawrence Buell's *New England Literary Culture* (Cambridge, 1986).

FREDERICK DOUGLASS

Narrative of the Life of Frederick Douglass: An American Slave
1845

Frederick Douglass (c. 1817–1895).

The *Narrative of the Life of Frederick Douglass: An American Slave*, an outstanding document of human liberty and stirring cry for freedom for *all* Americans, is also the best and earliest example of the slave narrative. The *Narrative* falls in this important nineteenth-century genre of American letters that arose after slaves achieved freedom, usually through flight. These biographies of former slaves were decisive in rallying public outrage against slavery in the decades before the Civil War.

"Am I Not a Man and a Brother?"

Frederick Douglass (c. 1817–1895) was the son of a slave woman and a white man, rumored to be his master. Separated from his mother at birth, he was never sure how old he was. He pondered this uncertainty in his *Narrative:* "By far the larger part of the slaves know as little of their ages as horses know of theirs, and it is the wish of most masters within my knowledge to keep their slaves thus ignorant."

Douglass escaped slavery when he was twenty one, moving from the Eastern Shore of Maryland to Massachusetts and changing his name from Bailey to Douglass. While there he became immersed in the abolitionist movement, delivering spectacular speeches in the Northern states and abroad. An imposing presence on the lectern, blessed with a booming voice and stately bearing, Douglass offered living proof that a black person could master English prose style as he sought to emancipate fellow human beings. The *Narrative* offers an endorsement for education ultimately as powerful as anything Benjamin Franklin or Ralph Waldo EMERSON ever wrote.

Douglass spoke against slavery for three years before writing his *Narrative.* Most slave narratives were transcribed by whites and thus their authority was often questioned, especially by Southern slave owners. To underscore authenticity when his *Narrative* was first published in 1845, the subtitle read *Written By Himself,* and the text was prefaced by testimonials from two major figures in the white abolitionist movement, William Lloyd Garrison and Wendell Phillips. Both point to Douglass's public lectures as a means of authenticating his narrative. Garrison argues that Douglass's case is representative: "The experience of Frederick Douglass, as a slave, was not a peculiar one; his lot was not especially a hard one; his case may be regarded as a very fair specimen of the treatment of slaves. . . . Many have suffered incomparably more. . . . Yet how deplorable was his situation!"

My long-crushed spirit rose, cowardice departed, bold defiance took its place; and I now resolved that, however long I might remain a slave in form, the day had passed forever when I could be a slave in fact.

—*Narrative of the Life of Frederick Douglass*

Telling a Free Story

Like other writers who depict slavery, including Harriet Beecher Stowe, Douglass conducts an encyclopedic tour of a hellish landscape, approached through what he calls the "blood-stained gate." His story details one hideous scene after another, such as when the child Frederick sees his cousin and his aunt savagely beaten and his grandmother put out into the woods to die. He himself struggles to survive hunger and cold, clad only in a tow shirt. Douglass writes in describing the harsh winters of his childhood, "My feet have been so cracked with the frost that the pen with which I am writing might be laid in the gashes."

Translating the codes of the slaves, Douglass teaches us how to hear the moving "sorrow songs" that whites until then had read as signs of contentment. "I have often sung to drown my sorrow, but seldom to express my happiness." The *Narrative* seems an extension of these spirituals; like the songs, Douglass's language is terse but often poetic. Throughout his account of a life of suffering, his poetic passages recall the Book of Job. For example, the white sails he sees on the Chesapeake Bay—images of sublime beauty and freedom—inspire a passionate outburst against his enslavement, akin to Job's laments:

> You are loosed from your moorings, and are free; I am fast in my chains, and am a slave! You move merrily before the gentle gale, and I sadly before the bloody whip! You are freedom's swift-winged angels, that fly round the world; I am confined in bands of iron! . . . O,

why was I born a man, of whom to make a brute! . . . O God, save me! God, deliver me! Let me be free!

But in his lament Douglass never loses sight of the brighter vision of humanity that is in line with the higher principles of the Christian faith he saw his masters abasing. His apt description of the dishonest man overseeing him illustrates this: "Poor man! such was his disposition, and success at deceiving, I do verily believe that he sometimes deceived himself into the solemn belief, that he was a sincere worshipper of the most high God."

Throughout the *Narrative* Douglass reveals how the slave owners blasphemously play God with their slaves. One owner paints the fence around his apple garden with tar to catch hungry thieves. The comparison with Eden seems unmistakable, but the symbolism of the supposed black "stain" that bars one from America's bounty emerges clearly as well.

This theme of power's corrupting poison weaves in and out of the narrative. Even formerly devout women can turn into monsters when they possess slaves; one once-kind mistress kills a young slave girl with a stick. Religion seemingly offers no remedy. Douglass's master, for example, undergoes conversion at a camp-meeting. Ironically, however, he becomes afterward even crueler to his slaves, citing biblical support for his harshness.

The tensions of despair and hope build to a climax when Douglass as a young man is hired out to the slave-breaker Covey for disciplining. In a powerful scene, Douglass, reinforced by a magic root sacred in African mythology, stands up to Covey and prevails in a grueling physical contest. In Douglass's words,

> This battle with Mr. Covey was the turning point in my career as a slave. It rekindled the few expiring embers of freedom, and revived within me a sense of my own manhood. It recalled the departed self-confidence, and inspired me again with a determination to be free.

For him, it is a "glorious resurrection," a Christian parable. "My long-crushed spirit rose, cowardice departed, bold defiance took its

Fugitive American slaves flee from Maryland to Delaware by way of the underground railway, 1850–51.

place; and now I resolved that, however long I might remain a slave in form, the day had passed forever when I could be a slave in fact."

Douglass had to omit the details of his escape, as others were still attempting to gain freedom as he wrote. The means therefore had to be concealed. But he shows how satisfying it is to hire *oneself* out in honest labor in the North, even though many of the same prejudices against blacks prevailed there as well.

Ultimately, the *Narrative* belongs with other jeremiads in American literature—those great works that chastise Americans for losing sight of their national ideals while urging them to seek a society that insures equal opportunity and participation for all its citizens. Douglass's *Narrative*, like the masterworks of his commanding contemporaries—Walt Whitman, Herman MELVILLE, and Henry David Thoreau—continues to span the years, urging Americans to meet the challenges of liberty, equality, and union.

Issues to Explore

Douglass's *Narrative* poses challenging questions, especially for the Christian. (1) How do Douglass's personal qualities mark him as a Christian? (2) How does the "Appendix" reveal the hypocrisy of many nineteenth-century American Christians? (3) How does the *Narrative* demonstrate that passivity—even in our

> *Mr. Covey's* forte *consisted in his power to deceive. His life was devoted to planning and perpetrating the grossest deceptions. Everything he possessed in the shape of learning or religion, he made conform to his disposition to deceive. He seemed to think himself equal to deceiving the Almighty.*
>
> —Narrative of the Life of Frederick Douglass

This battle with Mr. Covey was the turning-point in my career as a slave. It rekindled the few expiring embers of freedom, and revived within me a sense of my own manhood. It recalled the departed self-confidence, and inspired me again with a determination to be free.

—*Narrative of the Life of Frederick Douglass*

For Further Study

The *Narrative* is available today in many versions, including the recommended Benjamin Quarles's edition (Harvard, 1967). Penguin, New American Library, and Mentor also publish the text.

The *Narrative* was the first of several versions of Douglass's life. Of the others, the preferred version is *My Bondage and My Freedom* (1855), with the 1987 University of Illinois reprint containing an excellent introduction by William L. Andrews. Douglass's last autobiography, *Life and Times of Frederick Douglass* (1892), is available with an introduction by Rayford W. Logan (Macmillan, 1962).

Useful commentaries may be found in Eric Sundquist's *Frederick Douglass: New Literary and Historical Essays* (Cambridge, 1990) and in Sundquist's *To Wake the Nations* (Harvard, 1993). The standard biography is William S. McFeely's *Frederick Douglass* (Simon and Schuster, 1991). Also helpful is Nathan Huggins's *Slave and Citizen: The Life of Frederick Douglass* (Little, Brown, 1980).

own day—can lead ultimately to a slave-like existence? (4) How does it show that power can ultimately corrupt rather than facilitate self-development? (5) Discuss generally how religion functions in the lives of slaves.

(6) In a different vein, analyze how Douglass's actions coincide with other classical American writings, especially in terms of nonconformity, self-reliance, honesty, courage, and principles of justice. (7) Finally, literature is often said to provide a more accurate history than history books. In what ways does this seem true here? Why is it important to learn about slavery at all, and why must people attend to the voices of the slaves themselves?

—John Lowe

NATHANIEL HAWTHORNE
The Scarlet Letter
1850

When Nathaniel Hawthorne published *The Scarlet Letter* in 1850, he had no idea that his "tale of human frailty and sorrow" would become one of the most enduring classics in the American tradition. He set out to write a simple story about a poignant relationship in the distant past; what emerged was a profound meditation on the nature of guilt, the meaning of suffering, the struggle between freedom and authority, and the mysterious ironies of love and holy devotion. With the possible exception of Mark TWAIN's *The Adventures of Huckleberry Finn,* no other American novel has had a more enduring appeal or has assumed such a universally recognized status as a classic.

The Genesis of a Classic

The Scarlet Letter was published in a period when an extraordinary number of literary works of the highest order appeared in America. Some of those writings, such as Frederick DOUGLASS's *Narrative of the Life of Frederick Douglass* (1845)

Nathaniel Hawthorne (1804–1864).

and Harriet Beecher Stowe's *Uncle Tom's Cabin* (1852), dealt specifically with the pressing issue of slavery; others, such as Ralph Waldo EMERSON's *Representative Men* (1850) and Henry David Thoreau's *Walden* (1854), made more general calls to moral reform and personal perfection; yet others, especially Walt Whitman's *Leaves of Grass* (1855) and Herman MELVILLE's *Moby Dick* (1851), helped redefine the genres of the epic poem and the novel.

In many ways, *The Scarlet Letter* was the least innovative of these brilliant works. It neither challenged the conventions of the novel nor issued a call for dramatic social change. Instead, in this deceptively simple work, Hawthorne explored a series of perennial questions about guilt and grace, about the meaning of the Puritan past for the American present, about the nature of love and hate, and about the conflicts of interpretation that always come to the fore in American culture.

When *The Scarlet Letter* appeared, Hawthorne was already established as a major short-story writer. The novel was the first of four that he was to produce in the next decade. Following *The Scarlet Letter* came *The House of the Seven Gables, The Blithedale Romance,* and *The Marble Faun,* which was published in 1860. Hawthorne died in 1864.

Human Frailty and Sorrow

The Scarlet Letter has worked its way into the consciousness of American culture, so that even many who have not read it are somewhat

Thus, Hester Prynne, whose heart had lost its regular and healthy throb, wandered without a clew in the dark labyrinth of mind; now turned aside by an insurmountable precipice; now starting back from a deep chasm. There was wild and ghastly scenery all around her, and a home and comfort nowhere. At times, a fearful doubt strove to possess her soul, whether it were not better to send Pearl at once to heaven, and go herself to such futurity as Eternal Justice should provide.

The scarlet letter had not done its office.

—*The Scarlet Letter*

familiar with its plot. The novel opens in Boston in the year 1642. As punishment for her adultery, Hester Prynne must stand on public display on a scaffold in the center of town for three hours with her infant daughter Pearl in her arms and wear a large red "A" on her dress for the rest of her life.

By subjecting Hester to this particular punishment, the Puritan leaders set in motion the novel's central conflict between individual freedom and communal authority. Whatever the intentions of the Puritan authorities, however, the scarlet letter fails to "do its office." Hester's punishment brings her closer neither to God nor the Puritan community. Instead, in her isolation, Hester questions her community's most basic beliefs and even contemplates murdering Pearl and taking her own life.

Hester's partner in adultery is the Reverend Arthur Dimmesdale, the stellar young minister of the town. Hawthorne uses Dimmesdale's unwillingness to confess his sin to explore the torments of a guilty conscience. Dimmesdale's community and congregation are convinced of their own virtue and believe him to be a spotless pastor. Dimmesdale eloquently speaks of his general loathsomeness but remains silent about his specific sin of adultery. Hawthorne realized that a community that believes in its own purity and innocence can deal with its guilty practices only through hypocrisy.

The events of the novel unfold over seven years. Hester dwells on the outskirts of Boston, paying her penance and eking out a living as a seamstress. Dimmesdale flourishes as pastor but lives under the same roof with the physician Roger Chillingworth, whom the minister does not recognize as the husband of Hester Prynne. Having been separated from Hester for several years, Chillingworth arrived in Boston on the very day of her public humiliation. After intimidating Hester into remaining silent about his identity, Chillingworth pries into Dimmesdale's heart to learn its most guilty secret.

Hester eventually begs Arthur to run away with her: "What hast thou to do with all these iron men, and their opinions?" she asks. "They have kept thy better part in bondage too long already!" She pleads with him, "Preach! Write! Act! Do any thing, save to lie down and die!" However appealing Hester's plea might be, Hawthorne sees how it expresses the American belief that a change of place can lead to a change of heart. Like other great American fiction writers—including Herman Melville, Flannery O'CONNOR, and William FAULKNER—Hawthorne knew that we can never flee from the conflicts of history, because we carry history in our hearts.

After Hester's plea, Dimmesdale dies several days later in full public view in the arms of Hester Prynne and without having explicitly confessed his sin. Soon after this climax Chillingworth also dies, leaving Pearl a large estate. Pearl and Hester leave Boston, with Hester returning alone to the town years later. She is eventually buried near the remains of Arthur Dimmesdale. Though separated in life, they share in death a single tombstone with a brief inscription: "On a field, sable, the letter A, gules."

Perfection and Relevance

The Scarlet Letter has become a classic because of its formal perfection and perennially relevant subject matter. The work is framed by three scenes on the scaffolding at the novel's beginning, exact middle, and close. In each of

Hester Prynne is led to the pillory; an illustration by Hugh Tomson from *The Scarlet Letter.*

these scenes, the central characters—Hester, Arthur, Pearl, and Roger Chillingworth—are present. And in each instance, while Hester's guilt and shame are clear to her Puritan accusers, Dimmesdale's relationship to her remains shrouded in mystery. Hawthorne is extraordinarily economical in his telling of the tale. He employs a simple elegance to convey the passionate complexities of this drama.

Because it deals deftly and compellingly with questions of guilt and grace, of law and liberty, *The Scarlet Letter* continues to reveal the human condition in general and the conflicts of American culture in particular. In its depiction of the power of shame, the corrosive

effects of hypocrisy, and the ambiguities of love and hate, the novel explores timeless matters for all societies.

At the same time, Hawthorne is a skilled imaginative historian who raises many provocative questions about the Christian life in Colonial America. The opening chapter of *The Scarlet Letter,* for instance, points out that "the founders of a new colony, whatever Utopia of human virtue and happiness they might originally project, have invariably recognized" the need "to allot a portion of the virgin soil as a cemetery, and another portion as the site of a prison." In that single sentence, Hawthorne points to the enduring American conflict between the incredible expectations we hold for ourselves and our future, on the one hand, and the sober realities of our finite and fallen natures, on the other.

In *The Scarlet Letter,* as in much of his fiction, Hawthorne both admires the moral seriousness of the Puritans and abhors the suffering that their system of guilt brought on transgressors. In the opening scene, for instance, as Hester stands in shame on the scaffolding, Hawthorne writes, "there can be no outrage, methinks, against our common nature . . . more flagrant than to forbid the culprit to hide his face for shame." At the same time, he acknowledges that "the scene was not without a mixture of awe, such as must always invest the spectacle of guilt and shame in a fellow-creature, before society shall have grown corrupt enough to smile, instead of shuddering, at it."

Issues to Explore

As one reads *The Scarlet Letter,* such questions as the following arise: (1) What does Hawthorne admire about the Puritans? What does he deplore about them? About Hester? About Dimmesdale? (2) How do the Puritans fail to achieve their goals by making Hester wear her scarlet letter? (3) How does the letter affect each of the main characters in the novel, including the community as a whole? (4) Why does Dimmesdale refuse to confess his sin? What might happen to him if he were to do so? (5) Why is it that Chillingworth, who was truly the victim of Hester and Arthur's adultery, ends up ruined?

—Roger Lundin

For Further Study

The Scarlet Letter is available in a number of suitable, inexpensive editions. It is also included in the one-volume collection of Hawthorne's novels published by the Library of America (1983). Randall Stewart (Yale, 1948) and Arlin Turner (Oxford, 1980) have written reliable and readable biographies of Hawthorne. For critical background, F. O. Matthiessen's *American Renaissance* (Oxford, 1941) is still an excellent source. The chapter on Hawthorne in William Spengemann's *The Adventurous Muse* (Yale, 1977) lays out brilliantly the theological and interpretive issues at stake in the novel. For a splendid survey of the historical background to Hawthorne's fiction, see David Hackett Fischer's *Albion's Seed* (Oxford, 1989).

EMILY DICKINSON

The Complete Poems 1850–66

Emily Dickinson (1830–1886).

The family and friends who gathered for Emily Dickinson's funeral in Amherst, Massachusetts, on a sunny afternoon in May, 1886, had no idea that the woman they mourned was one of the greatest lyric poets in the English language. To the members of the group who assembled that day, Dickinson was a beloved sister and a dynamic, albeit eccentric, friend. All of the mourners knew that their reclusive neighbor had written poetry of a kind. Some were even aware that a very few of those poems had been published anonymously during her lifetime. None of them, however, had any real notion of the enormous scope of this woman's genius or the abiding power of the poems she had written. Yet within decades, Dickinson's daring and enigmatic poetry would secure for her a permanent place in the top echelon of poets in the English language

"Essential Oils —are wrung"

Emily Dickinson was born in Amherst in 1830. Her grandfather had been one of the founders of Amherst College, and her father became the College Treasurer and a member of the U.S. Congress. In adolescence Dickinson received a challenging education at the Amherst Academy and the Mount Holyoke Female Seminary. As a woman in mid-nineteenth-century New England, however, she found most professions closed to her.

When she returned home in 1848 after a year at Mount Holyoke, Dickinson faced the prospect of marriage or the single life. She chose the latter, and, years later, her brother Austin explained that "her curious leaving of outer life never seemed unnatural to him." Dickinson experienced a "normal blossoming and gradual retirement." Her later life was "perfectly natural," he told the first editor of her poetry.

Dickinson traveled once to Philadelphia and Washington, D.C., in 1855 to visit her father near the end of his term in Congress. In the mid-1860s she made two extended trips to Boston to receive treatment for a mysterious eye ailment. After that, for the last twenty years of her life, she never left Amherst again and only rarely journeyed beyond the grounds of her home.

The poetry Dickinson produced in her seclusion has appealed to a remarkably broad range of readers over the past century. Some find the verbal daring of her verse its most extraordinary quality; others find an unparalleled rendering of the great themes of love, suffering, joy, death, and eternal life in her poems; still others prize her poetry for its prophetic power to anticipate the

1433

How brittle are the Piers
On which our Faith doth tread—
No bridge below doth totter so—
Yet none hath such a Crowd.

It is as old as God—
Indeed—'twas built by him—
He sent his Son to test the Plank,
And he pronounced it firm.

—Emily Dickinson

tion, her habit of refusing to supply nouns, verbs, and key modifying words, and her frequently startling use of images combine to confound even as they delight.

A relatively early but unmistakably great Dickinson poem displays the beguiling mysteries of her work:

> Safe in their Alabaster Chambers—
> Untouched by Morning—
> And untouched by Noon—
> Lie the meek members of the Resurrection—
> Rafter of Satin—and Roof of Stone!—
>
> Grand go the Years—in the Crescent—above them—
> Worlds scoop their Arcs—
> And Firmaments—row—
> Diadems—drop—and Doges—surrender—
> Soundless as dots—on a Disc of Snow—
> [#216]

The opening lines are haunting in their depiction of tombs as "Alabaster Chambers" in which the "meek members of the Resurrection" wait patiently for their deliverance. Through images that speak of an excruciatingly tedious process, the second stanza shows how long these "meek" ones must wait. There is a certain kind of beauty in the description of constellations "scooping their Arcs" and "Firmaments rowing" their way across the heavens. The underlying note of these lines, however, is one of lonely resignation. The "Doges" of the last lines were rulers centuries ago in the Italian cities of Venice and Genoa; here they stand for all who inevitably fall silent before the indifferent power of death.

"Safe in their Alabaster Chambers" shares with many Dickinson poems a sharp sense of the vulnerability of the self. In some poems, she sees scientific discoveries about the vastness of space and time exposing that vulnerability; in other poems, changes in theological belief assail the self. For example, in a poem written late in her life, Dickinson explores the decline of faith in the modern world:

> Those—dying then,
> Knew where they went—
> They went to God's Right Hand—
> That Hand is amputated now
> And God cannot be found—

spiritual and emotional dynamics of twentieth-century experience. What Dickinson wrote in 1863 proved to be uncannily true about the fate of the poems that her sister Lavinia found bound together in packets in Emily's room not long after the poet's death:

> Essential Oils—are wrung—
> The Attar from the Rose
> Be not expressed by Suns—alone—
> It is the gift of Screws—
>
> The General Rose—decay—
> But this—in Lady's Drawer
> Make Summer—When the Lady lie
> In Ceaseless Rosemary—[#675]

Like perfume squeezed from rose-petals under great pressure, Dickinson's poems had been wrung from her experience and her suffering. And the poet was confident that long after she had died, and lay "In Ceaseless Rosemary," those poems would live on and "Make Summer" for readers through generations.

"It beckons, and it baffles—"

What Dickinson once wrote about heaven— "It beckons, and it baffles"—is also true about her poetry. It tantalizes and invites its readers in while simultaneously mystifying and perplexing them. Dickinson's unusual punctua-

The abdication of Belief
Makes the Behavior small—
Better an *ignis fatuus*

Than no *illume* at all—[#1551]

Here Dickinson gives a startling perspective to a comforting image from the Apostles' Creed. In the "Age of Belief," the way to "God's Right Hand" was clear for those who had "died in Christ." But with that hand "amputated now," and with belief abdicating its reign, human behavior seems dreadfully "small." The *ignis fatuus* of the last stanza is a "false fire," a "will o' the wisp," a delusive hope. In this poem, a belief of any kind seems preferable to the spiritual poverty of unbelief.

The struggles alluded to in these two poems—between despondency and hope, doubt and faith, hard truths and consoling fictions—are indicative of the tensions that appear throughout Dickinson's poetry. Some poems treat powerfully the conflict between her need for love and her fear of violation, some depict conflict between her longing for friendship and her adoration of solitude, and still others show evidence of the struggle between her joy of life and her fear of death. "The going from a world we know / To one a wonder still," Dickinson wrote only two years before her death, "Is like the child's adversity / Whose vista is a hill."

Behind the hill is sorcery
And everything unknown,
But will the secret compensate
For climbing it alone? [#1603]

Dickinson's love of life—of nature, familial affection, and the delights of friendship—was as powerful as her puzzlement over death's power to rob us of all we hold dear. One of her last poems brings together many of the themes that occupied her as she pondered the mysteries:

Of God we ask one favor,
That we may be forgiven—
For what, he is presumed to know—
The Crime, from us, is hidden—
Immured the whole of Life
Within a magic Prison

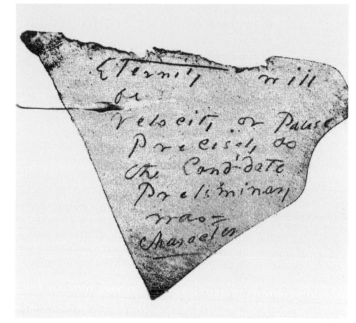

We reprimand the Happiness
That too competes with Heaven. [#1601]

Fragment of handwriting by Emily Dickinson.

Issues to Explore

"In every work of genius we recognize our own rejected thoughts: they come back to us with a certain alienated majesty," wrote Ralph Waldo EMERSON in his explanation of the workings and appeal of genius. This has undoubtedly been the case with the reception of Dickinson's poetry over the past century. The Amherst poet appears to have had an uncanny ability to capture the full range of human experience in an arresting manner. She speaks powerfully not only to women wrestling with issues of gender, identity, and power, but to all who have been wounded by intense suffering or sorrow. Dickinson voices the vexing uncertainties about faith and death that many feel in the modern world. She also reaches those who revere the fathomless mysteries of nature and common experience.

The Christian reader of Dickinson might ask the following questions: (1) Why does Dickinson call the very nature of God into

For Further Study

Dickinson's poetry appeared in a piecemeal, often poorly edited fashion until the middle part of this century when Thomas Johnson produced the first definitive collection of her poems and letters. It is best to begin reading Dickinson with a text edited by Johnson. This can be found in a three-volume edition of the poetry with scholarly notes (Harvard, 1955), in an edition complete in one volume (Little, Brown, 1960), or as a selection of poems entitled *Final Harvest* (Little, Brown, 1961). In addition to being a poet of the highest order, Dickinson was also a brilliant letter writer. The letters are available in a three-volume edition, also edited by Thomas Johnson (Harvard, 1958).

Richard Sewall's *The Life of Emily Dickinson* (Farrar, Straus, and Giroux, 1974) remains the definitive biography. For background to the history of the publication of Dickinson's poems, Millicent Todd Bingham's *Ancestors' Brocades* (Harper, 1945) remains instructive. For critical studies of the poet, see Albert Gelpi, *Emily Dickinson: The Mind of the Poet* (Harvard, 1966) and Jane Donahue Eberwein, *Dickinson: Strategies of Limitation* (Massachusetts, 1985).

question in some poems while in others she affirms the central tenets of the faith? (2) Does a pattern emerge in her poetic treatment of questions about the nature of revelation, the trustworthiness of the Scriptures, the meaning of suffering, and the existence of eternal life? (3) Dickinson looked unflinchingly at every aspect of human experience. How might her probing of perennial questions, as well as her exploration of the particular vulnerabilities brought on by modern realities, clarify and deepen the faith of modern Christians?

—Roger Lundin

HERMAN MELVILLE

Moby Dick
1851

"The great American novel": no work presents itself for this honor as readily as *Moby Dick*. Melville's masterpiece responds to two yearnings within the American psyche: one for a journey into the unknown and the other for an encounter with the powers of nature. *Moby Dick* achieves true greatness, however, not merely by gratifying these desires but by transforming them imaginatively into a powerful myth. Often ridiculed for the unlikeliness of many of its farfetched interpretations, its story is quite clear on the literal level while being remarkably suggestive of larger and deeper meanings occurring in different perspectives.

The fateful voyage of the *Pequod* epitomizes many themes—the perilous destiny of America in the world; Western civilization at a turning point in history; the mind encountering nature and alien peoples; the soul's quest for redemption while caught in the downward pull of the world; the demise of the person of ego and the rise of a new sensibility. Above all, in the midst of the torrent of

Herman Melville (1819–1891).

destruction wrought by the enmity between the human will and the natural order, *Moby Dick* presents an epic vision of a cosmos in harmony with itself.

The Restless Imagination

During the 1840s and 1850s, a time of growth and increasing crisis, America's changing conditions led her writers to a wealth of specula-tion. The revolution in thought and expression was centered in New England, where the mercantile class was reaching unprecedented heights of power. The expansionist concept of "manifest destiny" along with a growing sense of American leadership of the world spread through the country. Deepening the social rift was the conflict over slavery, which would soon transform culture and society on every level.

These developments elicited a complex imaginative response from EMERSON, Thoreau, Whitman, Poe, DICKINSON, and HAWTHORNE, each of whom became a distinctive voice and authority and made a lasting contribution. The writer who risked most and seemed to gain least in his time, however, was Herman Melville (1819–1891).

Although known through his first two works, *Typee* and *Omoo,* as primarily a writer on the South Seas, Melville defied a secure career and experimented increasingly with each novel. He began the 1850s, the great period of his restless imagination, with his sixth novel, *Moby Dick*. His masterwork was followed by *Pierre,* a probing,

Ah, God! what trances of torments does that man endure who is consumed with one unachieved revengeful desire. He sleeps with clenched hands, and wakes with his own bloody nails in his palms. . . . when this hell in himself yawned in him, a wild cry would be heard through the ship, and with glaring eyes Ahab would burst from his state room, as though escaping from a bed that was on fire. . . .

—*Moby Dick*

unsettling parody of romance and the quest for identity, and *The Confidence Man,* a satiric novel that outlines the deformation of the American soul by commercialism. All three were badly received, though his great tales "Bartleby the Scrivener" and "Benito Cereno," also written in this period, won him favorable comment but no fame. His last great short work, *Billy Budd,* an exploration of the tragic confrontation of innocence, evil, and law, came in the final years of his life and was published posthumously in 1924, during the resurrection of his reputation that began thirty-odd years after his death.

A Journey into Knowledge

Is nature benevolent or malevolent? This is the urgent question posed in *Moby Dick.* Centered on the *Pequod* and the mad quest of its captain to avenge his lost leg by hunting down a particular white whale, a "grand hooded phantom, like a snow hill in the air," the novel examines numerous ways of regarding the cosmos and its relation to humankind. Sailing aboard the whaling vessel on its doomed voyage is an ill-assorted group of crewmembers. Among them are Ishmael, a young schoolteacher "bitter about the mouth" who becomes the lone survivor and consequent narrator of the account, and a South-sea islander, Queequeg, whose mentoring of Ishmael changes Ishmael's outlook and enables him to survive. As Ishmael comments, "No more my splintered heart and maddened hand were turned

against the wolfish world. This soothing savage had redeemed it."

Ishmael's fateful and, by worldly standards, extremely foolish decision to sign on as crew member of the *Pequod* unfolds a chain of events constituting nothing less than a journey of the soul. He enters this spiritual pilgrimage not through piety but paradoxically through accepting danger and submitting to nature and community while being a passive part of Captain Ahab's "fiery hunt." Supposed to learn to hate the white whale, he instead learns to acclaim it as showing forth the magnificence of the created world. He describes his first sight of Moby Dick:

A gentle joyousness—a mighty mildness of repose in swiftness, invested the gliding whale. Not the white bull Jupiter swimming away with ravished Europa clinging to his graceful horns; his lovely, leering eyes sideways intent upon the maid; with smooth bewitching fleetness, rippling straight for the nuptial bower in Crete; nor Jove, not that great majesty Supreme! did surpass the glorified White Whale as he so divinely swam.

But the holy and awe-inspiring elements in nature, he learns, can be witnessed only at great peril; they reveal themselves in unexpected, grotesque, and threatening forms.

The Pacific islander Queequeg is the catalyst in Ishmael's transformation. As one from a primitive society, he manifests the power of imaginative strength over against civilized conventions—the freedom of imagination to look on culture with a renewed eye. Their friendship surmounts the barriers created by American exploitation and testifies at a deeper level to the uniting of the separated halves of the soul. More profoundly, Queequeg acts as rescuer and savior three times in the narrative, the last time by proxy as the caulked and intricately carved coffin in which he had planned to be buried becomes the lifebuoy for Ishmael after the sinking of the *Pequod* and its crew.

Captain Ahab's drama, related to the reader only through Ishmael's developing perspective, is the chief content of Ishmael's more encompassing story. The captain's pursuit of

PLATE 10.

Harpooning a sperm whale; hand-colored print published in 1837.

the white whale is a tragedy of will that gives an allegory of our modern world as it distills the aggressive, power-centered forces of domination characterizing the modern world in the last four centuries. Ahab's self-centered scheme to eliminate evil develops rather into a drama of isolation from the good. Certainly a descendant of MILTON's Satan, Ahab represents the part of Western man that seeks to dominate and control. But he is noble for his courage and the qualities of spirit he displays in attempting to reclaim his honor. "God help thee, old man," the narrator writes, "thy thoughts have created a creature in thee; and he whose intense thinking thus makes him a Prometheus; a vulture feeds upon that heart for ever; that vulture the very creature he creates." Yet Ahab is despicable for his active destructiveness toward nature and for using other human beings as mere tools. Finally, however, he is pitiable as he faces in momentary glimpses the abyss his own obsession has made.

Since its rediscovery in this century *Moby Dick* has appealed especially to existentialists who have seen Ahab as the "hero" of the novel and who hail him for noble rebellion. If the whale has struck Ahab without motive, then should not Ahab "strike through the mask" at the one who made the whale? Melville's letters, however, give us the key to the true significance of his work. He refers to the Sermon on the Mount and its unfamiliarity to most Christians. In Ishmael he has created a character who—poor in spirit, merciful, pure in heart, and meek—mourns and hungers after righteousness. And, at the end, after surviving the whirlpool created by the sinking ship, it is he who will symbolically inherit the earth.

On Ishmael's survival:

Buoyed up by that coffin, for almost one whole day and night, I floated on a soft and dirge-like main. The unharming sharks, they glided by as if with padlocks on their mouths; the savage sea-hawks sailed with sheathed beaks.

—Moby Dick

Ishmael on himself:

I felt a melting in me. No more my splintered heart and maddened hand were turned against the wolfish world. This soothing savage had redeemed it.

—*Moby Dick*

Issues to Explore

(1) Melville's use of biblical names and themes illumines a meaning that would otherwise be hidden. Is the whale Job's or Jonah's? That is, is nature friendly or unfriendly? (2) What is the significance of Ishmael's name? Of Elijah's? Of Ahab's? (3) Is Ahab a classical tragic hero for whom character is fate? Does fate dominate? Or is his destruction the result of a series of choices? What are the steps in the process of Ahab's loss of his soul? (4) What are the greatest dangers facing Ishmael? How has he changed from beginning to end? (5) What role does the supporting cast play? (6) What are the different ways in which the whale is viewed? Can the whale be both good and evil, or "beyond" both? (7) Does the work as a whole announce a shift in the pattern of the hero away from the aggressive and violent action of an Ahab toward the empathy and sensitivity of an Ishmael?

—Bainard Cowan

For Further Study

Moby Dick is an adventure in language as well as action, and the reader should resist impatience at the continual postponement of the main action and instead enter into an exploration of the reflective power of the imagination.

The authoritative text is *Moby-Dick or, The Whale*, eds. Harrison Hayford, Hershel Parker, and Thomas Tanselle (Northwestern University, 1976, 1988); editions published by the University of California (1981) and the Library of America (1983) are based on it. The edition by Luther Mansfield and Howard P. Vincent (Hendricks House, 1962) has extensive notes, and the Norton Critical Edition, eds. Harrison Hayford and Hershel Parker (1967), has useful materials and criticism following the text.

Interpretative criticism of *Moby Dick* can be found in Charles Olson, *Call Me Ishmael* (Reynall & Hitchcock, 1947); C. L. R. James, *Mariners, Renegades, and Castaways* (Bewick, 1978); James Baird, *Ishmael* (Johns Hopkins University, 1956); Maurice Friedman, *Problematic Rebel* (University of Chicago, 1970); Bainard Cowan, *Exiled Waters* (Louisiana State University, 1982); Douglas Robinson, *American Apocalypses* (Johns Hopkins University, 1985).

GUSTAVE FLAUBERT

Madame Bovary
1856

ustave Flaubert's *Madame Bovary* is one of the finest but most controversial novels ever written—the preeminent example of the impressionist style. This densely detailed work, upon which Flaubert's literary fame rests, chronicles the life of the beautiful young Emma from the time she meets her future husband, Charles Bovary, until her terrible death some ten years later. One of the most memorable characters in Western literature, Emma is beautiful and passionate in her desire to experience life to its fullest. But Flaubert depicts her as a tragic figure, cast into a world of mediocrity and dullness that discerns neither her suffering nor her corruption and finally observes her fall in helpless horror.

When *Madame Bovary* first appeared in 1856 it stirred up widespread controversy. Although his editors had censored certain sections, Flaubert was charged with writing an immoral novel and made to stand trial. He was acquitted, and in 1857 the uncut version was published to become a popular success. It has since

Gustave Flaubert (1821–1880).

enjoyed enormous acclaim as a supremely wrought, deeply moral work of art.

An Agonizing Process

Flaubert (1821–1880) was born into a France still feeling after-shocks from the Revolution that began in 1789. It had introduced the rise of the middle class, or

bourgeois, which Flaubert despised above all else, along with the dull provincial life that typified his own hometown in the farm country of Normandy. Wishing to avoid anything sentimental or mediocre, he said that he intended to arrive on the literary scene with a "thunderclap" that would change the literary world. Thus it is ironic that in 1851 he felt pulled almost against his will to write a novel about a young woman from the very part of France for which he felt such contempt.

For some five years Flaubert struggled with his "simple subject" (as he described the story in his letters). The writing was an agonizing process, and he came to see his goal of achieving a new objectivity for the novel as "attentive observation of the most unexciting details." Often in despair or frustration he doubted his work: "Personality of the author absent. It will be dismal to read; there will be atrocious things in it—wretchedness, fetidness." But he knew he was attempting something different, a story "suspended over the double abyss of lyricism and vulgarity. . . ."

Hopes for Passion
in a Life of Mediocrity

What makes *Madame Bovary* so powerful is not any mere accumulation of detail for its own sake. Rather its power comes through Flaubert's faithful observation of the *physical,* through which he mysteriously illuminates the *spiritual.* Every particularity lends insight either into the soul of Emma or the inadequacies of the world in which she lives. Herein lie the challenge and reward of the novel: nothing is superfluous; everything reveals meaning. Flaubert has composed his prose with the precision of poetry.

Early in the story, for example, we first glimpse Emma when Charles Bovary, a young country doctor newly established in a provincial town, is called to treat her father, a prosperous farmer who has broken his leg. Later, after Charles's wife has died, Emma's beauty draws him back to the farm. His encounter with her is rendered in a famous passage that reveals Flaubert's fundamental conviction that nothing exists in fiction until it has acted upon or been acted upon by some other object:

> One day he arrived about three o'clock. Everyone was in the fields. He went into the kitchen, and at first didn't see Emma. The shutters were closed; the sun, streaming in between the slats, patterned the floor with long thin stripes that broke off at the corners of the furniture and quivered on the ceiling. On the table, flies were climbing up the sides of glasses that had recently been used, and buzzing as they struggled to keep from drowning in the cider at the bottom. The light coming down the chimney turned the soot on the fireback to velvet and gave a bluish cast to the cold ashes. Between the window and the hearth Emma sat sewing;

her shoulders were bare, beaded with little drops of sweat.

Politely, Emma offers Charles a liqueur, filling one glass "to the brim" and pouring just a little in the other. "She touched her glass to his and raised it to her mouth. Because it was almost empty she had to bend backwards to be able to drink; and with her head tilted back, her neck and her lips outstretched, she began to laugh at tasting nothing; and then the tip of her tongue came out from between her small teeth and began daintily to lick the bottom of the glass."

In such descriptions Flaubert seems simply to record the physical details of life but actually reveals movements within the human soul: in just a few sentences we see Emma as a proper, restrained farm girl with a sensuous innocence and a strong desire to taste life in its fullness. Without hearing a single thought of Emma's we understand that she wishes to escape the "still life" of the farm, which has its own drama and beauty, for what she believes will be the "real life" of the outside world.

The rest of the novel concerns what Emma discovers in that world once she marries Charles. From this point onward Flaubert reveals Emma through her thoughts and emotions, her expectations and disappointments. His narrative technique creates a strong intimacy with her, drawing the reader into her aspirations and illusions.

Emma expects what the world can never seem to give her: love, happiness, nobility, a cause worthy of complete devotion. She anticipates that life will be so exciting and full that it will demand her passionate response. But she is disappointed. She finds herself surrounded by mediocrity and dullness—ordinary people incapable of lofty ideas and actions. Charles is boring and assumes that because he is happy, she must be too. The church is blind to her distress. Her attempts to do good and be happy all fall on barren ground.

Soon Emma's decline and corruption begin, including her unfaithfulness to Charles, her failure as a mother, her growing indebtedness to an unscrupulous merchant, and the gradual hardening of her heart. These events evoke disap-

. . . she wasn't happy, and never had been. Why was life so unsatisfactory? Why did everything she leaned on crumble instantly to dust?

—*Madame Bovary*
Francis Steegmuller, trans.

Jennifer Jones as Madame Bovary in the MGM film of the 1940s.

proval as we read but also the two deeper emotions of tragedy: terror and pity. Flaubert so expertly portrays Emma that we not only sympathize with how completely the world fails her but also experience horror as she allows that failure to destroy her. Yet Flaubert is mercilessly faithful to his vision of his heroine. After ingesting arsenic and placing the "most passionate love-kiss she had ever given" on the crucifix during her death-throes, she receives a disclosure of God at her window in the form of a blind beg-

Rodolph, Emma's first lover, thinks:

Emma was like all his other mistresses; and as the charm of novelty gradually slipped from her like a piece of her clothing, he saw revealed in all its nakedness the eternal monotony of passion, which always assumes the same forms and always speaks the same language.

—*Madame Bovary*
Francis Steegmuller, trans.

And Emma tried to imagine just what was meant, in life, by the words "bliss," "passion," and "rapture"— words that had seemed so beautiful to her in books.

—*Madame Bovary*
Francis Steegmuller, trans.

gar whom she has several times flouted—a hideous but very real figure that reveals the truth of her whole life of vanity and pride.

Issues to Explore

Readers are tempted to judge *Madame Bovary* as either a too attractive picture of sinful excess or a moral warning against lustful desires. But neither of these assessments penetrates the heart of Flaubert's novel. He himself said, "My gaze is fixed on the mould of the soul"; this is a good stance from which the Christian may reflect on Emma. (1) What is the progression of her fall from such hope and promise? (2) Is she destined to fall, or does she create her own destiny? (3) What is Charles's role in her story? (4) What effects does her presence have on the world around her, and what response does that world make to her? (5) More generally, how should her abundant feminine qualities influence society? What are the consequences when those qualities are lost?

It is also tempting to pronounce what Emma *should* have done; a better strategy, however, is to keep some detachment in order to grasp the significance of her life. (6) What does she search for? When she doesn't find it, how does she react, and why? (7) Should we simply "blame" Emma, or should we feel pity and even compassion for her situation? (8) At the end, does she experience insight and recognition that the Christian might relate to? (9) How should the Christian regard this life of "great promise" that seems to go so wrong?

—Larry Allums

For Further Study

Madame Bovary reads slowly in the beginning, but is easy to comprehend and becomes more and more engaging as it unfolds. The best edition is the 1957 translation by Francis Steegmuller in the Modern Library paperback series. Steegmuller also has written an intriguing account, *Flaubert and Madame Bovary: A Double Portrait* (Macmillan, 1939, revised 1977), and edited Flaubert's letters in two volumes (Harvard, 1980–82).

Victor Brombert's *The Novels of Flaubert* (Princeton, 1966) is a good general introduction with a helpful chapter on *Madame Bovary*. D. Roe's *Gustave Flaubert* (St. Martin's Press, 1989) is a more recent study. Several essays by various commentators can be found in *Flaubert: A Collection of Critical Essays* (Prentice-Hall, 1964), edited by Raymond Giraud, and *Critical Essays on Gustave Flaubert* (G. K. Hall, 1986), edited by L. M. Porter.

French Classics

The mark of French writers on world literature has been striking and pervasive. Although no Gallic author may show the magnitude of a DANTE or a SHAKESPEARE, the general influence of French ideas and styles on other nations far exceeds that of Italian and English writing. From the High Middle Ages to our own times, French literature has determined many of the intellectual preoccupations, stylistic innovations, and thematic directions of the prevailing literary currents in Europe from Spain to Russia. With the extension of European influence and colonization to the rest of the world, that impact has widened to include such cultures as the Japanese, Chinese, and African. Thus no student of Western literature can afford to ignore the major achievements of French letters.

The Medieval Period

One of the most striking aspects of French literature is its peculiar mingling of the sacred and the secular. Early medieval lyric poems are concerned with religious fervor on the one hand and erotic love on the other. At times the tension between these themes is considerable, becoming increasingly so from the sixteenth century on when the worldliness and skepticism characteristic of the modern sensibility begin to emerge. As a result, French writers have been responsible not only for some of the most fervent Christian literature but for some of the most virulently anti-Christian attacks ever written. Sometimes a sincere religious sensibility and a pervasive anti-clericalism reside in the same author.

The first great masterpiece of French letters, the *Chanson de Roland* (Song of Roland), written between 1075 and 1110, was based on an historical event, the defeat in 778 of the rearguard of Charlemagne's army by a Basque contingent in Spain. The *Chanson* introduces the character of Roland, peer and nephew of Charlemagne, whose valiant fight against a treacherous and numerically superior enemy makes him a hero. In the context of its period, the Chanson de Roland was understood as a document extolling Christian supremacy over the threat of Islam. In modern France, this medieval epic has gained new popularity in a nation that, paradoxically, has long viewed its identity in secular terms.

In the fifteenth century, François Villon (1431–1463), a graduate of the University of Paris and a convicted thief and murderer, wrote two collections of songs and ballads, *Petit Testament* (1456) and *Grand Testament* (1461). These he gave the form of a last will and testament, consisting of satirical analyses of the world. He broadened the range of literature by writing poems addressed to the Virgin Mary alongside others to executed criminals, occasionally using slang to describe the experiences of the lower classes. In Villon's groundbreaking work, the particular sacred-secular tension that permeates French literature first emerges.

Two prominent and influential sixteenth-century writers, François Rabelais (1494–1553) and Michel Eyquem, Seigneur de Montalgne (1553–1592), developed further the possibilities opened up by Villon, though in distinctly different ways. The former, author of *Pantagruel* and *Gargantua* (1532–52), wrote epic parodies with consciously ridiculous exaggerations to amuse his readers. The feather on Gargantua's cap, for example, weighs 103 pounds. But behind the satire and comedy, Rabelais's narratives contain the teaching of the budding Renaissance: the doctrines of individuality, of universal education, of a guilt-free love of life contrasted with medieval monastic regulations and church-orientated teaching. His wild and boundless fantasy, which we call "Rabelaisian," was inspired by the ribald comedy of ancient Greece and Rome, but his ideas were equally informed by the Christian perspective of the Dutch Renaissance humanist Erasmus.

Montaigne's famous *Essais* (1572–92) also reflect the Greco-Roman heritage. Writing in a nonspecialist, nontechnical language, Montaigne was a moralist who drew on everyday observations and experiences to describe an ever-changing society shaped by unique individuals. His powerful skepticism and ethical relativism helped to shield him against the political realities of the sixteenth century with its religious wars and social unrest. Although he held this attitude of reasoned neutrality that seemed beyond the reach of any school of religion, philosophy, or politics—which may explain his ongoing popularity among modern readers—he never renounced his personal commitment to the Christian faith. In reaction to Montaigne's pose of radical skepticism René Descartes (1596–1650), also a practicing Christian, sought to put philosophy on a more certain basis in the mid-seventeenth century. Paradoxically, Descartes's attempt gave rise to a rationalism that led directly to the skepticism and secularism that have dominated European thought since then.

Classicism

The seventeenth century, considered the classical period of French literature, was dominated by five other literary figures: the three playwrights Pierre Corneille (1606–1684), Jean Racine (1639–1699), and Jean Baptiste Poquelin, called Molière (1622–1673); a poet, Jean de La Fontaine (1621–1695); and a philosopher-theologian, Blaise Pascal

(1623–1662). *Le Cid* (1637), Corneille's most controversial and to this day most popular play, broke the accepted rules of French drama and introduced a new type of protagonist: one who tries to solve life's predicament by being both truly individual and truly political. Many of the dilemmas in Corneille's plays reflect a conflict between opposing sets of values—honor versus love, familial loyalty versus patriotism, religious conviction versus political expediency.

This conflict of values is continued by Racine, whose most famous tragedy, *Phèdre* (1677), employs a Greek setting to explore modern psychological conflicts.

Several of his other plays also use pagan settings as a means of sidestepping contemporary theological controversies concerning questions of grace and free will. These earlier tragedies engage little or no overt Christian dimension, but those written after his conversion, *Esther* (1689) and *Athalie* (1691), suggest that, in spite of redemption and reconciliation, the possibility of tragedy remains for those who disobey God's will.

In a certain sense the other three writers continue to support morality while criticizing religious hypocrisy. Molière confined himself principally to comedy, unlike his

Jean Baptiste Poquelin, called Molière (1622–1673).

illustrious contemporaries Corneille and Racine. Despite the patronage of the king, his profession as actor in a time when the stage was considered an immoral environment added to the risks he took as a playwright in his astute satirical thrusts at the fallibilities of pompous and egotistic people. One of his masterpieces, *Tartuffe* (1664/1667), attacks religious hypocrisy, but it was widely interpreted as an attack on the clergy in general. Writing in the wake of Rabelaisian satire, Molière caricatured all sorts of narrow-mindedness, as in *The Misanthropist* (1666) and *The Miser* (1668), and pretentiousness, as in *The Bourgeois Gentleman* (1670), *The Reluctant Doctor* (1666), and *The Imaginary Invalid* (1673).

La Fontaine's *Fables* (1667–94), versified stories based on Aesop, Phaedrus, and other writers from the ancient, medieval, and Renaissance periods, portray animals in human situations. Through this disguise the author is able to attack the social and political shortcomings of all times but particularly of his own. As a skeptic with leanings toward the free-thinkers of his day, La Fontaine came close to Montaigne's position, that of the wise person who renounces all forms of involvement in the body politic.

Pascal, on the contrary, held deep religious convictions as a mathematical genius with profound philosophical insights and elegant literary style. The lasting fruit of his endeavors are *two literary works, Lettres provinciales* (1656–57) and *Pensées* (Thoughts, 1670). The first work was appreciated (even by the atheist Voltaire) for its dazzling

The pillars of Nature's temple are alive
and sometimes yield perplexing messages;
forests of symbols between us and the shrine
remark our passage with accustomed eyes.

La Nature est un temple où de vivants piliers
Laissent parfois sortir de confuses paroles;
L'homme y passe à travers des forêts de symboles
Qui l'observent avec des regards familiers.

—Charles Baudelaire
"Correspondences"
Richard Howard, trans.

style and technique; the second, despite its fragmentary nature, continues to be read as a prime exploration of the human condition and the paradoxical relationship between faith and reason, grace and will.

The Enlightenment

During the period known as the Enlightenment, secular thought in the fullest sense began to develop in France. The major representatives of that thought, such as Charles Louis de Secondat, Baron de la Brède et de Montesquieu (1689– 1755); François-Marie Arouet, called Voltaire (1694–1778); his rival, Jean-Jacques ROUSSEAU (1712–1778); and Denis Diderot (1713–1784), were part of a small though vocal minority. But in the main the eighteenth century was a period of widespread conservative religious conviction and practice, with these men representing forces that found expression only at its end in the eruptions of the French Revolution.

Montesquieu's *Spirit of the Laws* (1748) directly influenced the U.S. Constitution. More representative of his perspective, however, is his epistolary novel *Persian Letters* (1720), which criticizes the powers allegedly behind the intellectual decay of his times: the church and the papacy, celibacy, and the doctrine of the Trinity. He meant for his often one-sided and knowingly biased approach to be read as a philosophical challenge directed against a providential interpretation of human history. The most sharp-tongued and polemical proponent of the new secularism was Voltaire, who began as a poet and a writer of tragedies and histories but later turned to prose narratives and essays. His combination of poetry and philosophy proved to be a successful means of propagating Enlightenment ideas. A lack of refinement, however, along with a propensity for vitriolic polemics prevented Voltaire from having the influence of Montesquieu or

Rousseau; but his spirited satirical tale *Candide or Optimism* (1758) has enjoyed continued popularity.

Rousseau's enormous influence was principally due to his activities as novelist. And as autobiographer and philosopher with a social and political message, he captured the attention of those searching for an optimistic view of society. In spite of his opposition to violence, Rousseau became something of a patron saint of the French Revolution after his death.

Finally, Diderot is noteworthy less for his novels and essays, often anti-religious in subject and tone, than for his editorship of the first encyclopedia. This truly comprehensive summary of human knowledge from the point of view of rationalism and empirical science played a key role in the propagation of a secular perspective in the modern world.

The Realistic Novel

Nineteenth-century French literature was dominated by the emergence of four great novelists and five great poets. Stendhal (1783–1842), the pen name of Marie Henri Beyle, wrote two novels that changed the course of French fiction: *Red and Black* (1830) and *The Charterhouse of Parma* (1839). Stendhal's analytical portrayals, dissecting romantic sensitivity and creating an atmosphere of disillusioned ambition that led to self-destruction, were admired by thinkers as different as Goethe and Nietzsche. He depicts a society in which the church has become a mere stepping-stone to worldly success.

Honoré de Balzac (1799–1850) was much like Stendhal in lacking

a religious perspective and thus remaining at the level of a secular Enlightenment sensibility. He created a whole universe of characters and later gave the title of *The Human Comedy* to his collected works. Balzac revels in the depiction of base human instinct and behavior, using the dark side of humanity to highlight the development of a new class, the bourgeoisie of a postrevolutionary society gone awry.

Gustave FLAUBERT (1821–1880), the third novelist, was the grand master of detailed realism and probing psychology that influenced whole generations of French, European, and American writers. In *The Temptation of St. Anthony* (1839–57) he uses the Christian mystic's struggle against temptation as a foil to portray the cruelty of a world guided by a decadent philosophy and the depravity of a ruling class sated with luxuries. The same outlook, though with a different character and setting, marks his masterpiece *Madame Bovary* (1856). His three short stories "Un coeur simple" (A simple heart), "St. Julien l'hospitalier" (St. Julien the hospitable) and "Herodias" (all 1876) show different aspects of piety at work. Nevertheless, it may be said of Flaubert that his religious themes serve a symbolic rather than a transcendental goal; his own personal perspective was, in the main, that of an informed secularist.

The century of the realistic novelists ends with Emile Zola (1840–1902), whose theory of hereditary and environmental influences on the success or failure, the strengths or shortcomings of people, can be seen in a novel such as *Nana* (1880). His social and

socialistic worldview became more stringent in his later works, most notably in a final, unfinished four-novel project.

Nineteenth-Century Poets

Victor Hugo (1802–1885), often called the last and greatest of the French romantics, is considered to be one of the major poets of the French language. He was prominent as a dramatist and also as a novelist, especially for *The Hunchback of Notre Dame* and *Les Misérables* (1860). In both roles he promoted liberal causes, but as a political essayist he was even more outspoken; and his criticisms of Emperor Napoleon III resulted in exile (1850–70). He was particularly interested in pursuing epic-length mythical-historical and religious themes with a visionary cast in such large-scale poetic works as *The Legend of the Centuries* (1859).

Charles Baudelaire (1821–1867), whom some call the inventor of modern poetry, was fascinated by the evil side of human nature. According to Baudelaire, where there is an angel, there must also be a devil; where there is hope, there must be despair; where there is love, there·must also be cruelty. Unlike his more optimistic contemporaries, he was convinced of the reality of original sin and the inevitable failure of all projects that presuppose automatic progress and the perfection of human nature. Where he sought perfection, in contrast, was in poetic forms as he explored such themes as the urban environment and the disorder and ugliness of the modern world. He transformed the range and depth of the sonnet and other traditional forms and meters in his major collection of poems, *Les Fleurs du Mal* (The Flowers of Evil, 1855).

Two poets who felt the impact of Baudelaire's startling explorations of new poetic themes were Paul Verlaine (1844–1896), noted especially for the musical quality of his poetry, and his younger friend and contemporary, Arthur Rimbaud (1854–1891), an astonishing prodigy who was writing mature poetry by the age of sixteen. Rimbaud is known for his dramatic vision, particularly in such verse poems as "The Drunken Boat" and collections of prose poems as *A Season in Hell* (1873) and *Illuminations* (1886). After considerable hallucinogenic and sexual experimentation (he called for a "long derangement of the senses and for the reinvention of love"), Rimbaud abandoned literary Paris at the age of twenty-two to become an adventurer abroad until his death at a fairly early age. On his deathbed he reconverted to the childhood Catholicism he mocked in his teens. Verlaine, in contrast, vacillated between Catholic mysticism and the decadence of the Parisian artistic subculture.

Stéphane Mallarmé (1842–1898), also influenced by Baudelaire, is the most difficult of the so-called symbolist poets. Convinced that people are trapped in a universe subject entirely to chance, he nevertheless saw immense grandeur in the human ability to dream. His poetry is rigorously dependent on formal constraints and exploits. In his most ambitious poem *A Throw of the Dice* (1897), he uses even the blank spaces on the page as means of aesthetic organization, anticipating twentieth-century experiments with language and poetic structures. At the end of the century, Mallarmé signals the modern predicament of a world that has lost its foundation of religious faith but cannot abandon the cultural underpinnings that give it meaning.

Modern Existence

Four authors, from a large number of possible candidates, typify the way the conflict between religious and secular forces took shape in early twentieth-century writers. Paul Claudel (1868–1955) wrote as a committed Catholic. His one drama written before his formal conversion, *Tête d'Or* (Head of Gold, 1891), already portrays characters torn between a world without God and the quest for meaning, while *L'Echange* (The Exchange, 1893) effectively criticizes the modern opinion that everything can be determined in

Victor Hugo (1802–1885), often called the last and greatest of the French romantics.

materialistic terms—even wives. In these and other early plays as well as in later masterworks such as *The Break at Noon* (1905), *The Annunciation to Mary* (1912), and *The Satin Slipper* (1919), Claudel contrasted French culture with biblical history, other European experiences, and elements of oriental and Asiatic cults he came to know as a diplomat. Thus his celebration of Christian truth in his plays, prose, and essays is based on a multicultural, international awareness.

André Gide (1869–1951), who received the Nobel Prize in 1947, was an avowed pederast who married his own cousin, torn between literary debauchery and the desire to shape a puritanical, strict, conscientious world. Claudel, who saw this inner struggle, tried in vain to convert him to the Christian faith. Gide's novels, among which are *The Pastoral Symphony* (1919) and *The Counterfeiters* (1925), exemplify his sincere if hopelessly egocentric quest.

Marcel Proust (1871–1922) created a world of his own in the seven-part novelistic sequence *A la recherche du temps perdu* (Remembrance of Things Past, 1913–27), which describes timeless observation and aesthetic awareness of language as the artist's tools for analyzing and overcoming existential problems. The memory of one's own history or that of one's family, country, or people becomes essential as one constructs an existence outside earthly confines. Proust's unfinished work, in its ambition, was an effort to create monuments in the human imagination to supplant those certainties lost in the collapse of traditional religious values.

Paul Valéry (1871–1945), a disciple and friend of Mallarmé, has been described as France's greatest twentieth-century poet; as a master craftsman, he wrote verses of finely tuned observation, analysis, and synthesis in such poems as "The Cemetery by the Sea" (1920). Such poems, the prose cycle "Monsieur Teste" (1894–1926), his collection of *Poesies* (1929), the drama "Mon Faust" (1940), and a large body of literary and cultural criticism made Valéry the most widely respected French author of the first half of the twentieth century. Like his master and many other writers after Baudelaire, he attempted to find a means of countering the apparent meaninglessness of modern existence.

Existentialist Influences

Later twentieth-century French writers offer an impressive range of perspectives and themes. Typical of mid-century concerns with the conflict between the religious and secular perspectives are the influential works of philosopher, novelist, and playwright Jean-Paul Sartre (1905–1980). His plays—*The Flies* (1942) and *No Exit* (1944)

For Further Study

Sources for further exploration of the French classics include:

Geoffrey Brereton, *A Short History of French Literature*, second edition (Penguin, 1976).
L. F. Cazamian, *A History of French Literature* (Oxford, 1955).

Wallace Fowlie, *French Literature: Its History and Its Meaning* (Prentice-Hall, 1973).
Denis Hollier, editor, *A New History of French Literature* (Harvard, 1989).
Will Grayburn Moore, *The French Achievement in Literature* (Barnes & Noble, 1969).

among others—and novels, such as *La Nausée* (Revulsion, 1934), did much to popularize existentialist notions that the human person is "a useless passion," "condemned to be free."

Albert Camus (1913–1960), who exhibited a similar literary versatility, was especially admired for the moral fervor he brought to his own existential atheism. In such novels as *The Stranger* (1940) and *The Plague* (1947), he held out the possibility for human action in a world that seemed devoid of meaning and order. His death at the age of forty-six and Sartre's turn to a variety of Marxism brought an end to the extraordinary vogue of postwar existentialism, but not to the dual concern with religious themes and

secular solutions that continues to characterize French literature to the present day.

Since the 1950s, French literature has been marked by the so-called "new novel" of Nathalie Sarraute, Michel Butor, and Alain Robbe-Grillet; the "theater of the absurd," as practiced by Eugène Ionesco, Samuel Beckett, and Jean Genet; and the structuralist movement, primarily analytical in focus, which was furthered by critic Roland Barthes and anthropologist Claude Lévi-Strauss. More recently, postmodernism and deconstruction have had a powerful impact on intellectual thought worldwide through the work of historian Michel Foucault and philosopher Jacques Derrida.

—Carsten Peter Thiede

CHARLES DICKENS

Great Expectations
1861

*E*ngland honors its writers
more than most countries
do, and except for
SHAKESPEARE, no writer has
captured the allegiance of the
nation more than Charles Dickens.
Dickens (1812–1870) was a
prolific practitioner of what
literary scholars call "the nine
teenth-century British novel" and
no novel exemplifies that vital,
jostling world better than *Great
Expectations.*

It has been said regarding
Dickens's nearly twenty novels that
"for all their strong plots and
distinct moods, the books coalesce
in memory into one huge Dickens
Novel, or Dickens Universe."
Here, then, are some typical
features of Dickens's novels that
will help readers find their way
through *Great Expectations:* realism
of setting and action; skill at
character portrayal and description
of scenes; evocation of atmosphere;
ingenious plot structure in which
multiple threads converge at the
end of the story; social protest
(denunciation of evil in society);
moral earnestness; interest in
human psychology; satiric
exposure of human vice or folly;

Charles Dickens (1812–1870).

comic spirit; and reliance on the
great archetypes (master images
and universal motifs) of the human
imagination—such patterns as the
journey, the wicked city, the
villain, and the hero.

An English Institution

No English author epitomizes the
quality of Britishness better than
Dickens. Part of the appeal of

reading his novels is simply the
holiday spirit that results from
being whisked away from our own
time and place to Victorian
England. There is no finer
introduction to things English
than *Great Expectations,* where we
encounter such distinctly English
themes as these: a strong sense of
place (of English landscape, place
names, local color, and weather);
class consciousness; formality and
love of privacy; the central
importance of London; provincialism (the sense of a self-contained
island country with its own
customs); the prominence of
nature; preoccupation with
character and personality; subtlety
of humor; and the omnipresence of
the pub as a social institution.

Storyteller Supreme

C. S. LEWIS remarked that such
authors as HOMER, Shakespeare,
and Dickens speak at once to every
reader's imagination. What, then,
does the popular imagination like
in a story? To answer that question
is to identify the ingredients that
make up the storytelling technique
of Dickens in such a novel as *Great*

The June weather was delicious. The sky was blue, the larks were soaring high over the green corn, I thought all that countryside more beautiful and peaceful by far than I had ever known it to be yet. . . . They awakened a tender emotion in me; for my heart was softened by my return, and such a change had come to pass, that I felt like one who was toiling home barefoot from distant travel, and whose wanderings had lasted many years.

—*Great Expectations*

for example, in the case of villains or underdogs), and comic or satiric portraits that make us laugh.

A Victorian Prodigal Son

The novel as a whole can be grasped quite simply. The title calls attention to the central action of the story—the acquisition and loss of the hero's "great expectations" based on the wealth he inherits from an anonymous benefactor (to reveal the identity of the benefactor would spoil the suspense and discovery that are leading elements in the story). Dickens divided the story into three clear stages—Pip's childhood and adolescence in the village, his living as a member of the leisure class in London for several years, and his return to a life of modest usefulness after he loses his inherited wealth. Pip's final state is a synthesis of the previous two: he retains something of the virtues that he absorbed during his childhood in the village but also the increased sophistication that he picked up in London. One of the strokes of genius in this novel is that it shuttles back and forth between the village and the city, with an accompanying sense of variety.

Expectations: heroes who elicit the reader's admiration and sympathetic identification; villains and villainy; romantic love; suspense and mystery (a typical Dickens novel is in effect a detective story); adventure; conflict and tension; poetic justice (good characters rewarded, evil characters punished); vivid characters; a happy ending; episodes of surprise, rescue, reunion, recognition; atmosphere and mood; dramatic irony (in which readers know more than characters in the story); at least one good chase scene; contrivance of plot to bring the plot threads ingeniously together at the end. All of these ingredients appear in *Great Expectations.*

Of course these elements can appear in stories that strike the sophisticated reader as amateurish and clumsy. A good Dickens novel rises to the status of a classic by including, in addition to the ingredients noted above, such qualities as subtlety, depth of human experience, moral and intellectual stimulation, fully developed characterization, and superiority of style.

Dickens is famous for his powers of characterization for several reasons. One is his ability to create universal character types, so that we have the feeling of meeting people in a Dickens story that we have also met in real life. Balancing this is his ability to create unique characters—so striking in their individuality that we feel we meet them only in the story in which they appear. Other qualities of characterization include vividness of description, ability to evoke strong reader involvement (as,

The circular pattern of the story is the parable of the prodigal son in a latter-day setting, as Dickens hints when Pip says late in the novel that he "felt like one who was toiling home barefoot from distant travel, and whose wanderings had lasted many years." The journey through false values and suffering to self-discovery and virtue is, in fact, found in the myths of many heroes. This is one of several ways in which *Great Expectations* fits comfortably in the mainstream of Western literature.

The novel traces the life of the hero from age seven to approximately age thirty-four. Pip is twenty-three when his life falls apart. Using the scheme of the well-made plot gives the story further shape. The first seven chapters are exposition—the background to the main action that places the youthful Pip in his hometown environment. The inciting moment is Pip's first visit to Miss Havisham's house, which propels the story into the rising action of Pip's quest to rise socially. His com-

Joe Gargery, the gentle giant, provoked to violence in his smithy. In the background his brother-in-law Philip Pirrip (Pip) works the bellows. Illustration by Charles Green (1840–1898).

ing into money is the key event in that quest. The turning point occurs in chapter 39, where Pip is forced to acknowledge the false premises on which he has based his life. The further complication consists of Pip's struggle against adversity to establish a new identity and help his benefactor. The climax is the arrest of Magwitch, a criminal whom Pip tries to help escape from England. The denouement (tying up of loose ends) consists mainly of pairing off various couples in marriage.

The implied message in all of this analysis is that *Great Expectations* exists first of all for the reader's enjoyment—of things English, of exciting action, of unforgettable characters, of comedy, and of Dickens's way with words. But the last page of the novel links the action to such masterpieces as the Old Testament book of Job, *Oedipus Rex,* and *King Lear.* The transformed Estella speaks of how "suffering has been stronger than all other teaching. . . . I have been bent and broken, but—I hope—into a better shape."

I took her hand in mine, and we went out of the ruined place; and, as the morning mists had risen long ago when I first left the forge, so the evening mists were rising now, and in all the broad expanse of tranquil light they showed to me, I saw no shadow of another parting from her.

—*Great Expectations*

Issues to Explore

On the tragic theme of wisdom through suffering: (1) What causes the suffering of various characters in the story? (2) What is the nature of their various sufferings, and what type of wisdom do the principal characters achieve?

The moral pattern of the story emerges if we are aware that the story is (like the parables of Jesus) a warning to avoid false values and an exhortation to embrace true ones. (3) What values does the story offer for approval and disapproval? (4) What virtues are espoused in the story? What vices are denounced? One pattern emerging from this analysis is that the *morality* of the story is in harmony with a Christian outlook, although the *values* ultimately are not.

The intellectual and moral depth of the story can be seen in the story's moments of illumination. It is a convention of storytelling to move the action toward one or more such moments relatively late in the story. Greater meaning will emerge when we start pinpointing the candidates. (5) For example, if Pip's moral development can be measured by the degree to which he finds his world picture inadequate, where does he most obviously reach this point? (6) If the index to Pip's maturity is his ability to feel for others, where does he most decisively show that ability? (7) If the essential development of Pip is his triumph over false values, where does he achieve that triumph?

Finally, although the book deserves praise for its ability to transport us to Victorian England, we should be aware of the contemporaneity of the novel—for its being truthful to reality as we know it in our own world. A beginning list of recognizable human experiences would include approximately what we find in the daily news: dysfunctional families; abuse of children and criminals; violence, fear, and other problems of city living; the failure of the judicial system; the psychological neuroses and psychoses of troubled people; worship of money and the success ethic, and the moral decay that such idolatry brings; the failure of life to match the ideal and an accompa-

For Further Study

Great Expectations is such a famous novel that many publishers print a paperback edition. Some examples include Penguin (with an excellent introduction), Bantam, Signet, and Rinehart. From time to time publishers produce inexpensive hardcover editions (usually as part of a series, such as the Courage Classics series by Running Press). Reading the novel in this format is even more delightful.

Scholarly sources also abound. A good first book to consult is Angus Wilson's *The World of Charles Dickens* (Viking, 1970), an illustrated biography that spans Dickens's life and writing. Harry Stone's *Dickens and the Invisible World* (Indiana, 1979) is superb on the story and fairy-tale qualities of Dickens's novels. A current vogue is for publishers to produce series in which individual books are devoted to the great masterpieces, and these are generally very helpful guides; publishers that thus far have produced critical books on *Great Expectations* include St. Martin's, Unwin, and Twayne.

nying restlessness of the human spirit; the snobbery of the powerful visited upon the weak; the power of love and infatuation.

This is only a beginning; the reader can continue the list by simply developing a knack for identifying the recognizable human experiences in the fictional. At the most general level, *Great Expectations* makes us think about the two issues that seem most relevant to our own moment in history: why do so many people make such a shambles of their own and other people's lives, and what is the exact nature of the good life that could serve as an alternative to the way most people live?

—Leland Ryken

JOHN HENRY, CARDINAL NEWMAN
Apologia pro vita sua
1864

*J*ohn Henry Newman's *Apologia pro vita sua* is one of the greatest spiritual autobiographies of all time and the central literary achievement of one of the commanding intellects of the nineteenth century. Its title, which can be translated "The Justification for His Own Life," is followed by a subtitle, "Being a History of His Religious Opinions." The account depicts the drama of a soul being drawn to God.

In describing the *Apologia* as a "spiritual autobiography," one should place as much importance on the word "spiritual" as on "autobiography." The autobiography gives little of Newman's conventional life story, but it does present his intellectual development in careful detail. It also relates the compelling narrative of Newman's sequence of conversions from a tepid, received, general Christian persuasion to a deeply held faith tied inextricably to the Roman Catholic Church.

Newman's Conversions

Saint Paul's experience on the road to Damascus set the pattern for

Statue of John Henry Newman (1801–1890).

virtually all subsequent accounts of Christian conversion. This pattern is the confounding of one's hostility and resistance by an unsettling experience, followed by a turning of the inner spirit to a new understanding of reality. The story of John Henry Newman (1801–1890) parallels the Pauline pattern, though Newman's presentation is so measured and

subtle that the underlying drama can be easily missed.

But underneath the factual surface a powerful emotional drama unfolds. First is the episode of individual conversion from casual to intensely held faith. Second is the episode of conversion from one religious body to another in an age when denominational allegiance was for many more important than theology. And third is the episode of a quest in which the protagonist searches for a final destination and a final truth. As Newman wrote in his most famous poem, something always beckoned:

> Lead, Kindly Light, amid the
> encircling gloom,
> Lead Thou me on!
> The night is dark, and I am far
> from home—
> Lead Thou me on!

These successive conversions marked Newman's life from his evangelical conversion in 1816, when he was fifteen, to his final conversion to Roman Catholicism in 1845, when he was forty-four. Though he did not fully discern the large design until 1845, each conversion pointed him in the same direction—toward an ever-

[My conversion at age fifteen had the effect of] making me rest in the thought of two and two only absolute and luminously self-evident beings, myself and my Creator.

—*Apologia pro vita sua*

deepening faith. He continued in the Catholic Church the remaining forty-five years of his life.

Newman's pattern of conversion provides the underlying intensity and forward movement of the *Apologia,* which could otherwise be obscured by the wealth of factual material, dates, and citations from letters. The key to understanding this larger movement can be found in following not only Newman's intellectual growth, but also his spiritual and emotional development. Such a reading best satisfies Newman's motto of *cor ad cor loquitur*—heart speaking to heart.

The Writing of the *Apologia*

Newman wrote the *Apologia* in 1864, almost twenty years after he had left the Church of England for the Church of Rome. The work grew out of religious controversy, namely the exchange between Newman and the Anglican clergyman and author Charles Kingsley, who cast a slur on Newman in a book review in *Macmillan's Magazine,* a prominent periodical of the day. Newman was provoked by Kingsley's assertion that he and Roman Catholic clergy in general had no regard for the truth. Newman's initial response and Kingsley's answer began a kind of pamphlet war. But as the exchange developed and Newman felt moved to write a justification of what he believed, his rejoinder turned into a full-scale narrative of how he came to hold his religious opinions.

The original form of the *Apologia* contained seven parts and an appendix. Subsequently, when the excitement over the exchange with Kingsley had subsided, Newman published the autobiography as the book now generally read. He omitted the polemic first two parts and substituted a preface to explain as much of the controversy as necessary.

The *Apologia* and the Oxford Movement

In the *Apologia* Newman tells the story of the Oxford or Tractarian movement, which he simply calls at the end of chapter 1 "the religious movement of 1833." It came to be known as the Oxford movement because it was centered at that university; it was known as the Tractarian movement from the *Tracts for the Times,* the theological pamphlets that Newman initiated at the start of the movement. It is also sometimes called the Catholic Revival, because it was a revival and reaffirmation of the traditional, historic, catholic, and apostolic character of the church—though within the Church of England.

To define the movement is almost to take sides. Supporters considered it a rediscovery of the English Church as a middle way between Rome and Protestantism, defined by the early church fathers rather than the medieval schoolmen. More decidedly Protestant opponents saw the movement as a subversive effort to transform the Church of England in order to surrender it to the domination of the pope. However it was viewed, it stirred a national ferment.

When Newman converted from this middle-way Anglicanism to Rome, many of his supporters followed. But others were regretful and many were deeply distressed. Opponents felt that Newman showed his true colors, revealing himself as the traitor he had been all along. It is important to bear in mind that the national church was widely viewed in a patriotic and theological light; the Roman Catholic Church was seen not only as theological error but also as a foreign despotism.

The intensity of feelings about Tractarianism and Newman's role in the movement had not much abated in the twenty years following Newman's departure from the Anglican Church. Those feelings went to the heart of what Newman's life stood for, not only for him

All Souls' College, Oxford.

but for the nation and Christian belief. Thus the *Apologia* carried great urgency for Newman, which it still communicates today. It speaks to such questions as what it means to believe in the Christian faith and what it means to adhere to a particular denomination.

Newman as a Religious and Literary Figure

Although he is best known today for the *Apologia*, Newman was a preeminent religious figure and one of the most prolific authors of his age. The first half of his life was dominated by his association with Oxford, where he matriculated as an undergraduate when he was only fifteen years old. At Oxford Newman gained prominence first as a fellow of Oriel College, later as the vicar of the university church, and ultimately as the national leader of the Oxford movement.

The second half of Newman's life was dominated by service in the Roman Catholic Church and by continued writing of all sorts. He wrote copiously—sermons, poems, religious tracts, histories, theological disquisitions, and even novels. His elevation to the position of cardinal came late in his life, in 1879 when he was seventy-four. Apart from the *Apologia*, the most important of Newman's works are his variously collected University and Parochial sermons from the 1820s and 30s, *Essay on the Development of Christian Doctrine* (1845), *The Idea of a University* (1852), *The Dream of Gerontius* (1865), and *The Grammar of Assent* (1870). Though unsuccessful in many of his undertakings during his lifetime, Newman's genius has been recognized increasingly since his death.

And I earnestly pray for this whole company, with a hope against hope, that all of us, who once were so united, and so happy in our union, may even now be brought at length, by the Power of the Divine Will, into One Fold and under One Shepherd.

—*Apologia pro vita sua*

I thought life might be a dream, or I an Angel, and all this world a deception, my fellow-angels by a playful device concealing themselves from me, and deceiving me with the semblance of a material world.

—*Apologia pro vita sua*

Issues to Explore

Newman's *Apologia* poses many questions. (1) He wrote: "The heart is commonly reached, not through reason, but through the imagination. Many a man will live and die upon a dogma; no man will be a martyr for a conclusion." To what extent does the *Apologia* illustrate those sentiments? (2) Does it appeal to the imagination more than to reason? (3) Is his assertion about their relative importance true for all Christians at all times? (4) How important for the individual Christian are articles of faith and particular denominations?

(5) To what extent is Newman's position peculiar to the circumstances of the nineteenth century and to what extent does it reflect today's Christian in the world? (6) Why did Newman wait twenty years to write his justification? (7) How important was Kingsley's role in provoking the *Apologia*?

(8) If Newman's primary purpose is to justify his own conduct, a secondary purpose is surely to justify the Christian faith in general and the Roman Catholic position in particular. Does the *Apologia* serve to persuade nonbelievers to accept the Christian faith as true? (9) Does it persuade Protestants concerning the positions of the Catholic Church? (10) Why do you think the Roman Church is considering the case for

For Further Study

Newman's vast corpus of writings has been collected in forty volumes (Longmans, 1914–21). His letters and diaries, still in progress, will run to thirty-one volumes (Thomas Nelson and Oxford, 1961–). The literature on Newman and the Oxford movement is so vast that the beginning reader should first consult one of the various editions of the *Apologia* that provide extensive commentary and support. The fullest of these editions is edited by Martin Svaglic (Oxford, 1967). There are also excellent editions by Wilfrid Ward (Longmans, 1912), A. Dwight Culler (Houghton Mifflin, 1956), Philip Hughes (Doubleday, 1956), and David DeLaura (Norton, 1968).

Beyond the *Apologia,* the chapters on Newman by Martin Svaglic and C. S. Dessain in *Victorian Prose: A Guide to Research* (Modern Language Association, 1973) are helpful, as is the bibliography of Newman's writings compiled by Vincent Ferrer Blehl (University of Virginia, 1978). For the Oxford movement itself, see the chapter in *Victorian Prose* by Howard Fulweiler and the compilation by Owen Chadwick, *The Mind of the Oxford Movement* (Stanford, 1960).

the canonization of John Henry Newman? Judging from the *Apologia,* should the decision be affirmative?

—G. B. Tennyson

SØREN KIERKEGAARD

Fear and Trembling
1843

øren Kierkegaard's *Fear and Trembling* is the best known work of the nineteenth-century Danish philosopher who is a founder of the twentieth-century existential movement. It gives a classical example of how existentialists convey philosophical themes through dramatic literary power. In this book Kierkegaard (1813–1855) makes a series of reflections and poetic musings on the biblical story in Genesis 22, in which God tests Abraham's faith by asking him to sacrifice his son Isaac. *Fear and Trembling* defies easy classification; it is an imaginative work that employs philosophical questions as it engages religious questions of a deeply personal nature. It is literature, philosophy, theology, and devotional writing all at once while never being any of these alone.

Søren Aabye Kierkegaard (1813–1855).

A Veiled Autobiography?

Many people have read *Fear and Trembling* as an autobiographical account of Kierkegaard's life in Copenhagen, Denmark. They see his telling of Abraham's willing-ness to sacrifice Isaac for God's sake as a disguised account of his own willingness to give up his love, Regine Olsen. They reach this conclusion because Kierkegaard had recently broken his engagement, at least in part because of what he perceived as a divine call to do so. Other people have read the book as a retelling of Kierkegaard's own relation to his father, with Kierkegaard himself as the "Isaac" who had been "sacrificed" by his father's stern and strange religious upbringing. Although such readings give the book poignancy, they fail to recognize the universal meaning Kierkegaard creates.

In literary terms, the book is best viewed against the background of German romanticism, with its fascination with fairy tales, legends, and myths. It also contains a polemic against the philosophical influence of Hegel, who had claimed to develop a philosophical system in which religion was recognized, but was subservient to philosophical reflection. *Fear and Trembling* pours relentless scorn on those who seek a deeper meaning in life beyond religious faith, and it endeavors to show that genuine faith is never an easy accomplishment. The work undermines the assumption that "we all have faith" by its contrasts between the struggles of Abraham, the father of faith, and the comfortable life of the contemporary intellectual.

An ethics that ignores sin is a completely futile discipline, but if it affirms sin, it has eo ipso *exceeded itself.*

—*Fear and Trembling*
Walter Lowrie, trans.

The Three Stages

Fear and Trembling is one of the many works Kierkegaard wrote in the early 1840s. These include *Either-Or, Philosophical Fragments, Repetition, The Concept of Anxiety,* and *Stages on Life's Way,* culminating with the great *Concluding Unscientific Postscript.* Kierkegaard himself describes these as belonging to his "aesthetic" works. By this he means that the works have a literary and artistic character, but embody viewpoints that may not agree with his own religious standpoint. He thus attributes these works to fictitious authors, who are best understood as characters in their own right. *Fear and Trembling* is ascribed to a character named Johannes de Silentio (John the Silent), who admires Abraham's faith but does not claim to have faith himself.

Kierkegaard accompanied these aesthetic works written pseudonymously (under an assumed name) with a series of sermon-like discourses published during the same period under his own name. Eventually these discourses took on a more decisively Christian tone in such books as *Works of Love, Practice in Christianity, For Self-Examination,* and *Judge for Yourselves.* But to complicate things still more, he attributed some of these last works to yet another fictitious character, the "super-Christian" Anti-Climacus. Kierkegaard's work culminated in a series of magazine and newspaper articles in which he attacked the state church of Denmark as a perversion of the true Christian faith.

The early aesthetic works are best seen as an attempt to move readers along the journey to the Christian faith. The works embody the "three stages on life's way." Humans naturally begin in the first stage as aesthetic creatures who live "immediately" so as to satisfy their natural desires. The second, or ethical, stage begins when people begin to recognize the role of responsible ethical choice in the self's formation. The third stage, the religious sphere, begins when people recognize their ethical guilt and their complete dependence on a higher power to become the selves they ought to become.

Kierkegaard's fictitious authors represent different "spheres of existence" and thereby hold up a mirror to readers whose own lives fall into one of the three stages. Kierkegaard does not assume, as some interpreters have thought, that the choice between these different views of life is arbitrary. Rather he hopes that readers who look into these mirrors honestly will come to understand the truth about their own lives.

When placed in the framework of Kierkegaard's "three stages on life's way," *Fear and Trembling* stands on the border between the ethical and the religious life. The work shows that the religious life cannot be understood, as many nineteenth-century theologians assumed, simply in ethical terms. Religious faith does not merely entail recognizing the "fatherhood of God and the brotherhood of man."

An "Absurd" Faith

The story of Abraham's willingness to sacrifice Isaac disturbs our genial assumption that religious faith simply means being a "nice" ethical person. In *Fear and Trembling* Kierkegaard reinforces this disturbance with a series of imaginative retellings of the biblical story. He contrasts the actual story with such variations as Abraham losing his faith, Isaac losing his faith, Abraham taking his own life, and Abraham repenting of his sinful willingness to kill his son. These variations all point to the way in which Abraham demonstrates his faith—not by conforming to the ethical conventions of his society but through an action that those ethical conventions would condemn as immoral.

The book thus can be seen as a treatise on the implications of God's possibly command-

The Exchange, Copenhagen, in 1864.

ing something immoral. But the deeper meaning of the book lies in its questions about the individual's relation to God. In the final analysis, can God be known only through universal moral laws that are understood as divine commands? If so, the individual has no personal relation to God, and God is seen as "an invisible vanishing point," the abstraction behind the moral law. On this kind of view, faith is equated with ordinary ethical life. This means that faith "has always existed," but in a deeper sense faith, as a uniquely religious phenomenon, has therefore never existed.

The story of Abraham raises the question of whether a person can relate to God as an individual. To use the abstract language of *Fear and Trembling:* Can the individual be related to the universal (the ethical) through the absolute (God), or must one relate to the absolute (God) solely through the universal (the ethical)? The pseudonymous author Silentio also asks whether Abraham, as a person of faith, can communi-

cate his dilemma to others concerning what his faith requires him to do. He suggests that Abraham's responsibility is a lonely one that cannot be shared or explained to others.

All of these questions are posed through reflection on a fictitious character Silentio calls the "knight of faith," who is contrasted with the "tragic hero" on the one hand and the

The difference between the tragic hero and Abraham is clearly evident. The tragic hero still remains within the ethical. He lets one expression of the ethical find its telos *in a higher expression of the ethical; the ethical relation between father and son, or daughter and father, he reduces to a sentiment which has its dialectic in its relation to the idea of morality.*

—*Fear and Trembling*
Walter Lowrie, trans.

"knight of infinite resignation" on the other. The tragic hero is "the beloved son of ethics" who must sacrifice his personal happiness for the sake of the greater social good; Abraham's willingness to obey God cannot be understood in this way. Nor is Abraham simply a knight of infinite resignation who represents an otherworldly religiousness that willingly sacrifices earthly hopes and joys for the sake of eternity. The paradoxical quality of Abraham's belief as a "knight of faith" lies in the fact that he continues to believe God's promises *for this life.* Even as he prepares to sacrifice Isaac he believes that his son is the child of promise and that through Isaac he will be the father of many nations. Abraham's faith in God is the sole basis of his life. His trust in God's character, power, and promises provides a basis for an action that the worldly mind sees as absurd.

Issues to Explore

Fear and Trembling is a relatively short work, containing many beautiful and memorable stories that make it gripping literature. Nevertheless, its philosophical depth and literary complexity render it a difficult book to read and understand. (1) Although *Fear and Trembling*'s fictitious, non-Christian narrator can only hint at this, Kierkegaard certainly intended the book to enlighten those who are confronted by the claims of the Christian faith. Do people come to know God through reason and ethical conscience alone, or can God be known in the particular historical claims of the individual made by Jesus of Nazareth? (2) Must a person come into relation with God simply by ethical striving, or can a person come

For Further Study

The best scholarly translation of *Fear and Trembling* is by Howard V. and Edna H. Hong (Princeton, 1983). Alastair Hannay's translation (Penguin, 1985) is very readable. Two collections of critical articles about *Fear and Trembling* warrant attention, both edited by Robert Perkins: *Kierkegaard's* Fear and Trembling: *Critical Appraisals* (University of Alabama, 1981) and *International Kierkegaard Commentary: Fear and Trembling* (Mercer University, 1993). Walter Lowrie's *A Short Life of Kierkegaard* (Oxford, 1944) is probably still the best biography of Kierkegaard. Bruce Kirmmse, *Kierkegaard in Golden Age Denmark* (Indiana University, 1990), is a fine attempt to set Kierkegaard's life and writings in the context of early nineteenth-century Denmark.

into a right relation to ethical goodness through a personal relationship with God in Jesus Christ? How does the latter alternative make possible a powerful argument against reducing the life of faith to the ethical life? (3) What if the individual cannot successfully carry out the ethical life? In this case, how does Abraham, who is counted righteous by virtue of his faith, become "the guiding star that saves the anguished"?

—C. Stephen Evans

GEORGE ELIOT

Middlemarch
1871–72

Middlemarch, the masterpiece of George Eliot, is probably the greatest novel ever written in the English realistic tradition. George Eliot is the pen name of Mary Anne Evans, a central figure in this tradition and a leading thinker in radical Victorian ideas. *Middlemarch* is a work of immense seriousness that Virginia Woolf said was written for "grown-up people." Subtitled "A Study of Provincial Life," it brings to life a community of characters who confront readers with a profound moral challenge concerning the consequences of human actions.

Goodness without God

George Eliot (1819–1880) was born in Warwickshire, England, the daughter of a land agent. She was a brilliant, sensitive, and intense woman who passionately embraced the evangelical faith in her girlhood but permanently rejected Christian dogma when she was twenty. She retained, however, a strong belief in the value of Christian ethics.

The conclusion of Eliot's first

George Eliot (1819–1880), after the portrait by F. d'A. Durade.

book of fiction (*Scenes of Clerical Life,* 1858) praises her hero, a brave, evangelical Christian "whose heart beat with a true compassion, and whose lips were moved by fervent faith." Such faith inspires many of Eliot's characters to make choices based on what Eliot calls the "divine" principles of sympathy and duty. She portrays acts of kindness motivated by the "sympathetic imagination" as

essential for the development, or evolution, of morality. Eliot, however, was an agnostic. And at first it is puzzling to reconcile the convincing Christian models in her novels with her own disbelief.

Eliot's belief that Christian ethics could bring about moral evolution derived from both evolutionary science and "higher criticism." She translated the first English editions of two key books of higher criticism, D. F. Strauss, *The Life of Jesus,* and Ludwig Feuerbach, *The Essence of Christianity*. These studies of the New Testament deny the supernatural Jesus and emphasize the human Jesus and the ethical and spiritual principles his life symbolized.

While editing a progressive intellectual journal, the *Westminster Review,* from 1851 to 1854, Eliot also promoted the publication of many important essays on evolution. George Henry Lewes, the man with whom she lived from 1854 until his death in 1878, was the author of several prominent studies. But Eliot's profound moral sense was not satisfied with the scientific explanations alone. For evolutionary theories to be plausible, they

[C]haracter too is a process and an unfolding. The man was still in the making, . . . and there were both virtues and faults capable of shrinking or expanding.

—*Middlemarch*

need not only scientific validity but the ability to account for the evolution of *morality*. Eliot's fiction therefore employs Christian ethics—as a form of goodness without God—to create a model in which morality evolves through suffering, sympathy, and duty.

In addition to *Middlemarch,* Eliot wrote six other novels. The first is the beloved story of *Adam Bede,* in which she develops the moral philosophy that inspires all her works. The two other best-known are *The Mill on the Floss,* Eliot's darkest novel, and the still-popular gem *Silas Marner.* In her last novel, *Daniel Deronda,* a massive undertaking on the scale of *Middlemarch,* Eliot creates her most visionary exploration of the moral potential of human community.

This Particular Web

Eliot called *Middlemarch* "this particular web" because a central feature of the novel is the complex interconnectedness of the people— and their choices—in the town of Middlemarch. *All* the major characters are related in some way. Even the minor characters, who gossip in the taverns and at work, influence the main players.

Middlemarch develops through two main plot lines—and multiple subplots. It follows the growth from egoism to altruism of two young, naive idealists, Dorothea Brooke and Tertius Lydgate. Eliot had originally planned two separate novels about Dorothea and Lydgate, which explains the novel's length—six to eight hundred pages, depending on the edition.

The well-intended yet errant idealism of these characters leads each into a bad marriage—Dorothea because she hopes to help an aging scholar with his lifework and Lydgate

because he believes he can separate his progressive medical practice from his life with a physically attractive but small-minded and vulgarly egotistic wife, Rosamond Vincy. The eventual success or failure of the characters depends on their ability, after great suffering and disillusionment, to act for the good of others in the community. When Lydgate pleads for sympathy from his wife, she recoils and whines, "What can *I* do?" In contrast, when Dorothea finds that Lydgate is in trouble, she asks, "What should I do—how should I act now, this very day?"

Dorothea rises above her own concerns, which include her fear that the man she truly loves, Will Ladislaw, loves Rosamond. After a dark sleepless night of internal conflict, Dorothea chooses to reach out to Rosamond in her efforts to help Dr. Lydgate. Rosamond perceives Dorothea's pains and temporarily overcomes her own self-centeredness to help Dorothea by revealing the truth that Will loves only Dorothea. Thus the suffering and self-sacrifice of one character uplifts and alters another, creating a rippling effect that could someday change the community.

The conflict between shriveling egoism and expansive sympathy, which occurs within the community and each individual, appears in images of webs and of vision. Webs connect the community, creating possibilities for sympathy, but they also enclose individuals, allowing egoism to thrive. For example, Nicholas Bulstrode, the man who is arguably the novel's most wicked character, spins rationalizations around himself "like masses of spider-web, padding the moral sensibility." Similarly, images of enhanced vision reveal the enlightenment of "vivid sympathetic experience." But the most famous image of vision—a candle held before a mirror—creates a parable of "the egoism of any person." The random scratches on the mirror seem "to arrange themselves in a fine series of concentric circles round that little sun."

Multifaceted images of webs and light reflect human tendencies to both selfishness and sympathy—tendencies that are expressed through the imagination. On the one hand, the *egoistic* imagination paints self-serving pictures that justify selfish actions. On the other, the *sympathetic* imagination extends vision beyond the self, lessening the sufferings it witnesses in others. Eliot calls suffering a "baptism" through which people grow from egoism to sympathy, as Dorothea does through her dark night of the soul. The memory of suffering "passes from pain into sympathy"; as we remember our own suffering we are enabled to imagine others' pain and sympathize with

I think we have no right to come forward and urge wider changes for good, until we have tried to alter the evils which lie under our own hands.

—*Middlemarch*

them. Thus we can choose to act sacrificially rather than selfishly and our actions will aid rather than hinder moral progress.

Dorothea finds her husband in the garden; an illustration by W. L. Taylor from *Middlemarch*, 1886.

[T]he growing good of the world is partly dependent on unhistoric acts; and that things are not so ill with you and me as they might have been, is half owing to the number who lived faithfully a hidden life, and rest in unvisited tombs.

—*Middlemarch*

Every human choice has consequences; some decisions cause pain, others grow out of pain to nurture moral growth. The novel's closing sentence illustrates Dorothea Brooke's effect on those around her as being "incalculably diffusive." She has affected the world: "for the growing good of the world is partly dependent on unhistoric acts; and that things are not so ill with you and me as they might have been, is half owing to the number who lived faithfully a hidden life, and rest in unvisited tombs."

Eliot thus believes in a radically nontraditional world that is evolutionary and unpredictable. She still relies, however, on such traditional values as kindness, sympathy, a fellowship of suffering, self-sacrifice, and duty as guides for living in that world.

For Further Study

One of the best editions of the novel is the Riverside, with its fine introduction by Gordon Haight; the Oxford and Penguin editions are also good, affordable paperbacks. Haight also wrote the excellent *George Eliot: A Biography* (Oxford, 1968). *George Eliot: Middlemarch* (Penguin, 1989), by Catherine Neale, is a helpful introduction to the novel.

Helpful background for reading Victorian novels appears in Julia Prewitt Brown's *A Reader's Guide to the Nineteenth-Century English Novel* (Collier, 1985) and Daniel Pool's *What Jane Austen Ate and Charles Dickens Knew* (Simon and Schuster, 1993). A good book on the intellectual climate of Eliot's sphere is *Making It Whole* (Ohio State University Press, 1984), by Diana Postlethwaite. Gillian Beer, in *George Eliot* (Indiana University Press, 1986), writes intelligently and wisely about Eliot as a woman writer.

Issues to Explore

Middlemarch reads slowly, but readers are rewarded with a story that vividly illustrates the difficulty of choosing to do good. They can thus respond to the book's moral challenge by examining more closely the selfishness and selflessness of their own actions.

Eliot called her novels "experiments in life." The success of a fictional experiment, however, lies in the reading. Does the experiment convince us? Several questions will help us explore this query, some of which are difficult and disturbing: (1) Throughout *Middlemarch* Eliot emphasizes the need to make wise moral choices. Do her characters have the *freedom* to make choices? (2) Eliot believes that human beings are the products of laws of inheritance. Can they have free will? (3) She insists that people should not allow "a fatalistic point of view to affect practice." Does she make her characters' freedom to choose believable in the context of a world determined by laws of social and biological inheritance? (4) Furthermore, can they as products of Darwinian struggle consciously and rationally choose to nurture feelings of sympathy rather than selfishness? Or do the characters' moral choices make an evolutionary ("survival of the fittest") model false? (5) Does Eliot's evolutionary model make the moral lessons too remote from a Christian notion of reality?

—Dean Ward

GERARD MANLEY HOPKINS
Poems
1874–89

Next to SHAKESPEARE, Gerard Manley Hopkins is arguably the most widely quoted English poet. His sonnet "The Windhover" has delighted and challenged many readers and has generated more written criticism than any other single English lyric. Such poems as "God's Grandeur," "Pied Beauty," *The Wreck of the Deutschland,* and the celebrated sonnets of despair have drawn almost equal attention.

Where to place Hopkins historically remains problematic. His poetry was not published until 1918, when his literary executor, the Poet Laureate Robert Bridges, felt that the poems would attract interest. By the 1930s a second edition was released, and a wave of interest in Hopkins broadened his reputation. That appeal comes from his linguistic freshness, rich symbols, and earnest wrestling with matters of faith and doubt. Today his work is a standard feature of any British anthology. Although representative of Victorian literature, his unique style influenced a number of modern poets, including W. H. Auden, William Empson, and

Gerard Manley Hopkins (1844–1889).

Dylan Thomas. Still, Hopkins's sensibilities and the issues he addresses (industrialism, faith and doubt, science, beauty) place him, if not so squarely, in the Victorian tradition.

A Short Life

Hopkins was born in 1844 in Stratford, Essex, the first child of a well-to-do Victorian family. He won an exhibition to Balliol College, Oxford, in 1863. There he experienced the wake of the Oxford movement, a religious and literary reaction to nineteenth-century rationalism and skepticism. John Henry NEWMAN began this movement, which sought to return rituals, ornaments, and neglected sacraments to the Church of England. Like Newman, Hopkins converted to Catholicism. His life as a Jesuit priest was marked by countless reassignments that took him to parish work in the indus-trial cities of England and finally to a professorship in the classics at Newman's University College, Dublin. Because of the city's poor drainage he contracted typhoid, to which he succumbed on June 8, 1889, at the age of forty-five.

Faith and Hope amidst Doubt and Despair

Hopkins's standing as a poet is remarkable given his limited literary corpus, a slim collection of fewer than two hundred poems. And his letters, diary, journal, and religious writings, though longer,

The world is charged with the grandeur of God.
*   It will flame out, like shining from shook foil;*
*   It gathers to a greatness, like the ooze of oil*
Crushed. Why do men then now not reck his rod?
Generations have trod, have trod, have trod;
*   And all is seared with trade; bleared, smeared with toil;*
*   And wears man's smudge and shares man's smell: the soil*
Is bare now; nor can foot feel, being shod.

—"God's Grandeur"

are slight when compared with those of other poets of equal reputation. His juvenile and Jesuit poems prior to *The Wreck of the Deutschland* show remarkable range. Such poems as "Heaven-Haven," "The Alchemist in the City," "Let me be to Thee," and "The Half-way House" are veiled autobiographical pieces, while "Myself unholy" and "My prayers must meet a brazen heaven" express the spiritual doubt characteristic of nineteenth-century poetry. Such traditional Catholic poems as "St. Thecla," "Margaret Clitheroe," "St. Winefred's Well," and "Lines for a Picture of Saint Dorothea" memorialize these martyred Catholic saints. These poems, like so many others, address spiritual crises, poetic creativity, and the value, if not the beauty, of suffering.

With the publication of *The Wreck of the Deutschland* in 1875, Hopkins ended his seven years of self-imposed poetic silence. This long elegy concerns a shipwreck at the mouth of the Thames in which five nuns exiled from Bismarck's Germany under the Falck Laws were drowned. The poem appeals to England to return to Christ through its ancient Catholic faith.

Hopkins's most fruitful period was from 1875 until his move to Ireland in 1884. In one single year (1877) he wrote such splendid lyrics as "God's Grandeur," based on Psalm 19; "The Starlight Night," a poem that beckons our adoration heavenward; "Spring," which declares that the way to secure eternal spring is through Christ; and "Pied Beauty," a psalmic poem that proclaims glory to God for the diversity of creation.

An equally fertile period was 1879, in which Hopkins composed the companion poems "Duns Scotus's Oxford" and "Binsey Poplars." The first complains about architectural modernization at Oxford and the second laments the senseless deforestation along Oxford's Isis River. Other poems written during this period include "Henry Purcell," a sonnet to the acclaimed seventeenth-century English composer; "The Candle Indoors," which asks us to mend our own "fading fire"; "The Handsome Heart," which locates true beauty within the heart; and "Andromeda," which warns against prevailing threats to the church in a poem built on the Greek myth as recorded in Ovid's *Metamorphoses*.

Hopkins was often disconsolate during his five years in Ireland. He lamented his health, the political weather, and his inability to revive the inspiration to write. Yet in this inhospitable environment he composed his most powerful expressions not only of doubt and despair but also of faith and hope. Of these Dublin sonnets, the one beginning "I wake and feel the fell of dark" concerns an unresponsive God, describing a neglect compared to letters sent to an absent lover. But although the poet sees his own condition as gloomy, even more hopeless is the lot of those spiritually lost; their "sweating selves" are "worse." Another sonnet, "Thou art indeed just, Lord," takes its epigraph from Jeremiah 12:1 to argue the apparent contradiction between a just God and the successes of the wicked. This age-old dilemma, also faced by Job and the Psalmist, remains unanswered in the poem. The poet asks only that he be granted the spiritual and poetic fruits befitting one whose request is just and who remains a friend of God.

Similarly brilliant are "Spelt from Sibyl's Leaves" and "That Nature is a Heraclitean Fire and of the comfort of the Resurrection." The first deals with the ancient Sibyl's oracle on the unfastening of heaven and earth with its threat to humans—the delicate ecosystem makes our existence an equally tenuous thing. The second poem uses Heraclitus's doctrine of the

The wreck of the Deutschland, December 6, 1875; on which Hopkins' poem is based.

earth incinerating to argue the refining properties of the resurrection. At a "trumpet crash," the body becomes imperishable and the individual, because of the incarnation, becomes "immortal diamond."

"The Windhover": An Allegory for Christ

"The Windhover," Hopkins's most celebrated sonnet (a fourteen-line poem in iambic pentameter with a fixed rhyme scheme), expresses a wealth of important ideas. Much of it, however, is not easily accessible except through the beauty of its language. The idea in the first eight lines (the octet) is not especially difficult. One early morning the poet catches sight of a speckled falcon. He calls it the darling of the morning because it is "drawn" by the dawn in the sense of being attracted to and silhouetted against the sky. Equestrian and skating images describe the bird's adroitness—in its "riding," "striding," and "gliding." It circles and then darts right and left as skaters propel themselves forward. The bird's riding of the wind is described as a knight on horseback; it becomes

an allegory for Christ, the poet's "chevalier," to whom the poem was later dedicated.

The poet's admiration of the falcon and desire to emulate its mastery continues in the final six lines (the sestet), the poem's most difficult section. He celebrates the bird's untamed beauty, bravery, and elegance and becomes imaginatively one with the bird. The bird's harnessing of its energy for a daring dive is described as "a fire that breaks from thee." That fearless, fiery descent, when retold, becomes "lovelier" and "more dangerous."

At this point the analogy to Christ becomes

Glory be to God for dappled things—
*   For skies of couple-colour as a brinded cow;*
*   For rose-moles all in stipple upon trout that swim;*
Fresh-firecoal chestnut-falls, finches' wings;
*   Landscape plotted and pieced—fold, fallow, and plough;*
*   And áll trádes, their gear and tackle and trim.*

—"Pied Beauty"

As we drove home the stars came out thick; I leant back to look at them and my heart opening more than usual praised our Lord to and in whom all that beauty comes home.

—*The Journals and Papers of Gerard Manley Hopkins*
Humphrey House and Graham Storey, eds.

For Further Study

Norman Mackenzie's *The Poetical Works of Hopkins* (Clarendon, 1990) is the definitive text of Hopkins's poetry. As useful and far less expensive, however, is Catherine Phillips's *Gerard Manley Hopkins* (Oxford Authors Series, 1986). Because of recent findings, earlier extant editions of the poems are not as reliable.

Critical sources abound. Norman Mackenzie's *A Reader's Guide to Gerard Manley Hopkins* (Cornell, 1981), with its lucid interpretations of the poems, is a practical handbook; Norman White's *Hopkins: A Literary Biography* (Clarendon, 1992) is the most useful biography of Hopkins, although Robert Martin's *Gerard Manley Hopkins: A Very Private Life* (Putnam's, 1991) will be preferred by casual readers of Hopkins; Walter Ong's *Hopkins, the Self, and God* (University of Toronto, 1986) is the most theological approach to Hopkins; and Jude V. Nixon's *Gerard Manley Hopkins and His Contemporaries: Liddon, Newman, Darwin, and Pater* (Garland, 1994) connects Hopkins to Oxford's ritualism, Tractarianism, the emerging science of Darwinism, and Victorian aesthetics.

more apparent. The bird's mastery of the heavens in the octet and its earthly plunge in the sestet create a joint image of the incarnation. Christ's fall, like the windhover's, grows lovelier the more the good news is recounted. Combined images create a picture of the incarnation and the shedding of the precious blood of Christ: ploughing of a field polishes the plough and reveals the sillion (silicon) in the soil in the same way that seemingly dead embers reignite when they "fall, gall themselves, and gash gold vermilion." The discipline of industry and self-sacrifice becomes redemptive.

In many ways the pattern in "The Windhover"—the poem's first part observing a natural phenomenon and the second applying it to some spiritual idea—is evident in any number of Hopkins's poems: "The Starlight Night," "Spring," "God's Grandeur," "The Caged Skylark," "The Lantern out of Doors," "Hurrahing in Harvest," and "Heraclitean Fire" to name a few.

Issues to Explore

When one reads Hopkins's poetry, it is helpful to consider the following questions: (1) Does the poet approach nature for its own sake or for its symbolic value? (2) Does language play a crucial role in providing access to meaning, or is language merely ornamental? (3) How crucial are rhythm and meter (sound) to meaning (sense)? (4) Are Hopkins's major symbols primarily natural, religious, or an unmediated vision of the two? (5) How would you characterize either the psychological condition of the poet or that of the character(s) in the poem? (6) And how do entries in Hopkins's diary, journals, essays, and religious writings shape his poetry?

—Jude V. Nixon

LEO TOLSTOY

Anna Karenina
1875–77

Anna Karenina (1875–77), the psychological novel of the nineteenth century, and *War and Peace* (1865–69) are the masterpieces of a literary giant, Leo Tolstoy. DOSTOYEVSKY called *Anna Karenina* a "perfect creation," speaking of it in his journal *Diary of a Writer* as a uniquely Russian response to the European attitude toward "human guilt and criminality." Perhaps even more than the mammoth *War and Peace*, *Anna Karenina* served to remind Europe—as it does people everywhere—that rationalist theories cannot explain the mystery of evil or grace.

Count Leo Nikolayevich Tolstoy (1828–1910).

The Winds of Change

Count Leo Nikolayevich Tolstoy was born on August 28, 1828, and died on November 7, 1910. He lived during a time of massive change in the world, being born soon after the Napoleonic wars and dying shortly before World War I and the subsequent Bolshevik Revolution. Although he lost both of his aristocratic parents when he was quite young, Tolstoy remained attached imaginatively to the ancient Mother Russia—in spite of his exposure to the flood of new political ideologies from abroad. The young Tolstoy held what were considered "progressive" ideas about land reform and the peasantry, like those of the character Levin in *Anna Karenina,* but his actual experience always held sway over unbridled idealism. His own tempestuous and tortured marriage, which produced thirteen children, continually reminded him that human existence is far removed from paradise.

Later in his life, when writing *Anna Karenina,* Tolstoy underwent a spiritual crisis he describes in *A Confession.* Rejecting orthodox doctrines such as the existence of a personal God and the divinity of Jesus, and developing a variant of the Christian faith that focused on the ethical teachings of Jesus, he turned away from writing fiction and attempted increasingly to live the life of peasant and sage. Hundreds of Tolstoy societies advocating nonviolence were formed across the world, his influence making him one of the world's most famous spiritual leaders.

Tolstoy's fiction, however, far surpasses his theories of morality. Emerging from the rich texture of his narrative and the complex humanity of his characters is a poetic universe that casts an ironic light on all the ideologies of his day. And his output was enormous, consisting of some ninety volumes of letters, journals, religious and philosophic tracts, novels, and short

All happy families are alike but each unhappy family is unhappy after its own fashion.

—*Anna Karenina*
Louise and Aylmer Maude, trans.

stories. Besides his two great novels, his fiction includes *Childhood* (1852), *Boyhood* (1857), *Youth* (1862), "Two Old Men" (1885), "The Death of Ivan Ilych" (1886), "The Three Hermits" (1886), *The Kreuzer Sonata* (1890), "Master and Man" (1895), and *Resurrection* (1899). Tolstoy's late parable-like stories, though intended for educational purposes to reach a peasant audience, remain aesthetic successes for all discriminating readers.

Fatal Passion and Sacramental Union

Anna Karenina begins: "All happy families are alike but each unhappy family is unhappy after its own fashion." In such a world, adultery represents a symbol of a perverted union based on passion rather than loving commitment, a lawless and fleeting pseudomarriage that destroys and undermines society even as it adversely affects the perpetrators. The epigraph for this powerful novel, "Vengeance is mine, I will repay," is a reminder of a moral law that exacts its toll, beginning with Anna's contempt for her husband, Karenin, once she has entered into an adulterous affair and ending with her final bitterness toward her lover. Yet the biblical passage is also an admonition to avoid usurping God's place at the throne of judgment. Anna too may receive mercy as well as justice in the divine scheme of redemption.

The novel focuses on parallel love stories, one of them adulterous and the other sanctified by marriage. Anna Karenina and Count Vronsky dominate the tragic stage while Kitty and Levin are the principal characters in the upward, comic movement. The novel's action moves between two great Russian cities, one sacred and the other profane. Moscow repre-

sents old Russia; a city where good and evil are recognizable. Thus Moscow can be the site of reconciliation and forgiveness as well as a community of faith. St. Petersburg, in contrast, is the city of facades—external forms that mask internal complexities.

Anna, the beautiful wife of Alexey Karenin, has been since her marriage a leader in Petersburg society. She appears first in the novel as an emissary of peace who has come to Moscow to reconcile her brother Stiva with his wife, Dolly. Anna restores unity in the family by persuading Dolly that her adulterous husband loves her. Ironically, however, Anna herself becomes enamored with the dashing Count Alexey Vronsky, a military officer who fails to foresee the spiritual consequences of an affair for a virtuous woman.

Vronsky has this blind spot because he has grown up in a corrupt society with few models to follow. The relatively new city of St. Petersburg, created unnaturally on a frozen swamp by Peter the Great, represents the plight of modern Russia, torn away from its roots in both the divine and earthly orders. Vronsky's own mother has led a life of discreet hypocrisy. Extramarital affairs, in her view, have no stigma if they are conducted without scandal. Sin does not enter her imagination as a prohibition against unlicensed pleasure. Anna is particularly vulnerable to Vronsky's infatuation with her beauty because her own marriage bears the stamp of Petersburg's degradation of the feminine role in marriage. Anna's beauty was bartered for familial and economic reasons into her marriage with Alexey Karenin, a government official who views her as a lovely decoration.

But Anna cannot initially escape her own sense of the immorality of her situation. Her instinctive remorse indicates that she is superior to the callous hypocrites, the "whited sepulchers" of Petersburg society. She weeps when Vronsky finally consummates their relationship. The narrator comments:

. . . she felt her humiliation physically. . . . He felt what a murderer must feel when looking at the body he has deprived of life. . . . There was something frightful and revolting in the recollection of what had been

Petersburg, Russia.

paid for with this terrible price of shame. The shame she felt at her spiritual nakedness communicated itself to him.

The biblical allusion to the sense of nakedness felt by the first parents after eating the forbidden fruit dominates this passage.

Tolstoy completes the unfolding of the relationship between Anna and Vronsky by relentlessly examining the consequences of their futile attempt to set up their adulterous love as a rival order to God's sacramental union. Only at the moment of her death, as she throws herself in front of a train but makes the sign of the cross and falls to her knees, does Anna ask forgiveness. Although the train, which symbolizes the relentless onrush of modern secular life, strikes her, the narrator seems to suggest that Anna has repented. And so the novel's final revelation for Anna puts a fragmented life into the context of a divine order that had been concealed by the frenzy of her passion and the hypocrisy of the society in which she lived.

Scenes of Kitty and Levin's story alternate with those of Anna and Vronsky's relationship. The young couple's progress toward happiness and illumination thus serves to counterpoint the tragic theme. Their growing mutual understanding, unlike adulterous passion, issues in a fertile and blessed union. Just as Vronsky and Anna go off to Italy in an illicit flight from the bonds of home, the narrator interjects the description of the young couple's nuptials in the Moscow cathedral. Into this image of communal and sacred marriage the narrator brings

Death, the inevitable end of everything, confronted [Levin] for the first time with irresistible force. And death, which was here in this beloved brother who groaned in his sleep and from force of habit invoked without distinction both God and the devil, was not so remote as it had hitherto seemed to him. He felt it in himself too. If not to-day, then to-morrow; if not to-morrow, then in thirty years' time— wasn't it all the same? And what this inevitable death was, he not only did not know, not only had never considered, but could not and dared not consider.

—*Anna Karenina*
Rosemary Edmonds, trans.

Vronsky, reflecting on Anna:

She was utterly unlike the woman she had been when he first saw her. Both morally and physically she had changed for the worse. She had grown stouter, and when she spoke of the actress a spiteful expression had distorted her face. He looked at her as man might look at some faded flower he had picked, in which it was difficult to trace the beauty that had made him pick and so destroy it.

—*Anna Karenina*
Rosemary Edmonds, trans.

representatives from all the levels of Moscow life: policemen, peasants, royalty. This wedding ceremony is full of vitality and promise for the future of the entire community.

Kitty and Levin quarrel throughout their married life, but their disagreements, in contrast to those of Anna and Vronsky, prevent them from growing apart. Though Levin is agnostic, Kitty's love is sacramental: marriage for her, as for St. Paul, is the metaphor for the relationship of Christ to the church. It therefore works consistently toward bringing Levin into the fold of divine as well as human love. At the end of the novel, after Anna's death and the birth of Levin and Kitty's child, the skeptical Levin begins his task of subordinating reason to faith. He resolves not to question religious forms and to give over to God any judgment concerning other faiths, even as he affirms his own. He is aware of a "feeling" that has "entered imperceptibly through suffering and is firmly rooted" in his soul. Though he knows that "his reason will still not understand why" he prays, Levin transcends the disintegration of both culture and the human psyche to see beyond "scientific explanations" into a realm of mystery that enlightens more than it obscures.

For Further Study

Anna Karenina is frequently taught in advanced courses in secondary schools; mature readers will delight in the intricate structure of this masterpiece. The most authentic translation is that of Louise and Aylmer Maude, which can be found in *The Norton Critical Edition,* edited by George Gibian (W. W. Norton, 1970), along with background materials and seminal essays on the work. *The Modern Library College Edition,* edited and introduced by Leonard J. Kent and Nina Berberova (Random House, 1965), is based on the famous Constance Garnett translation. The standard biography, Ernest J. Simmons's *Leo Tolstoy* (Little Brown, 1945), is currently out of print but can be found in most libraries. A. N. Wilson's biography, *Tolstoy* (Fawcett, 1988), is a readable but scholarly treatment of the writer's life and work; and Edward Wasiolek's *Tolstoy's Major Fiction* (Chicago, 1978) is a helpful exploration of Tolstoy's most important novels and short stories.

Issues to Explore

(1) The great theme of *Anna Karenina* is marriage. What does Tolstoy suggest by the contrast between the several examples of the sexual union between man and woman in the novel? What does he seem to imply about the basis of marriage, since even the superficial society of St. Petersburg will not tolerate its open violation? (2) A second important theme is the town-country issue. How does Tolstoy develop his defense of agrarian life? (3) How does Levin's path to faith contrast with Anna's agonizing disillusionment? Is Anna ultimately saved or lost?

—Dona S. Gower

FYODOR DOSTOYEVSKY

The Brothers Karamazov
1880

he *Brothers Karamazov*,
by Fyodor Dos-
toyevsky (1821–1881),
is one of the world's gravest and
most absorbing literary achievements, considered by many the
greatest novel ever written. From
the time the book was published it
has been recognized as a work of
genius, even though critics have
deplored, on the one hand, its
political conservatism and defense
of Russian Orthodoxy and, on the
other, its apparent rebellion against
political order. Further, the novel
has been frequently misinterpreted
as an intolerant piece of
slavophilism in its seemingly
exclusive love of Slavic culture
combined with fear and mistrust of
the West. Seldom has *The Brothers
Karamazov* been fully accepted for
what it is—a consummate work of
Christian imagination, as ornate
and involved as a Gothic cathedral.
But those readers who do approach
it on its own terms recognize that
its task is both memorial and
prophetic, giving form to a past
and predicting a future. That past,
for Dostoyevsky, is "Holy Russia";
the future is the hoped-for
communion of the human race to

Fyodor Dostoyevsky (1821–1881); sculpted
head by Dina Konenkova.

be brought about by a universal
belief in Christ.

Yet *The Brothers Karamazov* is
no devotional work. It treats theological issues but approaches them
through character and action,
maintaining the detachment and
impersonality characteristic of the
novel form. No explanatory omniscient voice provides an overview;
readers must scrutinize and interpret the narrator's statements as
carefully as they interpret other
elements of the work. The novel's

apparent objectivity, however,
along with its plurality of voices
and its paradox and irony,
strengthens rather than dilutes its
spiritual impact.

Earthly Imprisonment and Visionary Freedom

Fyodor Mikhaylovich Dostoyevsky
was born on October 30, 1821, in
a Moscow hospital for the poor
where his father was a surgeon.
The second of seven children,
Dostoyevsky grew up and was
educated in this urban environment. He has been called the first
writer to deal with the underlying
horrors and psychic ailments of
urbanization. His first published
work, *Poor Folk* (1845), seemed to
fit the critics' demand for humanitarianism; a subsequent novella,
The Double, however, revealed that
his primary genius lay rather in
the exploration of the unconscious
workings of the human psyche.

At this point Dostoyevsky's literary career was interrupted by an
event that changed the course of
his life. He and other members of
the Petrashevsky circle, a mildly
socialist group, were arrested after

> *"Karamazov," cried Kolya, "can it be true what's taught us in religion, that we shall all rise again from the dead and shall live and see each other again, all, Ilyushechka too?"*
>
> *"Certainly we shall all rise again, certainly we shall see each other and shall tell each other with joy and gladness all that has happened!" Alyosha answered, half laughing, half ecstatic.*
>
> *"Ah, how splendid it will be!" broke from Kolya.*
>
> —*The Brothers Karamazov*
> Constance Garnett, trans.

a meeting, imprisoned, and sentenced to be shot. On December 22, 1849, lined up for execution, they were saved at the last minute by a courier's message of commutation from the czar. Dostoyevsky was sentenced to seven years of hard labor in the Siberian prison camp at Omsk, where his epilepsy worsened, but where daily reading of the New Testament turned him to the words of Christ as sustenance. His thought and writing were permanently altered after those years of exile.

Dostoyevsky returned to Moscow in 1859 and published in 1861 *The Insulted and Injured* and in 1862 *The House of the Dead,* a fictional work based on his prison experiences, which reestablished him in Moscow literary circles. He edited the journal *Time* and later *Epoch* and in the midst of a serious depression began the serial publication of a novel that marked the turning point in his career. *Notes from Underground* (1864), an ironic first-person narrative, announced his vision of what the liberal gospel of reason and social improvement had effected. In it, as reprisal against the Enlightenment, his protagonist, a spiteful little "mouse" of a man, turns against his own self-interest and lives underground in his perversity.

From this point on, Dostoyevsky's writings depict the struggle between the communal faith of ancient Russia and the secular rationalism of the West. He foresaw the hor-

rors of the totalitarian twentieth century, with its lack of regard for human life and freedom. His later writings propose as remedy for the "age of positivism and science" a return to what Russians considered the sacredness of earth—an acceptance of human limitations and a recognition of mutual love and responsibility.

In 1866, Dostoyevsky completed two novels—*The Gambler* and *Crime and Punishment,* the latter probably his best-known work. *Crime and Punishment* details the course of a young rebel who withdraws into himself in contempt for his fellow human beings. This alienation eventually leads him to commit murder, which he defends as the exceptional person's right and even obligation. *The Idiot* (1869) and *The Devils* (1873), sometimes translated as *The Possessed,* are Dostoyevsky's most disturbing novels, difficult to interpret and yet conveying an unmistakably apocalyptic urgency concerning the collapse of the modern world. Soon after completing *The Devils* Dostoyevsky published the novel *A Raw Youth* (1875), which traces the psychological development of a young man as he moves into adulthood; and under the title *Diary of a Writer* (1876–77) he composed weekly essays for a conservative newspaper.

But his final novel, *The Brothers Karamazov* (1878–80), written during the last two years of his life, is a feat of consummation that reaches the calm and serenity of a long-pursued vision. In this magnificent work Dostoyevsky solved the problem on which he had been working during an entire career: the portrayal of a convincing positive character. Father Zossima, Christ-like in his healing power of love, is yet close enough to the earth and people to reveal the full dimensions of humanity.

Four Sons, Four Visions

The novel concerns the four sons of Fyodor Karamazov, born of three different mothers. In the course of investigating the father's murder, the reader is led to examine all the possible

Still from the 1958 MGM film *The Brothers Karamzov*, starring Yul Brynner.

paths for modern Russia—and therefore humankind. On one level the sons represent different "ways" for humanity: Dmitri, the eldest, depicts the way of the senses; Ivan, the intellect; Alyosha, the soul; and Smerdyakov—the illegitimate son—the debased way of skepticism and secularism.

Unjustly accused of killing his father, Dmitri and his trial make up a good portion of the novel. The second son Ivan is a Westernized intellectual who discovers that *he* has unconsciously caused his father's murder. His overt teachings that all things are permissible along with his covert hatred of his father have communicated to his bastard half-brother Smerdyakov the justification for murdering the dissolute old man. The third son, Alyosha, is a gentle boy apprenticed to Father Zossima, an elder in a nearby monastery. Father Zossima's unassuming but firm teachings mark the center of the novel, offsetting Ivan's famous Grand Inquisitor legend.

Dostoyevsky prefaces his book with a passage from the Gospel of John that constitutes the underlying theme of the work: "Verily, verily, I say unto you, except a corn of wheat fall into the ground and die, it abideth alone; but if it die, it bringeth forth much fruit." Each of the brothers must experience this cen-

tral pattern of falling to the earth and dying. In fact, the novel's chief action traces these experiences of rebirth.

The most famous section of the book is the dramatization of Ivan's anger at a God who has permitted innocent children to suffer. In a frequently excerpted section, the Legend of the Grand Inquisitor, Ivan recounts to his distressed brother Alyosha his case against Christ through the mouth of a worldly wise old Inquisitor during an *auto-da-fé*—a cere-

Father Zossima:

. . . love in action is a harsh and dreadful thing compared with love in dreams. Love in dreams is greedy for immediate action, rapidly performed and in the sight of all. Men will even give their lives if only the ordeal does not last long but is soon over, with all looking on and applauding as though on the stage. But active love is labor and fortitude, and for some people too, perhaps, a complete science.

—*The Brothers Karamazov*
Constance Garnett, trans.

monial public burning of heretics—in sixteenth-century Seville. In Ivan's account, a stranger whom the people identify as Christ appears in the village, raises a maiden from the dead, and is subsequently imprisoned. The Grand Inquisitor visits and reproaches the stranger, whom he plans on the morrow to burn at the stake. "Is it Thou?" the old man asks, declaring, "You had no right to come. We have corrected thy work." The Inquisitor charges that Christ's message is too difficult to follow; people cannot achieve his high demands. They do not want freedom; they want security. The Inquisitor offers Christ his liberty if he will go and "come no more." The Christ of the poem silently kisses the old man's pale lips as he leaves the prison and vanishes into the dark streets of the city.

Alyosha, however, has known Father Zossima and knows that the Christian faith is not so helpless, that it does not demand perfection, that it does indeed "work." The Elder's message of active love does more for the simple peasant women who visit him than all the bread they could receive from a totalitarian system such as Ivan has proposed.

The novel ends with the shout, "Hurrah for Karamazov!" This cry of joy is in praise of Alyosha, but in a larger sense it is an affirmation of the human race, for the Karamazov vitality is the positive force in humanity. Although this passion is subject to terrible sins of carnality and pride, nonetheless it is splendid in its vigor and exuberance and capable of Christlike love. It is the human nature Christ came to save.

Issues to Explore

In *The Brothers Karamazov,* Dostoyevsky sets in motion tenets of the Christian faith as Russian Orthodoxy embodied them, emphasizing the positive effects of suffering, a belief in the brotherhood of all people, and a sense of the ancient holiness of the earth. Yet the belief he expresses is not naive; as he has

For Further Study

The first translation of *The Brothers,* by Constance Garnett, is still the most easily approached; Ralph E. Matlaw has revised Garnett's translation in the Norton Critical Edition (1976). A recent translation by Richard Pevear and Larissa Volokhonsky (North Point Press, 1990), however, has a great deal of merit. For an understanding of Dostoyevsky's vision, see Nikolai Berdiaev, *Dostoevsky* (Meridian, 1957); Vyacheslav Ivanov, *Freedom and the Tragic Life* (Noonday Press, 1957); Konstantin Mochulsky, *Dostoyevsky, His Life and Work* (Princeton, 1967). Mikhail Bakhtin's *Problems of Dostoyevsky's Poetics* (University of Minnesota, 1984) marked a change in critical approaches to the novelist, focusing on his artistic innovations.

said, his "hosannah has come out of a furnace of doubt." Some questions to ponder follow: (1) In one of his letters Dostoyevsky maintained that his novel stands or falls on the effectiveness of the monk Zossima's last testament as an answer to Ivan's atheism. Is his picture of the saintly Zossima credible? (2) Father Zossima defines "active love" as opposed to love in dreams. Active love, he says, "is harsh and dreadful," requiring patience and even for some a "complete science." He thus defines love as something more than feeling, making of it a powerful force in the world. Could the entire novel revolve around this theme? (3) The novel is "open-ended," with many of its issues unresolved. What purpose might an author have in making use of this sort of ending?

—Louise Cowan

HENRY JAMES

The Portrait of a Lady
1881

*T*he *Portrait of a Lady* is a profoundly moral and compelling tale that supports Henry James's reputation as America's most sophisticated stylist and storyteller. As James's first long masterpiece, the novel stands as the culmination of his early work—and his most complex character study. Its fascinating heroine, Isabel Archer, explores questions of character and destiny, the consequences of marriage, and the subtlety of evil. More than the ideal work of art that James strived to craft, the novel's psychological and moral insight make it a major contribution to humanity's understanding of itself.

The Artist

The grandson of a rigid Presbyterian financier, the son of a thinker and theologian, and the brother of the influential psychologist and philosopher William James, Henry wanted only to be an artist, but one of great achievement. He brought to his art a talent for writing, a keen eye, and an acute moral sense.

1908 portrait of Henry James (1843–1916) by Jacques Emile Blanche.

Born in New York in 1843, James spent his formative years in Europe, including his childhood education. Only after returning to America did he seriously attend to his writing. As early as 1865, when he was only twenty-three, James was developing a distinct literary style and concern for form, which he explored in numerous book reviews and essays on literary criticism. He never married, dedicating his life to perfecting his writing.

In one sense James's religion was Art, but not Art for its own sake. His art is informed by his moral sensibility. From his New England ancestors James had inherited a highly critical moral perspective, but one that philosophers and scientists had robbed of any divine authority.

Like his father's friend, the romantic writer Ralph Waldo EMERSON, he believed that the poet should teach the reader by illustrating and interpreting life's experiences. Unlike Emerson, however, James did not think that trusting one's own intuitions would lead to truth. James was too keen an observer of people and society to accept the romantics' subjective view that the source for truth is in oneself. For him innocence must always be tempered by experience.

The Portrait

In *The Portrait of a Lady* James set out to draw "the character and aspect of a particular engaging young woman." She would include those distinctive qualities of American femininity that James refers to as "intellectual grace" and moral spontaneity." His heroine, Isabel Archer, is bright and good, but marked by a sense of superiority and too great a desire to control her own destiny. James takes this independent and naive young American to the corrupt Old World of aristocratic Europe, where her "sin of self-esteem," coupled with her independence and "nobleness of imagination," yield disastrous results. For although she spends "half her time thinking of beauty and bravery and magnanimity" and knows it is "wrong to be mean, to be jealous, to be false, to be cruel," she has

> *Recognising so promptly the one measure of the worth of a given subject, the question about it that, rightly answered, disposes of all others—is it valid, in a word, is it genuine, is it sincere, the result of some direct impression or perception of life?*
>
> —Henry James, from the Preface
> *The Portrait of a Lady*

seen "little of the evil of the world." Therefore she fails to recognize the evil she encounters in other characters.

Isabel had already shocked her aunt's family, with whom she stayed in England, by declining the marriage proposal of a handsome and intelligent English lord. This blatant show of independence fascinates her cousin Ralph Touchett. Because he wants to see what she will do with a "little more wind in her sails," he persuades his wealthy father to make Isabel an heiress. But Ralph's fascination turns to dismay when Isabel marries the fortune-hunter and American dilettante Gilbert Osmond. As she had thwarted her aunt's wishes by refusing Lord Warburton, she now rejects the advice of her wiser cousin.

Isabel believes that she is acting on her independent will and high ideals, but her will is neither fully independent nor her goals completely lofty. She has been subtly manipulated by the attractive and sophisticated but conniving Madame Merle, who has her own dark reasons for wanting Isabel to marry Osmond.

Osmond is poor but highly cultivated. To Isabel he appears high-minded, and she wants to use her fortune to further his artistic talents. But Osmond's only goals are a life of luxury and total dominion over his wife. Thus Isabel's proud independence and self-congratulatory generosity lead her, through the manipulations of others, into a loveless marriage with a man who shows her only jealous suspicion and harsh cruelty.

The novel raises the question of whether Isabel's destiny is self-determined or set by people and circumstances beyond her control. Ultimately she is brought through suffering to a truer understanding of her responsibility for her own life, from which vantage point she can make a wiser decision about her future. For in the end Isabel must decide whether to abandon Osmond or to return to the oppression of their marriage, if only to help his weak but essentially good daughter, Pansy.

Isabel's difficult decision is brought to a climax when a former suitor, Caspar Goodwood, offers a promise of total freedom from responsibility and contemporary conventions. Escape is alluring, but Isabel must face the consequences of her actions, including moral degradation. When she leaves Caspar's passionate embrace, Isabel is "set free," but not in the way that Caspar had hoped. She is now free to make her own choices because she knows all of her options. "She had not known where to turn; but she knew now. There was a very straight path."

Isabel chooses to embrace her duty and return to a life of responsibility, even though it entails considerable suffering. In the end her decisions are no longer based on her own proud notions; suffering and experience have transformed her spirit. Isabel is now more capable of helping the others who truly need her.

The Art and the Audience

The Portrait shows a highly polished mastery of literary form—a perfected and compelling psychological portrait—but to many of James's contemporaries the novel seemed incomplete. Although readers gain some sense of Isabel's final direction, they never see her actual efforts. This open-endedness results from James's deci-

Henry James's house at Rye, Sussex.

sion to conclude the novel when his character sketch seemed complete, rather than neatly wrapping up the details. Real life, like James's story, has few ideal endings.

To maintain the realism of the story's perspective James highlights the central character's point of view. The story unfolds mostly as Isabel sees it; the interpretation of events is limited to her own experience and individual understanding—and she learns just how limited her viewpoint has been. Because a naive person, such as Isabel, can easily misinterpret reality, the reader could be led astray by her perspective. But James's subtle narrative technique—for which his brother William first coined the phrase "stream of consciousness"—does allow other characters to discuss central events, such as Isabel's marriage, and proffer their own opinions. Thus James investigates

Joseph Conrad, commenting on the achievement of his friend and mentor:

A novelist is a historian, the preserver, the keeper, the expounder of human experience. As is meet for a man of his descent and tradition, Mr. Henry James is the historian of fine consciences.

all of the moral and psychological implications of a situation, affording multiple representations of the truth. The reader is led to understand the complication of moral choices.

James encourages his readers to examine themselves and their world honestly in order to perceive the good and the evil in both. Christian readers will recognize an accurate, but not oversimplified, depiction of human

[Ralph] observed, in petto, *that under the guise of caring only for intrinsic values Osmond lived exclusively for the world. Far from being its master as he pretended to be, he was its very humble servant, and the degree of its attention was his only measure of success.*

—The Portrait of a Lady

good and evil. James is concerned with what truly enhances human experience (his "good") and what diminishes it (his "evil"). He believes in living life to its fullest while acknowledging the boundaries of our own limitations and our duties to others.

Issues to Explore

A free spirit in her own time, Isabel is an appealing heroine to most modern readers. (1) For Isabel, absolute independence means relying on her own judgment. How should she, and we, balance our judgment against the advice of others? (2) What role does imagination play in the novel and in our lives? When does it help us soar and when does it create false expectations and illusions? (3) How much does character determine destiny? (4) How does Isabel's suffering alter or improve her character? (5) Although it is difficult to find a more fiendish villain in a realistic novel than Gilbert Osmond, in what ways are he and Isabel alike?

—Margaret Gardner

For Further Study

Henry James is the most prolific American author. His works comprise forty-four volumes of novels and short fiction, literary and art criticism, travel writing, plays, reviews, biography, and autobiography. A reader new to James could begin with his shorter novels, such as *The American* and *The Europeans,* which, like *The Portrait,* employ "the international theme," as does *The Ambassadors,* James's own favorite. *The Turn of the Screw,* a shorter work, offers an unusual psychological exploration.

James himself was the subject of what is probably the most comprehensive American literary biography ever written, Leon Edel's *The Life of Henry James.* Originally it was published in five volumes, but is now available in one definitive edition (Harmondsworth, 1977). Edel also edited the insightful *Henry James: A Collection of Critical Essays* (Prentice-Hall, 1963).

A good edition of *The Portrait of a Lady* is the Penguin Classics (1986). Roger Gard's *Henry James: The Portrait of a Lady* (Penguin, 1986) and Lyall Powers's *The Portrait of a Lady: Maiden, Woman, and Heroine* (Twayne, 1991) offer helpful studies of the novel. Also see *Twentieth-Century Interpretations of The Portrait of a Lady: A Collection of Critical Essays* edited by Peter Buitenhuis (Prentice Hall, 1968) and *The Merrill Studies in The Portrait of a Lady* compiled by Lyall H. Powers (Merrill, 1970).

MARK TWAIN

The Adventures of Huckleberry Finn
1885

Mark Twain, pen name for Samuel Langhorne Clemens (1835–1910).

Mark Twain's novel *The Adventures of Huckleberry Finn* is the quintessential American adventure story because of what it reveals about the human heart in general and, in particular, the American "habits of the heart." As an American odyssey in the tradition of the Homeric epic, the novel outlines the moral battle between generosity and greed, between salvation of the human soul and its capitulation to avarice. Its central action is Huck Finn's development of a moral code, based on his loyalty to Miss Watson's runaway slave, Jim. Moreover, the novel depicts the stunning variety of ways that the American spirit wrestles with the demons of slavery and the angels of freedom—going well beyond the liberation of an individual slave or issues of race.

Explorer of the American Character

In 1863 Samuel Langhorne Clemens adopted his pen name, Mark Twain, almost in jest to give himself a public persona. River-boat operators used the phrase as a warning cry for two fathoms (a fathom equals a depth of six feet). The pen name reflects Twain's love for the Mississippi River. And his trilogy—*Tom Sawyer* (1876), *Life on the Mississippi* (1883), and *Huckleberry Finn* (1885)—celebrates the life of youth along the banks of the great body of water that slices the heartland of America.

In his books Twain created an original depiction of American culture. A prior generation of American writers had published works that were steeped in the tradition of an earlier European fictional style but were partly led by a spirit of democratic independence. Twain, however, sought to examine and question through his sardonic and witty prose what gave America its particular character. Although moored in a deeply Puritan heritage, that character, Twain believed, tended to resist codes and civilizing strictures. For at the base of civilizations, Americans perceived an unacknowledged urge to harden the human spirit by institutionalizing its most benevolent impulses.

Twain was a prolific writer. Other noteworthy books of his include *The Celebrated Jumping Frog* (1867), *Innocents Abroad* (1869), and *The Gilded Age* (1873). He never tires of examining certain themes in his works: deceit and fraud, hypocrisy, gullibility, superstition, trickery, freedom and bondage, the heart's impulse to do good, and the innocence of the natural order. Twain especially explores the world of deception in

Huck:

You can't pray a lie—I found that out.

—*The Adventures of Huckleberry Finn*

Tom Sawyer and *Huckleberry Finn* to reveal the propensity for being fooled. And in the character of Huck he shows the innate desire of humanity to follow the heart despite the paralyzing aspects of "sivilization."

As such, Huck is an American-style hero—independent, resourceful, a trickster and consummate survivor—who is driven by love of adventure and a growing conviction of the heart. He is the kind of individual who, as William FAULKNER wrote in another context, is willing to be receptive to the "truths of the heart . . . love and honor and pity and pride and compassion and sacrifice." Twain reveals that sometimes the civilized order impedes rather than promotes such a moral and ethical disposition.

Banned but Important

Ernest Hemingway wrote, "All modern literature comes from one book by Mark Twain called *Huckleberry Finn.*" Yet no other American novel seems to have sustained such a long and battered history of rancor, banishment, controversy, and misinterpretation. Banned initially in Boston's library upon its publication, it is still withdrawn from many school classrooms today. One offensive aspect, critics cite, is the word "nigger," which appears over two hundred times in the speech of various characters. A further objection centers on what readers consider the racially stereotypical way that Jim is presented. But close scrutiny of the novel reveals its moral underpinnings. For underneath the caricature of Jim, Twain portrays him as a figure of moral strength and virtue.

Jim's enslavement is a poetic metaphor for the heart's enslavement to any number of maladies: bigotry, greed, violence, mob rule, pharisaical religion, alcohol, anger, fanatical ideas,

prudish language, ignorance, and self-righteousness. This American masterpiece examines these forms of moral enslavement through the formative—and at times satiric—mind and voice of a young boy. In the first-person vernacular narration, the seemingly uneducated Huck recounts his own moral and spiritual crisis. To obtain Jim's freedom he has to decide how to surmount these forms of bondage. Huck learns many lessons from Jim as they journey down the Mississippi. He learns how the actions of service and generosity, fidelity to one's mission, and magnanimity of heart and soul are the surest antidote against hatred, greed, and the many forms of slavery.

Journeying into the Dark Heart of Society

What Tom Sawyer develops as an ideal for adventure through reading romantic fiction, Huck lives out as real adventure. Tom is Huck's foil. Whereas Tom imitates bookish adventures to conform the present to the past in formula and style, Huck improvises stratagems to survive present ordeals. He is much more creative and resourceful than Tom. For example, Huck feigns his own murder to throw his father, pap, off his tracks. He joins forces on Jackson's Island with Jim, who embodies an old and mysterious world of superstition, witchcraft, charms, and portents.

In addition, Jim's acts of generosity and self-sacrifice give Huck new moral bearings. Throughout the river trip, Huck's moral dilemma is whether to choose friendship and fidelity or restore Jim to his owner. As he and Jim float down the Mississippi River through the dividing current of America, Huck begins to liberate himself from the influences of society. When Jim is recaptured, he makes his final choice. If returning Jim to Miss Watson as stolen property is the right thing to do, then Huck must forever be in the wrong: "All right," he declares, in what is actually a supreme triumph for good, "I'll go to hell." Here he reconfirms his overt mission: to free a person from slavery. His covert mission, however, is fidelity to the human heart.

The novel illustrates a moral journey into both the heart of one's own darkness and the communal soul of America with all its depravity: the senseless feuds between the Grangerfords and Shepherdsons; the duplicity of the duke and the dauphin as they bilk townspeople out of their money and divide the families of slaves for profit; the hatred, ignorance, and malice of people toward one another. Neither the raft nor the river is exempt from the intrusion of evil, as when Jim finds Huck's father, pap, dead in a house floating down the river, or when the duke and king muscle their way onto the raft to escape the wrath of the townspeople.

Surrounded by the world's deceptions, Huck must continually choose between the inclinations of his innate virtue and his civilized conscience. Like Hamlet, to whom references in the novel are frequent, Huck must negotiate moral choice and action even as truth is hidden or severely distorted. He must, for example, steal the money taken by the bogus actors to return it to the rightful owner Mary Jane Wilks. He must lie to protect Jim and himself from being imprisoned by the townspeople. And he must deceive to achieve a higher end—his and Jim's freedom.

The final quarter of the novel focuses on the efforts of Huck and Tom to free Jim from his latest captors. Tom steals center stage as he strives to turn Jim's escape into another storybook adventure. Once Jim is freed Huck chooses to "light out for the Territory ahead of the rest" to escape the trappings of being "sivilized," a condition he has brushed up against before. The novel illustrates the way in which virtue is most vital and efficacious when carried into action. A life of service, generosity, and loyalty to others is the strongest buffer between Huck and a world seemingly guided by gullibility, deception, and avarice. The protagonist confronts the dark side of human nature, the struggle giving rise to the virtues that sustain a soul in travail.

Criticism of the work's structure, especially the failure of the last twelve chapters, as many critics have written about it, centers on three issues: Tom's return to the narrative and his "cruelty" toward Jim and Huck through his elabo-

Huck Finn, orphaned waif of the backwoods.

rate scheme to free the already liberated slave; the change in Huck from an active, clever force to a passive spectator; and a failure of tone in the last chapters wherein Twain loses his nerve as a novelist. But what these arguments do not address sufficiently is the collision of two ways of knowing: Tom Sawyer's book knowledge and Huck Finn's experienced knowing. Twain's vision at the novel's end entertains the insoluble problem of whether art imitates life or life imitates art.

Tom Sawyer on doing everything by the book:

"Don't I tell you it's in the books? Do you want to go to doing different from what's in the books, and get things all muddled up?"

—The Adventures of Huckleberry Finn

Huck on Tom Sawyer:

He was always that particular. Full of principle.

—*The Adventures of Huckleberry Finn*

Issues to Explore

Twain wrote *Huckleberry Finn* with the use of multiple dialects in an engaging vernacular style in the tradition of oral literature. It reads as if the narrator is casually telling the story to the reader, ironically conveying more than he knows. Huck's disarming prose and language hide a sophisticated design in a complex interwoven plot. It alludes to many earlier stories, including several books of the Old Testament; SHAKESPEARE's plays, especially *Hamlet* and *King Lear*; the *Arabian Nights; Tom Sawyer;* and others.

When reading the text we should ask several fundamental questions: (1) Are human beings innately good though depraved by civilization? (2) What does Huck learn from Jim, the slave who speaks of prophecies and superstitions yet seems to have deep wisdom? (3) Are the wilderness and the river, as emblems of the natural order, superior to civilized or cultural order? (4) How can we interpret what we see or read to determine what is true? (5) How many different ways are enslavement and free-

dom explored in the novel? (6) What is the role of money in the economic life of the communities along the banks of the river?

—Dennis Patrick Slattery

For Further Study

For reading the novel only, a good edition is published by Bantam (1981). For a more inclusive edition with letters, reviews, and criticism, see the Norton Critical Edition, edited by Sculley Bradley (Norton, 1977). Biographical and critical works on Mark Twain include Henry Nash Smith, *Mark Twain: The Development of a Writer* (Harvard, 1962); Everett Emerson, *The Author Mark Twain: A Literary Biography of Samuel L. Clemens* (University of Pennsylvania, 1984); John Lauber, *The Making of Mark Twain: A Biography* (Houghton Mifflin, 1985); Hamlin Hillard and Walter Blair, editors, *The Art of Huckleberry Finn: Texts, Sources, Criticisms* (Chandler, 1962). An excellent sourcebook that outlines the controversy over the novel's end is a new edition of the novel: *Adventures of Huckleberry Finn: A Case Study in Critical Controversy,* edited by Gerald Graff and James Phelan (Bedford Books, 1995).

The Makers of the Modern World

The great works of modern poetry and fiction have been forged in a crucible of ideas and extraordinary events. Although they are central to our understanding of modern culture, these works of literature can be fully understood only in the context of the dominant intellectual trends of the era. Adam Smith helps make sense of Charles Dickens; Charles Darwin illuminates Henry James and Henry Adams; the work of Sigmund Freud paves the way for James Joyce and Virginia Woolf.

Relationships of this kind are legion, pointing to the intricate connection between theoretical reflection and imaginative literature. Just as changes in the understanding of the self, nature, and God have profoundly affected modern beliefs and actions, so too have they changed many of the ways in which poetry and fiction are written and read.

In trying to understand modern individualism, for instance, one could trace changing images of the self in literature from the time of SHAKESPEARE up through the romantic and Victorian periods; the history of these changes could be charted through exclusive reference to literary images, stories, and characters from literature. But an argument about modern individualism that excluded philosoph-ical ideas and economic forces would be partial and flawed at best. For the development of modern thinking about the individual, the economic theorist Adam Smith is every bit as important as, and arguably more influential than, William WORDSWORTH. Charles Dickens has brilliant insights into the complexities and injustices of a modern capitalist society, but it is Karl Marx who provides the more trenchant theoretical analysis of capitalism.

Charles Darwin (1809–1882) in 1840; watercolor after the portrait by George Richmond.

Adam Smith and the Capitalist Order

There is something fitting about Adam Smith's masterpiece, *The Wealth of Nations,* appearing in 1776, the same year that the American colonies declared their independence. Smith was a Scottish philosopher who lived from 1723 to 1790. What the Declaration of Independence did to shape the political future of the world, his *Wealth of Nations* did to direct the course of modern economies. What one observer has called Smith's "democratic, and hence radical, philosophy of wealth" paves the way for "the modern world, where the flow of goods and services consumed by everyone constitutes the ultimate aim and end of economic life." In Adam Smith's world an invisible hand governs the acquisition of wealth and the consumption of goods and services, miraculously coordinating the individual pursuit of self-interest for the well-being of the whole of society.

Under the guidance of Smith and others, in theory and in practice, capitalism focused unprecedented attention on the individual as an entity of production and consumption. In doing so, it preached an implicit gospel of radical egalitarianism, which in theory made matters of gender, class, and race irrelevant in the marketplace. The market economy's power, as much as any belief about the self or truth, subverted the customary hierarchies of social and spiritual life, isolating the modern individual. Traditional theories of the self, explains one historian, "begin with the person as a member of society born into a complex of obligations and identities." But in contrast, the

Adam Smith (1723–1790).

liberal individualism that both shaped and grew out of the development of capitalism "starts with the individual who possesses a common set of needs." Thus the desiring and acquiring self promoted in many contemporary theories of culture more than casually resembles the unit of consumption at the center of market economies and democratic societies.

The Marxist Critique

Abuses and excesses in the practice of capitalism led inevitably to a questioning of its theory. By the middle of the nineteenth century, a variety of radical alternatives to the capitalistic system had sprouted up across Europe. The most powerful critique came from the pen of Karl Marx, the founder of international communism who lived from 1818 to 1883. The work of this German philosopher was destined to become one of the dominant intel-

lectual and political forces of the twentieth century.

Marx and his collaborator Friedrich Engels built their system on the philosophy of G. W. F. Hegel, a towering figure in early nineteenth-century German philosophy. Hegel saw history as a series of monumental struggles between theses and their antitheses, which then produce higher syntheses. He termed the process *dialectical* because it involved the ceaseless give and take of opposing ideas. Marx and Engels adopted Hegel's idea of dialectical struggle but perceived different forces as generating that struggle. Instead of conflicting ideas, they saw competing social and economic forces as the great engines of historical change. In the Marxist vision, history is not a battle between rarefied, opposing beliefs; instead it is a brutal competition to control the means of economic production and exchange. For Hegel, history as dialectical development was to lead to the rule of Absolute Spirit; for Marx and Engels, the inevitable end of economic conflict was to be a utopian Dictatorship of the Proletariat.

Marxism has shaped the modern world in several ways. Although now thoroughly discredited as an economic practice, for the better part of this century it was the ruling ideology that governed the lives of a sizable portion of the earth's population. Marxism fueled the Russian Revolution of 1917, provided the theoretical underpinnings for the expansion of the Soviet empire, and in 1949 helped propel a small revolutionary sect to power in China, the largest nation on earth. To a lesser extent, Marxist political factions and parties have influenced developments in countries of the Third World and in Western democracies.

Modern Masters of Suspicion

Perhaps more important than Marxism's direct political influence, however, has been its dominant power as an intellectual force. Marxism attributed all historical change to the workings of economic forces, which it saw as working toward a blessed appointed end. It somehow combined modern scientific naturalism and determinism with the powerful Jewish and Christian traditions of millennialism. In doing so, it gave modern intellectual credibility to an ancient ethical and spiritual ideal.

Of the great intellectual figures of the late nineteenth century, Marx was virtually alone in retaining utopian hopes for a world that appeared to be governed by material drives and desires. For the other major figures of that period—particularly Friedrich NIETZSCHE (1844–1900), Charles Darwin (1809–1882), and Sigmund Freud (1856–1939)—neither history as a whole nor the lives of individuals were driven by rational or conscious purposes. Instead, these thinkers argued that powerful subterranean forces propel human life and that they do so without any transcendent destiny in mind.

One philosopher has brilliantly described Marx, Nietzsche, and Freud as masters of the "hermeneutics of suspicion"—that is, of a way of interpretation based on suspicion. These thinkers have taught us, he explains, to doubt human consciousness itself. Rather than viewing history as being

directed by divine providence or rational human choices, the masters of suspicion explain history and thought by powerful unconscious drives. As we have seen, for Marx the struggle to control the means of production provides the interpretive key for the actions of individuals, societies, and indeed the whole of human history; for Nietzsche, the irrational will to power on the part of individuals explains the entire course of human experience; for Darwin, the

struggles of species to adapt and survive govern human history and individual behavior; while for Freud, largely unconscious sexual drives determine everything from the clothes we choose to the theological systems we embrace.

The two major cultural developments of the twentieth century—modernism and postmodernism—can be seen as reactions to the intellectual movements that transformed Western thinking at the end of the nineteenth century.

Karl Marx, founder of international communism (1818–1883).

Through the likes of Marx, Freud, Nietzsche, and Darwin, that era bequeathed to the twentieth century a naturalistic understanding of the human condition. Like older Christian understandings of the self and its place in the scheme of things, the hermeneutics of suspicion sees the self as vulnerable and subject to overwhelming forces.

Nevertheless differences between modernism and postmodernism, on the one hand, and postmodernism and the Christian faith, on the other, are genuine and significant. When Christian theology describes the self as fragile and at the mercy of a power greater than itself, it believes that power to be personal, purposive, and loving. For the masters of suspicion, the governing powers are impersonal and chillingly indifferent to human desires or purposes. And while modernism looks to art for redemption and postmodernism finds salvation in ironic self-awareness, the Christian faith turns to other sources for its sustenance.

Christians in the Modern World

For the Christian trying to understand the modern world and bear witness to Christian truth in it, modern thought presents unique opportunities and challenges. On the one hand, by recapturing a sense of the vulnerability and fragility of the self, modern thinkers have overcome some of the naïveté in rationalist, Enlightenment, and romantic views of human nature and human des-

For Further Study

Resources abound for studying the making of the modern world. The single best comprehensive volume on the subject may be Franklin Baumer, *Modern European Thought* (Macmillan, 1977). Other outstanding recent books are Hans Blumenberg, *The Legitimacy of the Modern Age* (MIT, 1983); Jean-François Lyotard, *The Postmodern Condition* (Minnesota, 1984); Leszek Kolakowski, *Modernity on Endless Trial* (Chicago, 1990); and Louis Dupré, *Passage to Modernity* (Yale, 1993). The most trenchant assessment of the theological dimensions of modernity remains Reinhold Niebuhr's *The Nature and Destiny of Man,* two volumes (Scribner's, 1941).

tiny. Darwin, Marx, Freud, and others have dealt devastating blows to the early modern confidence in the power of the self to know all truths and to right all wrongs. Properly understood, the theories of these makers of the modern mind confirm what Christians have long believed about the finite and sinful nature of human beings.

Yet on the other hand these masters of suspicion have called into question the very ideas of God, providence, and redemption. More often than not, they construe the idea of God to be nothing more than the projection of human fears and longings upon a blankly indifferent universe. Having traced the source of ideas and values to the realms of economic, biological, sexual, and psychological drives, the modern mind can find no source for the idea of God outside of those inner realms. Not surprisingly, Marx interprets God as an idea that the powerful use to subject the weak, while Freud sees God as a projection of deep-seated sexual drives and anxieties.

In coming years, Christian

interpreters of culture and modern history will be challenged to incorporate the powerful insights of the hermeneutics of suspicion without denying the claims of the Christian faith. The dimensions of which Marx, Freud, and others have written so compellingly are elements of the complex life as led by finite, sinful men and women. One need not set a Christian understanding of life directly against a Freudian understanding of sexuality's power or a Marxist reading of the power of economic motivations. Rather than denying outright modern insights, Christians would do well to incorporate some of those insights into their own accounts of the gracious activity of God. In the coming decades, attempts to affirm truth by denying sexual, economic, or psychological reality could discredit the very truth Christians have set out to defend.

—Roger Lundin

FRIEDRICH NIETZSCHE

Twilight of the Idols
1888

*T*wilight of the Idols, by Friedrich Nietzsche, is one of the most famous works of a nineteenth-century philosopher who has been a decisive influence on twentieth-century thought and life. In his works Nietzsche was not content merely to document the bankruptcy of Western thought and culture. Rather he felt compelled to destroy the idols as well as expose them. The subtitle of *Twilight of the Idols* attests to this drive to destroy: "Or How to Philosophize with a Hammer."

Striking for their brilliant epigrams, rich in such famous ideas as "the superman," filled with a portion of everything—philosophy and theology, literary criticism and history, fiction and fable—the works of Nietzsche's final years were daringly conceived and executed with an impressive literary flair. And there is more than a little irony in the fact that such books as *Twilight of the Idols,* which set out to undermine many of the canonical assumptions of Western culture, have themselves assumed the status of canonical texts.

Friedrich Wilhelm Nietzsche (1844–1900).

Twilight of the Idols clearly shows some consequences of the rejection of God and truth in portions of the contemporary West. As a source and exemplar, Nietzsche is a central figure in contemporary debates about the existence of God, the nature of truth, and the nature of the self. In a fundamental sense, we cannot understand contemporary ideas of truth and interpretation without comprehending the work of Nietzsche.

Thinking with a Hammer

The son of a Lutheran pastor, Nietzsche (1844–1900) was devoutly religious in his childhood. As a young man, however, he was drawn away from the pastorate and the world of faith toward the scholarly profession. At the age of twenty-four, he was appointed to a chair in classical philology at the University of Basel. Within years he began to produce the revolutionary books that secured him a central place in the canon of contemporary thought. Not long after he completed *Twilight of the Idols* in 1888, Nietzsche went insane. He died in 1900 at the age of fifty-five.

A key to understanding Nietzsche is the fact that he was a convert. He exchanged the orthodox piety of his childhood for a revolutionary view of God and human nature. Like many converts, Nietzsche reserved his greatest scorn for the idols that he believed had long held him in bondage. "There are more idols in the world than there are realities," he wrote in the foreword to *Twilight of the Idols.* For that reason, it is essential "to pose questions here with a hammer and perhaps to receive for answer that famous hollow sound which speaks of inflated bowels." With an unprecedented fury, he set out to

For art to exist, for any sort of aesthetic activity or perception to exist, a certain physiological precondition is indispensable: intoxication. . . . *In this condition one enriches everything out of one's own abundance: what one sees, what one desires, one sees swollen, pressing, strong, overladen with energy. The man in this condition transforms things until they mirror his power—until they are reflections of this perfection. This* compulsion *to transform into the perfect is—art.*

—*Twilight of the Idols*
R. J. Hollingdale, trans.

smash the idols of his age. He saw the two greatest to be the bankrupt bourgeois culture and the life-despising God of historic Christian theism.

The Inestimable Value of Life

Twilight of the Idols is, as Nietzsche intended, an alternatingly infuriating and illuminating exploration of contemporary culture and its historical background. The work consists of pithy phrases interspersed among longer sections that have such titles as "Morality as Anti-Nature" and "The Four Great Errors." The many disparate observations and sections are unified by several convictions that shape not only the whole of this work but the rest of Nietzsche's writing in his final productive years as well.

Because *Twilight of the Idols* radically reinterprets the history of Western thought, to understand it we must grasp Nietzsche's view of history. Central to his vision is the conviction that *he* is one "in presence of whom precisely that which would like to stay silent *has to become audible. . . .*" Nietzsche sees himself as a preeminent interpreter to articulate the new meaning of the self, nature, society, and God.

Twilight of the Idols exposes the wicked "judgment on life" at the heart of Western experience. That judgment, Nietzsche concludes, is that life *"is worthless."* By equating reason with virtue and happiness, Nietzsche asserts, Socrates originally made reason the tyrant of life, condemning all who followed after him to repeat his error: "Socrates was misunderstanding: *the entire morality of improvement, the Christian included, has been a misunderstanding. . . .*"

These misunderstandings are rooted in what Nietzsche considers an arrogant failure to acknowledge *"that the value of life cannot be estimated."* It cannot be estimated "by a living man, because he is a party to the dispute, indeed its object, and not the judge of it." Having failed to grasp this fact about the severe limits of human knowledge, men and women throughout history have repeatedly created idols to worship.

Chief among these idols to Nietzsche is the belief that truth stands outside of life and must be revealed to humanity through the laws of nature, the lessons of experience, or scriptural revelation. Such a belief is an idol, Nietzsche would claim, because it ignores the fact that truth is entirely a human creation. Truth as the gift or creation of a transcendent God is nothing but an idol. Only when this idol has been broken may "the *innocence* of becoming [be] restored." And once we have been freed from idolatry, then we can see that *"nothing exists apart from the whole!"* and "that no one *gives* a human being his qualities."

Reflections on Perfection

Twilight of the Idols does not conclude with this assault on the "idol" of truth. Stripping humanity of the comforts of truth and eternity, Nietzsche offers instead the consolations of art. To Nietzsche, art is not an imitation of nature but an expression of the human will to power. In Nietzsche's world, *all* uses of language are forms of expressive artistic endeavor. Because there is no such thing as truth, all that we can ever know are willful *interpretations* of the meaning of a single event or the whole of life. All of us are interpreters, all of us are artists.

"Nature, artistically considered, is no model," *Twilight of the Idols* declares. "It exaggerates, it distorts, it leaves gaps. Nature is *chance.*" Instead of weakly studying "from nature," the self must become intoxicated with its own power. "The essence of intoxication is the feeling of plenitude and increased energy. . . . The man in this condition transforms things until they mirror his power—until they are reflections of his perfection. This *compulsion* to transform into the perfect is—art."

Nietzsche's definition of art helps explain the extraordinary influence of *Twilight of the Idols* and his other famous works, such as *Beyond Good and Evil* and *Thus Spake Zarathustra.* Whether his work is a primary cause or merely illustrates a trend, it points to the enormous appeal of the expressive view of the self and the centrality of art in contemporary culture. Under the influence of Nietzsche and others, the modern world has grown increasingly skeptical about the belief that truth can be discovered or revealed. Instead truth is something to be made and fabricated by the willful, creative self.

Nietzsche's philosophy offers comfort for those who celebrate the self's power even as they doubt its capacity to know the truth or do the good. For Nietzsche and his intellectual descendants, all knowledge is a matter of interpretation and all interpretations are lies. It would be impossible for matters to be otherwise, because the only relationship of language to reality is that established by acts of violence and power. As all uses of language involve deception, Nietzsche claims, a person can do nothing more than seek to dissemble with power and effectiveness. In articulating such a vision, Nietzsche gave voice to what would become in the twentieth century the master spirit of the age.

Issues to Explore

Considering Nietzsche's beliefs about God and truth, we can easily wonder why a Christian would bother to read him. Quite simply, *Twilight of the Idols* is important for the Christian reader because of the powerful—however par-

Friedrich Nietzsche (1844–1900).

tial—nature of the truth that it does tell. It poses various questions: (1) If Nietzsche is in the business of breaking idols, does he not have at least something in common with the Judeo-Christian tradition?

(2) In biblical history and the history of the Christian church, has it not been repeatedly necessary for prophetic voices to rise up to break the idols that falsely claim the allegiance of believers? For instance, in *Twilight of the Idols* Nietzsche criticizes the English Victorian novelist George ELIOT for believing that once she gets "rid of the God," she can still "cling all

For Further Study

Twilight of the Idols may present difficulties to the reader new to Nietzsche's work. It is available in an inexpensive edition, with a helpful introduction, from Penguin (1990). This volume includes another work from Nietzsche's final phase, *The Anti-Christ*. The *Portable Nietzsche* (Penguin, 1976), edited by Walter Kaufmann, contains *Twilight* and *The Anti-Christ* and several other works. Ronald Hayman has written a highly readable biography of the philosopher (Penguin, 1982). The secondary literature on Nietzsche is enormous and stands as a clear indication of his influence; for a good introduction to this literature see Alexander Nehamas, *Nietzsche: Life as Literature* (Harvard, 1985).

the more firmly to Christian morality." A Christian critic of culture might well sympathize with Nietzsche's attack on the modern idolatry of the self. It is Nietzsche who says in this passage on Eliot that "Christianity is a system, a consistently thought out and *complete* view of things. If one breaks out of it . . . the belief in God, one thereby breaks the whole thing to pieces." Nietzsche argues that there are no moral sources within the self. "Christian morality is a command; . . . it possesses truth only if God is truth."

—Roger Lundin

JOSEPH CONRAD

Heart of Darkness
1899

*S*ome of the greatest fiction in English was written by a Polish seaman, Joseph Conrad. Of all his works, *Heart of Darkness,* the journey not only into the jungles of Africa but into the human heart, is doubtless the best known. This novella (a short novel) has generated an enormous body of critical studies, which examine it from virtually every conceivable angle. It continues to have an enduring grasp on the modern imagination.

A Spinner of Sea Yarns and More

Putting to sea as a teenager, Jósef Teodor Konrad Nalecz Korzeniowski (1857–1924) learned English only when he was twenty-one, a language that he always spoke with a thick accent. It was his third language after Polish and French. He eventually settled in England, shortened his name to Joseph Conrad, and wrote fiction ranging from short stories to novellas to long novels. His rich, masterful prose style demands—but also amply rewards—slow reading.

Joseph Conrad (Jósef Teodor Konrad Nalecz Korzeniowski) (1857–1924).

Conrad's maritime career took him to the far reaches of the globe, and his travels were of immense importance to his writing. At first he was read merely as a spinner of sea yarns. But in reality Conrad sought to examine the moral issues of basic human nature stripped of the thin veneer of civilization. It is to this effect that he uses exotic settings for his writings: Southeast Asia for *Lord Jim, Victory,* and many short stories; Latin America for *Nostromo;* Russia for *Under Western Eyes;* Africa for "An Outpost of Progress" and *Heart of Darkness.*

Into the Jungle

In 1890 Conrad fulfilled a boyhood dream by taking a steamboat up the Congo River to the center of Africa, which, on the maps he had seen as a boy, was left as a blank spot. *Heart of Darkness* draws on this experience of the Congo. Though the novella is rich in characterization and theme, its plot is simple. Captain Charley Marlow, the chief narrator in four of Conrad's works, goes up river to fetch a cargo of ivory. Repeatedly he hears of Kurtz, the agent at the innermost station and the one who sends out the greatest loads of ivory. Everyone considers Kurtz an exceptional man, but something now seems wrong with him. As Marlow journeys up the river his steamer is shot at with arrows, but it gets through. Kurtz dies shortly after Marlow reaches him, but not before revealing himself to Marlow.

It turns out that, initially to further his work, Kurtz has allowed the natives to worship him

This is the reason why I affirm that Kurtz was a remarkable man. He had something to say. He said it. Since I had peeped over the edge myself, I understand better the meaning of his stare, that could not see the flame of the candle, but was wide enough to embrace the whole universe, piercing enough to penetrate all the hearts that beat in the darkness. He had summed up—he had judged. "The horror!" He was a remarkable man. After all, this was the expression of some sort of belief; it had candor, it had conviction, it had a vibrating note of revolt in its whisper, it had the appalling face of a glimpsed truth—the strange commingling of desire and hate.

—*Heart of Darkness*

as a god. Succumbing to a fascination with his primitive setting, he has taken up with a gorgeous native woman who symbolizes the wilderness itself.

He has also indulged in unspeakable rites, which are not described but signs of which remain, such as the human skulls on posts around his headquarters. He has indeed seen into the heart of darkness. Wishing to be left undisturbed, he had ordered his loyal natives to shoot at Marlow's steamer. Just before dying, Kurtz asks Marlow to report back to "the Intended," Kurtz's fiancée in Brussels. When she asks what his last words were, Marlow lies and says that they were her name. In actuality, Kurtz's last words were, "The horror! The horror!"

Point of view is always an important matter for Conrad. In this case, Marlow tells his story to four other trading-company men on a sailing yawl moored in the Thames River in England; one of them is the actual narrator, the "I." So Kurtz reaches the reader only after passing through various intermediate consciousnesses: Marlow, the narrator, Conrad. Thus Conrad forces us to wonder how accurate our understanding of Kurtz is, especially since Marlow himself seems unsure. Communication is difficult; the truth is hard to know.

Therefore it is easy to misunderstand this novella. Some say Conrad's very point is the impossibility of knowing truth. Others use the story to psychoanalyze Conrad. The most widespread misreading emphasizes politics. Thus some accuse Conrad of imperialism, racism, and sexism, though on each score he has more defenders than accusers. Ideological critics are guilty, at the least, of imposing current standards on prior ages. The best, and most common, approach to understanding the story emphasizes moral issues.

The Heart of *Heart of Darkness*

Although Marlow is the main and central character, Kurtz is the touchstone by which Marlow gauges his own moral being. Everyone agrees that Kurtz is "a special being"; they call him a "universal genius," a "gifted creature." A Russian disciple who lives at Kurtz's compound declares, "Oh, he enlarged my mind!" Kurtz is half English and half French with a German name. "All Europe contributed to the making of Kurtz." He comes to the heart of the Dark Continent as the best that Europe has to offer. And he "had immense plans": he himself declares, "I was on the threshold of great things."

But the primitive place "seemed to draw him to its pitiless breast by the awakening of forgotten and brutal instincts, by the memory of gratified and monstrous passions." Instead of conquering the wilderness, Kurtz is conquered by it. Like the surrounding cannibals, Kurtz loses any sense of restraint. Marlow judges, "He had kicked himself loose of the earth." In breaking the traditional bonds with humanity and nature, Kurtz abandons all limits to his freedom and descends into license. In the end, the man who would exalt himself goes on all fours in his death throes. He acknowledges his moral breakdown, and his final judgment of himself is of hellish horror.

One of Kurtz's assignments was to write a report to the International Society for the Suppression of Savage Customs. He writes seventeen tightly packed pages. The report opens with the notion that white men must appear to Africans "in the nature of supernatural beings." It ends with a postscript, added much later in unsteady hand: "Exterminate all the brutes!" As the report reflects, even his artificial bonds with the natives did not hold. He is isolated, alienated, despairing—as are many characters in modern literature.

Yet for all this, Marlow insists that Kurtz achieves "a moral victory." And he does, for he comes to know who he really is. He comes to understand that the very heart of darkness is the darkness of his very heart. Moreover, Marlow realizes that what is true of Kurtz is also true of him. And what is true of them is true of us all—the chief lesson in the novella. "The heart is deceitful above all things, and desperately wicked: who can know it?" (Jeremiah 17:9 KJV).

To think that Conrad locates darkness only in the Dark Continent would be a great mistake. At the outset, Marlow notes that England, too, "has been one of the dark places of the earth." About the Africans, he says that "what thrilled you was just the thought of their humanity—like yours." Conrad's eye is ever fixed on our common human nature. He is able to examine the primitive heart of humanity because Africa "still belonged to the beginnings of time." But even the most civilized people have those "brutal instincts" and "monstrous passions"; they, too, have a savage breast.

In Christian terms, Conrad grasps that all have sinned. *Heart of Darkness* examines this essential fact of our human nature. William Golding in *Lord of the Flies* focused on this essence by removing children from adult supervision; Conrad focuses on it by placing a highly civilized person among primitives. Like DOSTOYEVSKY, Conrad shows that no extraordinary people exist. We are all ordinary, all sinners. But unlike Dostoyevsky, who believed in Christ, Conrad sees no redemption available. His vision is very dark. It leaves behind the comfortable doctrines of progress and human perfectibility of the eighteenth-century Enlightenment, but is devoid of any good news.

T. S. ELIOT used the line "Mistah Kurtz—

John Malkovich in the Turner Pictures film of *Heart of Darkness*, 1993.

he dead" to introduce his poem "The Hollow Men." Enlightened Europe is dead. Humanity without God is hollow at the core. Without God all search for meaning in human life fails. This is where such believers as Eliot and such unbelievers as Conrad agree.

> *He struggled with himself too. I saw it—I heard it. I saw the inconceivable mystery of a soul that knew no restraint, no faith, and no fear, yet struggling blindly with itself.*
>
> —*Heart of Darkness*

Going up that river was like traveling back to the earliest beginnings of the world, when vegetation rioted on the earth and the big trees were kings.

—*Heart of Darkness*

Issues to Explore

Ideally, readers will find others with whom to discuss this remarkable work. Questions to ask include: (1) At every point in the story, how reliable are Marlow's judgments? (2) Although stopping short of the ideological critics' excesses, can we ask fairly what Conrad's view of human nature implies for colonialism? (3) What does it mean that Marlow remains "loyal to Kurtz to the last"? Was he right to do so? (4) Is Marlow's lie to "the Intended" a failure of nerve, the kindness of offering a saving illusion, or something else? And what should we make of her, perhaps in contrast to Kurtz's African queen? (5) Why is Brussels called a whited sepulchre? (6) Why do Marlow's listeners show such little reaction to his story?

—Edward E. Ericson, Jr.

For Further Study

Heart of Darkness is widely available in paperback editions, sometimes with other short Conrad works. The Norton Critical Edition of *Heart of Darkness* includes the text, background, and commentary. Most of Conrad's other works remain available in paperbound editions. A new collected-works edition of Conrad is in progress from Cambridge University Press. The standard biography is Zdzislaw Najder's *Joseph Conrad: A Chronicle* (Rutgers, 1983). Among the abundant scholarly studies, notable standards are Ian Watt's *Conrad in the Nineteenth Century* (California, 1981), Albert J. Guerard's *Conrad the Novelist* (Harvard, 1958), and Thomas Moser's *Joseph Conrad: Achievement and Decline* (Harvard, 1957).

JAMES JOYCE

Dubliners
1914

*D*ubliners stands as every aspiring writer's textbook in the craft of fiction; and its author, James Joyce (1882–1941), as perhaps the most innovative fiction writer in English of the twentieth century. Joyce began writing the first of the stories that compose *Dubliners* in 1904 and completed work on the last story, "The Dead," in 1907. Because of censorship concerns, *Dubliners* did not appear until the beginning of World War I in 1914, to little notice.

Also in 1914, Ezra Pound began to champion Joyce, publishing installments of his first novel, *A Portrait of the Artist as a Young Man,* in Pound's journal, *The Egoist.* But even Joyce admirers still viewed *Dubliners* as a mere collection of sketches. Then in the 1950s serious critics examined it more closely and found a masterpiece that is also highly useful for teaching purposes.

Joyce had discovered how to bring into prose fiction metaphorical uses of language and methods of construction previously associated with poetry. Like his later work *Ulysses* and even the

James Joyce (1882–1941).

extremely experimental *Finnegans Wake, Dubliners* unites surface details with underlying symbolism to combine portraits of separate lives into a map of a private universe. Along with W. B. YEATS, T. S. ELIOT, and Pound, Joyce wanted nothing less than to provide a prophetic vision for his time—"to forge in the smithy of his soul the uncreated conscience of his race."

A Writer's Calling

Joyce was born in Dublin on February 2, 1882, the eldest son of John Stanislaus Joyce, an unsuccessful tax collector, and a pious mother, Mary Jane Joyce. Educated in two different Jesuit boarding schools, he took his university degree at another Catholic institution, University College, Dublin.

Joyce rebelled against his Irish Catholic upbringing, yet this heritage informs his work and its purpose to a startling degree, if often ironically and paradoxically. Although he is best known for his technical innovations and supreme facility with language, Joyce himself spoke in spiritual terms of writing as his vocation. *A Portrait of the Artist as a Young Man* dramatizes how Stephen Dedalus, Joyce's literary alter ego, transcends an earlier calling to the priesthood through becoming a writer, which the novel presents as the true priestly role of its time.

Joyce's later works become increasingly complex. In *Ulysses,* he manipulates a "continuous parallel" between a contemporary middle-aged Dubliner named

Gazing up into the darkness I saw myself as a creature driven and derided by vanity; and my eyes burned with anguish and anger.

—"Araby"

Leopold Bloom and HOMER's Odysseus. The action takes place during one day in which past and future, events and imaginings, fuse into a vision of life's universals—our desire for home, our exile. *Finnegans Wake* takes this process of symbolic compression a step further, down into its very words. It cannot be read, only explained.

The Awakening to Spiritual Paralysis

The fifteen stories of *Dubliners* can be read as a collective novel. Joyce grouped the stories into four divisions: the first three treat childhood; the next three young adulthood; the next four are about mature men and women; the final four concern public life. The masterpiece "The Dead" closes the work, serving as a summary even as it introduces a refreshing new perspective.

At first view, the stories appear to be almost formless. In "Araby," for instance, the story appears to be an anecdote about young love. But Joyce uses the tradition of courtly love, specifically the Arthurian legends with their spiritual extensions, to inform almost every line. The narrator is at once seen as a twelve- or thirteen-year-old Irish boy, a representative of the knight who quests through a hostile world for his Holy Grail, and the courtly lover whose "adoration" of a Lady lifts him to a higher spiritual plane. Here Joyce uses the tradition of romance or courtly love to mock it. But this mockery has a serious purpose in its service of the final line's diagnosis of the boy's spiritual state. He is "a creature driven and derided by vanity"; these romantic traditions are nothing but adolescent pretension—a vain spiritualizing of desire.

In *Dubliners* Joyce intended to write a "moral chapter" on his race. "Araby" exemplifies this purpose, in that its treatment of contemporary experience and the traditions that inform and interpret that experience exposes what Joyce saw as moral poverty. He set out in *Dubliners* to render his neighbors' lives and his own with such "scrupulous meanness" that their spiritual paralysis would be revealed.

Joyce spoke of his stories as "epicleti." In the Orthodox Church, the *"epiklesis"* is the prayer for the Holy Ghost to transform the elements into the body and blood of Christ. "Epicleti" implies transformation but also judgment, for when we see things in their true nature we cannot help being repelled or attracted and thus instructed. Joyce wrote to his brother, "there is a certain resemblance between the mystery of the mass and what I am trying to do . . . to give people a kind of intellectual pleasure or spiritual enjoyment by converting the bread of everyday life into something that has a permanent artistic life of its own . . . for their mental, moral, and spiritual uplift."

Joyce also borrowed the Christian term "epiphany"—a showing forth or revelation—to describe the moments of insight he wanted to capture in his work. In "Araby," the narrator articulates what he learned through his "epiphany," but in other stories we must examine the evidence for ourselves. In this way, the stories become interactive.

Story after story in *Dubliners,* using similar methods, fills out our understanding of the spiritual poverty and moral bankruptcy afflicting Joyce and his contemporaries. "Eveline" portrays a young woman reduced by her abusive family to "a helpless animal"; she becomes paralyzed on the gangway of an ocean liner and cannot respond to her lover's invitation to a new life. "Counterparts" depicts a clerk, Farrington, who counters the ridicule of his boss, Mr. Alleyne, by beating his son. Another small man, Little Chandler in "A Little Cloud," explodes at his infant son when he realizes he has succumbed to a passionless life and a lifeless marriage. "A Painful Case" finds Mr. James Duffy at first unable to respond to a married woman who has fallen in love with him and then dumbfounded by the betrayed woman's throwing herself under the wheels of a train.

The stories are an unremitting exploration of the deathly life these Dubliners are living. The collection's finale, "The Dead," explores the same theme and then qualifies it. It reveals another Irishman as a "pitiable fatuous fellow"—Gabriel Conroy, a university graduate and teacher like Joyce himself. Gabriel, however, is allowed a new vision of human limitation to which he responds with compassion. He comes to see his own egotism and romanticizing much as the narrator in Araby sees his flaws. But Joyce allows Gabriel a profound epiphany. And in this moment of identification, Gabriel sheds his superiority and realizes his common humanity. The snow is falling outside the hotel window as he has a new vision of life.

> He watched sleepily the flakes, silver and dark, falling obliquely against the lamplight. The time had come for him to set out on his journey westward. Yes, the newspapers were right: snow was general all over Ireland. It was falling on every part of the dark central plain, on the treeless hills, falling softly upon the Bog of Allen and, farther westward, softly falling upon the dark mutinous Shannon waves. It was falling, too, upon every part of the lonely church yard on the hill. . . . It lay thickly drifted on the crooked crosses and headstones, on the spears of the little gate, on the barren thorns. His soul swooned slowly as he heard the snow falling faintly through the universe and faintly falling, like the descent of their last end, upon all the living and the dead.

Joyce's revolutionary methods of fictional construction have forever changed the literary landscape. *Dubliners* and especially *Ulysses* have helped form the systems of interpreting the world in which we live. But some critics have been so taken with Joyce's radical experiments that they have minimized the moral implications of his writing. Joyce's methods nearly always sacrifice the traditions on which they depend. "Araby," as mentioned, casts doubt on the tradition of courtly love. Another story, "Grace," broadly implies that no such thing could ever be found in the church. *Finnegans*

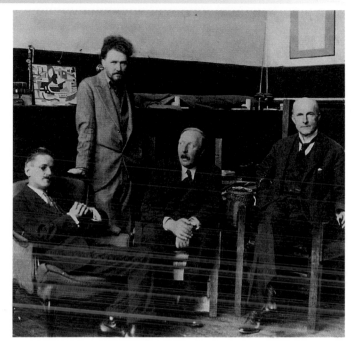

Wake shows Joyce as a high modernist and a self-ordained prophet of a new order who proposes to substitute the "secular scripture" of his writing for holy writ.

James Joyce with Ezra Pound, Ford Maddox Ford, and John Quinn in Pound's studio in Paris, 1924.

Her image accompanied me even in places the most hostile to romance. On Saturday evenings when my aunt went marketing I had to go to carry some of the parcels. We walked through the flaring streets . . . amid the curses of labourers, the shrill litanies of shop-boys. . . . These noises converged in a single sensation of life for me: I imagined that I bore my chalice safely through a throng of foes. Her name sprang to my lips at moments of strange prayers and praises which I myself did not understand. . . . I did not know . . . how I could tell her of my confused adoration. But my body was like a harp and her words and gestures were like fingers running up on the wires.

—"Araby"

He watched sleepily the flakes, silver and dark, falling obliquely against the lamplight. The time had come for him to set out on his journey westward. Yes, the newspapers were right: snow was general all over Ireland. It was falling on every part of the dark central plain, on the treeless hills, falling softly upon the Bog of Allen and, farther westward, softly falling upon the dark mutinous Shannon waves. It was falling, too, upon every part of the lonely churchyard on the hill where Michael Furey lay buried. It lay thickly drifted on the crooked crosses and headstones, on the spears of the little gate, on the barren thorns. His soul swooned slowly as he heard the snow falling faintly through the universe and faintly falling, like the descent of their last end, upon all the living and the dead.

—"The Dead"

Issues to Explore

(1) When reading *Dubliners,* notice that many of the stories take the form of short trips or journeys. Why would Joyce use this form? How does the form connect with the Western tradition in literature? (2) If the characters are suffering from a spiritual and moral paralysis, where are they going? Why? (3) Particularly in reference to "The Dead," does Joyce recommend journeying East or West? What values are associated with each direction? (4) What might Joyce's characters do to overcome their paralysis? Does he offer them any options?

For Further Study

The definitive edition of *Dubliners* is the Viking Critical Library Edition, edited by Robert Scholes and A. Walton Litz. It includes everything needed for a first and second reading. See also the Viking Critical Library Edition of *A Portrait of the Artist as a Young Man* edited by Chester G. Anderson. *Ulysses* (Penguin Classics, 1969) serves as the definitive text after long and arduous work by scholars.

For biography, Richard Ellmann's *James Joyce* (Oxford, 1959) is a masterpiece that raises the moral issues Joyce wanted addressed. Anthony Burgess's *Re-Joyce: A Guide to* Ulysses (Norton, 1968) is the best guide to an endlessly fascinating book by a writer who learned Joyce's lessons. And R. M. Adams's *After Joyce* (Oxford, 1977) proposes that most twentieth-century fiction writers have felt compelled to respond to Joyce's work. Adams explains why and how through astute readings of major writers.

(5) Why have the moral implications of Joyce's work been so neglected when he himself saw his work in analogous terms to Christian worship? (6) How does judging an author's work to be true, but not the whole truth, affect our literary appreciation?

—Harold Fickett

FRANZ KAFKA

The Trial
1925

Franz Kafka (1883–1924).

he Trial, along with the slightly more difficult novel *The Castle*, stands in the forefront of a slender literary production from which Franz Kafka has gained a secure place as one of the giants of modern literature, perhaps even its central figure. In the words of poet W. H. Auden, "Had one to name the author who comes nearest to bearing the same kind of relation to our age as DANTE, SHAKESPEARE, and GOETHE bore to theirs, Kafka is the first one would think of." His works, like much of modern literature, feature abandonment, estrangement, alienation, and isolation.

The alienation in Kafka's fiction is rooted in the triple alienation in his life. Born in Prague, Czechoslovakia, he was a German-speaking Jew among Yiddish-speakers. He lived as an agnostic among Czech-speaking Christians. And he passed almost all of his life under the roof of a domineering father. Though once in love, Kafka never married. He took a doctoral degree in jurisprudence and worked in a large insurance company until illness forced him to retire. Two years later, at age forty-one, he died of tuberculosis.

During his uneventful lifetime Kafka published a few short stories and novellas, most notably *Metamorphosis*. At his death he left behind three nearly finished novels, including *Amerika,* with strict instructions to his friend Max Brod to burn them. After much deliberation, Brod instead edited and published them.

A Journey into Nowhere

Kafka's life and work have been examined from almost every conceivable angle. But when Philip Rahv calls him "a man of religious temper," he speaks for the majority of Kafka critics. And this critic correctly names original sin as "the dogma closest to the thematic center of [Kafka's] work."

Kafka follows Dante in his depiction of the quest for the Absolute, from which meaning derives. In the medieval Dante, the pilgrimage moves from initial darkness to final light. The quest is purposeful and successful. In the modern Kafka, in contrast, there is a goal but no way to it. The quest shows the absurdity of the effort and issues only in despair.

Dante was a part of the great tradition of the West that had the Bible as its core text and assumed the universe to be orderly and meaningful. But Kafka writes on this side of NIETZSCHE's terrible announcement that God is dead, relentlessly showing us that with the death of God comes the death of humanity. Kafka's nostalgia for that old universe, with objective

With a flicker as of a light going up, the casements of a window there suddenly flew open; a human figure, faint and insubstantial at that distance and that height, leaned abruptly forward and stretched both arms still farther. Who was it? A friend? A good man? Someone who sympathized? Someone who wanted to help? Was it one person only? Or was it mankind? Was help at hand? Were there arguments in his favor that had been overlooked? Of course there must be. Logic is doubtless unshakable, but it cannot withstand a man who wants to go on living. Where was the Judge whom he had never seen? Where was the High Court, to which he had never penetrated? He raised his hands and spread out all his fingers.

—*The Trial*
Willa and Edwin Muir, trans.

meaning to which we can attach ourselves, simply cannot be satisfied. He makes the bleak assessment that our condition is absurd and that the only logical response is despair.

Kafka is unblinking in this conclusion. To reject all meaning is to be left with a great nothingness. The term for this worldview is *nihilism,* which Kafka encapsulates in his many parables. For example, "Atlas was permitted the opinion that he was at liberty, if he wished, to drop the earth and creep away; but this opinion was all that he was permitted." Or another, "The crows claim that a single crow could destroy heaven. This is undoubtedly so but proves nothing against heaven, since heaven means precisely: impossibility of crows."

Why would someone with such a closed and circular way of thinking even bother to write? Another parable gives what answer there is. "Previously I did not understand why I got no answer to my question; today I do not understand how I could believe I was capable of asking. But I didn't really believe, I only asked." Kafka never comes close to believing, but he can never stop asking.

Understanding *The Trial*

The anti-heroic hero of *The Trial* is called Joseph K., sometimes just K. This semi-nameless modern Everyman lacks distinct identity or personal worth. Like his creator, he is a small cog in a large bureaucracy—a recurring Kafkan image of hell.

In the opening sentence Joseph K. is arrested, but "without having done anything wrong." For the rest of the novel, the reader anticipates learning why K. was arrested. The trial would give answers, but it never comes about. Various events occur, but they do not move the story toward a climax. The only trial in the novel is K.'s trying to get to a trial.

Every story should have a beginning, middle, and end, according to ARISTOTLE. Actions have consequences, and once the consequences are enacted, the story is over. But all these classical requirements are gone with Kafka. Joseph K. experiences no character development, no attainment of insight; he remains perpetually in his initial situation. Time lacks its usual ordering power. There is no sense of an ending, or even a middle. Thus in editing the manuscript Max Brod was never sure in what order to place the unnumbered chapters.

Not only is time unreliable in *The Trial,* but so is space. The Court that would try Joseph K. meets in a stuffy apartment in a suburban tenement as the family continues with its business. Familiar rooms have wrong occupants in them. Other mergings and dislocations abound. In the Christian understanding, the time-space order is a gift from the Creator, which he validated by Christ's incarnation in a given body (space) at a given historical moment (time). But this trustworthy order is simply absent in *The Trial.* Instead, we enter a world devoid of familiar landmarks, a world described today by the adjective *kafkaesque.*

Joseph K. was arrested on his thirtieth birthday, the start of Jewish adulthood. He "cannot recall the slightest offense that might be charged" against him. The Inspector replies, "I can't even confirm that you are charged with an offense." Oddly, K. is to make his first court appearance on Sunday. He is told neither the time nor the place; he must guess. When he

St. Nicolaus Cathedral in Franz Kafka's birthplace, Prague.

arrives, he finds out that he is late. But K. is resolute, assuming that everything will be sorted out, although he is disconcerted by the raucous audience, all with cushions on their heads to keep from bumping against the low ceiling.

In scene after scene, familiar images of everyday life converge in an outlandish, nightmarish pattern. K. opens a lawbook and finds indecent pictures. He has unwelcome erotic encounters. He meets a tradesman, Block, who over five years has futilely spent all his money hiring lawyers. Titorelli, the Court painter, tells K. that one must be innocent for definite acquittal but that the Court is "impervious to proof." Personal intervention can move the judges but never achieve definite acquittal.

The theme of *The Trial* is justice. Kafka once wrote, "The state in which we find ourselves is sinful, quite independent of guilt." The issue with Joseph K. is not any specific act of sin but the state of sinfulness—he is under the curse of the fall. This novel is about the Law and one man's standing before it. And, as St. Paul tells us, the Law shows the sinfulness of

our condition. Paul adds that where sin abounds, grace much more abounds. But not in *The Trial,* where there is a Law but no Lawgiver who could personally extend grace.

In the next-to-last chapter, K. insists on his innocence to a priest: "And, if it comes to that, how can any man be called guilty? We are all simply men here. . . ." The priest, who also

> "... *the real question is, who accuses me?*
> *What authority is conducting these proceedings?"*
>
> —*The Trial*
> Willa and Edwin Muir, trans.

belongs to the Court, replies, "That is true, but that's how all guilty men talk." Then he explains that one seeking admission to the Law receives two statements from the doorkeeper: "that he cannot admit the man at the moment" and "that this door was intended only for the man." The priest denies any deceit or contra-

"So then I'm free," said K. doubtfully.

"Yes," said the painter, "but only ostensibly free, or more exactly, provisionally free. For the Judges of the lowest grade, to whom my acquaintances belong, haven't the power to grant a final acquittal, that power is reserved for the highest Court of all, which is quite inaccessible to you, to me, and to all of us."

—*The Trial*
Willa and Edwin Muir, trans.

diction. Again, only the Law is present; there is no grace and therefore no resolution.

In the final chapter two men come to kill Joseph K. As he is about to die, K. sees "a human figure, faint and insubstantial," leaning out a window and stretching out both arms. "Who was it? A friend? A good man? . . . Was it one person only? Or was it mankind? Was help at hand?" And he wonders, "Where was the Judge whom he had never seen? Where was the High Court, to which he had never penetrated? He raised his hands and spread out all his fingers."

In the Christian story, this is where grace enters. Christ steps forward as the substitute to die in K.'s place. But not in Kafka. K. is stabbed to death, "like a dog!" Human beings, once seen as a link in the Great Chain of Being connected both upward to God and downward to animals, are now connected only downward. Without the image of God, human beings are dehumanized. With the death of God has come the death of humanity. This is Kafka's central lesson.

For Further Study

The definitive edition of *The Trial* is available in paperback from Vintage Books. Recommended biographies are Ernest Pawel, *The Nightmare of Reason: A Life of Franz Kafka* (Farrar, 1984), and Frederick Karl, *Franz Kafka: Representative Man* (Ticknor & Fields, 1991). Good critical works are Erich Heller, *Franz Kafka* (Viking, 1984), and Anthony Thorlby, *Kafka: A Study* (Rowman & Littlefield, 1972).

Issues to Explore

As easy as *The Trial* is to read, the puzzles in it are endless, and endlessly discussable. (1) Christians can analyze the story through the lens of Scripture. For instance, what is the relationship between the Law in the novel and the Law in the Old Testament? How does the final chapter echo the crucifixion story? (2) Readers may wish to keep track of the many times when Joseph K. gives more than one possible explanation for the meaning of an experience. Is the difficulty caused by K. or by the experience itself? (3) Also, what do we take for granted about our lives that is simply not present in this novel? (4) Finally how would you imagine that Freudians, Marxists, and other secularists read Kafka?

—Edward E. Ericson, Jr.

WILLIAM BUTLER YEATS
Poems
1933

William Butler Yeats's poetry is the supreme accomplishment of one often called the greatest English-speaking poet of this century, a man of letters who had a decisive impact on the character of his native Ireland. Yeats spent his life in quest of spiritual wholeness. Though he never could embrace the Christian beliefs central to the Irish culture he helped reshape, he always knew of the need for faith in something greater than the merely human. His exotic verse portrays his creative genius in its attempt to unite historical, political, psychological, metaphysical, and literary concerns into a new whole.

Between Two Worlds

Yeats was born in 1865, the son of a distinguished Irish portrait painter, John Butler Yeats. The elder Yeats had reacted to the strict orthodoxy of his grandfather and father—both Protestant clergymen—by rejecting all religious belief. When William's turn came to react against his own father, however, he did not do so in the name of the orthodox Christian

William Butler Yeats (1865–1939).

faith. Rather, he engaged in a quest for the unknown that included secret societies, astrology, seances, and several other varieties of occult "mysticism."

Yeats's childhood was divided between the wild countryside of western Ireland in Sligo, where he spent holidays with his grandparents, and the urban environment of London, then the largest city in the world. Not surprisingly his early poetry is filled with longings for the landscape of Ireland and the mythic figures that populated it in the folk imagination.

Though Yeats's family moved back to Dublin during the poet's late teens, William remained a man who bestrode both worlds for the rest of his career. His family had some affinities with the "Ascendancy"—the powerful landowning class that was English in origin and Protestant in religion. Yeats, however, attempted to combine the world of the Catholic peasant, marked by earthiness and rich traditional Celtic lore, with the qualities of leadership, orderliness, and responsibility that characterized the Anglo-Irish aristocracy. Despite his fervent nationalist politics and support of Irish independence, he never rejected the English literary tradition.

By the time Yeats reached twenty he was convinced that Ireland offered a unique opportunity for a new kind of art that would change the world. Drawing on the richness of both folk and high culture, this art would overcome the materialism and abstract rationalism of nineteenth-century British civilization to bring about a renaissance of spiritual values. Irish culture, in his eyes, could show the world a way out of its malaise.

316 Invitation to the Classics

How but in custom and in ceremony
Are innocence and beauty born?

—"A Prayer for My Daughter"

Apart from Yeats's poetry—including some of the greatest lyrics in English—he also wrote essays, plays, and fiction. He received the 1923 Nobel Prize for his literary achievements. Indeed, for the last quarter century of his life he was a living legend in his native country.

The Public Stage

After Irish independence in 1922, Yeats was given an honorary position in the new Irish Senate. He remained uninterested in political activity divorced from art, however, because he believed that politics should serve art. This attitude resulted in continued tension between Yeats and the fiery, revolutionary activist Maud Gonne, whom he met early in life and with whom he was hopelessly in love. She is a major thematic figure in his poetry.

Another woman who played a crucial role in Yeats's life was Lady Augusta Gregory—playwright, translator, patroness. Lady Gregory supported him throughout his career and collaborated with him in a number of theatrical ventures, culminating in the famous Abbey Theatre. Yeats not only cofounded the Abbey, for which he created radically innovative poetic dramas, but also managed it for a significant period in its formative years. In this capacity he sought out and encouraged new dramatic talent and attracted patrons to keep the theater economically viable. Indeed, he and Lady Gregory created an Irish stage where none had existed before.

I must lie down where all the ladders start
In the foul rag-and-bone shop of the heart.

—"The Circus Animals' Desertion"

The Abbey Theatre was a key part of Yeats's artistic program for modern Ireland. It was a place where Celtic traditions could be brought to the attention of a modern, urban public. He was often disappointed in the results; even so, this dramatic movement was crucial in the emergence of modern Irish consciousness.

The Poet and His Stages

Though the main lines of Yeats's interests always remained the same, his poetry falls into several distinct stages. The early verse, which is romantic and dreamy in tenor, is filled with such exotic names of Celtic myth as Oisin, Aengus, Fergus, the Sidhe, and Cuchulain. It is a tribute to his imaginative genius that these shadowy remnants of the Irish past are more familiar now than a century ago. The magical lyricism of "The Song of Wandering Aengus" exemplifies the work of this period:

> Though I am old with wandering
> Through hollow lands and hilly lands,
> I will find out where she has gone,
> And kiss her lips and take her hands;
> And walk among long dappled grass,
> And pluck till time and times are done
> The silver apples of the moon,
> The golden apples of the sun.

Nevertheless, Yeats's first three poetic volumes do not neglect the present and the actual. The mythical figures are not mere nostalgic images of a half-forgotten past; they powerfully symbolize the human spirit and the dilemmas of mortal existence. Some of his poems most frequently chosen for anthologies are among those published between 1889 and 1904. Maud Gonne figures in a number of them, especially in the notable "The Folly of Being Comforted" and "Adam's Curse."

While preoccupied with the Abbey Theatre, Yeats was less prolific as a poet. Beginning in 1910, however, his poems underwent a marked shift in style. His language was sharpened and informed by a more mature perspective. He began to treat his earlier preoccupations (Maud Gonne, romantic Ireland, Celtic lore) with a slightly ironic detachment. He created succinct, powerful statements of

Maud Gonne
(1865–1953),
dedicatee of many of
Yeats's poems.

self-awareness in "No Second Troy," "The Cold Heaven," "That the Night Come," and "A Coat." In this last poem he abandons his "old mythologies" with the pronouncement that "there's more enterprise / In walking naked."

What followed was some of the major poetry not only of Yeats but of the twentieth century: "The Wild Swans at Coole," "In Memory of Major Robert Gregory," "Ego Dominus Tuus." This poetry culminated in "Easter 1916" with its famous refrain "A terrible beauty is born." In that poem Yeats confronts his inadvertent role in bringing to birth an Ireland racked by violence in the political struggle for independence, not one of artistic and spiritual wholeness.

Yeats's mature poems are not always easy. Lyrics like "Among School Children," "The Tower," "Sailing to Byzantium," and "Byzantium" require not only close attention to the text but also knowledge of details from his other writings. This is especially true of his famous "The Second Coming" with its apocalyptic and ambiguous vision of coming chaos:

> The darkness drops again; but now I know
> That twenty centuries of stony sleep
> Were vexed to nightmare by a rocking
>   cradle,
> And what rough beast, its hour come
>   round at last
> Slouches towards Bethlehem to be born?

The last poems, written during the final decade of Yeats's life, show undiminished powers of creativity and brilliance. They are marked by new, more insistently violent, concrete images and an almost terrifying energy. They

It's certain there is no fine thing
Since Adam's fall but needs much labouring.

—"Adam's Curse"

For Further Study

The definitive edition of Yeats's poetry is *Collected Poems,* Richard Finneran, editor (Collier Books, 1989). The most recent biography is by A. Norman Jeffares (Hutchinson, 1988), whose *New Commentary on the Poems of W. B. Yeats* (Stanford, 1984) is indispensable. Two comprehensive critical guides are John Unterecker, *A Reader's Guide to William Butler Yeats* (Noonday, 1959), and Hazard Adams, *The Book of Yeats's Poems* (Florida State University, 1990). For a sympathetic assessment of Yeats's occult interests from a Christian perspective see Kathleen Raine, *Yeats the Initiate* (Barnes & Noble, 1990).

celebrate the comprehensiveness of a tragic understanding that can still admit, in the midst of suffering, a strange joy in "ancient, glittering eyes."

Though Yeats could not embrace the Christian faith, he did not entirely reject it. Rather he presented it as part of his total vision. According to him, we must be prepared to be reborn not once, but at every stage of our lives. In one of his last poems, "The Circus Animals' Desertion," he accepts a fundamental humility in the face of inevitable human limitations: "I must lie down where all the ladders start, / In the foul rag-and-bone shop of the heart."

Issues to Explore

To the Christian, Yeats's attempts to find spiritual meaning in occult or other pseudoreligious activities may seem misguided and even a little dangerous. (1) Could his inability to find a solution in more orthodox beliefs suggest less a failing in the poet than in the religious alternatives available to him? (2) Could the Christian faith he experienced have come to seem too routine, too rationalistic and materialistic in day-to-day practice to attract someone of his imaginative gifts?

(3) Could Yeats's poems force Christian believers to reassess the degree to which spiritual values truly inform their own lives, as opposed to merely offering psychological comfort or minimal rules for correct social behavior? (4) Could his resort to myth at least reinforce a belief in good and evil forces beyond human control? (5) Does his poetry reveal the weakness as well as the glory of the human?

—Robert S. Dupree

T. S. ELIOT

Four Quartets
1935–41

*F*our Quartets, T. S. Eliot's series of lyric poetry, forms an undisputed literary masterpiece and a twentieth-century Christian classic. These poems reveal a striking message of redemption against the chaos of the modern world. Along with Eliot's entire body of work—essays, dramas, and lyrics—they have exerted an incalculable influence on the modern age, particularly on poetry and criticism.

Conversion of a Modernist

After moving from New England to England, T. S. Eliot (1888–1965) became a premiere advocate of modernism between 1917 and 1925. He applied the themes and style of modernism to both philosophy and literary practice. Philosophically, modernism assumes that we live in a post-Christian era. And in the more pessimistic form, which Eliot helped inaugurate, its adherents find few ordering principles for modern life, adopt a general mood of bleak disillusionment, and attack the fallacies and frailties of the day.

As a literary practice, mod-

T. S. Eliot (1888–1965).

ernism relies heavily on "imagism" and allusions. Imagism is the use of concrete images to incarnate human experience, with the absence of any editorial voice in the work of art. Imagist poetry holds up seemingly random images as mirrors to the modern spirit. Often they are in tension; sometimes they have a clear resolution; always they are evocative. Allusions are references to other works that appeal to the shared knowledge of the poet

and the reader. Much of Eliot's poetry is enriched by this echoing of other artistic works in his new poetic context. For example, the title "Four Quartets" alludes to music as a structural basis for the poem.

In 1917 Eliot published "The Love Song of J. Alfred Prufrock," which includes the much-quoted line, "I have measured out my life with coffee spoons." This is the first of what is commonly called Eliot's "Wasteland Cycle of Poems." It was followed in 1920 by "Gerontion," in 1922 by *The Waste Land,* and in 1925 by "The Hollow Men." Each poem portrays human experience by images, refusing to draw conclusions about those experiences. Written in a highly impersonal poetic voice, these lyrics ironically juxtapose a series of impressions filtered through the consciousness of the various characters.

Eliot's reputation as a poet would be secure on the basis of these poems alone. So startling were his techniques, so powerful his portraits of a lost humanity wandering a metaphysical wasteland, that they took the world of

Time present and time past
Are both perhaps present in time future,
And time future contained in time past.

—"Burnt Norton"

both specialized and common readers by storm. Eliot reshaped and restyled modern poetry, influencing its direction for years thereafter.

A curious twist appeared in the road, however. Eliot made a spiritual turn—he converted to the Christian faith. But his was not an instantaneous conversion. The troubled skepticism of the Wasteland Cycle was a manifestation of Eliot's own search for spiritual certainty. Raised in the Unitarian church, which he later dismissed as heretical, he sought a surer anchor for his faith. After systematically exploring Christian doctrine, he was baptized into the Anglican church in a private ceremony on June 29, 1927.

Eliot's conversion posed serious challenges to him as a poet. Having vividly portrayed spiritual skepticism and questioning, how was he to frame the answers? Having exposed characters as hollow as scarecrows, tossed in the winds of spiritual relativism, how was he to present characters redeemed, with a place to stand?

Eliot's first response appeared in "Journey of the Magi," published on August 25, 1927. This poem, as Eliot himself said, "released the stream" and rejuvenated his poetic artistry. Since "The Hollow Men" he had endured a two-year hiatus from writing any poetry. It seemed he was starting all over. "Journey of the Magi" was quickly followed by several more so-called "Ariel" poems and by *Ash Wednesday* in 1930. Then Eliot's restless imagination changed direction once more, this time to drama. With choruses written for a church pageant, *The Rock,* and then his first play, *Murder in the Cathedral,* Eliot pioneered a resurgence of Christian drama in the twentieth century.

Redeeming the Time

Four Quartets first appeared as a unified work in the United States in May, 1943, and in England in October, 1944. Although previously published independently between 1935 and 1941, the four individual poems are unified in several ways. First, each poem centers on an actual experience at a specific place. "Burnt Norton," the title of the first poem, is the site of a house and garden set on a hill in the English Cotswolds. "East Coker," the second poem, is a small, lovely village in Somerset, England, which Eliot visited in 1937. The location of the third poem, the "Dry Salvages," refers to rocks off the Cape Ann coast of New England where the Eliot family vacationed during the poet's youth. And "Little Gidding" is the site of a small chapel in Huntingdonshire, founded in 1625 by the Anglican spiritual leader Nicholas Ferrar. Eliot visited the chapel in May, 1936. The four poems are also unified by their common focus on the four elements: air, earth, water, and fire. Further, they share numerous formal and thematic patterns.

The general theme of *Four Quartets* may be summarized by the recurring line "redeem the time." Throughout the poetry Eliot speculates on both the nature of the present age and the impact of the eternal on the present.

"Burnt Norton" establishes this tension between the two ages. In this turning world there is a "still point," the point at which the divine and eternal intersect the human and temporal. This focal point is evidenced most dramatically in the incarnation of Christ. It is central to the lives of believers, redeeming human desire by redirecting it from the things of this world to the things of God.

"East Coker" immediately picks up the theme: "In my beginning is my end." Redemption from mere human desire begins by being committed to an end within the life of the spirit. This is a poem of darkness and horror; Eliot wrote it on the threshold of World War II, confronting the overwhelming terrors of the age. The central image is blood. But even this is a sign of redemption, for the blood and flesh are also those of the Lord's Supper, another "still point" at which the temporal and human intersect the eternal and divine. Eliot reverses the first line of the poem at its close: "In my end is my beginning." With the sense of an eternal goal one can actually begin to live anew.

"Dry Salvages" is the loveliest of the poems, written out of Eliot's lifelong fondness for the sea, for streams and rivers. But water, he asserts, is paradoxical, an image of both life and destruction. This is another tension that threads through the *Four Quartets* as a whole. The ceaseless flow of water figures the ceaseless flow of humanity's aspirations to know the divine in different ways and cultures. All such efforts—"hints and guesses"—point toward the fulfillment in Christ, a truth that Eliot suggests in the poem but deliberately understates.

Not so in "Little Gidding," the most overtly Christian of the four poems. From the outset, when the narrator makes a pilgrimage to the chapel of Little Gidding, the effort is toward communion with God. Eliot's communion occurs at the ruined chapel, but he makes clear that it can happen anywhere, at any time, for any believer—for it comes about through prayer and the work of the Holy Spirit. "Little Gidding," patterned on the element of fire, is essentially a Pentecost poem. As a fire warden when London was bombed during World War II, Eliot writes of the monstrous fires of the modern age—those of war and the human desire for things of the flesh. These destructive forces are offset by the cleansing, redemptive fire of the Holy Spirit. Eliot sets the argument like this:

> The only hope, or else despair
>   Lies in the choice of pyre or pyre—
>   To be redeemed from fire by fire.

At the heart of the poem Eliot suggests humanity's choice: either to be consumed by the fires of the age or by the fire of the Holy Spirit.

Although Eliot's poetry is overtly Christian, contemporary Christians may find his work difficult to comprehend. His oblique and indirect style goes beneath the surface to bring about in the reader a state of stillness and contemplation. *Four Quartets* is meditative poetry that shows the temporal world to be touched by sacramental grace through con-fronting divine revelation. In so doing, it highlights the fundamental choice of Christians—to be refined by the blazing presence of God or to be consumed by the burning conflicts of civilization.

Commuters on London Bridge remind us of *The Waste Land*.

> *Love is most nearly itself*
> *When here and now cease to matter.*
>
> —"East Coker"

We shall not cease from exploration
And the end of all our exploring
Will be to arrive where we started
And know the place for the first time.

— "Little Gidding"

Issues to Explore

Eliot's writing provides a rich resource for reflection and discussion. (1) Why does his poetry after his conversion remain as dark as his earlier poems in its depiction of the ills of the present era? (2) What characteristics of the modern age does Eliot unveil? (3) Can we see the world as a sort of "wasteland" and yet discern a redemptive presence in it? (4) Is it possible to live in two sorts of time: the chronological and the sacred? (5) Does an awareness of the spiritual realm lessen or heighten our appreciation for ordinary objects and events?

—John H. Timmerman

For Further Study

Eliot is among the most discussed authors of the twentieth century. The rows of books on his works in any library can be daunting. Nonetheless, several excellent guides can be a starting point. Grover A. Smith's *T. S. Eliot's Poetry and Plays: A Study in Sources and Meaning* (University of Chicago, 1956) remains one of the best introductions to Eliot's work generally. John H. Timmerman's *The Poetics of Recovery: T. S. Eliot's Ariel Poems* (Bucknell University, 1994) discusses the effects of Eliot's conversion on his poems. The best discussion of the *Four Quartets* appears in Helen Gardner's *The Composition of Four Quartets* (Oxford, 1978). The authoritative text for *Four Quartets* appears in Eliot's *The Complete Poems and Plays: 1909–1950* (Harcourt Brace, 1952).

ROBERT FROST

Poems
1913–1962

No American poet has had such popular acclaim in his lifetime and such an enduring critical reputation after his death as Robert Frost. His work is loved because of its accessibility, universal themes, and perfectly disguised art Children in elementary school, haunted by the peculiar magic of the language, memorize his apparently simple lyrics. Students in universities study the same poems, unveiling their guise of simplicity but not their magic.

Should Frost's poetry be studied? In the much-memorized "Stopping by Woods on a Snowy Evening," the practical-minded horse shakes his harness bells to ask the driver "if there is some mistake." In the same tenor, some early critics queried the importance of Frost's work because of its simplicity. How can we take him as seriously as T. S. ELIOT and Ezra Pound?

The answer lies in the poetry itself. Younger children might not consciously know it when they recite "Stopping by Woods," but a rare, deliberate pause for the silence of poetic hearing comes on the imagination. Child or adult, we

Robert Lee Frost (1874–1963).

listen not only to the snow but to the delicately crystallized language: "The only other sound's the sweep / Of easy wind and downy flake." Remembering or rereading this poem after many years—even decades—we might yet have a fresh intuition of what it means to be, in Frost's words, "entranced to the exact premonition."

The New England Sage and the "Other Frost"

Public adulation came to Robert Frost relatively late in his life. He was able to enjoy it largely because he lived on into an active and vigorous old age. When he read "The Gift Outright" at John F. Kennedy's Inauguration in 1961, he was in his late eighties, a beloved American icon of folk wisdom. Within a decade of Frost's death in 1963, however, this view of the gentle old New England sage was shattered by Lawrence Thompson's official biography. Reviewing the second volume of this work, *The Years of Triumph*, one writer described Frost as a "monster of egotism." This picture went largely unmodified until William H. Pritchard's *Frost: A Literary Life Reconsidered* was published in 1984.

Born in San Francisco in 1874, Frost grew up in New England and married his high-school sweetheart, Elinor White. Shortly after the death of their firstborn son, the Frosts moved to a farm in Derry, New Hampshire. They lived on those thirty acres for eleven years, and there Frost wrote much of the

Warren and Mary discuss the hired man Silas who has returned to their house, despite not being kin to them; Warren speaks first and Mary answers:

"Home is the place where, when you have to go there,
They have to take you in."
*   "I should have called it*
Something you somehow haven't to deserve."

—"The Death of the Hired Man"

poetry in his first three books. Yet, nearing forty, he was still virtually unknown. He boldly sold his farm and moved his family to England, where he achieved his first success. He published his first book of poetry, *A Boy's Will,* in 1913 and the great *North of Boston* a year later. From the time of his return to New Hampshire in 1915, Frost's reputation steadily rose.

The time when Frost emerged into public fame, however, was also the period of his greatest personal darkness. His favorite daughter, Marjorie, died from complications of childbirth in 1934, his wife Elinor died in 1938, and his son Carol committed suicide in 1940. Privately, Frost often felt like the man in "Home Burial" whose wife, not understanding his complex feelings, accuses him of not caring enough about the loss of their first child. He answers, "'I shall laugh the worst laugh I ever laughed. / I'm cursed. God, if I don't believe I'm cursed.'"

Ironically, inaccurate as it has proved to be, Thompson's biography helped to explain the poetry of "the other Frost" that some had written about as early as 1953 and that literary critic Lionel Trilling had described as "terrifying" in a controversial speech on the poet's eighty-fifth birthday. Neither a monster nor a gentle bard, Frost was a complex man whose personal life was touched with dark grief, harsh anger, and terrible guilt. He was one who faced his lot with courage and imagination.

The Scope of Frost's Poetry

Frost's work falls into three loosely defined categories. First are the shorter lyrics in stanza forms, such as "Acquainted with the Night," "The Road Not Taken," "Nothing Gold Can Stay," "Desert Places," and "Design." Second are the "looser" poems. They are often colloquial, sometimes dramatic monologues, and sometimes narratives. Usually they focus on some central thing or act revealed as symbolic. These include "Mending Wall," "After Apple-Picking," "An Old Man's Winter Night," "Out, Out—," "Birches," "The Wood-Pile," and "Directive." Third are the longer poems, which are monologues or dramatic narratives. Examples include "The Death of the Hired Man," "Home Burial," "A Servant to Servants," "The Fear," and "The Witch of Coös."

Except for "The Death of the Hired Man" and, increasingly, "Home Burial," Frost's poems of this third type are rarely included in anthologies because of their length. Critics despair because several of Frost's most magnificent, characteristic, and nearly incomparable poems are too long to cite—or even include in anthologies. "If I could quote 'Home Burial,' 'The Witch of Coös,' and 'A Servant to Servants,'" one critic says, "Pharisee and Philistine alike would tiptoe off hand in hand, their shamed eyes starry. . . ." To those first moving from the most familiar works into the *Collected Poems,* however, the longer poems are a revelation. Comic, tragic, memorable, always enigmatic, these poems and their characters open up a world of surprising dramatic reality and depth.

Frost and the Christian Reader

No one thinks of Frost as a religious poet like John DONNE, George HERBERT, Gerard Manley HOPKINS, or T. S. Eliot. But Frost does strike most of his readers, sooner or later, as *wise*. Biblically, Frost has a deeper affinity with the rich lyric pessimism of Ecclesiastes than the gospels. Literary critics have found an even darker note, most notably in the sonnet "Design." The poem makes the two options for nature seem to be either the "design of darkness to appall" or the terrifying absence of any governing order. But

The woods of New Hampshire in the fall.

even when Frost scares himself with his own "desert places," he nobly and patiently confronts darkness with his "momentary stay against confusion" that becomes a lasting poetic form.

Much of Frost's work is sheer poetic delight. Take, for example, the sonnet "Never Again Would Birds' Song Be the Same." The poem begins with a third-person description of Adam's cautious observations about the effect of his wife's voice on nature:

> He would declare and could himself believe
> That the birds there in all the garden round
> From having heard the daylong voice of Eve
> Had added to their own an oversound,
> Her tone of meaning but without the words.
> Admittedly an eloquence so soft
> Could only have had an influence on birds
> When call or laughter carried it aloft.

The birds have come upon what Frost elsewhere calls the "sound of sense" in Eve's speech. Adam, however, wants to resist being fooled by his partiality. But he seems increasingly willing to risk the disapproval of his own skeptical side. Frost's art emerges most characteristically in this

"trial by doubt." Precisely because of the logical qualifications, the images of Eve begin to reveal why Adam holds his fond opinion with such conviction.

Stubbornly, as though against stiff opposition, Adam carefully avoids any admission of the actual motive of his argument:

> Be that as it may, she was in their song.
> Moreover her voice upon their voices crossed
> Had now persisted in the woods so long
> That probably it never would be lost.
> Never again would birds' song be the same.
> And to do that to birds was why she came.

To hear a recording of Frost reciting this poem is to hear the amused, impertinent, and incontrovertible voice of the poetic imagination, transfigured in its praise of being by love.

> *Here are your waters and your watering place.*
> *Drink and be whole again beyond confusion.*
>
> —"Directive"

I'd like to go by climbing a birch tree,
And climb black branches up a snow-white trunk
Toward heaven, till the tree could bear no more,
but dipped its top and set me down again.
That would be good both going and coming back.
One could do worse than be a swinger of birches.

—"Birches"

Issues to Explore

Questions about Frost's poetry will help us penetrate its seeming simplicity. (1) Why does Frost insist that writing poetry without regard for traditional forms and meters is like "playing tennis without a net"? (2) Is it possible that the neighbor in "Mending Wall," although described as an "old stone-savage armed," is nevertheless right that "good fences make good neighbors"—as good form makes good poems? (3) Why do so many of the poems, such as "Birches," seem to adopt a skeptical attitude toward the imagination? (4) Is the evidence of

For Further Study

The standard edition of the poems is *The Poetry of Robert Frost,* Edward Connery Lathem, editor (Henry Holt, 1969). The two spirited essays by Randall Jarrell, "The Other Frost" and "To the Laodiceans," in *Poetry and the Age* (The Ecco Press, 1953; 1980), are still by far the best introduction to Frost's poetry. Those interested in another angle on Frost's biographical difficulties should read Donald Hall's essay "Vanity, Fame, Love, and Robert Frost" in *Their Ancient Glittering Eyes* (Ticknor and Fields, 1992). The *Voices and Visions* video on Frost (The Annenberg/CPB Collection, 1988) contains fine comments by Richard Wilbur, Seamus Heaney, and Richard Poirier, as well as readings by Frost himself.

the human capacity and desire for form the best answer to the questions posed in "Design"?

—Glenn C. Arbery

Modern Poetry in English

The first half of the twentieth century witnessed perhaps the greatest period for poetry in English, surpassing the other two strongest eras of lyric poetry, the early seventeenth century and the early nineteenth century—the romantic period. Never in English have there been so many poets of high quality, including W. B. YEATS, Ezra Pound, H.D. (Hilda Doolittle), T. S. ELIOT, William Carlos Williams, Robert FROST, John Crowe Ransom, Wallace Stevens, and Marianne Moore. But although modern poetry is brilliant, it makes unusual demands on the reader, often being strange in syntax, obscure, and sophisticated, requiring much study and knowledge. This difficulty has to some extent limited its audience. Yet many of the poems of Yeats, Eliot, and Frost come alive when read repeatedly and remain in the memory; these poets are, if not popular, at least widely known and quoted.

World War I German trench at the Somme, 1916.

Fortitude, Frankness, and Disillusionment

The first generation of modern British and American poets—those who came to maturity in the first two decades of the twentieth century—were highly conscious of their break with immediately preceding poets. Yet, though they were aware of the need, in Pound's words, to "make it new," they nevertheless saw themselves as recovering lost poetic traditions. They struggled to shape a poetry responsive to its time in the context of the intellectually turbulent, war-cursed, fragmented "modern" world.

These poets, like their revolutionary counterparts in painting such as Pablo Picasso and Georges Braque, share a cultural context in which no religious or moral truths can be taken for granted. The destruction of World War I, preceded by various revolutions in thinking and the arts, deeply affected people's sense of continuity with the past and undermined their trust in government and society. In "Hugh Selwyn Mauberley," Pound laments the carnage of the war, speaking of "fortitude as never before // frankness as never before, / disillusions as never told in the old days"; he wonders whether the death of a whole generation of young men "for a botched civilization" was worth the sacrifice. Though they could assume no common understanding among members of their audience, and though traditional moral convictions appear fragmentary, each of these early modern poets strives to suggest some version of a whole, an underlying integrity in nature and the human mind that goes beyond the fragments.

There died a myriad,
And of the best, among them,
For an old bitch gone in the
    teeth,
For a botched civilization.

—Ezra Pound
"Hugh Selwyn Mauberly"

The Need to Believe

The major early modern poets would each agree to some extent with Yeats's remark that a poet cannot write without belief, even if one's belief (as with Wallace Stevens) is in the impossibility of final belief. Few of these poets, however, adopt the Christian faith; it was rejected along with traditional certainties. Most encourage a variety of belief systems. Even Eliot, who after his conversion became one of the most Christian of modern poets, speaks in his poetry of other religious traditions, such as Buddhism and Hinduism.

At the turn of the century the flourishing of anthropology—the study of primitive cultures—made available for the first time a wealth of information about religious rites and cults throughout the world. Sir James George Frazer's *The Golden Bough* was the most influential of these sources. In this context the Christian faith seemed to be part of larger patterns of myth and religious practice. What seems important for modern poets, as for the romantics, was not so much the *object of belief* as the *capacity to believe* in an age debased in mind and feeling. This capacity to believe so that the world might have the potential for momentary miracles, they suggest, could be shaped and nourished by the imagination.

Poetic Belief

Each of the modern poets distinctly defines the character and focus of belief. Yeats himself, like the romantic poet William Blake, created his own metaphysical system from his study and practice of occult lore. Eliot fairly early in his career came to believe that the Christian faith provided the only sufficiently coherent myth within which to work and live. Ezra Pound, along with many others of his generation, such as D. H. Lawrence, H.D., and Robert Graves, was fascinated with the recovery of non-Christian sources, particularly of Greek deities and religious practices. Thus in his great epic poem, *The Cantos,* which he wrote throughout his career over a period of about thirty-five years, Pound structures the poem around three main "doctrines": the descent into hell, when one enters into the darkness of the soul; the idea of metamorphosis, the sudden change from one shape to another, such as beast or plant or human or god, taken from the Roman poet Ovid; and finally, the teachings of the Chinese philosopher Confucius, a kind of rational ethical guide to individual and political life. H.D., an early friend and colleague of Pound, also drew from ancient mystery religions as well as occult traditions to convey a visionary, erotic, psychological intensity in her lyric poetry and, later, in her *Trilogy,* a group of three long poems written in London during the Nazi aerial bombardment.

William Carlos Williams at-tempts an epic like *The Cantos* in *Paterson,* showing through complex allusion and layering of historical incidents the cosmic and timeless dimensions of an ordinary human city, Paterson, New Jersey. But Williams assumes another "belief" as a starting point. For him poetry must begin and end in rendering the ordinary; it must not be too abstract or elite—as he considered Eliot's poetry to be—or it will lose its very reason for being. Although Williams's credo was "No ideas but in things," for all the simplicity of this intention, his poetry is sophisticated, demanding, and in its own way obscure. This insistence on the ordinary and on rendering "the thing as it is" are convictions shared by many modern poets.

Another notable poet is Marianne Moore, whose poems consist often of intense, concentrated meditations on finite and particular things, often exotic birds and animals, such as the ostrich, basilisk, pelican, and elephant. She seeks to capture the essence and sharp beauty of each one as a creature, the way it speaks to the mind and imagination. Though strange and oblique, these meditations are finally moral in their implications, showing some dimension of value and relating to basic human ideals that the imagination finds in creatures and incidents of the world.

Two other important modern poets—the New England poet Robert Frost and the Southern poet John Crowe Ransom—represent another strategy similar to that of A. E. Housman and other British poets of the early twentieth century called the Georgian poets.

Housman and the Georgian poets, choosing not to embrace the complexity and confusion of their age, limited the settings of their poems to a certain rural landscape, celebrating the natural, moral simplicity of these contained places. Frost and Ransom differ from these poets, being entirely modern, their poetry suggesting a complex and sophisticated consciousness of modern problems. But they are like Housman in choosing to explore a limited and finite landscape. Unlike Pound and Eliot, whose poetry is cosmopolitan as it alludes to all times and places, Ransom and Frost make the part stand for the whole, the particular for the general. Frost, like his New England Puritan ancestors, explores the natural landscape as a constant revelation of interior states and dilemmas. Thus his poetry, for all its apparent straightness and simplicity, often raises troubling questions about the nature of reality and of good and evil.

Concerning the question of belief, no modern poet is more complex or more important than Wallace Stevens. Following the tradition of the romantics, his ultimate belief is in the imagination and its ability to testify to the "central man"—the full, godlike potentiality of the human. Imagination is actually the source of belief, the source of the stories by which we know ourselves. He would claim that "reality" and imagination are one—that the real does not exist apart from one perceiving and imagining. But although the poet "gives to life the supreme fictions without which we are unable to conceive of it," poetry is constantly pointing to the

Oh! Blessed rage for order, pale Ramon,
The maker's rage to order words of the sea,
Words of the fragrant portals, dimly-starred,
And of ourselves and of our origins,
In ghostlier demarcations, keener sounds.

—Wallace Stevens
"The Idea of Order at Key West"

Ezra Pound (1885–1972).

Shall I at least set my lands in order?
London Bridge is falling down falling down falling down.

—T. S. Eliot
The Waste Land

illusory or fictional nature of our beliefs. The fictions of belief with which poetry clothes the world are necessary to human life; poetry, however, also answers the human need to question and go beyond the known—in other words, to see the fictions dissolved in light of a greater imaginative necessity. In his late poem "Reality Is an Activity of the Most August Imagination," Stevens points to the paradox of human imagination, which is also a paradox of our limited and restless knowing of the world. Describing a stormy sky as an image of imagination, he says it is "An argentine abstraction approaching form / And suddenly denying itself away . . . an insolid billowing of the solid."

The Power of Imagination

In the words of one critic, echoing Pound, these modern poets attempt to find "a coherent splendor" in the given world. In this sense, they are like the romantic poets Wordsworth and Keats in seeing the imperfections of the world and life as possibly being healed by the loving vision bestowed by the imagination. These modern poets, like the romantics, give primacy to the imagination and the poet as guides to seeing, and thus to living, fully.

For the Christian, this serious modern poetry presents an antidote to the hardness of heart brought on by the dominant rationalism and utilitarianism of the

For Further Study

For an introduction to modern poetry, one could read Hugh Kenner, *The Pound Era* (University of California, 1971) and Albert Gelpi, *A Coherent Splendor: The American Poetic Renaissance 1910–1950* (Cambridge, 1987). The *Norton Anthology of Modern Poetry,* second edition, Richard Ellmann and Robert O'Clair, eds. (Norton, 1988), gives an adequate initial selection of poetry.

eighteenth and nineteenth century. These poems open the imagination to experience and celebrate life. Further, they bring back a sense of the sacred as, in T. S. Eliot's words, "some infinitely gentle, infinitely suffering thing" in the midst of a secular and uncaring urban civilization.

—Eileen Gregory

Modern Drama

Beginning roughly in 1880 with Henrik Ibsen (1828–1906) and ending in the 1950s in the fragmented vision of Samuel Beckett (1906–1989) and Eugène Ionesco (b. 1912), modern dramatists portrayed their various stories without a sense of a reigning benevolent power on earth or in heaven. Ordinary people therefore replaced kings and queens on the stage as the armchair took the place of the throne. Turning from traditional drama, which focused on the redemption of high-minded but fallen heroes, these playwrights depicted chaotic and meaningless experience with merciless clarity. Their plays are fueled by a strong social message, offering a disturbing picture of the philosophical, moral, and religious bankruptcy of modern life.

No longer did these modern dramatists share a common understanding of history or a common religious belief; instead they employed such widely differing forms as realism, naturalism, symbolism, and expressionism. One drama critic has commented on this lack of a unified view of the human image and history: "Human nature seems to us a hopelessly elusive and uncandid entity, and our playwrights (like hunters with camera and flash-bulbs in the

Norwegian dramatist Henrik Ibsen (1828–1906), in a cartoon published in London in 1902.

depths of the Belgian Congo) are lucky if they can fix it, at rare intervals, in one of its momentary postures, and in a single bright, exclusive angle of vision." These playwrights directed all their energies toward capturing an image so evocative that it reveals an otherwise inexplicable world. One family stands for all families; one living room for all places where

people struggle to understand what it is to be human.

A Sense of Loss

An emerging middle class is the subject matter of this group of modern playwrights who still influence the theater of our time. They depict a general loss of faith in a benevolent God; their characters instead look with hope to recent scientific advancements, despite the unfavorable living conditions brought about by the Industrial Revolution. Some writers also have seen the new interest in psychology as offering answers to questions about human behavior that classical writers had attributed to fate or to God's will.

By making drama out of daily life, deserting mystery, ritual, and symbol, modern playwrights set out in a direction from which the drama of our own day is only now beginning to turn. Their sense of abandonment is portrayed with an almost religious fervency and often harsh irony. In Samuel Beckett's bleak play *Waiting for Godot* (1952), for example, a mistreated servant (ironically named Lucky) delivers an incoherent speech dedicated to a "God who loves us dearly with some exceptions for reasons unknown."

The Well-Made Play

Not only the subject matter of modern drama but also its techniques evidence the flattened vision of the world known as "realism." Such dramatists as Ibsen were inspired to explore a new form when the French playwright Eugène Scribe (1791–1861) developed the "well-made play"— a phrase that describes careful plotting from the beginning of the work to a surprising but carefully prepared ending. Its "cause-to-effect" structure, though not inherently more lifelike than that of earlier forms of dramatic art, simulates real existence partly because of its closed form. It does not acknowledge the presence of the audience and thereby gives the

impression that viewers are unseen observers of real people enacting real events. Scenery and costume represent actual people and places; the box-set replaces the idealized palace and further particularizes the "reality" represented. What is required to appreciate these plays is a belief in the "truth" of the moment.

Dramas of Disillusionment

Ibsen's play *A Doll's House* (1879) uses the well-made-drama form to question the traditional definition of motherhood and the nature of family life. In response to the storm of criticism over the heroine's refusal to continue a marriage merely for the sake of appearances, Ibsen next wrote *Ghosts* (1881), which shows the result of a loveless marriage. In this play inherited syphilis was depicted on the stage for the first time, causing an outcry from audience members. Because these and other dramas of the realistic form were presented as overheard reality, their impact was disturbingly powerful on middle-class audiences.

Modern drama has never stopped disturbing its audience in ways previously unthinkable. Concern for the small, degrading events of daily life is what makes modern drama modern. The ancient Greeks, in contrast, came to the theater to celebrate a noble heritage. As masked performers sang their legends in poetic odes, the audience was further distanced from the ancient myths. No attempt was made to represent real life. Similarly SHAKESPEARE'S body of work examined topics inspiring to his audience but not of immediate concern to their lives.

And his actors spoke in an elevated style no groundling would mistake for ordinary speech.

The moderns, on the other hand, celebrate the inherent right to complain bitterly when leaders fail to protect and inspire their people. Deserted by myth and cut loose from national legends of their historic past, modern dramatists blame institutions and powerful men for their characters' arid lives. Two of England's most famous turn-of-the-century playwrights use comedy to convey the superficiality of its rigid class system. George Bernard Shaw (1856–1950) depicts the gullibility of its upper classes in *Pygmalion* (1912), a play in which a Cockney flower girl tricks the ruling classes into accepting her as one of their own by merely learning their manners and style of speech. Oscar Wilde (1854–1900) also uses humor to demonstrate the dangerous absurdity inherent in the manners of the rich. In his comedy *The Importance of Being Ernest* (1895), Wilde demonstrates his announced intent to "treat all the trivial things of life seriously, and all the serious things of life with sincere and studied triviality" and so show society its own foolish behavior. His light-headed characters enact the serious purpose of comedy in the hope that people will change direction once their folly is pointed out.

Taking a more serious point of view in his play *The Cherry Orchard* (1904), the Russian Anton Chekhov (1860–1904) writes about the lack of spirit among aristocrats who cannot muster the will to save their old home and its famous cherry trees. Even though opportunities exist to rescue the orchard and restore the family's fortune, the ancient grove falls to the axe of progress as the play ends. That a man whose father once was a servant on the estate buys and subdivides the cherry orchard into housing for the newly rich is particularly satisfying to middle-class audiences. With pathos and wry humor Chekhov renders a world that collapses of its own inertia.

Local Irish behavior offers sufficient color and variety to provide a genuine sense of drama in John Millington Synge's *Playboy of the Western World* (1907). This brilliant comedy concerns a young man who becomes a hero when he claims to have murdered his father. The inhabitants of a remote area of Ireland are so desperate for a sign of vigor that even such a despicable act becomes for them heroic. In the rich poetry of his dialogue Synge (1871–1909) has transformed the colorful speech of his native land into utterances "as fully flavored as a nut or an apple."

Modernist Experimentation

Realism and the well-made-play form, however, are not the only models for modern drama. In its attempt to hold a mirror up to life, many playwrights find realism inadequate to the task of capturing human nature. A person's dreams, visions, aspirations, and fears, for example, cannot be depicted by a mere glimpse of one's experience. Authors as diverse as August Strindberg (1849–1912), Bertolt Brecht (1898–1956), and Thornton Wilder (1897–1976) explored new forms more akin to those employed by modernist painters and poets about this same time:

PRODUCER: *Ah! There we have it! Your drama! Look here . . . you'll have to forgive me for telling you this . . . but there isn't only your part to be considered! Each of the others has his drama, too. . . . But it's here that we run into difficulties: how are we to bring out only just so much as is absolutely necessary? . . . And at the same time, of course, to take into account all the other characters. . . . And yet in that small fragment we have to be able to hint at all the rest of the secret life of that character. Ah, it would be all very pleasant if each character could have a nice little monologue. . . . Or without making any bones about it, give a lecture, in which he could tell his audience what's bubbling and boiling away inside him. You must restrain yourself.*

—Luigi Pirandello
Six Characters in Search of an Author

Picasso, Matisse, Braque, ELIOT, and Pound. Their experiments took them away from realistic scenery, linear plot development, and the notion of overheard reality as they expanded the very nature of the theatrical event. Strindberg wrote obliquely of people tormented by their dreams and visions. Brecht stripped his audience of the illusion that they were hearing a story and forced them to confront the horrors of their times. And Wilder's play *Our Town* (1938) shows a New England village as a notion in "the mind of God," whose inhabitants, after death, find that they have never "realized life" while they lived it.

For other American playwrights such as Eugene O'Neill (1888–1953), however, life was a torment that pitted aspirations against harsh economic and social conditions. Although he experimented with masks and interior monologues spoken aloud, O'Neill is best remembered for his autobiographical drama, *A Long Day's Journey into Night* (written in 1940, published in 1956), in which a family is damaged by its autocratic father. His voice, though authentically American, speaks of the same conditions about which the European authors write: poverty, self-deception, disease, alcoholism, and drugs.

The growing horror of people at their seeming inability to know or change the mind of God rendered them rudderless throughout modern drama. As a substitute for the belief that had sustained poets in the past, late nineteenth-century and early twentieth-century writers turned to introspection and the minute investigation of human consciousness. The entire movement led to the theater of protest in the thirties and forties and on, paradoxically, to the surrealism of "theater of the absurd."

Modern drama ended in the 1950s, after the atomic bomb

seemed to erase the sense that people could control even the most mundane aspects of their world. The theater that followed became a celebration of chaos in the early works of this postwar period. In it nonsensical dialogue, extreme actions and imagery, and end-of-the-world settings abound. Actors were forced to master nonrealistic styles of performance, such as dance, vaudeville, and mime, to meet the demands of a form of theater that draws on all art forms to evoke rather than explain its purposes. In Ionesco's *Rhinoceros* (1959), for example, people turn into rhinoceroses; in Peter Shaffer's *Equus* (1973) an actor portrays a horse; in Timberlake Wertenbaker's *Our Country's Good* (1988) each actor plays more than one character and women portray men without changing from their skirts; in David Henry Hwangs's *M. Butterfly* (1988) the audience is as surprised as the hero when a woman turns out to be a man.

Contemporary drama, in fact, is as identifiable by its lack of adher-

ence to one theme, form, style, or medium as modern drama has been by its insistence on a social message presented in a largely realistic setting. Theatrical experiments too far-ranging to group together are simply called "contemporary drama" because no more descriptive term has been coined. How this era will be perceived as a period cannot yet be determined. Perhaps the explosive nature of current theatrical events will be seen to mirror the lack of cohesiveness of our society. Or it may be that other entertainment media will characterize this age—we may

be known by the video games we play or the movies we watch.

Certainly the art of our time is as various as its practitioners. Artists of today have neither the singleness of purpose that drove the moderns nor the sense of artistic mission that sustained them. Their search for purpose delineates them best. Not yet blown apart by the bomb, our artists look intensely and in many corners for what they should be doing. The answer remains elusive.

—Mary Lou Hoyle

For Further Study

Many introductions to collections of modern drama provide insights into this body of work. One such anthology is *Modern and Contemporary Drama,* edited by Miriam Gilbert, Carl H. Klaus, and Bradford S. Field, Jr. (St. Martin's, 1994). Books on dramatic theory and criticism, such as Peter Brook's *The Empty Space* (Avon, 1968), Robert Brustein's *The Theater of Revolt* (Atlantic, 1964), Tom F. Driver's *History of the Modern Theater* (Dell, 1970), Martin Esslin's *The Theater of the Absurd* (Doubleday, 1961), and Francis Fergusson's *The Idea of Theater* (Doubleday, 1949), are helpful, as are individual commentaries on the playwrights themselves.

C. S. LEWIS

The Screwtape Letters
1941

*C*S. Lewis's *The Screwtape Letters*, considered to be his greatest work, is a brilliant transformation of an ancient literary form—the epistle—into a modern exploration of good and evil. The book was published in 1941 and soon became enormously popular throughout the English-speaking world, catapulting Lewis to worldwide fame. In fact, the very popularity of *The Screwtape Letters* points to one of the fundamental properties of the classics—they are written for and read by the general populace. The classroom is not their natural setting. Written from a devil's perspective, this classic explores the ramifications of the seemingly small decisions of everyday life in the battle between good and evil.

Using Dialogue to Expose the Inner Life

The Screwtape Letters does not easily fit in a specific literary genre. It exists completely outside the whole body of drama, fiction, and poetry that dominates Lewis's own century. *Screwtape* is unabashedly

C. S. Lewis at Magdalen College, Oxford.

hortatory—a work that earnestly advises and warns its readers. In direst terms it hails the readers with the nature and consequences of sin. This scarcely seems a recipe that would appeal to modern audiences, though it has many forerunners.

To place *The Screwtape Letters* among similar works we must reach back to late classical antiquity and the Middle Ages. It fits with the cautionary tales, dream visions, and morality plays

in which virtue, sin, judgment, heaven, and hell are addressed in highly explicit but highly imaginative ways.

The fifth-century Roman philosopher Boethius stands as a fountainhead for this kind of writing through his conversation with the Lady Philosophy in *The Consolation of Philosophy*. Here the subject of sin and judgment dims in comparison to the method, a searching scrutiny of the interior life in dialogue form. Plato had used this technique earlier, but Boethius became the primary source for it in the Christian West. The centuries following him in Europe and England poured out this robust prose and poetry of exhortation—of sin searched out and censured and virtue lauded.

The period of 1100 to 1400 is particularly rich in this literature, including such titles as *"Poema Morale,"* "Sinners Beware," "Handling Sin," and "The Prick of Conscience." These works vary in their literary appeal—some plod along stiffly—but the fifteenth-century morality play *Everyman* combines the baldly hortatory with dramatic merit. In all these works

It does not matter how small the sins are, provided that their cumulative effect is to edge the man away from the Light and out into the Nothing. Murder is no better than cards if cards can do the trick. Indeed, the safest road to Hell is the gradual one—the gentle slope, soft underfoot, without sudden turnings, without milestones, without signposts.

—*The Screwtape Letters*

the human imagination scrutinizes the whole of experience in starkly moral terms. The devil is the enemy; unrepentant sin is punished by damnation; joy and fulfillment are found in obedience to God's laws.

It is not surprising that C. S. Lewis wrote a work so grimly humorous as *Screwtape.* He was at home in the literature of the Middle Ages and the Renaissance. This was his field at Oxford and Cambridge, where he taught for the whole of his working life. He had published some poetry, a work of Christian apologetics (*The Pilgrim's*

The tomb of C. S. Lewis and his brother, Warren.

Regress in 1933), and scholarly and critical work before 1941, but he was catapulted to world fame with *Screwtape.* With his later works of apologetics and fiction he became one of the most famous Christian converts and most effective twentieth-century apologists. Between the years of 1938 and 1945 he published The Space Trilogy, a three-volume work of science fiction, and, between 1950 and 1956, his highly popular seven-book series for children, The Chronicles of Narnia. His most prominent work of apologetics, *Mere Christianity,* was published in 1952. Lewis's writings have become some of the best-selling Christian classics of all time; his ideas continue to be broadly influential today.

When Black Is White and White Is Black

Behind Lewis's artistry in *Screwtape* lies the whole tradition of epistolary works—novels in which the plot is unfolded through the exchange of letters. The book is a series of missives between two devils: the experienced tempter Screwtape as he writes to his nephew, the fledgling tempter Wormwood. Screwtape introduces Wormwood to the tactics of temptation. He responds harshly to Wormwood's reports of his progress in spoiling the newfound faith of a Christian. The point of view is hell's, which keeps the reader off balance because the letters extol all that is squalid, craven, cowardly, and niggardly. They abhor light, goodness, sweet reason, and charity. God appears as "Our Enemy."

This device of totally reversing all values is the book's great triumph as a work of imagination. By placing goodness in an unfavorable light and holding up evil as an admirable achievement, it jolts the reader into a fresh and vastly heightened moral and spiritual awareness.

The Screwtape Letters appeared during World War II. Some commentators criticized Lewis for focusing on minuscule and therefore seemingly inconsequential details of the inner life when war and conflict had burst on the world. How could anyone, they asked, speak of "evil" in such quibbling and minor terms when it was being unfurled with such titanic horror?

"The Kilns," Headington, Oxford, where C. S. Lewis lived with his brother, Warren.

The point of *The Screwtape Letters,* of course, is that the giant tree of evil flourishes only when tiny seeds have been planted. Where do Nazism and other global forms of conquest, greed, cruelty, and egoism come from if they do not germinate and sprout in the crannies of the human heart? The eyebrow lifted ever so slightly in a clever and haughty dismissal of a neighbor finds its ultimate expression in pogroms and Auschwitz. Hell plants and nurtures its crops with the most delicate assiduousness.

This attention to detail in the service of evil is the focus of the whole book. In letter after letter Screwtape concerns himself with the smallest nuances of attitude Wormwood should nourish in his client: get him interested in some fault of someone else; appeal to his self-respect; muddy the clear waters of disciplined reason with popular slogans; discourage him by making him struggle to *feel* a certain way in prayer; distract him; divert his attention from the immediate claim on him for some small act of kindness by hailing him with the supposedly bigger claim of the war; curry his desire to be sophisticated or to be thought clever. On and on goes Wormwood's schooling. And, as the readers are regaled by the letters, they find that the remorseless beam of charity's spotlight has been probing every cranny of their own inner beings all along.

The Dullness of Evil

Readers do not have to share Lewis's Christian point of view to recognize the baleful moral scrutiny at work in these letters. It cannot be dismissed as merely Christian piety. If goodness and evil do not look like this, then what would they look like in any conceivable world? But *Screwtape* is particularly significant for Christian

> *The Enemy wants him, in the end, to be so free from any bias in his own favour that he can rejoice in his own talents as frankly and gratefully as in his neighbour's talents—or in a sunrise, an elephant, or a waterfall. He wants each man, in the long run, to be able to recognise all creatures (even himself) as glorious and excellent things.*
>
> —*The Screwtape Letters*

Senior Devil Screwtape to Junior Devil Wormwood:

[The Enemy] cannot "tempt" to virtue as we do to vice. He wants them to learn to walk and must therefore take away His hand; and if only the will to walk is really there He is pleased even with their stumbles. Do not be deceived, Wormwood. Our cause is never more in danger than when a human, no longer desiring, but still intending, to do our Enemy's will, looks round upon a universe from which every trace of Him seems to have vanished, and asks why he has been forsaken, and still obeys.

—*The Screwtape Letters*

For Further Study

The Screwtape Letters is easily available through bookstores. A good edition is the paperback revised edition (Macmillan, 1982). Chad Walsh's *The Literary Legacy of C. S. Lewis* (Harcourt, Brace, Jovanovich, 1979) and the same author's *C. S. Lewis: Apostle to the Skeptics* (Macmillan, 1949) remain two of the best commentaries, along with Clyde Kilby's *The Christian World of C. S. Lewis* (Eerdmans, 1964). There is no booklength study of *The Screwtape Letters,* but the above-mentioned studies of Lewis's work include commentary on it. The best biography to date is George Sayer, *Jack: C. S. Lewis and His Times* (Crossway, 1994).

readers. Lewis, the great apologist for Christian faith, has driven home the point put forth by Scripture and the whole moral tradition of the church—the real struggle between good and evil comes down to the arena where attitudes, habits, and actions are formed. Mere assent to creedal propositions is the least of hell's worries. Further, Christians will find the ancient notion developed that evil is eventually *dull,* and that goodness finds its fruition in joy.

The work is short and can be understood and enjoyed by readers of many age groups. Although in one sense the style may be said to be Screwtape's, Lewis's renowned brilliance in his handling of the English language is clearly evident.

Issues to Explore

The Screwtape Letters can be read individually; it also lends itself to being read and discussed by small groups. Questions to explore include: (1) What sorts of attitudes is Screwtape most keen on getting Wormwood to foster in the man he is tempting? (2) In Screwtape's view, are there particularly crucial sins to be developed? (3) What reports from Wormwood worry Screwtape? Why? (4) How important is sex in the scheme of the book? (5) What qualities of "the Enemy" does Screwtape confess stumped him? (6) What rewards does hell offer over against those that heaven offers?

—Thomas T. Howard

WILLIAM FAULKNER

Go Down, Moses
1942

William Faulkner's *Go Down, Moses* is the acknowledged masterwork of a writer whom many consider the most powerful and accomplished American novelist. His fiction has brought American literature worldwide acclaim. Moreover, his scope and depth of vision rank him with writers of the highest stature—HOMER, DANTE, and SHAKESPEARE. Today contemporary novelists such as Toni Morrison and Gabriel García Márquez consider Faulkner their mentor, acknowledging a debt that goes deeper than mere innovative technique. Like all his work, the complex but vital *Go Down, Moses* is profoundly and explicitly rooted in three principal traditions: the classical Greek, the ancient Hebrew, and the Christian as the culmination and fulfillment of the earlier two.

The Southern Literary Renaissance

William Faulkner (1897–1962) is the preeminent figure of the twentieth-century's Southern literary renaissance, a movement that began in the 1920s with a group of poets

William Faulkner (1897–1962).

who called themselves the Fugitives: chiefly John Crowe Ransom, Donald Davidson, Allen Tate, and Robert Penn Warren. As Tate noted, Southern culture was set apart from much of the rest of the modern world through being based on an older model of society, recognizing the sacred in nature, the sinfulness of humanity, and the living presence of the past. The most important of the Southern fiction writers—Faulkner, Caroline Gordon, Eudora Welty, Katherine Anne Porter, and Flannery O'CONNOR—found this culture to be fertile ground for imaginative works of the highest order.

Faulkner was not overtly connected with other Southern writers, however, being always a very private person. He spent some time in New Orleans with Sherwood Anderson and other literary figures, and published during his time there his first novel, *Soldier's Pay* (1926), a dark parable of the decline of the West. His second novel, *Mosquitoes* (1927), was undertaken in that same atmosphere. But it was only after discovering what he called his "own little postage stamp of native soil" and inventing his mythical kingdom, Yoknapatawpha County (based on his own Oxford, Mississippi, and the surrounding Lafayette County), that he began the writing that was to make him famous. He began his Yoknapatawpha saga with *Flags in the Dust,* published during his lifetime as *Sartoris* (1929).

At first, however, his novels received more acclaim in New York and Paris than in his native region. Unlike most of the other Southern writers, he worked apart from the academic world. And although he

[Isaac] owned no property and never desired to since the earth was no man's but all men's, as light and air and weather were.

—*Go Down, Moses*

traveled in Europe and America and even wrote several (mainly unsuccessful) screenplays for Hollywood, he avoided the life of a celebrity, residing most of his life in Mississippi. But when he received the 1949 Nobel Prize, he accepted the responsibilities that come with fame and recognition. He gave lectures and interviews, took a position as writer-in-residence at the University of Virginia, and represented the United States on goodwill missions to Japan and Greece. Indeed, in the 1950s, Faulkner was honored more than any other American writer, receiving two Pulitzer Prizes, the Gold Medal from the American Academy for Arts and Letters, and numerous other awards and honors.

A Saga of the Human Heart in Conflict with Itself

As the author of nineteen novels and several collections of short stories, Faulkner's enduring stature can best be seen in his works as a whole, in which he evidences two discernible stages. In the first he is primarily concerned with the decline of a culture and the consequent tragic descent of civilization into decay and loss; in the second he portrays the triumph of the good in high comedy. Coming between the two stages, the epic *Go Down, Moses* marks the turn from tragic to comic.

The Sound and the Fury, his first major novel, is tragic in its outlook, with the quality of a poetic vision. Four times, and from four contrasting points of view, it tells the story of the decline of the once great Compson family. The first account, given by the mentally retarded Benjy Compson, is literally, in Macbeth's words, a "tale told by an idiot, full of sound and fury." The second and third sections are interior monologues by two other Compson brothers, Quentin and Jason. The last, re-

counted by an omniscient narrator, is the vision on Easter Day of Dilsey, the black servant who holds the family together.

Faulkner's succeeding novels—up until 1942, the date of *Go Down, Moses*—though not specifically tragic, take place within an environment that is hopelessly declining. Although the novels in this group anticipate the comedy of the later fiction, the hopeful signs are muted or distorted. Thus, while *As I Lay Dying* (1930) is often wildly funny, it is fundamentally grotesque, exhibiting very little hope for the future of humanity. *Sanctuary* (1931), another dark comedy, presents a kind of wasteland, where the only remaining arena of freedom seems to be outside the law. And though *Light in August* (1932) intertwines the tragedy of Joe Christmas with two stories of comic transformation, the question of whether "man will endure" is left largely unanswered. Each is a brilliant novel in its own right, but these early novels also share a view of society as riddled with the problems of the modern world: abstraction, fanaticism, radical individualism, the debasement of women, the desire for gain, the decline of faith.

In this first stage of Faulkner's writing, another novel (besides *The Sound and the Fury*) stands out in its tragic power. *Absalom, Absalom!* (1936) centers on Thomas Sutpen's ruthless yet somehow innocent attempt to carve out a dynasty, which turns out to be a mere counterfeit of the genuinely aristocratic Southern life. Like many of Faulkner's other novels, *Absalom, Absalom!* examines the very process of interpreting heroic action. Through retelling the story of Sutpen's vainglorious project, the various narrators attempt to comprehend the significance of such a man in their community. What is their responsibility for his presence? Through their reflection, they accept their own tragic fallibility.

In the novels after *Go Down, Moses,* the dominant concern of Faulkner's fiction is less with the nature of evil than with its actual defeat. The full extent of his comic vision is revealed in the massive Snopes trilogy. The first novel of the series—*The Hamlet* (1940)—however, retains the pessimistic outlook of his other

Working boat on the Mississippi, New Orleans.

early work. It shows respectability gradually replacing virtue as the old agrarian order is reduced to a stagnant remnant. It is ripe for takeover by members of the Snopes family, who hold the land financially captive. *The Town* (1957) and *The Mansion* (1959), on the other side of the dividing line, broaden in scope as Faulkner envisions the possibility of the world's renewal by the lowly of the earth through humility, work, forgiveness, and love.

The Reivers (1962), completed the year Faulkner died, presents a mellow and often hilarious world reminiscent of the comedies of ARISTOPHANES and DANTE. In this last novel the Yoknapatawpha cycle is gathered, completed, and verified. Faulkner shows that even as they seemingly regress, people may actually move forward in time. As he said in an interview, "we must take the trouble and sin along with us, and we must cure that trouble as we go."

Go Down, Moses—The Heroic Life

Although the most controversial of Faulkner's works, *Go Down, Moses* is the key to his overall vision. He himself spoke of the work as a novel; to some, however, it seems a collection of rather loosely related short stories. It traces the history—from 1859 to 1941—of the family of Carothers McCaslin, who, coming to Mississippi in the early 1830s, founded a dynasty of both white and black descendants. The novel focuses on Old Carothers's grandson, Isaac McCaslin, who in the first section—"Was"—has not yet been born and in the last section—"Go Down, Moses"—is no longer living.

Though the parts are not sequential and the characters seem at times unrelated to the large subject of the novel, readers who learn to assemble the different tales in their imaginations find their understanding of the moral and religious concerns of the novel deepened. The work is based on the black spiritual "Go Down,

> [Ike earned a living as a carpenter] *not in mere static and hopeful emulation of the Nazarene, but . . . because if the Nazarene had found carpentering good for the life and ends He had assumed and elected to serve, it would be all right too for Isaac McCaslin.*
>
> —*Go Down, Moses*

I like to think of the world I created as being a kind of keystone in the Universe; that, as small as that keystone is, if it were ever taken away, the universe itself would collapse.

—Faulkner, in *Lion in the Garden*

Moses," using the plight of the Israelites in their Egyptian captivity as the controlling metaphor. And though *Go Down, Moses* provides a searching examination of the sin of slavery, it gives no less attention to absolute ownership in general. The sections "Was" and "Pantaloon in Black" provide a comic and tragic account of the enslavement that results from the attempt to possess the earth and other people and thereby "dispossess" the Creator. Freedom, the novel shows, is to be found only in renunciation and love.

Isaac's decision to renounce his rightful inheritance of the McCaslin plantation in order to live a life of atonement for the wrong of slavery is the central focus of the novel. Every other chronicled event casts light on this act. Although Isaac forfeits his privileges, by the time he is in his eighties, as "uncle to half a county" he finds compensation in teaching young hunters who are "more his kin than any." Far from escaping the burdens of his heritage, he substitutes for familial responsibility a more universal stewardship.

Such generosity toward the world is also

If Sam Fathers had been his mentor and the backyard rabbits and squirrels his kindergarten, then the wilderness the old bear ran was his college and the old male bear itself, so long unwifed and childless as to have become its own ungendered progenitor, was his alma mater.

—*Go Down, Moses*

characteristic of the black woman Molly Beauchamp, an archetypal mother figure portrayed in the second section of the novel, "The Fire and the Hearth." She reappears in the last section, "Go Down, Moses," in which another guardian, Gavin Stevens, a local lawyer, becomes a partner in Molly's task of burying the grandson who was executed for killing a policeman in Chicago because "Pharaoh got him."

Isaac's renunciation of his birthright does not have immediately evident results; and most who benefit from his sacrifice fail to recognize their debt. But as with all great works, the large action of the novel encompasses more than any one character. Isaac, like Ishmael in *Moby Dick* and Alyosha in *The Brothers Karamazov,* demonstrates that the way of acceptance and love is more powerful than that of force. The last episode of *Go Down, Moses,* concerned with the proper burial of the young black criminal and hence his acknowledgment as a member of the community, thus manifests the deliverance that is the fruit of Isaac's faith and hope. This last section reveals something of the spiritual character of the "promised land," the redeemed community on earth, which, as the Moses of the title, Isaac is not allowed to enter.

The other large theme of *Go Down, Moses,* explored in the two central sections of the novel, "The Old People" and "The Bear," is the education that prepares a person for the calling of prophet and saint. Isaac's teacher is the part-Indian, part-Negro Sam Fathers, who initiates him into the life of the wilderness through hunting. The ritual of the hunt involves violence, but it is the violence of sacrifice and not slaughter. The commemorative action of the hunt gathers a community of men into a contemplative experience, into "the best of all talking," foreshadowing the brotherhood for which Isaac longs.

Isaac's education has two stages. At first, he learns skills so easily that he borders on pride. But through his encounters with the great bear Old Ben, who embodies the spirit of the place and seems almost immortal, he learns humility. Education, the central transforming force of *Go Down, Moses,* not only puts Isaac in com-

munion with the order of creation but joins him to the many peoples who have gone before him in history. Moving a sinful race toward the founding of an America that embodies "the communal anonymity of brotherhood" is Isaac's goal, though he does not live to see his yearning fulfilled. "Delta Autumn," the last section in which Isaac appears—now in his eighties—seems to point to the failure of his sacrifice to make any difference in the world.

But, as the last story of the novel shows, the community has indeed made an advance in its long journey toward justice and freedom. Paradoxically, at the heart of what moves the human enterprise toward redemption are the renunciation and heroic sacrifice of such characters as Isaac, Molly, Sam Fathers, and Gavin. These acts, though hidden, silently transform the earth.

Issues to Explore

In *Go Down, Moses* Isaac McCaslin's choice to renounce his inheritance follows the pattern of the Christian who chooses a dedicated life of poverty and detachment. (1) Isaac's decision, however, is considered questionable by many readers. Was it an act of self-sacrifice or cowardice? (2) Can the choice of such an apparently otherworldly dedication affect society? (3) How are the sections "Pantaloon in Black" and "Go Down, Moses" related to the action of the whole novel? (4) How is the guardianship exercised by Gavin Stevens related to the work of Isaac McCaslin?

(5) Faulkner's style has been related by many of his critics to an oral tradition; that is, his language and rhythm are not intended

You don't need to choose. The heart already knows. He didn't have His Book written to be read by what must elect and choose, but by the heart, not by the wise of the earth because maybe they don't need it or maybe the wise no longer have any heart, but by the doomed and lowly of the earth who have nothing else to read with but the heart. Because the men who wrote his Book for Him were writing about truth and there is only one truth and it covers all things that touch the heart.

—*Go Down, Moses*

For Further Study

Go Down, Moses is not difficult to read, although part 4 of "The Bear," which details Isaac's encounters with the commissary ledgers in which he uncovers the darkest aspects of his family history, may be confusing in places. And in the dialogue that follows between Isaac and his cousin Cass Edmonds, it is sometimes difficult to determine the speaker. A rapid reading, in which one absorbs the tone of the writing and subsequent reflection, however, should enable the reader to follow with certainty.

Of Faulkner's other novels, *The Sound and the Fury* is probably the most difficult to read. A more accessible introduction to the Faulknerian style is provided by *Light in August*. Although *Absalom, Absalom!* looks formidable at first glance, the episodes can flow in a surprisingly natural way especially if one takes into consideration which narrator is speaking. The stories "Barn Burning," "Mountain Victory," "Dry September," and "Turnabout" are good short introductions to Faulkner's work.

The most readily available editions of the novels and the collected and uncollected stories are published by Vintage Books. For helpful commentaries on each of the main novels, see Cleanth Brooks's *Faulkner's Yoknapatawpha Country* (Yale, 1963). Brooks analyzes some of the most difficult passages and outlines the complicated genealogies. Particularly helpful, in addition, are Michael Millgate, *The Achievement of William Faulkner* (Vintage, 1966), Warren Beck, *Man in Motion* (University of Wisconsin, 1961), and Edmond Volpe, *A Reader's Guide to William Faulkner* (Noonday, 1964). For some of Faulkner's own comments on his writing, see *Faulkner in the University,* eds. Frederick L. Gwynn and Joseph L. Blotner (Vintage, 1965), and *Lion in the Garden: Interviews with William Faulkner, 1926–1962,* eds. James B. Merriwether and Michael Millgate (Random House, 1968).

so much for the eye as for the ear. How does this affect the quality of the experience one gains from reading Faulkner? (6) Though Faulkner's fictional territory is the South, he himself would declare that he is not writing about the South, but about "the human heart in conflict with itself." Does this seem a possible attitude to take toward his writing? (7) In his Nobel Prize speech, Faulkner declared that he believed the human race would "not only endure, but prevail." What might he mean by these two terms?

—Mary Mumbach

SIMONE WEIL

Waiting for God
1950

Simone Weil (1909–1943).

*P*erhaps no other author in the twentieth century witnesses to the presence of the sacred with more searing testimony and intellectual honesty than Simone Weil (1909–1943) in *Waiting for God*. Weil was a religious genius who suffered the intellectual turmoil and historical torment of living as a French Jew in the shadow of the Third Reich. But as a disciple of Christ, she enshrined the experience of grace in language of simple and lucid beauty.

Waiting for God was not conceived as a homogeneous work. Rather it is a posthumous collection of Weil's writings edited by her friend and confessor, Father Jean-Marie Perrin. And yet overall this book stands as an organic unity and a supreme example of poetic art. For indeed *Waiting for God* should be seen as an autobiographical poem in which Simone Weil represents the Christian pilgrim.

Unconventional Believer

Christian mystics have traditionally fallen into two categories: those who embrace the *via positiva* and those who embrace the *via negativa*. The first experience an "orientation of the soul to grace" as they affirm mortal beauty and pass, by degrees, from the gift of the Lover to the love of the Giver. The second avoid the world of tangible objects altogether in order to contemplate the transcendent Being that is ultimately incomparable with any created thing. Despite Weil's preoccupation with the political and social nightmare of the Spanish Civil War and World War II, she still experienced the second approach by remaining focused on a God who supersedes the pain and chaos of this world.

Weil's Christian witness has been troubling to believer and unbeliever alike. Although she venerated the Catholic Church and was extraordinarily sensitive to the poetry of its rites and sacraments, she refused to be baptized into the church because of her conviction that she should share the lot of those afflicted by war, poverty, and bereavement who knew neither Christ nor the sacraments. For in these victims who suffered outrage uncomprehendingly she recognized the wounds of her crucified Lord. Consequently she has been described as a "saint for the churchless."

God created through love and for love. God did not create anything except love itself, and the means to love. He created love in all its forms. He created beings capable of love from all possible distances. Because no other could do it, he himself went to the greatest possible distance, the infinite distance. This infinite distance between God and God, this supreme tearing apart, this agony beyond all others, this marvel of love, is the crucifixion. Nothing can be further from God than that which has been made accursed.

This tearing apart, over which supreme love places the bond of supreme union, echoes perpetually across the universe in the midst of silence, like two notes, separate yet melting into one, like pure and heart-rending harmony. This is the Word of God.

—Waiting for God

For some, her refusal to enter a church—of any denomination—betrayed a spiritual unyieldingness incompatible with the corporate nature of the Christian faith. This intransigence was subsequently apparent when she died at thirty-four after virtually starving to death because she refused to eat more food than her fellow French citizens received during the German occupation. Actions such as these have made her—for all of her spiritual insight—a somewhat questionable and ambiguous figure, even to her most ardent admirers.

For others, however, her indeterminate stance "at the intersection of Christianity and everything that is not Christianity" reveals a discipline and obedience peculiarly appropriate to the times in which she lived. As she wrote to Father Perrin: "I have always remained at this exact point, on the threshold of the church, without moving, quite still . . .; only now my heart has been transported, forever, I hope, into the Blessed Sacrament exposed on the altar."

Meditating on the Incomprehensible Love of God

Waiting for God falls into two parts: the first consists of six letters to Father Perrin in which Weil describes her spiritual milestones and her reasons for abstaining from baptism; the second is a series of meditations that distill the essence of her devotional life in language of transparent grace and purity.

Among the letters, the most moving passage describes a decisive event in Weil's Christian journey. Having suffered from migraine headaches since childhood, she found, in her late twenties, that by reciting the devotional poetry of George HERBERT she could transcend the sense of physical pain as she contemplated the Christian mysteries. On one occasion she was reciting the poem, "Love (3)": "Love bade me welcome, but my soul drew back / Guilty of dust and sin. . . ." In doing so she experienced an encounter so overwhelming in its otherness that she became convinced that "Christ came down and took possession of me." She further observed, "in this sudden possession of me by Christ, neither my senses nor my imagination had any part; I only felt in the midst of my suffering the presence of a love, like that which one can read in the smile of a beloved face."

In the essays of *Waiting for God,* Weil, like the author of the Song of Solomon, uses the language of the nuptial chamber. Here her preoccupation with the experience of affliction reaches its highest level of expression and insight. Affliction is not accidental but natural to our life as we suffer here on earth and as God suffered in his incarnate Son. For Weil, those who experience this estrangement and affliction and still continue to hope and love share uniquely in Christ's crucifixion:

God created through love and for love. God did not create anything except love itself, and the means to love. He created love in all its forms. He created beings capable of love from all possible distances. Because no other could do it, he himself went to the greatest possible distance, the infinite distance. This infinite distance between God and God, this

FRANCE COMBATTANTE

LAISSEZ - PASSER

o. *1663*   Nom   *lle Weil*

Prenoms   *Simone*

Grade ou Profession   *Redactrice*

Bureau ou Service   *C. N. I*

Londres le   *30 Mars 1943*

Le Chef du Service de Sécurité

The French Resistance identity card of Simone Weil.

supreme tearing apart, this agony beyond all others, this marvel of love, is the crucifixion.

This passage epitomizes the heart of Weil's message. For her nothing is more contrary to human nature and yet more instrumental to Christian growth than the ability to attend to the afflicted: for, in doing so, we are actually attending to Christ.

Another dimension of Weil's religious thought is found in her meditation on "the implicit love of God." Because God can never be known as he is in himself—in the center of his divine essence—we must experience his presence indirectly through those encounters in which a portion of his infinite love is mediated to our finite senses. In the rites and ceremonies of the church, the beauty of art or nature, and the love of our neighbor, we can glimpse a portion of the divine glory. But we must cultivate the capacity of attention; our own efforts are not enough: "We cannot take a single step toward heaven. It is not in our

power to travel in a vertical direction. If, however, we look heavenward for a long time, God comes and takes us up. . . ."

One pitfall that attends the implicit love of God for Weil is the confusion of the object that mediates that love with its source. We must, therefore, give up the belief that happiness, security, or joy are ultimately attainable here below. But most people cannot make such a renunciation and therefore spend their lives pursuing objects that invariably impoverish or

Christ came down and took possession of me. . . . in this sudden possession of me by Christ, neither my senses nor my imagination had any part; I only felt in the midst of my suffering the presence of a love, like that which one can read in the smile of a beloved face.

—*Waiting for God*

The longing to love the beauty of the world in a human being is essentially the longing for the Incarnation. It is mistaken if it thinks it is anything else. The Incarnation alone can satisfy it. It is therefore wrong to reproach the mystics, as has been done sometimes, because they use love's language. It is theirs by right. Others only borrow it.

—Waiting for God

disappoint. Waiting patiently and uncomplainingly for God in the midst of dearth and famine is the highest state we can reach on earth: "If after a long period of waiting God allows [us] to have an indistinct intuition of his light or even reveals himself in person, it is only for an instant. Once more [we] have to remain still, attentive, inactive, calling out only when [our] desire cannot be contained."

Waiting for God concludes with a meditation on the one prayer that Jesus expressly instructs his followers to repeat, the "Our Father." Exploring each clause for its spiritual import, Weil compels the reader to reexamine and reestablish a connection with words too often blunted by repetition and custom.

Issues to Explore

(1) The line between humility and humiliation, adoration of God and gratuitous wounding of the self is sometimes very fine. Does Weil, in her ethic of renunciation, cross over the line and blur the distinction between the humility of the saint and the pathological thirst for self-torture? (2) Weil herself confessed that she committed the sin of envy in contemplating the crucifixion. Does such an admission show

For Further Study

Waiting for God, with an excellent introduction by Leslie Fiedler, is available from Harper Perennial (1951). Students desiring a more extensive knowledge of Weil's writings should consult *The Simone Weil Reader* edited by George A. Panichas (David McKay Company, 1977). Its introduction and commentary is extremely searching and insightful. As a supplement, one should also consult "The Christ of Simone Weil," reprinted in George A. Panichas's *The Critic as Conservator* (Catholic University, 1992). To explore Weil's problematic relationship with the faith of Israel, see Martin Buber's "The Silent Question" in *At the Turning: Three Addresses on Judaism* (Farrar, Straus and Young, 1952).

us the need to discriminate between moments of genuine illumination that transfigure her work and unconscious compulsions that may distort her message? (3) In short, does she demand more of holiness than is humanly possible—or desirable—even for a saint?

(4) Should a Christian believer challenge Weil's repudiation of the institutional church because too frequently it has mirrored less of the kingdom of God than the majoritarian tyranny of the secular state? (5) Should Weil have emphasized more strongly the fact that the church, in preserving and transmitting the gospel, has upheld the standard by which all institutional and personal aberrations—including its own—must be judged?

—Stephen Gurney

DIETRICH BONHOEFFER

Letters and Papers from Prison
1951

As Dietrich Bonhoeffer was being led away to his execution on the morning of April 9, 1945, his last reported words were, "This is the end—for me the beginning of life." Bonhoeffer was referring, of course, to his belief in the resurrection. But in ways that he never could have fathomed, he was also uttering a prophetic truth about his own theological legacy. Within years after the end of World War II, this German Lutheran pastor had become widely venerated as a modern martyr and as a theologian of incalculable influence.

The meteoric rise in Bonhoeffer's reputation can be traced in large measure to one remarkable book, *Letters and Papers from Prison,* first published in English in 1953. This collection brought together the letters, poems, and meditations that Bonhoeffer wrote during his two years in a Gestapo prison. Several generations of readers have discovered in these documents an inspiring model of contemporary Christian courage, a testimony to the power of grace in extreme adversity, and a host of challenging reflections about the meaning of

Dietrich Bonhoeffer (1906–1945).

the gospel in a secular age. The unique impact of Bonhoeffer's life and work together make it likely that *Letters and Papers from Prison* will have the lasting status as a classic of Christian autobiography and theological reflection.

Born in 1906, Dietrich Bonhoeffer early displayed an affinity for theology. By the age of twenty-five, he had received a professorship in

the discipline at the University of Berlin. During the 1930s, drawn into the church's resistance movement against the Nazi regime, he was the leading author of the celebrated Barmen Declaration. In the middle of the decade, he was appointed to head the seminary of the Confessing (Dissenting) church and continued in that capacity when persecution forced the seminary underground. Eventually he became involved in a movement to overthrow Hitler and was arrested in April 1943. More than a year later, documents were discovered connecting him to the failed plot to assassinate the Führer on July 20, 1944.

From Prison

Letters and Papers from Prison appeals to readers on several distinct levels. The letters reveal Bonhoeffer's pain over separation from his family, his longing to be free to marry, and his alternating moods of elation, despondency, and patience. In the very first letter written only days after his arrest, Bonhoeffer told his parents of his anguish over "the

Who stands fast? Only the man whose final standard is not his reason, his principles, his conscience, his freedom, or his virtue, but who is ready to sacrifice all this when he is called to obedient and responsible action in faith and in exclusive allegiance to God—the responsible man, who tries to make his whole life an answer to the question and call of God. Where are these responsible people?

—Letters and Papers from Prison

thought that you are being tormented by anxiety about me," his apprehension over the fate of his young fiancée, his delight in the impending wedding of his niece, and his simple pleasure provided that "here in the prison yard there is a thrush which sings beautifully in the morning, and now in the evening too." At one level, the entire work can be read as a gripping drama of the suffering and broken relationships faced by countless individuals during World War II.

If *Letters and Papers from Prison* were only a series of intimate reflections, however, it would hardly have acquired its vast influence. The book's documentation of Bonhoeffer's profound sacrifice and its revolutionary theological arguments give it a greater depth and resonance. A pacifist by conviction, Bonhoeffer joined the Resistance movement as an act of solidarity with the German people who opposed Hitler.

In the book's opening meditation, written only days before his imprisonment, Bonhoeffer speaks of how "it is infinitely easier to suffer in obedience to a human command than in the freedom of one's own responsibility" and "infinitely easier to suffer with others than to suffer alone." Yet the truth of the gospel is that "Christ suffered as a free man alone, apart and in ignominy, in body and spirit; and since then many Christians have suffered with him."

While shunning morbid introspection in *Letters and Papers from Prison*, Bonhoeffer nonetheless repeatedly undertakes frank assess-

ments of himself. "Who am I?" he asks in one of the poems he wrote in prison.

> Who am I? A hypocrite before others,
> And before myself a contemptibly
>   woebegone weakling?
> Who am I? They mock me, these lonely
>   questions of mine.
> Whoever I am, thou knowest, O God, I am
>   thine.

The Suffering God

Over the course of Bonhoeffer's two years in prison, his writings on suffering deepened considerably as he meditated on the suffering of God himself in Jesus Christ. "Christians and Pagans," a particularly moving poem, begins by describing the habit all humans have of going "to God when they are sore bestead." But to be a Christian is to "go to God" because he is

> poor and scorned, without shelter or
>   bread
> Whelmed under weight of the wicked, the
>   weak, the dead;
> Christians stand by God in his hour of
>   grieving.

As one of Bonhoeffer's later letters puts it: "Man's religiosity makes him look in his distress to the power of God in the world. . . . The Bible directs man to God's powerlessness and suffering; only the suffering God can help."

Bonhoeffer's meditations on human and divine suffering lead to the most crucial theological reflections of *Letters and Papers from Prison*. In letters written to Eberhard Bethge, his friend and future biographer, Bonhoeffer ponders a problem that he said was "bothering [him] incessantly." It is "the question of what Christianity really is, or indeed who Christ really is, for us today." Bonhoeffer finds himself absorbed with the question of how to follow Christ in a world grown increasingly "religionless." Following the lead of his theological mentor Karl Barth, Bonhoeffer distinguishes religion in general from the Christian faith in particular. The former is the product of human efforts to reach God; the latter is the story of God coming to save humanity.

Dachau Concentration Camp, Germany.

Though confined in prison with few books at his disposal, Bonhoeffer nonetheless set out to rethink nothing less than the whole of modern history. The argument that emerges in his letters has exercised vast influence over the development of theology in the postwar years. For centuries, Bonhoeffer explains, Christians have responded to advances in knowledge by trying "to use God as a stop-gap for the incompleteness of our knowledge." But by using God as nothing more than a "god of the gaps," the Christian church pushes him further and further to the periphery of human life. "We are to find God in what we know, not in what we don't know," Bonhoeffer asserts. It is God's "will to be recognized in life, and not only when death comes; in health and vigour, and not only in suffering."

Again and again in his final letters Bonhoeffer returns to his basic theme of "Christ and the world that has come of age." Under God's providence, human history has reached the point where "we live as men who manage their lives without" God. Rather than condemning this development, Bonhoeffer asserts that "before God and with God we live without God. God lets himself be pushed out of the world on to the cross." The hope of the resurrection especially drives "a man back to his life on earth in a wholly new way. . . ."

Before he could develop these thoughts, or write the book he outlined for his friend Bethge, Bonhoeffer was hung by the Nazis only weeks before the Allied liberation.

Issues to Explore

Bonhoeffer's theological reflections in *Letters and Papers from Prison* are as sketchily incomplete as they are bold. He raises more questions than he resolves. So, not surprisingly, his thoughts have been taken toward widely conflicting conclusions.

For the Christian reader, *Letters and Papers from Prison* raises the issue about the degree to which Christian profession should be bound to a specifically religious language. (1) Is the Christian vocabulary—of guilt and grace, sin and redemption, death and resurrection—an essential element of the faith, or a time-bound form of expressing a timeless truth? (2) As the church tries to communicate the gospel to a secular culture, how far should it go in adopt-

For Further Study

Though the reader of *Letters and Papers from Prison* is not likely to arrive at easy answers to the questions it raises, the book is readily accessible to the average reader. Because it is mostly letters, it has a tone of familiarity and reads with a degree of ease. There are cultural, historical, and theological references that present occasional obstacles to the lay reader, but the standard English edition has ample explanatory notes. Whatever its difficulties, Bonhoeffer's classic richly rewards its readers at several levels.

Letters and Papers from Prison is available in a standard paperback edition (Macmillan, 1972). Several of Bonhoeffer's other works merit special attention, particularly *The Cost of Discipleship* (Macmillan, 1959) and *Ethics* (Macmillan, 1964). Eberhard Bethge's *Dietrich Bonhoeffer: A Biography* is the definitive study of the life (Harper & Row, 1970).

ing that culture's vocabulary? (3) Can we have a meaningful understanding of the gospel without employing a historically grounded, explicitly Christian vocabulary?

These matters raise other questions about the nature of Bonhoeffer's reading of history. (4) Should the church embrace or resist the process of secularization? (5) Does Bonhoeffer's celebration of human autonomy rightfully acknowledge the state of affairs that God has brought about in history? Or does it unwisely grant a privileged status to the prideful rebellion better known as the Fall?

—Roger Lundin

FLANNERY O'CONNOR

"A Good Man Is Hard to Find" (1953)
"Greenleaf" (1956)
"Revelation" (1964)

Flannery O'Connor's thirty-three short stories and two brief novels have a perfection of art and form that few other writers achieve.

One critic has considered her fiction a twentieth-century version, in words, of a medieval cathedral. It is populated with gargoyles and peculiar-seeming, haloed saints.

O'Connor's use of the grotesque, which she defines as "the good under construction," highlights the plight of modern humanity while illustrating moments of grace. Her stories dramatize moments of crisis that can catch people offguard, leaving them in dangerous and awkward positions—moments when grace can intervene.

On sending one of her stories to a friend, O'Connor herself called it a morality play. One of the great masters of the short story, she enlarges the moral boundaries of that medium while simultaneously exploring the farthest reaches of comedy. Her writing surveys reality from the vantage of the end of time, in light of final things.

Flannery O'Connor (1925–1964).

A Life Cut Short

O'Connor's work marks the end of the Southern literary renaissance, confirming with finality its loving yet unsentimental vision. She herself knew that her work represented a late stage of this flowering. Asked about William FAULKNER's work, she said that it "makes me feel that with my one-cylinder syntax I should quit writing and raise chickens altogether."

Above all, O'Connor was fiercely opposed to nostalgia. She once compared sentimentalism to pornography, pointing out that both lead to cynicism by giving only a one-sided view of a complex experience. Like other Southern fiction writers—Faulkner, Caroline Gordon, Eudora Welty, and Katherine Anne Porter—she maintained that the real heritage of the South was grounded in "a shared past, a sense of alikeness, and the possibility of reading a small history in a universal light." In some ways she seems the least Southern of all the Southerners, for she sees their territory as transparent, revealing what she called the "true country."

Flannery O'Connor (1925–1964) spent most of her life at home in Savannah, Georgia. She was a prodigy who, after her first story was published when she was twenty-one, began immediately to work with established writers. But suddenly at twenty-five an attack of lupus, a severe immune disorder, brought her close to death. Because of its disabling symptoms, O'Connor lived and worked the rest of her mere thirty-nine years

The death of Mrs. May:

She continued to stare straight ahead but the entire scene in front of her had changed—the tree line was a dark wound in a world that was nothing but sky—and she had the look of a person whose sight has been suddenly restored but who finds the light unbearable.

—"Greenleaf"

on the family farm near Milledgeville. She was not in isolation, however: she sent her typescripts to the novelist Caroline Gordon, whom she called her "mentor," kept up a rich correspondence with a wide circle of friends, and was often able to travel to give lectures.

Grace through Violence

"I have found that violence is strangely capable of returning my characters to reality and preparing them to accept their moment of grace. Their heads are so hard that almost nothing else will do the work," says O'Connor. Three of her representative stories, taken from the beginning, middle, and end of her career, focus on the crises three women experience when they encounter death and unlooked-for love.

In her first well-known story, "A Good Man Is Hard to Find," the protagonist, a grandmother, learns that being a "lady" is no shield from harm. On the contrary, it makes her vulnerable to unimaginable danger. Within seconds of her own death, this elderly lady, half-delirious from shock and not even suspecting her own responsibility for her family's murder, begins to redeem the life of a hardened criminal. As she relinquishes all self-concern in bestowing compassion and love on this man, known as the Misfit, she instantaneously changes the shape of both their lives. The grandmother hallucinates and imagines him as her own child, speaking to him with sudden tenderness. He reciprocates by shooting her.

The Misfit's desperation and helplessness are unveiled in his conversation with the elderly woman before her death. "Jesus thrown everything off balance," he complains. If Christ is true, he acknowledges, then people must leave everything and follow him. If he is not, then people must simply take whatever pleasure they can find in life. And as he explains, "No pleasure but meanness." But now the grandmother's testifying to love has thrown *him* off balance. Though he has just practiced the extraordinary meanness of killing a helpless family, he admits there "ain't no real pleasure in life." Where will he turn now?

The central character in the second story, "Greenleaf," does find pleasure in meanness for most of her life. Like the Misfit, Mrs. May believes herself self-made. Embittered at an apparent lack of appreciation by those around her, she refuses all offers of communion or care. But the gentle tone of the narrator indicates that, without recognizing it, she has been continually gazed at and waited on by some invisible but all-seeing presence, if she would only notice. Her world seems harsh because she has made it so through blindness and ingratitude. She scorns the prayer of the healer Mrs. Greenleaf: "Oh Jesus, stab me in the heart!" But at last Mrs. May's own heart is pierced by a strange agent of grace, a bull likened to "a gentleman" and to "some patient god come down to woo her." The runaway bull she has ordered to be killed gores her in a violent death that has the character of a courtship. As she dies, she appears "to be bent over whispering some last discovery into the animal's ear."

Unlike Mrs. May, Ruby Turpin, the protagonist in the third story, "Revelation," claims to see everything in her life as a sign of God's favor. She often asks her Lord about the ranks various people and classes occupy in the hierarchy of virtue. She little suspects how he will reply through his chosen agent, a disturbed student from a northern college. To her credit, Mrs. Turpin insists on learning the truth from this young woman, who calls her a "wart hog from hell." She is troubled, questioning, "How am I saved and from hell too?" Standing in her immaculately clean pig sty, she finally cries out in protest to the Lord.

A farmstead in Georgia.

Her answer is a vision of the redeemed souls proceeding into heaven, the disreputable and dispossessed in the front ranks. She and her husband are in line, but last. In the purifying action of the revelation, she sees that "even their virtues," which they were so thoughtfully cultivating, "were being burned away." In that new world, it seems, nothing less than charity abides.

The Two Novels

O'Connor's short stories are distinguished by their uncompromising apocalyptic revelation. They present moments in which the veil of worldly appearances is torn apart to reveal eternal realities that demand immediate and ultimate choices. Her two novels, in contrast, depict the slow growth, step by step, toward a self-annihilation that the protagonist long ago sensed but does everything in his power to prevent. In *Wise Blood* (1952) Hazel Motes resists his call to be a preacher by establishing a "Church without Christ" and finding that he must finally deny everything, even blasphemy. He blinds himself, winds barbed wire around his waist, and walks on broken glass; ulti-

mately, however, his dead body and empty eye-sockets witness to that reality he sought all his life to evade.

Of the two novels, though *Wise Blood* has attained a greater renown, *The Violent Bear It Away* (1960) is more approachable. It traces the path of a rebellious young man named Francis Marion Tarwater, who having lived at a place called Powderhead with his great-uncle, Mason Tarwater, a self-styled prophet, refuses to follow in his elder's footsteps. The old man, knowing that he is near the end of his life, begs the boy to bury him after his death. Realizing his own power, the boy refuses to promise; and one morning, finding the old man dead, he sets fire to the house and takes off for the city. He is gradually pulled against his will into the tasks assigned him by his uncle, chief among

Some people have the notion that you read the story and then climb out of it into the meaning, but for the fiction writer himself the whole story is the meaning, because it is an experience, not an abstraction.

—*Mystery and Manners*

The meaning of a story has to be embodied in it, has to be made concrete in it. A story is a way to say something that can't be said any other way, and it takes every word in the story to say what the meaning is.

—*Mystery and Manners*

them the baptism of his half-witted nephew. The path leading to Tarwater's submission to his vocation is grim and harrowing; but finally, after being unable to eat (out of hunger for what his uncle had spoken of as the "living bread") and having been raped by a young man who has given him a lift, he returns to the burnt-out home at Powderhead, finding that the nearby Negroes have buried the old man. Lying on his uncle's grave, he hears the command, "as silent as seeds opening one at a time in his blood": "GO WARN THE CHILDREN OF GOD OF THE TERRIBLE SPEED OF MERCY." The novel ends with Tarwater's turning toward the sleeping city.

O'Connor's writing is startling and disturbing: in its movement toward grace, conversion, and prophecy, it deals not only with violence but with the demonic. The profoundly shocking quality of her fiction, however, is never mere sensationalism. Rather, it represents the abrupt invasion of absolute love into a fallen and therefore distorted world.

Artists with faith, O'Connor insisted, have an even more serious responsibility to work at perfecting their craft than do unbelieving artists: "your beliefs will be the light by which you see, but they will not be what you see and they will not be a substitute for seeing." The higher the vision, then, the more determined the artist must be "to convince through the senses."

For Further Study

Of Flannery O'Connor's fiction, readily available are *Three by Flannery O'Connor* (Signet, 1983), which contains the two novels, and *The Complete Stories* (Farrar, Straus and Giroux, 1981). *Mystery and Manners,* edited by Sally and Robert Fitzgerald (Farrar, Straus and Giroux, 1969), is the posthumous collection of her essays and talks and contains her reflections on the art of writing and its relationship to belief and to life.

Commentaries on O'Connor's fiction are numerous, considering that it is a small, recent body of work. A good study (except for what seems a serious misreading of "Parker's Back") is John Desmond's *Risen Sons: Flannery O'Connor's Vision of History* (University of Georgia, 1987). *Critical Essays on Flannery O'Connor* (G. K. Hall, 1985) gives a helpful survey and sampling of interpretations. For readings on the sacramental vision in literature, see Allen Tate's "The Symbolic Imagination" in *Essays of Four Decades* (Swallow Press, 1959).

Issues to Explore

Some questions to ponder include: (1) What is the value of the grotesque and violent as O'Connor uses these qualities? How do they affirm grace and love? (2) What is the difference between sensationalism and O'Connor's use of unpleasant and repulsive material? (3) How would one defend her writing against the charge that it is too dark? (4) How does her comic vision shed light on all the details of her stories, even their most serious aspects?

—Mary Mumbach

ALEKSANDR I. SOLZHENITSYN
One Day in the Life of Ivan Denisovich
1962

*A*leksandr Solzhenitsyn's *One Day in the Life of Ivan Denisovich* is a short, dramatic lightning bolt of a book that lit up the horrors of the Soviet concentration camps. Through Soviet leader Nikita Khrushchev's decision to allow its publication in 1962, Solzhenitsyn—then an unknown high-school teacher of mathematics and physics—entered the limelight of world attention and raised a cry that set off a political avalanche. This most-celebrated survivor of the Soviet concentration camps remains famous today and seems destined to be known for generations. Already Solzhenitsyn's work appears in anthologies of world masterpieces. His memorable name for the system of prison camps, the *Gulag Archipelago,* along with the word *holocaust,* has come to serve as a shorthand term for our modern inhumanity to fellow human beings.

An Exile Returned Home

Solzhenitsyn was born on December 11, 1918. Although he learned about the Bible and the Christian

Aleksandr Isayevich Solzhenitsyn (b. 1918).

faith as a boy, his Soviet schooling trained him to believe in Marxism-Leninism. While serving in the Red Army during World War II, he was arrested for making critical comments about Joseph Stalin in a private letter to a friend. During his eight years of imprisonment, he met many Christians whose words

and examples gradually brought about his move from Marx to Jesus. Importantly, his turn, or return, to the Christian faith preceded all his writing.

Solzhenitsyn's development as a writer in the camps and the ingenuity with which he preserved what he had written make an awe-inspiring story of human courage. His initial acceptance by the Soviet authorities quickly turned to disapproval and, by the late sixties, to a campaign of vilification and slander in the Soviet press. His award of the Nobel Prize for Literature in 1970 was some guarantee of his relative safety from harm. In 1972, with all hopes dashed of ever being published in the Soviet Union again, Solzhenitsyn went public with what he had kept private: his faith. He published the first version of his most overtly Christian novel, *August 1914.* He circulated an open letter to Patriarch Pimen, scolding the Russian Orthodox Church for cooperating with an atheistic government. And he released a prayer that begins, "How easy it is to live with you, O Lord."

Pursuing a rumor in 1973, the secret police—the KGB—located a

Ivan Denisovich:

"Can a man who's warm understand one who's freezing?"

—*One Day in the Life of Ivan Denisovich*
H. T. Willetts, trans.

copy of Solzhenitsyn's history of the Soviet concentration-camp system entitled *The Gulag Archipelago*. Solzhenitsyn had not planned to publish the manuscript until much later. To forestall the authorities from dishonestly quoting fragments out of context, he gave the word and the Western presses rolled. The book's impact was sensational. No other single piece of writing did as much as *Gulag* to undermine the authority of the Soviet regime. It was especially decisive for the Soviet readers who obtained copies published underground.

In early 1974 the Soviet officials sent Solzhenitsyn into exile in the West. This was almost surely the most clever way to deal with him, for he deeply feared how being cut off from his homeland would affect his writing. He and his family moved to Vermont in 1976. After accepting some speaking invitations during his first few years in exile, culminating in his controversial commencement address at Harvard University in 1978, he settled into the quiet life of writing.

Shortly after his exile, the Western press, which had initially lionized Solzhenitsyn, largely turned against him. The media discovered from his speeches and essays that he was not the liberal they had assumed him to be. For some he proved to be an unwelcome guest, especially as he wrote warnings to the West, mainly about its spiritual decadence. Admittedly, some of his fears about Western weakness, though sound in principle, did turn out to be exaggerated.

Nevertheless, Solzhenitsyn's general understanding of the modern world and especially the nature of communism was confirmed by the passage of time. Hardly anyone sensed as surely as he that the Soviet Union's days were sharply numbered. He arrived in the West at

age fifty-five, predicting that he would return to Russia during his lifetime, even though his homeland would have to change drastically for his homecoming to occur. He returned to his native soil in 1994, twenty years after his exile.

Solzhenitsyn's Prolific Writing

The Gulag Archipelago is Solzhenitsyn's most celebrated work today. It has sold millions of copies and has been translated into as many languages as Shakespeare's plays. But Solzhenitsyn has never seen this work as his most important, for he views himself as primarily a novelist. Two rich novels that draw upon his life experiences are *The First Circle* and *Cancer Ward*.

Solzhenitsyn planned from his teenage years onward to write a series of novels about what he considered the most important event in modern world history, the Bolshevik Revolution of 1917. After he became a Christian, his attitude toward the first officially atheistic regime in history changed. But he saw the events of that era as central to our century. The expanded *August 1914* is the first volume in this sequence entitled *The Red Wheel*. The others have been written, but their translation moves slowly, especially into English.

One Day in the Life of Ivan Denisovich

Of all Solzhenitsyn's works, *One Day in the Life of Ivan Denisovich* continues to be most read and taught. Khrushchev sought to use it to establish his own niche in Soviet history through his campaign of de-Stalinization. The novel, however, is not only anti-Stalinist but anti-Soviet—and most broadly, a protest against the inhumanity of totalitarianism. For its hero, a simple peasant unjustly imprisoned, shows that he will retain his basic humanity no matter what the authorities do to him.

The literary excellence of this short novel lies in its deceptive simplicity. Solzhenitsyn resorts to the old-fashioned dramatic unities of time, place, and action to focus our attention on one character during one day in one prison camp. Yet readers understand the story to rep-

resent all the prisoners in all their days in all the camps. The description of suffering and degradation is rendered in a seemingly impassive voice that underlines the rigid injustice of the system. Thus, although Ivan Denisovich does not tell his own story, the subtle handling of point of view makes it seem as if the readers are inside his mind. The simple peasant is accorded the respect of being addressed by first name and patronymic (John, son of Denis).

Similarly, the suffering the prisoners endure is described mostly in terms of physical deprivation. ("Can a man who's warm understand one who's freezing?") But readers perceive it also to be psychological and spiritual; they experience not only the cold but the moral outrage. This effect is achieved through the book's most memorable technical device, understatement. If readers find this day almost unbearably painful and can hardly imagine facing another, Ivan Denisovich judges that it was almost a happy day. Understatement reaches its climax in the final lines: "Just one of the 3,653 days of his sentence, from bell to bell. The extra three were for leap years." From one day we feel every day.

Humanity Resisting Dehumanization

The collectivist ideology of the Soviets imposes a regimented life. Arbitrary regulations are designed to break down individual dignity and human solidarity. Sometimes they succeed; sometimes, as with Ivan, they do not. Such is the mystery of human suffering. Still, nothing inside his own worldview explains why he endures. For this explanation Solzhenitsyn needs another character.

This character is Alyoshka the Baptist. A good worker and kind person, Alyoshka draws his strength from the New Testament, which he has shrewdly hidden in a chink in the wall. In the climactic conversation of the novel, he explains his Christian faith to Ivan. Alyoshka is the only character who can give a positive meaning to his prison experience: "Be glad you're in prison. Here you have time to think about your soul."

Ivan and Alyoshka are brothers under the skin. Both are apparently insignificant persons who somehow are able to withstand everything that a soulless tyranny inflicts on them. By

Alyoshka:

Be glad you're in prison. Here you have time to think about your soul.

—*One Day in the Life of Ivan Denisovich*
H. T. Willetts, trans.

himself, Ivan suffices to show us the possibility, despite all, of moral heroism. Nevertheless, our understanding of Solzhenitsyn's Christian outlook concerning the ultimate source of human dignity remains incomplete until we come to know Alyoshka, the man of faith.

Issues to Explore

(1) Why does Solzhenitsyn choose a naive, superstitious peasant for his hero? (2) By what details does Solzhenitsyn show his hero to be life affirming? (3) Why does Solzhenitsyn choose a Baptist, rather than a Russian Orthodox, believer to articulate his Christian worldview? (4) How would the novel be different if Alyoshka the Baptist were not in it?

—Edward E. Ericson, Jr.

For Further Study

The authorized translation is Aleksandr Solzhenitsyn, *One Day in the Life of Ivan Denisovich,* H. T. Willetts, translator (Farrar, Straus and Giroux, 1991).

For collections and discussions of Solzhenitsyn's writings, refer to John B. Dunlop, Richard Haugh, and Alexis Klimoff, editors, *Aleksandr Solzhenitsyn: Critical Essays and Documentary Materials,* second edition (Collier, 1975); John B. Dunlop, Richard Haugh, and Michael Nicholson, editors, *Solzhenitsyn in Exile: Critical Essays and Documentary Materials* (Hoover Institution Press, 1985); and Edward E. Ericson, Jr., *Solzhenitsyn: The Moral Vision* (Eerdmans, 1980).

For a thorough examination of his ideas and surrounding controversies, see Edward E. Ericson, Jr., *Solzhenitsyn and the Modern World* (Regnery Gateway, 1993). One biography, which is strong on the early life, but unfortunately weak on the later life and controversies, and very poor on religion, is Michael Scammell, *Solzhenitsyn: A Biography* (Norton, 1984).

Contemporary Writers

In an unprecedented volume of activity, contemporary world literature offers daring and authoritative new ways of viewing the human situation. Writers around the globe are committed to presenting the distinctiveness of diverse cultural traditions in juxtaposition with the modern West—and often in conflict with it. Setting their actions amid multiple cultures, they intermix fantasy and myth with everyday life. Though not incapable of realism, they turn away from the narrow confines of rationalism and reopen the world to a sense of wonder. The "marvelous reality" these writers depict evokes a mysterious order larger than the human, finding in it an endless source of complexity and fertility.

The Rebirth of the Fabulous

The literary form at the center of these international developments is the novel, a medium open to change and exportation. To be sure, important novels continue to be written as social and political critique and commentary, as intense descriptions of personal struggle, and as explorations of the nature of consciousness; in Africa alone, Chinua Achebe, Nadine Gordimer, and Naguib Mahfouz are honored practitioners of these novelistic traditions. But the most dis-

Italo Calvino (1923–1985).

tinguished of those who write in what might be called the line of the marvelous—including several Nobel laureates in recent years—encompass new and larger purposes as well. An additional dimension that qualifies their writings as potential classics is their poetic authority; their works explore good and evil not as exercises in nostalgia but as

surprising discoveries in a complex world seen once again to be animated with both heavenly and hellish powers.

Two precursors have led the way in these trends. The stories of Argentinian Jorge Luis Borges (1899–1986), with their concise explorations and impasses, strike a contrasting note to the dominant "neo-realism" introduced by Ernest

Hemingway and Italian filmmakers. Borges also adapts the spellbinding style of the fable to a complex world of intellectual paradoxes. Several brilliant Latin American successors and a host of academic novelists in the United States have been influenced by his style and facility with ideas; this tendency, however, has sometimes led toward a cynical and narcissistic interpretation of the world.

A truer inheritor of the genuine spirit of fable is Italian novelist Italo Calvino (1923–1985), who took up Borges's dominant themes—the infinite, strange inner life; the figure of the labyrinth; the intellectual world as cerebral game—and cast over them an attitude of wonder and delight. Discovery is often the underlying structure of his fictions, as in *The Baron in the Trees* (1957), in which the young scion of a wealthy family retreats to the trees to escape his family. Instead of coming back down, he launches himself from tree to tree into a vivid life of interaction with the changing Europe of the French Revolution as he corresponds with thinkers and even organizes military raids and meets with Napoleon. He becomes, finally, a guiding spirit to his people. In *Cosmicomics* (1965), a whimsical account of the creation of the universe, and in such later works as *Invisible Cities* (1972), Calvino expands this attitude to a celebration of the unpredictability and beauty of the natural and human worlds.

Magical Realism in Latin America

The major twentieth-century novels of Latin America share a style of portrayal that has been called "magical realism." Characterized by the inclusion of the spiritual world as a legitimate presence in the secular world, magical realism emphasizes the extraordinary and experiments with the order of time and space. Facilitating this departure from traditional realism is the incorporation of folk forms—myth, legend, fable, superstition—into the framework of the modern novel. Julio Cortázar of Argentina (1914–1984), Carlos Fuentes of Mexico (b. 1928), and Jorge Amado of Brazil (b. 1912) are all major practitioners of this important mode.

The most prominent among them, however, is Colombian novelist Gabriel García Márquez (b. 1928). Beginning with *Leaf Storm* (1955), extending through more than a dozen stories, and culminating in *One Hundred Years of Solitude* (1967), he has produced a body of work that views with wonder the tragic drama of the New World family set against the brutal action of Latin American history. Drawing inspiration from Faulkner's universe in his single county of Yokna-patawpha, García Márquez's fictional world is concentrated in the imaginary village of Macondo. His method is to present cata-strophic events that are unique yet typical in encapsulating the fate of whole historical epochs. Marked by the arresting image and the still moment, his writing often begins in the recollection of wonder, as in the first sentence of *One Hundred Years:* "Many years later, as he

Gabriel García Márquez (b. 1928).

faced the firing squad, Colonel Aureliano Buendia was to remember that distant afternoon when his father took him to discover ice." Later works, such as *Love in the Time of Cholera* (1985), encompass broader themes but also revisit his continual concerns: history, violence, solitude, and love.

The remarkable first novel of Isabel Allende (b. 1942), *The House of the Spirits* (1981), focuses on the vast suffering of Chile from its oppression by landowners to the violent, CIA-induced overthrow of its socialist government. But the Trueba family is redeemed and its house literally transformed by three generations of clairvoyant women who take upon themselves others' suffering and their need for imagination and healing.

Exodus and Promised Land in African-American Literature

In the first half of the twentieth century, African-American authors emphasized their alienation from the main line of American culture. Such poets as Jean Toomer (1894–1967), Langston Hughes (1902–1967), and Countée Cullen (1903–1946), along with such novelists as Richard Wright (1908–1960), Ralph Ellison (1914–1994), and James Baldwin (1924–1987), each depict from their individual perspective the "invisible" plight of blacks unable to enter white culture on an equal basis.

In their works they use as a frequent point of reference the ancient pattern of exile and freedom, drawing on the long-standing parallels of black liberation in the United States to the biblical exodus and America's

> *What* was *strange was that the spectators did not see the butterflies, or what they did next. But Mirza Saeed clearly observed the great glowing cloud fly out over the sea; pause; hover; and form itself into the shape of a colossal being, a radiant giant constructed wholly of tiny beating wings, stretching from horizon to horizon, filling the sky. . . . "Clouds take many shapes," he shouted. "Elephants, film stars, anything. Look, it's changing even now." But nobody paid any attention to him; they were watching, full of amazement, as the butterflies dived into the sea.*
>
> —Salman Rushdie
> *The Satanic Verses*

struggle for freedom from Britain. The poetic imagination of these accomplished writers reverberates with the story of forced exile, captivity, struggle inspired by vision, and perpetually uncertain entry into the land of promise.

The poetry of Robert Hayden (1913–1980), especially his distinguished "Middle Passage" (1944), incorporates all these motifs and in so doing transforms the language from clichés of thoughtless adventure and conquest to idioms of suffering, defiance, and hope.

Contemporary African-American literature, led by novelist Gloria Naylor (b. 1950), poet Rita Dove (b. 1952), and other women authors, has built on and expanded this perspective. Their writings encompass the elements of human community in personal and familial relationships as affected by the black experience. The works of Zora Neale Hurston (1891–1960), including *Their Eyes Were Watching God* (1937), constitute a significant precursor for this new attitude among African-American

authors. It is Toni Morrison (b. 1931), however, who has entered most fully into some of the darkest episodes of this journey, renewing and redeeming the "unspeakable" through language. Her fifth novel, *Beloved* (1987), brings forth a mysterious young woman who "walked out of the water" to possess the life and house of the novel's heroine, the escaped slave Sethe. Called Beloved and adopted by Sethe to replace her own child whom she had killed in a frenzy to prevent recapture, this spirit embodies the trauma of history as a tragic curse passed down through the generations.

Myth, Ritual, and Remembrance in Africa

Critics have cited West African culture as an enlivening influence in the work of Morrison and other contemporary African-American writers. Africa below the Sahara remains most fully in touch with traditions, orally transmitted through countless stories, that celebrate the continuity of the

IYALOJA: . . . *There lies the honor of your household and your race. Because he could not bear to let honor fly out of doors, he stopped it with his life. The son has proved the father, Elesin, and there is nothing left in your mouth to gnash but infant gums. . . .*

—*Wole Soyinka*
Death and the King's Horseman

divine and human worlds. Wole Soyinka (b. 1934), perhaps the world's greatest living dramatist, has rejuvenated the theater through the presentation of the multidimensional Yoruba world of his native Nigeria. Although he gives a strong critique of Western exploitation and Westerners' rationalist mentality, his elegant dramas such as *A Dance of the Forests* (1963) and *Death and the King's Horseman* (1975) return ritual to the experience of tragedy.

Like Soyinka, Kenyan novelist Ngugi wa Thiong'o (formerly James Ngugi, b. 1938) was "detained"—the title of his prison diary—for his political views. Perhaps the most politically engaged of these authors, he is also in some ways the most spiritual. Ngugi's novels depict the struggle for Kenya's nationhood as concerning not only political freedom but also the moral and spiritual freedom that alone can give meaning to political independence. Ngugi's pervasive metaphor of "homecoming" envisions the restoration of Africa's psychological, moral, and spiritual integrity. His portraits of the organized church and its adherents are harsh, but his imagery and language invoke the Christian tradition, and his central focus is the development of community through suffering and love.

Petals of Blood (1977), Ngugi's fourth novel, is set in a newly liberated Kenya that has fallen into degeneracy, poverty, and mutual exploitation. Its title refers both to the violence suffered by the Kenyan people and to a red flower that was the traditional source of liquor used in their sacred rituals. The ancient liquor is replaced by alcohol produced by a distilling factory, which has become the symbol of their spiritual debasement. The town of Ilmorog is tied symbolically to Eden, and its degradation by the

Cover of *The Satanic Verses* (1988).

factory and other modes of international exploitation propels the novel's grim drama. In the course of the action, Wanja, a woman, comes to embody the spirit of Kenya itself—its beauty and kindness, dignity and decency even in the midst of degradation.

A World without Frontiers

Salman Rushdie (b. 1947) has commented that magical realism expresses a consciousness belonging to all the countries struggling with modernization, for "it deals with what [novelist V. S.] Naipaul has called 'half-made' societies, in which the impossibly old struggles against the appallingly new." Naipaul in Trinidad and Rushdie in Britain were both born in India; Rushdie has called their experience a central theme of twentieth-century life: the migrant's loss of home and culture. An understandable outcome of this loss is the pessimism and isolation prevalent in Naipaul's novels; in contrast, Rushdie's exuberant inventiveness seems all the more daring.

Rushdie's own quest has changed from the nostalgia for a true country, expressed so explosively in *Midnight's Children* (1981)—his allegory of the birth of an independent India—to the acceptance of nationlessness and a personal reawakening in his great novel *The Satanic Verses* (1988). This exuberant work, for whose deeply spiritual vision Rushdie has spent years in hiding from a formal death sentence, begins with two Indian actors falling out of the sky and changing, respectively, into winged and horned beings; it ends with a miraculous pilgrimage and the reconciliation of a long-estranged father and son. Rushdie recovers Calvino's sense of wonder, situated not in a faraway time, however, but in the contemporary world. He combines dark humor and biting satire with a tender love for the human race and its daily struggles. He seems especially to honor the virtues of faith, hope, and love, which shine forth through landscapes blighted with poverty, luxury, and danger.

Poetry

Outstanding contemporary poets form a kind of international community along the frontiers of the developed world, using their own cultural traditions to reinterpret the human condition. Octavio Paz of Mexico (b. 1914), Adrienne Rich of the United States (b. 1929), Derek Walcott of St. Lucia in the Caribbean (b. 1930), Seamus Heaney of Ireland (b. 1939), and the expatriate Russian Joseph Brodsky (1940–1996) are new voices of a decentered and disseminated culture. Paz depicts the return from solitude as a passage through a maze created by myth, poetry, and ritual. All of these, he says, permit people to "become one with creation."

The literature that we call classic partakes of the unrest of its times, offering insight into what is valuable and what, as Toni Morrison has said, "must be discarded." But the particular challenge of reading contemporary literature is to be ready for a

For Further Study

The recommended editions of the works follow:

Jorge Luis Borges: *Labyrinths: Selected Stories and Other Writings,* Donald A. Yates and James E. Irby, editors (Penguin, 1976).

Italo Calvino: *The Baron in the Trees,* Archibald Colquhoun, translator (Harcourt, 1977); *Cosmicomics,* William Weaver, translator (Harcourt, 1968); and *Invisible Cities,* William Weaver, translator (Harcourt, 1974).

Gabriel García Márquez: *Leaf Storm and Other Stories,* Gregory Rabassa, translator (Harper, 1972); *No One Writes to the Colonel and Other Stories,* J. M. Bernstein, translator (Harper, 1968); *One Hundred Years of Solitude,* Gregory Rabassa, translator (Harper, 1970); and *Love in the Time of Cholera,* Edith Grossman, translator (Penguin, 1989).

Isabel Allende: *The House of the Spirits,* Magda Bogin, translator (Knopf, 1985).

Robert Hayden: *Collected Poems* (Liveright, 1985)

Zora Neale Hurston: *Their Eyes Were Watching God* (Harper, 1990).

Toni Morrison: *Beloved* (Knopf, 1987)

Wole Soyinka: *A Dance of the Forests* (Oxford, 1963) and *Death and the King's Horseman* (Norton, 1975).

Ngugi wa Thiong'o: *Petals of Blood* (Dutton, 1977).

Salman Rushdie: *Midnight's Children* (Knopf, 1981) and *The Satanic Verses* (Viking, 1988).

Octavio Paz: *The Collected Poems of Octavio Paz, 1957–87,* Eliot Weinberger, editor and translator (New Directions, 1987).

Adrienne Rich: *Adrienne Rich's Poetry and Prose,* Barbara Charlesworth Gelpi and Albert Gelpi, editors (Norton, 1993).

Derek Walcott: *Collected Poems, 1948–1984* (Farrar, Straus, Giroux, 1986).

Seamus Heaney: *Selected Poems, 1966–1987* (Farrar, Straus, Giroux, 1990).

Joseph Brodsky: *A Part of Speech* (Farrar, Straus, Giroux, 1980).

Selected criticism includes: Lois Zamora and Wendy Faris, editors, *Magical Realism* (Duke, 1995); Kathryn Hume, *Calvino's Fictions: Cogito and Cosmos* (Oxford, 1992); George R. MacMurray, editor, *Critical Essays on Gabriel García Márquez* (Twayne, 1987); Terry Otten, *The Crime of Innocence in the Fiction of Toni Morrison* (Missouri, 1989); G. D. Killam, editor, *Critical Perspectives on Ngugi wa Thiong'o* (Three Continents, 1984); E. M. Santí, *Rights of Poetry: An Intellectual Biography of Octavio Paz* (Harvard, 1995).

struggle not just of two orders—impossibly old and appallingly new—but of styles and cosmic visions in which the ancient dreams of the human race may return to assist the arrival of new and unconventional forms.

—Bainard Cowan

Index

Italicized page numbers indicate illustrations.